Pauper's Gold
and
Wish Me Luck

Margaret Dickinson is the author of nineteen
novels including most recently *Without Sin*, *Red Sky in
the Morning* and *Twisted Strands*. She is married with
two grown-up daughters, and lives in Lincolnshire
where the majority of her novels are based.

Margaret Dickinson

Pauper's Gold
and
Wish Me Luck

PAN BOOKS

Pauper's Gold first published 2006 by Pan Books
Wish Me Luck first published 2007 by Pan Books

This omnibus first published 2008 by Pan Books
an imprint of Pan Macmillan Ltd
Pan Macmillan, 20 New Wharf Road, London N1 9RR
Basingstoke and Oxford
Associated companies throughout the world
www.panmacmillan.com

ISBN 978-0-330-50791-2

1 3 5 7 9 8 6 4 2

A CIP catalogue record for this book is available from
the British Library.

Typeset by SetSystems Ltd, Saffron Walden, Essex
Printed in the UK by CPI Mackays, Chatham ME5 8TD

Pauper's Gold

For David and Una Dickinson,
my brother and sister-in-law

Acknowledgements

I am very grateful to David and Mavis Holmes for their kind permission for me to use Cressbrook Mill in Derbyshire as the inspiration for part of this story. The former cotton mill has now been beautifully transformed by them into apartments – a far cry from the conditions in which spinners, weavers and apprentices once worked.

Because I never use real people as the basis for the characters in my novels, I always change the names of small towns and villages deliberately. But with larger towns and cities like Macclesfield, a town with a fascinating social history, I like to keep its rightful name. Although I mention the workhouse there, I must stress that the characters and story are entirely fictitious and have no relation whatsoever to any real inmates or staff. Similarly, I have named actual streets and buildings, but have peopled them with my own imaginary characters.

My grateful thanks to Professor Chris Wrigley of the School of History at Nottingham University, who recommended that I should read *The Hungry Mills* by Norman Longmate (Maurice Temple Smith, 1978). This story of the Lancashire cotton famine, 1861–5, was indeed inspirational. I also consulted several other books and papers in my research, the most noteworthy of which were *A History of Macclesfield* edited by C. Stella Davies (E. J. Morten, 1976) and *Life & Labour in Victorian Macclesfield* by George Longden (Neil Richardson, 1986).

Very special thanks to members of my family Helen and

Mike Lawton, Carole and Paul Cairns and David and Una Dickinson, who gave generously of their time and knowledge, supplied books, maps and photos, and took me on tours of Macclesfield. Thank you too to the staff of Macclesfield Library, the Silk Industry Museum and West Park Museum for their interest, practical guidance and help. And not forgetting other members of my family and friends who have also read and commented on the script: Robena and Fred Hill, Pauline Griggs and Linda and Terry Allaway. The help and encouragement of all of you means more to me than you can ever know.

One

May, 1854

'We'll get rid of her. That girl's been nothing but trouble since she came in here.' Cedric Goodbody belied his name for there was nothing 'good' about the man. He was thin and wiry with a rat-like face. His grey eyes, sharp and piercing, missed nothing. His frown deepened. 'If I'd known what I know now, I'd never have admitted her. Her or her mother. The woman had the gall to refuse to pick oakum, on the grounds that she's a silk worker and the rough work might injure her hands.'

He drummed his fingers impatiently on the desk in front of him. The room around him was cluttered with files and ledgers. Papers were strewn over the surface of his desk and piled in untidy heaps on the floor. He was sitting in the only chair in the room. Any visitor – even his wife, Matilda – was obliged to stand. Hands folded in front of her, she was facing him now across his desk. She was no better than her husband. Thin and gaunt with a waspish tongue, she took a malicious delight in the misfortunes of others. Together – as master and matron – they ran the Macclesfield work-house just within the rules laid down by the Board of Guardians, and outside them if they were sure they would not be found out.

'The girl's got spirit,' Matilda admitted grudgingly. 'I'll give her that. Nothing seems to depress her for long.'

'Can't you try punishing her? I'm sure you can find a reason,' Cedric growled. 'She's too pretty for her own good. That long, blonde hair and those bright blue eyes—'

'My word, Cedric, I've never known you to be so observant.' Matilda pursed her mouth.

Cedric ignored her sarcasm. 'But it's her singing all the time that gets on my nerves. I can't abide cheerful inmates. In all my years running workhouses, I've never known an inmate to *sing*!'

Matilda shrugged. 'There's no stopping her even when she's locked in the punishment room on bread and water.'

Cedric smiled cruelly. 'Well, I've an idea that'll put a stop to it. Critchlow's sent word he wants four more paupers. She can be one of them.'

Matilda raised her eyebrows. 'Is he *still* managing to keep that system going? I thought all the cotton mills'd given up having pauper apprentices.'

'Most of them have. With all the new laws about the employment of children, it was becoming uneconomic. But not for the Critchlows. Tucked away in that Derbyshire dale, they don't get many visits from the authorities. They just ignore any law that doesn't suit them. I'm just thankful they have carried it on. They've always been fair in their dealings with me.' He cast her a shrewd glance. He'd never actually told his wife about the money he received from the Critchlows in exchange for a steady supply of strong, healthy orphans to work long hours in their cotton mill. But he was sure she had guessed.

It seemed she had, for, 'You want to mind the Board don't find out,' was her tart reply.

'They won't as long as you don't tell 'em.' His eyes narrowed. 'There's only you 'n' me know about it. So watch that tongue of yours, woman.'

'But I thought Nathaniel Critchlow—'

'Oh, Nathaniel!' Cedric was scathing. 'I don't deal with him any more. He's getting past it. Going soft in his old age. No, it's Edmund – his son – I need to keep in with.'

'Well, you'll be sending him a barrel of trouble with that girl. Besides, I don't reckon the mother'll let you send young Hannah all the way into Derbyshire.' Matilda smirked. 'Whatever fine tales you tell her about how wonderfully her daughter will be looked after and taught a trade that'll be the making of her.'

'The mother'll have nothing to do with it. If I say the girl goes . . .' Cedric banged his clenched fist on the desk and papers fluttered to the floor, 'then she goes. She's young and strong. Just the sort Critchlow wants.' He ran his tongue around his thin lips, greedily anticipating another generous payment.

'Maybe,' Matilda murmured. 'But she's not biddable. She's a mite too much to say for herself.'

'Edmund Critchlow's got his methods of taming the wilful ones. He's got a punishment room just like us.'

Matilda sniffed. 'Well then, young Hannah will likely be spending most of her time there.'

The subject of their conversation was at that moment working in the laundry. Little light penetrated the filthy windows, and the huge room was filled with steam and the sharp smell of disinfectant. Three other girls and two older women besides Hannah toiled over the wash tubs. Their hands were wrinkled from the hot water, their faces red and their clothes drenched with sweat. Hannah was hanging dripping clothes onto the slats of a wooden rack, which she then hoisted to the ceiling for the clothes to dry. Above the noise of the sloshing water, Hannah's voice trilled pure and clear. 'How sweet the name of Jesus sounds . . .'

'Ah, bless 'er,' one of the women at the tubs murmured. 'That was me mother's favourite. Eh, but it brings back the memories.'

Rebecca, Hannah's mother, looked up worriedly. 'I'm sorry if it upsets you. I'll tell her to stop—'

'Don't you dare. You let your little girl sing,' Alice answered. 'I might shed a tear or two, but me memories're happy ones. I'll tell you summat, Rebecca. She brightens our days with her sunny smile and her merry singing. Come on,' she raised her voice. 'Let's all sing. Let's show 'em . . .' And in a raucous, tuneless voice she joined in the words of the hymn.

Rebecca shook her head in wonderment and smiled softly, marvelling at the way her twelve-year-old daughter could spread even the smallest spark of joy in this cheerless place. There were few occasions in the workhouse when the inmates felt like smiling – some had almost forgotten how. But since Rebecca and her daughter had arrived, there'd been more smiles and fond shaking of heads than ever before, as they heard Hannah's piping voice echoing through the vast building. She led the other youngsters in games in the women's exercise yard and, for a few minutes each day, she made them forget the drudgery and misery of their lives. With her blue eyes full of mischief and daring, the young girl had become the darling of all the inmates. For, though the men and boys were strictly segregated from the women and girls, they could still hear her over the wall from their yard, could hear the sound of playful laughter.

The women in the laundry room were startled into silence by a loud banging and only Hannah was left singing at the top of her voice.

'That's enough, girl,' the matron snapped, grasping Hannah's arm in a painful grip. 'The master wants to see you.'

'Why?' Hannah ceased her singing and dropped the rough blanket she was washing back into the tub. It splashed soapy suds onto the matron's pristine apron. Matilda shook the girl roughly. 'Now look what you've done. My word, I'll be glad to see the back of you.'

Hannah's eyes shone. 'We're leaving? Mam,' she called, 'we're getting out. We—'

'Not your mother, just you.'

Hannah's eyes widened. 'Oh no, I'm not going without me mam.'

'You'll do as you're told.'

Drying her hands on a piece of rough cloth, Rebecca came towards them. 'What is it, Matron?' she asked in her soft, gentle voice.

Before Matilda could reply, Hannah said, 'She says the master wants to see me. I'm leaving. Just me, not you. But I'm not going without you, Mam, I—'

The matron gave an exasperated sigh. 'You'd better both come along to his office. He can deal with the pair of you.'

Moments later, mother and daughter stood before the master's desk, but it was the young girl who fired the questions. 'Has someone come for us? Is it me Uncle Bill?'

Cedric smiled cynically. 'And which uncle might

that be?' He leered at Rebecca, standing quietly beside her daughter. 'I expect you had a lot of them, didn't you?'

The older woman blushed and hung her head, but Hannah's clear, innocent gaze darted between them. 'No,' she retorted. 'I've only one uncle. He's not me real uncle—'

'I bet he isn't,' Cedric muttered.

'He lived next door to us. He and me Auntie Bessie—'

'Hush, Hannah dear,' Rebecca said softly, touching the girl's arm. 'Let the master tell us.'

Hannah pressed her lips together, but her blue eyes still sparkled with indignation.

Cedric shuffled some papers in front of him. 'I've found the girl a position working in a cotton mill in Derbyshire. A lot of the youngsters go from here.' He stared hard at Rebecca, daring her to argue. 'She'll be well looked after, I assure you.'

Hannah spoke up again. 'What about me mam? Is she coming an' all?'

'No, there's no place for an older woman. At least, not ones with no experience.' He glanced at Rebecca again. 'You haven't worked in a mill before, have you?'

'Only in a silk mill here.'

'That'd be near enough, wouldn't it?' Hannah put in before the master could answer.

Cedric glowered. 'No, it wouldn't. Not the same thing at all.'

She opened her mouth to retort but Cedric held up his hand. 'I don't want to hear another word from you, girl. And if you take my advice, you'll learn to curb that runaway tongue of yours. It'll get you into a lot of trouble where you're going, if you're not careful.'

For once, Rebecca dared to question the master. 'I thought you said she'd be well treated?'

'She will – if she behaves herself. Mr Critchlow, the owner of the mill, is a good master, but he expects loyalty and obedience from *all* his workers.'

Rebecca bit her lip. 'I don't want her to go. She's too young to go all that way.'

'You have no say in the matter.' Cedric's lip curled. 'If you and your – er – offspring . . .' he laid insulting emphasis on the word, implying so much more, 'allow yourselves to become a burden on the parish, you have to pay the price. You're no longer free to decide your own future. You'll do what the Board of Guardians tells you. And they always take my recommendations.'

Again, Rebecca hung her head.

Cedric turned to Hannah. 'You're to be ready to leave tomorrow morning. You'll be going on the carrier's cart as far as Buxton and then he'll arrange for you and the others to be taken on to Wyedale Mill.'

It was an arrangement that had worked well for Cedric in the past. For a few coins the carrier would take the orphans part of the way and then pay a local carter to take them the few extra miles.

'Others?' Hannah piped up again. 'Who else is going?'

Cedric stood up, dismissing them curtly. 'You'll see in the morning. Just you mind you're ready and waiting.'

Two

It irritated Cedric Goodbody that he knew little more about Rebecca Francis and her daughter than he had on the day they'd knocked on the door of the workhouse and begged admittance. Rebecca was a quiet, reserved young woman, well liked by the other inmates and staff yet not forthcoming about her life before that day.

It was shame that stilled Rebecca's tongue. The humiliation of entering the workhouse lay heavily on her. Once, she too had laughed and sung – just like her lively, innocent daughter did now – but then she'd made the mistake of falling in love and everything had changed.

Rebecca had been born in a street of garret houses, three storeys high, occupied by weavers. Her father, Matthew, had his workroom in the top storey, its long window giving him light to carry on the trade of his father before him. Her mother, Grace, had worked in a silk mill. Though the family – like every other family around them – had suffered the ups and downs of the silk trade, Rebecca's young life had been a happy one. When her parents had married they'd lived with Matthew's widowed mother, and when Rebecca was born one year later Grandma Francis had looked after the infant whilst Grace returned to work in the mill.

At ten years old, Rebecca went to work eight hours a day in the mill.

'Hello there, young 'un,' James Gregory, the man who was the supervisor over the workforce of women and children, had greeted her. 'Going to be as good a worker as your mother, are yer?'

Rebecca, with her shy, brown eyes, her soft dark hair hidden beneath her bonnet, had nodded, gazing up at him in awe. James had bent down and touched her cheek. 'Don't be afraid of me, young 'un.' Gently he'd traced his finger round the outline of her face. 'You're far too pretty to be afraid of anyone.'

From that moment, Rebecca had been James Gregory's willing slave. She idolized him. Through the years as she grew, the other women teased her. 'Mr Gregory's little sweetheart, ain'tcha? But just remember, girl, he's got a wife at home and there's a little 'un on the way.'

By the time Rebecca was fifteen she had the shape and demeanour of a woman. Working alongside adults all day long – women who talked and laughed and joked, and who didn't trouble to curb their raucous tongues before the youngsters in their midst – Rebecca could not be ignorant of the facts of life. She knew full well that it was wrong to meet James Gregory in secret, knew it was dangerous to give herself to him.

But Rebecca was hopelessly, helplessly in love with James's blond, curling hair and merry blue eyes. He was tall and broad shouldered, with slim hips, and he carried himself proudly as if he truly believed he was destined for better things. Rebecca was utterly, selflessly loyal to him and when, inevitably, she found herself carrying his child, she refused to name him as the father. Gossip was rife through the mill, but Rebecca stubbornly refused to blame anyone but herself. When her daughter, Hannah, screamed her arrival into the cramped bedroom of the terraced house, there was no loving father present to welcome her, only a reluctant grandmother. Even the grandfather had disappeared to the nearest pub to be with his cronies and to try to blot out all thought of his daughter's shame. Tactfully, his friends asked no questions. What was going on in Matthew's home at that moment was women's business.

Overcrowded and at times a hotbed of gossip though the houses in their street might be, there was nevertheless a deep sense of neighbourliness, of protecting their own. As news of her arrival spread quickly, there was soon a constant stream of visitors at the door. Some bore gifts, others came just to see the child and the young mother, yet more with an excuse to wet the baby's head.

'She's a bonny 'un,' was the unanimous verdict. But, tactfully, they made no comment on the child's wispy blonde hair and bright blue eyes. Only amongst themselves, they nodded their heads and said, 'No mistaking whose kid she is.'

Kept in ignorance, Hannah's early life was happy. She lived in the close-knit community, was protected by it, too young to remember when her grandfather, Matthew, died only three years after her birth. Rebecca's wage now supported them, with a little help from the work Grace was able to do at home. Their landlord rented out Matthew's garret workroom to another weaver. For a while, Grace and Rebecca were terrified they would be turned out of their home. Thankfully, the weaver lived elsewhere and was happy to walk the couple of streets to his new workroom.

Of Hannah's father not a word was ever spoken.

Not until she was old enough to play in the street with the other children did she begin to understand the circumstances of her birth. Slowly, it dawned on her why her surname was the same as her mother's and her grandmother's. Cruel names were hurled at her and sometimes she found herself excluded from the other children's games. Hannah would toss her bright curls and smile at those taunting her. And beneath her breath she would sing to comfort herself. Little by little, she won them over and when the day came that her mother and grandmother insisted she should attend school, it was now the children from her own street who defended her against curious strangers.

The first really harsh blow to disturb her childhood came when Hannah was eight years old. Her grandmother, Grace, was taken ill with distressing sickness and diarrhoea and terrible leg cramps. Rebecca stayed at home from work to nurse her mother but after only three days Grace died. After a simple funeral attended by their neighbours, Rebecca and Hannah returned to the home that now seemed empty and soulless without the old lady who had been its centre.

'I'll have to go back to work,' Rebecca said in her soft voice. 'I'll see if Auntie Bessie next door will take care of you.'

'I can take care of meself, Mam,' Hannah had declared stoutly, but Rebecca had shaken her head. 'No, no, I won't have you left alone. Bessie won't mind.' Rebecca had smiled gently. 'She'll never notice another one amongst her brood.'

So Hannah had become a daily visitor to the overcrowded house next door where Bill and Bessie Morgan, their three sons and two daughters lived. The Morgan children were all older than Hannah but they took the lonely child in and treated her as if she were another sister. Peggy, the youngest at twelve, was the closest in age, but even she was already working at the mill. Bill and two of his sons worked in the top floor garret of the house and Bessie had her hands full caring for them all.

''Course she can come to us. She can 'elp me with me washing,' Bessie had said at once when Rebecca tentatively broached the subject. It was from Bessie Morgan, who sang all day long in her loud, tuneless voice, that Hannah, amongst the soap suds and steam of the back yard wash house, was to learn the words of all the hymns.

'We'll mind her,' Bessie had promised. 'You get back to your work, Rebecca, while you've still got a job to go to.' She had cast a knowing look at Rebecca, and the younger woman had felt the flush of embarrassment creep up her neck.

In the uncertain silk industry, Rebecca had kept her place at the mill even through hard times when many had been laid off. She was well aware it was whispered that it was only because she was James Gregory's mistress that she had kept her job. And, in a way, Rebecca had to admit that it was true. Whilst he'd never openly admitted to being the father of her child – and Rebecca maintained her steadfast silence – James Gregory had always made sure she'd a job at the mill. And though she was no longer his mistress – hadn't been from the day he'd learned she was pregnant – he still favoured her, much to the irritation of the other workers. If she was feeling tired or unwell, he'd find her easier work. He allowed her time off – with no questions asked – if Hannah was ill. The other women grumbled, but there was little they could do about it

12

other than to ostracize Rebecca. It was a lonely time for the young woman but she stuck it out. She'd no choice – hers was the only income her family had.

Hannah's time with the Morgan family was short lived. Life swiftly dealt Rebecca another harsh blow. In less than a year, James Gregory had left the mill. She had heard the news from the gossip that rippled amongst the mill workers.

''Ave you 'eard, 'ee's got himself another fancy piece. Daughter of a mill owner, no less. And her father's made him manager of one of his mills.'

'What about his wife and family? Gregory's married, ain't he?'

'Oh, didn't you know? His wife and kiddie died with the cholera last year. So he's fancy-free.'

'Is 'ee, by God! So, he's not marrying that girl – what's 'er name?'

'Rebecca Francis. Oh no. 'Ee's set his sights higher than 'er. And let me tell you something else. Once 'ee's gone from here, that little madam 'ad better watch out.'

And soon after James's departure, Rebecca was told that her 'services were no longer required at the mill'.

For a few months, she managed to pay the rent, though she grew thinner from worry and tramping the streets in search of work. By the January of 1851 there was no food in the house, no fuel to keep them warm, their winter clothes had been pawned, and she was hiding when the rent man called. Two months later, Rebecca and her young daughter were evicted from their home.

The workhouse was the only place they could go.

Three

'Now, have you got everything? How generous Mr Goodbody has been.' Rebecca fingered the clothes lying spread out on Hannah's bed. The garments – two shifts, two frocks, two aprons and two pairs of stockings – were not new, but Rebecca had washed and lovingly ironed and mended them. It was the final motherly act she was to be allowed to do for her daughter. 'And you must take care of this money. Two whole guineas,' Rebecca told her, handing her a cloth purse. 'Tie it round your neck for the journey, but you'll have to give it to . . . to whoever's in charge of you . . .' Her voice threatened to break, but she smiled bravely and added, 'Mind you're a good girl, won't you? Do as you're told and—'

Hannah's blue eyes brimmed with tears. She flung her arms around her mother's slim waist and hugged her tightly. 'I don't want to go. Don't let them send me away. I – I might never see you again.'

Though Rebecca embraced her fiercely in return and her voice trembled, she tried valiantly to make the words cheerful and hopeful. 'Of course you'll see me again. Once you've got settled in, you ask around. There might be a job for me there. I'm sure my experience in the silk mill will count for something, whatever Mr Goodbody says. You just mind you tell them about me. Don't forget, now will you?'

'Oh no, Mam. 'Course I won't.'

The cart pulled to a halt at the top of a steep hill.

'Right, out you get.' The old driver dropped the reins and climbed stiffly down from his seat. He walked to the back of the cart. 'Come on,' he said roughly. 'I ain't got all night.'

Three of the four children riding in the back scrambled out. Only Hannah made no move to obey him. 'You're not leaving us here. There's no sign of the mill and you were paid to take us all the way.'

The old man coughed juicily and wiped the back of his hand across his mouth. 'Well, this is as far as I'm going, missy. I'm on me way back to Buxton now. You do as you please. This is as far as I can take you. My old girl wouldn't make it back up this 'ere hill if I teks 'er down. You'll have to walk rest of the way. It's down there.' He pointed to the road, disappearing steeply down into the dale below them. 'Just follow that road. Mill's at far end. You can't miss it.'

As Hannah climbed down, she looked about her and, suddenly, she smiled. The sun was setting behind the hills, casting a golden glow over the slopes and glinting on the trees. Even the rough road on which they were standing was bathed in golden light.

'It's a pretty place,' Hannah murmured.

The man climbed back onto the front of his cart and picked up the reins. 'Aye, missy, take a good look at the sunshine. Pauper's gold, they call it. I reckon that's the only gold you'll ever see. And you won't be seeing much of that either – not in Critchlow's dismal mill, you won't.' He laughed loudly at his own joke and flapped the reins. The horse, as if knowing it was homeward bound, moved forward with an eager jerk. Within moments the cart was rattling back the way it had come, leaving the four youngsters standing forlornly in the road. Far below them a river wound its way through the deep valley between hills that seem to fold in on each other. They could see houses dotted here and there, and sheep in a line following a track along the hillside, making for home. But there was no sign of a building large enough to be a mill.

'Should we ask the way?' Luke jerked his thumb over his shoulder towards the Wyedale Arms behind them. Hannah glanced at it, but the door was shut and there seemed no sign of life. She was the eldest of the four – and the boldest – and the others were looking to her to take the lead. She felt a tiny, cold hand creep into hers and looked down into the small, white face of the youngest. Jane was only ten and small for her age. She had been born to a young widow in the workhouse who had died at her birth. She was truly an orphan. She looked exhausted by the day's travelling, her eyes huge in her pale, gaunt face. Tears were close. 'Are we lost?'

Hannah gave the child's hand a comforting squeeze. 'No, 'course we're not.' She glanced round at the two boys – twin brothers, Luke and Daniel Hammond – trying to instil confidence into her voice. 'Come on, you lot. It's down this hill, the man said. We'd best get going if we're to find it before dark.'

With more purpose in her step than she was feeling inside, and still holding Jane's hand, Hannah strode down the hill, the other two falling in behind them.

'Lead us, heavenly Father, lead us . . .' she began to sing.

She'd sung the hymn through once and was about to start again, when Luke said, 'How much further is it?'

'Dunno,' Hannah said cheerfully. 'Maybe we'll see it round the next bend.'

They walked on beneath the canopy of trees overhanging the lane as the shadows lengthened and the sun dipped out of sight. Dusk settled into the dale.

'I'm tired and me leg hurts,' Jane murmured.

'I'm hungry,' Daniel moaned.

Luke and Daniel had been left at the workhouse door five years earlier when their mother had died and their father couldn't cope with the lively six-year-olds. They hadn't seen him from that day to this and had given up hope of him ever coming back for them. Now, coming up to twelve years old, they were excited at the prospect of a real job. They were small and thin like most of the children in the workhouse, but they were fit and healthy with the same mop of unruly light brown hair, hazel eyes and cheeky grins. Their teeth were surprisingly good, white and even. Just the sort of boys that Mr Critchlow was looking for, Cedric Goodbody had assured them.

But now, they too were tired, their excitement waning.

'It can't be much further,' Hannah said, almost dragging the weary little girl alongside her.

The shape of a house loomed up on the left-hand side of the road.

'Is that it?' Jane pointed. 'Is that the mill?'

Hannah eyed it doubtfully. 'I don't think so. It's not

17

big enough.' She paused and added, 'Is it?' She wasn't exactly sure just how big a cotton mill was, but she imagined it must be at least the size of the silk mill where her mother had worked.

'That's a farm,' Luke said scathingly and his twin nodded. 'It smells like one.'

Hannah glanced at them. She'd only known town streets with no trees or fields. The only animals she'd seen had been scrawny dogs and cats and most of them had been strays. So, she didn't argue, aware that the boys had known six years of life before coming into the workhouse. Who was she to say that they hadn't seen a farm?

As if answering her unspoken question, Luke said, 'Our dad worked on the land, but he moved about from job to job.'

Daniel nodded. 'Every Lady Day, we'd be packing up and moving to a new farm.'

She saw the two boys glance at each other and knew they were remembering happier times.

'Come on, then. Best walk a bit further,' Hannah said briskly, trying to inject some encouragement into her tone. But they'd gone only a few yards further when they came to a crossroads. The lane to the left led to the farm, but they'd no idea which of the other two roads they should take.

'Which way now?' Luke asked

'I don't know.' Perplexed, Hannah glanced this way and that.

'Let's ask at the farm,' Luke suggested. 'They'll know where the mill is.'

Hannah pulled a face, reluctant to knock on a stranger's door, unsure of the welcome that four work-house brats would receive. 'All right then,' she agreed diffidently, aware of how tired they all were. They were hungry and thirsty too. She turned and frowned at the two boys behind her. 'But just you two mind you behave yourselves.'

They grinned up at her with identical saucy expressions. 'Yes, miss,' they chorused.

The four of them trooped through the gate, the boys closing it carefully behind them. 'You always have to shut gates on a farm,' Luke said.

'Oh – yes – right,' Hannah nodded. She wasn't sure why it was necessary. There was no one about in the yard but, again, she didn't argue.

As they neared the back door, there was a scuffle, and a black and white collie appeared out of a kennel set to one side of the back door and began to bark.

Jane gave a terrified scream and clutched at Hannah's skirt, hiding behind her. Even the two boys took a couple of steps backwards. Hannah too jumped, but she pulled in a deep breath and held out her hand. 'Here, boy. Good dog. Nice dog.'

'He might not be as nice as you think,' Luke muttered. 'He's a sheepdog. A working dog.'

'And a guard dog,' Daniel added.

But the animal ceased its barking, whined, wagged its tail and licked Hannah's outstretched hand.

'Well, would you look at that!' Luke grinned at her. 'Charm the birds off the trees, you could.'

In the workhouse, males, females, girls and boys had been strictly separated, but on the few occasions they had glimpsed one another, Hannah and Luke had liked what they'd seen. And now here they were, having travelled together all day, standing outside the back door of a farmhouse seeking help.

'Go on then,' Luke encouraged. 'Get on with it.'

Hannah glanced at the other three as she raised her hand to knock, seeing a mixture of trepidation and hope on their weary, pinched faces. It was exactly how she felt as she turned to face whoever should open the door.

They heard heavy footsteps and then the door was pulled open. A tall, well-built, red-faced woman wearing a white bib apron stood looking down at them.

'Come away in.' She smiled and held the door wider open.

It seemed they were expected, yet Hannah still hesitated. 'Is this the mill?'

'Lord bless you, no. This is Rushwater Farm. The mill's further on . . .' She jerked her thumb over her shoulder. 'Along this road.' Her smile broadened so that her round cheeks almost made her eyes close. 'I guessed that's where you're heading. I'm used to youngsters coming to my door. Eh, dear me—' She shook her head and her smile faded. 'If I'd a pound for every child who's knocked at my door to be fed, I'd be a wealthy woman.'

'Oh, we . . . we only wanted to ask the way. We weren't sure, you see, which road—' Hannah began.

'Come along in, all of you,' the woman stood back and beckoned. A mouth-watering smell wafted from her kitchen and the two boys, forgetting their promise to Hannah, pushed forward.

Drawn by her own hunger and encouraged by the woman's kindly, beaming face, Hannah stepped over the threshold. Jane, still clutching Hannah's hand, followed.

'Sit down, sit down. You've had a long journey, I'll be bound, sitting in Bert Oldfield's draughty cart.'

The four children gaped at her. 'How . . . how did

you know . . . ?' Hannah began, but the woman chuckled. 'You're from Macclesfield workhouse, aren't you? You've come on the carrier's cart to Buxton and then Bert's brought you to the top of the hill. But the wily old bird won't bring you all the way down in case his scrawny horse can't get back up again. Am I right?'

The children glanced at each other and then smiled. 'How d'you know all that?' Luke asked.

'Because it happens every year, that's why. When Mr Critchlow wants more children to work in his mill, he sends word to the master of the workhouse and along you all come. Bin happening for years.'

'Why . . . why does he need so many?' Hannah asked. A sudden shiver ran through her. She wasn't sure she should have asked the question. She might not like the answer.

'Ah well, now,' the woman turned away, busying herself over a huge pan of stew sitting on the hob of the kitchen range, 'I wouldn't know about that.'

Hannah stared at her stooping back. She had the feeling that the woman knew only too well, but didn't want to tell them. She sighed, but as a plate of stew and dumplings was set before her, she forgot about her worries and concentrated on filling her empty belly.

The farmer's wife sat down opposite. She let them eat their fill before she asked, 'Now, tell me your names. Mine's Mrs Grundy.'

'This is Jane Pickering and these two are twins.'

Mrs Grundy nodded. 'Aye, I can see that. Like as two peas in a pod, aren't you?'

'Luke and Daniel Hammond and I'm Hannah. Hannah Francis.'

The woman smiled at them and nodded, 'I'm pleased

21

to meet you all. And don't forget, if you want to visit me any time – any time at all – there'll always be a welcome for you at Rushwater Farm. You'll not meet my husband today. He's busy with the evening milking now, but he'll be pleased to see you an' all. He loves children too.'

Hannah rose from her chair. 'You've been very kind, Mrs Grundy,' she said politely, 'and we'd love to stay longer, but perhaps we'd best be going. Could you please tell us which road we should take to the mill?'

''Course I can,' the woman said, heaving herself up from her chair and leading them to the back door. She walked out of the yard to the road and then pointed. 'Take the road on the left here and just keep on. You'll soon see it. Mind you,' she went on, 'you'd be best to go straight to the apprentice house. Go up the steep slope at the side of the mill to the row of houses directly behind it. It's the third building along. A white house. Ask for Mr or Mrs Bramwell. They're the superintendents. Now, off you go. They'll be expecting you and it'll be dark soon.'

She stood watching the children walk along the lane until they were out of sight.

'God be with you, my dears,' she murmured, thankful that the youngsters couldn't see the tears in her eyes.

Four

'Is . . . is that it? Is that the mill?' Luke's voice was suddenly scared. 'It's awfully big, isn't it?'

The four children stood in the pillared gateway and looked at the place where they'd come to live and work. There were three huge buildings. The biggest was rectangular and set with its back against a steep hill, its rows of numerous small-paned windows facing down the dale. Set at right angles to that was another oblong shape, and the third, a square building, stood at the end of the second one.

'Look at those houses built on the hill behind it,' Luke murmured. 'You'd think they'd fall off, wouldn't you?'

'I can hear water,' Daniel murmured.

Luke turned suddenly and darted across the road. 'There's a big pond here and a stream that goes under the road.' He re-crossed the lane. 'And it comes out here. Then it goes in front of the mill.' He pointed to the bubbling brook. 'And joins the river over there. On the far side of the mill. See?'

They were all silent, staring about them. Jane, white-faced, cowered behind Hannah.

'Come on,' Hannah said briskly at last. 'We'd better go and find this Mrs Bramwell.' She smiled down at the younger girl and gave her cold hand a comforting squeeze. Jane dragged her feet, and glanced apprehensively over her shoulder. 'I don't like it,' she whispered. 'It's so big. I want to go home. I want to go back to the workhouse.'

'We can't,' Hannah said. 'There's no one to take us back. Besides, we've been sent here. At least let's give it a try. It might be better than the workhouse.'

'Anything's got to be better—' Luke began.

'Than the workhouse,' Daniel finished.

They climbed the steep hill to the first row of houses perched just above the mill.

'This end one looks like a school,' Luke said excitedly. He grasped hold of the high window ledge and hauled himself up to peer in the window. 'There's boys and girls sitting at desks.'

'At this time of night?' Hannah stood on tiptoe, trying to see in, but she was too low down, and she had no intention of scrambling up the side of the rough wall and tearing her clean dress.

'It'll be after they've worked at the mill,' Luke said. 'There's a boy asleep at his desk. Oh!'

Suddenly, he let himself drop to the ground.

'What? What is it?'

Luke was laughing. 'The master saw him sleeping and cracked his cane on the desk. The lad didn't half jump. He thought he'd been shot.'

'Do you think we'll go to school?' Jane asked quietly.

'I don't know,' Hannah said. 'Maybe for a few hours a week.' She sighed. 'But what I do know is – we've been sent here to work.'

They moved on, dragging their feet now that they had seen the other children. Suddenly, however strict school life might be under a cane-wielding teacher, they yearned to join those children instead of entering

24

a new and frightening world. At least a classroom –
even a different classroom with strange children – was
a familiar world to them. There had been a schoolroom at the workhouse with a master for the boys and
a school-marm for the girls. Of the four of them, only
Jane couldn't read or write. She'd been a sickly child,
and her schooling, even in the workhouse, had been
spasmodic.

They knocked on the door of the white house, next
door but one to the school, and waited. A girl, not
much older than they were, opened it.

'Come in, the missis is waiting for you.'

They trooped after her, through the large kitchen
and a hallway, and were shown into a small, stuffy
room where a woman was sitting at a desk going
through some papers.

The girl bobbed a curtsy. 'The new ones have
arrived, Mrs Bramwell.'

'Thank you, Mary.'

The girl left the room, closing the door quietly
behind her, leaving the four new arrivals standing
nervously just inside the door. The woman didn't even
look up but continued to write notes at the edge of
one of the sheets of paper. They waited for what
seemed an age, until Jane tugged at Hannah's hand
and whispered urgently, 'I need the privy, Hannah. I
need it now.'

'Hush,' Hannah whispered. 'You'll have to wait.'

'I can't.' Jane's voice rose in a wail. 'I'll do it. Oh –
oh, I am . . .'

The woman looked up. 'Take her out this minute.
It's out the back.'

Hannah pulled open the door, dragging Jane with
her. She rushed back the way they had come, startling

25

the young girl, Mary, as they hurried through the kitchen. Hannah paused briefly. 'Where is it? Where's the privy?'

Mary pointed. 'Out the door and down the path to the left. It's the—'

Hannah waited to hear no more but hustled the unfortunate Jane out of the door and along the path. 'There it is. Hurry up.'

Moments later, Jane emerged from the wooden hut. She was calmer now, but tears ran down her cheeks. 'I'm sorry, Hannah.'

'Yes, well, you should've said you wanted to go before we went in.'

Jane sniffed loudly. 'Sorry.'

Hannah took her hand and smiled down at her. The little girl was obviously weary from the journey and fearful of the strange place and people. They all were. 'Come on, we'll have to go back.'

Mrs Bramwell was a tall, thin woman. In her early forties, she nevertheless looked old to the young children. She had a long, straight nose and grey eyes. Her mouth was small, with thin lips that rarely smiled. She was wearing a black dress with a white apron, and her hair was hidden beneath a white cotton bonnet tied beneath her chin, its white frill framing her face.

When they entered the room once more, Hannah saw the telltale puddle on the polished wooden floor. Mrs Bramwell rose from her desk, and, standing before them with her hands folded in front of her, she scrutinized them slowly.

'Well now, so you're the four urchins Mr Goodbody's chosen to send us this time.' Her gaze rested upon Luke and Daniel and she sniffed. 'Hmm. Boys, eh? And twins by the look of you. Mr Critchlow prefers girls. So much less trouble.'

Luke dared to laugh out loud. 'Her won't be.' He jerked his thumb towards Hannah. 'Her's as bad as any boy. Worse.'

Mrs Bramwell's glance swivelled to Hannah.

'Well, we'll see about that, young lady, won't we?'

Hannah bobbed a curtsy as she had seen this woman's maid do. 'I'll be as good as gold here, ma'am. I promise.'

Mrs Bramwell nodded. 'You certainly will,' she said firmly. Her words had an ominous ring. 'Now,' she went on briskly. 'I expect you're hungry after your journey.' She paused and there was the briefest flicker of amusement as she added drily, 'Or has the good Mrs Grundy been feeding you her stew and dumplings?'

The four youngsters glanced at each other.

Hannah's honest gaze met the woman's eyes. 'Yes, ma'am. We stopped – just to ask the way – and she was very kind . . .' Her voice trailed away. Had they done wrong? Were they all in trouble already?

But the stern-faced woman was nodding. 'It does you credit, girl, that you haven't lied to me. For that, you'll all still be given supper.' She sniffed. 'I doubt that skinflint Goodbody ever fed you properly. You'll find Mr Critchlow – Mr Nathaniel Critchlow, that is – a fair man, a caring man, but in return he demands hard work and utter loyalty from all his employees, *especially* from his young apprentices.'

The four youngsters stared at her, and then murmured in chorus, 'Yes, ma'am.'

'Very well then. Come along and I'll show you where you're to sleep.'

As the four children began to troop out of the room, Mrs Bramwell pointed down at the floor. 'You!' She prodded Jane with a sharp finger. 'When I've shown you the dormitory, you can fetch a bucket of water and a cloth from Mary and wash this floor.'

'I'll do it, ma'am,' Hannah began. 'Jane's only little and she's tired. She—'

'Did I ask you to do it, girl?'

'No, ma'am, but—'

'Then you'll oblige me by holding your tongue.'

Jane began to cry, and Hannah faced the superintendent, her mouth a determined line. She was about to protest further, but she felt Luke tug on her arm and hiss, 'Leave it, Hannah.'

Mrs Bramwell led the way up the stairs, keys jangling from a chain around her waist. First she took them to the boys' dormitory, where Luke and Daniel were shown the square wooden box-like bed, set on legs, with a straw palliasse and one blanket.

'You sleep two to a bed. Clean clothes every Sunday and clean sheets once a month. You wear your best clothes for chapel service on Sunday morning, after which you come back here for your dinner. We haven't got a chapel in the village, but a preacher comes to the schoolroom. In the afternoon, I teach the girls to sew, and the boys have more schooling. Unless, of course, there's work to be done in the mill, cleaning machinery and such, that can only be done on a Sunday.'

Hannah was scandalized. 'Don't we get any free time?'

'The devil finds work for idle hands. That's Mr Critchlow's motto. We live by it.' A note of bitterness crept into the woman's tone as she added, 'We all do. Now, you girls follow me.'

28

She led the way to a door, unlocked it, ushered the girls through it and then re-locked it.

'Boys and girls are separated.'

'Nothing new there, then,' Hannah muttered.

'What?' Mrs Bramwell snapped.

'Nothing, ma'am,' Hannah said brightly.

'Hm!' Mrs Bramwell frowned doubtfully. She was going to have to watch this one, she was thinking. A mite too much to say for herself had Hannah Francis.

'Here we are – this is your dormitory.' They entered a long room containing beds, just like the boys' room, but there were even more here. On each side of the long room was a row of ten truckle beds, set side by side, with scarcely an inch of space between them. There was even a row of five beds set end to end in the centre of the room. Twenty-five beds, Hannah counted. There was only one girl there, sitting on a bed at the far end of the room. She looked up apprehensively, and when she saw Mrs Bramwell she bit her lip.

'What are you doing here, Hudson?'

The girl ran her tongue nervously around her lips. 'I didn't feel well, ma'am. Mr – Mr Edmund said I could come home early.'

Colour suffused Mrs Bramwell's neck and crept up into her face. 'I – see,' she said tightly. She hesitated for a moment, then she moved towards the girl, leaving Hannah and Jane standing near the door.

Mrs Bramwell spoke to her in tones so low that Hannah couldn't hear what was said. Then she saw the girl shake her head, her eyes lowered.

'Very well, then,' Mrs Bramwell said on a sigh as she came back to Hannah and Jane. 'Hudson will tell you anything you need to know.' Drily, she added,

'Since she's here, she can make herself useful.' She walked towards the door leading to the stairs, turning back only to point at Jane. 'And don't forget to mop my floor.'

Jane gave a tearful hiccup.

When the superintendent had left the room, Hudson came bouncing towards them, her hazel eyes sparkling, her wide mouth smiling a welcome. Her hair, a mousy colour, was none the less curly and shining with cleanliness. She was a pretty girl, Hannah decided, and probably two or three years older than they were, for already she had a womanly body that was still evident beneath the long skirt and shapeless white cotton smock. But she didn't look ill, Hannah thought fleetingly, and couldn't resist saying, 'Are you feeling better?'

The girl threw back her head and laughed aloud. 'I wasn't ill. Mr Edmund sent for me and then let me leave work early.'

Hannah was curious. 'Why did he do that?'

Hudson stared at her for a moment and then grinned. 'You ask too many questions for a young 'un. Don't worry, he'll not bother with you. Not for a few years, anyway. Mind you,' the girl murmured thoughtfully, 'you're just the type Mr Edmund likes. You'll be a beauty one day, an' no mistake. Then you'll have to watch out. Know what I mean?'

Twelve-year-old Hannah wasn't sure that she did. So far, her mother and grandmother had sheltered her, protected her. With the strict segregation of the sexes in the workhouse, the longest time she'd ever spent in the company of boys had been on the journey here with Luke and Daniel. But, not wishing to appear ignorant, she smiled and nodded.

Briskly, Hudson changed the subject. 'You can sleep over here,' she went on, leading them to a bed next to hers. 'You have to share. We all do.' She paused and eyed them up and down.

Nettled by the girl's scrutiny, Hannah lifted her chin. 'Will we do, then?'

For a moment the girl looked startled. She put her head on one side and said offhandedly, 'Yeah. You look all right.' Then suddenly she grinned, and to Hannah's surprise flung her arms around each of them in turn. ''Course you'll do. We all get on well together.' She pulled a wry face. 'Most of the time, anyway. Case of having to, really, when we're living and working so close. Still, we're pretty well treated here – if we behave ourselves,' she added with a note of caution. 'What's your names? Mine's Nell. Nell Hudson. Put your things over there and we'd best go down for supper. The others'll be coming from school in a minute.'

Hannah introduced them both and then added, 'Jane's had a bit of an accident. Where can she rinse her underclothes out?'

Nell pulled a face. 'She can't. She'll have wear them until we get our clean clothes on Sunday.' She smiled down at the little girl. 'Don't worry. They'll soon dry. Come on, let's get down to supper. I'm starving. Mind you, I'm always starving.'

Jane tugged at Hannah's arm and whispered, 'What about her floor?'

'Yes, yes, we'll see Mary when we get downstairs.'

'You'll come with me, won't you, Hannah?' the little girl begged.

Hannah sighed. It would likely get her into trouble, but she said, 'Yes, 'course I will.'

31

When Jane knocked timidly on the door of Mrs Bramwell's room, with Hannah close on her heels carrying a bucket and floor cloth, there was no answer.

'Go on,' Hannah whispered. 'Open it. Maybe she's not there.'

The girl opened the door and peeped inside. 'No, she isn't.'

'Come on, quick then. Let's do it before she comes back.'

Jane opened the door wider and they crept into the room. Hannah dropped to her knees and began to mop the floor, wringing out the cloth in the bucket of hot water.

'Do hurry,' Jane urged, hopping from one foot to the other. 'She might come back in a minute.'

'There, that's all done,' Hannah said, throwing the cloth into the bucket. 'Come on, let's—'

She was in the act of scrambling up when the door opened, and Hannah saw a pair of feet – surprisingly dainty feet in button boots – then the hem of a long black skirt. Up and up to the trim waist and gently rounded bosom. Then she was looking into Mrs Bramwell's severe face.

'So – you disobeyed me.' Ethel Bramwell sighed. She and her husband were strict in their running of the apprentice house – they had to be – but they always tried to be just and fair. She didn't want to punish this new girl so soon. She liked to give all the youngsters time to settle in, time to learn the rules. But this girl had deliberately flouted her direct instruction, and couldn't be allowed to get away with it. If Ethel Bramwell or her husband Arthur relaxed their authority even for a moment, these unruly little tykes would take advantage, and mayhem would result.

'You, child,' she pointed at Jane. 'Take that bucket back to Mary and get your supper.'

Jane picked up the bucket and scuttled out of the room. As Hannah made to follow her, the superintendent put a heavy hand on her shoulder. 'Not you. You and I, girl, need to have a little chat.'

She shut the door and propelled Hannah to stand in the centre of the room. Then she sat down on a couch, spread her skirt, folded her hands in her lap and looked up at the girl.

'What am I to do with you, miss?'

Hannah smiled, her blue eyes sparkling with mischief. 'Well, if I was still at the workhouse, I'd be given no supper.'

Mrs Bramwell fought to keep a straight face. 'Full of Mrs Grundy's excellent stew, that would be no hardship, would it?'

Hannah wrinkled her brow, giving the matter serious thought. 'No, I don't suppose it would. In that case, then, I'd be sent to the punishment room. D'you have one here?'

'Indeed we do, miss. So, is that where you think I should send you?'

Hannah gave an exaggerated sigh. 'I suppose so, ma'am.'

'Then you'll spend the next hour in the punishment room whilst everyone else has their supper. It'll give you a taste of what to expect in the future, should you choose to disobey me again.'

'Yes, ma'am,' Hannah said meekly.

Mrs Bramwell rose from the couch, her keys jangling. For a moment she stood looking down at the girl. 'Why did you do it, Francis?'

As in the workhouse, Hannah realized that they would

33

all be addressed by their surname. But, just as she always had, she refused to refer to her friends in such a way.

'Jane's ten, ma'am, but she's small for her age an' very shy and frightened. I was just trying to look after 'er. She's got no mother or father.'

'So, why does that make her different? You're all orphans.'

Hannah shook her head. 'I'm not. I've got a mother. She—'

Mrs Bramwell's mouth dropped open. 'You – you've got a mother?' Hannah blinked. The superintendent made it sound as if it were another crime. 'But – but you're all supposed to be orphans. From the workhouse. Paupers.'

Hannah smiled. 'Oh, we're from the workhouse, and we're certainly paupers. But my mam's still there.'

'Is she indeed?' Mrs Bramwell murmured.

'Yes, ma'am, and . . .' Hannah took the plunge. 'And I was wondering if there was any work here for her. She's worked in a silk mill, but I'm sure—'

Hannah got no further. Mrs Bramwell shook her head vehemently. 'Oh no. We can't have any relatives of the apprentices here. It'd lead to all kinds of trouble. Oh no, it's out of the question, and if you take my advice, you'll keep it very quiet that you've got a mother. Mr Edmund wouldn't like that at all. Goodbody's only supposed to send orphans.'

'Why?' Hannah asked candidly.

Ethel gasped. 'You've got some cheek, girl. You'd better learn to watch your tongue, else you'll find yourself spending more time in the punishment room than out of it.'

'But why should he only send orphans?' Hannah persisted.

Mrs Bramwell gripped her arm. 'Never you mind that, girl. Just learn to do as you're told and not ask so many questions.'

The superintendent marched the girl up the stairs to a little room at the end of the attic storeroom. She opened the door with a key on her bunch and thrust Hannah inside. 'We'll see if an hour or so in there'll teach you a lesson.'

The door slammed, the key turned in the lock, and Hannah was alone. The whitewashed room was completely bare except for a rough blanket thrown in one corner on the cold, bare floor. Hannah went to the window and looked out. Night had fallen in the dale. There was no pauper's gold illuminating the hillside now and sparkling on the river. The blackness was complete.

She pressed her forehead against the cold pane and began to sing softly. 'Abide with me; fast falls the eventide . . .'

About to turn away, Ethel Bramwell paused in astonishment and stood still. 'Bless me,' she murmured. 'The child is singing.'

Never, in all her born days, as she would tell her husband later, had she ever heard any child sing when locked in the punishment room. Cry, scream, rage, bang on the door to be let out, but never, ever, had she heard them sing!

Five

Hannah was let out in time to go straight to bed. When she entered the dormitory, Jane ran straight to her, arms stretched wide, tears running down her face. 'Oh, Hannah, I'm so sorry, it was all my fault.'

Hannah hugged the girl. 'Don't worry,' she said, kissing the top of Jane's head and stroking her long brown hair, now released from its plait for the night. 'It's not as bad in there as the room at the workhouse. At least there's a window. I 'spect it's quite a nice view in the daytime.'

'But aren't you hungry?' Jane's mouth still trembled. 'You missed supper.'

Hannah laughed and rubbed her stomach. 'What, with all that stew Mrs Grundy gave us? No, I'm fine. Now, let's get you into bed. Dry your tears and we'll snuggle down together.'

As they began to undress down to their shifts, some of the other girls clustered around them, staring at the newcomers. Nell shouldered her way through and began the introductions, reeling off names so fast that after a moment Hannah laughed. 'Oh, stop, stop. I'll never remember.'

'You'll get to know us all soon.' Nell laughed good-naturedly. 'You'll be sick of the sight of us all in a bit 'cos we never get away from each other.'

Again Hannah nodded, but silently she was thinking, *Well, I will. I'll get out of here sometimes. Walk down the lane to see that nice Mrs Grundy. Climb the hills and . . .*

'Come on, we'd best get into bed,' Nell shooed the others away. 'She'll be up in a minute.'

The 'she' was Mrs Bramwell, who walked through both the girls' and the boys' dormitories to make sure they were all in bed, to make sure they were all still there.

The only segregation between the boys and the girls in the apprentice house was in the sleeping arrangements. Everywhere else they mingled freely. It was still dark when the door of the dormitory was flung open and a tall, broad-shouldered man with a stick walked between the beds, banging the end of each one to wake them.

'Time to get up.'

Dragging themselves out of bed and shivering in the cold, the girls dressed hurriedly.

'Quick as you can,' Nell whispered, 'else you'll not get a turn in the privy before we have to leave for the mill.'

'What about breakfast?' Hannah asked.

'They bring it to the mill at eight o'clock. We can't stop working, you just have to snatch it when you can.'

Summoned by the bell in the tower on the roof of the main building, they hurried down the steep hill towards the mill, following the clatter of the other children's clogs.

Hannah greeted Luke and Daniel. 'You all right? Sleep all right?'

'Not really,' Luke yawned. 'There was a boy in the next bed to us. Joe, I think his name is. Well, he—'

'Snored,' Daniel added.

'How about you?' Luke asked.

'Slept like a log. We were both tired.'

Luke grinned. 'Is it true you were sent to the punishment room last night?'

Hannah laughed wryly. 'Yeah. Made a good start, didn't I?'

'Whatever did you do? You've only been here five minutes. I'd've thought even you could've kept your nose clean for that long.'

Hannah pulled a face and murmured, 'I'll tell you sometime.' With her eyes, she gestured towards Jane running alongside her.

Luke glanced from one to the other. 'Ah, right.'

Jane said nothing. She was still clinging to Hannah's hand as if she would never let it go.

'Don't we get breakfast before we start work?' Daniel grumbled as they passed through the gate into the mill yard.

Hannah repeated what Nell had told them, and Luke murmured, 'You know, I reckon this could be worse than the workhouse.'

For once, Hannah said nothing. She had a feeling that he could well be right.

A man was standing by the door into the nearest building. At the sight of him, the children behind them began to run forward, passing the four newcomers until they were left at the back, the last to arrive before him. He was more smartly dressed than the workmen hurrying into the mill from all directions. He wore black trousers, a waistcoat and jacket, with a crisp, white shirt and red necktie. Whereas all the workmen wore caps, this man wore a black top hat.

'Ah, you're the new ones. How do?' As he stroked his drooping moustache and long sideburns, Hannah noticed that the third and fourth fingers on his left hand were missing. His voice was gruff and his face pock-marked, but she thought his brown eyes were kindly.

The four youngsters stared up at him wordlessly, until Hannah shook herself, cleared her throat, and said politely, 'Good morning, Mr Critchlow.'

The man stared a moment and then threw back his head. His laughter echoed through the morning mist shrouding the hilltops. 'Lord bless you, I'm not Mr Critchlow. I'm his overlooker, Ernest Scarsfield. I work for him just the same as you're going to.'

Hannah's gaze travelled upwards to marvel at the grand hat he was wearing.

Reading her thoughts, he laughed again. 'Ah, now you're admiring my top hat, aren't you?' Hannah grinned and nodded. The man's eyes twinkled and he bent forward, resting his hands on his knees. 'Well, you see, that's my sign of authority in this place. When folks see my top hat coming, they know they've to be working hard.' He winked and chuckled. 'But I'm sure I'm not going to have any trouble from you four, now am I?'

They smiled a little uncertainly as Mr Scarsfield scrutinized them. *Dear me*, he was thinking as his glance rested upon Jane, *they're sending them younger and younger. This little one looks no more than eight years old*. 'From the workhouse, are you?'

'Yes, sir,' Hannah answered, once again taking the lead.

'You needn't call me "sir", lass. You call Mr Critch-low "sir".' He sniffed, 'And Mr Edmund too, I sup-pose. But you call me "Mr Scarsfield". Now, follow me and I'll take you to Mr Critchlow's office. You have to sign a paper first and then we'll see what jobs we can set you to do.'

They followed him across the yard and in through a door at the end of the main building, up spiral stone steps to the first floor.

At another door, Ernest Scarsfield paused and turned to say, 'This first room is what we call the counting house. It's where Mr Roper sits to do all the bookwork. Beyond that is the master's office. Mr Nathaniel Critchlow is the owner of the mill, but his son, Mr Edmund, is in the business too now. He's the manager of the mill, really.' He leaned a little closer and lowered his voice, as if imparting a confidence. 'The old man still likes to keep his hand in, but it's really Mr Edmund who runs the place.' Ernest straight-ened up and winked. 'With me to help him, of course.'

The children smiled dutifully, yet they were all feeling apprehensive, not knowing what to expect. Even Hannah felt her knees trembling.

Ernest knocked on the door, and, hearing a murmur from within, opened it, standing aside to usher the children ahead of him. Finding herself once more in the lead, Hannah took a deep breath and stepped into the room. Jane, though still clinging to her hand, managed to hide behind Hannah. The two boys fol-lowed, with Mr Scarsfield bringing up the rear and closing the door behind him.

A man – thin, sour-faced and already balding though only in his thirties – was perched on a stool at a high desk, hunched over it, and writing in a thick, leather-bound ledger. He was dressed in sombre black from head to foot, the only relief being his stiffly starched white collar and blue silk cravat.

'Morning, Roper,' Mr Scarsfield said cheerfully, but he didn't pause in moving the children on towards a door halfway down the left-hand side of the room.

The man at the desk glanced at the children with grey, lifeless eyes over the top of his small, steel-framed spectacles. His only reply to Ernest Scarsfield's greeting was a disapproving sniff.

Mr Scarsfield opened the door to the inner office and stepped in first this time.

'Good morning, sir,' he greeted the man sitting behind the desk in the centre of the room. This time, Hannah noticed, his tone was far more deferential.

'Morning, Scarsfield.' His glance rested on the four youngsters. 'Well, well, and who have we here?'

The portly man, with a red face, thinning grey hair and long bushy side-whiskers, spread his podgy hands on the desk in front of him. He was dressed in a black frock coat, dark grey trousers and a light grey waistcoat, with a black stock knotted beneath a white, stand-up collar. Hannah had never seen anyone dressed so grandly in all her life.

'Mr Goodbody's latest arrivals, sir,' Ernest Scarsfield said. 'Now, tell Mr Critchlow your names. You first, lass.' He tapped Hannah's shoulder.

The children spoke in turn. Jane's voice was scarcely audible and Daniel mumbled, but Hannah and Luke spoke up fearlessly.

'Have they brought everything they should have?' Mr Critchlow glanced towards his overlooker.

'I'm sorry, sir. I haven't checked with Mrs Bramwell. They only arrived late last night.'

Mr Critchlow looked impatient. He turned back to Hannah. 'You've been given some clothes?'

She nodded.

'And two guineas?'

Reluctantly, Hannah nodded.

'Have you got it with you?'

The four youngsters glanced at each other and then nodded. All of them had had the sense to carry it, fearing that if they left it in the apprentice house, it might disappear. They'd no way of knowing at this moment just how honest their fellow apprentices were. If their life in the workhouse was anything to go by, then they should trust no one.

'It's to be handed to my clerk, Mr Roper, as you go out.'

'But it's ours,' Hannah burst out.

Mr Critchlow frowned. 'It's to pay for any fines you might incur.'

'Fines? What – what fines?'

'We call them stoppages. We fine you for bad behaviour, lateness or poor work.' He frowned at them over his bushy eyebrows. 'And of course, the more serious the crime, the more you will have to pay. Mr Roper keeps a ledger. Now,' Mr Critchlow went on briskly. 'We've a paper for you to sign. Has it been explained to you what this paper is?'

Four heads shook in unison.

Nathaniel Critchlow reached into a drawer in his desk, and brought out eight sheets of paper covered in small, neat writing. He cleared his throat. 'This is what we call an indenture. It's a legal piece of paper. We each have a copy and we each have to sign both copies.' He pointed a finger towards them and then at himself. 'You and me. You' – his finger pointed again at the children – 'are promising to bind yourself to me and my heirs for a fixed term of years – usually that's until you reach the age of eighteen. You're promising me that you will be a good and faithful apprentice, that you will not leave or absent yourself from your place of work without my consent. You will not steal, damage or destroy anything that is my property. You will obey all the rules and behave at all times in a manner befitting your station as an apprentice. And providing that you keep your side of the agreement, in return, I' – his finger now turned towards himself – 'and my heirs promise to employ you for that number of years in a suitable occupation and teach you all you need to know. Now,' he smiled down at them. 'Is that all clear?'

'Please, sir,' Hannah asked. 'What wages do we receive?'

'Wages?' Mr Critchlow frowned. 'We don't pay wages to apprentices.'

'Then – then how are we to live?'

His face cleared. 'Oh, I see. Didn't I say? We provide you with accommodation and all your food – and clothes.' The last item was added as if this were a great benevolence.

Ernest Scarsfield leaned forward. 'You can earn a bit doing overtime. You'll be paid for that.'

'A-hem, oh yes, of course. But it'll be a while before they're useful enough to do that, Scarsfield. Don't mislead them.'

'No, sir, of course not,' Ernest said dutifully, but out of sight of his employer, Hannah felt him squeeze her elbow and understood that, as soon as he could, he would likely put some work their way so that they could earn a few coppers.

But Mr Critchlow's next words dampened even that hope. 'And don't forget the stoppages ledger, Scarsfield. Make sure they understand that anything they break or do wrong will have to be paid for.'

'Sounds as if we'll end up paying to work here,' Hannah muttered. She felt a sharp dig in the ribs from Luke and another squeeze on her elbow from Mr Scarsfield. This time it was a warning.

'What? What did you say, girl?' Mr Critchlow demanded.

'Nothing, sir,' she replied, but she was thinking quickly, debating whether to sign the paper that would bind her here for six long years. She thought of her mother, who had begged her to behave, to work hard and learn a skill. 'It's a great chance for you, Hannah,' Rebecca had said in her gentle voice. 'Take it.' And it was a chance too, the young girl reminded herself, to find employment for her mother. Then they could be reunited.

Hannah smiled brightly and stepped forward. 'Where do you want me to sign, sir?'

A few moments later, when they'd each laboriously scratched their names (or, in the case of Jane, made her mark – an untidy, squiggly cross), they watched whilst Mr Critchlow filled in their names in the appropriate blank spaces in the document. At the bottom of the paper he added the date, his signature and a big, red seal of wax.

'There, that's all done, and now Mr Scarsfield will show you around the mill and then what work he would like you to do.' He looked up at his overlooker. 'Come back here later, Scarsfield. We've matters to discuss.'

'Yes, sir,' Ernest Scarsfield nodded as he led the

children out of the room, Hannah once more bobbing a polite curtsy and bestowing her most beaming smile on the man whom she was now bound to serve for the next six years.

Six

'Now,' Mr Scarsfield said, smiling down at them as they clattered back down the stone steps and into the yard once more. 'We'd better find you all a job to do.' He looked them over, assessing them. 'We usually start the apprentices off just sweeping up and keeping the place tidy. After a while, we'll try you on other jobs so's you work your way up, see?'

Four heads nodded.

'You three' – he pointed to the twins and Jane – 'are small enough to crawl under the machines to sweep the fluff up, but you . . .' Now he pointed at Hannah. 'You're a bit tall for that. I don't want any accidents.' He frowned. 'The mill is a dangerous place, 'specially for you youngsters and 'specially' – he laid emphasis on the word – 'when you're crawling about under the machines. Watch your heads and your backs and you, Pickering, mind your hair is plaited and covered by your bonnet.'

'What about me?' Hannah asked. 'What am I to do?'

'I think I'll try you scutching.'

Hannah blinked. 'Whatever's that?'

Ernest laughed and his brown eyes twinkled. 'It's part of the preparation of the raw cotton. Come on, let's set these three to work and then I'll take you and show you.'

He led the children into the mill. Now the noise of machinery was much louder, and the newcomers were tempted to put their hands over their ears to block out the din.

'You'll get used to it,' Ernest mouthed at them. 'And you'll soon learn to lip read an' all. It's the only way you can hold any sort of conversation in here. Mind you, don't let me catch you chatting, though.'

'Fat chance,' Luke muttered, though above the noise, the overlooker didn't hear him.

Ernest led them into a long room where dozens of machines were working. The noise was now deafening, but the workers standing before the machines didn't seem to mind. Ernest was pointing at a small girl darting between the machines and then crawling beneath them to sweep the dust and fluff collecting under each one. The newcomers stood watching for a moment and then the two boys picked up a brush and emulated the girl.

Jane clung to Hannah, whimpering. 'I can't do that. I'm frightened.'

The overlooker put his hand on the young girl's shoulder, but she cringed away from him, burying her face against Hannah.

'Don't be frightened of me, young 'un. I'll not 'urt yer.' He bent closer so that she could hear what he said. 'Look, just today, you can sweep the floors all round the machines, but mind you don't get in the way of the operators. They'll likely box yer ears if yer do.'

Jane trembled and tears ran down her face.

'Come on,' Hannah coaxed. 'You know we've got to work. We signed that paper and Mr Scarsfield's trying to find you something easy to do to start off.'

Jane sniffled and nodded. She took hold of the broom that Ernest held out to her.

'I'll just have a word with one of the women. Ask her to keep an eye on the little one.'

He glanced beneath the machinery before adding, 'The lads look to be doing fine.'

After a few brief words with the woman at the nearest machine, Ernest nodded to Jane, who began to sweep the floor with tentative strokes. The overlooker cast his eyes to the ceiling as if in despair, but then smiled as he and Hannah left the room.

Away from the noise, Hannah said, 'She's only ten and small for her age. She'll be all right once she gets used to it.'

'Aye well, we'll see,' Ernest said, sounding none too hopeful.

He led the way out of the main building again and across the yard into the one set at right angles. As they walked he said, 'The bales of raw cotton are stored in a room on the ground floor beneath the counting house. It's Mr Roper's job to check them all in. Then the lads carry them across the yard to this building. This is where the preparation is done.'

They entered a room where other children were working; some of them Hannah had seen in the apprentice house. They were unpacking bales of raw cotton, pulling it and then sorting it into different piles.

'That's called "blending",' Ernest explained. 'They're sorting into different qualities so that each pile consists of the same quality of cotton.'

Hannah nodded.

'Now, what I want you to do is to remove all the

seeds and the dirt from the cotton. It's a boring job, but you've got to start at the bottom, luv. But I reckon you're bright and quick and I'll keep me eye on you. You'll soon be moving on, I've no doubt.'

'That's "scutching" then, is it?'

'Aye, then the cotton's spread into a flat sheet before it goes into the next room where there's a carding engine. I'll show you that another time. Bentley!' Ernest raised his voice and beckoned one of the girls over. 'This is Francis. She's to start with the scutching. Show her what to do, will yer?'

'Yes, Mr Scarsfield,' the girl said meekly.

Just as he turned to go, Ernest reminded Hannah, 'Oh, and tomorrow morning, make sure Pickering plaits her hair and puts it up under her bonnet.'

Now it was Hannah who nodded, and said, 'Yes, Mr Scarsfield.'

'D'you know, I can't hear a thing,' Luke began as the four of them walked home after their first day's work in the mill.

''Cept them machines,' finished Daniel. 'I can still hear 'em banging in my head even now we're out in the open.'

'It hurts my ears,' Jane murmured, slipping her hand into Hannah's. 'And everybody shouts so.'

'They have to, don't they, to make themselves heard above the noise.' Luke grinned and added, 'There's one good thing.' He poked Hannah in the ribs. 'We can't hear your singing no more.'

Playfully, Hannah punched him on the shoulder.

At that moment there was a clatter of clogs behind

them and they heard Nell's voice. 'Come on, you lot. You've got school for two hours now and jobs to do before any of us get any supper.'

'School?' Luke said. 'Now? After working all day?'

'Jobs?' Daniel added.

'I'm tired,' Jane whimpered. 'I want to go to bed.'

Hannah squeezed her hand. 'Come on, Jane. Let's go and meet the teacher.'

'I don't want to. I don't want him rapping me with his cane.'

'You 'ave to go until you're thirteen. I don't any more. I'm fifteen. But you'll be in trouble if you don't go. It's the law and even the Critchlows have to abide by it,' Nell said. She sniffed. 'Mind you, I reckon they'd get out of it if they could. A schoolmaster needs paying, and the Critchlows don't like parting with their money.'

'Does the master teach the girls an' all?' Hannah asked as they neared the schoolroom.

Nell nodded. 'There used to be a schoolmarm for the girls, but she left, all sudden like.' She cast a swift glance at Hannah as if trying to convey some sort of message, but Hannah was mystified. No doubt the teacher had found better employment, she thought. 'And they didn't appoint anyone else,' Nell went on. 'So now Mr Jessop teaches everybody.'

For the next two hours the weary children were obliged to sit on the long benches behind the tables and draw letters in the sand trays. The more able were given slates. Several of the children's heads drooped until they were resting on the desk. Until, that is, Mr Jessop brought his cane down with a sharp crack.

Hannah kept nudging Jane, trying to keep her awake, but the child was so tired that at last Hannah let her sleep. The schoolmaster came to stand over her. He raised his cane and Hannah held her breath. Mr Jessop bent down, looking closely at the pale, drawn face of the little girl. He lowered his cane and turned away, leaving her to sleep. Hannah smiled to herself. Perhaps this place wasn't so bad after all. There seemed to be one or two people prepared to be kindly now and then – Mrs Bramwell, Mr Scarsfield and now the schoolmaster. But she doubted there was much compassion in Mr Roper, and she feared that Mr Critchlow would be a greedy taskmaster. Perhaps his son, Mr Edmund, would be nice. She daydreamed until her wandering thoughts were brought sharply back to her work by the crack of Mr Jessop's cane on her desk.

After the requisite two hours, the children were released to return to the apprentice house.

'Come along, come along. There's work to be done.' Ethel Bramwell was standing at the back door, clapping her hands to hurry them along.

'Do we really have to do jobs now?' Hannah asked Nell. 'Before we get any supper?'

''Fraid so. The boys have to sweep the yard and fetch logs and coal in, and we have to sweep and tidy the dormitories and Mrs Bramwell's private rooms. Then there might be darning and mending to do. On Monday and Tuesday nights, we have to do the ironing.'

'What about Mary? Doesn't she do all that?'

'She does the washing on a Monday, but she has to do all the cooking for about eighty of us. There's fifty girls and twenty-nine boys as well as the Bramwells and Mary herself. I tell you, I wouldn't swap jobs with her, even if it is hard in the mill.'

51

'What do you do, Nell?'

'I'm a piecer.'

'Oh!' Hannah was about to ask more, but Jane was tugging at her arm.

'I'm tired, Hannah.' Hearing the list of chores recounted by Nell had made her feel even more exhausted. 'I just want to go to bed.'

'Maybe Mrs Bramwell won't make you younger ones do jobs,' Hannah began, but Nell laughed.

'Don't you believe it. If she thinks Jane's trying to get out of any work, she'll give her the hardest job that'll take her twice as long.' Nell smiled down at Jane and took hold of the child's other hand. 'Come on, little 'un. We'll help you if we can, but it won't do you any good, or us, if we're spotted.'

'Let us with a gladsome mind . . .' Hannah sang as she knelt and scrubbed the floor, summoning up all the energy she could muster.

'And just what do you think you're doing, girl?'

Hannah looked up to see Mrs Bramwell standing over her.

'Washing your floor, ma'am.'

'I can see that,' the woman said testily. 'But this task was given to Pickering. Why are you doing it?'

Hannah stood up. 'She's dead on her feet, ma'am. I've told her to go to bed and that I'd do it for her. I've finished the job you gave me.'

'You've no right to say who may go to bed and who may not.' Ethel Bramwell pursed her thin lips. 'I can find another job for you if you've finished the one I set you.'

'Why? Why can't I help Jane?' Hannah was almost shouting now. 'She's only ten.'

Ethel's lip curled. 'That's nothing. In the past children have worked in this mill from the age of eight.' She sniffed and beneath her breath muttered, 'And younger, if the truth be known.'

Open-mouthed, Hannah stared at her and Ethel continued. 'Pickering must learn to do her share.' For a moment, she seemed to soften, even using the girl's Christian name for once. 'I know you mean well, Hannah, but you're not doing the girl any favours.'

'But she's tired, exhausted and, and . . .' Hannah faltered. She'd been going to say that the child was homesick. How anyone could be homesick for the workhouse was beyond Hannah, yet she knew that Jane was missing her friends from the only home the little girl had ever known. But maybe, given time, this house might be more of a real home than a workhouse could ever be. She would try to make Jane see that. But, just now, all she could do was to help the child physically.

Suddenly, Hannah put her head on one side and smiled. 'Please, Mrs Bramwell, won't you let me help her just tonight? Just this once? And then I'll tell her she'll have to manage. And I'll do the other job too. Whatever it is.'

Ethel Bramwell stared at her. She'd never met a girl like this before. Usually, it was a battle of wills to get any of the children to do the household chores after long hours in the mill and two hours' schooling too. And now here was a new arrival begging to do even more work than she'd been asked to do. The girl was slim and dainty, yet she must have an inner strength that was not immediately apparent. There were dark shadows of weariness beneath her own eyes, yet Hannah had the will power to drive herself on – just to help another. The sound of this girl singing in the punishment room had stayed with the superintendent, and she was sure she'd heard her again just now.

'Is Pickering a relative of yours?'

Hannah shook her head. 'No, but we're best friends. I've known her ever since we went into the workhouse.' At the reminder of the workhouse, the sudden longing to see her mother threatened to overwhelm her. But she lifted her chin and met the superintendent's gaze. 'We went in three years ago, but Jane'd been there all her life.'

'I see,' Ethel said, relenting. 'Well, all right then, but mind you make sure she understands that it is just this once.'

Hannah beamed. 'Thank you, ma'am.' She knelt down once more to finish her work, but then looked up to ask, 'What's the other job you want me to do?'

Now Ethel smiled, and some of the severity left her face. She waved her hand. 'Oh, never mind about that.'

As Hannah left the room a few moments later, Ethel gazed after her and bit her lower lip. That girl would be a beauty one day, she thought with a sudden shudder of apprehension. And that day wasn't far away. God help her then when Mr Edmund laid eyes on her.

'Well, I never,' Nell remarked, staring down at the sleeping Jane when the other girls trooped wearily upstairs to their beds. 'She'll be in trouble in the

morning when Mrs Bramwell finds out she's not finished her work.'

'No, she won't,' Hannah said, 'because I've done
it.'

Nell stared at her. '*You've* done it?'

Hannah nodded.

'Then you'll be in trouble an' all.'

'No, I won't. Mrs Bramwell knows all about it. She
let me do it. Just this once, she said.'

Nell gaped. 'She – she *let* you?'

Hannah nodded.

'Well – well . . .' For a moment the girl was lost for
words, then with a shrug she said, 'She must be going
soft in her old age.' She laughed. 'Well, now we know
who to come to if we want to get round her.'

Hannah grinned. 'I don't think it will work very
often.'

'Oh, I don't know. Mrs Bramwell has her favourites. You tek Joe Hughes – you know, the lad your
friends said was in the next bed to them?'

'The one who snores?'

Nell giggled. 'That's him. The whole dormitory
complain about him. Well, he's one of her favourites.
The things he gets away with, you wouldn't believe.
If the rest of us did half what he does, we'd end up in
the punishment room.'

Hannah laughed. 'Don't forget I've been in there
already. I quite expect to spend half me life in there.'

Nell shuddered. 'That time was just a warning. You
wait till they decide to really punish you.'

Seven

Hannah met Joe Hughes the next morning as they all hurried down to the mill.

'Is this the girl you were telling us about?' he asked Luke.

'Yeah. This is Hannah. Hannah – Joe Hughes.'

Hannah smiled at him, but none of them slowed their pace. Already they could see Mr Scarsfield waiting by the door.

'Pleased to meet yer, Joe Hughes.'

'And you, Hannah. Come for a walk up the hills on Sunday afternoon, will yer?'

Hannah glanced at the hills, shrouded in early morning mist. But she'd already seen how beautiful they were when the sun shed its golden light upon them.

'Yeah. All right. We'll come.'

'Oh, I didn't mean—' the boy began, but they'd reached the door and Ernest Scarsfield said, 'No talking now. Get to your work and look sharp about it.'

The children parted, the twins and Jane going into the main mill. Hannah skipped across the yard to the preparation room in the nearby building with Joe Hughes trotting beside her. He worked the carding machine in the room next door.

However boring the job, Hannah was meticulous in her work, but it wasn't long before she noticed that the other girl was not as careful to get every seed and bit of dirt out of the cotton.

'You've missed some bits there, Millie,' she pointed out.

The girl looked up at her, her dark eyes flashing anger. Her lips twisted as she said, 'Oh, got a boot-kisser here, 'ave we?'

Hannah gasped. 'How dare you? I was only trying to help.'

'I'm supposed to be the one helping you – not for you to come in here trying to lord it over me. Reckon you know better than me how to do it, d'yer?'

Hannah nodded towards the pieces of raw cotton the girl had put on the heap that was supposed to have been cleaned. 'If that's the way you do your job, then yes, I do.'

The girl leaned towards Hannah. 'Well, I can make your life a misery in here – and in the house. No one likes a bootkisser.' She smiled maliciously. 'That's what I'll call you. "Boot". And if anyone wants to know why, then I'll tell 'em.'

For a moment Hannah stared at her. The years rolled back and once again she was a bewildered little five year old standing in the street near her home, being taunted with cruel names. Only at that time she hadn't known the meaning of the names they called her. But she recalled how she had learnt to deal with the insults.

She threw back her head and laughed aloud, amused at the look of confusion on Millie's face. Then Hannah began to sing, but this only incensed the other girl further. She shook her fist in Hannah's face. 'Aye, go on sing. Sing your heart out, girl, 'cos when you've been here a bit, you won't feel like singing. I promise

57

you that.' She flung a handful of cotton in Hannah's face. 'And since you're so clever, you can do all the scutching on yer own. I'll do the blending and spreading.'

Hannah's only reply was to sing louder than ever.

About mid morning, the door to the preparation room opened and three men came in. Hannah knew two of them: Mr Critchlow and the overlooker, Ernest Scarsfield. Her gaze rested briefly on the third. He was a tall, handsome man with dark curly hair, his age about forty or so, she guessed. He walked with a graceful ease and held his head in a proud manner. Expensively dressed in a maroon frock coat, fawn trousers and matching waistcoat, he had high cheekbones above a firm, square chin and thick, black eyebrows that shadowed his dark brown eyes. He had neatly cut sidewhiskers but, though his mouth was well shaped, there was a discontented downturn to his lips.

For a brief moment their eyes met, and Hannah saw his eyebrows draw together in a frown. He strode towards her, his face thunderous.

'What's all the noise? Concentrate on your work, girl.'

Ernest was beside her at once. 'She's new, Mr Edmund. Only arrived yesterday.'

'That's no excuse. She should know her place, and her place is attending to her work, not singing.'

'I'll see to it, Mr Edmund.'

'Mind you do, Scarsfield.' He was about to turn away when his glance rested on some of the raw cotton that Millie had been working on. He picked up a

handful. 'And what's this? Supposed to be finished is
it?' He flung it at Hannah. 'You'd better learn to do
your work a lot better than this, else you'll be back
to the workhouse. And Goodbody will *not* be pleased to
see you. Scarsfield, you're to stop her a shilling from
her pay—'

Hannah's blue eyes flashed. 'How can he stop
money out of my pay? I don't get paid.' She pointed
her finger at the older man. 'Mr Critchlow said so.'

There was a breathless silence whilst everyone in
the room stared at her.

The tall man stepped close to her, glaring down at
her from his superior height. He grasped her chin with
strong fingers, forcing her head backwards. He held
her like that for several moments, gazing into her eyes,
his glance roaming over the whole of her face.

'Answer me back would you, girl? We'll see what a
night on the floor of the punishment room will do for
you.'

He released her suddenly so that she staggered
backwards. He turned away. 'See to it, Scarsfield. No
supper and you can take a shilling from the money she
brought with her.'

Hannah opened her mouth to protest, but she
caught Ernest's warning shake of his head. The angry
stranger brushed imaginary fluff from his jacket and
strode into the room next door, followed by Mr
Critchlow.

'I'll see you later, Francis,' Ernest said before he
hurried after them.

Spreading out the cleaned cotton fibres into a flat
sheet, Millie smiled triumphantly. 'Serves you right.
You should know better than to cheek Mr Edmund.'

59

So, Hannah thought as she picked up the cotton he had flung at her, that was Mr Edmund Critchlow. The man she had been warned about.

A little later, Ernest Scarsfield came back alone. He stood with his arms akimbo, glancing between the two girls. 'Now, which of you two was supposed to have scutched that piece of cotton the young master found? Come on, I want the truth.'

Hannah met his gaze fearlessly, but she said nothing.

'It weren't me, mester,' Millie whined. 'I've put 'er on the scutching. I'm doing the blending and the spreading now.' She cocked her head on one side and smiled winningly at the overlooker. 'If that's all right with you, Mr Scarsfield. See, you 'ave to know what you're doing with the blending, don't you, Mr Scarsfield? We don't want all different qualities mixed up together do we, sir?'

Shocked, Hannah gaped at the girl. Millie was lying quite blatantly. She pressed her lips together and shot the girl a vitriolic glance, but still she said not a word.

'Hmm,' Ernest said thoughtfully, stroking his moustache. 'Very well then, but you'd better both mind what you're doing. I don't want any slacking else I'll have to fine the pair of you.'

With a stern glance at each of them in turn, Ernest Scarsfield left the room, banging the door behind him.

Once she was sure he was out of earshot, Hannah turned on the girl. She grasped her arm and swung her round to face her. 'Don't you dare tell lies about me again. I don't tell tales on others and I always tell the truth about meself. If it'd been me that'd sorted that cotton, I'd've owned up.'

Fear flickered in Millie's eyes. 'Le' go, you're hurting my arm. I'll tell—'

'No, you won't. You hear me. You won't tell any more tales about me – or anyone else – and if I hear you have . . .' Her grip tightened until the girl cried out in pain. Then Hannah released her grasp, flinging Millie away from her. 'If it's anyone slacking around here, then it's you.'

Hannah returned to her work. Not another word passed between them for the rest of the day. And Hannah was too angry to sing.

Sunday was the only day of the week when the mill workers were allowed any time off. The adults who worked there mostly lived locally and had the day to be with their families. They were expected to attend the Methodist service held in the schoolroom at the mill, but afterwards there was time for the younger men and women to go courting.

The apprentices, though, were still under Mr and Mrs Bramwell's authority. They too had to attend the morning service, but afterwards there was more schooling and household tasks for them. Pauper apprentices, it seemed, had no free time at all. Even in the workhouse, Hannah thought truculently, there had been exercise time. Though they were not allowed outside the confines of the workhouse walls without permission from the master or the matron, at least all the inmates went out each day into the fresh air to walk, to chat or just to sit in the sun on warm days.

'You know you asked me to go walking with you on Sunday afternoon?' Hannah said to Joe as they fell into step on their way to work the following morning.

Joe grinned at her. 'Yeah.'

'Well – how? Or when? We don't seem to be given any time off.'

Joe shrugged. 'We just go.'

'And end up in the punishment room when we get back, I suppose?' Hannah had spent an uncomfortable night there. Given no supper, she had lain on the bare floor with only one blanket to wrap herself in. She had hardly slept and this morning she was both tired and ravenously hungry.

'We can either sneak off after the service – there's an hour or so before dinner – or we can go after.'

Hannah pulled a face. 'Mrs Bramwell says she teaches the girls sewing on a Sunday afternoon.'

He grinned. 'And that's going to stop you?'

Hannah laughed. 'Not really, no. I'll risk it.'

'Tell you what, we'll just have a short walk between chapel and dinner.' He winked at her. 'Don't want you moving into the punishment room permanently.'

Hannah pulled a face. 'Me neither.'

Eight

'I don't want to come, Hannah,' Jane said, when told of the proposed outing with Joe Hughes as they came out of the schoolroom after the service on the first Sunday morning. 'I'm so tired I could cry.' Indeed, tears of exhaustion filled the young girl's eyes. 'I just want to go home and sleep.'

'I know.' Hannah hugged her. 'You go on then. I'll wake you up for dinner when I get back.'

'Where are you going?' Jane asked worriedly. 'You'll be in trouble again.'

'Only for a little walk. Joe's promised to show me the waterfall behind the mill.'

Jane returned her hug fiercely. 'You don't mind me not coming,' she said, her voice muffled against Hannah's shoulder.

''Course not.'

They pulled apart and smiled at each other. 'Besides,' Jane said, coyly, 'I think that Joe Hughes wants you to himself.'

'Eh?' Hannah was startled, then she laughed. 'Don't be silly.'

'I'm not.' Jane yawned, already thinking of their bed in the dormitory with longing. 'I reckon he likes you.'

'Don't be daft, he . . .' Hannah started to say, but Jane was already walking away from her, too tired to stand talking any longer.

'There you are!' Joe came towards her, walking with a swagger, his hands in his pockets. 'Just walk slow, so we end up at the back. Then, when we get to the bottom of the hill, there's a little path that runs at the back of the mill just below the cliff. If no one's watching, we nip through there.'

Hannah nodded, her eyes shining at the thought of an hour or so of freedom.

'Hey, Hannah, wait for us.'

'Oh no,' Joe muttered. 'Not that pair.'

Hannah turned and saw Luke with Daniel trotting close behind him.

'Off for a walk, a'yer?'

'How did you know?' Joe said belligerently.

'Heard you ask her the other day.' Luke grinned.

'Yeah. I asked her,' Joe glowered. 'Not the whole blooming lot of yer.'

Hannah laughed and slipped her arm through theirs. 'Oh, come on, let's all go. It's too nice a day to argue. Let's just enjoy ourselves while we can.'

'I'm tired, Luke,' Daniel muttered. 'I want to go home.'

Luke glanced at his twin. 'All right. See you later.'

Daniel blinked. 'What – what do y'mean?'

'You go and have a sleep. I'm going with these.'

Daniel glanced from his brother to Hannah. He and his brother were never apart. They went everywhere together. But now, Luke was choosing the company of others rather than him. Daniel didn't like it, and he was blaming Hannah. She could see it in his eyes.

'All right,' he muttered sulkily. 'I'll come an' all.'

'No, you go back if you want to—'

'I don't,' he snapped back. 'Not on me own.'

Joe was disgruntled too now. He'd wanted to walk out with Hannah on his own, not have the twins tagging along. Joe was older than the other three. At fourteen, he fancied himself old enough to start courting. He liked the look of this new girl whose blue eyes sparkled when she laughed. She'd left her long blonde hair flying loose this morning, cascading down her back in golden waves and curls that glinted in the sunlight. She was lively with boundless energy and she laughed often. And sing! He'd heard singing in the room next door to where he worked in the carding room. In the service that morning, her voice had risen, clear and pure, above all the others. She was a bit young yet, but she'd grow, he told himself, and he reckoned she'd grow into a beauty an' all.

'Come on then. Here's the path . . .' He caught hold of Hannah's hand and was elated at the look of fury on Luke's face.

They skirted the base of the cliff on which the row of houses containing the school and the apprentice house stood, and came to a place where a stream ran under the path to the waterwheel, whose power turned all the machinery in the mill.

'They call this the "head race",' Joe told them importantly. 'They constructed this to run from the mill pool down to the wheel.'

Hannah's gaze followed the line of the man-made stream that surfaced beyond the path and ran towards the paddles of the great wheel, which stuck out like sharp, hungry teeth. The wheel was silent today.

'So how do they stop the water,' Luke asked with boyish curiosity, 'when the mill's not working?'

'There's an iron hatch at the top of the race where it leaves the pool. When they want the wheel to work they just open the hatch. The water flows down the race to work the wheel and then it comes out the other side and flows down the tail race back into the river.'

'But where does the water go when the hatch is closed?' Now Daniel took up the question.

'There's a weir out of the pool straight back into the river. I'll show you.'

A few paces further on they came to where the River Wye widened out into the huge lake that Joe called the mill pool. Then, walking to the left, they stood a moment on the narrow footbridge watching the white foaming water cascading over the edge of the weir and rushing on down the rocky riverbed. Ahead of them was a steep climb up rocks to the hillside above.

Joe, still holding Hannah's hand, began to climb, pulling her after him. 'From up here you can see all the mill and some of the village.'

They climbed, puffing and panting, until they gained a narrow path running along the hillside overlooking the mill. Far below them now, it seemed small. They walked on along the sheep tracks, climbing higher.

They stood a moment to catch their breath.

'That way,' Joe waved to their right, 'is up to the Wyedale Arms.'

'We saw that the day we came,' Luke said.

Joe ignored him as if he hadn't spoken. 'And the other way,' he pointed in the opposite direction, 'leads to another mill about a couple of miles away.'

'Another mill!'

'Yeah. You can walk to it by a path on the other side of the mill pool.' He squeezed Hannah's hand and lowered his voice. 'I'll show you that another time. It's a lovely walk by the river. Very quiet and peaceful.' He glanced about him and then added, 'But we ought to go back now. If we're late for dinner, we'll all be in trouble.'

'Don't expect *you* will be, though,' Luke sparred. 'Not with Mrs Bramwell, anyway.'

Colour suffused the other boy's face. 'Have it your own way then,' he muttered moodily and looked directly at Hannah. 'I was only thinking of you. You've been in trouble already, haven't you?'

Hannah lifted her face to the sunshine, closing her eyes and luxuriating in the feel of the breeze on her face, rippling through her hair. 'You're right, Joe. But it's so lovely out here. It's almost worth risking a spell in the punishment room just for an hour or two of freedom.'

'Well, I'm going back now.' Joe let go of Hannah's hand. 'I don't fancy a beating from Mr Bramwell. You lot can please yourselves.' He thrust his hands in his pockets, turned and began to walk back the way they had come.

Worriedly, Daniel said, 'Come on. We ought to do what he says.'

'I'm not going back just 'cos *he* says so,' Luke scoffed. 'Come on, Hannah, let's walk a bit further. It's a great view from up here. Much better than walking on the road. You can see everything.'

'I don't think we ought to,' Daniel murmured, frowning.

Now it was Luke who grasped her hand. 'Well, you go, Dan. We'll see you later,' he called back cheerfully to his twin. Now – just as he'd wanted all along – he had Hannah to himself.

Joe Hughes had spent most of his life in the work-house and then in the mill. Places where segregation was the rule. And although he was younger than Joe, from his early years spent on a farm Luke, even at eleven years old, probably knew more about the natural instincts of animals – and human beings – than the older boy did. And Luke's natural instinct was to contrive to be alone with a pretty girl, to hold her hand, to put his arm around her. Even, if he was greatly daring, to kiss her.

And the prettiest girl he'd ever seen in his life was walking beside him right now.

'D'you like Joe?' he asked her suddenly.

'He's all right,' she said carefully. 'Why? Don't you like him?'

Luke pulled a face. 'He's a bit of a know-all.'

'Well, he's been here a few years now. I think he's only trying to be friendly.'

'The other lads say he's Mrs Bramwell's favourite.'

Hannah laughed. 'That's what Nell said an' all.'

Suddenly, Luke grinned. 'Mind you, it might do us a bit of good – to be on his right side.'

'Oh, Luke! How could you possibly think such a thing?' Then she giggled deliciously. 'But you could be right.'

'Look,' Luke said suddenly. 'Isn't that the Grundys' farm down there?'

'I think so. Yes, it's near the crossroads, but doesn't it look small from up here.' She laughed. 'And look at the cows in the field. They look like ants.'

'And look up there. Joe's right, that is the Wyedale Arms where the carter dropped us off.'

'Mm.' Hannah's voice was suddenly wistful. 'I wonder,' she began, and then stopped.

'If you could get a lift back again one day?'

Her eyes widened. 'How – how did you know?'

Luke's expression softened, and he was no longer teasing as he said, 'Because if I had a mam back there, then I'd be wanting to go back to see her sometime.'

'You would?' Hannah breathed.

Luke nodded. 'And if you ever want to – *really* want to – then I'd help you do it.'

'Even if . . . even if you got into trouble?'

'It'd be worth it – for you to see your mam,' he told her earnestly.

Hannah felt a blush creep up her neck and into her face. Tears prickled her eyelids. 'Oh, Luke,' was all she could say.

He squeezed her hand. 'We'd best be getting back an' all now. Look, there's a path here going right down to the farm. I 'spect it's one the sheep have worn on their way back home. Let's follow it. We'll go back this way. It'll be quicker. We can run on the road.'

Feeling a thrill of daring, they followed the path down the hillside towards the river. Hand in hand they ran across the footbridge over the water and up the lane bordered by the Grundys' farm. A man stood in the yard, watching their approach. He took his cap off, scratched his head and replaced it. He moved towards the gate and leaned on his arms on the top of it.

'Now where're you two off to in such a hurry? What've you been up to, 'cos you've got "guilt" written all over your faces.'

'A' you Mr Grundy?' Luke said as they stopped by the gate.

'Tha's right. And who're you then to know my name?'

'Your wife was very kind to us when we arrived the other day,' Hannah said. 'She gave us some lovely stew.'

'Ah,' said the burly man as understanding dawned. 'From mill, a' yer?'

The two youngsters nodded.

His expression softened. 'Out for a bit of an airing, a' yer. 'Spect there's not much fresh air in that place.'

'It's very dusty, isn't it?' Hannah said. 'With all the cotton bits floating in the air.'

The man nodded. 'I'll give you a tip. Whenever you wash, bathe your eyes with clean water. A lot of the youngsters get trouble with their eyes. And if they get very sore, you come and see my missis. She'll give you some eye lotion to use, 'cos that old skinflint won't spend an 'apenny on having a doctor visit if he can avoid it.'

'Thank you, Mr Grundy. That's very kind of you.'

The man smiled. 'Coming in to see the missis, 'a you? Nice joint of lamb we've just had for dinner.'

The children's mouths watered, but regretfully Hannah said, 'That's ever so kind of you, but we ought to get back. If we're missed, we'll be in trouble. And it's the best meal of the week today. Boiled pork and potatoes.'

'On yer go then. I'll tell the missis I've seen you.'

Bidding him goodbye, Hannah and Luke began to run. They didn't stop until they were in sight of the mill.

'I reckon Joe and Daniel'll both be in a huff with us.' Luke grinned, looking not particularly bothered.

'They'll get over it.' Hannah laughed. 'At least, Daniel will. He'll not stay mad at you for long. As for Joe – he can please himself.'

Luke felt a warm glow. When they arrived at the back door of the apprentice house breathless from running, Hannah turned to Luke.

'That was wonderful.' Her cheeks were pink, her bright eyes glowing and her hair flying free. Luke caught hold of her and gave her a swift, fumbling peck on the cheek.

Then, as they opened the door and burst into the kitchen, eighty or so pairs of eyes turned in their direction.

Near the range, with her hands folded and her mouth pursed, stood Ethel Bramwell. Slowly, she walked towards them. There was not a sound in the room. The children, seated on benches on either side of the four long tables, stopped eating to watch what was about to happen.

Ethel Bramwell reached them. 'And where might you two have been when there's work to be done? You're not allowed out of this house without permission. You should have come straight back here after the service. Why didn't you? I know you are both comparatively new here, but you know the rules, don't you?'

Hannah and Luke glanced at each other. 'Yes, ma'am,' they murmured in unison.

'If it hadn't been for Joe telling me that he'd seen you going up the hill,' Mrs Bramwell went on, 'I might've thought some accident had befallen you and sent people out to look for you. You'd've been in serious trouble then.'

Hannah felt a flash of anger. So, Joe was a telltale an' all, was he? It seemed there was no one here she could trust, except the three children who'd come with her from the workhouse. And maybe Nell. She liked

71

Nell. Daniel would never in a million years tell tales about his twin. He'd rather take punishment himself. But Joe, it seemed, had no such scruples. Hannah guessed that he was miffed at Luke having taken Hannah away from him on the walk *he* had planned. And now, he'd taken revenge.

Her glance raked the tables until she saw him. He was the only one with his gaze averted. He dared not look her in the eyes. Well, Hannah promised herself, she'd sort him out later, but her attention was dragged back to what Mrs Bramwell was saying.

'I can't let this go unpunished even so. There'll be no dinner for either of you. You' – she pointed at Hannah – 'will spend the rest of the day in the punishment room on bread and water.' Her glance turned to Luke. 'And we'll see what a beating will do for you.'

She stepped between them and laid a hand heavily on their shoulders. 'Come along.'

As they were led away, Hannah caught sight of the tears coursing down Jane's face, of Nell's anxious look and Joe's scarlet cheeks.

Not until the next morning as they hurried to work were Hannah and Luke able to speak to each other.

'Was it very bad, Luke? Did she hurt you?'

'It was him – Mr Bramwell – not her. He beats the boys and she punishes the girls.'

'Did it hurt?'

'It wasn't too bad. I've 'ad worse from old Good-body.' The lad grimaced and Hannah knew he was being brave. 'I'm sorry I led you into trouble, Hannah, but it was great out there on the hills, wasn't it?'

'Yeah, it was. And it's not the first time I've been in trouble and I doubt it'll be the last.' She grinned at him. 'I'm just sorry we didn't stop and have Mrs Grundy's roast lamb, aren't you?'

As they parted in the yard to go to their separate places of work, Ernest Scarsfield saw them laughing together. He'd heard about the previous day's escapade and now he shook his head in wonder. Was there nothing that would tame this girl? Because the way she was going on, she was going to spend half her days in trouble. And the more trouble she got into, the harsher the chastisement would become. He didn't want to see a pretty, bright little lass like her forever being punished, yet he couldn't help but secretly hope that her spirit would never be broken. He'd seen it all over the years. Undernourished, overworked children cowed and old before their time, many of them never even reaching adulthood. The work was arduous and only the strongest endured. He devoutly hoped Hannah was a survivor.

Nine

The following Sunday as they walked back from the morning service in the schoolroom, Luke whispered, 'Are we going out again?'

Hannah shook her head. 'It's not that I don't want to, or that I've suddenly turned into a bootkisser like Millie calls me.'

Luke grinned. 'Fat chance!'

Hannah smiled too. 'But I do want to keep in Mrs Bramwell's good books for a bit, if I can. You know what she's like.' Suddenly, Hannah clapped her hands and mimicked the superintendent. ' "Come along, come along. There's work to be done." Well, I'm going to do whatever she asks me. You see, I want to go and see me mam. And they won't let me if I keep getting meself into trouble, will they?'

Luke pulled a face. 'I don't think they will anyway. 'Specially not yet. We've only been here a couple of weeks.'

'Well, I'm going to try in another two weeks' time,' Hannah said determinedly. 'But in the meantime, I'm going to behave myself.'

Luke laughed aloud. 'I'll believe that when I see it. By the way,' he added, 'have you seen Joe?'

'Not to speak to. I've seen him in the yard but he scuttles out of my way whenever he catches sight of me.' Her eyes sparkled with mischief. 'Reckon he's scared to face me.'

74

'Me an' Daniel thought about giving him a thumping—'

'Oh, don't do that, Luke. You'll end up in more trouble.'

He nodded. 'That's what Daniel said. So instead we've got all the other lads to ignore him for a bit. None of 'em can stand him, so maybe that'll teach him a lesson.'

Hannah laughed. 'Poor Joe,' she said, but there was not much sympathy in her tone.

The four children had been living and working at the mill for a month. Apart from still trying to help Jane with the evening's household chores when the younger girl was almost dropping on her feet with tiredness, Hannah had been a model of good behaviour. Every day, except Sunday, was the same. All the children, regardless of their age, were woken at five thirty in the morning and had to be at work by six. Their breakfast of porridge and oatcake was brought to them in the mill by the overworked Mary from the apprentice house, but the children were allowed an hour at mid-day to go back to the house for their dinner. They then returned to the mill and worked until six o'clock in the evening, followed by two hours' schooling, household chores, supper and bed. The food was reasonable – better than the fare in the workhouse. There was a regular supply of fresh vegetables from the field in front of the mill, in which the boy apprentices worked on Sundays under Arthur Bramwell's instruction whilst the girls sewed and darned under his wife's direction. They were given meat two or three times a week and there was plenty of milk from the Grundys' cows.

Hannah remained fit and healthy. She'd taken Mr Grundy's advice and bathed her eyes night and morning, which seemed to prevent her suffering from the eye infections that plagued many of the mill's workers. And sometimes, when the atmosphere became dense with the floating dust from the cotton, she would tie a piece of clean rag around her mouth and nose.

'Look at Lady Muck here,' Millie would jeer, but it wasn't Hannah who went home at night with rasping breath and her mouth caked with fuzz.

At the end of Hannah's fourth week at the mill, Mr Scarsfield came into the preparation room. 'I'm going to try you as a piecer, Francis. You've made good progress in here and—'

Overhearing, Millie piped up. 'What about me, Mr Scarsfield? I've been here longer than Boot. I should be—'

Ernest Scarsfield frowned. 'Boot? Why on earth do you call her Boot?'

Millie blushed. She'd called Hannah the derogatory name ever since that first day. Usually she remembered to call her by her proper name in front of their superiors, but in her indignation at being passed over, as she thought, the nickname had slipped out.

'I – I . . .' the girl faltered, but Hannah laughed.

'It's nothing, Mr Scarsfield. It's only a bit of fun. I've got a name for her, an' all.' Her eyes twinkled with merriment. 'But I'm not going to tell you what it is.'

The overlooker glanced between the two girls. He was well aware that there was animosity between them; he'd seen it from that first day. That was partly why he was looking to move Hannah to another job.

He'd taken to this girl. She was a willing worker and a quick learner, even if she was a bit rebellious at times.

'Hmm,' he glanced at Millie. 'I'll think about it. Maybe I'll try you as a tenter working on the carding machine with Hughes. In the meantime, I'm putting a new girl with you. You can teach her to do your job and then we'll see.' Millie's eyes flashed resentment but she had the sense to keep silent. The overlooker's voice took on a note of warning. 'She's come from the village, not from a workhouse. Her *parents* work here in the mill and they've apprenticed her.' Without saying so, he was indicating that it would be unwise to try bullying the new girl; she was not alone in the world. 'She starts on Monday, so you,' he turned back to Hannah, 'come to me first thing on Monday and I'll take you to Hudson. She'll show you what to do.'

Hannah smiled broadly. 'Thank you, Mr Scarsfield.' She liked Nell Hudson. The bed she shared with Jane was still next to Nell and her sleeping companion, and there were often muffled giggles in the night between the four of them.

'It's all right for some,' Millie muttered begrudgingly. 'I've been here a lot longer than you. I should be getting a better job, not you.'

'Who says it's a better job? It's not bad in here. At least it's away from all that noise.'

'You'll've more chance of being offered overtime, that's what,' Millie spat. 'You'll be able to earn money instead of just your keep and a new set of clothes once a year.'

'Well, if you weren't such a slacker, you might get the chance. The bosses aren't stupid, y'know. Keep yer nose clean and you might get the chance to work with Joe next door.'

'I don't want to work with *him*. Mrs Bramwell's pet. I'm no bootkisser,' Millie sneered. 'You 'n' Joe Hughes make a good pair.'

Now Hannah didn't respond. Since the day he'd carried tales to Mrs Bramwell, Hannah had heard it from some of the other children that he was not only the woman's favourite but that he deliberately sucked up to her. Joe still attempted to be friendly with her, but Hannah gave him the cold shoulder. Luke, she'd decided, was the one she wanted as her friend.

'Come to think of it, that Hudson girl's one an' all.'

Hannah's eyes widened. 'Nell? Never!'

'You'll find out. Only it's not boots she's kissing,' Millie said smugly and refused to say more.

The rest of the day passed in silence between the two girls, but at six o'clock, Hannah ran out of the yard and up the hill, excited to tell her good news to Jane and Nell.

'I'm coming to work with you,' she cried, grabbing hold of Nell about the waist and whirling her around. 'Mr Scarsfield says I can be a piecer and you're to teach me what to do.'

Nell's dark eyes lit up. 'That's wonderful. Marvellous!' She flung her arms around Hannah and they danced the length of the dormitory, laughing and singing together.

'What's got into you two?' one of the other girls asked as, one by one, they trudged wearily into the room. 'Come into a fortune, 'ave yer?'

'They're leaving. I bet that's what it is,' said another.

'Nah.' Millie, coming into the room, overheard the remarks. 'They're a couple of bootlickers, the pair of 'em. 'Er,' she pointed at Hannah, 'has got Mr Scarsfield wrapped round her little finger. And as for 'er – well, we all know who'd she'd lift her skirts for, don't we?'

The two girls stopped dancing and looked at each other, their merriment dying. Hannah made to pull away from Nell and lunge herself at the smirking Millie, but Nell caught hold of her. 'No. Leave it. She's not worth it. Not worth losing this chance over. You come and work with me. We'll be all right together.'

'Yeah, 'course you will,' Millie sneered. 'His pimp now, a' yer?'

Hannah started forward again, but Nell's grip tightened. 'I said, leave it.'

The rest of the girls averted their eyes or hurried out of the room. Hannah said no more, but the vindictive Millie had spoiled her exciting news.

'Mrs Bramwell, please may I go to see my mother one Sunday?'

The superintendent stared at Hannah in amazement. 'Go – to – see – your – mother?' she repeated.

'Yes. I haven't heard from her since I came here.'

Mrs Bramwell sat down suddenly, her shocked gaze still fastened on Hannah's face. 'Well, I never heard the like.'

Hannah put her head on one side and stared at her, puzzled by the woman's reaction to what, to the girl, seemed a simple, straightforward question. 'May I go? Please?'

'Oh no, no.' Mrs Bramwell shook her head. 'It's out of the question. Dear me. The very idea.'

Now Hannah frowned. 'Why? Why can't I go? It's not so far. I could do the journey in two days. There one day and come back the next. I just want to see her.'

Mrs Bramwell laughed wryly. 'Oh, my dear child, don't you know what signing that indenture means?'

'What's an in – indenture?'

'The piece of paper you were asked to sign when you arrived here.'

'Oh, that. I'd forgotten what it was called.'

'Yes, that.' Mrs Bramwell's tone was flat. 'Signing that paper means that you're bound to Mr Critchlow until you're eighteen. And he doesn't allow anyone to leave here. Not even for a day.'

Shocked, Hannah stared at Mrs Bramwell. 'You mean – you mean I can't go to see my mother for – for *six years*?'

Mrs Bramwell nodded.

The twelve-year-old child felt a lump in her throat and her eyes smart with tears. 'Why? Why not?'

Mrs Bramwell bit her lip as she considered her answer. This young girl was spirited, some might say wilful. If she put ideas into the girl's head, then . . . 'It's – it's the rules here,' she said lamely, ducking giving a full answer.

Now Hannah was angry with the uncontrolled rage of a young girl. Her blue eyes sparkled defiantly. 'Then they're cruel rules that keep a child from its mother. *For six years!*' She whirled around and ran from the room, and though Mrs Bramwell called after her, the girl didn't stop, ignoring the possibility of a night in the punishment room for her disobedience.

Left alone, Ethel Bramwell sighed. For once, she'd take no action against the girl. For once, she sympathized with her.

Hannah ran on, out of the house and down the hill to the mill. She would see him. She would seek out Mr Critchlow – the man who made these harsh rules. She'd tell him exactly what she thought of him.

Moments later she was banging on the door of the outer office. When a voice bade her enter, she thrust open the door and marched into the room. The clerk, Mr Roper, looked up from his desk. He blinked at her over the top of his spectacles.

'What do you want, girl?' he asked gruffly. 'You've no right to be in here. Have you been sent for? In trouble, are you?'

'No, but I want to see Mr Critchlow.'

'See – Mr Critchlow?' Mr Roper was startled, just as Mrs Bramwell had been, at the girl's audacity. Hannah thought for a moment that he was going to say, just like Mrs Bramwell, 'Well, I never heard the like.' But instead, he pursed his mouth. 'You've got cheek, I'll give you that. But in this place, that'll only earn you a punishment – not admiration.'

Hannah bit back a hasty retort. She swallowed her anger, realizing suddenly that belligerence would gain her nothing.

'Please, sir,' she said, modifying her tone, her whole attitude. 'Please, could I see Mr Critchlow?'

'He's not here. He's gone for the day.' Mr Roper paused and then added, slyly, 'but Mr Edmund's here. You could perhaps see him, if you like.'

In her innocence, Hannah nodded. 'Yes, please.'

Josiah Roper was a strange, complicated character. He had been born into relatively privileged circumstances.

81

He'd attended private schools and had been set to enter Oxford or Cambridge University until the day he'd learned that the family fortunes had been drunk and gambled away by his ne'er-do-well father. Josiah had been obliged to seek gainful employment. He was intelligent and able, but the doors that once might have been opened to him by way of his family's standing were now slammed in his face. Seventeen years earlier, as a desperate young man of eighteen, Josiah had sought out Edmund Critchlow, who'd been one of Josiah's father's more fortunate gambling cronies. Mistakenly, Josiah believed the man might feel some pangs of guilt, perhaps some sort of responsibility that he'd been involved in the downfall of the Roper family. Whilst Edmund did persuade his own father to employ Josiah as their clerk, his reasons were far from charitable. Edmund was ambitious. He couldn't wait to take over the running of Wyedale Mill from his father. Roper, he assumed, would be eternally grateful and utterly loyal to him. The impoverished young man, Edmund believed, would be his eyes and ears throughout the mill. People would tend to ignore the quiet man, to look upon him as a mere clerk. But they would be mistaken, Edmund schemed, for there would be nothing happen in the mill that he wouldn't hear about from Roper.

Josiah was indeed grateful to take the position, but his appreciation was short-lived. Though he did his job conscientiously, he was resentful of his benefactors, seeing his lowly position as an insult to his intelligence and none of his own making. In his twisted, embittered attitude, he took a perverse delight in hearing the quarrels and troubles that took place within his hearing in the inner office. As he went about the mill, ostensibly on office business, he picked up titbits of gossip, overheard private conversations, witnessed quarrels between workers and saw problems arise. And all of this he carried back to his office to calculate how he could best use such information. If he could manipulate a situation to cause trouble for someone – anyone, it didn't matter who it was – then his day was all the brighter. It relieved the monotonous drudgery of his enforced servile position. Yet, with his tale-bearing he was unwittingly fulfilling the very act that Edmund wanted of him.

And now here was this girl, who'd been in the mill but a few weeks, standing in his office demanding to see the master. Josiah's lip curled. It lightened his day. Well, she could see the young master. That'd stop her gallop and no mistake. She was a bit young at the moment, but Edmund would mark her out, and in three or four years' time . . .

Josiah rose slowly from behind his desk and straightened up. 'I'll ask if Mr Edmund will see you.' He moved deliberately slowly towards the door to the inner office, knocked and entered without waiting for a reply. He closed the door behind him and Hannah was left alone. She looked about her.

The offices were on the top floor of an annexe attached to the main mill. As she looked out of the windows, Hannah could see the building at right angles to this one and then, directly in front of her, the third one. The room itself was dark and dreary, furnished only with Mr Roper's high desk and an odd chair or two. A candle stood on the corner of his desk to give him a little extra light by which to write in his fine, spidery hand. The walls were lined with shelves, overflowing with ledgers and files and papers. No

83

doubt Mr Roper knew where everything was, but to her, the place looked a muddle.

After what seemed an age, the door opened again, and Josiah beckoned her inside. Nervous now – the waiting had robbed her of her daring – Hannah stepped forward until she was standing before the man she'd seen only a few times walking through the mill. Mr Roper retreated from the room and softly closed the door.

Mr Edmund kept her waiting several minutes whilst his pen scratched across a sheet of paper before him. At last, he looked up, his thick, black eyebrows meeting in a frown. Then, as he realized who it was, he leaned back in his chair and linked his fingers.

'Well, well, well, the little blonde girl whom Scarsfield thinks fit to promote to piecer, even though she couldn't do her first job properly.'

Hannah's chin lifted defiantly. 'I hadn't done the piece of cotton you picked up.' She paused deliberately before adding, 'Sir.'

Edmund's eyes glittered. 'Hadn't you, indeed? Are you telling me that the other girl had done it?'

Hannah shook her head. 'No, sir. I'm just saying that you picked up a piece that I hadn't worked on.' She met his gaze, outwardly fearless yet inside she was quaking, her knees trembling uncontrollably.

He was a frightening figure, tall, commanding, and he held her life in his hands. His power was absolute and yet here was this slip of a girl daring to stand up to him. Strangely, it amused Edmund. He leaned forward, resting his arms on his desk. 'So – to what do I owe this pleasure?'

84

Hannah ran her tongue around her dry lips. 'Please, sir, I would like permission to visit me mother.'

Edmund frowned. There was a long pause, before he said slowly, 'Your – mother? You have a mother?'

'Yes, sir.'

'Goodbody told me you were orphans. The four of you.'

'The other three that came with me are, sir. But I've still got me mother.'

'And where is she?'

'At the Macclesfield workhouse, sir.'

'And how do you propose to go all that way to visit her?'

'I . . . I thought if I went on a Saturday afternoon and came back on Sunday night—'

He smiled sarcastically. 'You think you could walk all that way in that time?'

Hannah shook her head. 'I thought I could get a lift with the carter who brought us.'

'That costs money, girl.'

'But I have money, sir. The two guineas—'

'Ah yes. The two guineas.' His cruel smile broadened. 'That money is to pay for any stoppages you incur. It is not to be frittered away.'

'And that's frittering? Wanting to see me mother?' Hannah cried rashly, growing red in the face.

Edmund regarded her. *This girl is a little wild-cat*, he was thinking. *And wouldn't I just like the taming of her.* He smiled, but his smile was at his own thoughts. He was imagining Hannah a few years older . . .

He shook his head, pretending regret. 'I'm sorry, my dear, but it will not be possible to allow you to travel all that way to visit your mother.'

'But, sir—'

He held up his hand to still her protest. 'Perhaps, by now, she may have moved on. Found employment—'

'She'd've let me know. She'd've written to me.'

'Would she, indeed? She can write, then?'

'Well, no, but she'd've got someone else to do it for her. She'd've let me know somehow.' Hannah was insistent and incensed enough to demand boldly, 'Why can't I go to see her?'

'Because you signed a paper promising to be a loyal employee.'

'But I am a loyal employee. I'm not trying to leave. Just to go and see me mother. Just for a day. Other children see their parents. Several go home on a Sunday even though they live in the apprentice house in the week.'

'Not the workhouse paupers.'

She flinched to hear herself described that way.

'You see,' he went on, 'those other children live locally. They've been apprenticed by their parents, who've signed the paper on their behalf. So it is the *parents* who are legally bound to ensure their children keep to the agreement. Now, in the case of children from the workhouse, we have only the signatures – or the crosses – of the apprentices themselves. If we were to allow them to go wandering all over the country, well, we'd have no way of knowing if they'd come back.'

Hannah gaped at him. 'But of course I'd come back. I've promised you, and I don't break my promises.'

'Very laudable, I'm sure.' Edmund leaned back again. He regarded her thoughtfully for a moment. 'And do you know,' he said, sounding as if the admission actually surprised him. 'I think I believe you. But it's not possible. If we were to allow one to go, then all the others would want to go too.'

'But most of them don't have family. Most of the children, who've come here from the workhouse, don't have anyone. They're orphans. I'm not.'

'But you should be,' Edmund said. 'Goodbody is supposed to send only orphans.' His face darkened. 'Otherwise we encounter this very problem.' His lip curled. 'Children wanting to see their parents.'

Hannah bit her lip. 'Then – will you let me write to her? Will you see that my letter is sent?'

Edmund looked at her thoughtfully. He felt the familiar stirrings. One day, he promised himself, he would have this girl. Deciding to appear benevolent, he smiled, 'Of course, my dear. You write your little letter and bring it to Mr Roper. He'll make sure that it's sent to your mother.'

There was no more to be said. Hannah could see that no amount of pleading was going to change his mind. If only, she thought, she could have seen the older man, Mr Critchlow senior, then . . .

As if reading her mind and without looking up, Edmund added, 'And don't go asking my father if you can visit her. The answer would be the same.'

As she turned and marched towards the door, his final words followed her. 'And don't think about running away, will you? Our punishments are very severe for runaways.'

Hannah looked back over her shoulder, staring at him for a moment.

She hadn't thought of doing any such thing. At least, not until he had put the idea into her head.

Ten

'So.' Nell smiled. 'Are you ready to become a piecer?'

Hannah nodded. The previous evening she'd written her first letter to her mother. It was nestling in her skirt pocket. She planned to take it to Mr Roper at dinnertime. But for now, she must concentrate on what Nell was telling her.

'We work for the women who operate the spinning machines – mules, they're called. You'll be with me and Dorothy Riley to start with. Then, when you're good enough, you'll work with someone else.'

Hannah smiled. 'What do we have to do?'

'When a thread breaks we have to twist the ends back together again. But you have to be quick, 'cos they don't stop the machine.'

'Isn't it dangerous?'

Nell shrugged and pulled a face. 'Not if we're quick. And the women are good. They shout a warning.' Nell leaned forward and lowered her voice. 'The women get paid for every piece they produce, and if we can mend the broken threads without the machines having to be stopped, they can earn more. Sometimes, at the end of the week, they'll give us a few pence out of their own wages 'cos we've helped 'em earn more, see? We'll be working with Mrs Riley. She's ever so generous. She'll see us right. And you need nimble fingers.'

She flexed her own long, slim fingers and laughed. 'Mr Edmund says I've got nimble fingers.'

'Mr Edmund? I thought it was Mr Scarsfield who told us what work we're to do.'

Nell stared at her for a long moment, then seeing the genuine look of puzzlement on the younger girl's face, she gave a small sigh and said flatly, 'Yes, yes, of course it is. That's what I meant to say. Mr Scarsfield.' She smiled and linked her arm through Hannah's as they moved into one of the spinning rooms, where the clatter of machinery was deafening. Hannah grimaced but she saw Nell was laughing. 'You'll soon get used to it,' the girl mouthed at her.

For the morning, Hannah just observed Nell watching the rows and rows of yarn being drawn and twisted. The girl never took her eyes off the machine, and the moment a thread snapped, she swiftly twisted the broken ends together. By dinnertime, Hannah had a slight headache from staring at all the fine strands of cotton and the noise all around her, but she kept the fact to herself. Not one word of complaint would pass her lips. The job was a good one for a child of her age and – like Nell said – she was sure she would get used to it. Nevertheless, she was pleased to escape into the fresh air in the hour's break for dinner. She ran lightly across the yard and up the stone steps to the counting house. At his 'come in' in answer to her knock, Hannah opened the door and stepped inside to stand meekly before Mr Roper's desk, waiting until he should condescend to look up and acknowledge her presence. He kept her waiting – deliberately, she thought – for what seemed an age, until Hannah was afraid she'd be late back to her work.

'Don't fidget, girl. What is it you want?' he snapped, looking up at last.

'Please, sir, Mr Edmund said you'd see that a letter's posted for me.'

Hannah gave him what she hoped was her most winning smile, but it was lost on the embittered man. He merely glanced at her briefly over his spectacles and grunted sourly, 'Leave it there. I'll see to it.'

'Thank you, sir. Thank you very much.'

As Hannah left the office, Josiah Roper picked up the letter and, for a moment, weighed it in the palm of his hand. He glanced at the door, listening to make sure she had gone. He could hear her footsteps clattering down the steps and her sweet voice echoing back up the stairs. Josiah's mouth curled with disdain. Singing, indeed! How anyone could feel like singing in this place he couldn't imagine. He unfolded the letter to read her neat, childish handwriting.

'*Dearest Mam, I hope you are well. I am fine and now working as a piecer with Nell, who is my friend.*' The letter went on to describe the apprentice house and Mr and Mrs Bramwell and some of the other children. She made no mention, Josiah noticed, of the Critchlows or the fact that she'd already been confined to the punishment room on several occasions and that stoppages had been made out of her precious two guineas now in Josiah Roper's keeping. He smiled wryly. The child made this place sound idyllic, but, he realized, the girl wanted her mother to believe her well and happy.

Perhaps she was, Josiah thought, surprised. If her wretched singing was anything to go by.

The letter finished with a plea. '*I do wish you would write to me. I long to hear from you and know that you are all right. Perhaps matron would write a letter for you.'*

Josiah frowned thoughtfully. The matron. Matilda Goodbody. Ah, now there was an idea – if it should become necessary. He glanced at the door once more before slowly tearing the letter into small pieces. He was not taking this action on his own initiative; Edmund had given the instruction.

'Destroy them, Roper,' he'd said. 'And make sure no incoming letter reaches her.'

Josiah smiled cruelly, deliciously anticipating what the girl might do when no answer to her letters arrived.

As Hannah and Nell left the mill that evening and crossed the yard, they passed a boy talking to Ernest Scarsfield. The newcomer was tall and very good-looking in Hannah's eyes. He had dark brown hair and eyes to match. He looked a little solemn, but then, she thought, he might well if he had any idea what he was coming to. She bent towards Nell to whisper, 'Do you think he's come for a job?'

'Eh?' Nell gaped at her in surprise. Then she laughed. 'Don't you know who that is?'

Hannah shook her head.

'That's the next Critchlow. Adam. He's Mr Edmund's son. We don't see much of him though. He's away at school most of the time. Just now and again he comes to the mill when he's home for the holidays.' She grinned. 'To check his inheritance, I expect.'

Hannah glanced back over her shoulder and stared at the young man. He looked a little older than she was. Fourteen or maybe fifteen, she thought. She could see now that he had the look of his father, the same dark colouring. Yet there was a marked difference: the boy had no cruel, sardonic twist to his mouth. As if feeling her scrutiny, Adam Critchlow turned and their eyes met. Embarrassed, a faint blush crept up Hannah's face and she looked away swiftly.

'Well, I'm off to the schoolroom,' she said, deliberately changing the subject.

'Not for much longer you won't be. You're not allowed to go after you're twelve.'

'Oh.' Hannah bit her lip. She was twelve already, almost thirteen, but she loved the two hours in the schoolroom after work each day. It was the only place she never got into trouble. Though the master was strict, Hannah so enjoyed soaking up the knowledge that her attention never wavered. She could write neatly, spell reasonably well and was above average at arithmetic. Some of the children, even at her age, still couldn't write their name in the sand tray, let alone be allowed to move on to use a slate. But Hannah was surprisingly alert even after long hours in the mill.

For the teacher, who laboured with children too exhausted to take in anything he was telling them, Hannah was a joy to teach. The elderly schoolmaster found his stern ways softening towards this able pupil. He had never before encountered such an enthusiastic child amongst the pauper apprentices at the mill. So, when later that same evening Hannah approached him as the other children escaped the classroom, he smiled at her. The girl didn't return his smile.

'What is it?' he asked. 'Something amiss?'

'Please, sir, I understand I'm not supposed to come to school any more. I'm thirteen next month.'

'Ah.'

'But I don't want to stop coming for lessons, Mr Jessop. That book you're reading to us – *Swiss Family Robinson* – I love it. I want to know what happens. I want to hear the end.'

The man was thoughtful for a moment. 'Has anyone said anything to you? Mr Critchlow, Mr Edmund or the Bramwells – about you not being able to attend classes any more?'

Hannah shook her head.

A twinkle came into Mr Jessop's eyes. A twinkle that very few of his pupils ever saw. He leaned towards her. 'Then we'll carry on until someone tells us to stop, eh?' He pointed his forefinger at her. 'You don't know the rule about stopping at twelve, and I,' now he pointed towards himself, 'don't know how old you are.'

Hannah's eyes shone. 'Oh, thank you, Mr Jessop.'

'Just one thing, mind,' he added. 'You won't be able to tell anyone that it's your birthday.'

'I don't mind. I'd rather keep coming to school.'

Mr Jessop nodded. 'Very well, then. Our little secret, eh?'

It would be six months before anyone realized that Hannah should no longer be attending the school, but in that time Mr Jessop had finished reading the story and started another. When she was forced to stop attending, he lent her books from the schoolroom. And whenever Hannah found herself destined for a spell in the punishment room, she hid the current precious book beneath her skirt and was lost in another world away from the stark confines of the bare room.

Little did anyone know that, apart from constant hunger, Hannah now quite enjoyed her spells of solitary confinement.

As Nell had said, Dorothy Riley was more than just 'nice', she was generous with her pay at the end of the week.

'There you are, my pets,' she said, slipping a few coppers into the girls' hands outside the mill gates. 'Can't promise it every week, but you've done really well considering it's your first week. Mind you,' she laughed, eyeing them, 'I don't think you'll be at the job long. You'll soon be a mite too big to nip in and out. Besides, old Scarsfield's got his eye on you two to go up in the world.'

Nell and Hannah exchanged glances. 'You think so, Mrs Riley?'

'I know so, luv. So, you keep on the way you are and you'll soon be earning proper money of your own.'

Hannah pulled a face. 'Well, Nell might. She's older than me, but I've a long way to go before I'm out of my indenture.'

Dorothy laughed. 'Don't you worry about that, luv. Our Ernest has ways and means of getting round that if he finds a really good worker amongst the apprentices.' She tapped the side of her nose knowingly. 'You mark my words.'

The two girls were to find that Dorothy Riley was even more generous in sharing her knowledge and experience with her two young piecers. When the machine was running smoothly, she made them watch her every move and explained everything she did and everything that happened. Before long, Hannah was working with another woman, Mrs Martin, who was as generous as Dorothy Riley.

'And when we get a machine of our own,' Hannah asked Dorothy, 'might we get paid then?'

'You should do, but now *he's* running the mill, he's put a stop to all that. Ernest told me himself. He's mad about it an' all, but there's nowt he can do. Sorry, luv.' Hannah pulled a face, knowing Dorothy was referring to Mr Edmund. 'Ah well, what you never have, you never miss, eh?'

Dorothy laughed. 'So they say, but I've never quite believed it myself.'

Hannah had settled in quickly to her new work and, whilst she still sang, no one else could hear her now above the noise of the machinery. Hannah sang on, hopeful every day that word would come from her mother. But the days and weeks turned into months, and still no answer came to her letters. At last, worried out of her mind and longing to see Rebecca, Hannah made up her mind to go back to Macclesfield to the workhouse and find out for herself.

'Oh no, Hannah, don't do that. You'll get into such trouble.' Jane's eyes filled with tears and she clutched Hannah's hand. 'They put children who run away into that awful room for a week. And they might beat you.'

Hannah wished she had not confided in the younger girl.

'I know you must want to see your mam,' Jane

went on. 'But she wouldn't want you to get into such trouble. You know she wouldn't.'

Hannah bit her lip. That much was true, but she was so worried about her mother now. Why had she not heard from her? Something must be wrong. After the conversation with Mr Edmund three months ago now, she'd written four letters, dutifully taking each one to the office and handing it to Mr Roper. She was not to know that, as with the first, moments after she'd left the room her loving letter lay in shreds in the bottom of Mr Roper's waste paper basket.

'I have to go,' was Hannah's simple answer to Jane. 'But forget I ever told you. And don't tell anyone else. If they ask, you mustn't tell them anything.'

Miserably the younger girl nodded. 'I wish you hadn't told me,' she whispered.

So do I, Hannah thought, and vowed not to tell anyone else.

Eleven

'Coming for a walk this afternoon?' Luke asked her as the apprentices trooped back from the schoolroom one Sunday morning. The service was not just for the apprentices, but for the whole village. Sometimes a man who lived in the village led the worship, and sometimes they had a visiting preacher. Hannah's favourite was the local doctor who lived in the next village. Dr Barnes was a portly figure with a round, red, beaming face and bushy side-whiskers. He was a benevolent preacher, gently exhorting his congregation to try to lead a blameless life. He didn't make Hannah feel sinful by just being alive like some of the other preachers did, thumping poor Mr Jessop's desk and shouting at the cowering youngsters in a thunderous voice that echoed to the rafters.

'I'd like to, Luke,' Hannah said, 'but I've got something else I have to do this afternoon.'

'What?'

She grinned at him. 'Never you mind.'

'I do mind. I thought you was my girl. You meeting some other feller, then? It's that Joe, I bet.' His jealousy was real. If an adult had overheard them, they might have roared with laughter at such a conversation taking place between two children. But the twelve-year-old boy (the twins had had a birthday since their arrival at the mill, though, like Hannah's, it had passed

97

unnoticed) and the thirteen-year-old girl, working as hard as they did in the mill, considered themselves more grown up than others thought them.

'I talk to everybody, haven't you noticed?' Hannah said saucily.

He grinned ruefully. 'Yeah. All right, you do.' He paused and then asked, 'What's so important then that you won't come out, though? Got my socks to darn, 'ave yer?'

Darning socks was one of the many tasks Hannah had to tackle in Mrs Bramwell's sewing class. Strangely, the woman turned a blind eye if some of the girls did not present themselves in the kitchen every Sunday afternoon. It was the only occasion on which she showed leniency. Earlier that morning she'd called Hannah into her sitting room. The girl had stood in front of her, sighing inwardly and raking through her mind to think what she was in trouble for this time. But Ethel Bramwell was smiling. 'I don't mind you going out on a Sunday afternoon, Francis. In fact, if I'd my way, you children ought to be encouraged to walk out on a Sunday afternoon.' She sighed. 'But I have my orders as I'm sure you know.'

It was the closest the superintendent would come to criticizing their employers to one of her charges. But for some reason, Ethel Bramwell trusted this girl. She couldn't explain why. Maybe it was the girl's spirit that refused to be cowed or her open honesty. Whatever Hannah did, she would always own up to it and take her punishment cheerfully. She had even been known to take the blame for something someone else had done – if that someone was one of her close friends.

'But,' Mrs Bramwell was saying, 'you're one of the

neatest workers I've got. Your darning is as good as mine. The simple truth is, Hannah, I need your help.'

Hannah, noticing the woman's use of her Christian name, knew her words were sincere and her praise genuine.

'So,' Mrs Bramwell went on. 'How about you and I strike up a bargain? You come to my sewing classes on alternate Sundays and you're free to go out into the hills on the other days.'

Hannah beamed, delighted that, for once, she was not going to have to break the rules.

'Thank you, ma'am,' she said simply, and vowed to work twice as hard as anyone else on the days she tackled the piles of mending that Mrs Bramwell laid in her lap.

Now, Hannah punched Luke playfully on the shoulder for his impudence. Impulsively, and breaking her promise to herself, she turned to face him. 'Luke, don't tell a soul, but I'm so worried about me mam. I've written four times and not a word's come back. I have to go and see her.' Her words came tumbling out. 'I went to see Mr Critchlow – to ask permission – but there was only Mr Edmund there and he wouldn't let me go.'

Luke shook his head. 'The old man wouldn't't've done either. Don't do it, Hannah. Please. It's not that bad here if you behave yourself, but they're devils if you don't.' He was still remembering the beating he'd had.

Anguished, Hannah cried, 'But what else can I do? I've got to know if me mam's all right.'

Luke bit his lip, thinking. 'Why don't you ask Mrs Bramwell to see if she can find out for you?'

Hannah shook her head. 'She'd only say the same

as Mr Edmund. "If we do it for one, they'll all want it." That's what he said about letting me go to see her.'

'Oh.' Luke had run out of ideas. He bit his lip worriedly. 'So – what're you thinking of doing then?'

'Going anyway,' she said firmly.

'What? This afternoon?'

'No – I was going to see Mrs Grundy. See if she'll help me. She might know if I can get a ride to Buxton . . .'

Luke shook his head. 'It might make things awkward for her.'

'How . . . how do you mean?'

'She'll know we're not supposed to run away. She wouldn't help you do something wrong like that.'

'She's nothing to do with the mill, is she?'

Luke shrugged. 'They supply the milk and other food. The Critchlows might cause trouble for her.'

'Oh,' Hannah said. 'I hadn't thought of that.'

They walked on in silence.

'Look,' Luke said. 'We could still go and see her this afternoon. I'll come with you. We could sort of bring the talk round. Tell her you're that worried about yer mam. She might think of something.'

Now Hannah stopped and turned to face him. 'You really mean you'll help me? You'll not try to stop me going?'

Luke regarded her solemnly. 'I don't think you should go. You'll get caught and brought back here and punished. You might not even get as far as the workhouse to see yer mam and then it'll have all been for nothing.'

'But I'll have tried, won't I?'

Luke nodded. 'Yeah, and I can't blame you for trying. If I was in your shoes, I'd do exactly what you're doing.'

Hannah squeezed his arm in gratitude.

'Hello, my dears. This is a nice surprise. Come away into the warm. Blustery old day even for October, isn't it? Winter's coming early this year, I reckon. There's a nice piece of beef and roast potatoes left from our dinner.' Lily Grundy reached out and pinched Luke's cheek playfully. 'You must have known there were leftovers.'

She chuckled as she ushered them into her warm kitchen and sat them at the table. Though the fare at the apprentice house was adequate, it was never enough to assuage growing appetites, and the two youngsters fell to eating the food she placed in front of them with gusto.

'Where's the mester?' Luke asked, his mouth full and gravy oozing out of the corner of his lips.

'In the front room fast asleep. Just like he always is on a Sunday afternoon. You'll see him later,' she laughed. 'If you can stay long enough.'

'He works very hard. I 'spect he deserves a sleep on a Sunday,' Luke remarked, popping another loaded forkful into his mouth.

'This is wonderful, Mrs Grundy,' Hannah said. 'I haven't tasted meals like this since – since . . .' Her voice faltered and for a moment tears filled her eyes. She blinked them back hastily, but not before both Luke and Mrs Grundy had noticed.

'It's because of Hannah we've come to see you,'

Luke rushed in. 'See, her mother's still in the work-house we came from, but Hannah's never heard word of her since we left. She's worried about her.'

Mrs Grundy's face sobered and she looked first at one and then the other anxiously.

'Hannah asked for permission to go and see her mother,' Luke went on. 'But—'

Mrs Grundy's generous mouth pursed as she finished his sentence. 'They won't let her go.'

'I asked Mr Edmund,' Hannah said, trying to keep her voice steady. 'But . . . but he said no.'

'Huh! Him! He would!' Mrs Grundy's tone was scathing and there was a bitter note to her words. She sighed heavily and sat down at the table, resting her arms on its surface. 'I don't often talk about this, but you both seem nice enough young 'uns.' Her glance roamed over Hannah's face as if assessing her.

Hannah dropped her gaze in embarrassment. Not so bashful, Luke grinned. 'We are.'

Mrs Grundy gave a faint smile, but it faded as she went on. 'We've never been blessed with children, me and the mester, but we've nephews and nieces. My brother's got a boy and a girl, but they live away. Right down south, so we don't see much of them. But Ollie's sister lives up the hill.' She nodded her head in the direction of Millersbrook, the village perched on the hillside above the mill. 'She'd a lad and – and a little lass.' She paused a moment and wiped a tear away with the corner of her apron. 'The lad – Ted – works here on the farm with Ollie. He's a good boy and – because we've no family of our own – this farm'll be his one day.' For a moment she pressed her lips together to stop them trembling. 'But their Lucy, she went into the mill.' She paused again as if the telling of this tale was painful. 'She was apprenticed and, just like you are I expect, she was given all the rotten jobs to start with. She had to crawl under the machinery. One day, there was an accident and her lovely hair got caught.' The woman closed her eyes, screwing up her face as she relived the agony. 'Tore it off her head, it did. Scalped her.'

The two youngsters stared at her with absolute horror. 'Did she – I mean – was she . . . ?'

Mrs Grundy nodded and her voice was a whisper. 'Yes, she died. Poor little mite. Only twelve, she was.'

There was silence between them, the only sounds the singing of the kettle on the hob, the settling of coal in the grate and a sudden flurry of sparks up the chimney.

At last Mrs Grundy cleared her throat and, her voice stronger now, said, 'So, if you want any help, Hannah, any time, you come to me and Ollie. We'll help you. We've no time for them at the mill. No time at all.'

'But . . . but I thought you supplied the milk an' that?' Luke asked.

Mrs Grundy's mouth was grim. 'We do. It goes against the grain, in a way, but we argued it out. One,' she ticked the reasons off on her fingers, 'it's business. We've a living to make. Two, we've nowt against the Bramwells. In fact, I'm quite friendly with Ethel Bramwell, and Ollie has a drink in the Wyedale Arms with Arthur. They were as upset as anyone over the accident. And three, we reckon if we supply the house, then we know you youngsters are getting good food. We . . . we reckon it's what our little Lucy would've wanted.'

There was logic in their reasoning, Hannah supposed,

though she thought she'd have been hard put to have anything further to do with the place if that had happened to one of her relatives or someone she cared for.

She said nothing as Mrs Grundy repeated, 'So, we'll help you whenever you need it – if we can.'

Luke spoke up for Hannah. 'She wants to go and see her mother. She knows that she'll probably be caught and punished, but she'll risk that, if she can just find out if her mother's all right.'

Mrs Grundy eyed Hannah. 'So, what do you want to do exactly?'

For a moment, Hannah gazed at her. Could she really trust this woman? Would she and her husband really help her or would they take her straight back to the apprentice house where she'd be locked in the punishment room? Luke, sensing her misgivings, reached across the table and touched her hand. 'It's all right, Hannah. Go on, tell Mrs Grundy.'

The woman's eyes softened. 'It's all right, dear. We won't let you down, I promise.'

'I . . . I thought if I left late one Saturday after work and walked through the night to Buxton, I could maybe get a lift on the carrier's cart from there. But I don't know the way. I know we came from Buxton to here, but I don't know which road to take to get back there.'

'All them corners and hills, I 'spect you lost your sense of direction,' Mrs Grundy said.

Hannah wasn't quite sure what she meant, but she nodded.

''Course,' the woman went on, musing aloud. 'If you was walking, the best way is up through the village and go by the country roads. But a little lass, on your own and in the dark, you could easy get lost.'

'I could go with her,' Luke began, but Hannah interrupted swiftly.

'No, I won't have you getting in trouble because of me. Thanks, Luke, but I've got to do this on me own.'

'Well,' Mrs Grundy said slowly. 'There's another way. Ollie could take you as far as Buxton in the cart and then you could make your way from there. Mebbe you could catch the coach from there. Or beg a lift with a carrier going to Macclesfield.'

The two youngsters stared at her. 'Would Ollie – I mean, Mr Grundy – do that for me?'

Mrs Grundy shrugged. 'I dunno, but we could ask him.' She began to rise as if to go and ask her husband there and then, but Hannah touched her arm, 'No, please, don't wake him.'

Lily Grundy sat down again, smiling comically. 'P'raps you're right. He'd not be in the best of moods to be woken from his Sunday afternoon nap.' She thought for a moment before saying, 'I tell you what you could do. You might beg a lift with the chap who fetches our milk every morning. Mind you, he's here early. One or two folks from the dale beg a lift with him now and again. He won't charge you anything and he'll take you nearly to Buxton. You could walk the rest of the way. Mind you –' she was thinking aloud now – 'you'd need some money to get a ride from there to Macclesfield.'

Hannah pulled a wry face. 'I haven't got any.'

'You've still got your two guineas from the work-house, ain't yer?' Luke reminded her.

'Well – yes, but . . . but Mr Critchlow,' she smiled

105

ruefully, 'or rather Mr Roper has charge of that. They'd likely demand to know what I wanted it for. Besides,' she grimaced ruefully, 'Mr Edmund said it's to pay for stoppages and I reckon Roper's taken some out of it already.'

'I'll lend you some, luv,' Mrs Grundy offered. 'And then you pay me back when you can. Few pence a week. I wouldn't mind.'

Hannah's eyes filled with tears at the woman's kindness. Mrs Grundy scarcely knew her, yet she was offering her far more than anyone at the mill would. She hesitated, but Luke urged her to accept. 'Go on, Hannah. You've got the chance of earning a bit now you're a piecer, and Mrs Grundy wouldn't offer if she didn't mean it.'

'It's very kind of you and I will pay you back. Every penny.'

Mrs Grundy patted her hand. ''Course you will, luv. I know that. So, when are you going to go?'

'Next Saturday,' Hannah said firmly, before she could lose her nerve.

'Right. Well, you'll need to be up at the top near the Arms by five o'clock in the morning. Ollie always takes our churns up there for him. And I'll get you the money now. Enough for coming back, an' all.'

'I don't know how to thank you.' Now Hannah allowed the tears of gratitude to spill over.

Twelve

'What are you two whispering about?'

Hannah and Jane looked up guiltily at Nell's question. The older girl's smile faded when she saw their expressions. 'Hey, I was only joking, but you really are up to something, aren't you?' She pursed her lips. 'I just hope it's nothing that's going to get us all into trouble, that's all.'

Hannah forced a laugh. ''Course it isn't.'

Nell moved closer. 'What then? What's going on? Is one of you in trouble already? Is that it?'

'No, but she will be if she does what she says she's going to,' Jane burst out, her face red.

'Jane!' Hannah cried, but the damage was done. Now Nell wouldn't let the matter drop.

Suddenly, she was very anxious. 'You're not going to run away?' This was the unthinkable. It was what carried the severest of punishments. Even a girl could be beaten for that.

'No,' Hannah said reluctantly. 'I'll come back.'

'So – what are you going to do?'

'She's going back to Macclesfield to see her mam,' Jane blurted out. 'She's never heard from her all the time we've been here.'

Nell looked at Hannah with a mixture of pity and fear. 'I can understand you wanting to go, but you won't half be in for trouble when you get back. And you probably won't even make it to Macclesfield. They'll catch up with you long before you get there and they'll never believe that you meant to come back.' She pulled a face. 'Not many of us would, if we once got out.' She paused, hoping she'd made the girl change her mind, but seeing the determination on Hannah's face, Nell sighed and asked flatly, 'So, when are you going?'

Hannah put her hand warningly on Jane's arm to stop her saying any more and faced Nell. 'It's best you don't know.'

Now Nell was indignant. 'Don't you trust me?'

Hannah was quick to say, ''Course I do, but – like you say – there's no need for anyone else to be in trouble. Only me.'

Nell nodded towards Jane. 'Well, she will be. She sleeps with you, and the rest of us can hardly say we haven't noticed you're missing.'

'I'll go early, while you're all still asleep. All you've got to do is to know nothing when they ask you.' She laughed. 'You can say you thought I was in the punishment room. I spend enough time there.'

Nell snorted. 'You'll be spending a lot more in there an' all when they catch you.' Then she sighed and relented. 'But we could cover for you for a bit. Give you time to get right away.'

Hannah shook her head. 'It's good of you, Nell, but I'd rather none of you knew. There's just one thing. I've decided to go early on a Saturday. It'll give me two days. I know how I can get a lift part of the way and I'll get back – somehow – on Sunday night. Thing is, Mr Scarsfield'll miss me at work.'

'He might not. He doesn't come round so much on a Saturday. Spends the morning with the bosses in the office. Planning next week's work. I know, 'cos—' Nell stopped suddenly and bit her lip. A faint blush tinged her face. 'Anyway,' she went on swiftly, 'me and Jane'll play dim, and the rest of them really won't know anything. And I'll cover your machine for Mrs Martin. I'll tell 'er you're not well or summat.' Now Nell glanced severely at Jane. 'So don't go telling anyone else, see.'

Jane shook her head, red-faced and tearful that she had given away Hannah's secret. 'I'm sorry, Hannah.'

Hannah put her arms around her and hugged her. 'It's all right. No harm done.'

She hoped fervently that she was right.

On the Saturday morning, very early, Hannah slipped out of the bed she shared with Jane, managing not to disturb the sleeping child. Carrying her clothes, she tiptoed out of the room and dressed on the landing outside the dormitory. It was still dark as she crept down the stairs and into the kitchen. The noise, as she opened the back door, seemed to echo through the house. She held her breath a moment, listening, but there was no movement from above that might mean someone had heard her. As quietly as she could, she pulled the door shut behind her and set off down the hill, then along the wall side and past the pillared gate leading into the mill. Once clear, she began to run up the lane. Passing the Grundys' farm, she could hear sounds from the cow shed but she didn't dare to linger. She wasn't sure of the time and she didn't want to miss the man who collected the milk.

At the top of the hill she bent over to catch her

breath but was relieved to see that Mr Grundy's churns were still standing against the low stone wall. She sat down beside them, leaning her back against the rough stones. As she waited she watched the dawn streaking the sky with a rosy peach colour and the world around her grew lighter. She listened, straining her ears for the sound of the rattling wheels of a cart that might herald the carrier's arrival.

She had no means of telling the time and she began to worry that she'd missed him. Perhaps the churns were empty, returned for the farmer to refill the next day. She tapped the side of the one nearest to her and heard the dull sound that meant it was full of milk. She breathed a sigh of relief. But then she heard another sound – a sound she dreaded hearing. Footsteps were coming up the last stretch of the hill, nearer and nearer. Someone else was coming from the valley to beg a lift too. She watched as a figure, climbing the last few feet, appeared. Hannah drew in a startled gasp. The man was walking with his head bowed. She couldn't see his features, but there was no mistaking his hunched stance. Shocked, she couldn't move. And then it was too late to run as he lifted his head and saw her.

'You!' Josiah Roper came towards her slowly, his beady eyes never leaving her face. As he drew closer she could see that he was smiling with sadistic pleasure. 'Running away, are you?'

Now her boldness returned. She stood up, facing him and saying stoutly, 'No, I'm not. I'm coming back tomorrow tonight. I'm going to see my mother in Macclesfield.'

For a brief moment even Josiah Roper seemed fazed by her bold, yet polite retort. But he recovered quickly to say, 'I thought I heard Mr Edmund tell you distinctly that you couldn't go?'

There was a brief silence before Hannah muttered, 'He did. But,' she added, more strongly, 'I mean to come back. I'm not a runaway, Mr Roper, truly I'm not.' She stepped closer, trying to appeal to the man's better nature – if he had one. 'I have to see my mother. I have to know if she's all right. I haven't heard a word from her ever since I came here. And you know I've written four times.'

'That's as may be, but you cannot go without the master's permission . . .'

At that moment, they both heard the sound of the carrier's rattling wheels.

'Oh, please, Mr Roper, let me go. I beg you. I swear on my mother's life that I'm coming back tomorrow night. I *promise* you.'

But he was smiling nastily. 'I don't believe you. I'll have to take you back.'

'But – but you'll miss your ride too. Please, Mr Roper . . .'

But delivering an errant child back to the punishment that awaited her would bring Josiah Roper far more satisfaction than his monthly weekend trip to Buxton to see his widowed mother.

'Mr Roper.' Mrs Bramwell's face was puzzled as she opened the back door of the apprentice house to the man's loud knocking. Then her glance travelled down a little to see the girl standing beside him and saw that he was gripping Hannah's arm tightly. For a clerk who sat hunched over a desk all day, Josiah was surprisingly strong.

111

'Francis?' Now there was an anxious question in her tone as if she already knew – and feared – the answer.

'I found this girl at the top of the hill, waiting – would you believe? – for a ride with the milk cart. And where, I'd like to know,' Josiah put his head on one side and smiled accusingly, 'did she get the money to take a trip all the way to Macclesfield?'

Mrs Bramwell's mouth dropped open and she glanced from one to the other. 'Well, you needn't look at me like that, Mr Roper. I know nothing about this, believe me.'

Josiah grunted. 'Really. Then in that case you've shown a serious dereliction of your duties, Mrs Bramwell. Because you should've known and put a stop to it.' He gave a mock sigh, pretending that what he was about to say pained him. 'I shall be obliged to report the matter to Mr Edmund.'

Ethel Bramwell stared at him before saying bitterly, 'Oh, I'm sure you will, Mr Roper. Nothing'll give you greater pleasure, will it?'

'It's not Mrs Bramwell's fault,' Hannah cried. 'She knew nothing about it. No one did.' She looked up at Ethel. 'And I wasn't running away, Mrs Bramwell. I was coming back tomorrow night. I was only trying to see my mother.'

'A fine tale,' Josiah snorted. 'Since when did any child voluntarily come back if they once got away from here?'

'Me.' Hannah glared up at him. 'If I say I'll do something, then I'll do it.'

The adults looked down at her. She could see that Mrs Bramwell wanted to believe her, but there was no softening in Josiah Roper's attitude. 'Where did you get the money? Did you steal it?'

'No,' Hannah gasped, horrified that anyone could think such a thing of her.

His grip tightened painfully on her shoulder and he bent menacingly towards her. 'Then where did you get it?' His face close to hers, Hannah stared into his beady eyes and shivered fearfully.

But now Hannah couldn't answer truthfully. She wouldn't involve Mrs Grundy. 'I . . . I saved it. It was mine.'

'Saved it? How? You came from the workhouse and all they give you is the two guineas you handed to Mr Critchlow.' He smiled maliciously. 'And I still have that in my safekeeping.'

'That he took off us, you mean,' Hannah said rashly and earned herself a clout across the side of the head from Josiah.

'I asked you where you got the money,' he shouted, but now Mrs Bramwell intervened.

'That's enough, Mr Roper. You've no right to touch this girl. No right at all. She's my responsibility.'

Josiah turned on the woman. 'Then you'd better start doing your job, Mrs Bramwell, or else—'

'Oh yes, Mr Roper, or else – what? You lay another finger on this girl – or any of the children in my charge – and I'll be the one doing a bit of reporting to the master. To Mr Nathaniel Critchlow.'

They glared at each other, whilst Hannah stood watching, biting her lip and chastising herself for her wayward tongue. It'd got her into trouble before and it looked as if she'd made matters worse now.

Josiah turned away, but as he did so, he wagged his

finger in Mrs Bramwell's face. 'You watch out, Ethel Bramwell. You just watch your step, that's all I'm saying.'

As he turned to go, Mrs Bramwell reached out and dragged Hannah into the kitchen and slammed the door. 'And now, young lady, I'll deal with you.'

Thirteen

'It's out of our hands. There's nothing we can do about it, Arthur.'

Mr and Mrs Bramwell were standing either side of the kitchen table, arguing over the girl who sat between them calmly eating her porridge. They glanced at Hannah with expressions of anger tinged with pity. They were cross with her for – as they believed – attempting to run away. They, as well as she, would be in trouble. But more than the concern for themselves, they pitied the golden-haired girl for the punishment they knew awaited her – a punishment of which she was, at this moment, blithely unaware.

'Roper knows. He brought her back. He'll waste no time in telling the master or Mr Edmund.'

Arthur Bramwell regarded the girl sorrowfully. 'The old man's away. It'll be Mr Edmund he tells.'

'Ah!' Ethel let out a deep sigh and murmured, 'Poor child.'

Arthur leaned on his hands on the table, large, capable hands that had never been afraid of manual work, hands that were just as ready to caress as to chastise the apprentices in his care. He was a big man, broad and strong and quiet, and when he could he protected the youngsters. Sometimes he had to beat them, but he made sure he did not damage them physically. It was humiliation he wished to inflict rather than actual hurt. Just to make them toe the line. But when it came to the matter of a child running away, he was powerless to prevent the inevitable punishment.

'Why did you do it, Francis? Why did you try to run away?'

Hannah swallowed the last mouthful and laid her spoon in the empty bowl. She looked up at them both, first at Mrs Bramwell's anxious face and then at the big man's. During the time she'd been here, she'd come to like and respect this couple. They were strict, but fair, and she knew they really cared about all the children. She was sorry to have caused them trouble and said so, adding, 'But I wasn't running away. I just had to go and try and find out how me mother is. I asked for permission, but Mr Edmund refused me.'

'So,' Arthur said in his deep rumbling voice. 'You went anyway?'

Hannah bit her lip and nodded. 'I'm sorry,' she said huskily. 'But you've got to believe me, Mr Bramwell, I was coming back.'

'Do you really mean that?' It seemed as if Arthur Bramwell couldn't quite believe what he was hearing.

Hannah nodded. 'I like it here. The work's hard, but I don't mind that. And I like the people.' She pulled a face. 'Well, most of them. All except Mr Roper.'

She didn't like Mr Edmund either, but she thought it wise not to say so at this moment.

Husband and wife glanced at each other and, though they said no more, Hannah could see that neither of them really believed her. And if they didn't, then there was not the remotest chance that either of the Critchlows would, especially Mr Edmund.

'Well, we'd best get it over with,' Ethel Bramwell said. 'Come on, girl.'

'Want me to go with her, Ethel?' Arthur straightened up and looked across at his wife, but she shook her head. 'No, no, Arthur. The girls are my responsibility. It'll not be the first time I've had to stand there and take his abuse – nor will it be the last.'

Again they both looked down at Hannah. 'Mebbe he won't be so hard on her,' Arthur murmured, intending that Hannah should not hear him, but her sharp hearing caught every word. 'She's a pretty little thing.'

But Ethel answered swiftly, 'I'd sooner see her spend a week in the punishment room than anything else he might have in mind.'

'Well, keep your eye on her. She's just the sort he goes for. Give her another year or two and – well . . .'

His voice petered out as Mrs Bramwell took hold of Hannah's shoulder and propelled the girl in front of her. 'He'll have to get past me first. He can get up to his tricks with the mill girls from the village if he likes. They'll have to look out for themselves, but he's not having his way with any of my girls. Not if I can help it. Mind you,' she lowered her voice. 'I don't seem to be managing it with young Nell.' She raised her voice. 'Come on, you. Let's get it over with.'

Hannah wasn't sure who was trembling the most as they stepped into the inner office.

Even though it was Saturday morning, Edmund Critchlow was sitting behind his desk, leaning back, rocking slightly as he regarded them through his dark, hooded eyes.

'So, girl, you thought you could defy me and get away with it, did you?'

'Mr Edmund—' Mrs Bramwell began, but the man

held up his hand to silence her, his glance never leaving Hannah's face.

'Well, what have you to say for yourself?'

Hannah lifted her chin and met his eyes boldly. Inside she was quaking, but she was determined not to let this man see her fear. 'I'm truly sorry, Mr Edmund, that I disobeyed you. I just wanted to see my mother.'

'Don't you think all the children here would like to see their mothers? Why should you be different?'

With an outward calmness, Hannah answered, 'Most of the children in the house have no mothers – or fathers. They're orphans. I'm not. I have a mother. I wanted to see her. I've written to her four times – like you suggested – and brought the letters to Mr Roper to send, but I've not had a word back. I just want to know she's all right. That's all.'

It was quite simple to the girl's mind. She couldn't understand why no one else could see it. And worse still, she couldn't understand why anyone would deliberately want to keep a child from its mother.

Edmund leaned forward, tapping the desk with his forefinger. 'I thought I'd made it clear last time. When you came here, you signed a paper. You remember?'

'Yes, sir.'

'And do you know what that paper was?'

'An indenture, sir.'

'Quite right. And what did it mean?'

'That I'm apprenticed to you for six years.'

'Exactly. Six years. And that means you do not run away during that time.'

'I wasn't running away, sir. I keep trying to tell you – and everyone – I was coming back tomorrow night. As soon as I'd seen my mother.'

For a moment, Edmund stared at her and then his lip curled, 'You really expect me to believe that?'

Hannah met his gaze steadily. 'Yes,' she said simply, 'because it's the truth.'

'She's a good girl usually, sir,' Mrs Bramwell began but Edmund snapped.

'Hold your tongue, Bramwell. I'll have more to say to you later. I hold you responsible for all this.'

'Mrs Bramwell had nothing to do with it, sir,' Hannah spoke up. 'She knew nothing about it. I let myself out of the back door this morning, really early. Before anyone was up.'

'That's no excuse. You shouldn't have been able to get out. The door should have been locked and the key hidden.'

Mrs Bramwell opened her mouth to protest, but at the sight of the young master's glowering face, she closed it again.

His mouth was tight, his thick black eyebrows drawn together almost hiding his cruel eyes. 'Well, we have a way of dealing with runaways here.'

Hannah opened her mouth to say, 'I'm not a runaway,' but further protest was useless. No one would believe her.

Hannah roused to hear a soft tapping on the door.

She was lying on the cold hard floor of the punishment room with not even the rough blanket for covering. There was nothing in the room now except a jug of water to drink and a bucket for her to relieve herself in. She pulled herself up slowly. Every bone in her body ached, every muscle screamed for relief and her buttocks stung from the wheals inflicted by the thin cane. Mr Edmund had delivered the beating himself, despite Mrs Bramwell's valiant protests.

'You've no right, sir,' Ethel had cried. 'Not a girl.'

'No right? No right, you say. I've every right, Bramwell. I own her – body and soul. I own all of them, every last one, and I will do with them as I please.'

With that, Edmund had grabbed hold of Hannah and hauled her towards his desk. Swinging her round, he had grasped the back of her dress, and in one swift movement torn it open to reveal her naked back and bottom.

'No, sir, no,' Ethel had tried in vain, terrified by the madness in the man's eyes. He had raised the cane, and though she lunged forward, trying to wrest it from his hand, he had pushed her roughly out of the way so that she overbalanced and fell to the floor. Then with a vicious delight he had brought the cane down on the girl's pink young flesh again and again until her skin was raw and bleeding.

Ethel had sat on the floor where she had fallen, closed her eyes and moaned aloud. But there was no sound from Hannah. Not a whimper, not a word of protest or entreaty. She had stood with her face buried against her arm as she was held over the desk, and made not a murmur. It had incensed Edmund further. 'I'll teach – you – to run – away,' he had shouted between each cutting stroke. 'We'll see how you – sing after this – eh?'

On and on he had gone, stroke after stroke, until Hannah's legs had given way and she had crumpled to the floor. At last, he had stopped, standing over her, breathing hard whilst Ethel Bramwell scrambled across the floor to gather the girl into her arms.

At last Hannah had made a sound. Quite plainly they had both heard her trembling words.

'Rock of ages, cleft for me . . .'

Ethel Bramwell had looked up at the man towering above them both, and almost laughed hysterically to see the incredulous look on his face.

'Hannah? Hannah – you there?' The voice came again, rousing her.

Despite her terrible state, Hannah wanted to laugh and reply, 'Where else do you think I'd be?' But she quelled the retort and struggled to the door. She pressed her face to it and whispered, 'Luke?'

'Yeah, it's me. I've brought you some food, but there's no key. I can't open the door.'

Again a sharp retort sprang to her lips but remained unspoken. Instead, she said, 'That's nice of you, but I can't open it either.'

There was a long silence and Hannah thought he had gone, but then she heard Luke say, 'Can you open the window?'

'I . . . I'm not sure. It's so cold in here, I haven't tried.'

'Well, have a go because . . .' His next words were lost to her as, stiffly, she moved across the small room and pushed at the window. She pushed and shoved, and slowly, protestingly, it opened. She went back to the door.

'Yes, I've opened it, but why?'

'Listen, when it's dark tonight I'll get a rope and throw it up to you. Then I'll tie a cloth with some food wrapped in it and you can pull it up.'

121

'Oh, Luke, you'll be in trouble if you're caught.'

'Ne'er mind about that. You're hungry, aren't you?'

At the mere thought of food, Hannah's stomach rumbled, but Luke was whispering urgently, 'I'll have to go. But watch out tonight.'

She heard a brief movement on the other side of the door and knew he was gone. Now she felt lonelier than ever.

It worked better than Hannah had imagined it possibly could. The punishment room was at the top of the house in the attic, but she'd reckoned without Luke's determination. It took four attempts before she caught hold of the rope and hauled it into the room.

'Wait a bit,' Luke called up in a loud whisper. 'I've got to tie it on this end.' A moment's silence and then she heard him say, 'Right, pull away.' Slowly and steadily she hauled on the rope until the bundle came level with the window.

'And what, may I ask, is going on here?'

Hannah gasped, startled by the voice that came up through the darkness from below the window. Oh no! she thought. Not him again. Swiftly she dragged the bundle in through the window and squatted down out of sight. She held her breath, listening intently through the open window.

'Evening, Mr Roper,' she heard Luke say brightly, but Josiah Roper was not to be fooled so easily.

'I asked you what you were doing, boy?'

'Tekin' a stroll like you, Mr Roper. Nice evenin', ain't it?'

There was a moment's silence when Hannah visualized Josiah glancing up towards the window of the punishment room. His next words confirmed her fears. 'I hope you're not communicating with that girl?'

'What girl, Mr Roper?'

Despite her pain, Hannah had to stuff her fist into her mouth to silence the laughter bubbling up inside her. Luke sounded so innocent.

'You know very well "what girl",' Josiah snapped. 'I think I'd better report this to Mrs Bramwell . . .'

Hannah heard no more. Swiftly she opened the bundle to reveal a piece of cold meat pie and some bread and cheese. This wasn't the sort of fare the apprentices were given. She hoped Luke hadn't stolen it. He'd be next in the punishment room if he had. She heard them move away, and now, ravenous, she stuffed it into her mouth.

By the time footsteps sounded outside the room, the door flung open and light from the lamp that Mrs Bramwell carried flooded the room, making Hannah wince against the sudden brightness, all trace of the food was gone and the cloth it'd been wrapped in hidden beneath her clothing. The rope was the only thing that might have given them away, but she'd thrown that out of the window, hoping that Luke would have the sense to retrieve it as soon as he could.

Ethel glanced round the room and then, seeming satisfied, she nodded, 'You'll be coming out in the morning. Mind you're ready for work.'

The light disappeared and the door slammed shut again. Hannah sighed and lay back on the floor trying, in vain, to find a comfortable position. Tomorrow night, she thought, she'd be back in her own bed snuggling close to Jane.

*

When she appeared in the dormitory the following morning, Jane ran to her and hugged her hard. 'Oh, I've missed you so.'

Hannah hugged her in return and then said, 'Come on, we'd best hurry. I don't want to be late on me first morning back.'

Hand in hand they left the house and ran down the hill, joining the other apprentices already making their way through the early morning mist, scarcely awake and rubbing their eyes with weariness.

Ernest Scarsfield counted them in. 'Oh, you're back with us, Francis, are yer? Not do that again in a hurry, I'll be bound.'

Hannah glanced up at him. 'Why will no one believe me, Mr Scarsfield?'

'Eh?'

As she explained, his blank look turned to one of incredulity. He laughed. 'You trying to tell me you really meant to come back?'

Hannah nodded. 'Yes, I am.'

Ernest pushed back his hat and scratched his head. 'Well, if that don't beat all. I've never heard the like.'

'It seems as if no one expects someone to come back if they once get away,' Hannah said solemnly.

Ernest nodded. 'That's about the size of it, lass.' He paused and then stared at her again. 'You really did mean to come back once you'd seen yer mother?'

'Yes, I did.'

For the first time someone really seemed to believe her. The overlooker smiled and bent towards her. 'Look, I'll try to see what I can do to help yer. I've got a mate in the village who goes through to Macclesfield about once a month. Would yer like him to ask around for yer? See if he can find out about yer mother?'

Ernest Scarsfield was rewarded with Hannah's wide smile. Her blue eyes sparkled with grateful tears. 'Oh, thank you, Mr Scarsfield. You're so kind. I don't know how to thank you.'

He straightened up, feeling an unaccustomed lump in his throat. 'There, there,' he said awkwardly. 'Don't fret. I'll see what I can do.' He patted her shoulder. 'Run along into work now.'

As he watched her go, Ernest stroked his moustache, still marvelling over the child. Not only had the young girl done something remarkable – she'd made him involve himself in the life of one of the workers, a thing he'd vowed he'd never do – but for some reason he couldn't explain, he believed her story. He actually believed the child had meant to return to the mill.

And that, to him, was the most incredible part of it all.

That morning, despite the soreness of her back that would take some time to heal, Hannah sang at her work.

At last, someone really believed her.

Fourteen

Hannah had to be patient – something she wasn't very good at. Ernest Scarsfield had said he'd try to make enquiries for her and she believed him, but the wait was agonizing. She busied herself with work, trying to keep her mind off thoughts of her mother, even asking Mrs Bramwell for extra chores in the evening. 'Jane's so tired. Please let me do her jobs.'

Ethel Bramwell was amazed at the resilience of this girl. After a beating like she'd taken, many another would have moaned and begged to be excused from work for weeks. But Hannah made no complaint even though her back was smarting and she would always bear a faint scar or two where the cane had cut the deepest. Ethel believed Hannah's story now and was secretly trying to think of a way to help the girl find out about her mother. They were all supposed to be orphans that came from the workhouse. It was Goodbody's fault for sending Hannah, no one else's and certainly not the girl's.

'Can we do something, Arthur?' Ethel asked her husband. 'I can't help liking her. I know she's a bit of a rebel.' She smiled with something approaching fondness. 'But I have to admire her spirit. We don't get many like her in this place. You should have seen that beating he gave her.' The woman shuddered. 'He was like a man possessed.'

Arthur's kindly face was grim. 'I expect there was a bit more to it than that.' He nodded knowingly at his wife. 'You know what I mean, love. Beating a young girl. Gave him a thrill, I expect. By, he's a nasty piece of work and no mistake.'

'I know she's a handful, but she didn't deserve that. She's a funny little lass. She's – she's . . .' Ethel sought the appropriate way to describe Hannah. 'She's rebellious for the right reasons.'

Arthur nodded. 'I know exactly what you mean.'

'So?' Ethel prompted. 'Is there anything we can do to help her?'

'I'll have a word with Ernest. He's a decent bloke. Mebbe he can think of something.'

Ethel smiled. 'D'you know, she's still doing all her little friend's chores at night? The little pasty-faced one. Pickering.'

'And you let her? Spoiling the other lass though, isn't it?'

Ethel grimaced and shrugged. 'Like Francis says, the other child's dropping on her feet when she gets back from the mill. It's plain to see and I can't argue with it. I have to let the little 'un rest else she'll not be fit for the mill and then you know what'll happen. It'll be us to blame. As usual.' They exchanged a glance, then Ethel asked, 'D'you know what job Pickering's doing?'

Arthur shrugged. 'No, but I'll mention it to Ernest. See if he can put her on something a little less tiring.'

They met in the Wyedale Arms at the top of the hill – Ernest Scarsfield, Arthur Bramwell and Ollie Grundy. Several of the male mill workers also climbed the steep slope two or three times a week. The ale was worth the tough climb and the walk back home was easy, unless of course one too many had been imbibed and then there was the danger of falling and rolling home quite literally.

The three of them tucked themselves away in a corner and almost before they'd got settled with their pints in their hands, Arthur said, 'Now, Ernest, my missis has made me promise to ask you about that little lass who's desperate for news of 'er mother. You know, the one that ran away and spent a week in the punishment room for her trouble.'

Ollie Grundy pricked up his ears, knowing at once that it was Hannah they were talking about.

Ernest was nodding soberly. 'He beat her himself, didn't he?'

'Beat her? Who?' Ollie had spoken aloud before he could stop himself.

'One of the lasses tried to run away,' Arthur explained. 'She *said* it was to see her mother in the workhouse, that she meant to come back—'

'Oh, she did,' Ollie said, without thinking. 'She did mean to come back.'

'Eh?' Ernest stared at him.

Ollie sighed, realizing he'd said too much. Now he'd have to explain. 'My missis helped her. Lent her some money. Lily trusted her – believed her.' He faced the other two fiercely. 'And so do I.'

Ernest and Arthur exchanged a glance.

'But who beat her?' Ollie persisted.

'Mr Edmund,' Arthur said. 'Thrashed her till she bled, my missis says. I've never seen the wife so upset over any of the young 'uns.'

Ollie's face was grim and Ernest shook his head sadly.

'But d'you know what?' Arthur said, leaning forward. 'Ethel said that he only stopped when the little lass fell to the floor almost in a faint, but she was still trying to defy him. She was still trying to sing.'

The three of them sat in silence, until at last Arthur said, 'Well, then, is there anything we can do to find out about her mother for her? She's a good worker – at least she is at the house. Even does some of the jobs for her little friend. And that's another thing – that little girl Pickering is fair done in when she gets home at night. A' you working 'er too hard, Ernest?'

'I wouldn't be at all surprised,' Ernest remarked, drily. 'But you know I don't make the rules, Arthur.'

There was silence between the three of them whilst Ernest took a long swig of his ale. Ollie was saying nothing now, but he was listening intently. His Lil would certainly want to hear about all this. Ernest wiped his mouth with the back of his hand and then twirled the ends of his long moustache. 'As a matter of fact, I've already asked a pal of mine to inquire at the Macclesfield workhouse about her mother.'

Arthur beamed. 'That's good o' yer. The missis'll be pleased.' He shrugged and gave a wry laugh. 'Don't know why 'cos Francis is a troublesome little baggage, but the missis has taken a liking to her. I 'ave an' all, if truth be known.'

Ernest laughed. 'I know what you mean.' He leaned towards Ollie. 'D'yer know, she sings hymns. All day long while she's working.'

'Aye. She does at the house, an' all,' Arthur put in.

Ollie, who had promised himself to say no more,

could contain his curiosity no longer. 'Sings, you say? In that place? What on earth has the poor little lass got to sing about?'

'Francis is a good little worker,' Ernest said. 'I've already set her on as a piecer alongside Nell Hudson. You know Hudson, don't you, Arthur?'

'Oh aye. I know her,' Arthur said wryly.

'And the two lads that came at the same time – the twins,' Ernest went on. 'They're doffers now. But that other little lass you're on about – Pickering. She's not making much progress. She's still sweeping up.'

Ollie's face was grim. 'What, under them machines?'

The two mill employees glanced at each other uncomfortably. They remembered only too well what had happened to Lucy Longmate, Ollie's niece.

'I'll watch out for the little lass,' Ernest said gently.

Two days after this conversation had taken place, Hannah woke with a start as Arthur came into the girls' dormitory, banging the ends of their beds with his stick as he always did. She sprang up, wide awake at once. She never seemed to suffer the weariness that the others did. Some had to be fairly dragged out of their beds every morning. And Jane was one of them.

'Let me be,' she whimpered as Hannah shook her awake. 'I can't get up. Not today. I really can't. I'm so tired.'

It was the same complaint every day and Hannah took no notice. 'Come on. Up you get. If you want me to plait your hair, you'll have to get up now.'

There was no answer – Jane was asleep again.

With a sigh, Hannah ran to the bowl and ewer at

the end of the dormitory and splashed her face with the cold water. She liked to be first to use it; by the time fifty girls had washed their sleepy faces in it, the water was cloudy with scum. Hannah dressed quickly and tied up her own long hair. Then she bent once more over the sleeping girl. 'Do come on, Jane. We'll be late.'

'I'd leave 'er,' Nell commented. 'Let Mrs Bramwell find her. She can deal with her. She's a pain, that one.'

'She's just tired out.'

'So's a lot more that work in the mill. She's nobody special.'

'She is to me,' Hannah snapped back.

'Oh, sorry I spoke, I'm sure.'

'No, I'm sorry, Nell,' Hannah said quickly, not wanting to fall out with the girl who had become such a friend to her. To them both, if it came to that. 'It's just that I don't want to see her in trouble. The work's more than she can manage without being put in the punishment room.'

Nell moved to the other side of the bed. 'Come on, then. I'll give you a hand.'

Together, they pulled back the thin grey blanket, grasped Jane on either side and hauled her upright. The girl's head lolled to one side.

'Come on, you,' Nell said sharply. 'Up with you, else I'll throw that bowl of mucky water all over you.'

They got her standing, and Nell held her whilst Hannah pulled on her skirt and blouse. Jane just stood there, swaying limply, her head down, her eyes closed. If they hadn't held on to her, she'd have fallen over. She was quite literally asleep on her feet.

Hannah grasped hold of her hair and began to separate it into three hanks ready to plait it.

'You haven't time to do that now,' Nell said. 'We'll all be late. Everyone else's gone already.'

Hannah bit her lip, but she couldn't argue.

'Put her bonnet on and tie it tightly. That'll have to do her today.'

Together they dragged the girl out of the room, stumbling awkwardly down the stairs with Jane between them.

The blast of cold morning air seemed to wake her, and she pulled herself free of Hannah and Nell to walk on her own. She pulled her shawl closely around her and hurried into the mill.

'Thanks for your help,' Nell muttered sarcastically, her eyes following Jane, but it was said with a grin. She linked her arm through Hannah's. 'Come on, there's a lot of broken threads waiting for our fingers.'

'They're late with the breakfast, aren't they?' Nell said, when they had been worked for over two hours.

'I dunno, I left me gold watch at home this morning,' Hannah mouthed.

'Oh, very funny, but I wish they'd hurry up. Me stomach thinks me throat's been cut.'

'You carry on here,' Hannah suggested. 'I'll just pop me head outside and see what's happened.'

To her amazement, groups of workers were standing about the yard, whispering together, their faces solemn. But there was no sign of Mr Scarsfield. She saw Luke and ran to him. 'What's going on? Why's everyone out here? And where's breakfast?'

As Luke turned to face her, Hannah was shocked to see tears in his eyes. Fear gripped her insides. 'What is it? What's happened? Is . . . is it Daniel?'

Luke shook his head. He took hold of her hand. 'It's Jane. She . . . she got her hair caught in one of the machines . . .'

Hannah felt as if the breath had been knocked from her body. The colour drained from her face, and her legs gave way beneath her. If Luke hadn't caught hold of her, she would have crumpled to the ground.

There was no hope that the child could survive. Though she was mercifully unconscious now, her injuries were so terrible, the loss of blood so much that by the time the doctor arrived, Jane was slipping away. Her unplaited hair had escaped from beneath her bonnet, and as the exhausted child had crawled beneath the clattering machines, she'd failed to keep her head low enough. The cruel machine had caught at her hair and whipped it up. Jane's petrified screams had been heard even above the machine noise. The operator had stopped the machine immediately, but the damage was done. They had pulled her out to find hair and skin torn from her scalp and blood flowing everywhere. Luke had been there when it had happened. He'd been the one to crawl underneath to release her. His eyes were dark with the horror of what he'd seen as he told Hannah about it.

Then, for the first time since he'd known her, Luke saw Hannah cry. She burst into noisy sobs and clung to him. 'It's my fault. It's all my fault. I didn't plait her hair. We were l-late and I . . . I didn't do it. And . . . and I always do it. Oh, Luke – Luke – it's all my fault.'

He put his arms around her and held her close, not caring who saw them. But everyone was dealing with their own shock at the horrifying accident.

'Of course it's not your fault. It's not up to you to look after her.'

'Yes, it is. It is. I always look after her. She's so little and pale and gets so tired.'

'That's not your fault. It's them. They shouldn't work her so hard. A little thing like her. And if anyone should see she's got her hair plaited, it should be Mrs Bramwell.'

Luke's words were meant to comfort her, but they didn't. Hannah blamed herself and there was nothing anyone could say to her that would ever take away her guilt.

Fifteen

'I want to see her. Let me be with her.' Outside the room where Jane lay, Hannah tussled physically with Mrs Bramwell, who was trying to restrain her.

'You can't do her any good, Hannah.'

'She's going to die, isn't she?'

The woman nodded.

'Then let me be with her,' she begged. 'Let me hold her hand. Please!'

Mrs Bramwell was firm. 'Promise me you'll stay here if I go and ask the doctor.'

Hannah swallowed and nodded reluctantly. 'All right,' she said hoarsely. 'Tell him . . . tell him that I'll do whatever he says, but if she's going to die, I want to be with her. I'm her best friend. She'd like me there. I know she would. Even though . . . even though . . .' Fresh tears welled.

'Even though – what?' Mrs Bramwell asked gently.

Hannah pulled in a deep shuddering breath. 'Even though it's all my fault.' The words came out haltingly and Ethel Bramwell could see the agony haunting the girl's eyes. 'I didn't plait her hair this morning like I always do. She was so tired – she wouldn't get up. Me and Nell had to drag her out of bed. It made us late and – and . . .'

'And you didn't plait her hair because you were so

afraid of being a few minutes late,' Mrs Bramwell finished softly.

Miserably, Hannah nodded.

For the first time ever, Ethel Bramwell was moved to enfold one of the pauper children into her arms. Hannah leaned against her and closed her eyes. For a moment she could imagine it was her mother holding her, Rebecca who was comforting her. She laid her head against the older woman's shoulder and wept silently. She was no longer hysterical, just dreadfully sad and burdened with a heavy weight of guilt.

At last, Mrs Bramwell patted her back, trying to give a little comfort, even though she realized the gesture was futile. She released Hannah and turned away, wiping a tear from the corner of her eye. She'd never met a girl like Hannah before. Most of the children who came here were just out for themselves. They'd rob each other of their last piece of bread, their last ha'penny, given half a chance. But here was Hannah Francis caring for a weaker child more than she cared about herself. Look how she'd done the younger child's household chores just because little Jane had been dead on her feet after her first day in the mill. And she'd gone on doing Jane's work whenever the child couldn't cope with the tasks. Ethel Bramwell felt a shudder of shame. It should've been her looking out for the younger, weaker ones. And now here Hannah was again, bravely wanting to sit beside the dying child, even though she was blaming herself for the accident. She was ready to put herself through the torment of seeing her friend die before her eyes, just to bring whatever comfort she could to the little girl.

As Ethel entered the room, Dr Barnes turned to her

and shook his head gravely. 'I'm sorry. She's so badly injured—'

'I know,' Ethel whispered and then swiftly explained Hannah's request.

'I don't want an hysterical child in here.'

'She won't be. I promise you. She – she . . .' Ethel paused, searching for the right words to describe Hannah to the doctor. 'She's a remarkable girl. I've never met anyone quite like her – not one so young, anyway. She's been punished recently.' Ethel dropped her gaze in shame. 'Most severely, I'm afraid – for running away to try to see her mother, who's still in the workhouse. But Hannah's adamant she wasn't running away, that she intended to come back. But, of course, no one believed her.'

The doctor said bluntly, 'Well, if this place is run so badly that you all can't believe anyone would voluntarily return if they once got away, then it's high time things were changed. That's all I can say.' He nodded grimly towards the bed. 'And if this sort of thing can happen to a child, if we can kill a little mite by tearing her to shreds all in the cause of making money . . .' The usually genial doctor spat out the words with a bitterness that made Ethel Bramwell flinch. 'Then what is the world coming to?'

She was obliged to agree. 'You're quite right, of course.' Mrs Bramwell sighed. 'It's high time there were some changes. But it'll never happen. Old man Critchlow – Mr Nathaniel – just carried on running the mill the way his father did.' She shrugged. 'Oh, he abides by the law – or nearly so.'

Dr Barnes eyed her keenly. 'Are you quite sure about that? This wretched pauper apprentice system has been abandoned in most of the mills. New laws made it too expensive, as I understand it. Mind you, the new laws are better for the children, aren't they? They raised the minimum age and cut the number of daily working hours. So why not here, I'd like to know? How come the Critchlows are still running the scheme?'

Ethel Bramwell ran her tongue around dry lips. She was sailing in deep waters now, risking her own livelihood and that of her husband's by speaking her mind. But she rarely got the chance to unburden her deep anxieties to someone who understood, to someone who wouldn't betray her confidence. Though she didn't know the doctor well – the Critchlows were too mean to call upon his services except in the direst emergency, even for their staff – Ethel felt she could trust him. 'Some mills are running twenty-four hours a day, with a shift system. That's never happened here, though. Mind you, when me 'n' Arthur first came here more than twenty years ago, children as young as nine used to work eight hours a day in the mill – longer if they wanted to do overtime to earn a few pence. And that left very little time for any education. By the time they were thirteen they worked twelve hours a day and no more schooling.'

The doctor grunted. 'Hmph, still not good enough in my opinion. What's the law now? No child under eight can work at all, is it?'

The superintendent nodded. 'And youngsters can only work between six in the morning and six at night and for no more than ten hours a day.'

'Oh, that's spoiling them rotten,' Dr Barnes said sarcastically. He glanced at the still form of Jane in the bed. His tone softened. 'And this poor creature? She only looks seven or eight. How old is she?'

'Ten. At least, that's what Mr Goodbody said.'

'Goodbody? Who's he?'

'The master of the workhouse where . . . where the children come from.'

The doctor's expression hardened. 'So – it really is still going on here then?'

'The pauper apprentice system? Oh yes,' Ethel Bramwell said bitterly. Then she sighed. 'I've very mixed feelings about it all, Doctor, I don't mind admitting. We haven't quite so many as we used to have. At one time we had over a hundred children; now there's only about eighty.' She smiled thinly. 'Of course if they close the house, Arthur and me will be out of a job, but even so . . .' She bit her lip. Ethel was warming to something that had bothered her and the kindly Arthur for years, yet it was the first time she'd ever dared to voice her misgivings to anyone apart from her husband. 'I don't like being part of something that could be described as – well – as cruel. Of course, I have to be strict with the children. Eighty youngsters all living together – they can get out of hand. It's part of my job to keep them in line, but in here . . .' She laid her hand over her heart. 'I do feel for them. I . . . I try to be fair. That's why when the girl you're about to meet always did little Jane's household chores for her after work at night – well – I let her. The – little one,' she gestured with a trembling hand towards the child in the bed, 'was always so exhausted.'

The doctor grunted. 'Well, if they'd let me see the children now and again, I could maybe have helped. They do it in some mills, y'know. There's one in

Cheshire that's got a marvellous reputation for caring for its workers.'

Ethel sighed. 'Yes, I've heard of it too, but there's not an earthly chance that Mr Edmund would ever agree to anything like that here.'

'Well, sadly, I don't believe there's a law – yet – that says they have to provide regular medical checks for their workers, but,' he eyed her keenly, 'are you telling me, Mrs Bramwell, that the Critchlows do bend the law when it suits their own purpose?'

The woman, torn between telling the truth and yet risking her own position by doing so, nodded. Casting caution aside now, she went on heatedly. 'They work the children far longer than the hours they're supposed to. They get less schooling than is laid down by the law. They're supposed to get at least three hours a day until they're twelve, but it's only ever two at the most. And whilst they're apprentices, bound to the Critchlows by that wretched bit of paper they're made to sign when they arrive, they only get their bed and board. The only way they can earn money for themselves is by doing overtime on top of the already long hours. And believe me, Doctor, most of them don't even understand what that paper really is that they're signing.'

'And how are the children treated?'

'If they do anything wrong, the boys are beaten, the girls locked in the punishment room and half starved for days. And on rare occasions – very rare, thank the Lord – a girl will be beaten.'

'On whose orders?' Dr Barnes barked. 'I didn't think Mr Critchlow was a bad master.'

'Oh, he's not so bad. But his son – Mr Edmund – is another matter.' Her voice dropped to a whisper. 'He's

... he's evil, Doctor. The day he takes over the running of this mill, may God help us all.'

There was a long silence whilst they both pondered the appalling prospect. Then, as the child in the bed stirred and whimpered in pain, the doctor cleared his throat. 'Fetch this remarkable young lady in then, but I suggest you stay with her, Mrs Bramwell. It's a hard thing to do. To sit and watch your friend die.'

When Mrs Bramwell opened the door and beckoned Hannah inside, the doctor looked up, intrigued to see this unusual girl of whom the superintendent had spoken. At once he was struck by the young girl's demeanour. She walked into the room, her head held high, her face calm. It was only on closer inspection that the doctor could see the anguish in her blue eyes and the blotchy marks on her cheeks of recently shed tears. Hannah wished herself anywhere – back in the mill, even back in the punishment room – anywhere but here. Nevertheless, she sat down beside the bed and gently took hold of Jane's hand, steeling herself to face the terrible sight – the blood-soaked bandages, the scarcely recognizable face.

'I'm here, Jane,' she whispered, swallowing the bile that rose in her throat. 'I'm here now. It'll be all right. Don't be frightened. I'll stay with you. I won't leave you.' She whispered the comforting, reassuring words with such mature composure that the two listening adults glanced at each other.

'See what I mean, Doctor?' Ethel murmured, and the man nodded, 'Indeed I do, Mrs Bramwell. Indeed I do. A most remarkable child.'

He took out his pocket watch and murmured. 'I think I'll stay a while. I've more calls to make, but they'll wait.'

'I'll get another chair. We can sit over here in the corner, but we'll be close by if . . .'

She stopped and faced the awful truth. It wasn't a matter of 'if' but 'when'.

Mrs Bramwell slipped quietly out of the room and returned with a chair. Then she and the doctor sat in the far corner of the room, silently watching.

Jane stirred and opened her eyes and Hannah leaned closer. 'I'm here, Jane. I'm here.'

Weakly, the girl whispered, 'It wasn't your fault, Hannah.'

'It was. I should have plaited your hair. I—'

Jane tried to shake her head and then winced at the terrible pain. She cried out and screwed up her face. 'No, no, I . . . I don't want you to blame yourself. You . . . you've always been so kind to me. Looked after me. Please, Hannah, sing to me. I want to hear you sing my favourite . . .' It seemed as if she might have said more but the effort was too much, the pain unbearable. Her eyelids closed and she drifted away.

Her voice shaking and with tears streaming down her face, Hannah began to sing, 'The Lord's my shepherd, I'll not want . . .'

Mrs Bramwell wept openly, and even the doctor wiped a tear from the corner of his eye as the little girl's life ebbed away.

As Hannah's voice faded away at the end of the hymn, the doctor rose quietly from his chair and went to the other side of the bed. He felt the child's pulse and then looked down into Hannah's upturned face.

His voice deep with emotion, Dr Barnes said, 'I'm sorry, my dear. She's gone, but she's out of pain now. That's how you must think of it. She's at peace.'

Hannah laid her cheek against Jane's hand and

sobbed. She could not in all honesty have prayed for her friend to survive. Jane was hurt beyond all hope, so dreadfully injured that any life would have been a living hell. Better that her little friend was, like the kindly doctor said, at peace.

They gave her a few moments, and then it was Dr Barnes who put his hand on her shoulder. 'Come, my dear. Mrs Bramwell will look after her. There are things she must do. But she'll be gentle with her.'

Hannah knew what that meant. She had to lay out Jane ready for the rough pauper's coffin. She pulled herself up and bent over to kiss Jane's cheek one last time. Already, it felt cold beneath Hannah's lips, but perhaps that was her imagination.

The doctor's arm supporting her, she stumbled from the room. Outside the door, Luke was waiting and she fell into his arms. Above her head, Luke and the doctor exchanged a glance.

'Look after her, son. She's a very special girl.'

Luke, unable to speak for the huge lump in his throat, nodded.

'Come on,' he whispered at last. 'Let's get out of here. Let's go up on the hill.'

'What . . . what about Daniel?' Even in her distress, Hannah spared a thought for the shy boy. He depended on his twin just like Jane had depended on her. But she'd let her little friend down. She didn't want to be the cause of trouble between the brothers.

'He's still working. He'll be all right. Just this once. Come on.'

They left the house and began to run down the hill and along the path leading to the weir. Then, turning away from the mill, they scrambled up the rocky track, slipping and sliding, to the narrow steep path on the hillside high above the mill pool and the river. Luke took hold of her hand and held it tightly as they walked on in silence. Before they rounded the curve of the hill that would take them out of sight of Wyedale Mill, they paused and looked back.

'It don't look such a bad place,' Luke murmured.

Hannah sighed. 'It's not the place. The mill's – what's the word? – majestic. Yes, that's it, the mill's a majestic building.' Her glance roamed away, down the dale, following the winding river. 'And the valley's lovely. So peaceful, so . . .' Tears blurred her eyes. The terrible sight of her friend was still so fresh in her mind. It would haunt her for ever. She swallowed hard and said huskily, 'It's the people who run it. The Critchlows. It's all their fault. But it's such a shame. It could be such a happy place. The workers are good people.'

'It'll never be a happy place with Mr Edmund around. And I 'spect his son'll be just like him when he grows up.'

Hannah thought about the young, solemn-faced, dark-haired boy she had seen just the once. She'd've liked to have thought that he might grow up to be different. But it wasn't very likely.

She sighed sadly. 'Yes, I expect you're right.'

They turned their backs on Wyedale Mill and walked on, following the winding path worn into the steep hillside by the sheep that grazed there.

'See that big house across there.' Luke pointed to the cliff on the opposite side of the dale. 'That's the Critchlows' place. Millersbrook Manor.'

The house was perched halfway down the steep hillside a little way from the village itself.

'Do they all live there, then?'

'Yeah. The old man, Mr Edmund and Master Adam – when he's home.'

'From school, you mean?'

'That's right. He's away at some fancy boarding school. That's why we never see him much. He only comes home in the holidays.'

'How do you know all this?'

Luke forced a grin. He was trying hard to draw Hannah's thoughts away from the sadness they were both feeling, take her mind off what was happening back at the apprentice house. ''Cos I'm a nosy beggar.'

'Who else lives there, then? Is there a Mrs Critchlow?'

Luke shook his head. 'No. The old man's wife died years ago and Mr Edmund's wife died having another baby.'

'Oh yes. I'd heard that.'

'It's a houseful of men.'

'They've got servants though? They'll have a house-keeper, surely?'

'Oh aye,' Luke said airily. 'But servants don't count, do they?'

'No,' Hannah said soberly and her thoughts came back to Jane. The little girl's life hadn't counted with the Critchlows.

Sixteen

By a strange coincidence, it was Adam Critchlow whom they saw first when they dragged their feet reluctantly back to the mill.

'What's he doing here?' Luke muttered.

'He must be home from school,' Hannah said.

The young man was standing in the middle of the yard looking up at the mill. At the sound of their footsteps, he turned. He didn't say anything until they drew level with him. They were about to pass by, but he spoke, bringing them to a halt.

'I heard about the little girl.' His voice was soft, gentle almost, though Hannah could hardly believe such a word could describe any of the Critchlows. She pressed her lips together to stop the tears flowing again, yet her action had the look of disapproval.

Adam's eyes clouded. 'Tell me,' he said suddenly, his gaze on Hannah's face. Luke was ignored. 'What happened? Tell me it all. I want to know.'

Hannah did so, sparing him nothing. She was gratified to see him wince, yet at the same time his response surprised her. Perhaps this Critchlow did have some feelings. If so, he was the only one who did, she thought bitterly.

But it seemed that Adam believed differently about his family. 'My grandfather's distraught.'

Hannah's eyes widened in disbelief and, beside her, she heard Luke give a derisory snort. Adam glanced at him briefly, but dismissed his presence. His attention returned to Hannah. 'He is,' he persisted. Even though Hannah had not spoken, he could read her thoughts plainly written on her face. He stepped closer to her, cutting Luke out. 'I know perhaps he seems harsh to you, but there are other mills a lot worse than this one, you know. They don't have good food or the medical attention we provide.'

'Medical attention? What medical attention? We never see a doctor from one month to the next. They only called him in this time because they had to. Because . . .' Her tears spilled over again. 'Because they knew she was going to die. He couldn't save her. No one could have done except not to've let it happen in the first place.'

Adam dropped his gaze and shuffled his feet. 'I know and I'm sorry.' He lifted his head again and stared into her face, holding her gaze. 'But one day it'll all be different. One day – when the mill's mine – it'll be very different.'

'Aye,' Luke spoke for the first time. 'But how long have we to wait before that day comes? And in the meantime, once the old man's gone, it'll be your father in charge.' He paused and added pointedly, 'Won't it?'

To this, it seemed, Adam had no reply.

News of the child's accident and subsequent death spread through the mill, and a sadness descended over the workforce. Though everyone carried on with the work expected of them, there was an undercurrent of resentment flowing beneath the surface. The workers were suddenly not as biddable. There was a feeling of unrest, and Nathaniel Critchlow was alarmed by it.

'It's just like that other time when a little girl got killed. What can we do?'

'Do?' Edmund snapped at his father. 'Why, nothing, of course. As long as they're doing their work. And Scarsfield will see to that, else he'll have me to answer to.'

Nathaniel spread his hands. 'But I like my workers to be happy. They work better. Maybe we should have a doctor visiting the apprentices regularly. I've heard there's a mill in Cheshire where—'

'Nonsense, Father. You're too soft. They respect a firm hand, not a weak one.'

Nathaniel regarded his son soberly and not without a little disappointment. 'There's a vast difference between a firm hand and a callous one, my boy. It'd be no bad thing to look after their health. And,' he added pointedly, 'to be seen to be doing so.'

Edmund's mouth twisted. 'I'm not one for philanthropy.'

His father shook his head. 'Outsiders – and even the workers themselves – might see it as philanthropic. But think about it for a moment, Edmund. A healthy, happy millhand will work better. We need to keep them on our side.' He frowned worriedly. 'It's what your grandfather believed and so do I.'

'Our side,' Edmund scoffed. 'Workers will never be on "our side", as you put it. It's us and them, Father. Always has been, always will be. And for most of them, the more they produce, the more they earn. Isn't that incentive enough?'

'Not for the apprentices. They're not paid at all unless they do overtime.'

'Huh! We feed and clothe the little brats. And we have to educate them – thanks to all the blasted new laws they keep bringing in.' Edmund wagged his finger at his father. 'Their lives are better here than if they were still in the workhouse, but as for pandering to them with regular health checks, well, that's an unnecessary expense to my mind.'

'It's not pandering to them. They have a right to—'

Edmund stepped closer to his father's desk and leaned across it. Prodding his forefinger on the surface of the desk, he said, slowly and deliberately, 'They have no "rights". When they work in this mill, when they sign their indenture, they belong to us. We *own* them. Body and soul.'

Edmund swung round and marched out of the room, slamming the door behind him.

Nathaniel stared after him with a growing sense of foreboding. How, in God's name, he asked himself, had he reared such a heartless and, yes, he had to admit it, cruel son? A shudder of apprehension ran through him. He had a sudden, awful, premonition of how the mill would be run after his own demise. It was a picture that filled him with fear. He sighed deeply. We should be looking to improve conditions, not going back into the past, Nathaniel thought. It's bad enough I've let him persuade me to carry on the scheme with Goodbody long after every other mill owner has abandoned it. They were breaking the law, he knew. The children in Wyedale Mill worked longer hours, had less schooling than anywhere else. If a government inspector should call . . .

'There's only one thing for it,' he murmured aloud. 'I'll just have to live long enough to see Adam grown up and come into the business.' But then his musings came to a halt. The boy was certainly tender-hearted, but would Adam be strong enough to stand up to his ruthless father?

Nathaniel groaned aloud and, resting his elbows on the desk, dropped his head into his hands. He felt suddenly dizzy and sick at the thought of what might happen to the mill his own father had begun.

From boyhood, the mill had been Nathaniel's life. He could still remember so vividly the day they had found Wyedale. They'd been touring the Derbyshire countryside on horseback, just he and his father, Moses, looking for a place to build a cotton mill.

And they had found it. At the end of the long, curving valley where the River Wye tumbled in a natural waterfall, Moses had found the perfect place to build a mill for his son to inherit. And it would pass down the generations, Moses had dreamed. From father to son with always a Critchlow at the helm.

Nathaniel could still remember that day so clearly – his father sitting astride his horse, his tall and imposing figure hiding a stern yet kindly disposition. At the top of the hill, he had taken off his hat and waved it in the air, his dark brown hair blowing in the wind. They had ridden down the steep mud track, past the smattering of houses – the farm and a few cottages – right to the end of the dale, where there was room to build a mill beside the river that would provide the power for the great wheel.

'This is it, my boy,' Moses had cried jubilantly. 'This is where the Critchlows' mill will stand for generations. For you, Nathaniel. For your sons and even for their sons.'

'But, Father,' Nathaniel had said, looking around

him at what appeared to him to be a bleak and desolate place. 'There are no houses. Where will you get the people to work in the mill?'

Moses had laughed, the wind whipping away the sound and carrying it through the dale. 'We shall build houses. Up there.' He had pointed to the cliff face rising steeply at the end of the valley. 'We'll bring workers from the city slums. From the workhouses. We'll give them a good life – a better life than they've ever known or ever expected. And in return,' Moses had smiled down at the young Nathaniel, 'they'll work hard for us and make us rich men.'

And everything that Moses had promised had come to pass. He'd built his fine mill and the houses on the cliff for the workers, and Millersbrook village above Wyedale Mill was born. He had built an apprentice house and a schoolroom and brought pauper orphans from the workhouses in the nearest towns and cities. And many had stayed on to work in the mill as adults and to live in the cottages in the village, to marry and bring up their families there.

Moses was a strict but fair employer. The list of rules and the fines posted up about the factory were those he had drawn up, and they were still in force to this day.

Remembering all this, Nathaniel groaned aloud.

The sound carried through the door to the outer office, and Josiah Roper smiled.

Three days later, though he was quaking inside, Mr Critchlow stood up to his son. 'You're to let anyone who wants to go attend that child's funeral.'

Edmund glowered and opened his mouth to speak, but Nathaniel Critchlow held up his hand. 'We'll have a rebellion on our hands if you don't.'

Edmund appeared to think for a moment. 'I'll allow her closest friends to go and the Bramwells. Maybe Scarsfield as well, but no others. We'll have the whole mill grind to a halt if they think they can all wangle time off.'

'Very well, then,' Mr Critchlow agreed to the compromise. 'Are you going?'

Edmund laughed without humour. 'Me? Attend a pauper's funeral? Hardly!'

Nathaniel's hand shook visibly. 'I should go,' he murmured. 'But . . . but I can't face it. I don't feel well.' He passed a hand over his forehead as he felt the dizziness and the headache he had been experiencing for the past few days – ever since the child's accident – sweep over him.

But to everyone's surprise, there was a Critchlow at the funeral.

As Arthur Bramwell and Ernest Scarsfield pushed the coffin on the handcart up the steep hill to the burial ground beyond the village, the few – the pathetically few – mourners fell into step behind them. Mrs Bramwell, Hannah and Nell in the front, followed by Luke and Daniel, as ever walking side by side.

As they began to move off from the apprentice house, Adam Critchlow stepped out from behind the mill's pillared gateway and fell into step at the back. Hannah didn't notice him. Walking between Ethel Bramwell and Nell, she kept her eyes firmly fixed on the small coffin and quietly prayed that her little friend had truly found peace.

'Did you see him?' Luke asked her later when it was

all over and they were sitting in the kitchen at the house, drinking tea as a special treat on such a dreadful day.

'At the back,' Daniel put in. The four youngsters were sitting together whilst the three grown ups had gone into the Bramwells' sitting room to partake of something a little stronger than tea.

'Who?' Hannah asked listlessly, cupping the mug in her hands to warm them. She was still shivering, though it was more from her inner misery and the terrible burden of guilt rather than from the cold day.

'Master Adam,' Luke said. 'He followed us all the way to the cemetery.'

'At the back,' Daniel repeated. 'He walked behind us and then stood at the back when we was all round the grave.'

'Did he?' Hannah was surprised and, even against her will, a little moved. She wanted to think badly of the Critchlows, yet was there one amongst them who was actually showing some compassion?

'Did you speak to him?'

'No,' Luke said and Daniel shook his head.

'I wonder,' she mused, 'just why he came?'

No one could answer her.

'I'm sorry, Francis,' Ernest Scarsfield stopped Hannah as she was leaving the mill three days after Jane's funeral, 'but my mate can't find out anything about yer mother. He went to the workhouse, but they wouldn't tell him anything. He saw someone called – now, what was it? – Good, was it?'

'Mr Goodbody,' Hannah said, the disappointment

spreading through her already. She'd had such hopes that word would come any day from Mr Scarsfield's friend. Since Jane's death, Hannah had not felt like singing – not once – and news from her mother had been the only thing she'd looked forward to.

'Aye, that was it. Well, he more or less ordered him out of the place. "Can't divulge information about inmates," he said. Miserable old bugger. It wouldn't've hurt him to send word to a little lass about her mother, now would it?' He looked to Luke for agreement. Luke was always at Hannah's side these days with Daniel never far behind.

Luke nodded. 'He's a right bastard.' And Daniel nodded grim agreement.

For a brief moment, Ernest Scarsfield looked taken aback, then he frowned. 'Now then, lad, none of that sort of language here. You know the rules. By rights, I should fine you thruppence for that.' Then, realizing that he had just been swearing himself, Ernest smiled. His admonishment was gentle. These three had been through enough already in their young lives. He ruffled Luke's hair as he added, 'But I know what you mean.' He turned again to Hannah. 'I'm sorry, lass.'

Hannah tried to smile, but her voice wobbled as she said, 'Thank you for trying, Mr Scarsfield.'

She turned away, but Ernest called after her. 'You could see Mr Critchlow. The old man, that is. He *might* help. He's not a bad old stick – most of the time.'

'Thanks. I will.' But she didn't hold out much hope.

*

'We'll have to go and see Mrs Grundy. I haven't dared go yet, but I should,' Hannah told Luke and Daniel the following Sunday.

Luke nodded. 'You'll have to tell her that they've taken the money she lent you. And kept it.' He paused a moment. 'It'll take you years to pay it back.'

'I know,' Hannah said miserably. 'I'll be old and grey by the time I do.' She sighed. 'Still, let's get it over with. Let's go and see her.'

'Can I come an' all?' Daniel asked.

Luke's face sobered and he shook his head, but not, as Hannah thought at first in answer to his brother's question, but to her suggestion. 'We can't go. None of us.'

Hannah stared at him. 'You ... you mean you won't come with me? Oh, Luke!'

'No, no, it's not that. Of course I'll come with you.' He paused, then added, 'When you can go.'

'But I want to go today. Now.'

He shook his head. 'You can't.'

'What do you mean? It's Sunday. We'll go this afternoon. Mrs Bramwell will understand.'

'You can't. You're not allowed out. Not even to go to the service with the rest of us.'

'Not – allowed – out? Nobody's said anything to me.'

'I heard Mrs Bramwell telling Mary that you'd be staying with her this morning and that she'd tell you to help get the dinner ready.'

Hannah, angry now, whirled around. 'I don't believe this. I'll go and ask her myself.'

'Hannah, don't . . .' Luke called after her, but Hannah paid no heed.

She knocked sharply on the door of Mrs Bramwell's sitting room, indignation lending her boldness.

'Come in.'

Hannah flung open the door and marched into the room. 'Is it true?' she burst out. 'Is it true I'm not allowed out? Not even to go to the service?'

Ethel Bramwell sighed, rose and came to stand in front of the girl. 'I'm sorry, Hannah. Truly I am. But that's Mr Edmund's orders. We're under his strict instructions, see. Me, Mr Bramwell and even Mr Scarsfield. We've not to let you out of our sights, so to speak. I'm to keep you here and Mr Bramwell's to see that you go to the mill every morning. Then Mr Scarsfield's to keep his eye on you all day until you come back here at night.'

Hannah's gasped and her eyes widened. 'But . . . but that's like being in prison.'

'Aren't we all?' the older woman murmured.

'Well, I won't be a prisoner. Not here. Not anywhere.'

'You've no choice, child.' Ethel Bramwell said, but there was sadness in her tone. 'None of us have. The Critchlows own us – all of us.'

Hannah frowned. She knew she was fastened to the Critchlows for the term of her indenture, but surely the Bramwells weren't.

'Why do you say "all of us"? You and Mr Bramwell can leave any time you like, can't you? You're not under any kind of indenture, are you?'

Mrs Bramwell shook her head. 'No, but think about it, Hannah.' Without realizing it, Ethel Bramwell called the girl by her Christian name. 'How would we find other employment? If we just upped and left, where would we go? How would we ever get another position without a reference?' She leaned closer. 'And how would we get a reference? Mr Critchlow would

156

never give us one in a month of Sundays if we said we wanted to leave even though we've served him for over twenty years.'

Shocked, Hannah stared at her. She hadn't realized that everyone here – including the Bramwells, even Ernest Scarsfield and Mr Roper – were all virtual prisoners of the Critchlows.

'Now, you be a good girl and do what they say for a week or two and then we'll see. Likely, they'll've forgotten all about you by then.'

Hannah pursed her lips and shook her head. 'I'm not staying locked up in here even for a week or two. First thing tomorrow morning, I'm going to see Mr Critchlow.' Then she swung round and marched from the room again, leaving Ethel Bramwell staring after her and sighing deeply. 'Oh, my dear child. You don't understand what you're doing. You really don't.'

Seventeen

Hannah ignored their warnings. She paid no heed to Mrs Bramwell or to Luke. Not even to Ernest Scarsfield. They tried to stop her – tried to warn her.

'And if you run into Mr Edmund, well . . .' They all said exactly the same thing, and all left the sentence hanging in the air unfinished. Hannah was determined, but she was trembling as she knocked on the door of the outer office and stepped in to face Mr Roper.

Josiah Roper did not, of course, try to dissuade her. He had good reason not to. He wanted a few fireworks to brighten his dull routine. He didn't care if this wilful child, who'd spoilt his weekend away from this place, was locked in the punishment room again. He was smiling as he ushered her into his master's office and closed the door behind her. He didn't return to his desk, but leaned close to the door to listen.

Inside the inner office, Hannah faced Mr Nathaniel Critchlow. She breathed a little easier to find him there and not his son.

'Please, sir, I'd like your permission to go to morning service with the others on Sunday.'

The old man frowned at her. 'So you can run away again, eh?'

Hannah shook her head. 'I wasn't running away, sir. I keep telling everyone, but no one will believe me. I just wanted to find out how my mother is, that's all.

I haven't heard from her since I came here even though I've written several letters to her. I was coming back, sir. Truly I was.'

The man gazed at the young girl's fresh face, at her clear blue eyes, at the golden hair cascading down her back. He sighed. She was going to be a real beauty in a few years' time. She was now, but she was not quite old enough . . . He shuddered. Maybe he shouldn't keep her here. Maybe he should let her go back to the workhouse. He could tell Goodbody that she wasn't suitable, even though she was actually one of the best child workers they had. She was shaping up very nicely. Soon, she would be shaping up in an entirely different way and then his son would really start to take notice of her . . .

With unaccustomed impetuosity, he said, 'Would you like to go back to the workhouse, my dear – for good?'

'Oh no, sir. I signed that piece of paper for you and I intend to keep my promise. I mean to stay here. But all I want is to know how my mother is.'

Now Nathaniel Critchlow stared at her in amazement. 'You want to stay here?'

Hannah nodded. 'I didn't – when Jane—'

'Yes, yes,' Nathaniel said and his own voice was husky. He hated any kind of accident in his factory. And this had been a bad one – the very worst. Though he'd shied away from seeing the child for himself, he still trembled at the mere thought of Jane's injuries.

'I wanted to run away then,' Hannah was saying, 'because I blamed myself for not tying her hair up properly for her like we'd been told.' The man and the girl stared at each other, their faces filled with sadness at the tragedy. They each felt a sense of guilt that the accident could have been avoided.

'I just can't understand why my mother hasn't answered my letters. She can't write herself, but she'd have got someone to read them to her and then sent me word.'

Nathaniel leaned forward and rested his elbows on his desk, linking his fingers to stop their shaking. 'I'll tell you what I'll do,' he said slowly, 'but first, you have to give me your word that you won't try to run away—' As Hannah opened her mouth to protest once more, he held up his hand. 'Not even just for a day.'

Hannah took a deep breath. 'It depends what you're going to do.'

Nathaniel smiled wryly. The boldness of this girl was truly amazing and yet it was not insolence. Even from his lofty position as her master – the man who owned her body and soul now – he had to admit that she was only standing up for what she considered her rights. Her rights, indeed! Edmund would say that she had none and Nathaniel was tempted to tell her as much. But as he gazed again on her pretty, open face, the retort died on his lips.

'Well, providing I have your promise, I'll write to Cedric Goodbody myself and ask for news of your mother. We might even arrange for her to visit you here.'

The ecstatic delight on the young girl's face was like the appearance of the sun after storm clouds. 'Oh, sir, would you really do that for me?' She clasped her hands in front of her. 'Oh, thank you, *thank* you.'

Nathaniel cleared his throat and said gruffly. 'So, will you give me your promise? No more trying to sneak off to see her for yourself.'

'I promise, sir. Oh, I promise.'

'Now, just to show me that you mean what you say, you're to stay in for another two weeks. Then you can go to the Sunday services again.'

Hannah nodded and thanked him again. At that moment she would have done anything he asked her. Anything at all.

'I'm so sorry, Mrs Grundy, about the money. But I will pay you back every penny.'

Three Sundays later, the three youngsters – Hannah, Luke and Daniel – were sitting in the warm kitchen at the farm.

Mrs Grundy shrugged. 'Don't worry about it, love. I shan't lose any sleep over it. I'm just sorry you didn't get to see your mother.' Her usual merry face clouded. 'That Josiah Roper – he's a nasty piece of work. He could've turned a blind eye. Could've let you go when he found you at the top of the hill. I remember our Lucy hated him. He was always creeping about the mill, watching an' listening and then telling tales to Mr Edmund.'

She looked into the sad faces opposite her. 'I heard about your little friend,' she said gently. 'Just like our Lucy, weren't it?'

Hannah nodded, looking stricken.

Lily Grundy sighed heavily and heaved herself up to get them a drink and fetch a fruit loaf from her cake tin. Changing the subject away from matters that grieved them all, she said, 'So, what are you going to do now about yer mam?'

'Mr Nathaniel's been quite good,' Luke said taking up Hannah's tale. 'He's promised—'

161

'To write to Mr Goodbody himself,' Daniel finished.

For a moment, Mrs Grundy glanced between the three of them, with a puzzled expression. Then her face cleared. 'Oh, him at the workhouse, you mean? Where you came from? But I thought you'd already written to him.'

'Not exactly. I wrote to me mam.'

'And she's never replied?'

'Well, no. She can't write. But I know she'd've got one of the others to write for her.'

Mrs Grundy handed round mugs of thick creamy warm milk and slices of cake before she spoke again. She sat down and pulled her cup of tea towards her, stirring it thoughtfully. 'I don't suppose that someone along the way has been stopping your letters. Either going out or coming in.'

The three youngsters stared at her. 'Would . . . would they do that?' Hannah asked indignantly.

Mrs Grundy snorted and took a sip of her tea. 'I wouldn't put anything past that lot up at the mill – if it suited their purpose. Anyway, love, it'll soon be Christmas. Maybe your mother will send you a letter then, eh?'

'Do you think anyone would really do that?' Hannah asked the two boys again as they walked back to the apprentice house as dusk descended into the dale. 'Stop someone's letters?'

'Mr Edmund would,' Luke said.

'And Mr Roper,' Daniel volunteered.

'But I don't think old Mr Critchlow would, do you?' Hannah said. 'I'm sure he wouldn't.'

The two boys glanced at one another but did not

answer, and the three of them walked the rest of the way in silence.

Christmas came and went, marked only by a little more food at dinnertime and a couple of hours' free time in the afternoon. The pauper children in the apprentice house scarcely noticed the difference, though the feasting at the Manor lasted three days and left Nathaniel Critchlow suffering from severe indigestion and an even worse headache from the drink he had consumed.

Struggling to his office at the mill on the fourth day, he sat at his desk, his head in his hands. 'I don't know what to do,' he murmured.

Josiah, hovering on the other side of the desk, asked, 'Can I help, sir? You don't look too well. Perhaps you should go home.'

'I should speak to Edmund,' the old man murmured.

'Mr Edmund won't be back from Manchester until late tonight.'

It was from the merchants in Manchester that the Critchlows bought the bales of raw cotton, that started life on the *Gossypium* plant in the southern states of America, its fluffy bolls picked by slave labour and transported all the way to Liverpool and by canal to Manchester. Edmund was a shrewd and clever negotiator – no one could deny that – and Nathaniel had been happy and relieved to hand over that side of the business to his son.

'Are you sure I can't help, sir?' Josiah asked again. His seeming concern was persuasive. Nathaniel sighed and confided, 'It's the girl.'

163

'Which girl might that be, sir?' Josiah feigned ignorance, yet he'd already guessed.

'Francis.'

'Ah!' Josiah said, a wealth of understanding in that simple utterance. 'She is somewhat – er – wilful. What has she done now?'

'It's not so much what she's done as what's happened.'

Nathaniel Critchlow raised his head slowly and sighed deeply. 'When she ran away that time, it seems that all she was trying to do was to see her mother. She's not had word from her mother – or even *of* her – since she came here. And the child's worried. It's only natural, I suppose. She's written several times, she says, but no word has come.'

Josiah smiled but said nothing. All Hannah's letters had been unanswered because they had only left his office in shreds.

'Until now,' Nathaniel finished heavily. He picked up a sheet of paper and held it out for Josiah to read. 'This arrived this morning. It's from Goodbody. The child's mother died only a few weeks after the girl's arrival here. All this time and no one thought to tell us so that we could tell the poor child.'

Nathaniel's face crumpled and he dropped his head into his hands once more. Brokenly, he said. 'It's all getting too much for me. I can't bring myself to tell her.'

Josiah looked down at his master and felt a thrill of jubilation. The old man was past it. High time he retired and handed over the running of the mill to his son. And with Edmund in charge – Edmund, who was Josiah's mentor and friend, then . . .

'Why don't you leave this to me, sir? I'll attend to what needs to be done.'

Nathaniel looked up gratefully. 'You will? Thank you, Roper. You're a good man.'

He pulled himself up and stood swaying unsteadily. Josiah put out his hand and took hold of his arm. 'I think you should go home, sir. I'll get one of the hands to bring the pony and trap to the door. Here, let me help you with your coat.'

Solicitously, Josiah helped the old man shuffle to the door, down the stairs and into the trap.

'See him right home, Baldwin,' he ordered one of the mill workers. 'Mr Critchlow isn't well.'

'Your father doesn't seem well, Mr Edmund,' Josiah greeted him on his return late that night. Knowing Mr Edmund's habit of returning straight to his office after a successful buying trip to the city, the clerk had stayed late in the office deliberately. Sitting there in the semi-darkness, Josiah had hatched a plan. But it would need careful handling.

'You still here, Roper?' Edmund said, shrugging himself out of his coat and striding into the inner office and towards the waiting whisky bottle in his cabinet. He poured himself a double measure and sat down in his father's chair. Leaning back, he rested his feet on the corner of the desk, crossing his ankles. 'What's the matter with him?' His eyes gleamed, matching the excitement glittering in Josiah's eyes. 'Serious, d'you think?'

'I hope not, sir,' Josiah said dutifully, but they both knew it to be a lie. They both wanted the same thing – Edmund to be in full control of the factory.

By God! they were each thinking. *Then we'll see things happen.*

'This letter,' Josiah went on, holding out the piece of paper, 'seemed to upset him. It's from Goodbody. About the Francis girl. It seems your father wrote to him to make enquiries. At the girl's behest.'

Edmund dropped his feet to the floor with a thud and sat up. 'Did he, b'God?'

'It seems,' Josiah went on smoothly, 'that the mother died only a few weeks after Francis came here. And – um – nobody seems to have thought to let us know.'

'I see.' Edmund's eyes narrowed as he regarded his clerk thoughtfully. Josiah licked his lips before saying carefully, 'I think your father was reluctant to tell the child. Didn't want to distress her further. She . . . she's a trifle wilful, I believe.'

Edmund snorted and took another mouthful of the burning liquid. 'She's trouble. I've a good mind to send her back to the workhouse and let her stay there.' He was silent for a moment, thoughtful. Despite the trouble Hannah had constantly caused, Edmund was no fool. The girl was a good worker. Scarsfield had said so. Soon, she would be capable of carrying out an adult female's work at no extra cost. Besides, he was confident that the Bramwells or Scarsfield fined or punished her appropriately for her misdemeanours. And now, she was truly an orphan.

Josiah's humble tones cut into his thoughts. 'If you'll permit me, I'd like to make a suggestion, Mr Edmund.'

'Eh?' Edmund roused himself from his thoughts. 'Of course, Roper.'

Josiah licked his lips again. 'I've been thinking over

the problem, sir. You see, if the girl finds out her mother's dead, she could do anything. Cause a riot amongst the apprentices, run away. She might,' he emphasized, 'even take the matter to the authorities. Anything . . .'

Edmund's eyes narrowed. 'So – what is your suggestion?'

'That we don't tell her.'

Edmund pulled a face. 'But won't she go on asking? Won't she try to run away again to find out for herself? Just like she says she did the last time?'

With smooth deliberation, Josiah said, 'Not if she starts to receive regular letters from her mother.'

'Eh?'

'If I may be so bold, I believe your – er – relationship with Mr Goodbody is such that the man would be prepared to participate in a little harmless deception. I say harmless, sir,' he hurried on, 'because, after all, we have the child's best interests at heart, don't we? We want her to be happy and settled in her work. And I'm sure she would be, Mr Edmund, if she were to receive a letter every now and again from her mother telling her to be a good girl and not to even think of running away.' Warming to his theme, Josiah hurried on. 'She'd be reassured that her mother was in good health and . . . and I think she'd be obedient to her mother's wishes as expressed in the – er – letters.' He cleared his throat. 'It seems, sir, that the girl's mother cannot read or write and would have to ask someone to write for her. So, there is no chance, you see, that she'll question why someone else has written in her mother's stead.'

Edmund stared at the man in front of him. 'Well, well, well, Roper. What a devious mind you have.' His eyes gleamed and he smiled. 'But a clever one, even I have to admit. And yes, you're quite right. Goodbody will do whatever I ask him. I'll write to him. But not a word to my father, mind.'

'Of course not, sir,' Josiah said with a little bow. He laid the letter on the desk in front of Edmund. 'If there's nothing else, then I'll bid you goodnight, sir.'

'Goodnight, Roper,' Edmund murmured absently, as he picked up the letter from the master of the workhouse and began to read it for himself.

The following week, Josiah Roper sent for Hannah.

'Come in, girl, come in.' He beckoned her forward and motioned her to stand in front of his tall desk.

'Mr Critchlow has asked me to tell you—'

'Has he heard from Mr Goodbody? Is my mother all right?'

Josiah frowned. 'If you'll give me time, girl, I'm getting to that.'

'Sorry, Mr Roper,' Hannah smiled at him winningly, but her prettiness was lost on the cold-hearted man.

'Mr Critchlow – Mr Edmund Critchlow, that is – has asked me to see you. His father is unwell at the present time and all correspondence is now being dealt with either by Mr Edmund or – myself,' he added loftily. He was deliberately dragging out getting to the point. He was enjoying the girl's agitation. She was hopping impatiently from one foot to the other and pressing her lips together as if to prevent further questions bursting forth.

Slowly, he held up a piece of paper. 'This letter purports to be from your mother, child. Mrs Goodbody, I understand, has been kindness itself in undertaking to write to you on behalf of your mother.'

Joseph believed that in matters of deceit, the nearer the truth one could keep to, the better the chance there was of the lies being believed. Mrs Goodbody had indeed penned the letter, but under the instruction of her own husband, who'd explained tersely the necessity of keeping on the right side of Edmund Critchlow.

Hannah sprang forward and snatched the sheet of paper from Josiah's bony fingers. She scanned it eagerly and, as Josiah watched closely, a smile spread across her mouth. There were tears in her eyes as she looked up at him.

'Oh, thank you, Mr Roper. You don't know how much this means to me. Please – will you thank Mr Critchlow for me? I don't know how I can ever repay him.'

'You can repay him, girl, by working hard and keeping yourself out of trouble. And no more thoughts of running away, eh?'

'Oh no, Mr Roper.' Her bright blue eyes were glowing with a happiness that had been missing for weeks, ever since Jane's death. She'd never forget her little friend and she would always carry the feeling of guilt. But with news she believed to be from her mother, Hannah could allow herself to look forward again.

'Fall for it, did she?' Edmund demanded, opening his door as soon as he heard Hannah leave the clerk's office.

Josiah smiled maliciously. 'Oh yes, sir. She fell for it.' *And so*, he thought as the young master's door closed again, *have you. Another Critchlow secret in my keeping.*

At that moment, Hannah was skipping down the stairs back to her work, the precious letter clutched against her breast and, for the first time since Jane's tragic death, she was singing at the top of her voice.

But the next day, a rumour flew through the mill that struck dread into the heart of each and every worker. Mr Nathaniel Critchlow had suffered a serious seizure. For days, his life hung in the balance, but when the news came that he would live, there was little rejoicing. The man was paralysed and would never again sit behind the desk in the mill office. From that moment, Mr Edmund was in full control of Wyedale Mill, and there was only one person who revelled in the news.

Josiah Roper.

Eighteen

As the months and years passed, Hannah moved from job to job in the mill, working as a bobbin winder and then as a drawer.

'I could leave you on the mule with Mrs Martin,' Ernest told her, 'but you're a quick learner and I want you to learn as many jobs as you can. Then, if I'm short anywhere, you can always fill in for me, lass.'

Hannah beamed at him and nodded. She always found a new interest in her work, always found something to sing about. On alternate Sundays, she, Luke and Daniel climbed the hills above the mill, to breathe in the fresh air and taste freedom, even for only an hour or so. When it snowed and the hillsides were clothed in white, they still climbed, slipping and sliding and clinging on to each other, laughing and shrieking in delicious enjoyment. Most weeks they called to see Mrs Grundy, Hannah taking a few of her hard-earned coppers whenever she could. Slowly, the debt was being repaid.

And still the letters that she believed were dictated by her mother to Mrs Goodbody arrived regularly. Hannah could imagine her mother speaking the words aloud – she could almost hear Rebecca's gentle, loving voice exhorting the girl to be good and to stay at the mill.

'*Don't be trying to come to see me,*' the letters

always said. '*I'm well and happy to know that you are too. You are so fortunate in your position. It was so kind of Mr Goodbody to arrange it all for you and we don't want to upset either him or Mr Critchlow, who has been so good to you too, do we?* She signed all her letters, *Your loving mother*, and this was followed by an untidy cross.

Hannah would hold the place where she imagined her mother's fingers had touched the paper against her face, close her eyes and pretend that her mother was tenderly caressing her cheek.

'Mrs Goodbody must write them all for her,' Hannah told Luke and Daniel as the three of them stood on the top of the hill overlooking the dale. She showed them the growing bundle of precious letters from her beloved mother that she carried in her pocket.

'They're all in the same handwriting.' She paused and then added wistfully, 'It's lovely to hear from her and know she's all right, but it's not the same as being able to see her and talk to her and . . . and hug her.'

With one accord as if pulled by the same string, the two boys turned and Daniel began to run down the hill, slipping and sliding in his haste to get away. Luke paused for a moment to look back at her.

'At least you've still got a mam,' he said harshly and then he ran after his brother.

Hannah stared after them, tears welling in her eyes. 'Oh, how stupid I've been. How unkind. I never thought . . .'

At suppertime, she sought them out. Never one to shirk doing the right thing, she stood in front of them. 'I'm so sorry. It was thoughtless and hurtful of me to keep going on about my mother. You helped me so

much at first when I was so worried about not hearing
from her that I hadn't realized every time I talk about
her it must remind you of . . . of . . . Well, I'm sorry.'

The two boys glanced at each other and then looked
at her with identical grins on their cheeky faces. ''S all
right,' Luke said. 'We were being daft an' all. It's not
your fault we've no mam and dad.'

'And we are glad for you that your mam's all right,'
Daniel added.

'Friends then?'

''Course,' the twins chorused.

Summer came round once more, Hannah's fourth in
Wyedale. Letters from her mother came spasmodically,
but Hannah wrote faithfully every month. On alternate Sundays, whatever the weather, she roamed the
hills or walked beside the river with Luke and Daniel,
and her friendship with Nell, too, deepened. Ernest
Scarsfield had noticed how well the two girls worked
together, so when it was time for them to learn yet
another job, he put them together once more.

'We're to learn to be throstle spinners,' Nell told
her excitedly. 'Oh, I've always wanted to do that.
We're to work on one of the machines that produces
the warp thread.' Nell hugged her. 'We're going up in
the world, Hannah. Just like Mrs Riley said we would.
You'll see. I must remember to be specially nice to . . .'
She broke off. 'Come on, let's go and find your Luke
and tell him.'

'*My* Luke,' Hannah laughed.

'Oh yes.' Nell's face was serious. 'He's in love with
you. Hadn't you noticed?'

'Well, I love him. And Daniel and you, of course.' She skipped ahead of Nell, singing a song of her own making this time. 'We're going up in the world.'

Nell smiled and shook her head in wonder. Was Hannah still so innocent and naive as she made out? She frowned. Maybe she should have a little talk with the younger girl, explain just how boys, and men in particular, could be – once you started to grow up.

'Quick, she's coming,' Luke hissed. 'Get ready. The minute she opens the door we all shout "Happy Birthday".'

The giggling children lined up around the long bench tables in the kitchen. It was suppertime on a Saturday evening in August, the evening of Hannah's sixteenth birthday. In the middle of the table stood a birthday cake, which Mrs Bramwell had made herself. It was something she and Arthur did on an apprentice's sixteenth birthday. Although it meant no legal coming of age, to the Bramwells that particular age seemed to mark a turning point in the lives of the youngsters in their charge. If a child had already worked four or five years – or even longer – in the mill, by the time they reached sixteen they were doing the work of an adult and the Bramwells believed they should be treated as such. And if anyone had earned that right, it was Hannah Francis. She was a hard worker and always cheerful – well, almost always. Mrs Bramwell was well aware that the girl still carried a sadness in her heart over the death of her little friend, and daily she still longed to see her own mother. During the three years and three months that Hannah had been at the mill, it had never been possible for Rebecca to travel to see her, and the girl – of course – had never been granted permission to return to the workhouse.

Ethel Bramwell understood that part of it. What she didn't understand was why the mother had never been allowed to visit. Parents who'd agreed to their children being apprenticed to the Critchlows were allowed to visit often.

'I expect the guardians won't pay for her fare to get here, if she's still in the workhouse,' Arthur had remarked reasonably when Ethel broached the subject with him earlier that day.

Ethel had sighed. 'It's not right. Keeping a girl from her mother for all that time with only letters to keep them both going.' Her voice had faltered a little over speaking of what was a great sadness to both her and her husband. 'If we'd been blessed with children, I know I couldn't have borne to've been separated from them in such a way.'

'No, love,' Arthur had agreed quietly. 'No more would I.' He had sighed. 'But that's the way it is. At least she's been well treated at this mill. It'd be a different story at some of the others.'

Ethel had shaken her head. 'If Mr Nathaniel had still been at the helm, then I might've agreed with you, but not now. Not with *him* in charge. I hear the children talking. The tales they're bringing back, Arthur. Things are getting worse and they'll go on getting worse now he's got no one to curb him.'

'It's been happening for years, Ethel. Let's face it, Mr Nathaniel was weak. He rarely stood up to his son even when he was still coming to the mill, now did he?'

Ethel Bramwell had shrugged. 'But when he was

still here, Edmund was away a lot in Manchester on business. Things didn't seem quite so bad then, but now he's here more of the time . . .' Her voice had trailed away.

Arthur Bramwell's face had been solemn. There was something he'd heard that had filled him with deep foreboding. He'd put off telling his wife until he knew if the rumour was true. Yet then, he had felt he must tell her. 'I'm sorry to say,' he had said slowly, 'that things are about to get worse.'

Ethel had stared at him. She held her breath, knowing she was not going to like what he was about to say.

'It seems that Mr Edmund wants to resume handling the business side of things. He'll be spending more time away just like he did before.'

Ethel had begun to smile hopefully. 'Well, that'll be better—' Seeing her husband's expression, she stopped.

Bluntly and in a flat, hopeless tone, Arthur had said, 'Ernest reckons he'll make Roper manager of the whole mill when he's away.'

Ethel's eyes had widened. 'Josiah Roper! Why him? He doesn't know the first thing about the workings of the mill. He's just a clerk. Why not Ernest or one of the other overlookers?'

With a puzzled frown, Arthur had said slowly, 'I don't know.'

'Well, if it does happen, if Roper's put in charge, then may God help us all. That's all I can say. But let's not say anything to the children,' Ethel had begged. 'Not yet. Let's not spoil Hannah's day. You can tell them when we know it's really going to happen.'

Now, as they stood waiting for Hannah, they

pushed aside all thoughts of the mill. Tonight, they would have a party for all the children in their care. For a few precious hours they'd try to help them forget the drudgery of their working days.

'She's coming,' Luke said again. 'I can hear her singing.'

A ripple of soft laughter ran amongst the children. 'We can always hear where Hannah is,' Daniel said, and everyone laughed.

'Shh,' Luke hissed, and everyone tried to stifle their laughter.

The door opened and Hannah stopped in surprise, the words of her song dying on her lips, her mouth wide open in astonishment as everyone chorused, 'Happy Birthday.'

She put her hands over the lower part of her face to hide her blushes, but her eyes sparkled with tears of surprised delight. As their voices died away, Luke and Daniel moved forward and stood on either side of her.

'Mrs Bramwell's made you a cake.'

'And now you must cut it and make a wish.'

For the next hour laughter and singing filled the kitchen of the apprentice house. At last Arthur rapped on the table for silence. 'Now, we've all had a good time, but it's time the younger ones were in bed . . .' This was greeted with a chorus of protests, but they rose obediently, helped to clear away the remains of the feast, and climbed up the narrow twisting staircase, still laughing and talking.

Hannah put her arms around Ethel Bramwell's waist. 'Thank you. Thank you so much for a lovely party. It was just like my mother used to do for me. I only wish . . .' The girl's voice broke and she buried her face against the superintendent's breast.

Ethel put her arms about Hannah. Though kindly towards all the children in her charge, she was rarely demonstrative. But her lack of any show of affection was deliberate. It didn't do to become too attached to any of the children. Her position demanded aloofness, and besides, that way lay hurt. How could she have borne to watch poor little Jane die in agony if she'd allowed herself to love the child? How could she – each and every day – watch the little ones toil to and from the mill, dragging their weary feet, coughing and spluttering as the fluff took hold of their lungs, watching as their eyes became sore, their ears hard of hearing? No, Ethel Bramwell couldn't allow herself to become a proper mother to the children. She dared not. But tonight, just for a moment, the barriers were down and she hugged Hannah to her. 'I know, my dear, I know how you must feel.'

Hannah lifted her face and smiled through her tears. 'But I wouldn't want you to think I'm ungrateful. My mother would love to've been here to join in the fun, but when I write to her, I'll tell her everything. It'll make her so happy.'

Ethel, who knew nothing of the deception being carried on by Josiah Roper and Edmund Critchlow, smiled. 'I'm sure it will. And she should be very proud of her grown-up daughter. You're a credit to her, Hannah. Now,' she said briskly, gently easing herself out of the girl's arms, 'help me clear up and then you can get to your bed.'

As the room began to empty and Ethel bustled about clearing away the last few crumbs of the demolished cake, Luke grabbed Hannah's hand. 'Come for a walk,' he whispered. 'Now you're an old lady of sixteen, you don't have to go to bed for another hour.'

Hannah giggled. 'Oh, the freedom. It'll quite turn my head.' Then impishly she added, 'But you're not sixteen yet. You'd better go to bed, little boy, or you'll be in trouble.'

'I'll risk it,' Luke grinned, but as he pulled her towards the door, Hannah glanced back. 'What about Daniel?'

'He'll be all right. I want you to meself for once.'

Hannah's eyes widened and she laughed, a faint pink tingeing her cheeks as they slipped out of the back door and into the velvet blackness of the night. 'Come on. Let's go into the wash house.'

'I thought you wanted to go for a walk.'

Through the darkness, she heard his soft chuckle. 'Not really. I just wanted to get you to meself.'

They crept into the building across the yard and shut the door behind them. Hannah shivered and Luke put his arm about her, drawing her close.

'Enjoyed your birthday, have you?'

Hannah rested her head against his shoulder and sighed. Although a year younger, he was as tall as she was now. 'Of course I have. It was lovely of the Bramwells to arrange it all.'

'With a bit of help from me an' Daniel.'

Hannah put her arms round his waist and hugged him. 'I thought as much. Thanks, Luke. You and Daniel are my very best friends besides Nell.'

His arms tightened around her. Against her hair he whispered huskily, 'I . . . I'd like to be more than friends. Hannah – I want you to be my girl.'

179

She drew back a little. 'Oh, Luke, I'd love that, but you know it isn't allowed. We'd be in such trouble—'

He laughed so loud now that she put her finger against his lips to quieten him. 'Since when,' he mocked her fondly, 'has that ever stopped you?'

Hannah laughed softly and leaned forward, until their foreheads were touching. Thinking back over the time she'd been here, she seemed to have been in trouble more times than not. Most of the time her misdemeanours had been nothing very serious. The worst had been the time she'd tried to visit her mother. But since letters had come frequently, she'd been, if not happy, then content to do as her mother asked her in every letter. '*Be a good girl, work hard and be a credit to me.*'

'We'll have to keep it secret, then, won't we?' Luke was saying. 'Folks are used to seeing us together. They know we're good friends. We'll just have to mind they don't guess it's a lot more now.' He paused and there was an unaccustomed hesitancy in his tone as he added, 'It *is* a lot more now, isn't it, Hannah?'

'Yes, oh yes, Luke.' She wound her arms around his neck as he leaned forward and tried to kiss her. But they bumped noses and ended up convulsed in laughter. 'Reckon we need a bit of practice,' Luke whispered. Then he bent his head to one side and his lips touched hers in their first tentative kiss.

They stood whispering and giggling and kissing until at last, Luke said reluctantly, 'We'd best go back in. I don't want Mr Bramwell coming after me with a big stick. Come on,' he grabbed her hand and together they sneaked out of the wash house once more. 'Now,' he said, letting go of her hand near the back door. 'Remember, no one must know.'

'Not even Daniel?' Hannah said.

'Daniel?' Luke was surprised that she should even ask. 'Oh, he knew how I felt about you even before I realized it meself.'

Hannah collapsed in gales of laughter and clung to him for a moment, and that is how Mrs Bramwell saw them as she opened the back door.

'There's something going on between those two,' Ethel told her husband as they undressed for bed that night.

'Which two?'

'Luke Hammond and Hannah.'

'Going on? Naw. They're just friends, that's all.' He laughed, a deep, low rumbling sound. 'Can't be much going on when the three of them go everywhere together. Can't do a lot when his twin's tagging along, can he?' He sobered suddenly. 'Unless you're implying—'

'No, no, of course I'm not suggesting anything like that,' Ethel said hurriedly.

'Thank God for that,' her husband muttered.

'But you know the Critchlows make their own rules. If word gets out they'll be sacked. One, if not both of them. Ne'er mind their so-called indenture.'

Arthur made a dismissive sound as he said, 'Ach, I know the rules, woman. But it goes on. You know it does. We see the lads and lasses walking back up the hill to the village at night after work hand in hand, now don't we?'

'There's not much he can do about those who live out, but what he doesn't like is it going on here in the apprentice house. Old man Critchlow might've turned a blind eye, but his son certainly won't. And I'll tell you something else, an' all. It'll make Mr Edmund notice *her*. She's growing up fast. And if he starts to notice her, you know what might happen then.'

For a moment, Arthur stared at his wife across the width of their double bed, then he shrugged. 'I don't think it's Hannah you've to worry about. If anyone, it's Nell.'

As Arthur Bramwell climbed into bed, lay down and closed his eyes, his wife sighed heavily. 'I've been worried about Nell Hudson for years.'

In the dormitories, most of the children were asleep, but two were wide awake, thinking of each other. Hannah snuggled down in the bed she no longer had to share, feeling the happiest she'd been since she'd come to the mill.

'Nell?' she whispered. 'Nell, are you awake?'

When there was no answer, she reared up and squinted through the darkness to the bed next to hers. To her surprise, it was empty. But far from being concerned, Hannah only chuckled. Maybe Nell's got a sweetheart too, she thought happily.

Nineteen

The day that Edmund became bored with spending most of his days at the mill, Josiah Roper believed it might be the happiest day in his life.

'I'm not getting the best prices for cotton,' Edmund ranted, pacing up and down his office.

'There's no better negotiator than you, sir.' Josiah gave a small obsequious bow as he hovered in the doorway. 'The figures certainly aren't as good as when you were doing the buying in person.'

Edmund grunted and continued to pace. 'There's nothing else for it, Roper, I'll have to start going to Manchester and Liverpool again myself. I can't trust anyone else to do it. Not properly.'

I could do it, Josiah was thinking. *I could barter just as well as you.* But the clerk held his tongue. He was an expert book-keeper – no one could ever deny that. He knew how to make the figures add up to a healthy profit on the bottom line in his numerous, neatly written ledgers. Yet no one realized that during the years he had, on the surface, faithfully served the Critchlows, Josiah Roper had been garnering a wealth of knowledge about the cotton industry. He'd learned all he could about the financial side of the trade – and so much more. He could recognize the best quality of the cotton and where it came from. On the pretext of checking deliveries, he'd seen for himself the bales of raw cotton that Edmund had bartered for and bought. He'd listened at doors, subtly questioned the workers as they passed in and out of his office. And when the machines fell silent late at night, Josiah would pass like a shadow through all the floors, seeing for himself all the processes needed to turn the raw cotton into a finished, saleable product.

But he could reveal none of this to Edmund Critchlow. He had to wait. He had to bide his time . . .

Edmund stopped his pacing and faced his clerk. 'What I need, Roper, is someone to be manager of the mill whilst I'm away.' His lip curled. 'Scarsfield would be the obvious choice, but he's far too soft. He'd have the hands running circles round him. No, I need someone with a firm hand. Someone who'll stand no nonsense.'

Josiah cleared his throat. 'Does it have to be someone who actually works in the mill itself, sir? I mean, surely, it should be someone who understands the business side too. The – er – financial side. They would know what needed to be done and merely be capable of passing on those requirements to the various overlookers.'

He fell silent, waiting for his words to permeate Edmund's mind. He watched the fleeting expressions on his employer's face. Saw the light beginning to dawn. Hardly daring to breathe as excitement flooded through him, he wondered briefly if this feeling was akin to the thrill his own father and Edmund had felt at the gaming tables. If so, then for the first time in his life, he could understand his father's addiction. The fast-beating heart, the clammy hands, the beads of sweat on his forehead.

Edmund was staring at him. 'You mean – you?' There was sarcasm in his tone.

Again the deferential bow. 'You know you can trust me implicitly, Mr Edmund. You surely cannot doubt my loyalty to you and your family.'

'But you know nothing about the workings of the mill.'

'Perhaps not,' Josiah said meekly, preferring not to divulge the extent of his acquired knowledge. 'But – like I said – is that strictly necessary?' Daringly now, he put it into words. 'I'm sure I could see that the overlookers carry out all their duties. If, of course,' he added slyly, 'you were to give me the authority.'

'Hmm.' Edmund pondered for a moment and then his face brightened. 'I've a better idea. I'll bring Adam home from school. Make him manager of the mill.'

Josiah's hopes faded. Yet he was not quite ready to give up. 'But Master Adam's only sixteen—'

'Seventeen. High time he was here learning the family business instead of idling away his time at school.'

'But won't he be going to university?'

Edmund let out a loud guffaw. 'Adam? Go to university? He's not clever enough, Roper. He'd never get in. Besides, he'd be far better here. After all, the mill will be his one day. The sooner he starts learning his trade, the better. He's too soft, of course. He's like his grandfather. But with me to guide him, he'll toughen up. I'll write to his headmaster at once.' Edmund rubbed his hands, gleeful that his problem had been solved. 'Of course,' he said offhandedly as he sat down behind his desk and picked up a pen, 'you can hold the fort until Adam gets home.'

Josiah Roper almost spat in the other man's face. He glared at Edmund's head bowed over the letter he'd begun to write. If he'd had a weapon to hand at that moment, Edmund Critchlow might not have lived to see another day. As it was, Josiah turned on his heel and left the room, his only outward show of displeasure being to bang the door behind him.

One day, he promised himself. Oh, one day, Mr Edmund Critchlow . . .

'Nell – where were you last night? Oh, you weren't in the punishment room, were you? Surely Mrs Bramwell couldn't have been so mean. Not after my party. She couldn't have been—'

'Hannah, just shut up, will you? And stop asking so many questions.'

Hannah gasped. 'But . . .'

'But nothing. Just mind your own business. All right?'

Hannah stared at her friend. Nell avoided meeting her eyes and pushed past her to get to her bed. Hannah's mouth tightened. She picked up her shawl and her clogs. 'Well, if that's the way you want it,' she said stiffly, and began to follow the others rushing to get to work. The bell had gone already. At the door, she paused. 'You'd better get a move on. You'll be late and then you'll be fined . . .'

'Just go, Hannah. Leave me alone.'

To Hannah's surprise, Nell made no attempt to follow, but climbed onto her bed and lay down, curling herself into a ball, hugging herself.

Hannah bit her lip, hesitating. 'Nell, are you ill? Do you want me to fetch Mrs Bramwell . . .'

Nell sat up suddenly, and leaned over the side of her bed to pick up her clogs. Hannah felt a wave of relief.

'Come on, then,' she began, but her relief turned to horror as Nell flung one of her clogs straight at her, narrowly missing her head. The clog banged against the wall and fell to the floor with a clatter.

'Get out!' Nell screamed. 'Just get out and leave me alone.'

Hannah went, almost falling down the stairs, gulping back the sobs. Whatever was the matter with Nell? She rushed to find Mrs Bramwell, not caring if she was late and incurred a fine.

'There's something the matter with Nell,' she burst out. 'She wasn't in bed last night before I fell asleep and she's just come in like a bear with a sore head. She's lying in her bed and won't come to work.'

Mrs Bramwell's face was grim. 'Is she indeed?'

It was a strange thing to say, Hannah thought. The woman didn't seem concerned that Nell might be ill. Just that she was not going to work.

'I think she's ill, she's holding her tummy and—'

'Leave her to me and you get to work, Francis.'

Hannah ran out of the house and down the hill, only just managing to clock in half a minute before the bell in the tower stopped ringing.

The whole day passed with Hannah having to run between the two machines, doing her own work and Nell's, trying to keep her friend out of trouble.

The day passed quickly. As she was leaving by the gate, hurrying back up the hill to the house to see how Nell was, she heard a shout behind her and saw the twins running towards her.

'Have you heard the news?' Luke began.

'Master Adam's back,' Daniel continued.

'He's to be manager—'

'Of the mill—'

'When Mr Edmund's away—'

'On business.'

As always when they were together, the two boys imparted the information in turn.

Hannah glanced from one to the other in amazement. 'Master Adam? But . . . but he's only a boy. How can he be manager?'

'Because he's a Critchlow—'

'That's why.'

'And he's about seventeen now, isn't he?'

'Oh.' Hannah wrinkled her forehead. 'Oh well, I don't suppose it will make much difference to us. Will it?'

Luke grinned. 'Things might be better. Word has it that Mr Adam is much nicer—'

'Than his father.'

'More like—'

'His grandfather.'

Hannah smiled at them in turn and then stepped between them, linking her arms in theirs. 'Come on, let's go and tell the others. And I want to find out how Nell is.'

There was excited chatter amongst all the apprentices at the news. Only Mr and Mrs Bramwell seemed preoccupied and anxious.

'Don't you think it's good news about Master Adam being made manager, Mrs Bramwell?' Hannah asked.

'What? Oh yes, I suppose so. Don't bother me now, Hannah. I've enough on my mind.'

'How's Nell? Where is she? Can I see her?'

'No,' Mrs Bramwell snapped. 'You can't. Nor will you. She's gone.'

Hannah's mouth dropped open. 'Gone? What do you mean, gone? Gone where?'

'How should I know?'

'But . . . but . . . you should know. You're the superintendent, you're—'

Mrs Bramwell rounded on her. Now she was nothing like the kindly woman who'd hugged Hannah on her birthday only yesterday. Now she was like a screaming banshee. 'Is it my fault if the stupid girl gets herself into trouble and gets sent away? Is it? Is it?' Mary, the kitchen maid, stopped and turned to stare at her mistress. Even she, who worked for her all day and half the night too sometimes, had never seen Mrs Bramwell in such a temper.

Hannah blinked and opened her mouth to speak, but at that moment Mr Bramwell came into the kitchen and hurried towards his wife. 'There, there, Ethel,' he soothed, putting his arm around her shoulders. 'You mustn't blame yourself. Or the poor girl, if it comes to that. We know who's to blame, now don't we, but there's not a thing we can do about it.'

To Hannah's horror, Ethel turned her face away and wept against her husband's shoulder. 'But what'll become of her? What'll happen to her?'

Hannah began to feel frightened. 'Mr Bramwell, what's happened? Please – won't you tell me?'

Arthur Bramwell looked down upon the innocent face upturned towards him. He sighed inwardly. He would dearly like to tell this honest, hardworking child the truth, but he had been sworn to secrecy and so had his wife. He'd like to warn Hannah too, but he dared not do so.

Instead, he said sternly, 'It's not your place to ask questions. Hudson's gone and she won't be coming back. That's all you need to know. Now, get about your chores else you'll find yourself in the punishment room for insolence.'

For once Hannah did as she was told, and the following morning she sought out Dorothy Riley, but the woman only shrugged. 'Best not to ask, love. Know your place, that's my advice to you.' She glanced at Hannah and then touched her face with callused, work-worn fingers. 'You're a pretty lass, more's the pity, so keep your head down. Do your work and try not to get noticed. Now come on, we've all got work to do, else we'll have Mr Scarsfield after us. And he's in a bad mood this morning, now he's a throstle spinner down.'

Again Hannah worked the two machines all day, though it wasn't easy. Tired, hot and dirty by the end of the day, she was still determined to try to find out what had happened to her friend.

The overlooker was standing next to the time clock when the bell sounded for the end of the day.

'Mr Scarsfield,' Hannah asked after she had stamped her card and returned it to its holder. 'What's happened to Nell?'

The man stared at her in surprise for a moment and then frowned. 'Ah,' he said. 'I see you don't know.' He glanced away, avoiding her clear, straight gaze.

'All I've been told is that she's gone away and won't be coming back. What I don't know is why. No one will tell me.'

'She's been sacked,' Ernest said bluntly. 'She's displeased the master and he's sacked her.'

'But . . . but how? Why?'

190

Ernest looked at her strangely for a moment and then muttered bitterly, 'You'd better ask him.'

'Oh, I will.' Hannah began and turned away as if to go that very minute, but Ernest caught hold of her arm and held her fast. He shook his head, his eyes full of concern for her now. 'No, lass, don't. I shouldn't have said that. That's the last thing you should do. Promise me you won't go asking any more questions.'

Hannah stared at him for a moment before saying solemnly, 'I'm sorry, Mr Scarsfield, I can't give you that promise.'

He released her with a click of exasperation. 'On your own head be it then, girl. But don't say I didn't warn you.'

Twenty

Now, on Sundays, Luke and Hannah walked alone.

'I feel awful leaving Daniel,' she said more than once. 'He hasn't any other friends.'

But Luke only grinned 'He doesn't mind. I've told him – time he got himself a girl an' all.'

'Is there anyone he likes?'

'Don't think so.'

He glanced behind him. They were out of sight of the mill now, walking round the edge of the mill pool beneath the cliff and alongside the river. Green-headed mallards, uptailed as they searched the depths for food, swam close by. Coots and moorhens darted about the surface and every so often they heard the plop of a jumping fish. Overhead, leafy trees sheltered them from the hot sun. Luke put his arm about her waist and they walked on, matching their steps to each other.

'So – what do you think to our new young master then?' Luke asked her.

'He's all right. I haven't seen much of him.'

'Haven't you? Well, I've seen him watching you at work'

'I hadn't noticed.'

'No, he minds to keep himself well back in the shadows. But he stands watching you and listening to you singing.'

Hannah laughed. 'I shouldn't think he can hear much above the noise all that machinery makes.'

'No – but he can look at you.'

Hannah teased him. 'A' you jealous?'

He grinned at her. ''Course I am. I don't like anyone eyeing my girl up, even if he is the boss's son.'

Hannah tweaked his nose playfully. 'Just so long as it isn't Mr Edmund. He sends shivers down my spine every time he looks at me.'

Now Luke wasn't laughing any more. He'd heard the tales about Mr Edmund and he didn't like them one little bit. And he didn't want Hannah asking him about them, especially if the latest rumour about Nell was true. Deliberately, he changed the subject. 'Have you heard from your mother lately?'

Hannah didn't answer immediately. Ever since that day on the hillside when the twins, younger then, of course, and feeling more vulnerable, had been so upset, she'd avoided talking to them about her mother. In fact, she scarcely spoke to anyone at the mill about her now. She was conscious that many of the children she lived and worked with were orphans. But now, as Luke asked her directly, she frowned and said, 'No, not since before my birthday. In fact, I didn't get a letter then and I know she wouldn't have forgotten it. She . . . she always used to make a big thing of anyone's birthday.'

Gently, Luke said, 'Hannah, you didn't get a letter last year for your birthday. You were upset about it then.'

Hannah stared at him. 'You're right. But I got such a lovely one a week later that I forgot all about it. I . . . I just thought that . . . well . . . being in there, she'd lost track of the date.' Her voice trailed away, her heart aching at the thought of her mother still imprisoned in the workhouse.

'Have you written to her?' Luke prompted.

'Yes. Twice – but she's not written back.'

They walked on in silence. Luke couldn't think of any useful suggestion, and though Hannah was busy with her own plans, she had no intention of telling Luke what they were. It had been two months since Nell had disappeared so suddenly and Hannah still didn't know what had happened to her, and now she wanted to find out why the letters from her mother had stopped. And so, despite her declaration that she tried to avoid Mr Edmund, there were now two very good reasons why she needed to seek him out deliberately.

'May I see Mr Edmund, please?' Hannah asked Josiah Roper politely.

'What about?'

'I – it's a personal matter.'

The man's mouth twisted slyly. ''Bout you and young what's-'is-name, is it? Want to get married, do you?'

Hannah gasped and couldn't stop the flush rising in her face. 'I don't know what you're talking about.'

'Oh, I think you do. You'd better be careful. If Mr Edmund gets wind of it, that lad'll be out on his ear, indenture or no indenture. He'll be gone.' His impudent glance raked her from head to toe. 'Mind you, he'll not sack you. Oh no, he'll likely keep you for himself.'

'It's nothing like that. There's nothing between me and Luke—'

Josiah raised his eyebrows. 'So you do know who I was talking about then?'

Hannah's blush deepened. 'Stop trying to put words in my mouth,' she cried angrily. 'Is Mr Edmund here – or not?'

'No, he isn't.'

'Thank you,' she said, her tone heavy with sarcasm. She turned to go. As she pulled open the door to leave, Josiah said airily, 'Not had a letter lately, have you?'

Hannah stopped in her tracks and looked back at him. 'What . . . what do you mean?'

'Oh, nothing.' He paused and then added, calculatingly, 'I expect Mrs Goodbody has got sick of writing. It can't be easy making up lovey-dovey letters, pretending to be your mother.'

'Whatever do you mean? *Pretending* to be my mother?'

Josiah's lip curled. Still harbouring bitterness at Mr Edmund's decision to pass him over and bring home a mere youth to be manager of the mill, he said, 'Those letters aren't from your mother, girl. Mrs Goodbody wrote them all. Every last one of them.'

Hannah was still puzzled. 'My mother can't write herself, but—'

'Of course your mother can't write now – even if she ever could. She's dead.' Hannah clutched at the door to steady herself as Josiah continued vindictively, 'She's been dead for three years. Ever since a few months after you came here.'

Hannah felt the colour drain from her face, and felt her legs tremble weakly as if they would no longer support her. 'But . . . but Mr Edmund . . . ?'

'He deceived you. Him and Mr Goodbody wanted to keep you here. Keep you happy. They cooked up the little scheme of Matilda Goodbody writing to you – just so you'd think that your dear mama was still well and happy.'

Hannah gasped. 'I don't believe you. You're a wicked liar, Mr Roper.'

Josiah shrugged. 'Think what you like. It doesn't bother me. But what would I have to gain by telling you lies?'

She stared at him for a long moment, her thoughts in turmoil. 'I . . . I . . .' she began, but she could think of nothing to say, so she turned and ran. Ran to find Luke, all thoughts of the second reason for her visit to the office – to ask about Nell – driven from her mind.

It was not Luke she found, but Adam Critchlow.

Running wildly across the yard towards the gate, she ran smack into him and would have lost her balance and fallen had he not caught hold of her.

For a moment he held her close and then, when she was steady on her feet, though gasping for breath through her sobbing, he held her a little from him and looked down at her. His eyes darkened as he saw her distress.

'Hannah, what is it? Whatever's the matter?'

'You – you and your family. He's . . . he's lied to me. All this time, I believed him. I've been loyal. I've worked hard – and all I get in return is lies and deceit.'

'Whatever do you mean? I don't understand what you're talking about.'

'My mother's dead. And he never told me. He's lied to me. Kept me believing she was alive and well and . . . and happy and all the time . . .'

She broke into fresh, hiccuping sobs.

'No! I don't believe it. My grandfather wouldn't do something like that.'

'It wasn't your grandfather – it was your father.'

'My *father*?' His look was incredulous.

Hannah nodded grimly. 'It was all a plot hatched up between him and the master of the workhouse to keep me quiet.' Her voice broke and she sobbed afresh.

'You're saying my father did that?' Adam asked slowly.

'You don't believe me, do you? Why will no one ever believe me?' she cried passionately. She realized he was still holding her and she tore herself free. 'Let me go! Let me go! You're – you're all the same. *You'll* be just the same.'

Adam's face blanched. 'No, I won't. I promise I'd never do anything like that.' She could still hear the doubt in his voice. He couldn't believe such a thing of his own father.

Her eyes blazing now, rage drying her tears. 'Oh yes, you will. You'll be just like him. You won't be able to help yourself. When you have us all in your – in your power, you'll be as bad as him. He'll *make* you just like him. There's a lot you don't know about your father. You've not been here to see it. But things are very different for us workers since your grandfather was taken ill. Very different.'

Then she ran. Out of the gate and up the steep slope, not stopping until she'd rushed into the apprentice house and slammed the kitchen door behind her. She leaned against it, sobbing and breathless.

'What on earth . . . !' Ethel Bramwell began angrily, but when she saw the state of the young girl, she laid down her rolling pin at once and, wiping her floury hands on her copious white apron, she hurried forward. 'Oh, my dear, what's happened? Don't tell me there's been another accident.'

She led Hannah forward and pushed her into a chair near the kitchen range and then poured a cup of tea from the huge teapot sitting in the hearth. 'There, there. Tell me all about it.'

The story flooded out and even Ethel Bramwell, who'd worked for the Critchlows for years, was astonished.

'Mr Critchlow? Old man Critchlow?' Her tone was disbelieving. 'He was party to this?'

Hannah shook her head. 'I don't know. Maybe. It was Mr Edmund mainly and Mr Roper was in on it too. It . . . it was always him who gave me the letters an' . . . and posted mine. If he ever did post them,' she ended flatly. It didn't matter now whether he had or not. Her loving letters would never have reached the person for whom they were intended anyway.

Mrs Bramwell sighed. 'I don't like to think the old man knew about it. I'd've thought better of him.'

Hannah's face hardened. Her blue eyes turned cold. 'They're all the same. Every one of them. Master Adam'll be just the same, when he's older.'

Once, Ethel would have leaped to the young boy's defence. But now she could think of nothing to say.

Twenty-One

'So, you're causing trouble again are you?'

Early the following evening, Hannah was making her way round the back of the mill along the path towards the waterfall where Luke would be waiting for her. The mill was still working, the millhands trying to catch the last of the daylight. The huge wheel thundered round and round, the water rushing along the race to feed its hungry teeth. Suddenly, a figure loomed up out of the shadows, and before she could step around him, Edmund Critchlow had grasped her arm in a vice-like grip. 'You need teaching a lesson, girl.'

'You're hurting.' She tried to twist herself free, but he held her fast.

'Oh, I'll hurt you girl. I'll give you a lesson you won't forget in a hurry. Now Nell's no use to me, you can take her place. I fancy me a young tender piece . . .'

Hannah struggled, trying to free herself, trying to get away. She twisted and lashed out at him with her free hand, but he caught hold of that too. Then she kicked out, catching him on the shin. He let out a yelp of pain, but instead of releasing his hold, he gripped her even more tightly. She screamed, but no one could hear her cries above the roar of the churning water. Edmund raised his hand and dealt her a stinging blow to the side of her face. She reeled and would have fallen if he had not still been holding her. 'You little bitch,' he snarled.

The last vestige of her resistance was almost gone; he was too strong for her. And then suddenly, miraculously, a figure hurtled towards them, waving his arms and yelling, 'Let her go. Leave her alone.'

'Oh, Luke, Luke,' Hannah sobbed thankfully.

He'd been standing on the path leading to the waterfall, watching for Hannah and had seen it all. Now he stood a yard away from them, his hands clenched at his side, every sinew in his body poised, tensed to spring, but he did not touch either Hannah or Edmund. Instead, his steely eyes bored into the older man's. 'Let – her – go,' he yelled.

Edmund threw back his head and laughed. 'And who's going to stop me?' He pointed at Luke with a derisory gesture. 'You?'

Luke took a step towards them. 'Yes. Me.'

He was not as tall as Edmund or as strong. He was still only a youth, but at this moment he was defending the girl he loved. And his anger lent him strength.

For a brief moment, a flicker of uncertainty crossed Edmund's face, but then it was gone and he was once more the master, the powerful owner of the mill who ruled all their lives. But in that brief moment, Hannah had felt the tiniest relaxation of his hold on her and she twisted herself out of his grasp.

'Run, Hannah,' Luke ordered. 'Go home – to the house and stay there.'

'No – I—'

'Go!' Luke's tone was a whip crack, demanding obedience.

Hannah went, running along the path and up to the

house. 'Oh, please, please come and help Luke,' she cried as she fell into the kitchen, panting and breathless.

'What's to do?' Arthur Bramwell strode towards her and grasped her arms to steady her.

'It's Luke and . . . and Mr Edmund. Fighting,' she gasped.

'Fighting?' Arthur Bramwell was incredulous. It was unheard of – an apprentice fighting with the master. Even strong Arthur Bramwell quailed at the thought. He released her and rushed from the house. Several of the boys and a few of the girls followed, chattering excitedly. 'A fight. There's a fight between Luke and the master.'

Hannah followed, pushing her way through them to get there first.

There were other figures, looming out of the shadows coming from the mill to stand watching – and waiting. But no one moved forward.

'He'll be for it, fighting with the master.'

'Where's Mr Scarsfield? He might be able to—'

'Mr Bramwell's there. Look.'

'He'll not step in. This is mill business.'

'But the lad's from the house.'

'Help him,' Hannah begged. 'Please – help Luke.'

But no one moved.

'We'd like to, lass,' one of the men murmured. 'But it's our jobs – our homes. We daren't.'

'He's right,' another muttered. 'I'd like to give that Mr Edmund a taste of his own medicine. Been wanting to punch him in the face for years, but I've me wife and young 'uns to think of.'

'I'm sorry, lass. The lad's on his own.'

Hannah cast about wildly, but no one moved. No

one went to Luke's aid. But there was one who she knew would come running.

'Where's Daniel?' she cried.

'Working. He's on the late shift. Best leave him, Hannah. If you fetch him here, he'll be in trouble too. Luke wouldn't want that. He'll deal with this on his own.'

She tugged at Mr Bramwell's arm. 'Stop them. Oh, please, stop them.'

The big man shook his head sadly. 'I can't. It's out of my hands.'

Hannah bit her lip and a sob escaped her. She stood with her hands over her mouth, watching the scene with terrified eyes.

'Oh, please, Luke, don't,' she cried.

The muttering fell silent as the onlookers watched the two figures stalking each other like a pair of fighting cocks.

'Taking wagers, are we?' someone murmured, but no one took him up on the suggestion. No one spoke. All eyes were riveted on the two men. This was a serious business.

Edmund, six inches taller than Luke, looked down at him disdainfully. Above the roar of the water, he shouted, 'Go on, then. Hit me. If you dare.'

Luke's eyes were glittering with hatred and loathing. He would've liked nothing better than to smash this man's face to a pulp. Yet he held back. He had rescued Hannah. That was what mattered. They'd have to think what to do next – after this – but for the moment, she was safe.

'I've no wish to hit you, sir, but you've no right to touch the girls. Specially not my Hannah.'

Edmund laughed humourlessly. 'Oho, your Hannah, is she? Well, well. We'll have to see about that. Fornication in the apprentice house? Dear me. The Bramwells have been neglectful in their duties. They'll be out on their ear—'

'There's been no . . . no fornication. I love Hannah. *I* wouldn't hurt her.'

Edmund thrust his face close to Luke's. 'You won't get the chance. You're sacked. You'll be on your way back to the workhouse before this night's out. Back where you belong. You and your mealy-mouthed brother.'

It was the insult to his twin that finally tipped Luke over the edge. He swung an ungainly right hand at Edmund's chin and caught him a glancing blow as Edmund ducked. Though a big man, Edmund was quick and light on his feet. Rumour had it that as a young man at university he'd indulged in all the raffish pursuits: drinking, gambling and a little bare-knuckle fighting. And anyone who'd had a wager on Edmund Critchlow to win had always gone home a happy man at night.

Now, Edmund's fist landed in the centre of Luke's face with a sickening crack. Bone splintered and blood spurted from the younger man's nose. Luke tottered backwards, but then the vision of Edmund grasping Hannah so roughly, dragging her along, swam before his eyes. He straightened up and lunged at Edmund, but he was no match for the older, stronger man. Luke had little knowledge of fighting. In the odd boyish scrap in the workhouse yard, there had always been the two of them. Him and Daniel against the world.

Where was Daniel? Why wasn't he here, standing shoulder to shoulder with his twin?

Edmund's blows rained thick and fast. Two more

to the head, one just below Luke's ribs, knocking the wind out of him and causing him to bend double. And each blow drove him backwards. There was no let up. A blow to the side of his head sent him reeling, closer and closer to the edge of the bank above the wheel. The watchers moved forward, shouting, but above the roar of the churning water neither Edmund nor Luke could hear them. Luke was almost senseless, still on his feet but only with tremendous willpower. And on Edmund's face was murderous intent.

The watchers knew it was going to happen. They could see it. Hannah, Arthur Bramwell and one or two others ran forward, shouting a warning, but it was too late. With one last vicious blow, Edmund sent Luke flailing backwards over the edge and down, down into the cavernous centre of the giant wheel. His body was tossed and tumbled until his features were scarcely recognizable.

The wheel ploughed on relentlessly, but Edmund stood on the edge looking down, watching with fists clenched, jaw hard and unrepentant, and making no move to stop it.

Hannah rushed towards the edge and would have fallen in too, but Arthur Bramwell caught hold of her. She struggled against him, screaming, 'Stop the wheel. Stop it.'

Others arrived at the edge, staring helplessly down at Luke being thrown around the inside of the wheel.

Arthur's grasp tightened on her arms briefly. 'Stay here,' he ordered and then he ran into the mill.

The wheel was slowing, the water settling. A gasp rippled amongst the onlookers as they saw Luke's battered body fall to the bottom and lie there, a mass of blood and shattered bone.

And then Hannah began to scream as if she would never stop.

'It's all your fault. If it hadn't been for you, I'd've been with him.'

Hannah gasped. Her eyes were blotchy from two days of constant weeping. She was inconsolable, but Daniel was angry, vitriolic.

'And now he's dead – all because of *you*!'

She had no answer.

'I'd've been with him,' he ranted on. 'We were always together. Always. Until you came along. Then he'd rather be with you than with me.' He glared at her, hatred in his eyes. 'I 'spect you were making a play for the master, were you?'

Now, Hannah was startled out of her lethargy. 'No.' She was horrified. 'How can you even think such a thing of me? I loved Luke. You know I did.' Tears welled again in her eyes and she covered her face and sobbed. 'How can you even think that, Daniel?'

He was silent, unapologetic. He was hurting, just like Hannah, and his only weapon was to lash out at her to try to assuage his own guilt at not being at his twin's side when Luke had needed him the most. But it wasn't working. He could not pass the guilt onto her shoulders. Daniel would carry the burden for the rest of his life. And so would Hannah, for she blamed herself just as much as Daniel did.

Her sobs quietened and for the first time since the tragedy, calmness came over her. 'It wasn't your fault,' she said in a flat, emotionless voice. 'And it wasn't really mine, even though I shall feel it was for the rest of me life. There's only one person to blame and that's

Edmund Critchlow, and as God is my witness, I'll pay him back for this.' Her tone took on a steely edge and even Daniel was forced to believe her. 'I'll never forgive and I'll never forget. And one day, I'll make him pay.'

Twenty-Two

Luke was buried in a pauper's grave alongside Jane.

The mill worked on as usual and no one was granted official leave to attend the funeral. Only those who dared to defy the rules and take time off from their work were there. Daniel, Hannah and Ernest Scarsfield together with Ethel and Arthur Bramwell, even though they all knew they'd be fined for doing so.

They'd thought that no one from the Critchlow family would have the audacity to show their faces, yet as they followed the coffin on its final, sorrowful journey, another figure fell into step at the very back just as he had at Jane's funeral.

Adam Critchlow.

He was an unwelcome presence, but later, as Arthur Bramwell remarked, 'The lad was brave to come. Think about it. His father caused Luke's death. We all know that. And there were enough of us there to bear witness, yet there's been no inquiry. It's all been hushed up. There's a few bribes changed hands, if you ask me.' It was the first time that Hannah had ever heard the taciturn Arthur Bramwell speak out against his employers. 'The poor lad's been pushed into a pauper's grave and forgotten about. The Critchlows haven't even had the decency to pay for a proper burial for him.'

Listening to the conversation, Ethel put in, 'I 'spect they thought it'd be like admitting guilt if they did.'

Arthur glanced at his wife and nodded. 'You've a point there. Aye, I see what you mean.'

There was silence for a moment before Hannah said softly, but in a tone that was like a vow, 'Well, he won't be forgotten about. Not by me.'

'No,' Arthur agreed. 'Nor by us. And he'll never be gone whilst Daniel's around, will he? Like two peas in a pod they are. I could never tell the difference between them. I'd never have believed two people could be so alike.'

Hannah said nothing. To her the two boys had been very different. Daniel was nothing like the merry, outspoken Luke, but a mere shadow of his brother. But she felt for him. What was poor Daniel going to do now without his twin?

Mrs Grundy wept openly. 'Another death. When are the authorities going to do something about that place?'

'There's not much they can do, love.' Ollie Grundy patted his wife's shoulder and glanced sympathetically at Hannah.

'Well, there ought to be. Isn't there someone we can report it to?'

Ollie shrugged his huge shoulders. 'I wish there was. D'you know, I'd even risk that part of our livelihood – losing that trade – if it meant saving them poor children up there any more hurt.'

Hannah, believing him, smiled weakly. 'It wasn't so bad when old man Critchlow still ran things. It's only since *he's* taken over.' She paused and then added,

'You've heard the news, I suppose, about Mr Nathaniel?'

The Grundys glanced at each other. 'No.'

'When he heard the news about Luke, he had another seizure. A really bad one. He's not expected to live.'

'Aye,' Lily Grundy said bitterly. 'Well, there you are then, that puts Mr Edmund in full control an' no arguing with it now. And he's likely to be there for years to come.' She paused and looked directly at Hannah. 'You ought to get away from that place – from *him* – whilst you've the chance. We'll help you, won't we, Ollie?'

Hannah stared at them, glancing from one to the other in amazement. 'But . . . but I haven't even paid you all the money back you lent me last time. With all the stoppages I get, I haven't been able to manage even a few pennies recently. I still don't get proper wages.'

Lily flapped her hand. 'Don't think any more about that. We've got it all planned, me and Ollie.' Husband and wife glanced at each other like conspirators. 'He'll take you to Buxton on the cart on Friday morning and you can get a ride from there on the carrier's cart – or the coach, whichever you like – back to Macclesfield. There must be folks there you know who'd help you.'

Hannah was doubtful. 'We were in the workhouse. I daren't go back there. Mr Goodbody'd have me sent straight back here.'

'What about where you lived before you went into the workhouse? Can you remember?'

Hannah sought back through her mind to being eight years old and even before that. 'I can remember me gran – just. She looked after me when me mother went out to work. I . . . I can remember her dying and the coffin outside our house in the street, on a cart – a handcart – and the men pushing it. And . . . and the neighbours. They all came out and I watched me mother walking behind it down the street. I wanted to go with her but I wasn't allowed and . . . and someone was holding onto me to stop me running after her . . .'

'Can you remember who that was?' Lily tried to prompt her memories.

'I . . . I think she lived next door. I called her Auntie – Auntie – oh, I can't remember.' Hannah rubbed her forehead in frustration as if the action would massage her brain to work better.

'Can you remember where you lived – the name of the street? She might still be there.'

Hannah shook her head. 'It was a narrow street with tall terraced houses.'

'Well, there'll be dozens of streets just like that one in a place like Macclesfield,' Lily said. 'That don't help much.'

'Is there anything else you can remember?' Ollie pressed, trying to help. 'Did you live near anything like a church or the place your mother worked or . . . ?'

Hannah frowned. 'I . . . I think we lived a couple of streets away from the mill where Mam worked.'

'The mill? Your mother worked in a mill?'

'Oh, not like the one here. It was a silk mill. I do remember that.'

'A *silk* mill! Well, I never.' Ollie was thoughtful for a moment before he said, 'That might help. You could ask at the silk mills. There might be people there who'd remember her.'

Hannah smiled wryly. 'There might well be, but I don't know if they'd kill the fatted calf, exactly.'

Ollie and Lily glanced at each other. 'What do you mean, lass?'

Hannah pulled a face. 'I think the reason we ended up in the workhouse was because we lost the house after me gran died.'

'Why?'

'Me gran was the tenant – not me mam.'

'Couldn't your mother have taken it on?'

Hannah shook her head. 'No – she was sacked from her job.'

Gently, Lily asked, 'Do you know why?'

'No. Not really. But . . . but . . . I always thought it had something to do with me.'

'With you?'

Hannah nodded, the shame flooding through her as she whispered, 'I haven't got a dad, you see.'

Lily laughed, and it was a genuine laugh – the first Hannah had heard since Luke's terrible death. 'Well, there's plenty of your sort about, love. I shouldn't let that worry you. Most o' them orphans up at the mill'll be just like you, I'll be bound.'

Hannah smiled weakly. 'Well, yes, they are. And there were plenty of us in the workhouse. It . . . it was only then I realized I wasn't the only . . . only bastard in the world.'

'Aw, lovey.' Lily gathered Hannah to her bosom. She rocked her and the girl felt comforted. 'There's one thing though, lass, that perhaps you hadn't thought of. *Somewhere* you've got a dad. How about trying to find him, eh?'

Hannah drew back from the woman's embrace and stared up at her in surprise. 'I – I'd never thought of that.'

211

'Now, hang on a minute,' Ollie said, suddenly concerned. 'D'you think that'd be wise? I mean – there might be all sorts of complications.'

Lily's face was set. 'Such as?'

'Well,' Ollie floundered, glancing helplessly from one to the other. 'I dunno. I just think—'

'I'm not suggesting she should go marching up to his door demanding to be taken in as his daughter. But if she could find him, he just might be willing to help her. She can only ask.' They were talking now as if Hannah was not in the room. But she was and hanging on every word.

'Aye, and how will she feel if he sends her off with a flea in her ear? She'll be hurt all over again.'

'Not if she prepares herself that that might happen. She'd be no worse off than she is now.'

'Huh! Just rejected again, eh?'

'Oh, Ollie, you're a lovely man.' Lily reached up and patted his cheek. 'But sometimes, just some-times—'

'Yes, you are, Mr Grundy.' Hannah smiled. 'But Mrs Grundy's right. I've nothing to lose. That's what I'll do. I'll find my father.'

Over the next few days, Hannah made her plans carefully. She was determined not to be caught this time. There was only one person she confided in. Daniel. Though he was still offhand with her, she still counted him as her closest friend in the house now. How she wished Nell was still here. She would have helped her, advised her. But Nell was gone and no one would tell her where or why.

'You'll only be caught and brought back like last

time,' Daniel muttered morosely. 'And don't expect me to be passing up food to you in the punishment room like Luke did.'

'I'm not going to get caught. Not this time. I've got help.' She bit her lip, not knowing if she could trust him enough to confide in him that much. He was still very bitter. But he guessed anyway. He stared at her for a moment and then gave a little nod. 'Oh aye, the Grundys, I suppose.'

Hannah caught hold of his arm. 'Don't tell a soul. Please, Daniel.'

'All right,' he agreed grudgingly, and she had the awful feeling that if he'd dared, he would dearly like to give her away.

'Why don't you come with me?' she said rashly. 'Get away from this place? Surely, you don't want to stay here now? Not after what's happened?'

He glared at her. ''Course I'm staying here. I can't leave Luke here all on his own, can I? I can never leave here. Not now. But you go. Oh yes, you go and forget all about us.' He jerked himself out of her grasp, turned and hurried away.

'Oh, Daniel,' Hannah whispered, tears in her eyes.

Hannah couldn't follow the same escape pattern as on the previous occasion. Security at the house was much tighter since that time, but she planned to leave late one Thursday evening and go to the Grundys' farm. Then early on the Friday morning, before she was missed, Ollie would take her to Buxton. So, when everyone else was in bed, Hannah took a blanket from the bed that had been Nell's and bundled it beneath her own to look as if she was sleeping there, nestled down beneath the covers for warmth. Then picking up the bundle of her few belongings, she slipped down the stairs and into the kitchen.

Ethel Bramwell was busy in front of the range, her face red from the heat. For a brief moment, Hannah hesitated, wishing she could say goodbye. Ethel and her husband had been as kind to her – and the others – as their position allowed. She was surprised to realize just how fond she'd become of them both.

Ethel straightened up from bending over the fire and was about to turn around as Hannah slipped unnoticed out of the back door. She hurried along the path and down the steep slope, past the gate into the mill. Even from here she could hear the rhythmic clatter of the machinery as it worked through the night. From the rumours she'd heard, it seemed Edmund had plans to have the mill running non-stop – twenty-four hours a day, seven days a week, even on a Sunday.

'He's got young master Adam drawing up plans to have us working in relays,' Hannah had overheard Ernest Scarsfield telling Arthur Bramwell one night over a tankard of ale at the kitchen table. 'And he's lengthening the hours we've to work. Breaking the law, he is, but what can any of us do about it?'

Nothing, Hannah thought bitterly. *Mr Edmund considers himself above the law, even that of murder.*

'Sit down, sit down,' Lily Grundy greeted her, bustling about the warm kitchen.

'I ought to hide,' Hannah said anxiously, standing just inside the doorway, still holding her bundle. 'If they come after me—'

'Look, love, sit down. I've something to tell you.' Mrs Grundy was avoiding looking directly at her, and

Hannah felt a moment's panic. Then she calmed herself. If the worst came to the worst, she could always go back now, before she was missed. No one would be any the wiser.

'My Ollie had a bit of an accident. Hurt his leg, silly man – stabbed himself in the foot with a pitchfork.'

'Oh, I'm so sorry. Is it bad?'

'He'll be all right, but he'll be laid up for a day or two.'

'Tell him not to worry. I'll go back now – this minute. We'll wait till he's better.'

'No, no, our Ted's going to take you. He'll be here early in the morning. And in the meantime, we'll hide you here. In the hayloft, if necessary. They can't come searching our place. Oh, they can come and ask, but that's as far as they'll get.' She sniffed. 'They'll get short shrift from me if they try searching my place without so much as a by-your-leave.'

She was so adamant, so sure, that Hannah believed her.

'Now,' Lily said briskly, as if it was all settled. 'Sit down and eat your supper. I'll just take a plate up to his lordship and then you and me can sit down and have ours together. That'll be nice, won't it?'

'Yes,' Hannah said meekly, and sat down.

As they finished their meal, they heard the dog begin to bark. Hannah leaped to her feet. 'It's them. I know it is. They've come after me.'

'Quick. I'll let you out the front door. They'll likely come to the back. I'll ask 'em in and you nip round to the barn and up the ladder into the loft. I'll hide this,'

Lily said, snatching up Hannah's bundle of belongings from the floor and moving with surprising agility. 'Look sharp, now.'

Hannah ran. Out of the door on the opposite side of the house and around the corner. Here she paused, listening to the voices as Mrs Grundy opened her back door and ushered the visitors into her kitchen. Then Hannah ran softly across the yard to the barn. Inside it was gloomy, but she could just see the ladder up to the hayloft. Gathering up her long skirt, she climbed up. Her knees were shaking, not from the climb up the rickety ladder, but the fear of being caught by the ankles and dragged down again. She reached the top and scrambled across the hay-strewn floor to the furthest, darkest corner, where she huddled into a ball, her heart beating so loudly, she was sure that if they came into the barn below they would hear it.

Minutes passed and she heard voices. Voices that came nearer and nearer.

'She's not here, I tell you. What would she come here for, I might ask?'

'You helped her before. And you've helped others an' all.' Hannah recognized Arthur Bramwell's voice. 'Don't think we don't know, Lily. It's only 'cos we've kept it from the master that he hasn't stopped you supplying us.'

'Huh!' was Lily's scathing reply.

'Look, love,' Ernest Scarsfield's tone was placating. 'We're mates, me 'n' Arthur here and your Ollie.'

'Aye, drinking mates,' Lily put in, but there was amusement rather than resentment in her tone.

Hannah heard the two men chuckle. 'Aye well, mebbe so, mebbe so, but we wouldn't want to do anything to harm your living. You know that, so if you know anything about the girl, tell us.'

'I don't.'

'If you see her, you'll let us know?'

'I'm sorry, Ernest. I know you mean well, and I 'preciate it, but, no, I won't come telling tales to the mill about her or anyone else from that place. You know full well what happened to me niece and I've no time for the Critchlows, not one of 'em. So there you have it.'

'Well, you're straight, Lily Grundy, I'll give you that. But it'd be the best for the girl herself. Where's she going to go? Back to the workhouse, eh? She'll not get a welcome there, I can tell you. The Critchlows and Goodbody have got a nice little scheme still going that they're not about to let go of. She'll be sent right back here to spend a week in the punishment room. And God knows what else Mr Edmund might think up to punish her.'

'He's evil, that one,' Lily spoke up. 'The old man was bad enough, letting accidents happen and young lasses get killed, but he was a saint compared to that son of his.'

To this, the two men made no reply.

Hannah held her breath as she heard a scuffling in the barn below and then, when they spoke again, their voices were further away and she began to breathe more easily. Several minutes passed before she heard Lily below calling up. 'Come on down, Hannah. Coast's clear. They've gone.'

Hannah peered down from the hayloft. 'They might come back.'

'No, I don't think so.' Lily chuckled. 'I reckon they

know very well you're here. Maybe, deep down, they sympathize with you, love. Come on down, they're not coming back. I'm sure of it.'

Reluctantly, Hannah climbed down and, as she reached the bottom of the ladder, Lily put her arm around the girl's shoulders. 'Now come on, you snuggle down in the bed in the spare room and I'll bring you up a nice mug of cocoa.'

Impulsively, Hannah hugged her. 'Oh, Mrs Grundy, you spoil me.'

Embarrassed, Lily patted her shoulder. 'Aye well, mebbe so. But it's nice to have someone to spoil and I reckon you deserve it, love.'

Hannah couldn't remember when she'd last slept in such a comfortable bed nor been cosseted and pampered by anyone. Her memories of life with her mother and grandmother when they'd lived in their own home were dim and fleeting. It was as if all the traumas of the past three and a half years had blotted out some of her happy memories – more, if she counted her time in the workhouse too. But she fell asleep in the soft feather bed dreaming of soft hands and gentle voices and the shadowy unknown figure of a man – her father.

Twenty-Three

The Grundys' nephew, Ted, arrived the following morning as the first fingers of light crept over the top of the hills. He was fair-haired, small and wiry, with a grin that seemed to stretch across the whole of his face. He reminded Hannah poignantly of Luke.

'Hello there,' he greeted her, and held out his hand to help her onto the seat on the front of the cart. 'Aren't I the lucky one? It's not every day I get to drive a pretty girl into the countryside.'

Lily Grundy bustled up. 'Now then, Ted, none of your flirting with this one. She's special, she is.'

Ted's grin widened even further if that were possible. 'I can see that.'

'And just mind you get her well away from here before anyone from the mill is likely to be about. I don't want her running into Roper – not this time.'

The young man's face sobered and his tone became serious. 'I know, Auntie. I've put a pile of sacks in the back. If the worst happens, she can hide under them.'

Lily smiled and patted his shoulder. 'Good lad. I've packed some food up for you both and mind you let her take some with her when you drop her off in Buxton, Ted. We don't know if she's going to get anywhere to sleep tonight. And I want you to have this, Hannah.' Lily unfolded a thick, warm shawl and tucked it around Hannah's shoulders.

219

'Oh, Mrs Grundy—'

'Now, now, none of that. It's a gift. I don't want it back.'

Ted's face was a picture of concern as he glanced up at Hannah sitting, a little impatiently, on the front of the cart. 'Haven't you got anywhere to go?'

'Only the workhouse – and I don't fancy going back there. Mr Goodbody will send me straight back to the mill.'

'She's going to try to find the street she used to live in years ago,' Lily put in. 'There might be a neighbour there who'll remember her and give her a bed for the night.'

Ted glanced worriedly from one to the other. 'Wouldn't it be better if I took her all the way to Macclesfield? Stayed with her till I see she's got somewhere?'

Lily frowned and glanced up apologetically at Hannah. 'I'd like to be able to say yes, lass, you know I would. But I need him back here. With Ollie laid up, I can't manage everything on me own.'

Hannah smiled down at her. 'Of course you can't. It's very good of you to let him take me at all. Come on, Ted, the quicker we get off, the quicker you can get back.'

He gave a mock sigh and climbed up beside her. 'Oh well, I'm no match for two determined women.' He pulled a comical face. 'I never was for me auntie anyway.' He picked up the reins and slapped them against the hind quarters of the huge carthorse between the shafts. 'We'll be off then. See you later, Auntie Lily.'

The horse climbed the steep hill steadily, its great shoulders pulling strongly on the harness. Their progress was laboured and slow, and Hannah bit her lip, expecting any moment to hear a cry from behind them and running footsteps. Once or twice she glanced back anxiously, but the road sloping away behind them was empty.

As they reached the top of the hill, Hannah took one last glance back at the hills and the river winding through the dale – the place where she and Luke had escaped from the daily grind of the mill to snatch a few hours of freedom and real happiness. The early morning sun cast pale light on the hillsides and touched the trees with delicate fingers, but it was not the glorious colour she'd seen on the day she'd arrived here. Pauper's gold the man who'd brought them had called it. Well, she'd known some golden days with Luke and Daniel and little Jane. If she closed her eyes now, she could still see the four of them running alongside the river, or racing each other up the steep slopes, to stand at the top looking down on the mill below them. It had been like standing on the top of the world and they'd thrilled at the feeling of freedom, even if only for a few precious hours.

But already two of her friends were dead and Daniel had turned his back on her. She couldn't stay, didn't want to stay, for she feared Mr Edmund's vindictiveness. Even those who might try to protect her were helpless against his authority. If Master Adam were older, it might be different. But he wasn't. He was little more than a boy himself and as much in his father's power as the lowliest pauper apprentice.

It would be so easy to turn her back on it all, to set her face forward and never think about Wyedale and its mill again. At that moment as she looked back and said her silent goodbyes, she was very tempted to do

just that. But instead, Hannah made a vow to herself.
*I'll come back one day, Luke, I promise. Mr Edmund
might have wriggled out of the law with the help of all
his cronies, but he's not going to get away with what
he did to you.*

*One day, I'll pay him back. I don't know how and
I don't know when. It might take a lifetime, but one
day, I'll bring him down. I'll see him rot in Hell!*

The road levelled out and the horse picked up a little
speed.

'Why are you leaving now, 'cos you've been there
for a few years, haven't you?' Ted asked conversation-
ally. 'I'd've thought you'd have gone a long time ago.'

'I did try. Once. But not to run away, just to go
back to . . . to see me mother.'

'Oh aye, me auntie told me about that. You ran
into Roper, didn't you? Bit of bad luck, that.'

There was silence for a moment before Ted prompted, 'So did you ever get to see your mother?'

Hannah bit her lip and didn't answer immediately.
'No,' she said huskily. 'I . . . I never saw her again.'

'Is that why you're going now then? To try to find
her?'

Hannah pressed her lips together to stop them
trembling. She shook her head. 'She – I think she's
dead now. That's what I've been told. Unless, of course
it's another lie.' She'd like to hope it was, but she
didn't dare.

Ted was apologetic. 'I'm sorry, I shouldn't have
asked.'

Hannah sighed. 'It's all right.'

There was a pause, but the young man could not hold back his curiosity. 'So why are you going now?'

Hannah was silent again for a moment and then, haltingly, she began to explain. And then it all came in a torrent, like the waterfall behind the mill, the words just came flooding out. She told him everything, finding it strangely easy to talk to a comparative stranger. She told him about her early life, how she had vague memories of a much happier time and then how she and her mother had gone into the workhouse.

'I don't really understand what happened then. I know me gran died – I remember that.' She wrinkled her brow. 'I ought to remember more. I was eight when that happened. I *ought* to remember, but all I can think of is the time in the workhouse.'

'Why did you end up in the workhouse?'

'Mam lost her job at the mill.'

'The mill? What mill?'

'One of the silk mills in Macclesfield.' She went on then, describing her life in the workhouse. 'It was hard, but it was the same for everyone and there was a sort of . . . a sort of friendliness amongst the inmates.'

'Inmates? Is that what they called you?'

Hannah smiled. 'Mm, but it wasn't so bad in a lot of ways. If you were young and strong and could work, you were all right.' Her face clouded. 'But if you were ill or old, it must've been terrible to think that you were going to spend the rest of your days in there.'

'Bit like the mill, then?' Ted was referring to the Critchlows' mill – the only one he knew. 'That's what they all say about the mill. Once you get in there,

223

there's no way out.' He was silent for a moment, before he said seriously, 'I do know how lucky I am that me uncle's given me a job. And he's promised me the farm. He's got no kids of his own, you see, and auntie's no family to speak of. I think she had a brother but he lives down south and they've lost touch. Sad, that, isn't it? So, there's only our family. Uncle Ollie is me mother's brother.'

Hannah nodded. 'I know. It was your sister that . . . that—'

'That got killed in the mill? Aye, it was.' Ted's voice hardened in just the same way that Lily Grundy's tone always did when she spoke of the mill. 'Poor little Lucy. She was a lovely little kid. Bright and merry – you know – real fun to have around. We still miss her.'

'I know how you feel. I expect you heard about my little friend, Jane?'

Ted glanced at her. 'Yeah. Same thing that happened to our Lucy, weren't it?'

Hannah nodded and they travelled for a while without speaking, each lost in their own thoughts.

'I suppose you had a rough time when they caught you that time you tried to go to see yer mother,' Ted broke the silence at last.

'He beat me.'

'Never!' Ted was scandalized.

'And then I was put in the punishment room for a week. Mind you, it wasn't so bad. Luke sent food up to me on a rope.'

'Luke. Who's Luke?'

Tears sprang to her eyes and the sudden lump in her throat stopped Hannah answering for a few minutes.

'He . . . he was my friend. My . . . my very *best* friend.'

'Was?' Ted prompted, but his tone was gentle.

'Mmm,' Hannah nodded. Tentatively, at first, but then with a growing need, she confided some more in this friendly young fellow, ending, 'I thought your auntie would've told you.'

Ted shook his head. 'We don't talk about the mill in our family. Not unless we really have to because of the business side.'

'I'm sorry, Ted. Here I've been rattling on. I never thought. I'm so sorry. I didn't stop to think how painful it must still be for you.'

'And you, too. You've had a rotten time there. Losing your friends, an' all.' He glanced at her. 'And I don't mind you talking about it, Hannah. Not if it helps you.'

Gratefully, she touched his arm. 'Thanks. You're kind. Just like your auntie and uncle.'

The young man felt a warm flush rise in his neck. 'Go on with you,' he said, suddenly embarrassed. 'I'm just nosy. Me auntie's always telling me to keep me nose out of other people's business else I'll get it chopped off one of these days.'

Hannah laughed and their mood lightened. With every stride of the horse's long strong legs, she began to feel safer. As the sun rose higher in the sky, Ted glanced up. 'I don't know about you, but I'm hungry. Shall we stop for a bit? It's time the horse had a rest and a nosebag or a graze on the side of the road.' He glanced at her, reading the anxious look that flitted across her face. 'We're far enough away now, I reckon.'

Hannah nodded and climbed down. 'Yes, I'm hungry

too and I could do to nip into that field behind a bush.'

Ted laughed and covered his eyes. 'I promise not to look.'

'You'd better not,' Hannah said spiritedly.

It was a warm, bright day for October and later, having eaten, they lay back in the grass and dozed a while. When they aroused, they had no idea of the time, but Ted squinted up at the sun. 'Must be nigh on midday, I reckon. Come on, we'd best be on our way, if I'm to get back home tonight.'

'How much further is it?'

Hannah had only travelled this road once before and she'd no memory of the distance. She hadn't even known on that occasion exactly where they were going. It saddened her to realize that of the four of them that had travelled together that day, two were already dead and the remaining two were left with the bitter taste for revenge.

'Not far.' Ted interrupted her thoughts.

Just over an hour later, they reached the outskirts of the town.

'Where is it you want to be? The railway station?'

'No. Your auntie said I'd best find a carrier or a coach. She's given me some money to pay someone.'

'There's often market traders travelling between the two places, I've heard tell. There's a chap who travels here from Macclesfield every Monday morning, his cart loaded with goods. He stays the week and then goes back at the end of the week and loads up ready to come back on the Monday morning. He might be leaving today. If we could find him . . .'

Hannah's expression was doubtful, but Ted was full of bright ideas. 'If we ask at some of the shops in the

town, mebbe someone will know him – know where
we might find him.'

Hannah didn't hold out much hope, but she supposed it was possible. 'All right then. Where do we
start?'

'Town centre, that's where,' Ted said, slapping the
reins. 'Come on, we've a man to hunt down before it
gets dark.'

Twenty-Four

Hannah had not believed it possible, but they found the man, a Mr Dawkins, who lived in Macclesfield, but who travelled between the two towns just as Ted had said. It took an hour of trekking round several shops but at last they met someone who knew him.

'Aye, tha's right,' the burley shopkeeper said. 'Bin here less than half an hour ago. He's tekin' a load back to Macclesfield for me. Me son's got a shop there and we often use old Dawkins to take stuff back'ards and for'ards for us. Only just missed him, you 'ave.' At the sight of the two youngsters' crestfallen faces, the man laughed. 'But I can tell you where he is. In the pub, that's where. Likes to wet his whistle before he travels home on a Friday night. Reckon that horse of his knows the way home better 'n he does.'

'Come on,' Ted said, grabbing her hand. 'Thanks, mister.'

'Don't mention it, lad. Want him to tek summat for yer, d'yer?'

Ted grinned. 'This lass needs a lift to Macclesfield and I remembered hearing about this feller. D'you think he'd take her?'

'Should think he'd be glad of the company of a pretty young wench.' He winked at Hannah. 'But don't worry, luv. He's a good family man, is Dawkins, with lasses of his own. He'll look after you all right.'

They found him sitting in the corner of the smoky tavern, a kind-faced man in his forties.

'Aye, that'll be all right, duck,' he said at once. 'You just wait outside whilst I finish me pint and me bit of baccy and I'll be with you. We'll be travelling through the night, but you can bed down in the back of the cart under the horse blanket.' He laughed. 'That's if you don't mind the smell.'

As they waited outside, Ted said, 'Now, are you sure you've got enough money? 'Cos me auntie'd box me ears if I let you go without enough. I can lend you a couple of shillings, if that'd help.'

'You're very kind, but your auntie's already given me some. I'll be all right.' She touched his arm. 'But thanks all the same.' Her face clouded. 'It'll be finding somewhere to stay that'll be the problem. I daren't go to the workhouse, and apart from that I don't really know where to start.'

'I'll tell you where. The police station.'

Hannah's eyes widened in sudden fear. 'The . . . the police station. But . . . but wouldn't that be dangerous? I mean – if the Critchlows have reported me running away.'

Ted threw back his head and guffawed. 'The Critchlows report you? Not likely. They'll not want the police sniffing around. Making inquiries.' As Hannah looked mystified, Ted went on. 'Look, we've always reckoned that the Critchlows and that fellow at the workhouse . . .'

'Mr Goodbody.'

'Yes, that's him. Well, we reckon they had a good thing going between them, but maybe it wasn't exactly legal, if you know what I mean.'

Hannah shook her head. 'No, I don't.'

229

'All them little pauper apprentices coming to the mill. Well, years ago it was a common practice with all the mills, but not lately. With all the changes in the laws, it became too expensive. Yet the Critchlows kept the system going. Now, why do you suppose that is, eh?'

Hannah shook her head. 'I don't know.'

'Somehow, they were making themselves a bit of money. I reckon Critchlow was paying Goodbody to provide him with cheap labour.'

'Cheap labour? How do you mean, cheap labour?'

'You were signed up for so many years, when you got to the mill, weren't you? I bet he made you sign a paper, didn't he?'

Slowly Hannah nodded. 'Yes, I was bound to him for six years.'

'Thought so. And I bet he doesn't pay you anything – still being an apprentice – even though you've been there over three years.'

Her eyes widened, as realization began to dawn.

'*And* I dare bet you're doing an adult's work now, aren't you? Same as some of the women from the village that work there?'

Hannah nodded and now her lips tightened.

Ted shrugged. 'There you are then. Cheap labour, 'cos he'll have to pay the women. But you're an apprentice and will be for the six years. And even then, you'd be lucky if you could get him to give you a proper wage. 'Specially now Mr Edmund's in charge. So, like I said, go to the police station. They might be able to tell you where to find a lodging house. And if they can't,' he grinned suddenly, 'they might let you sleep in one of their cells.'

'Oh, thanks.' Hannah laughed.

'No, I'm serious. A mate of mine got stuck in Manchester one night and couldn't get home so he went to the police and they let him sleep in one of their cells – just for the night. Honest,' he added as he saw Hannah's sceptical look. 'And besides, they wouldn't want a young lass like you roaming the streets at night.'

'Yes, well, I'll see.' Hannah was doubtful but his suggestion sounded sincere enough. And, after all, the police were supposed to be there to help you. They weren't just about catching criminals.

'Besides,' Ted went on, warming to his theme. 'They might be able to help you find that long-lost neighbour of yours.'

But that, it seemed, was beyond the burly policeman who stood behind the desk in the station. He scratched his head as he looked down at the slim young girl standing before him.

Hannah had enjoyed the ride through the spectacular countryside, passing from Derbyshire into the county of Cheshire. She'd slept for the first part of the way, but in the early hours of the morning, the cold had woken her and she'd clambered up to sit beside the carter. They'd chatted amiably but she'd not been drawn to confide much in him. All she'd told him was that she was returning home after some years, but that her mother had died and she needed to find a place to stay until she could find work.

'Ted – that's the young feller who brought me to Buxton – reckoned I should ask at the police station. Do you think that's a good idea?'

'I do, duck. They'll know of reputable lodgings for

a young 'un like you. They might even know if there's jobs going somewhere.' He sniffed. 'Surprising what the peelers on the beat know. A mite too much sometimes.' He paused and then asked, 'Where did you live before?'

'That's just the trouble, Mr Dawkins,' Hannah said. 'I don't know. I *ought* to remember, but I just can't.'

As they came down the last hill, Hannah was fascinated by the sight of the town spread out below them. A feeling that she was coming home flooded through her as her gaze took in the huge, square buildings and tall chimneys, church towers and spires and the roofs of hundreds of houses. She sighed as she swept her arm in a wide arc. 'I used to live somewhere down there – if only I knew where.'

Beside her, Mr Dawkins laughed. 'Well, I don't reckon it was anywhere near us, duck. I'm sure I'd've remembered a pretty little thing like you. But your friend had the right idea. The police'll help you. I can't take you right there – it's up the hill, near that church with the square tower – St Michael's. See?' He pointed with his whip. 'But I'll show you how to get there.'

They travelled another half a mile or so in silence until Mr Dawkins asked, 'Recognize anything yet?'

Hannah bit her lip and shook her head. She was disappointed. She'd so hoped that once she saw the town again, her memories would come back. But nothing looked familiar.

'Do you remember the railway?' Mr Dawkins asked. 'Or the Bollin? The river?' he explained when she looked puzzled.

'No.'

'We're just passing over the Bollin now, but you can't see it. It was covered up along here when they built the railway. There's still places where you can see it though. Now, this 'ere's the Waters. It's where I live.'

She looked at the wide open space surrounded by houses and larger buildings with tall, smoking chimneys. In the centre stood a square public house with a sign outside – the Cross Keys. A coach, drawn by two horses with prancing hooves, rolled by. Men on horseback clip-clopped past and two men driving four cows tipped their caps to Mr Dawkins, who waved in return to their greeting

'Why's it called the Waters?'

Mr Dawkins pulled a face. 'Place floods from time to time. It's by the river. If we get heavy rain, this whole area's like a lake.' He laughed and pointed at the Cross Keys. 'I remember a few years back, before the railway came, the pub getting flooded. Lost all their barrels of beer in the cellars, they did. A right to-do there was.'

Hannah frowned. She couldn't remember anything like that happening in her childhood.

'But we're used to it,' he went on, grinning like a man completely happy with his lot.

Pulling his cart to a halt at the bottom of a long flight of stone steps, he said, 'If you go up these, duck, you'll come out near the church, and the police station is on the other side of the church in the basement of the Town Hall. You can't miss it.'

He glanced at her apologetically. 'I wish I could take you home with me, duck, but our little house is fair bursting at the seams already. I've four young 'uns and another on the way and what the missis'd say if I turn up on the doorstep with a pretty young wench like you in tow, I daren't think.'

'It's all right, Mr Dawkins, honestly. And I can't thank you enough for bringing me this far. Are you really sure you won't let me pay you?'

'I wouldn't dream of it. It's been my pleasure. I've enjoyed your company.'

Hannah climbed down, and picked up her bundle from the back.

'I hope you've got plenty of puff, lass. There's an 'undred and eight of them steps. I know, 'cos I counted 'em as a lad.'

He was still laughing as the cart rattled away and Hannah turned to begin the long climb. Just as he had said, she was breathless by the time she arrived at the top of the steps. Before her was the dark stone of the church and, walking round it, she found the pillared entrance to the Town Hall and her way into the basement beneath it.

So here she was standing in front of the desk and looking up into the fatherly face of the constable.

'Well, love, if you don't know the street you lived on, nor your neighbour's name, then you've set me a real problem. Can't you remember anything about where you lived?'

Hannah frowned. She felt rather foolish. After all, she'd been nine years old when they had finally been forced into the workhouse. She ought to be able to remember where she'd lived before that. But for some reason, it was all very hazy. Just flashes came back to her, but nothing that seemed helpful. Now she knew what the phrase 'racking her brains' meant. Her head almost hurt with trying to think, trying to remember. Then suddenly, her face brightened. 'There was a pub just round the corner down the next street.'

'Ah, now we're getting somewhere. What was it called?'

'I – um – I don't know.'

The big man smiled at her. 'Oh dear, I thought we had it then. You see, love, there's lots of streets with pubs just round the corner. If we was to tramp round them all, we could be a week or more. Now, best thing you can do today is to have a wander round the town. See if anywhere seems familiar. But if you don't find somewhere to stay, then come back here. Now promise me you'll do that before it gets dark. I don't want to think of you wandering about the streets at night.'

'Do you know of a lodging house?'

The big policeman scratched his head. 'I know of a few, but some you wouldn't be able to afford. No offence, luv.'

'None taken.' She grinned ruefully at him as she hitched her bundle onto her shoulder. 'I'll go and have a look round then.'

'You do that,' he nodded, 'and yer can leave yer bundle here if you like. Pick it up later. No need to be carrying that around all day.' He stowed it safely in the back room as he added, 'Good luck.'

'Thanks. I think I'm going to need it.'

His gaze followed her as she left the station. He was curious about her. He'd already guessed she was a runaway, probably from a bad home or a harsh employer, but his instinct and his experience told him that she was no criminal on the run.

It was no surprise to Constable Robinson to see Hannah standing before his desk once more just as it began to turn dark. In a way, he was pleased to see her. For one, it meant she'd nothing to hide from the law, and secondly, she'd had the sense to come back where she would be safe.

'Now, love, no luck then?'

Hannah shook her head. She'd tramped the streets all day and now she was tired and hungry and frightened. Frightened that she would not be able to find a place to stay or work and that she would be sent back to the mill. Tentatively, she asked, 'Er – I don't suppose I could sleep in a cell tonight, could I?'

He blinked at her, obviously surprised by her request, yet, as he thought about it, he nodded slowly. 'I don't see why not. I'll have to check with my superior, because things can get a bit busy here on a Saturday night. But you sit down over there, love, and I'll go and ask.'

Hannah sank wearily onto the bench and leaned her head against the wall. It had been a long day and she hadn't slept well for the last two nights, but now that there was a good distance between her and the Critchlows, she could relax – a little, at least. And, ironically, if they let her stay, she'd be safe in the police station.

The officer was back in only a few minutes. 'Yes, that's all right. One night only, though, he says. But he don't like to think of a young girl like you wandering the streets. We've both got daughters of our own. Come on then.' He lifted the hatch in the counter and beckoned her through. 'You can share my bread and cheese with me.' He chuckled and patted his rotund belly. 'The missis always makes me too much anyway.'

The back room was a hive of activity. Two men were packing papers and books into crates whilst

Hannah sat and ate the policeman's crusty bread and creamy cheese.

He sat down too. 'Now then—' His tone was still kindly and concerned, yet there was a trace of firmness too. 'Are you going to tell me who you're running away from?'

Hannah stopped chewing for a moment and stared at him. 'How . . . how did you know I was?'

He chuckled. 'I've been in this job a few years now, love. A young girl like you doesn't just turn up in a place for no reason.' He glanced her up and down, taking in the state of her boots, the hem of her dress. 'You've not travelled far, nor have you been sleeping rough. So, where have you come from and why?'

'Are you going to make me go back?'

He shrugged his huge shoulders. 'Depends, love. I can't break the law, however much I might want to help you. And I do. Let me tell you that here and now, I do want to help you best I can.'

As Hannah munched, she eyed him speculatively. She was trying to decide whether to trust him or not. The very worst that could happen was that he would have her sent back to the mill – and the waiting punishment room. She gave an involuntary shudder.

The kindly man must have noticed for he asked gently, 'So very terrible was it?'

She sighed and decided that she had little choice. And there was just the chance that – for once – she'd found someone who might believe her.

So, she told him everything. At the end of her tale, the officer sat looking at her and stroking his chin thoughtfully.

'Well, by rights, you should go back to the mill, love. You've broken the terms of your indenture and I think I'm right in saying that this Critchlow fellow has the right to make you complete the term you signed up for.'

'I know,' Hannah said sadly, 'but surely, there's some law to say that they shouldn't lie to you about your mother. And I can't understand why more wasn't done to look into Luke's death. Jane's accident, I can understand. There's always accidents and that's exactly what it was – an accident. But Luke falling into the wheel wasn't. Edmund Critchlow struck him and he fell backwards.'

The policeman shook his head. 'Ah well now, I'd be inclined to agree with you there, but since it's outside our area and it's all been done and dusted, I don't think there's much we can do. Won't bring the lad back, will it?'

'No,' Hannah said grimly, 'but it won't make Mr Edmund pay for what he's done either.'

Constable Robinson eyed her as he said softly, 'I reckon you've got it in mind to see that he does – one day – haven't you?'

Hannah stared at him. Was he a mind reader?

He chuckled. 'It's written all over your pretty face. "I'll get him back one day," that look says.'

Hannah smiled a little sheepishly. 'I'll have to mind what my face is showing then, won't I?' And they laughed together. But more seriously, the man said gently, 'Well, love, just mind how you do it. Don't break the law, will you? Now then,' he went on more briskly as he pulled his huge frame to its feet. 'Let's get you settled in a cell before I go off duty. I'll make sure they leave the door open so's you won't feel you're being locked up for the night. And in the morning – well – we'll see, eh?'

It was strange lying alone on the hard bed in the tiny room. She was so used to sleeping in a large room with lots of other people, hearing their snuffles and snores. Yet it was far from quiet in the cell; sounds from other policemen on night duty drifted down the corridor. And from a neighbouring cell came the raucous singing of a drunk, arrested for disturbing the peace. Hannah smiled to herself in the darkness. He was still disturbing the peace in here – her peace. Yet gradually, the volume of his singing decreased and he murmured the words softly to himself.

It was strangely comforting for the girl who'd always loved to sing, even if it was the ramblings of a drunk.

Finally, wearied by the events of the long day, Hannah drifted into sleep, lulled by the crooning of her companion in the cell next door and wondering what the next day would bring.

Twenty-Five

The following morning, having shared in the station's breakfast in the back room, Constable Robinson introduced her to a young, fresh-faced officer. 'This 'ere's Jim Smith. How would you like to walk along with him on his beat and see if you recognize any of the streets?' He turned to the young man putting on his tall hat and straightening his knee-length blue frock coat. 'Now, Jim, if it gets to afternoon and you haven't found the place this young 'un is looking for, take her to Ma Boulton's. She takes in lodgers and she keeps a decent house.' He glanced archly at the young fellow. 'If you know what I mean.'

The young constable grinned at his superior and then swivelled his glance to include Hannah. 'I'll look after her, sir. Come on, then – Hannah, is it?'

She nodded.

As they came out into the street, the young man confided, 'You've done me a favour. I'm glad to get out of there. The station's moving to new premises with accommodation for our inspector so's he can live above the shop, you might say. We're all getting roped in to help pack everything up. So,' he winked at her, 'thanks for giving me a proper job to do. Right then,' he went on briskly, 'I reckon the best place to start is right here in the Market Place. Something might look familiar.'

As they began to walk along, Hannah kept silent, knowing that the young man was on duty, but he opened the conversation. 'Constable Robinson says you can't remember much about the place you used to live.'

Hannah frowned, trying again to drag up her childhood memories. 'I can't remember the names, but I've got a sort of picture in my mind. I . . . I think I might recognize the street.'

Jim pulled a wry face. 'If we can find it. Macclesfield's a big place.'

'I know,' Hannah said quietly. 'I'm sure I tramped most of it yesterday.'

'But you didn't see anything familiar?'

Hannah shook her head.

'Mr Robinson said your mother worked in one of the silk mills. Did you live near where she worked?'

'I think so. Just a couple of streets away.'

'Which mill was it?'

'I can't remember.'

'Did you ever go to the place where she worked? Would you recognize the mill?'

'I – don't think so. I used to stay home with my gran.'

'Did you go to school?'

'Oh yes. Me gran used to give me a penny and I'd go on a Sunday.'

'Ah, now that gives me a bit of a clue. Come on. I've got an idea.'

The tall young man began to lengthen his stride and Hannah had to trot to keep up with him. But she was smiling now. Suddenly, thanks to the kindly constable in the station and now this nice young man, she had real hope.

They'd walked quite a distance from the Market Place along a main street before Jim turned right into a narrower street. Still he said nothing until they came to a halt before a large building.

'This is the Sunday school,' Jim said.

Hannah stared up at the long rows of windows. Her mouth dropped open. 'That's it! That's it! This is where I went to school.'

Jim grinned down at her. '*Now* we're getting somewhere. So, can you remember your way home?'

Hannah's face fell as she looked wildly about her. There was a catch in her voice as she said, 'No, no, I can't.'

'Don't worry,' Jim said calmly. 'We'll do what Constable Robinson calls "acting it out".'

Hannah looked up at him, puzzled, but Jim's grin only widened. 'It's what we do when we want to try to figure out how a crime happened.' He leaned closer and, his eyes dancing as he teased her, added, ''Specially if it's a *murder*.'

If he was aiming to shock her, he was trying the wrong person. Hannah grinned at him and despite her anxiety, said impishly, 'I bet that's exciting – when you get a murder.'

He blinked and then laughed. 'By heck, you're a feisty little piece, aren't you? Most girls go all daft and squeamish when I talk about it.'

'So, what do I have to do to "act it out"?'

'Go right up to the main door there and pretend you're just leaving at the end of the day.'

Hannah looked at him blankly for a moment, then shrugged her shoulders and did as he suggested. She walked to the main door and then turned and looked back towards the young man standing at the gate.

Vague memories stirred in her mind. She closed her eyes a moment and she could almost hear the sound of other children, laughing and shrieking as they ran, pell-mell, towards the gate. She opened her eyes and began to run too. Reaching the gate, she didn't pause, but ran on, turning to the right and on up the street.

'Hey, wait for me.' Grinning, the young policeman took off his hat and pounded after her. Hannah glanced back and laughed aloud, realizing what it must look like to passers-by. She was hurtling along the street being pursued by a policeman. She slowed her pace and stopped to wait for him. When he reached her, she was bending forward, catching her breath but still laughing.

It was the first time she'd laughed with such abandon since Luke's death. Somehow, being miles away from the place where it had happened made it possible to put it out of her mind for a short while. But not for long; she couldn't imagine ever being able to forget about Luke for very long.

Puffing, Jim said, 'By heck, you can't half move for a girl.'

She chuckled. 'I thought I'd better stop. Folks might think you were trying to arrest me.'

He laughed too. 'You're right at that. But as long as it hasn't stopped you remembering where you're headed.'

Hannah straightened up. 'Oh no. I can remember very clearly now. We go right to the end of the road and then turn left.' She frowned. 'But I can't remember anything after that.'

'You will when you get there,' Jim said confidently. 'Come on. It sounds as if it's Bridge Street we're wanting.'

But when they turned the corner, Hannah was still puzzled.

'This is a silk mill on the left here,' Jim prompted helpfully. 'Is this where your mother worked?'

Hannah stared up at the building. 'I . . . I seem to remember it. I suppose it could be.'

'Maybe it's only familiar because you walked past it on your way home from the school.'

They walked a little further, and then suddenly, Hannah stopped on a corner where another street crossed Bridge Street. She stood looking down the sloping street to her left.

'This is Paradise Street,' Jim said. He waved his arm to the other side of the road. 'It carries on up there as well.'

Her voice was little more than a whisper, but there was no denying her excitement. 'This is the street where we used to live.'

'You sure?'

She nodded. 'It was very clever of you to suggest retracing my footsteps like that.'

He smiled and shrugged off her compliment, yet she could see he was gratified. Her face sobered and she frowned. 'You'd've thought I ought to've remembered the street names. After all, I lived here till I was nine. And I ought to remember the people we lived near. How dim am I?'

'Well, mebbe you sort of . . . sort of blocked it out. Didn't want to remember it. You know?'

She wasn't sure she understood what he meant, but he continued, trying to explain. 'Folks sometimes try to forget unhappy times in their lives.'

'But I wasn't unhappy. Not here.'

'But when you left here,' Jim persisted, 'you went into the workhouse, didn't you?'

'Yes,' she said slowly.

'Well, that's not a very happy experience, is it? Maybe you've tried to blot that out from your mind and the rest's gone as well.'

'There's worse things that can happen,' she murmured. There was suddenly a bleak, haunted look in her eyes. The last few weeks at the mill had been far more traumatic than life at the workhouse, grim though that had been. Luke's death had been the worst thing – the very worst thing – that had ever happened to her. Guiltily, she realized that his death had affected her far more deeply than hearing that her own mother had died. She supposed she could accept the death of her mother – although not the fact that it had been kept from her – because it was the natural progression of life. What was hard to bear was the loss of her young sweetheart, the boy she'd hoped to marry one day.

Jim glanced at her and saw the tears brimming in her eyes. 'Yes,' he said softly. 'I'm sure there is.'

Hannah took a deep breath and brushed her tears away with an impatient gesture. 'But I see what you mean. And maybe you're right.' She lifted her face and smiled bravely. 'It's all coming back now and it's thanks to you.'

Hannah stood a moment, gazing down the street at the terrace of tall, three-storey houses. The longer, small-paned windows on the top storey were the telltale sign that they were weavers' garret workshops. One of those very rooms had been where her own grandfather had worked, Hannah thought.

Children played in the roadway and women stood in front of their houses, keeping an eye on the youngsters and gossiping with their neighbours. Suddenly, Hannah's glance came to rest on a woman standing at the bottom of the three steep steps in front of her house and leaning against the railing, a small, round woman with her arms folded across her ample bosom. She was chatting to another woman standing on the pavement beside her.

'Auntie Bessie,' she whispered, then louder and louder until she was shouting and running down the street, her arms outstretched. 'Auntie Bessie, *Auntie Bessie*!'

She flung herself against the woman, who, taken by surprise, sat down suddenly on the bottom step.

''Ere, what d'you think you're . . . ?' the woman began indignantly as she grasped the railing and hauled herself up. But Hannah put her arms around the woman's plump waist and hugged her hard, pressing her cheek against her.

'What a' you doing?' The woman grasped Hannah by the shoulders and prised her away. She did not throw her off entirely, but held onto her, looking down into her upturned face. Behind them Jim had caught up with Hannah in time to hear the woman add, 'Who are you?'

He stood quietly, watching and waiting.

Hannah opened her mouth but before she could speak, the thin, grey-haired woman who had been gossiping with Bessie suddenly cackled with laughter and prodded Hannah with a bony finger. 'I know who you are, girl. I'd know you anywhere.' She glanced at her friend. 'Can't you see it, Bess? You know who she is, don't you?'

Bessie stared at her friend. 'No, I don't know.' She glanced between the thin woman and Hannah, seeming not to know quite which of them to ask. In the end, she asked them both. 'Who is she, Flo?' And turning again to the girl, 'Who are you?'

'It's as plain as the nose on her face,' Flo piped up, and cackled again with laughter at her own joke. 'Though it's a pretty little nose. Good job you didn't get his nose as well as his blond hair and blue eyes.'

'Flo,' Bessie was becoming impatient now, 'just cut the funning, will yer, and tell me who she is?' She turned back to Hannah and, still holding her shoulders, gave her a little shake. 'Or you tell me.'

Hannah grinned up at her. 'It's me, Auntie Bessie. It's Hannah. We used to live next door to you. I used to come into your house when me mam was at work.'

'Hannah,' Bessie said wonderingly. '*Hannah!* Aw, love—' Suddenly, Hannah was swept into the woman's arms and pressed against her softness. 'Fancy me not knowing you. Aw, I'm sorry, I'm sorry.' She held her at arm's length again. 'Let's 'ave a proper look at you.'

Hannah had no choice but to submit to her scrutiny. Beside them, Flo said softly, 'See what I mean, Bess? You remember *him*, don't you? She's his kid, all right, even if Rebecca would never say. There's no mistake now. Not now, there ain't.'

Hannah glanced at Flo, the question written on her face.

Bessie frowned. 'Shut up, Flo,' she muttered. 'You've said enough. More than enough, by the look of it.'

'Oh, sorry, I'm sure,' Flo said huffily. Then she bent towards Hannah. 'You remember me, ducky, don't yer? I'm yer Antie Flo.'

Hannah stared into the thin face, the grey eyes, the gaunt cheeks, the beak-like nose and the thin-lipped mouth. Oh, she remembered her all right. She remembered Florence Harris. How she'd called after Hannah and her mother, calling them names as they walked down the street. 'No better than you ought to be, Rebecca Francis. And that girl of yours'll be the same. It's in the breed. Her father's a good-for-nothing woman-izer and you're nothing better than a whore!'

Oh yes, Hannah remembered her now, but instead, she smiled sweetly into Flo's face and said, 'No, sorry. I don't. I only remember Auntie Bessie. She was always so kind to us.'

Flo straightened up and with a disgruntled 'Huh!' turned away. She began to walk back to her own house, next door, but with a parting shot, she pointed at the young constable and said, 'What's he doing here, then? In trouble already, is she? It'll be no more than you could expect. You want to be careful of her, Bess. Bringing trouble to your door. That's what she'll do.'

But Bessie was chuckling softly. 'That's put 'er nose out of joint. You come along in and tell me what's been happening to you. But first,' she glanced up at Jim. 'What is this bobby doing here? Are you in bother?'

'No, no, Auntie Bessie. He's been helping me find you. Well, helping me find where I used to live. I . . . I couldn't remember . . .' Her voice faltered and faded.

'Couldn't remember?' Bessie seemed shocked.

Jim stepped forward and, clearing his throat, he spoke for the first time. 'I think she's blotted a lot out of her mind. She – well, she'll no doubt tell you herself – but she's not had it easy . . .' Now, he too stopped, unsure what to say next.

'Ah,' Bessie said and nodded, catching on quickly. 'Well, let's go inside and we'll all 'ave a nice cup of tea and a bit of a chat, eh?' She grinned at the constable, her merry eyes almost lost in her round, red cheeks. 'You too, young feller. I ain't never 'ad no cause to be frightened of the bobbies and I ain't goin' to start now.'

Jim smiled back. 'Ta all the same, missis, but I'd best be getting back on me proper beat, else it'll be me in the trouble.' He nodded towards Hannah. 'But I'll keep in touch. I'd like to know how she goes on.'

Bessie chuckled inwardly. *I bet you would*, she thought, as she saw the way the young man's eyes rested on Hannah's pretty face. *Oh, I bet you would.* Aloud, she said, 'Well, lad, like I say, you're welcome in my house any time you like. In or out of your uniform.'

Hannah turned to him. 'Thank you so much for all your help. You . . . you've been wonderful. And please – thank Mr Robinson for me too, won't you?'

'I will, miss. And . . . and good luck,' he added as he put on his hat and turned away, raising his hand in farewell as he strode away up the street. 'By the way, don't forget to collect your bundle of things from the station, will yer?'

'I won't. And thank you.'

'Now, love,' Bessie said, putting her arm around Hannah's shoulders. 'Come along in. It's high time you and me did some catching up.'

Twenty-Six

Two hours later they were still sitting either side of Bessie Morgan's table, tea grown cold before them, exchanging their stories of the years since they'd last seen each other. Hannah had poured it all out – every bit of it – and she, in turn, had listened to Bessie's tale.

'Your gran was always good to me, love, 'specially when I lost one of me little 'uns with the scarlet fever.'

'I remember that,' Hannah said gently. 'I wasn't allowed to play with Peggy for weeks.' She leaned forward. 'Is . . . is Peggy all right? I mean . . .' She faltered. It was difficult asking about Bessie's large family. Perhaps there had been more tragedies. There had. Bessie wiped her eyes with the corner of her apron. 'She's all right.' Bessie's generous mouth was suddenly tight. 'Far as I know, that is.'

'Far as you know . . .' Hannah began and then stopped. But she had gone too far to pull back now. 'What . . . what do you mean?'

'I don't see her. I don't even know where she's living. Not for sure.'

Hannah waited. The questions were tumbling around in her mind, but she held them in check, waiting for Bessie to continue in her own time. 'Peggy was always a wild one,' Bessie was saying, and Hannah was remembering the bright, fair-haired tomboy she had played with. 'She met this lad when she was fifteen. I didn't like him. He was an idle beggar. Into all sorts, he was. Him and all his family and not always on the right side of the law. But she wouldn't listen to me. It was about – about the time I lost my Bill.'

Hannah gasped. She hadn't thought to ask about Bessie's quiet, unassuming husband, Bill.

'Oh no, not Uncle Bill.'

Bessie nodded and her eyes filled with tears again. 'He got injured at work in 'fifty three and died just before Christmas.'

'That was just before they sent me to the mill,' Hannah murmured, but Bessie was lost in the telling of her own tale now.

'What I'd have given to have your gran and your mam still living next door,' she went on, 'I can't tell you. And that was when madam,' Hannah guessed she was referring to her wayward daughter, Peggy, 'decided to up sticks and leave. Packed 'er bags, she did, and off she went with 'im. Went to live with his parents in Davies Street. Well, I say parents. His dad's in gaol, by all accounts.'

Hannah touched the woman's hand. 'Oh, Auntie Bessie, I'm so sorry to hear all this. You've had it worse than me.'

'No, love, no. Things like that shouldn't happen to a young girl. When you get older – to my age – well, you expect to 'ave to take a few knocks.' She smiled through her tears. 'Worst of it is, though, they've all left home now. The lads are working away. Ben is in Manchester and Micky went to London. Doing very well, he is. Got a job in an office, so he says. He writes regular, but he can't get home much. Neither can Ben, even though he's only in Manchester, it might as well be a million miles away.

'What about the others?' Hannah asked tentatively, fearing more bad news.

'Young Billy's at sea. Joined the navy, 'ee did, and Sarah's married.' Bessie was smiling now. 'Got a babby. Bonny little girl. Called her Elizabeth after me. Beth for short. But they live in Liverpool. Her husband works on the docks, so I don't see a lot of them either.' Her face fell again. 'It's hard, you know, Hannah, when you've had a house full of family and then, all of a sudden, you turn round and there's no one left but you.' Bessie forced a smile as she added, 'But I should count my blessings. The landlord let me stay in me home, even though I don't work in the weaving trade any more. Not now poor Bill's gone. There's a nice feller rents the garret.' She jerked her thumb upwards, indicating the attic rooms of her house. 'But he's a quiet sort. Comes and goes and I never see him.' She pulled a face. 'No company there, if you know what I mean.'

Hannah could hear the loneliness in Bessie's voice. She held Bessie's hand and leaned forward. 'Well, I'm hoping to find a job in one of the silk mills and stay in Macclesfield.' She pulled a wry face. 'As long as Edmund Critchlow doesn't catch up with me and have me dragged back to serve out my term. Anyway,' she went on briskly and with more hope in her tone than she was feeling inside. 'I'll come and see you often. I promise.'

Bessie smiled. 'Where are you living?'

'Nowhere yet. That's me next job. Find lodgings.'

Bessie's face lit up. 'Then you've found 'em, love. You can stay here and I won't take no for an answer.'

Now it was Hannah's eyes that filled with tears.

'Oh, Auntie Bessie, I'd love to,' she cried and, hugging her, Hannah felt as if she had come home.

With her husband and one of her boys dead and the rest of her family gone, Bessie's only source of income was to take in washing. But those who lived nearby were as hard up as she was and the work was spasmodic.

'We're doing each other a favour,' she assured Hannah. 'If you get a job and pay me a bit of board each week, you'll be saving me from the workhouse.'

Hannah's eyes widened in disbelief, but Bessie nodded, 'You will, I tell you, you will. The lads send me money now and again, but it's not fair to expect it.' She laughed suddenly. 'You don't see the chick scratching for the old hen, do you?'

Hannah put her arms around her and murmured, 'I'll scratch for you, Auntie Bessie, just like I'd've done for me mam, if only . . . if only . . .'

Bessie hugged her close. 'Aye, love, I know. I know.'

Hannah settled in quickly with Bessie Morgan. For the first few weeks they decided she should not go in search of work.

'You keep your head down, just for a week or two. There'll be time enough for you to look for a job after Christmas. In the meantime, you can help me with the washing and ironing. I reckon everyone's decided to have their sheets and blankets washed for Christmas. I've even got three pairs of curtains, would you believe? I don't know where all the work's coming from all of a sudden. I really need your help, Hannah. You couldn't have turned up at a better time.'

'What about Mrs Harris? You . . . you don't think she'll report me to Mr Goodbody, do you?'

'Not if she knows what's good for her,' Bessie said grimly. 'Don't you fret, love. I'll have a word with her. Make sure she keeps that runaway mouth of hers tight shut, else she'll have me to reckon with.'

Hannah smiled, suddenly feeling a lot safer. She wasn't sure whether Bessie was telling the truth about needing her help, but she worked hard alongside the older woman over the copper and the tub in the wash house in the back yard. At night, when Bessie put her swollen legs up, Hannah tackled all the ironing. The next day, she tramped the streets to return the fresh laundry and collect more work.

It was on a cold January morning, when she walked to the very end of Bridge Road, turned left into Chestergate and continued out onto the Prestbury Road, that she saw the workhouse. She stood before the main entrance, looking up at the imposing stone building, at the plaque above the door bearing the date that building began – 1843 – and up again to the clock tower and the weather vane on the very top. Then her glance took in the numerous windows and the tall chimneys. Hannah shuddered. She remembered this place all too well.

She wondered if the Goodbodys were still there and asked herself if she dared to knock on the door and ask for the truth about her mother. Hannah bit her lip and turned away, her eyes filling with tears. Though she longed to find out about her mother, it was too big a risk.

*

'What's the matter, love?' Bessie asked. Hannah had hardly said a word since her return from taking and fetching the laundry and now she was picking at her supper with little or no appetite. 'Are you poorly?'

Tears spilled down Hannah's face.

'Aw, love, what is it?' Bessie was round the table in a trice and enfolding the girl in her loving embrace.

'I . . . I saw the workhouse today and . . . and it brought all the memories about Mam back. I know they said she was dead, but was it true? Perhaps it was another lie.' She lifted her tear-streaked face. 'Auntie Bessie, what if she's still in there?'

'Well, we'll go and ask, but don't get your hopes up, love, will you? Because, to be honest, if your mam was still alive I reckon she'd've got in touch with you somehow. I can't believe she'd let nearly four years go by without a word.'

'But they stopped my letters.'

'Aye, I know. You told me,' Bessie said grimly.

'You see,' Hannah said, 'I want to find out the truth but I daren't go to the workhouse in case Mr Goodbody's still there. He'd have me sent back to the mill. I know he would.'

Bessie beamed suddenly. 'Then leave it with me, love. I've nothing to fear of that place – only of having to go in it to stay. But not now. Not now you're here. So I'll find out about your mam for you.'

'But . . . but what will you say? Won't he suspect I'm with you? He might already have heard from Mr Edmund that I've run away.'

Bessie frowned thoughtfully. 'Aye, well, I won't mention you . . .' she began, but then a gleam came into her eyes. 'Tell you what – it might be better if I *did* mention you.'

Fear crossed Hannah's face. 'Oh, Auntie Bessie, please don't—'

'No, no, love, listen a minute. If I go to Goodbody and ask where your mam *and you* are, then he won't suspect I've seen you, will he? I'll just say I'm trying to find out about my old friends.' Her face was suddenly sad. 'It broke my heart the day you left to go into that place, Hannah, but there was nothing we could do. We'd've helped you if we could've done. We 'adn't the room to take you in here.'

'I know, Auntie Bessie, I know you'd've helped if you could've. But,' she went on, coming back to the idea of Bessie visiting the workhouse, 'what if the master asks you outright if you've seen me?'

Bessie looked her straight in the face and said, 'I'll say I haven't set eyes on you from the day you left our street to enter the workhouse.' Suddenly she beamed, 'I'll just not add, "until now".'

Hannah's mouth twitched, she smiled and then she laughed out loud. 'Oh, Auntie Bessie!' And then suddenly, out of the past came the phrase that her gran had used fondly when speaking of Bessie Morgan. 'Oh, Auntie Bessie, you're a caution, you are.'

But the following day, when Bessie put on her best hat and coat and set off for the workhouse, Hannah was on tenterhooks. She couldn't settle and paced about the house like a caged animal. At last, with nothing to occupy her, Hannah picked up a parcel of clean laundry and set off to deliver it.

As she retraced her steps to the terraced house she

now called home, Hannah paused again outside the school. She wondered if there were any of the teachers there who would still remember her. She almost stepped into the building, but then turned and hurried away, realizing that the more people who knew she was back here, the more chance there was of Goodbody finding out about her. And then . . .

Hannah bent her head and hurried home.

'There you are.' Auntie Bessie was at the door, looking anxiously up and down the street. 'You had me worried.'

'Oh, sorry, Auntie Bessie, but I was that restless after you'd gone. I just had to get out for a bit. I've delivered Mrs Brown's laundry.'

Bessie nodded. 'That's all right then. Now come on in and we'll have a nice cup of tea and I'll tell you all about it. I'm parched, I am. It's me one bit of luxury. Tea.'

Hannah laughed. 'We only got given it in the apprentice house if we were ill.'

Bessie chuckled. 'Well, I hope you didn't get it very often then.'

Hannah had to hold in her impatience for Bessie's news just a little longer, until the older woman had lowered herself into her chair and drunk half her cup of tea. 'There, that's better.'

'Did you see Mr Goodbody? Did he ask about me?'

Bessie shook her head. 'I didn't see him, but I saw his wife.'

Hannah pulled in a startled breath. 'Oh! Oh dear!'

But Bessie was smiling and leaning towards her. 'I'll tell you something, Hannah. She's far more frightened of you than you are of them.'

'Eh?' Now Hannah was mystified.

Bessie sat back and said triumphantly, 'She was real jittery when I asked about you and your mother.'

Hannah shook her head wonderingly. 'Why? Why ever should she be frightened about me?'

'Because they lied to you, didn't they? Kept you thinking your mother was still alive and well and writing to you? I expect if you were to ask your policeman friend about that, you might find that it was against the law in some way. I don't know what they'd call it, but I'd call it criminal, wouldn't you?'

'I suppose so.' Hannah was doubtful. She'd lived her whole life under the rule of others and she couldn't imagine having any power over anyone else. Others wielded the power in Hannah Francis's world – not her. But a tiny sliver of determination and hope began to grow. 'What did she say, Auntie Bessie?'

'Well, when I got there I asked the porter if I could see Mr Goodbody, and he said he was away, but would I like to see Mrs Goodbody. "She's the matron," he said. "She can admit folks when the master's away."' Bessie sniffed. 'Likely he thought I was wanting to go in to stay.' She paused a moment, reflecting how close at times she'd come to having to do just that.

'And did you see her?' Hannah prompted.

Bessie nodded. 'Oh, I saw her all right. She soon came off her high horse when she realized I wasn't another pauper at her gate. And when I said I was inquiring after my old friend, Rebecca Francis, and her daughter, Hannah, she went white.'

Hannah's mouth dropped open. Bessie nodded, 'Oh yes, believe me, Hannah, she went white. She's frightened of her part in the deception coming out, I could tell. I don't reckon you've much to fear from her.'

'Maybe not,' Hannah murmured, finding her voice through her surprise. 'But that's not him, is it?'

'True, but I don't reckon they've heard about you running away. She told me that Rebecca died only a few months after you were sent to the mill. That seemed genuine, but then she seemed to get nervous. Just said that as far as she knew you were still there. When I pressed her and asked if she'd sent word to you that your mother'd died that was when she went white and began to stutter. "My husband deals with all that sort of thing," she said.' Bessie laughed aloud. 'Oh, Hannah, I couldn't resist it, I said, "I'd've thought that you being the matron, like, that it'd've been your job to let the poor girl know."' Bessie rocked with laughter until the tears ran down her cheeks. 'Oh no, no, she said. That was her husband's job. She was quick to put the blame on his shoulders, I can tell you.' Bessie wiped her eyes. 'Anyway, love, as I was coming out, this young woman comes running after me across the yard. She said she'd heard I was asking after Hannah Francis and her mother. Goodness only knows how she knew.'

Though she now had to accept that her mother was truly gone, it was no great shock. Deep inside, she'd known it to be the truth. 'News travels fast in there,' she said with a small smile. 'I reckon the inmates know what's happening even before the master does. Go on, Auntie Bessie.'

'This girl said she'd known you at the mill and that the last time she'd seen you, you'd been fine but that you'd been anxious about your mother as you'd never heard from her. She said she'd written to you herself after she heard in the workhouse that your mother had died. But she didn't know if the letter had ever reached you as you'd never replied.'

'No, it didn't,' Hannah said grimly.

'Doesn't surprise me,' Bessie said. 'I expect with their little scam going on between Goodbody and this Critchlow fellow, they intercepted *any* letters addressed to you.'

'Mmm,' Hannah frowned. 'I wish I knew who'd really done that. I can't believe it of old man Critchlow. He seemed so nice . . .'

Bessie snorted. 'Huh! They all do, until it comes down to money. You were money to them, love. The Critchlows likely paid Goodbody a handsome sum to apprentice you for the pittance it cost them to keep you. Neither of them would want to lose it.'

Hannah was silent for a moment, then she asked curiously, 'Who was the young woman who said she knew me?'

'Nell Hudson.'

'Nell!' Hannah stared at Bessie. 'Nell is in the workhouse?'

And when Bessie nodded, Hannah breathed, 'Oh no! Not Nell. Oh, Auntie Bessie!' She clasped Bessie's hand across the table. 'I have to get her out of there. I just have to.'

Twenty-Seven

'But I don't know what you can do,' Bessie said, though her eyes were full of sympathy for the girl. 'You haven't got a job yet yourself.'

'I will do and I won't be long about it.'

Bessie smiled at the young girl's confidence, marvelling at her determination, her resilience after all the cruel blows that life had dealt her. 'No, love, I'm sure you won't. You're young and strong and willing, and anybody'd be a fool not to employ you, but – but you can't expect to support a household of four on a woman's wage. Your friend could come here and with pleasure, but—'

'Four? What do you mean – four?'

'Didn't you know? Your friend Nell has got a baby. A little boy. He's about a month old.'

Hannah stared at her for a moment and then nodded slowly. 'Yes, yes, it all fits now. No wonder Mrs Bramwell wouldn't tell me why she'd gone away.' Her eyes filled with tears as she remembered. 'And why Nell was so short with me the very last time she spoke. She must've known, must've realized what they'd do. Oh, poor, poor Nell. But I wonder who—?' Then shook herself. 'No time for that now. I have to think of a way to get her out.' She looked Bessie straight in the eyes as she asked, 'So, if we could get enough money to support ourselves, you'd have her here? As another lodger? Her and her baby?'

'Oh yes.' Bessie smiled without hesitation. 'It'd be lovely to have a little one about the place again.'

'And supposing, just supposing that both Nell and me could get work, would you . . . would you look after her child?'

Bessie's eyes sparkled. 'Oh, I would. I would.' And the lonely woman clasped her hands together in thankfulness, blessing the day the young constable had helped Hannah find her old neighbour.

The very next day, Hannah tramped the streets looking for work but she returned home at night disappointed and dispirited.

'Did you try all the silk mills?' Bessie asked.

'Well – one or two,' Hannah said vaguely. She'd wanted to avoid mill work if she could, but it seemed if that was all that was left open to her, she'd no choice. At least she could offer some kind of experience that was allied to that trade. Silk work couldn't be so very different from cotton, could it?

'Anybody home?' came a voice from the door, and Bessie cast her eyes to the ceiling.

'Yes, come in, Flo – if you must.'

'Well, that's a nice greeting, I must say.' Undeterred, Flo Harris entered and sat down at the table. She reached across for a cup and saucer, picked up the teapot and poured herself a cup of tea.

''Elp yourself, why don't you?' Bessie muttered. 'As if I've the money to buy luxuries for half the street.'

Flo cackled with laughter. 'I will, ta, Bessie.' Then

she turned her attention to Hannah. 'Well, girl, gettin' yer feet well and truly under Bessie's table, a' yer?'

Refusing to be daunted by the woman's sharp tongue, Hannah grinned. 'That's right, Mrs Harris. Just like you.'

Now it was Bessie who roared with laughter. 'Now, now, come on you two. Let's not be 'aving any bickering. And as for you, Flo Harris, Hannah's living here with me now, so you'd best get used to the idea.'

Suddenly, Flo smiled. ''S'all right by me. It'll be summat to keep the neighbours gossiping about for a week or two. Gregory's whore's daughter back home. She comin' an' all, is she? Rebecca?'

Bessie banged her fist on the table so hard that the cups rattled in their saucers and the teapot lid bounced. 'Now, look here, Flo. There's no call for you to talk like that. Whatever happened in the past, it's not young Hannah's fault anyway, now is it?' She paused, waiting for Flo's agreement. When it was not forthcoming she banged the table again, demanding loudly, 'Is it?'

Flo jumped and blinked. She could see that Bessie meant business and if she wanted to keep on the right side of her neighbour then she'd better alter her tune. 'No – no, you're right, Bessie,' Flo said, calling upon all her acting skills. ''Course you are.' She turned to Hannah. 'Tek no notice of me. It's just my way. I don't mean no harm.'

Hannah was not taken in by Flo's apology, which had been dragged out of her by Bessie – she remembered her of old – but she smiled thinly and nodded.

'And in answer to your question,' Bessie said quietly now, 'no, Rebecca won't be coming back. She died in the workhouse.' She glared at Flo. 'And I reckon we're all a bit to blame for that happening when we didn't lift a finger to help when she was forced to go in there along with her little girl.'

Flo opened her mouth to make some retort but, seeing the look on Bessie's face, thought better of it. Instead, she turned to Hannah and muttered, 'I'm sorry to hear that.'

Now Bessie cleared her throat and changed the subject. 'Well, Hannah's been job hunting today, but she's not 'ad much luck. Do you know of anywhere where they're taking folk on, Flo?'

The woman appeared to give the question thought, but then pulled a face. 'Sorry, I don't.' Then a sly look came across her face. 'Why don't you go and ask your father to give you a job?'

'Now that's enough, Flo,' Bessie said, and Hannah could see that she was angry now. 'I'm warning you.'

'Oh, sorry, I'm sure.' Flo pretended huffiness. 'I was only trying to think of something to help. Forget I said anything.'

But Hannah was not about to forget. 'My father? You *know* who my father is?' She turned from Flo to Bessie and asked, almost accusingly, 'Do you know him?'

Bessie shifted uncomfortably. 'Well – er – you see, love . . .'

'Auntie Bessie, do you know him?'

There was a brief pause whilst both Hannah and Flo stared at Bessie, who, at last, sighed and said flatly, 'Yes, love. I know him.'

'We all know him,' Flo added triumphantly. 'We've always known who he was, even though Rebecca

would never say.' She touched Hannah's hair with
bony fingers. 'And now there's no mistaking it. You've
got his hair colouring and his bright blue eyes. Oh,
there's no mistaking Jimmy Gregory's bastard.'

Hannah flinched, not at Bessie's sudden banging on
the table once more but at the cruel name Flo had
called her.

'Now that is enough, Flo Harris,' Bessie roared. 'If
you can't keep a civil tongue in your head, you're not
welcome in my house no more.'

Flo knew that she'd gone too far this time. She'd no
wish to fall out with Bessie. Oh, they had their spats
and Flo was renowned for her sharp tongue, but they'd
never really fallen out – not seriously. Now, however,
it looked as if young Hannah was a serious threat.

'I'm sorry, Bessie,' Flo whined. 'I meant no harm.'

'Well, mind you don't,' Bessie snapped. Then she
was silent for a moment, thinking. 'Mind you,' she
said slowly at last, 'you've got a point – even though
you could've found a kinder way to say it.'

'How do you mean?' Hannah pushed aside the
insult. It wasn't the first time she'd had the cruel name
hurled at her and she doubted it'd be the last.

'Well, I suppose you *could* go and see your father.'

'See my father? Why?'

'He's manager at Brayford's silk mill.'

'And he married Brayford's daughter,' Flo put in.
'Oh, done very nicely for himself has Jimmy Gregory.'

Bessie cast her a warning glance but said, 'Yes, she's
right. Your father is now in a position of importance.'
She leaned towards Hannah. 'He's in a position to
help you, love.'

'If he will,' Hannah said bitterly. 'He evidently

didn't want to help my mother when she was expecting me, did he? Or later, when we were turned out of our home.'

There was a strained silence in the room whilst Bessie and Flo exchanged a look. Then came the words that shocked Hannah and broke her heart.

Bessie touched her hand gently and said softly, 'He couldn't, love. He was already married.'

Twenty-Eight

'I'm sorry you've had to find out, love,' Bessie was still trying to console Hannah late that evening. The girl had not cried, but she had gone very quiet, withdrawn into herself, and the older woman was distraught to think that she'd been the cause of the sparkle dying in the girl's eyes. Hannah was only just coming to terms with the death of her childhood sweetheart and the news of her mother, and now here was Bessie being the cause of further grief.

But Hannah took a deep breath and summoned up a tremulous smile. 'It's all right, Auntie Bessie. Honestly. I'd've had to've known sometime and if I'm to go and see him then . . . then I'd better know what to expect.'

Bessie chewed at her bottom lip, but nodded. The girl was right. Painful though it might be, it was better that she knew the truth, especially if she was to meet him.

'Will you do something for me though, Auntie Bessie?'

'I will if I can, love. You know that.'

'Will you tell me everything you know? About me father?'

'Aw – well – now, I don't—'

'Please. I need to know. It can't harm Mam now. If she was still alive, I wouldn't be asking. But I need to know.'

267

Bessie let out a huge sigh. 'Aye, well, I suppose you've a right to know – now you're older. Trouble is, love, I don't know very much really. See, your mam would never tell anyone who your father was. We *think* we know, but I have to say, it's all guesswork on our part.' She paused and her glance roamed over Hannah's face. 'But looking at you now, love,' she murmured. 'It does look as if we might be right.'

'Just tell me, Auntie Bessie.'

Bessie took a deep breath. 'There was this chap at the mill where your mam worked. Jimmy Gregory.' A small smile played on her mouth. 'Handsome devil, he was, I have to admit. But a one for the ladies. You know what I mean.'

Hannah nodded. She knew only too well what 'a one for the ladies' meant. Unbidden, the image of Edmund Critchlow was in her mind.

'By all accounts,' Bessie went on, 'there was something going on between him and yer mother. Folks used to see them together. And she used to stay late at work sometimes – I know that for a fact. Of course she could have been working . . .' Bessie's voice trailed away. Hannah could tell she didn't really believe that.

'But you think she was meeting him?'

Bessie nodded. There was silence until Hannah prompted, in a flat, unemotional tone, 'And he was married? To the boss's daughter.'

'Oh no, not then. He was only the supervisor then and married with a child, I think.'

'So,' Hannah mused, 'somewhere I have a half-brother or sister.'

'His first wife and the child died. It was the cholera.

268

Like your Gran Grace died of. And about the same time too. But you have got a half-brother and a half-sister by his present wife.'

Hannah digested this. From thinking herself an orphan and completely alone in the world, she was now having to come to terms with the knowledge that she had a father and siblings.

'But he didn't come looking for my mother then? When his wife died, I mean?'

'No,' Bessie said grimly. 'But I've a feeling your mother went looking for him.'

'How . . . how do you mean?'

'I think she expected that he would marry her, now that he was a free man.'

'But, obviously, he didn't want to know.'

Bessie sniffed disapprovingly. 'No. I remember her coming home, her face swollen with crying. Bless her. She really hoped—'

'Why do you think he didn't want to marry her?'

'By then, he reckoned he had better fish to fry. No disrespect to your mam, love, but you know what I mean.'

Hannah nodded. 'He'd got his eye on the boss's daughter had he?'

'Not the boss at the mill where he and your mother worked. No. He left there and went to work for Brayford's as manager. That's when he got to know Miss Emmeline Brayford. And, of course, after he'd left, your poor mam got finished at the mill. Her protector had gone.'

'You wouldn't have thought her father – Miss Emmeline's, I mean – would have allowed it. I mean, he can't be considered to be in the same class as her. Can he?'

Bessie shook her head. 'No, but by all accounts, Miss Emmeline is a very spoilt young woman. Her mother died when she was a baby and her father indulges her. Whatever she wants, she gets. And she wanted Jimmy Gregory.' Bessie laughed wryly. 'Mind you, I bet he's had his wings clipped since he married her. He'll not get away with any of his hanky-panky now.'

'I don't suppose his new wife will take very kindly to his bastard knocking on his door.'

Bessie put her arm around Hannah. 'Don't call yourself that, love.'

'But it's what I am, Auntie Bessie.' She lifted her chin and added, defiantly, 'And she'll just have to get used to the idea. And he will, 'cos that's just where I'm going. Knocking on his door. I need a job. It's the least he can do for me. The very least.'

Hannah stood in the pillared porch of the imposing house. Her courage almost failed her. Almost, but not quite. Indignation carried her up the step to lift the heavy knocker and let it fall with a resounding thud. She waited for what seemed an age, hopping nervously from one foot to the other. The door opened and a maid looked her up and down. 'You should've gone round the back. What do you want?'

'I want to see your master.'

'Who shall I say it is?'

'Never mind that.' Hannah was reluctant to give him advance warning. He might refuse to see her at all. 'Just tell him it's a personal matter.'

'Are you one of the mill girls? He'll not see you here. You'll have to see him at work.'

'No, no. I'm not.'

'You after a job then? Because if you are, he'll only see you at the mill—'

'There are reasons why I think he would prefer to see me here.'

The girl blinked. 'Oh. Oh, all right then. I'll ask him. You'd better come in, I suppose. Wipe your boots.'

While she stood in the hallway waiting for the maid to return, Hannah heard the sound of children's laughter and footsteps pounding on the staircase. She looked up to see two youngsters, a boy of about five and a girl a year or so younger, chasing each other down the stairs.

'Wait for me, Roddy. Wait for me,' the little girl cried plaintively.

'Come on, Caroline. Keep up.'

At the bottom of the stairs, the boy looked up to see the stranger standing there. The little girl cannoned into him from behind and then she too saw Hannah.

The boy smiled. 'Hello. Who are you?' He was dark-haired with hazel eyes, but it was the little girl who caught and held Hannah's attention. Startled, Hannah let out a little gasp and covered her mouth with her fingers. The child had long, blonde curling hair, and the eyes that were regarding Hannah curiously were bright blue. Even her features strongly resembled Hannah's own. There was no denying that this child was Hannah's half-sister.

But before either of them could say more, the maid returned to say, 'The master says you're to come this way.' She turned to the children. 'And you two, go and see cook in the kitchen.'

With one last glance at Hannah, the two children

clattered down the passageway leading to the rear of the house, the visitor forgotten, chattering in their high-pitched voices.

The master and mistress of the house were still at breakfast. He was seated at one end of the table, his wife at the other end. As Hannah followed the maid into the room, they both stared at her. Hannah's heart fell. She hadn't wanted to meet his wife. Indeed, she hadn't wanted to meet his children – especially one that looked so like her. She hadn't wanted any of his family to be present when she said what she had to say.

She bobbed courteously towards the woman. 'Begging your pardon, ma'am. I – I just wanted a word with the master.'

The woman was beautiful – there was no denying it. Her skin was flawless and her hair was a glorious colour – a bright red. It was not a colour Hannah had ever seen before and she was fascinated by it. The woman's mouth was perfectly shaped, though to Hannah's mind, her lips were a little thin. Her hazel eyes were cool and she raised one clearly defined dark eyebrow quizzically.

'And to what do we owe this intrusion? One of your mill girls in trouble, is it, James?' She rose gracefully from the table and moved towards the door. 'I hope this has nothing to do with you.'

As she passed close by Hannah, she glanced down, and then she faltered on her path out of the room. A small frown puckered her smooth brow as she stared into Hannah's face. Then her glance swivelled towards her husband and Hannah saw the fleeting anger cross the woman's face. Through gritted teeth, Emmeline muttered, 'Quite obviously, it has.'

Then with an angry swish of her long skirts, she left the room.

'I'm sorry,' Hannah faltered. 'I shouldn't have come.'

'Then why did you?' the man asked harshly, standing up and throwing the newspaper he had been reading at the breakfast table to the floor. He strode towards her to stand over her, angry and intimidating. But Hannah stood her ground.

She looked up into his face, into the bright blue eyes, sparkling with anger. And whilst his hair was thinning now and greying at the temples, she could see that it had once been thick and golden and curly.

There was no point in prevaricating. Even his wife had seen the striking likeness of this stranger to her own daughter. Another daughter who also took after her father.

Hannah licked her lips. 'I . . . I believe you are my father.'

James frowned. 'Do you indeed? And what makes you think that?' He was trying to avoid the obvious and they both knew it.

'Because my mother was Rebecca Francis.'

James looked startled. 'Was?' His surprise was not at Hannah's existence, but at her use of the past tense when speaking of her mother.

'She's dead,' Hannah said baldly, and was gratified when he winced. 'She's been dead for almost four years, but a fat lot you cared.'

'I . . .' he began and then stopped. He could not deny his callous treatment of Rebecca, and his defiant, stony-faced daughter, now standing before him, was living proof.

Put on the defensive, he said harshly, 'So, what do

you want now? To be welcomed into the bosom of my family, I suppose. Well, you can think again. My wife—'

'Ah yes, your wife. She seemed to suspect the truth very quickly, didn't she? And I've just seen your children.' Hannah put her head on one side, regarding him with calculated impudence. 'I think she saw the likeness between me and your daughter. Your *other* daughter.'

He stared at her. 'You're out to make trouble, I can see that.'

But Hannah shook her head. 'No, I'm not and – you probably won't believe me – but if I'd known that I would run into your wife and that she would see the likeness, I wouldn't have come here. Really I wouldn't.'

'So – why did you come?'

'I need a job. That's all I want from you – a job. Nothing more. Except maybe—'

'Ah – I thought there would be more.'

'Except maybe a job for a friend of mine. A girl called Nell. We've both worked at—' She had been about to state the name of Wyedale Mill, but then something held her back. Maybe he knew the Critchlows. Maybe in his anxiety to be rid of her, he would send word to Mr Edmund.

'In a cotton mill,' she went on. 'I'm sure the work can't be so very different.'

'You expect me to give you a job in my mill?' His tone was incredulous. 'And have all the workers gossiping. Have you any idea what you're asking?'

'Yes. I'm asking you to make up for getting my mother pregnant when you were already married. For not marrying her when you could've done. For letting her – and me – be sent into the workhouse without lifting a finger to help us. For letting her die there.'

James flinched and glanced away. 'Well,' he said gruffly, 'when you put it like that, I suppose I do owe you something.' For a moment, he was thoughtful. 'I'll see what I can do. It won't be at my mill. I can't have that. But I do have contacts at other mills in the town. I'll ask around.'

'Thank you. And don't forget – something for my friend too.'

He stared at her. 'By, you're a feisty little thing, aren't you?'

'I've had to be,' she told him grimly, and James Gregory had the grace to look ashamed.

'So – how did you get on?' Bessie was anxious to know. 'Tell me all about it.'

So Hannah told her it all in detail. 'And his little girl. She's the image of me. Can you believe that?'

'Aye well, it happens, love. I've known cousins – and distant cousins at that – be like two peas from the same pod.'

'I asked him to get Nell a job an' all.' Hannah bit her lip and looked at Bessie worriedly. 'Do you think I should've done that? D'you think I've pushed me luck?'

'Nah, love. It's no more than he owes you. You could have demanded a lot more. Just mind you stick to your side of the bargain, though. Once you get your job – and one for Nell – you keep right away from him and his family.'

'Oh, I will. There's nothing more I want from him,' Hannah declared stoutly. But deep in her heart, she knew that there was. She wanted him to be a father to her. A real father. But, young though she still was, life's knocks had put an old head on her shoulders. Hannah knew that her dearest wish could never be.

Smiling bravely so that this kindly woman would not guess her heartache, Hannah asked, 'So, when can we fetch Nell and her little boy?'

Bessie beamed. 'How about right now?'

Twenty-Nine

'Do we have to pay anything to get them out, Hannah, 'cos I haven't any money?'

It was the only thing worrying Bessie. As far as having them come to live with her, she couldn't wait. Especially having a little one running around again. Children had been her life and she missed them dreadfully. To Bessie, life had no meaning without a child about the house.

'I don't know,' Hannah said. 'Goodbody's a grasping devil. I think there was some sort of "arrangement" between him and the Critchlows – if you know what I mean.'

'I can guess,' Bessie said grimly, as she rammed her Sunday-best hat on her head and stuck a hat pin in it to hold it firm. She squared her shoulders as if ready to do battle – as indeed she was. 'Right then, I'll be off.'

Hannah hugged her. 'Oh, Auntie Bessie, you don't know how much this means to me. Nell was so good to me – to us – when we first arrived at the mill. I do so want to help her now. I only wish I could come with you, but I daren't. I just daren't. If Goodbody was to recognize me—'

'No, no, love. You stay here. I'll do my best.'

'I know you will.'

*

After Bessie had left, Hannah roamed around the house, once more restless with anxiety. In her mind, she travelled every step of the way with Bessie. She imagined entering the gates of the workhouse and being met by an unhelpful and belligerent master. She could see him shaking his head and ordering Bessie off the premises. Already she could see Bessie trudging home alone, defeated and dispirited. But Hannah's imagination was running riot and Bessie was faring better than the girl feared. Getting Nell and her son out of the workhouse was easier than either of them had anticipated.

Bessie's determination carried her all the way to the back gate of the building where she demanded admittance. 'You again!' the porter greeted her. 'Taken a liking to this place, 'ave yer?'

Bessie's answer was a derisive snort. 'Not likely. I ain't coming in, if that's what you're thinking. I've come to get someone out.'

The old man laughed. He still had enough spirit to joke with her. 'Aw, teken a fancy to me, 'ave yer? Come to tek me home with yer?'

Bessie smiled. 'I wish I could, love. I wish I was a millionaire and could tek the lot of you in here home with me. 'Cos if I could – I would.'

The porter's face softened, his expression wistful. 'Know what, missis. I believe yer.' He sniffed, drew the back of his hand across his face and said, 'So, how can I help you? 'Cos if you're fetching just one poor sod out of this place, I'll help you in any way I can.'

'It's two. At least, I hope so. A girl called Nell and her little boy.'

The man's face brightened even more. 'Aw, that's grand. She's a lovely lass and he's a grand little babby.

Shouldn't be in here. Shouldn't have been born in here. No one should.' He sighed. 'But there, that's how it is. Poor girl got taken in by some bastard, I suppose, who didn't want to know?'

'That's about the size of it,' Bessie murmured.

'Well, you're a good 'un to take 'em on.' He nodded at her. 'Relation of yours, is she?'

Bessie shook her head and pressed her lips together. She was on the point of telling him everything, all about Hannah and Nell and even about the master and mistress of this place, but it wouldn't do. Instead, she smiled. 'But I'm hoping we'll be like family.'

'She's a lucky lass,' he said gruffly. 'I hope she's properly grateful to you.'

Now Bessie said nothing. She didn't know Nell, didn't really know how they'd all get along together. But she was fond of Hannah, very fond, and she was doing this for her.

'Right then, I'll take you across to see the master.'

Bessie followed him as he hobbled painfully across the yard, into the back door of the building and through what seemed like a maze of dark passages until they came to a door. The porter raised his hand and knocked sharply. On being bidden to enter, he opened the door and poked his head around it.

'Someone to see you,' he said curtly. Bessie could tell at once that there was no love lost between this man and the master of the workhouse.

'Show them in then, man,' Bessie heard the thin, high-pitched voice demand from beyond the door.

Bessie stepped forward, nodding her thanks to the porter as she passed into the room. As she heard the door close behind her, she moved towards the desk. Sitting behind it, crouched over papers spread out upon its battered surface, was the man Hannah had described to her. Thin, hunch-backed with a rat-like face, beady eyes and a sharp nose. This was Cedric Goodbody.

Bessie licked her lips. 'Good morning, Mr Goodbody.'

The man grunted, pulled a blank piece of paper towards him and reached for a pen.

'Another mouth to feed,' he muttered. 'Name?'

'Mrs Elizabeth Morgan,' she said and he began to write.

'Age?'

'Why do you need to know that?'

He looked up and smirked. 'You drop your pride at the door when you come in here. Age?'

'But I'm not coming in here. I've come to get someone out.'

The man's eyes glinted. 'Have you indeed? And who might that be?'

'Nell Hudson and her son.'

A strange look crossed the man's face. 'Have you indeed?' he said again, but there was a different intonation in his voice now: surprise and a curious kind of wariness, as if he'd never expected anyone coming to ask for Nell Hudson.

He cleared his throat, dipped the pen into the ink once more and said, 'Well, I'll still need to ask you a few questions. Er-hem – for the information of the guardians, you understand.'

That's a lie for a start, Bessie thought, but she held her tongue and merely nodded.

'Where will the girl and her child be living?'

'Here in Macclesfield.'

'Can you support her?'

Now it was Bessie's turn to lie. 'Yes.'

He eyed her keenly. 'You have a husband? A man to support you?'

Now she couldn't lie. 'No, but I work.'

'Oh yes. Where?'

Again, she felt unable to lie. 'At home. I take in washing.'

The man's thin lips curled.

'And . . . and I have a lodger. She works and . . . and she's found a job for Nell an' all.'

'Ah, now that does throw a different light on the matter.'

Cedric bowed his head for a few moments. He was in a quandary. Nell Hudson had been orphaned and brought to the workhouse at the age of eighteen months. At ten she had been dispatched to the Critchlows' mill, but had recently been sent back to the workhouse when she had become pregnant. Though he had never been told officially, he suspected that Edmund Critchlow was the child's father. Nell had been the second girl to be returned to the workhouse from Wyedale Mill, heavy with child and calling Edmund Critchlow all the filthy names she could lay her tongue to. But Cedric Goodbody was beholden to the Critchlows. He'd taken the girls back into the workhouse and held his tongue, silenced by a nice little sum that passed each time from Edmund Critchlow into Cedric's bony hands.

'And you make sure they stay there,' Edmund had warned. 'It'll be the worse for you, Goodbody, if I ever set eyes on them again.'

Now Cedric raised his beady eyes and glared at Bessie. 'And where is she going to work?'

Bessie swallowed. Her throat was painfully dry. All this lying was hard work. 'At the mill.'

'What mill?' Goodbody snapped.

'One of the silk mills.'

'Here? In Macclesfield?'

When she nodded, he seemed to relax a little, though a deep frown still rutted his forehead. At last, after several moments of deep thought, which seemed an age to the waiting Bessie, he said, 'Very well, then. I will release her into your care. But you'll have to sign a paper that you take full responsibility for her.'

Now it was Bessie's turn to be anxious about what she was taking on. Then she shrugged her shoulders. Oh well, what did it matter. She'd been heading for the workhouse in her old age anyway before Hannah had appeared. If they all ended up in here, so what? It was no more, no less than she'd expected would happen one day. And in the meantime, well, she'd have a family of sorts to care for again.

That, more than anything, was worth the risk.

'Where do I sign?' She beamed at him.

'But I don't know who you are.' Nell's eyes were wide with fear. Much as she wanted to get out of the workhouse, this was like taking a blind leap off a mountain into the unknown. 'You . . . you could be anybody.'

Bessie chuckled, not in the least insulted by the girl's misgivings. She'd feel exactly the same in Nell's shoes. 'You'll just have to trust me, love, that's all. There's a home and a job waiting for you. Tek it or leave it,' she added, hoping that the girl wouldn't take her at her word and refuse to go with her. She couldn't explain it all, for Goodbody was still in the room. And even if he hadn't been, walls had ears as far as Bessie was concerned. She'd no intention of so much as mentioning Hannah's name until they were well clear of this place.

But Nell was still hesitating and Bessie began to grow a little impatient. She'd've thought the girl would have jumped at the chance to get out of the workhouse. She knew she would've done.

Then suddenly, Nell said, 'Wait a minute. I've seen you before. You came here the other day—'

Bessie gave a little shake of her head, trying to warn the girl to say no more. Swiftly, she interrupted. 'No, no, that wasn't me. Never been here before in me life, and I'd rather not have to come again, if it's all the same to you.'

'Oh,' Nell murmured, still staring at her. 'I was sure . . .' Then she shrugged. 'I must have got it wrong.' There was a pause before Nell went on, 'But why me? You don't know me. Why do you want to help *me*?'

'Well – er – see, it's like this. Me own family's all gone. Left the nest. And I'm all on me own.' It was the truth but not the whole truth.

Nell was still suspicious. 'Last time I left here, I thought I was going to be set up for life. Going to be well looked after in a good job. And look where that got me. Back here in a few years and ruined. Oh aye, ruined. I love me little baby, I won't let anyone say I don't, but I'd've sooner he'd never been born than end up in here.' She thrust her face close to Bessie's. 'Has Edmund Critchlow sent you? Is there a gang of thugs waiting for me outside to make sure I'm put out of harm's way for good? Me and little Tommy?'

Bessie was appalled. 'No, love. I promise you. Nothing like that.' She bit her lip. This girl wasn't about to go willingly with her unless Bessie confided a bit more. But how could she with Cedric Goodbody's ears flapping? She touched the girl's arm. 'Look, you'll just have to trust me, that's all I can say.'

Nell glanced at Goodbody. 'Can I leave Tommy here whilst I go and see what this is all about? Can I come back for him?'

Cedric hesitated. He wanted the girl gone. In fact he couldn't understand what was holding her back. For a young 'un, she had a very suspicious mind. But he could see that for two pins she'd refuse this woman's offer. Cedric couldn't care less what was going to happen to her or her bastard. He just wanted them both out of here so that when he reported the fact to the guardians that there were two fewer mouths to feed he would receive their smiling approbation. And maybe that approbation would take the form of a monetary bonus. It had in the past.

He smiled thinly, but there was no warmth in his eyes, only swift, self-interested calculation. 'Of course, my dear. Very sensible of you. You go with this – er – lady and see what she's offering. Then, if all is well, come back and fetch your little one.' If she didn't come back, he was thinking, even if she left the boy here, at least it was one gone. And the baby would probably soon pine away without his mother.

'Right, I will.' Nell turned to Bessie. There was still wariness in her eyes as she said, 'Let's be seeing what this is all about then.'

They walked outside into the yard and then, with a cheery wave to the porter, they were outside the gate and walking down the path. Nell was nervous, glancing anxiously about her, and when Bessie took hold of her arm, the girl actually flinched with fear. 'It's all right, love. Honestly, it is. Just a few more yards away from this place and I'll explain it all.'

'Explain?' Nell came to a halt, wrenching her arm out of Bessie's grasp. 'I knew it. There is more to this than you've said. I knew this sort of luck doesn't happen to someone like me.' There were tears in her eyes. She'd dared to hope. How foolish she'd been.

Bessie leaned close, keeping her voice low. 'D'you remember someone called Hannah at the mill?'

'Hannah?'

'Shh, keep your voice down,' Bessie hissed, glancing nervously up at the high windows.

Nell lowered her voice. 'Of course I remember Hannah.'

'Well, let's just keep walking and I'll tell you.'

Still a little reluctantly, but now with increasing curiosity, Nell fell into step beside Bessie.

'Hannah and her mother used to live next door to me,' Bessie began. 'Years ago, before they came into the workhouse.' Her face fell into sad lines. 'I only wished I could've prevented that, but I had all me own brood at home. I couldn't.'

Nell said nothing, so Bessie continued. 'I didn't know what'd happened to them. Hannah and her mother. I didn't know Hannah'd been sent away to that mill in Derbyshire. I didn't know Rebecca – her mother – had died in the workhouse. I knew nothing at all until Hannah turned up on my doorstep.'

Again Nell stopped and turned to face Bessie. 'Hannah? Hannah's here? In Macclesfield?'

Now Bessie stopped too and turned to face the girl. Smiling, she nodded, 'Yes, and waiting like a cat on hot bricks at my house. It's her you've got to thank, love. Soon as I said I'd seen a girl called Nell here – and yes, it was me that came the other day.'

'I thought it was. I thought I wasn't losing me marbles already. Mind you,' she added tartly, 'that place is enough to make you.'

'I came to ask about poor Rebecca for Hannah. She wanted to know. And when I got back home, I said I'd seen you. Spoken to a girl called Nell, I told her. Well, you should've seen her face. A picture, it was. "Oh, I've got to get her out of there, Auntie Bessie," she said at once. "I've just got to."' Bessie smiled gently at the girl. 'She said you were so good to her at the mill. She's not forgotten that.'

'So is it Hannah who's fetching me out?'

'That's it.' Swiftly, Bessie went on to tell Nell all that had passed between her and Hannah, all the plans they had. 'Hopefully, she'll've got a job for you an' all, but I had to lie through me teeth in front of old Goodbody there. I didn't want him finding out about Hannah. We're not sure what he'd do if he found out she'd run away from the Critchlows.'

Tears were in Nell's eyes. 'Oh, how good, how kind of her. But,' she shook her head and the tears flooded down her cheeks, 'but I can't. I can't come. Tell her I'm grateful. Ever so grateful. I'll never forget what she tried to do for me. And her secret's safe with me. Tell her that. Be sure to tell her that. I won't give her away to Goodbody.'

Bessie stared at the girl in disbelief. 'But why? Why won't you come?'

Nell shook her head. 'Tommy. My baby. I couldn't leave him behind.'

Bessie stared at her for a moment and then she

threw back her head and laughed aloud. 'Aw, love, we wouldn't expect you to do that. We wouldn't want you to do that. Of course, Tommy's to come an' all.' She threw her arms wide and enfolded the girl whilst Nell sobbed against her shoulder. But now her tears were of happiness and relief.

And there were yet more tears when they turned into the street and saw Hannah waiting outside Bessie's front door.

'Hannah, oh, Hannah,' Nell cried, and began to run.

'Nell!' Hannah spread her arms wide and ran towards her friend. They met and hugged each other, dancing and swinging each other round in sheer joy, whilst Bessie waddled down the street towards them, beaming from ear to ear.

Thirty

Two hours later, Nell had fetched her son from the matron's care and, together with their few belongings, they were installed in Bessie's second best bedroom. Hannah was to have the tiny boxroom next to it.

'It doesn't seem fair, us taking this room and you crammed into there,' Nell said.

'It's all I need,' Hannah reassured her, hugging her swiftly. 'It's so lovely to have you both here. I don't care where I sleep. Besides, you and Tommy are having to share.'

'Do you think I mind that? I've been separated from him ever since he was born. I'm not going to let him out of my sight now.'

'Oh er – well, I know how you feel, but we'll both have to work.'

Nell laughed. 'Oh yes, but you know what I mean.'

Hannah smiled with relief. For a moment she had thought that Nell had meant it literally.

They waited impatiently for two days but no word came from James Gregory.

'I'll just have to go and see him again,' Hannah said.

'Give him time, love,' Bessie said. She refused to worry. She was happier than she'd been for years. A lot of laundry work had come her way again in the last two days and now she had two strong lasses to help her, it was done in half the time.

'It's the fetching and taking back I can't do. All the walking. Me legs are getting bad.'

'Well, me an' Tommy can do that,' Nell offered. 'The fresh air'll do him the world of good.' The smile that hardly left her face now broadened. 'He's never seen the outside world much. High time he did.' She glanced from Hannah to Bessie and back again. Her face sobered. 'I can't tell you what this means to me, you know. I'll never, ever be able to repay your kindness.'

'No need, love,' Bessie said. 'You two have made my life worth living again. It's me should be thanking you both.' Her eyes softened as she glanced down at Tommy lying kicking on the hearthrug. 'And that little man there.'

'And it's me who should be thanking both of you. Nell was like my guardian angel when we first arrived at the mill. Showed me the ropes. And now you, Auntie Bessie, taking in a waif and stray. How can *I* thank *you*?'

The three of them clutched at each other, laughing together.

'Now then,' Bessie said at last, wiping the tears of laughter from her eyes. Oh, how good it was to laugh again and to have someone to laugh with her. She'd always loved the company of young people; preferred it to the likes of Flo Harris any day. And these two lasses were as bright as buttons and sharp as a packet of needles. 'I'd best get started else Mrs Montgomery won't get her washing delivered back by tonight and she's a tartar an' no mistake.'

'Right, I'll get the copper going,' Hannah volunteered and Nell said, 'I'll clear away the breakfast things and then I'll help.'

About mid-morning the door from the passageway into Bessie's back yard opened and a grubby urchin poked his head round it. 'A' you Hannah?'

Nell, pegging washing onto the lines stretched across the yard and with her mouth full of pegs, flicked her head towards the wash house.

The lad grinned and, weaving his way through the wet clothes, stood in the doorway and repeated his question.

Hannah, elbow deep in soap suds, glanced up. 'Yes.'

'Message from the mister.'

Hannah paled and her heart thudded. 'The . . . the master?' Her first thought was that Cedric Goodbody had found out that she was back here, but as the boy spoke again her heart slowed in relief and colour flooded back into her face. 'Yeah, the master. Mr Gregory. He's sent word you're to go to see a Mr Boardman at the mill in Brown Street. There might be a job going there for you.'

Hannah smiled. 'Thanks.'

'And there was summat else.' The boy frowned, trying to recall the rest of the message. 'Oh aye. Your friend is to go to the house. His house. Not you, he said, just your friend.'

'Nell?'

The boy shrugged. ''Ee didn't say her name.'

'No,' Hannah said slowly and thoughtfully. 'No, I don't think I told him it.' Then she roused herself from her wandering thoughts enough to say, 'Thanks for coming.' She paused, taking in the boy's skinny legs and thin wrists, the grubby bare feet. She smiled. 'Would you like a bowl of soup?'

The child's eyes widened. 'Ooh ta, miss.'

Hannah dried her hands on a rough piece of cloth and led him towards the back door of the house and into the kitchen. Nell followed them in as Hannah led the boy to the table, her hand resting on his shoulder. 'This young man's earned himself a bowl of soup, Auntie Bessie. He's brought us some good news. I'm to go to the mill just round the corner and you, Nell, are to go to my – to Mr Gregory's house.'

'His house? Why to his house?'

They all looked towards the boy, but he was now so intent upon slurping the soup into his mouth that he didn't even notice them looking at him.

'I don't think he knows,' Hannah murmured. 'But Mr Gregory's made it clear that I'm not to set foot near his house again.'

There was no mistaking the edge of bitterness in Hannah's tone.

Mr Boardman, the supervisor, turned out to be a tubby, jovial man.

'Worked in a cotton mill 'afore, I hear. Where was that, then?'

Hannah bit her lip. She was sure the man was just asking out of interest, to find out what her previous experience was. So, she answered swiftly. 'A mill in Derbyshire. I don't expect you know it.' She rushed on, telling him about all the jobs she had done, not giving him time to ask for the actual name of the place. 'I was a scutcher, then a piecer and a bobbin winder for a short while. The last job I had there was as a throstle spinner.' As she rattled on, he nodded, seeming pleased with her knowledge and the skills she'd learned. At last he said, 'Well, Mr Gregory has vouched for you. Says he'd employ you himself, but he's no vacancies at the minute and you need a job now.'

Hannah nodded. 'If you please, sir.'

'Right then. I'll take you on a month's trial and see how you go, eh? You'll be winding the skeins of silk onto bobbins.' He told her the wage and all the rules and conditions. 'And you can start tomorrow morning. How about that?'

'Thank you, sir. Thank you very much.'

For the first time in months, Hannah sang out loud as she hurried home to share her good news with the two most important people in her new life – three if you counted little Tommy.

But there was still one person she would never forget. The memories of Luke were locked away deep in her heart: poignant, heart-wrenching memories of a tender, innocent love that had never been given the chance to blossom. Cruelly cut down by a tyrant. And she could never forget him either. One day, she promised, her vow burning as strongly as ever. One day, I'll have my revenge on you, Edmund Critchlow.

'So, what did he want? What did he say to you? Why did he want you up at the house instead of at his mill?'

Hannah's questions tumbled over each other as Nell stepped in the back door.

'Hey, give me a minute to catch me breath,' Nell laughed, but her eyes were sparkling.

Hannah grinned and pulled a wry face. 'Sorry, but I can hardly wait to hear all about it.'

'I gathered that,' Nell teased.

'Here's a cup of tea, love. Special treat.' Bessie was no less anxious to hear about it all than Hannah but her approach was more patient. 'Tommy's fine. He's having his afternoon nap upstairs.'

They sat around the table, waiting whilst Nell had taken a sip of her tea.

'Do you know,' she began, surprise in her voice as she glanced at Hannah, 'he's quite nice?' Hannah smiled thinly but said nothing. 'I'd expected someone like Mr Edmund, but he wasn't a bit like that.' She nodded at Hannah. 'But no wonder he doesn't want you up there – at the house. You can see in a minute that you're his daughter. You've got his hair and his eyes, haven't you?'

Now Hannah nodded and said huskily, 'And did you see his little girl?'

Nell shook her head.

'She's about three or four and she looks just like me. I'm sure his wife saw it too. Anyway, what did he say? Is he giving you a job at his mill?'

'No, he's no jobs going there at the minute. But . . .' Nell paused dramatically, 'He's offered me a job as nanny to the children.'

Hannah's mouth fell open and Bessie murmured, 'Well, I never.'

'But – but – I thought – I mean,' Hannah spluttered, 'I thought he didn't want us anywhere near his house?'

Nell touched her hand and said gently, 'It's you he doesn't want there, not me.'

'But surely, you'll remind him – and her – of me.'

'Ah, now,' Nell glanced away, suddenly embarrassed. 'Well . . .' She paused, not knowing quite how to put the next bit.

'Go on,' Hannah prompted.

'I'm sworn to secrecy. I'm not to let on that I've anything to do with you, that I even know you. And I'm sorry, Hannah, but you must never visit me there or try to contact him again in any way.'

The look on Hannah's face was bleak. If she'd secretly hoped for any kind of relationship with her father, then those dreams were dashed.

'He did say one thing though.'

'Go on,' Hannah muttered through gritted teeth. She was trying desperately not to let the tears that were welling up behind her eyes come spilling out.

'He said, "The reason I'm offering you this job is . . ." now what word did he use? Ah yes, "twofold". Yes, that was it. That's what he said. "The reason I'm offering you this job is twofold." '

'What on earth does that mean?' Hannah cried.

'Means he's got two reasons,' Bessie put in. 'Go on, Nell.'

' "My wife," he said, "can be a bit difficult to work for. And the two children aren't easy. We've had more nannies than I've got workers in the mill." ' The three of them smiled thinly at his wry witticism, then Hannah's smile faded. 'Oh, Nell, you don't want to be working for someone like that.'

'Wait a minute, wait till I've finished telling you. You see, the other reason was that he said it would be a link between you and him. "If ever she needs anything," he said, "you'll be able to let me know." '

Hannah stared at her. 'He never said that.'

For a moment, Nell looked hurt that her friend

could think that she would lie to her. But then, she imagined herself in Hannah's place. The girl's father had never shown the slightest interest in her, had deserted her mother and left them to fend for themselves, had never lifted a finger to help them in their direst need. And even when they'd finally met a few days ago, he'd forbidden her to try to see him again. Why, then, should she believe that he'd had a change of heart? No, she wouldn't have believed it either. So she said gently, 'That's what he said, Hannah. I wouldn't lie to you.'

Now Hannah was contrite. 'Oh no, no, I'm sorry. I shouldn't have said that. It . . . it just came out because . . . because I couldn't believe it.'

'Mebbe when he saw you, love, he had a change of heart,' Bessie suggested softly.

'Huh! It was a big one then, 'cos the other day he didn't want to see hide nor hair of me ever again.'

'Well, that's what he said, Hannah, I promise you.'

Hannah was torn now. 'But I still don't like the thought of you working for a tartar just so that I've got a link with my father. I'd sooner you got a job alongside me at the mill.'

'Wait a bit. There's more.'

'More? Go on, then.'

'I was honest with him. I didn't think there was much point in being anything else. I told him I'd got a little boy and he said that would be fine. I could take him with me sometimes if I wanted.'

'By heck,' Bessie blurted out. 'They must be desperate for a nanny if he offered that. But you know you can leave him with me, love. You don't need to take him there unless you want to.' Suddenly, her face fell. 'Oh – you mean, they want you to live in?'

'Not exactly. I'll be given a room of my own there – and a bed in it for Tommy too – and they might want me to stay so many nights of the week, two or three maybe.'

Bessie was struggling with her feelings. It was like being desperately thirsty and being handed a cup of water only to have it snatched away again before being able to take even a sip. Yet she couldn't stand in the girl's way and little Tommy would live in the lap of luxury compared to her humble home.

She felt Nell's touch. 'I'm not going to live in, Auntie Bessie. I don't want to. She'd have me at her beck and call all day and all night too. And I don't want Tommy learning those kids' bad ways, 'cos they must have got a few if they can't keep a nanny for long.'

'Are you sure, Nell? I mean it'd be much better for you both living in a nice house.'

'Maybe,' Nell agreed. 'But there'd be no laughter, no fun – and no love.'

Bessie was thoughtful for a moment. 'Have you thought, Nell, that that's probably what those kiddies need? A bit of love? Children are sometimes naughty just because they want someone to take a bit of notice of 'em.'

Hannah and Nell glanced at Bessie and then at each other.

'You know, she could be right, Nell. Folk like them don't have much to do with their children. Look how the Critchlows sent Adam away to school. He was hardly ever at home, now was he?'

Bessie gave a snort of laughter. 'Well, Jimmy Gregory wasn't born into that sort of class, but I expect he thinks he's one of them now.'

'Yes,' Hannah said slowly. 'I expect he does.'

'Well, I'm going to give it a go,' Nell said. 'If it doesn't work out, I can always leave. One more to add to the long list of nannies who didn't stay long. I'll tell you one thing though,' she ended as, hearing Tommy's cries from the bedroom, she levered herself up from the stool to go to him. 'I shan't stand any nonsense from the kids – or from Lady Muck, whoever she thinks she is.'

Thirty-One

The sight of a policeman knocking at one of the doors in Paradise Street was unusual on a Sunday afternoon. Though it was not one of the wealthier streets in the town, the residents were, in the main, God-fearing and law-abiding. A wayward youngster was dealt a cuff around the ear by his father or a neighbour – or even the local peeler on the beat – and no ill-feeling resulted. The community watched out for each other, helped one other, laughed, quarrelled and made up to laugh together again. But when a young constable was seen visiting Bessie's house, that was cause for Flo's curtains to twitch and the tongues to wag.

'Come away in, lad,' Bessie welcomed, and ushered Jim into the kitchen where the two girls were sewing. Little Tommy was lying on the hearthrug, looking about him and gurgling with glee.

'I was just passing.' Jim smiled, tucking his hat under his arm. 'Constable Robinson put me on this beat special-like, so's I could call in and see how you are.'

Hannah threw her sewing aside and jumped up to pull out a chair for him. 'Oh, how kind of you – and Mr Robinson. I'm fine. I've got a job at one of the mills. Been there for two months now. And this is my friend, Nell, and her little boy, Tommy. They've come to live here as well. Nell's got a job as a nanny.'

'Sit down, lad, sit down,' Bessie waved him into the

chair. 'Now, I don't 'spect your superior would mind if you had a cuppa with us, would he?'

Jim grinned. 'Not if he doesn't know, missis.' And they all laughed.

He laid his hat on the table and squatted down to Tommy to tickle his tummy. 'You're a grand little chap, aren't you?'

Tommy looked up at the tall man, startled for a moment. His baby round chin trembled and he screwed up his eyes, about to cry.

'Aw, I'm sorry. I must've frightened him. Must be the uniform. I'm usually quite good with little ones. Got nephews and nieces of me own.' He stood up and backed away, but continued to smile down at the little boy.

Nell picked Tommy up and held him against her shoulder, patting his back comfortingly.

'It's not your fault. He's not used to men, see. In the workhouse, we were segregated. He's only been around women, really.'

The smile faded from Jim's face to be replaced by a look, not of disgust or censure, but of concern. He sat down in the chair Hannah had pulled out for him. 'I'm sorry to hear you was in there. Very long, was it?'

Nell pressed her lips together. 'Since just before Tommy was born.' Tears hovered in her eyes but she smiled at Hannah. 'But thanks to my friend here – and Mrs Morgan – we're out. And,' she said firmly, 'I mean to stay out. I don't want my son growing up in that place.'

The household soon settled into a happy routine. Hannah loved her job at the mill. The other workers there were friendly and helpful and she soon fitted in. And the conditions were much pleasanter than in the cotton mill. No fluff or dust floated in the air and Hannah revelled in the sight and the touch of the silk.

'It's so shiny and all the pretty colours they dye it,' she enthused to Bessie and Nell. Bessie nodded and smiled sadly. She fondly remembered watching Bill in his garret working with the lovely yarn.

As for Nell, forthright, no nonsense Nell, she soon had the Gregory youngsters eating out of her hand.

'You were absolutely right, Auntie Bessie.' Already Bessie Morgan was 'Auntie' to Nell too, and to little Tommy she was 'Nanna'. 'Those poor kids,' Nell went on indignantly, 'are just starved of attention. That's all they need. Mind you, this job's not long term anyway. They've hired a tutor for the little boy for two years and then he's going away to boarding school when he's seven.' Her eyes darkened. 'Fancy choosing to be separated from your kids. I can't believe it. They don't know how lucky they are.'

'But there'll still be the little girl to look after,' Bessie put in, trying not to get her hopes up that Nell and Tommy would be coming back to live all the time with her.

'Not really, 'cos when the boy goes to school, they'll get a governess for the girl. Madam told me so.' She laughed. 'That's what I have to call her – "Madam". And she can be a right "madam" an' all. Mind you, I don't stand no nonsense from her. I tell her exactly what I think. She keeps asking me to go and live there full time, but I keep giving her the same answer. I'll stay there some nights but I want to keep coming home.' She glanced at Bessie. ''Cos this *is* home to me an' our Tommy. I told her I don't want him growing up thinking he's part of that household – that he belongs there. It wouldn't do, wouldn't do at all. Funny thing is, she seems to take it from me whereas her poor lady's maid gets shrieked at from morning till night. It's a wonder she doesn't up sticks and leave. I reckon she would if she could get another position. Trouble is, she doesn't get any time to get out and look for another job. Madam keeps her working day and night. She never seems to get any time off. And the poor kid hasn't got the guts to stand up to Mrs Gregory. She's a mousy little thing – from the workhouse, so I suppose she's used to taking orders and never thinks to answer back.' She laughed. 'Not like us, eh Hannah? Old Goodbody and his missis couldn't wait to ship us out of the way, could they?' Her laughter died. 'But I turned up again on their doorstep like a bad penny and about to give birth. He wasn't best pleased, I can tell you.'

Nell chattered on about her life with 'the upstarts', as she referred to the Gregorys. 'She might've been born to that life,' she would say, 'but he certainly wasn't. He's no better than you and me, Hannah. He was just lucky enough to be born good-looking.'

'Yes,' Hannah said bitterly. 'A curse on all good-looking men.' And she knew that Nell was aware she was including Edmund Critchlow. But then Nell countered her remark by saying softly, 'He asked after you today. Mr Gregory. Asked if you were all right – if there was anything you needed.'

Hannah stood up suddenly and turned away. 'What did you tell him? It'd've been nice to've had a father when I needed one. His concern comes a bit late in the day.'

She left the kitchen, slamming the back door and leaving Nell staring sadly after her.

'He's here again,' Bessie called from the front doorstep as she saw Jim coming down the street. 'And on his day off, an' all, by the look of his clothes. That's not his uniform or I'm a Dutchman.'

Hannah poked her head out of the door, looking over Bessie's shoulder.

'This is the third time he's come.'

'I reckon he's got his eye on you.'

'Oh no, Auntie Bessie,' Hannah lowered her voice as the young man came closer. 'It's Nell. Haven't you noticed how he looks at her?' She raised her voice, 'Hello, Jim. She's not here. She's at work.'

There was no mistaking the faint flush that coloured his face nor the fleeting look of disappointment.

'You're right, Hannah,' Bessie muttered, but then raised her voice too. 'But we're glad to see you. Come away in.'

He stayed an hour, but Nell was still not home by the time he rose reluctantly and said, 'I'll have to go. I'm on duty at six.'

'Nell will be sorry to've missed you,' Hannah said archly.

'Come an' have your Sunday dinner with us tomorrow, lad,' Bessie invited. 'She'll be here then. It's her day off.'

'Mine too.' There was no denying the sparkle in his eyes. 'Do . . . do you think she'd go for a walk with me? See . . .' He was embarrassed now, but pressed on. 'See I've got something for her. A perambulator. The lady my mother cleans for has one to sell. It's a bit battered.' He smiled. 'It's been well used, but little Tommy must be getting heavy for her to carry far now. I thought it'd be just the thing for him.'

Bessie and Hannah glanced at each other. 'That's really thoughtful of you, lad, but I don't think we could afford—'

'Oh, it's a gift,' Jim interrupted swiftly. 'I want to get it for her.' The colour on his face deepened. 'Unless you think she'd be offended.'

'Offended?' Bessie laughed uproariously. 'When it's a gift for her little Tommy? Oh no, lad. You couldn't have thought of anything better,' she assured him, and the young man went away beaming.

'It can't be me he's coming to see, Hannah, it'll be you.' Nell, when they told her that evening of Jim's visit, was adamant. 'I'm not 'alf as pretty as you and besides, I'm a fallen woman.' She gazed down fondly at her child as if the thought didn't worry her too much now that she had him. But her tone was a little wistful as she added softly, 'No one'll want me now.'

'Well, you'll see for yourself tomorrow, love,' Bessie said, winking at Hannah. They hadn't told Nell of the gift Jim intended to bring. They wanted that to be a surprise – a surprise that, in their eyes, proved his growing fondness for Nell and – best of all – for her little boy too.

When a knock sounded on the door at eleven o'clock the following morning, Bessie shouted. 'Answer the door, Nell, will yer? I'm peeling the 'taters.' She was doing no such thing; both she and Hannah were hiding in the back scullery, stifling their laughter as they listened to Nell opening the door.

'Oh – hello, Jim.'

'Hello, Nell.'

There was silence whilst Bessie whispered impatiently, 'Get on with it then, lad,' to be shushed by Hannah.

They heard Jim speak again, nervously. 'Mrs Morgan – er – invited me for dinner.'

'So she said,' Nell answered. 'You'd best come in.'

'Well . . . um . . . I was wondering if – after dinner, like – you'd come out with me. For . . . for a walk?'

'Oh!'

Though they couldn't see her, Hannah and Bessie could imagine Nell's face growing pink.

'That's very kind of you,' they heard her say, 'but I couldn't leave Tommy. I only get to spend time with him on me day off and—'

'Oh, I meant Tommy too.'

'Oh . . . oh.' Now they could hear that Nell was truly flustered. 'But . . . but he's getting too heavy to carry very far.'

'That's why I've brought this.'

There was a pause and Hannah and Bessie held their breath. Then they heard Nell's gasp of delight. 'Oh, Jim. A baby carriage.'

'I've brought it for Tommy. To keep, I mean. It'd be so much easier for you when you take him to work than having to carry him. Oh, Nell, do say you're not angry or offended.'

'Come on.' Bessie gripped Hannah's arm. 'Time we lent the poor lad a hand.'

Together they stepped out of the scullery and into the kitchen.

'Now isn't that kind of you, Jim? Now bring it in. We'll make a space for it here in the kitchen and he can sit in it like the little lord he is.'

The perambulator was a box-like contraption sitting on two huge rear wheels and two smaller ones at the front, with two long curved handles to push it with. Nell still hadn't spoken, and Jim was eyeing her anxiously as he manoeuvred it in through the door and set it against the wall in the space that Bessie had already cleared.

'Oh, just look, a mattress and pillow and even blankets. Put him in it, Nell, do.'

Moments later, Tommy was lying in the pram looking very much at home and beaming up at the four grown-ups watching him.

'He likes it. What a grand present,' Bessie patted Jim on the shoulder. 'And you shall carve the joint of beef I've got in special.'

As Hannah and Bessie went back to the scullery, this time no longer pretending to prepare the meal, they glanced back to see Jim taking Nell's hands in his and she looking up into his eyes.

'Now mebbe she'll believe us,' Bessie said happily.

As she stood at the sink to peel the potatoes, Bessie began to sing, and just as so many years ago, Hannah joined in.

'Let all the world in every corner sing . . .'

Thirty-Two

'Oh, my lor'! What have you done to your hair?' Bessie threw her hands in the air as Nell stepped through the back door.

They'd been sharing the house now for a year. Hannah continued to be happy working at the silk mill, though, unlike her time at Wyedale Mill, her co-workers had not taken the place of her family. Home was now with Bessie, and Nell and Tommy when they were there. Those were the best times, when the door was closed, the curtains drawn against the world and there was just the four of them. Though more often than not, it was five, for Jim was now a regular visitor to the terraced house. He and Nell had been officially 'walking out' together for most of that time.

At Bessie's exclamation, Hannah straightened up from where she had been bending over the fire in the range. At the sight of her friend, she gave a little cry, but her surprise soon turned to admiration. 'Oh, Nell, it's lovely.'

'Lovely? Lovely, you say? I'll give her lovely,' Bessie was shouting and waving her arms about. 'Spoilt her pretty hair. She looks like a whore!'

There was a sudden stillness in the room as Bessie stared at Nell in horror and clapped her hand over her runaway mouth. But the sight of Bessie's horror-struck face was so comical that Nell, far from being offended, collapsed against the doorframe, laughing helplessly.

'If I look like one, then . . . then so does she,' she spluttered. 'So does his wife. Mrs Gregory.'

'Aw, I'm sorry, love.' Bessie was mortified. 'I shouldn't have said that. It's nowt to do wi' me. But . . . but I look on you – on both of you – like you was me own daughters.'

Hannah, recovering from the surprise, moved forward to examine Nell's hair that was now a bright shade of rich auburn that shone and glowed in the lamplight. Quite seriously, she said, 'It looks even better on you than on her. D'you know, I thought when I saw her that day, it didn't look quite natural. But it is a lovely colour.'

'I've been acting as her lady's maid for a few weeks,' Nell went on. 'That poor little creature finally plucked up enough courage to give in her notice. I hope she's found someone nicer to work for,' Nell murmured, sparing a thought for the young girl, who had suffered so under Mrs Gregory's sharp tongue. 'Anyway, madam wanted me to help her dye her hair one day and she suggested I should try it. You won't believe it, but she helped me do it. I've never like my mousy coloured hair, so I wasn't going to say no, was I? She seems to've taken a liking to me. She's given me some of the clothes her children have grown out of for Tommy. And they're hardly worn. He'll look a little prince in them. She's not so bad when you get to know her. D'you know, I think she's lonely. You'd think she'd have lots of friends, wouldn't you, but she doesn't seem to have any.'

'Maybe they think she married beneath her. The so-called gentry can be a snobby lot,' Hannah remarked.

She touched Nell's hair. It felt soft and silky. 'Well, I like it, Nell.'

She turned to Bessie, who had now sunk into a chair beside the table and dropped her head into her hands. Heaving sobs shook her shoulders. The two girls glanced at each other and then hurried to her, standing one on either side and bending over her. Tommy, who had come in with Nell, pushed his way between Hannah and the table to lay his head on Bessie's lap and clutch at her knees. 'Nanna, Nanna . . .' His chubby face threatened to dissolve into tears too.

'Auntie Bessie, don't take on so,' Nell tried to reassure her. 'I'm not offended, honestly I'm not. I'd sooner you told me the truth an' if that's what you think then . . .'

But Bessie was shaking her head violently. She sat up, dabbed her eyes with the corner of her apron and pulled the little boy onto her knee to cuddle him. 'There, there,' she crooned. 'It's only your old Nanna being silly.'

Hannah poured out a cup of tea and set it on the table. 'Here, drink this. You, too, Nell. Sit down, supper'll soon be ready.'

'I should explain,' Bessie said supping her tea.

'No need,' Nell said, patting her hair with pride. 'I'm taking no notice of you anyway.'

With that, they all laughed again, but Bessie couldn't let the matter rest there. 'No, no, I shouldn't have blurted it out. Not like that, but you see it – it reminded me . . .'

She glanced uncomfortably at Hannah, took a deep breath and said, 'I wasn't entirely truthful with you, love, when you first came back. Oh, I don't mean I lied to you, but . . . but I just didn't tell you everything about my own family.' She rested her cheek against the top of Tommy's dark head and closed her eyes. 'I was too ashamed,' she whispered.

'Ashamed? You, Auntie Bessie? Whatever do you mean?'

'Do you remember, when you first came back 'ere you was asking about all my family and what had happened to them and where they were?'

Hannah nodded.

'And I told you about our Peggy running off with a young lad, going to live with his family and that I hadn't heard anything about her from that day to this?'

'Yes,' Hannah whispered.

'Well, that was the bit that wasn't quite true. She did run off with him and she did move in with him, but only for a while.' She was silent for a long moment whilst Hannah and Nell waited. 'I . . . I saw her just the once about two years later, hanging around in a rough part of the town. I wasn't sure it was her at first, because . . . because she'd dyed her hair.' She glanced apologetically at Nell once again. 'That same colour.' Bessie paused again and then continued. 'I was just about to go up to her and say, "Come home, love, and we'll say no more about it," but . . . but just before I could, I saw her go up to this toff, smiling all coyly at him, bold as yer like. They spoke for a minute and then . . . then she put her arm through his and they . . . they went off together.' Bessie closed her eyes at the agony of her memory. 'I should have chased after her. Stopped her there and then. Dragged her home by her awful hair and locked her in. But I didn't. I couldn't take it in. Not then. And then it was too late. I couldn't find her again even though I tramped the streets for several nights looking for her. But do you know the worst thing?' Her voice fell to an unhappy whisper. 'I couldn't help thinking that I was glad my Bill wasn't alive to see what his daughter had become. Now how could I have thought such a thing? How *could* I have ever been glad he wasn't here any more?' Fresh tears flowed as she looked up again at Nell, seeking her understanding, her forgiveness. 'I'm sorry, love.'

Nell smiled a little pensively now. 'It's all right, Auntie Bessie.' She sighed heavily. 'Maybe I'm not much better. I'm a fallen woman, after all.'

'No, no, don't say that,' Hannah cried, putting her arms around her friend. 'I won't let you. You must have loved Mr Edmund and thought he loved you. Just like my mother believed Jimmy Gregory loved her.'

Nell laughed wryly. 'Aye, but I should've known better. I knew I wasn't the first, but you always think it'll be different for you. That they really love you, that you can change them. But you can't,' she added bitterly. Then raising her cup, she echoed Hannah's favourite saying. 'A curse on all good-looking men.'

'And does that include Jim?' Hannah put in slyly, her blue eyes sparkling with mischief.

'Oh, my goodness,' Bessie cried. 'Whatever will he say when he sees you?'

And with that, the three of them burst out laughing, with little Tommy chortling too – even though he didn't understand a word of what they'd been saying.

To Bessie's surprise, Jim was full of compliments for Nell's new hair colour. 'I like it,' he told her truthfully. 'It suits you.'

And though they all heard Bessie's disapproving sniff, this time she kept her lips firmly pressed together.

'You don't think I look like a . . .' Nell cast a wicked glance at Bessie. 'A lady of the night?'

'Wha—?' Jim's eyes widened and for a moment he looked angry. 'Well, if you do, then so do my mother and my sister, because their hair's that colour. Only difference is, they were born with it. All you've done is to give nature a helping hand.' His tone became firm, indignant. 'Don't ever say that about yourself again, you hear me?'

'Yes, Jim.' Nell lowered her head, hiding her bubbling laughter as she saw the consternation on Bessie's face.

And there the matter might have ended, if it hadn't been for Jim's final remark on the subject. 'It does make you look different. I almost didn't know you when you opened the door.' Then he touched her cheek with a gentle gesture. 'But you're still my Nell.'

Hannah stared at her friend, seeing her suddenly through the eyes of others. Yes, it had altered her. If someone who hadn't seen her for a few years met her now, would they even recognize her? Hannah wondered. And without her being conscious of it, the germ of an idea – a daring, dangerous idea – was implanted in Hannah's mind.

Thirty-Three

Hannah, Nell and Tommy had been living with Bessie for almost two years when Jim finally proposed to Nell.

'You're a lucky girl,' Bessie assured her. 'He's a fine young man and . . .' She had been about to say more, but bit her lip and looked away.

Gently, Nell added, 'And he's a good 'un to take me *and* Tommy on. Is that what you were going to say, Auntie Bessie?'

'Well . . .' the older woman was embarrassed, flustered now.

'But you're right,' Nell said. 'To take on Edmund Critchlow's bastard as his own takes a real man, a good man. I know that. And when we're married, he's going to adopt Tommy, all legal like, so that he'll have Jim's surname.'

'Aw, Nell, love. That's wonderful. Have you . . . have you . . . ?' Again Bessie's voice faltered. Whilst she was happy for the young couple and for the child, their marriage would take them away from her. She'd come to love them as her own, especially the little boy whose endearing ways had won her heart. It'd be another loss that would be hard to bear.

'In about a month's time. We thought on Tommy's second birthday in December. Just a quiet do. After all, I've no family and Jim's only got his mother and his sister and maybe his colleagues from the station.'

Bessie tried to smile, but she couldn't hide the bleak look in her eyes. But Nell was grinning broadly. 'Oh, you're not going to get rid of us that easy, if that's what you're hoping,' she teased, knowing full well Bessie was wishing for anything but that. She moved and put her arm around Bessie's ample shoulders and hugged her close. 'There's a house down the end of this very street to rent. It's belongs to a mill owner, of course, but the old lady who lived there's just died and—'

Bessie nodded. 'Oh yes, I know who you mean. But her son works in the garret, doesn't he? What's going to happen to him?'

'He's married and they live next door to his wife's parents.' Nell's eyes sparkled. 'Luckily for us, she doesn't want to move, so he can still go on renting the garret and we can live downstairs. Jim's sorted it all out with the mill owner and he's paid a month's rent up front and it's ours from the first of December. We'll be married on that very day. Just think,' she went on, her eyes sparkling. 'We'll be in our very own home for Christmas, and you and Hannah must spend Christmas Day with us.'

As Bessie opened her mouth to protest, Nell added, 'And we won't take "no" for an answer. So there!'

Bessie's face was a picture of happiness. 'Then I'll still see Tommy if you're only down the street. You'll still let him come and see me?'

Nell laughed. 'More than that. I was going to ask you if you'd look after him whilst I carry on working for a bit.'

Bessie's eyes widened. 'Jim doesn't mind you still going to the Gregorys?'

'Not if Mrs Gregory will let me go just daily.

313

Besides, it's not long now until the lad goes to school and they get a governess for the little girl. I always knew the job wouldn't last for ever. Mind you, madam asks me to do a lot more for her now. Says I have a way with clothes and such.' She touched her hair a little self-consciously. 'So she might want me to continue as her lady's maid. The one she's got at the moment is less than useless – worse than the girl that was there. You should hear her shouting at her.' She laughed. 'But she never shouts at me.'

Listening to the conversation, Hannah pulled a face. 'She wouldn't dare!'

Nell had the grace to nod and say, 'That's true, 'cos I'd only shout back and walk out, and one thing she can't abide is having to look after the kids herself.'

Bessie gave a snort of disapproval. 'Some women don't know when they're well off. She doesn't know how lucky she is.'

Nell's face was sober. 'They tried to take Tommy away from me, y'know.' Hannah and Bessie stared at her. 'Told me it would be a lot better for him if I let some nice, well-to-do family adopt him. That he'd have a much better chance in life than being brought up in the workhouse.' Bessie and Hannah exchanged a glance but said nothing, allowing Nell to unburden a guilt that had lain heavily on her. 'Maybe I should've done.' She looked at the other two, tears in her eyes. 'Was I being selfish, hanging onto him?'

'No, no, you weren't,' Bessie was swift to reassure her. 'You have to do what you think best. A lot of girls in your position would've let him go and who's to say they weren't right?' Her mouth tightened. 'A lot of 'em are forced into it, either by their families or by the authorities. They don't want to give up their babies, but they're left with no choice. In fact, they're not *given* the choice.'

'I know,' Nell nodded. 'There was one poor girl in there who was desperate to keep her baby, no matter what, but they actually snatched him out of her arms and carried him off to give to some well-off pair.'

'Huh!' Hannah said bitterly. 'Another of Goodbody's schemes. I dare bet he was paid handsomely.' She glanced at Nell. 'How come he let you keep Tommy then?'

Nell smiled sheepishly. 'He knew who the father was. It was Edmund Critchlow had me sent back to the workhouse when I told him I was carrying his child. I think Goodbody was a bit unsure what to do to be right. Whatever he did could've put him on the wrong side of Edmund. So he chose to let sleeping dogs lie. He did nothing. Oh, he tried to persuade *me* to give Tommy away, but no, he didn't force me.'

'Well, you've turned out lucky, Nell. You've found a good man who'll love you *and* your son.'

'Yes, yes, I have,' Nell said, 'But I'd never've had the chance to meet him if it hadn't been for you and Hannah getting me out of that place.' Her voice was soft with love and gratitude not only for Jim, but for Bessie and Hannah too.

'Oh, go on with you.' Bessie flapped her away, pretending embarrassment, but secretly she was heart-warmed. Then, playfully, she wagged her forefinger at the girl. 'Just so long as you don't ever take little Tommy away from me.'

*

Nell's wedding was a quiet affair, but Bessie and Hannah had managed to scrape enough money together to give Nell a wedding breakfast at home, and to Nell's astonished delight, Mrs Gregory had given her one of her old dresses to turn into a grand wedding dress.

She and Hannah sat far into the night, cutting and fitting and stitching.

It was a merry party that returned to the house in Paradise Street, where Bessie and Hannah had put on a spread fit for a queen.

'Going to invite the neighbours in then, Bessie?' Flo Harris was hovering on the doorstep.

''Course we are,' Bessie said happily.

Flo sniffed. 'Thought the likes of us weren't welcome, seein' as how we didn't get an invite to attend the service.'

'You didn't need no invite if you'd wanted to come. Free entrance at the church,' Bessie retorted. Then she relented, adding, 'Oh, come on in, Flo and stop moaning for once in your life. And tell anyone else down the street, they're very welcome if they want to come in.'

'Ta, Bessie.' Flo smiled. 'I will.'

Half an hour later, it seemed as if half the street was crammed into Bessie's terraced house. But her neighbours came with whatever little gift they could spare: pots and pans, bed linen for the young couple's new home and all sorts of useful items. One old man, a widower, gave Nell an apron that had been his wife's. Handing it to her, he said, 'If you look after your man as well as my dear wife cared for me and our young 'uns, you'll not go far wrong, lass.'

With a lump in her throat, Nell kissed the old man's leathery cheek.

When they'd all eaten and drunk their fill and tottered back through the dusk to their own homes, there came a moment of awkwardness.

'Well, be off with you then, the pair of you,' Bessie said with brusque fondness. 'You can leave Tommy here for the night. He'll be all right with me 'n' Hannah. It won't be much of a honeymoon, but you ought to have your wedding night to yourselves.' She pulled the little lad onto her lap and cuddled him close. 'You'll be all right with your Nanna, won't you, my little man?'

The little boy, wearied by the day's excitement, put his thumb in his mouth, leaned against her and promptly fell asleep. The grown-ups chuckled softly and Jim, with a tender gesture, touched the boy's hair. 'That's good of you, Mrs Morgan. We'll fetch him in the morning.'

'No hurry,' Bessie said.

Nell laughed softly. 'For two pins I reckon she'd keep him.' Above the child's head Bessie and Nell exchanged a fond look. They both knew there was more than a mite of truth in Nell's teasing statement.

Jim put his arm around his bride's shoulders. 'Come on then, Mrs Smith. High time I carried you across that threshold.'

There were kisses and farewells all round and Nell joked, 'Anyone'd think we were emigrating to the other side of the world.' But even so, she gave Hannah an extra fond hug.

'Thanks, Hannah, for everything,' she whispered. 'But for you I'd still be locked up in that place.'

'And but for you,' Hannah murmured in return, 'I might not have survived those first few weeks at the mill, especially after Jane . . .'

'You would. You're a fighter. A survivor. Whatever you want in life, you'll get. Just be careful that you don't get hurt yourself, that's all.' She pulled back a little and looked into her friend's eyes. 'There's something still brewing in that head of yours. Something that one day you're going to do. I can see it. Sometimes you get this far away look in your eye and it frightens me, Hannah, 'cos when it happens you look so grim and determined, I know someone, somewhere, is in for it.'

Hannah tried to laugh it off, but she was startled at her friend's perception. Oh yes, she had a secret and yes, someone was going to be in for it, as Nell said. In for it good and proper, if Hannah had her way.

One day, Edmund Critchlow was going to be made to pay.

'You know, it surprises me that you haven't found yourself a boyfriend before now,' Bessie said as she and Hannah sat before the range late that night with just the glow from the fire to light the room. After an exciting and busy day, they were content to sit warming their feet against the fender. Tommy was fast asleep upstairs and they would soon be joining him. But for the moment they were enjoying the cosiness of there just being the two of them. 'If I'm honest –' Bessie chuckled – 'I'd've thought you'd have found a feller before Nell. 'Cos when young Jim first started calling, I thought it was you he was coming to see.'

'I think he did at first, but only out of kindness. I think him and that nice constable at the station wanted to know I was all right. But once he set eyes on Nell . . .' Hannah laughed.

'And you don't mind?' Bessie asked seriously.

Hannah shook her head. 'Oh no. Not a bit. I like Jim ever so much, but . . . but he wasn't for me.'

For a brief moment she closed her eyes and she could see Luke's face in her mind's eye, see them running hand in hand up the hills above the mill, could almost feel the wind in her hair.

'You still haven't forgotten that lad at the mill, 'ave you?' Bessie said softly. Her face, illuminated by the soft glow from the fire, was full of sympathy.

'No,' Hannah said huskily. 'I don't suppose I'll ever forget him.'

'Don't spend your life grieving for him, love. He wouldn't have wanted that, would he?'

Hannah sighed. 'I don't suppose so.' She was on the point of confiding in Bessie, on the point of confessing that one day she intended to go back to the mill, when a knock came at the back door.

Bessie gave an irritated tut. 'Now who can this be at this time of night?'

'Sit still,' Hannah said, jumping up. 'I'll go. And whoever it is, they'll get a piece of my mind, disturbing folks this late.'

She threw the door open, an angry remark ready on her lips. Flo Harris, her arms folded across her thin chest, stood there. 'Is Bessie still up? There's summat I have to tell 'er.'

'Can't it wait till morning? We're both dead on our feet. We've been up since five.'

'No, it won't wait. An' she won't want it to when she hears what I've got to tell her.'

Hannah sighed. 'You'd better come in, then.'

Flo marched into the house, pushing her way past Hannah. There was a strange air of suppressed excitement about her. Whatever it was, she couldn't wait to tell it, but, following her into the room, Hannah had the uncomfortable feeling that this was not going to be pleasant news for Bessie. Flo was triumphant. Yes, that was the word. Triumphant.

'Hello, Flo.' Bessie, despite her tiredness, raised a cheery smile of welcome for her neighbour. 'What brings you round at this time of night when most good folks are in their beds?'

'Ah, now you've hit the nail right on the head there, Bessie Morgan.' Flo stood on the hearthrug in front of Bessie. 'When all *good* folks should be in their beds.'

'Oh, sit down, do, Flo. I'm getting a crick in me neck looking up at yer.'

Hannah closed the door quietly and came to stand behind Bessie's chair whilst Flo took the one near the fire where Hannah had been sitting.

'So? What's this important news that won't wait till morning?'

Flo leaned forward and her eyes gleamed with jubilance. 'I've seen your Peggy.'

Thirty-Four

For a moment there was utter silence in the room, then Bessie gave a cry and fell back in the chair. Swiftly, Hannah knelt beside her. 'Auntie Bessie, are you all right?' Even in the shadowy light from the fire, the girl could see that Bessie had turned pale and she was holding the palm of her hand flat against her chest as if she had a pain.

Angrily, Hannah turned to Flo. 'Why did you blurt it out like that? You could've been a bit more tactful.'

'Huh! Sorry, I spoke,' Flo said, making as if to get up and leave, but Hannah stood up and pushed her back into her chair. Standing over her, she said in a threatening tone, 'Oh no, you stay right where you are and tell us it all.'

'When . . . when did you see her?' Bessie gasped, still holding her chest. 'And where?'

Flo settled back, enjoying her moment of glory. She was sure of their full attention now. 'It was near the pub. I'd just gone to fetch Harry his pint. He has one every night 'afore 'ee goes to bed. Just the one, mind you, I wouldn't like you to think 'ee's a drinker.'

If the situation had not been so fraught, Bessie might well have laughed out loud at this. The whole street knew that Harry Harris spent most evenings in the pub and only staggered home at closing time. The

321

jug of beer that Flo fetched most nights from the pub in the street round the corner was for herself.

'Get on with it,' Hannah muttered through clenched teeth.

'She was hanging about outside the pub. Waiting for the fellers to come out.'

'What feller?' Hannah snapped.

Flo smirked. 'Any feller'd do, long as 'ee'd still got the price for a bit of you-know-what left in his pocket. Shouldn't be allowed. This is a decent neighbourhood, this is.'

'I know very well what my daughter is,' Bessie retorted, 'but you can't resist any chance to rub it in, can you?'

Flo laughed. 'Not my fault if I've heard tales, is it? She's been seen in some of the worst parts of Manchester and—'

'I think you've said enough, Mrs Harris,' Hannah interrupted. 'We'll bid you goodnight.' She grasped the woman's arm and hauled her to her feet.

''Ere, 'ere, what do you think you're doing?'

'I'm showing you the door, that's what I'm doing. Now you've done your dirty work, you can go.'

'Dirty work, is it? It's not me doing the dirty work. I thought Bessie would want to know.'

'Mebbe she does and mebbe she doesn't. Like I said, you could've done it in a lot kinder way. You've about given her a heart attack, by the look of her. So I'll be obliged if you'll leave. Now!'

Flo thrust her face close to Hannah's. 'You're a fine one to be handing out your orders like Lady Muck. Just remember who *you* are. Your mother weren't no better than her Peggy.'

'My mother's dead and buried. You leave her out

of this,' Hannah spat back. 'And I don't need no reminding of what I am, so there's nothing you can say that can hurt me. But you've hurt Bessie, so I hope you're proud of yourself. Go on, get out of here.'

'I'm going. And don't ask any favours of me again.'

'There's no fear of that.'

When the door banged behind her, Hannah turned to bend over Bessie. 'You all right?'

Bessie struggled to sit up. 'Aye,' she said heavily. 'Right as I'll ever be.' She clutched Hannah's hand. 'Oh, Hannah, love. Go up the street and see if you can see her, will yer?' Tears spilled down Bessie's face. 'Bring her back here, Hannah. If you find her, bring her home.'

Hannah patted her hand. ''Course I will.'

She hurried to take down her shawl from the peg behind the back door and run round the corner and along the street towards the Brewer's Arms. But there was no one standing in the shadows near the doorway. Hannah looked up and down the neighbouring streets, searching this way and that. But there was no one that could possibly be Peggy. The dark, wet streets were deserted except for the distant figure of a man, weaving his way unsteadily homewards.

Hannah bit her lip. It was almost closing time and she didn't want to be caught hanging about on the street corner. Then she made a sudden decision. She marched boldly up to the door of the tavern, pushed it open and stepped inside into the fog of pipe smoke, into the midst of the raucous laugher and the smell of ale.

Only women of a certain sort ever entered a public bar. Even Flo would go to the back door of the public house with her jug and wait there for the landlord to serve her nightly pint to her. The conversation stuttered and died, and Hannah found that every eye in the room full of men turned towards her. The big landlord stepped out from behind the bar and came towards her.

'Now, love, no offence, but I don't allow your sort in my pub. Out you go.'

He made to take hold of her arm, but Hannah said, 'I just came in to look for someone.'

'I bet you did, but like I say—'

'No, no, you don't understand. I'm looking for a girl.'

'Well, she's not here, love. I promise you that.'

Another man reeled his way towards her. ''Sall right, Dan. I'll look after her. And yes, yes, I'll tek her out. Now, my pretty one,' he leered at Hannah. 'Looking for company, are yer?'

The landlord turned away with a shake of his head and the buzz of conversation rose again, as the drinkers lost interest.

Hannah eyed the man now holding her arm with distaste and then suddenly, an idea came to her. She smiled. 'Isn't that what I'm supposed to ask you?' she said pertly, putting her hand on her hip and swaying provocatively. The man's smile broadened, showing a mouth of blackened and missing teeth. He put his arm around Hannah's waist and pulled her to him. Sickened by the stench of body odour and sour breath, she steeled herself not to repulse him. 'I'm looking for a friend of mine. Peggy. Someone told me she was here. Have you seen her?'

The man shook his head. 'Naw, but don't let's bother about her, my beauty. Let's go out the back.' He gave a sniff. 'Some places'd let us go upstairs. But not this landlord. Won't 'ave no goings-on on his premises, he says. He keeps an orderly house, does Dan.'

Hannah could not prevent the gleam in her eye at being given such information, but the man misunderstood it and made to pull her towards the door.

'But there's a nice little backyard 'ee's got, and whilst he's busy in 'ere . . .'

Hannah smiled into his face. 'Let me go first and see if the coast's clear.'

He grinned again. 'Tha's a good idea. Don't want to disturb anyone,' he leered. 'Or be disturbed, my lovely, do we?'

She pulled herself from his grasp and made for the door. Ribald laughter followed her, but, her heart thumping, she hurried round the corner and into the back yard of the pub. She leaned against the wall for a moment, her heart pounding, her palms sweating. The stench of the man still in her nostrils was making her want to retch. But her concern, her love, for Bessie drove her on into untold danger. If the man should choose to come after her, she was trapped with no one to lift a finger to help her.

As her eyes became accustomed to the darkness, she could see that there was no one there. There were two doors leading into low buildings across the yard and she opened each one, peering inside. They were cluttered storerooms but there was no one there.

Like a thief in the night, Hannah stole back round the corner. Not daring to linger, she picked up her skirts and ran past the barroom entrance and all the way back to Bessie's house, not feeling safe until she was inside and leaning against the closed door.

'Hannah? Is that you?' came Bessie's anxious,

quivering voice. Hannah moved forward into the room. 'Yes, it's me. I'm sorry, Auntie Bessie, but she's gone. I couldn't find her.' Swiftly, without dwelling too long on the detail of the man accosting her, Hannah explained. 'I went into the pub and even round the back, but she wasn't there.'

Bessie lay back in her chair and groaned. 'So close, so close and we've missed her.'

'Maybe she'll come another night. I . . . I could go again.' She didn't relish the idea, but she would do anything for Bessie.

Bessie let out a long, hopeless sigh. 'I don't reckon she'll come again. Maybe . . . maybe she came to . . . to look for her dad. He used to go on down to the pub sometimes. Just on a Saturday night. Maybe . . . maybe she hoped to see him.'

'Her dad?' Hannah was shocked. 'But . . . d'you mean she doesn't know about . . . about her dad?'

Bessie shook her head. 'Far as I know, she doesn't know he's dead. She'd gone before then.'

'Oh.' Hannah was thoughtful. An idea began to form in her mind, but she forbore from telling Bessie.

She had the feeling that the older woman would not be happy about it. Not happy at all.

'I need your help. I'm sorry to ask and if you feel you can't do it, Jim, because of your position an' all, I'll understand.'

'This sounds very mysterious, Hannah. Come inside and have a cup of tea with us. Nell is just home from work and I'm not on duty until ten o'clock tonight. Tommy's in bed, so you can talk freely – whatever it is. Is it Bessie? Not ill, is she?' All the time he was asking questions he was ushering her through from the front door, through their parlour, at present sparsely furnished, into the cosy kitchen at the back of the terraced house.

'Hannah!' Nell exclaimed, hugging her as if she hadn't seen her for weeks instead of only days. Whilst Nell excitedly showed her round the house and all that they had done in the short space of time, Hannah held herself in check, even though she was bursting to confide in Jim and ask his advice, ask for his help.

At last they sat down, grouped in front of the cosy fire in the range.

'Now,' Jim said, gently but firmly interrupting his wife's prattling. 'How can I help you, Hannah?'

'I'd better tell you the whole story . . .' Launching into her tale, she began by telling Jim about the night Nell had come home with her hair dyed and Bessie's outraged reaction. Nell nodded, taking up Hannah's story. 'She scared me a bit. I really thought I looked like some woman of the streets, but it turned out it was because her daughter, Peggy, had dyed her hair and . . .' Nell shot a look at Hannah. 'By all accounts, that's exactly what Peggy had become. Bessie said she'd heard bits of gossip over the years and, you could tell, she was so sad about it.' Nell paused and looked questioningly at Hannah. 'So, has something happened?'

Hannah nodded. 'The day you got married. We were just going to bed after a lovely day.' She smiled fondly at the happy couple, who exchanged a bashful glance. 'And who should come knocking at the door but Flo Harris. She couldn't wait to impart a juicy bit of gossip. She said she'd seen Peggy hanging around near the Brewer's Arms, waiting for the fellers coming

327

out, she said. Her and her vicious tongue . . .' Hannah paused a moment, imagining what she'd like to do to Flo Harris, given half a chance. Then she went on, recounting the events of that night. 'And since then,' she ended, 'Bessie's been sunk in despair. It's awful to see her. I just want to do something to help her. I want to find Peggy.'

Jim was thoughtful. 'If she's still here in the town, it mightn't be too difficult. We know most of the girls, but there's not many stay long.' He grinned. 'Not much business in this town. We move 'em on as quick as they come, that's if we can't actually arrest them. Now, if you were to say she'd been seen in one of the big cities . . .'

'She was – I mean Flo reckoned she'd been seen in Manchester.'

'Mmm, now that might be more difficult, 'cos it's a big place.'

'Bessie said she might have been looking for her dad. He used to go to that pub when . . . when he was alive.'

Now it was Nell's turn to be shocked and she repeated the very same words that Hannah had said to Bessie. 'You mean she doesn't even know her dad's dead?'

Hannah shook her head. 'Bessie thinks not.'

Nell turned to Jim. 'Oh, poor Bessie – and poor Peggy. Never mind what she's become. She was hurt by some feller and too proud to come home, I bet.' Nell touched her husband's hand. 'Not everyone's been as lucky as me,' she said huskily, 'to find someone big enough to forgive past mistakes. Jim, we have to help Hannah find her. For Bessie's sake, if nothing else.'

'But I do understand, Jim, if you can't,' Hannah put in, anxiously. 'I wouldn't expect you to risk your job.'

'No, no, I'll mind I don't do that. We're not just there to run folks in, you know. We try to help where we can.'

Hannah smiled. She, more than anyone, knew that. 'And if it's helping some poor girl off the streets, then I suppose it could be classed as part of my job.' He grinned, his kind face crinkling. 'I'll ask around. Ask my colleagues. I'll look at the charge book, an' all. See if she's ever been brought in.'

'Do you think she might be using another name though?' Hannah suggested. 'I know I would if I'd . . . if I'd . . .' She faltered. Far from condemning Peggy, Hannah was thinking, *there, but for this kind policeman and Bessie, I might have gone*. She saw, so clearly, that if she hadn't had a little help from caring people at the right moment, her life now might be very different.

Jim was wrinkling his brow thoughtfully. 'You could be right at that. D'you have a description of her? D'you know what she looks like?'

Hannah shook her head. Nell, despite the gravity of their conversation, couldn't help laughing. 'I know one thing, she's got red hair.' The other two stared at her for a moment and then joined in her laughter. It eased the tension and drove away some of the sadness. They were suddenly filled with more hope. The two girls had more faith in Jim than perhaps he had himself, but in turn, he had colleagues he could enlist in his search.

'We'll find her,' he said. 'We'll bring her home. But not a word to Bessie, Hannah. I don't want to raise her hopes until we have definite news.'

Thirty-Five

The days passed with agonizing slowness for Hannah and Nell, but each time when Jim returned home, he shook his head sadly. 'No news, love. I'm sorry, she must have left the town. The lads have kept an eye open for her, but she's skipping out of sight as soon as a policeman comes along. They do, you know, they just melt away into the shadows. I don't know how they do it.'

Nell sighed sadly. 'If you ask me, their whole lives are spent living in the shadows. I suppose the only alternative for them is the workhouse and they chose the way they did.' She paused a moment and then added bitterly, 'Can't say I blame 'em in some ways.'

Jim looked at his wife thoughtfully. Nell was loved and cared for now. She was plump and rosy cheeked, with her shining hair neatly coiled, her apron crisply starched. But it hadn't always been so. He knew a little about her past, as much as she had been able to bring herself to tell him. But he never pried, never demanded explanations. He loved her unconditionally for the girl she was now. But even though he had no conceit, he could see that her life could have been very different.

Silently, Jim vowed to redouble his efforts to find the missing Peggy. There was only one way he could think of; he would go out on his nights off in his own clothes. He would act like a man in search of female company, the kind of company to be found waiting on street corners.

But first, he knew he must confide in his older colleague. Much as he wanted to help find the girl, he was determined not to risk his career and the happiness of his little family to do so.

'Ah, well, now lad, I don't know about that,' Constable Robinson said when Jim told him of his plans. 'You could be getting yourself into a bit of bother doing that.' He chewed on his lower lip thoughtfully. 'Does it mean so much to Hannah and this – er – Mrs Morgan, is it?' He still remembered Hannah with affection. He'd been taken with the golden-haired girl with the startlingly blue eyes.

'Yes, it does,' Jim answered. 'Peggy's Mrs Morgan's daughter.'

'Ah.' The older man was suddenly full of understanding. He had daughters of his own and whilst he was obliged in his job to take a firm line with prostitutes, he was often filled with a great sadness. Some of them were hard-nut cases, loud-mouthed, vulgar and beyond sympathy, but for a few, it was the only way they knew how to survive and he could find it in his big heart to pity them. 'Tell you what, lad. I'll have to clear it with the inspector, but I don't want you going out on your own. I'll fix it so you an' me get some nights off together and I'll come with you.'

Jim stared at him. 'You'd do that?'

'Aye lad, I would. Call it my good deed for the day.' He grinned 'But not a word to the wife, mind. Far as she need be concerned, it's all in the line of duty.'

*

Jim and Constable Robinson tramped the streets on their nights off for several weeks. Not knowing anything of the efforts going on to find her daughter, Bessie grew more and more despondent, sinking further into silent misery.

Christmas had come and gone. Bessie had made a valiant attempt to rouse herself for the sake of the others, but her heart wasn't in merrymaking. And despite their own efforts, Bessie's sadness put a damper on all their spirits. Hannah, Nell and Jim discussed the matter endlessly, but they could think of nothing else to do other than what was already being done.

'I was so hoping she'd appear again at the pub round the corner on a Saturday night. But maybe, if it was her dad she was looking for, her courage failed her to do it again.'

'Or maybe someone at the pub told her he's dead,' Jim suggested.

Hannah sighed. 'I never thought of that. You could be right.'

There was silence until Jim said, 'Well, we're not giving up hope just yet. Mr Robinson is willing to carry on a bit longer and so am I.'

'Thank him for us, won't you, Jim?' Hannah said quietly.

Jim smiled and nodded.

On the next Saturday night following their talk, Hannah was restless. She couldn't explain why, but she couldn't sit still. She had to get out of the house. She felt stifled and edgy. She reached for her shawl from the peg. 'I'm just going to get a breath of air, Auntie Bessie, and I might pop into Nell's for half an hour, so don't wait up for me.'

Bessie, sitting staring into the fire, didn't seem to

hear her. Hannah sighed. Normally, such a remark might have been met with a teasing, 'Now don't you go keeping those lovebirds from their bed,' but now, there was nothing. Not even a warning to be careful out and about in the frosty darkness of the January night.

Hannah slipped out of the house and, pulling her shawl closely about her, walked around the corner. For some inexplicable reason she was being drawn towards the pub. She saw a figure walking towards her and her heartbeat quickened. But then, with a stab of disappointment, she saw that it was Flo.

''Evenin', Mrs Harris,' she forced herself to say cheerily, and she heard the woman sniff.

'Going to work, are you, love?' Flo asked sarcastically.

'Not tonight. Too cold to be hanging around street corners. Thought I'd give it a miss tonight.'

To her delight, she heard Flo gasp, 'Well, I never . . .'

In the darkness, Hannah grinned and walked on. It'd be all round the street tomorrow.

As she drew nearer the pub, her steps slowed, but taking a deep breath, she approached the door and pushed it open. Once more she was met by the stale smell of smoke and drink. One or two glanced up to see who'd come in, but this time the buzz of conversation never faltered. Hannah glanced round swiftly, anxious not to linger. She was about to turn and scan the other side of the bar room when she felt someone take hold of her arm and a rough voice speak close to her ear.

'I wondered when I'd catch up wi' you. Run out on me, would yer?'

Hannah twisted round to face the ugly face of the man from whom she had escaped the last time.

'Hello.' Hannah smiled brightly. 'Where did you get to?'

'What d'yer mean – where did I get to? It was you scarpered. I waited ages. Right till closing time.' His grip on her arm tightened. 'You want teaching a lesson, that's what you want.'

Hannah tried to twist herself free, but his grip was as tight as a man-trap as he began to drag her towards the door. Now Hannah was really frightened. 'Let go of me. I'm not what you think. I won't—'

'Oh yes, you will. Lead me on, would yer?'

'Let me go,' Hannah shouted now, her voice rising above the babble of conversation, which at the sound of her terrified tones lessened, and Hannah felt everyone's eyes turn in their direction. 'Let me go!'

'Old Sid 'aving to drag 'em in off the streets now, is he? He's too ugly even for the regular girls,' someone guffawed.

'Get 'er out of here, Sid,' the landlord called, but before he could weave his way amongst the tables to reach them, another voice spoke from behind, a soft, much younger voice.

'Let her go, Sid. She's not one of us.'

Sid gave a growl and turned to face the red-haired girl standing behind him. Hannah glanced at her too and her heart skipped a beat. The girl's face was unnaturally white and her cheeks were reddened. She wore a low-cut silk dress that had once been rather grand, but was now grubby and stained. But it was her eyes that tore at Hannah's heart. They were lifeless, defeated and hopeless. Here was a girl who had sunk to the very depths of degradation and could see no way out, except death. The girl smiled at Hannah, but the smile did not reach her eyes. 'I saw you come in here and knew you'd be in trouble. The landlord doesn't allow women in here. Go on, love. Go home. This is no place for you.'

Her voice faltered and now she stared hard at Hannah, almost as if she half recognized her. But Hannah had already guessed who she was. 'Peggy? It is Peggy, isn't it?'

The girls gasped in surprise. Beside them, the man was forgotten as the two girls stared at each other. 'Hannah? Is it – Hannah?'

'Yes, yes, it is.' Scarcely aware that the man still had a firm grasp on her, Hannah touched Peggy's arm. 'I'm so glad I've found you. We've been looking for you.'

'Looking for *me*?' She was shocked to think anyone could care enough.

'Yes,' Hannah said gently. 'We – we heard you'd been here. Some weeks back. We've been looking for you ever since.'

Tentatively, afraid of the answer, Peggy said, 'Who's "we"?'

'Your-mam and me. And two other friends, an' all.' She forbore to say that one was a policeman. She was afraid that Peggy would disappear into the night without a trace.

Peggy was shaking her head. 'No, you can't mean that. They can't want to know me. Not now,' she added sadly.

'Look, are you two going to stand gossiping all night? This girl—' Sid began, but Peggy rounded on him.

'Leave go of her, Sid. Like I said, she's not one of us. I'll see you later.'

'Oh no, you won't,' Hannah said firmly. 'You're coming home with me.'

'Oho, party time, is it?' Sid leered. 'I could fancy a threesome.'

Now the two girls faced him together. 'Go away, Sid.'

Those sitting close by, listening with avid interest to what was going on, laughed. 'Come on, Sid, leave 'em alone. You're not going to get anywhere.'

Grumbling to himself, the man at last released his grip on Hannah's arm. Absentmindedly, she rubbed her arm where his fingers had bitten into her flesh. She'd have a right old bruise there tomorrow, but she didn't care.

She'd found Peggy.

'Come on,' she said, taking hold of Peggy's arm, gently but firmly. 'You're coming home.'

As they walked along the street, Peggy said hesitantly, 'Are you sure this is a good idea? They won't want me. None of 'em. And my brothers will kill me.'

'Then why did you come to the pub so close to home? You must have been hoping for – for something.'

'I just wanted to see me dad. Not to speak to him, just to see him. I heard he'd been hurt at work not long after – after I left. I just wanted to know if he was all right.' Hannah stopped and touched the girl's arm. 'Peggy – there's something you should know. There've been a lot of changes since you left.'

Peggy stared at her through the darkness. 'Oh no!' she breathed, guessing at once that it was bad news. 'Me dad, don't say me dad . . .'

'I'm afraid so. I'm so sorry. And all the rest of the family've left home. Your mam's living on her own. At least, she was until I came back.'

It took Peggy, reeling from the shocking news, a few moments to realize what Hannah had said. 'Oh yes, I remember now. You and your poor mother got turned out of your house. Mam was distraught about it.'

Hannah sighed. 'There's a lot happened in the last few years. An awful lot to tell you, but come on.' She linked her arm through Peggy's and drew her towards her old home. 'Your mam is going to be so happy to see you.'

'Are you sure, Hannah?' Peggy said doubtfully. 'Are you really sure?'

Hannah was sure and her certainty was rewarded the moment she opened the door and pushed a hesitant Peggy into the room. 'Look who I've found,' she called out. Bessie looked round and her eyes lit up. She levered herself up and lumbered, arms outstretched and tears pouring down her cheeks, towards her daughter. 'Oh, Peggy! Peggy, love.'

The girl gave a sob, 'Oh, Mam,' and fell into her arms.

Quietly, Hannah turned and slipped out into the night again, but this time she turned down the street towards Nell's home. She must tell them the good news.

Thirty-Six

Bessie was happier than she had been in years. She still mourned her beloved husband, but now she had her daughter returned to her as if from the dead. And she cared not one jot for the gossiping neighbours.

It soon became apparent that Peggy's way of life had affected her health: her skin was sallow and blotchy and she was painfully thin.

'She's nowt but skin and bone,' Bessie whispered to Hannah. 'We'll have to feed her up. Look after her.' Bessie glanced at Hannah, a question in her eyes. 'You don't mind, Hannah, do you?'

Hannah gaped at her. 'Mind? Why on earth should I mind?'

'Well, she . . . she's not going to be able to work for a while, and besides, when folks know what she's been doing, she . . . she might find it hard to get proper work. When you've led that sort of life, it . . . it's difficult to get out of it.'

Hannah touched Bessie's hand and said softly, 'About as hard as getting out of the workhouse once you're in there. Auntie Bessie, of *course* I want to help Peggy. We'll manage. When she's feeling better, she'll be able to help you with the washing.'

'As long as none of my customers know. You know what folks are like. They'll treat her like a leper for a while.'

'I can still collect and deliver for you in the evening and Nell'll still help out, I'm sure. Don't you worry, Auntie Bessie, we'll manage.'

Hannah was not feeling as confident as she made out. There was now an extra mouth to feed on her one wage. Whilst Bessie still did a lot of washing, Hannah was sure that once word got out that her wayward daughter was home, folks might well take their washing elsewhere. Bessie would suffer the stigma of the life her daughter had led. And now she was married, Nell's contribution to the household budget had gone too.

And worse than all this, Hannah, though eternally grateful to Bessie, felt the trap closing in on her. Her own plans would have to wait for a while.

The weeks and months passed, and Hannah had been working at the silk factory for almost three years. Peggy's recovery had been painfully slow, but at last her skin was clearer, she had put on a little weight, and though the haunted look would never quite leave her eyes, at least she was able to smile now. She rarely ventured out of the house – the gossips had long memories. But after she had been home almost a year, Hannah determined it was high time the girl put the past behind her and held her head up high.

As she breezed into the house one evening after work, she called out, 'Peggy, Auntie Bessie where are you? I've got some good news.'

'In here,' came Bessie's voice from the kitchen where she was laying the table for their evening meal. As she stepped into the room, Hannah lifted her face and sniffed the air. 'Mmm, something smells good.'

'Sit down. It's all ready. Come on, you too, Peg. Leave that ironing, you can do it later.'

'But, Mam, me irons are hot . . .' Peggy began, but nevertheless she set her irons back on the hob and came to the table.

'So, love, what's your news?' Bessie said.

'I've got Peggy an interview for a job at the mill.'

Peggy's mouth dropped open in surprise, but then doubt and fear crossed her face. 'Oh, Hannah, it's good of you, very good, but I don't know if I'm ready to face folk. What if—'

'Take it a step at a time, Peg. See how it goes, eh? You can pull out any time you like. Just go for the interview with Mr Boardman. If you get the job, give it a try. If it doesn't work out, you've lost nothing, have you?'

'No, but what if folk know about me? They'll likely hound me out of the place.'

'No, they won't. Not while I'm around anyway.'

Both Bessie and Peggy smiled at the little firebrand. Slim, blonde and blue-eyed, Hannah had the looks of a china doll, but her spirit was like steel. 'Look,' she went on, 'there's a girl just started in our workroom and there's been a lot of gossip about her. They say she's been on the game, got two kiddies and she doesn't even know who their fathers are. Oh, there was a lot of gossiping and nudging when she first started, but I made a point of being friendly with her and one or two more followed suit. One or two who have no reason to be calling others names, I might tell you. But it's fine now. You'll just have to brave it out for a while until it all dies down. You'll be a nine-day wonder and then they'll find summat else to gossip about.' She smiled. 'Or someone.'

'Well . . .' Peggy said doubtfully, but Bessie urged, 'Oh, go on, love, give it a try. Like Hannah says, you've nothin' to lose. And the washing's not coming in like it used to. And to tell the truth, it's getting too hard for me now. With two proper wages coming in and the little bit that Nell gives me for looking after Tommy, we could live like kings.'

Hannah bit her lip. She couldn't let Bessie go on thinking she would have her wage coming in for ever. 'Maybe there's something I should tell you. I've got plans. I – I might be leaving.'

Bessie's face fell and Peggy looked worried. 'Is it because of me, Hannah, now I've come back? Because, if it is—'

'No, no,' Hannah reassured her swiftly. 'It's something I've wanted to do for a long time. But the time's not been right. I've had to wait a while anyway, and then I wanted to be sure Bessie was all right before I left. I thought I could leave when Nell and Tommy were here.' Her smile widened. 'But then she had to go an' get married, didn't she?'

'You're going back, aren't you? Back to that mill. Why, Hannah? It'll only cause you more heartache. Put the past behind you, love. It's what you're telling Peggy to do.'

'I know – and maybe you're right. Maybe I should. But I just know that I have to go back first, before I can get on with my life.' Her mouth tightened. 'I've unfinished business there.' Her face brightened. 'But so long as I know that I can always come back here if—'

'Of course you can,' Bessie and Peggy chorused.

*

To Hannah's delight, Peggy was offered the job, and despite having to run the gauntlet of the gossiping for a couple of weeks, the girl soon settled into the routine of mill life. She was a quick and willing learner. She was quiet and unassuming, and with Hannah as her champion, she was soon accepted by the others.

Now, at last, as winter turned to spring once more, Hannah felt free to make definite plans to return to Wyedale Mill.

'Nell, can you get me some of that hair dye you use?'

Nell's eyes widened. 'Whatever for? You've got beautiful hair.'

'I'm going back.'

'Back where?'

'To the mill.'

For a moment Nell looked puzzled and then she gasped. 'To Wyedale? Whatever for?'

'I'm not going to let Edmund Critchlow get off with causing Luke's death, even if his cronies fixed it for him so he did.'

Nell's eyes were troubled. 'Oh, Hannah, do be careful. He's so powerful. What're you going to do?'

'I don't know. Not exactly. Not yet. But I don't want anyone to recognize me. I've altered a lot while I've been away. I've grown taller and filled out.'

Nell chuckled as she let her glance run up and down Hannah's shapely figure. 'And in all the right places, too.'

'And if I dye my hair, I think I'll look very different.'

'Well, yes,' Nell said doubtfully. 'But you can't hide those lovely blue eyes can you? And don't forget, blue eyes don't very often go with red hair.'

'That's a risk I'll just have to take.' Hannah was

determined, and once she set her mind to something, there was no one who could dissuade her. No one.

That night, fully grown and aged nineteen with bright red hair and blue eyes, Anna Morgan was born.

Thirty-Seven

Hannah paused at the top of the hill, looking down into the dale below. The spring sunshine slanted on the hills, tipping the trees with its golden glow.

Hannah smiled. It was just like the day she had first arrived here as a child of twelve almost seven years earlier. Pauper's gold the driver who'd brought them had called the sunlight. The scene was unchanged, but the girl who now stood at the top of the steep slope was very different from the skinny pauper child.

Today Hannah was dressed in good clothes, with sturdy new boots on her feet. She carried a heavy bag of belongings and she had money in her pocket, money she'd earned. Money that no one was going to take from her. Not this time.

Excitement fluttering just below her ribs, she set off down the hill. There was just one person in whom she was going to confide. Or rather three people. Lily and Ollie Grundy and their nephew, Ted. She couldn't bring herself even to try to deceive them. If it hadn't been for their help, she'd still be slaving in the mill, only just having completed her indenture. She wouldn't have known the happiness of the last three and a half years with Bessie. Nell and Tommy would still be in the workhouse, and Peggy . . . Well, she dared not think what might have happened to Peggy by now. She marvelled at the way people's lives were intertwined with others. If it hadn't been for the Grundys' help, none of the good things of the past few years would have happened to others as well as to her.

Oh yes, she owed it to the Grundys to be honest with them if with no one else. But first, she smiled, she would have a bit of fun. She would test out her disguise on them.

At the gateway into the farmyard, she paused and looked about her again. The mill was still not in sight. It was set right at the end of the dale, around the next bend. Her heart was beating faster at the mere thought of stepping through its pillared gate once more. She wasn't quite ready to face that yet, so instead she stepped across the cobbled crewyard and knocked on the back door of the farmhouse, just like she had all those years earlier. Time seemed to tilt; for a moment it was as if the years between had never happened and she was once again that little girl, the leader of the four waifs from the workhouse, knocking on a stranger's door. She glanced over her shoulder, half-expecting to see the others, Luke, Daniel and Jane, standing behind her, scruffy, dirty urchins . . .

The door opened, pulling her back to the present. Lily Grundy had changed little; the intervening years had been kind to her. Perhaps there were a few more grey hairs, one or two more lines in her face, but the smile was still there. The welcome in her eyes, even for a stranger knocking at her door, was the same as ever it had been.

'Yes?'

'Can you tell me the way to the mill?' Hannah asked, and now she knew her voice sounded different too. When she had last said those very same words it had been with the piping tones of a child. Now her voice had deepened. It was low and husky and, though she was quite unaware of it herself, appealing.

'It's further on, love. Just keep on the way you were going. It's at the end of the dale.'

'Thank you.'

She made as if to turn away, but, as Hannah had known she would, Lily said, 'Perhaps you'd like a cup of tea and a bite to eat? You must have come a fair way.'

Hannah smiled. 'I have,' she said, but saying no more for the moment, she stepped over the threshold and into the kitchen she remembered so well. Nothing, not one thing, had changed. The smell of freshly baked bread still hung in the air. The kettle still sang on the hob near the blazing fire in the range, and Lily bustled about setting cups and saucers and a plate of home-made biscuits on the table.

'Sit down, do. Make yourself at home. It's a while since I had anybody calling on their way to the mill. Since they stopped the paupers from the workhouse coming here as apprentices, I don't get many waifs and strays passing my door.' She paused before adding simply, 'And d'you know, I miss them. Poor little mites.'

Hannah tried to hide the surprise from showing on her face. 'The . . . the pauper apprentices? What . . . was that?'

'Ah well now,' Lily settled herself down opposite and began to pour the tea. 'It began years and years ago, but it stopped . . . ooh let's see, in the late forties, I reckon, in most places, but the Critchlows kept it going at their mill –' she nodded, gesturing towards the mill further along the dale – 'for several years after that.' She leaned closer, confiding. 'We all reckon he had this scheme going with the master of a workhouse who used to send the children. They made them sign a paper binding them here for years. Poor mites didn't know what they were letting themselves in for. And then, of course, they was trapped here. They had no one to fight for them, no parents, and because they'd signed an indenture, the law was against them an' all. There was no escape, only to run away, and if they was caught, well, I hardly dare tell you some of the punishments them Critchlows meted out.' She pursed her mouth and shook her head and Hannah wanted to jump up and hug her.

'And did many run away?'

Lily smiled grimly. 'One or two. We – that's my husband, Ollie and me – and our nephew that works for us – Ted – we helped a little lass once. Nice little thing she was. Been through a lot, if you know what I mean. She deserved a bit of help.' She chuckled. 'We was risking a fair bit ourselves, mind, 'cos we supply the mill with produce – milk, butter, cheese, eggs – and it gives us a regular bit of income. But it was worth the risk – just to get one back on them Critchlows.'

'And the girl you helped?'

Lily's face lit up. 'Oh, she's all right. Wrote to us, she did. Don't know where she is, mind you,' she tapped the side of her nose, 'I've a good idea, mind, but it wouldn't do to say. Went back to where she came from and found an old neighbour who remembered her. Far as I know, she's fine.'

Hannah's smile broadened. 'She is.'

'Eh?' Lily gaped at her. 'You ... you know her? You know Hannah?'

Hannah could not stop the laughter bubbling out now. 'It's me, Mrs Grundy, don't you recognize me?'

Lily's mouth dropped open. 'Hannah? You're . . . Hannah? But she . . . she had lovely blonde hair . . .' Her voice petered away as she stared. Then slowly she nodded. 'Yes, I see it now. You can't hide those pretty blue eyes, can you? Aw, but lass, what have you done to your hair?'

Now Hannah's face sobered. 'It's not because I wanted to. Not out of vanity. I wanted to come back, but I didn't want anyone to recognize me.' Her mouth tightened into a grim line. 'I mean to get my revenge on Edmund Critchlow. I don't know how, but I have to try. I . . . I can't lay the past to rest until I do.'

'Well I never,' Lily was still staring at her, shaking her head in disbelief. But as she took in Hannah's words, she added, 'Well, I can't blame you for that, lass. I've a few scores I'd like to settle with the Critchlows myself, but I don't expect I'll get the chance.' Her eyes gleamed. 'But if there's any way I can help you, you just let me know. All right?' She paused and reached across the table to touch Hannah's hand. 'It's grand to see you. Wait till Ollie and Ted know. I reckon Ted took a shine to you. He was always asking after you for quite a while after you went. Oh – I can tell them, can't I?'

Hannah nodded. 'Just so long as they don't tell anyone else. I'm calling myself Anna Morgan now.'

'Oh, they'll not say a word. I'll make sure of that. But you just be careful, Hannah, that's all.' Then she smiled. 'Need a bed for a few nights, do you? You're very welcome to stay here.'

Hannah's heart was thumping madly as she neared the mill. What if someone recognized her? She wasn't sure of the law regarding the indenture she'd signed. She hadn't completed it. And even though she was now nineteen and legally out of it, could they still force her to complete a further number of years because she'd run away with still three years to serve? But what did it matter if they did? she answered herself. She intended to seek work here anyway, intended to stay to exact some kind of revenge on Edmund, and that wasn't going to happen overnight. She had to move slowly and make careful plans.

As she entered the gate, she saw a young man crossing the yard, and her heart skipped a beat. For a moment she thought it was Edmund, but as he heard the sound of her footsteps and turned to face her, she could see that he was much younger, yet he had the look of Edmund Critchlow. His black hair was smoothed back from his forehead. Straight, dark eyebrows overshadowed his deep set brown eyes. His jaw was square and resolute, but his firm mouth had nothing of the cruel twist of the man who was so obviously his father. This young man's mouth curved up in a smile as he paused and then came towards Hannah.

'Adam,' Hannah murmured to herself. 'Adam Critchlow.' The boy she remembered had grown in to a man. A very good-looking young man. And what was it she'd always said? A curse on all good-looking men. The thought made her smile.

'Can I help you, miss?' he asked in a deep, friendly tone, returning what he took to be her smile of greeting.

Huskily, Hannah replied, 'I . . . I'm looking for work. I've worked in a mill before. Over . . .' Now the lies must begin in earnest. 'Over Manchester way.'

'What work have you done – exactly?'

Hannah reeled off all the jobs she'd done in this very mill. She was about to add that she'd worked in a silk mill too, but then thought better of it. If she told as little about herself as possible, there was less chance of slipping up.

'You need to see Mr Scarsfield. He's the overlooker, but you'd have a final interview with my father.' His smile widened. 'Or with me.'

Hannah had to press her lips together to prevent herself asking the questions that tumbled around her mind. Was he – Adam – working at the mill now? Of course! She remembered now. He'd been brought home from school and made manager of the mill just before she'd left. So he was still here and in a position of importance, it seemed. What had happened to the old man, Mr Nathaniel Critchlow? she wondered. And Mr Edmund? Was he the sole owner of Wyedale Mill now?

But there was one good thing she'd learned already. Mr Scarsfield was still here. And yet, was it so good? Ernest Scarsfield might recognize her.

Adam broke into her thoughts. 'Come along, I'll take you to see him. This way.'

As Hannah followed him into the building, she realized this wasn't going to be quite as easy as she'd imagined. For one thing, she must remember to act like a complete stranger. She couldn't be seen to know her way around the building, along passages and through workrooms that were so familiar to her. And the people that would still be here whom she knew – she must remember not to greet them, not even to smile at them.

Adam led her towards the main mill and, as he held

open the door for her to precede him into one of the
workrooms, the very person she most dreaded meeting
was working at the nearest machine.

Daniel Hammond.

Thirty-Eight

Daniel looked much older than the eighteen years he was now. The clatter of the machine hid the sound of their approach and Hannah was able to study him as they passed by. To her relief, he didn't even look up. The same mop of curly brown hair was still there, of course, but cut shorter now. He was still thin, and his shoulders and back stooped from long hours bending over a weaving machine. She couldn't see into his eyes from where she was standing, but his mouth was sullen and down-turned. There was no sign of the cheeky grin that had so epitomized Luke and the twin who'd copied his every move.

But the young man still reminded her so much of her lost love. Hannah felt a lump in her throat and she almost stumbled. Adam caught her arm and steadied her.

'Be careful,' he mouthed. 'The floor's uneven and it's a bit of a mess.' He pulled a face. 'It's the one thing we can't seem to do – keep the place clean and tidy.'

Hannah forced herself to smile up at him, anxious that he should not suspect the reason for the tumult of emotions coursing through her. Being back here in the dusty atmosphere, amongst the noise and, most of all, seeing Daniel was causing her a heartache she hadn't envisaged. For a moment, she wanted to turn and run. But she gritted her teeth and allowed Adam to lead her through the mill, showing her the workrooms on each floor. She tried to concentrate on what he was telling her as he put his mouth close to her ear, shouting above the din. At last he led her back out into the yard and towards the door at the end of the building that led up to the offices.

They climbed the stone steps and came to the outer office where Mr Roper had his domain. Hannah found she was holding her breath as Adam opened the door and ushered her inside. Josiah Roper was little changed, perhaps a little more bent as he hunched over his ledgers, his features even sharper and his eyes filled with the bitterness and resentment that the passing of the years had only increased. He glanced up, inquisitive as ever he had been. But Hannah deliberately kept her eyes downcast.

'This young lady is looking for a job,' Adam explained cheerily. 'Is my father in?'

Josiah sniffed with disapproval; Hannah remembered the sound so well, she almost laughed out loud. 'Do you know her?'

'No, she's just turned up at the gate.'

'We don't usually employ folks without a reference of some kind,' Josiah said loftily. 'She could be anybody.'

Indeed I could! Hannah thought wryly.

'Oh, we'll go into all that,' Adam said.

'Well, he's not here.'

Adam turned and winked at Hannah. 'Fine. Then I'll interview her.'

Josiah made a movement, but Adam glanced at him. 'Any objections, Roper?'

The man faltered, muttered something under his breath and turned back to his books.

'Good. Come along in, then, Miss – er . . . ?

'Morgan,' Hannah said firmly. 'Anna Morgan.'

He drew her into the inner office and closed the door. 'I'm Adam Critchlow. Sorry about old Roper. He's been here a long time. He and my father have known each other for years and he seems to think he half-owns the place. Sit down, please,' he added, indicating a chair in front of the desk, the very same desk on which Hannah had painstakingly signed the indenture that had bound her to the Critchlows for six years. As she sat down, she felt a sudden stab of indecision. Was she being foolish, trying to retrace the past? Would it have been better to let it all go and move forward with her life? Was she stacking up a whole load of trouble for herself by coming back?

'I'm sorry my father, Mr Edmund, isn't here. He'd like to have seen you himself, I'm sure.'

At the mention of his name, all Hannah's doubts disappeared and her resolve strengthened. *I bet he would*, she thought. *But not if he knew who I really am and why I've come back.*

'You've worked in a mill before, you say?' Adam was beginning the interview in a businesslike manner, though if she could have read his mind, Hannah would've known that already he intended to employ her. There was something about this pretty girl with startling blue eyes and red hair that he found appealing; he wanted to know more about her, wanted to get to know her. And what better way than to have her working here, where he could find an excuse – a legitimate excuse – to see her every day?

Hannah licked her lips. Lying had never come easily to her, but it was a means to an end. It had to be done. 'Yes. It . . . it was a small mill in Lancashire. They . . .

they had to close.' It was the only thing she could think of to say that would stop the Critchlows trying to make contact with a former employer.

Adam pulled a sympathetic face. 'Yes, business has been difficult of late and some of the smaller mills have found it difficult to keep going. We've been lucky. My father has good contacts and work has been plentiful here. But with this war brewing in America . . . Ah well.' He smiled. 'Let's not get too pessimistic before we have to, eh? Have you brought any kind of reference?'

Hannah smiled. 'I'm sorry, I haven't got it with me. I really only came to the mill today to make an appointment to see someone. I didn't think I'd get an interview so quickly.'

'No matter,' Adam said, waving it aside as of no particular importance. 'I think I can trust my own judgement.' He smiled at her, drinking in her appearance. She smiled back, just a tentative, shy smile. Nothing too bold, she warned herself.

'Right, then. We'll go and find Scarsfield. He'll have a word with you and probably set you on for a trial period. Just to make sure you can do the job, you understand.' Suddenly, it was Adam who was nervous, at pains to make sure she understood that this was no reflection upon her as a person.

'Thank you, sir,' she said, rising and following him to the door. He opened it for her and, head held high, she swept through it, just like any lady of quality. Once more, she kept her glance averted from Josiah Roper as they passed through the outer office, and when they were in the workrooms again, Adam led her in search of Ernest Scarsfield. The overlooker hadn't changed at all. He smiled kindly at Hannah and stroked his moustache with the very same gesture she remembered so well. But thankfully, he didn't recognize her.

'Aye, Mr Adam, we'll be glad of her if she can do all she says. I've a girl gone off sick and I doubt she'll be coming back.' A meaningful glance passed between the two men and Hannah wondered what it meant. Not so naive now, Hannah could think of one or two reasons why the poor girl might not be resuming her work. She could have been badly injured in yet another accident or – as seemed more likely – she was yet another whose life had been ruined by the attentions of Edmund Critchlow, and sent away in disgrace.

Ernest Scarsfield turned to Hannah. 'Can you start in the morning, lass?'

Hannah nodded. 'I think so, if I can find some lodgings close by.'

'Try in the village. Go out of here and up the hill. Several houses take in lodgers – all mill workers.'

'Oh, what about—' Hannah bit her tongue. She'd almost asked about the apprentice house, but had remembered just in time. She stumbled for a moment and then altered her words to ask, 'My . . . my hours of working and . . . and my wage?' It seemed reasonable to ask and when Mr Scarsfield answered, she nodded and said, 'I'll be here in the morning, sir.'

'Oh, you don't call me "sir".' Ernest laughed and, just as he'd told her before, he added, 'You call me "Mr Scarsfield".'

She smiled at him. 'Thank you, Mr Scarsfield.' Then she turned to Adam and held out her hand. 'And thank you too, Mr Adam. I'll not let you down.'

He took her slim hand in his in a warm, firm handshake. 'I know you won't,' he said softly.

As she turned and walked away from them, Hannah was well aware that both men stood gazing after her, the one with admiration, the other with a puzzled look on his face.

'Mr Grundy – how lovely to see you again. And you too, Ted.'

The big man held out his arms and, without thinking, Hannah ran into his rough embrace.

'Eh, what about me? I wouldn't mind a bit of that, if there's hugs being given out.'

Hannah leaned back to look up into Ollie's face, her eyes twinkling with mischief. 'Seems your nephew wants a hug off you, an' all . . .'

'Not off him, silly. You!' Ted was quick to say, but then he saw she was teasing him and they all laughed together. Releasing herself from Ollie Grundy's strong arms, she hugged Ted too. He held her close and buried his face against her hair.

'It's great to see you again. But what's with the hair colour change? You had lovely fair hair.'

Hannah pulled away, almost having to prise herself out of his embrace. Ted was reluctant to let her go. The feel of her young, firm body in his arms had set the young man's pulses racing and his senses reeling.

'I didn't want anyone to recognize me.'

'Not recognize you? Some hope!' he laughed. 'I'd've known you anywhere, blonde or redhead. You can't hide them lovely eyes or that smile.'

Hannah's face fell. 'Really? Do you really think people will know me?'

''Course they won't,' Lily said, placing a meat and

potato pie on the table. 'Now come and eat – all of you. There's my special treacle tart for afters.'

'I don't suppose,' Hannah said as she sat down, suddenly feeling very hungry, 'that you know anyone in the village who'd take a lodger, do you?'

'You're staying then?' Lily's face lit up.

Hannah nodded. 'I got meself a job at the mill this afternoon. I start tomorrow morning.'

'And did anyone recognize you?' Ted asked, passing his plate to his aunt to be loaded up with a generous helping of pie and vegetables.

Hannah shook her head, but a fleeting anxious look was in her eyes. 'No. But then I only saw Mr Adam and Mr Scarsfield. Oh, and Mr Roper, but I kept my head turned away from him. I . . . I saw Daniel – you know, Luke's brother – but he never looked up from his work.'

'He'll know you.' Ted nodded with certainty.

'Mmm, maybe, but I think Daniel will keep my secret. He'll understand – if anyone will – why I've come back.'

Ted gaped at her, his fork suspended midway between his plate and his mouth. 'Why have you come back?' He grinned suddenly. 'I thought it was to see me.'

'Well, of course it was.' She smiled, playing up to him. Then her smile faded. 'But there's a much more serious reason.'

'Yes, and I'm not too happy about it,' Lily put in. 'I reckon the lass could be stacking up a load of trouble for 'erself.'

'Why?' Ollie and Ted chorused the question.

'She wants revenge on Mr Edmund, because of the accident and the death of her . . . well . . . of Luke.'

358

'More than just that,' Hannah said quietly and found that, suddenly, her appetite had left her. 'There's Nell too.'

'Who's Nell?' Ollie asked, still eating heartily but listening nonetheless.

'She came from the same workhouse as me, but a few years earlier. I never knew her there, but we got friendly at the mill. Then suddenly, she disappeared. None of us in the apprentice house knew what had happened to her, though I have a feeling Mrs Bramwell did. I mean, she hadn't even served out her indenture. One or two thought she'd run away.'

'And had she?'

'No.' Hannah's mouth was tight. 'She'd been sent back to the workhouse in Macclesfield because she was expecting a child.' She paused and added significantly, '*Mr Edmund's child.*'

To her surprise, Lily only shrugged and the two men looked down at their plates. 'Aye, well, she wasn't the first and I don't suppose she'll be the last.'

'Well, it's high time she was. It's high time something was done about that man. That's how Luke was killed, because he was trying to protect me. Mr Edmund was after *me*.'

Now all three looked at her.

'Trouble is, love,' Ollie said in his growly voice. 'He will be again, if you don't watch out.'

'That's just what I think, Ollie,' Lily remarked, triumphant to hear her husband agree with her.

'Then he'll have me to deal with,' Ted said stoutly and flexed his muscles.

The other three stared at him and then burst out laughing. Pint-sized Ted, though strong and sturdy, would be no match for the tall, well-built Edmund

Critchlow, but Hannah was touched by his chivalrous gesture. Wiping the tears from her eyes, she touched his arm. 'Thank you, Ted. I'll not forget that.'

The tension in the room broken, Hannah picked up her knife and fork. All at once her hunger had returned. 'By the way,' she asked as she ate, 'what happened to the Bramwells?'

'He sacked them,' Lily replied tartly. 'They'd run that apprentice house for over twenty years for the Critchlows, and just because Mr Edmund gave up the system about two years ago, they was out on their ear. He didn't even try to find them work in the mill. And I'm sure Arthur could've turned his hand to something, don't you, Ollie?'

''Course he could.'

'Where are they now?'

'Went away. To Manchester, I reckon. I 'ad one letter off Ethel, but things didn't sound too good and I've never heard again.'

'What happened to all the apprentices? Come to think of it,' she stopped eating, 'd'you know, I never thought about it before, but there weren't as many apprentices in the house by the time I left as there had been when we came. And there were no more paupers from the workhouse came after us. We were the last. I'd never realized it before, but now you mention it . . .'

Lily shook her head. 'No. As they finished their term, he didn't replace them and the last few that were there still with time to serve, he found lodgings for them in the village when he closed the house.'

'Poor Mr and Mrs Bramwell,' Hannah murmured. 'I quite liked them, you know.'

'So did we,' Lily agreed. 'I just hope they're all right.'

There was only one more thing that had to be done that night and Lily settled it as she rose to clear the table. 'You don't need to go looking for lodgings in the village. Not unless you want to, of course. You can stay here. Ollie and me's agreed. We had a little chat while you was up at the mill, when I told him you was back an' that you might be stayin'.'

'Oh, thank you, Mrs Grundy. That'd be perfect.'

Behind her, Ted beamed.

Hannah slipped into the work she was given with ease; it was as if she'd never been away. Several of the youngsters – now young men and women like herself – who'd been apprentices at the house when Hannah had lived there still worked in the mill, but no one seemed to recognize her.

There were now only two people she dreaded coming face to face with: Daniel and Mr Edmund Critchlow. And she wasn't sure which incited the most fear in her.

There were one or two other people she'd recognized, but no one to whom she'd been close. She hadn't seen Joe or Millie, and of course she couldn't ask about them. Maybe they'd left when they'd served their term.

Despite the reason for her return, Hannah was happy. She'd always liked the work at the mill, and now she was older, it was much easier. She was treated by the Grundys as a daughter and she had Ted as a friend, though he, she thought with a frown, might be trying to become a little too friendly. And her ruse seemed to be working: no one had recognized her.

But then, she met Daniel.

She was running up the stone stairs to the work-room early one morning, holding her skirts high so that she did not trip. And she was singing just as she used to, her pure voice echoing clearly up the staircase. Daniel, coming down, stopped and stared at her climb-ing towards him, her eyes downcast. He stepped in front of her, barring her way, and she would have cannoned into him and might have fallen backwards down the stairs if he hadn't grasped her strongly by the shoulder. She gave a little cry of alarm. As she looked up and saw who was holding her, her heart sank.

How could she have been so foolish as to be singing? Daniel, more than anyone else, would remem-ber her singing. It'd been a joke between the three of them – four counting poor little Jane.

Daniel wouldn't have forgotten the girl who sang.

Now he was looking down into her face, into her clear, blue eyes.

'You! It *is* you. I thought I was hearing things.' He flung her away from him so that she stumbled and fell heavily against the wall and only just prevented herself from tumbling down the stairs. 'Why've you come back?' he asked bitterly. There was no pleasure in his tone at seeing her, no welcome in his eyes.

Hannah's eyes glinted and her mouth tightened. 'I've unfinished business. I told you I'd come back one day. That he wouldn't get away with . . . with what he did.'

Daniel's face was a sneer. 'Oh aye? And what d'you reckon you can do to a powerful man like Edmund

Critchlow? Don't you think that if there'd been a way, I'd've found it?'

Now that she was close to him, she could see that the years had treated Daniel harshly. His grief at the loss of his twin and the bitterness in his heart had twisted his handsome, boyish features, had eaten into his soul and made him older than his years. He was only eighteen, yet he could have been mistaken for thirty.

'Oh, Daniel,' Hannah said sadly.

He saw the sympathy in her eyes and spat, 'Don't pity me. I don't need your pity or anyone else's. You shouldn't have come back.'

'You told me before that I shouldn't be going away.'

'No, you shouldn't. Not then. You left me to cope alone.'

'But . . . but you blamed me. Said it was my fault. I . . . I thought it was better if I went.'

Daniel ran his hand through his hair. He was unsure now what he really felt. Seeing Hannah again had confused him and awakened feelings in him which he'd worked so hard to bury. But seeing her again – the girl his brother had loved, the girl that Luke had given his life to protect – had brought back all the pain and suffering. He hated her. She'd ruined his life. He'd never been able to love another human being the same as he'd loved his brother. He would never love anyone else the way he'd loved Luke.

The way he had loved Hannah.

Unbidden, the realization came to him with a jolt.

He'd watched them together and been consumed with jealousy. Older now, he recognized the feeling, and those old emotions were flooding through him again at the sight of her. He'd never known – and with a shock he realized that he still didn't know – whether the jealousy was directed at her because Luke had loved her and she'd come between the twins, or whether it was because she'd loved Luke and not him. Had be been jealous of his own brother?

Even after all these years, Daniel still did not know.

'Get out of my way,' he growled, and pushed past her to continue on his way down the stairs. 'And if you know what's good for you, you'll stay out of my way.'

Stricken, Hannah stared after him for a moment. Then lightly she ran down the stairs after him and caught hold of his arm. 'Daniel, wait a minute. Please.'

He stopped. 'What?'

'Please, Daniel, don't give me away.'

He stared at her for a long moment, gave a brief nod, pulled himself from her grasp and continued down the stairs without another word.

Hannah leaned against the wall, closed her eyes and breathed a sigh of relief.

Now – there was only Mr Edmund to face.

Thirty-Nine

'So – how's it going?'

Adam was smiling down at her as she stood in front of her machine. As she glanced up at him, she was struck once more by his likeness to his father and yet there was a difference. A very important difference. His brown eyes were warm and friendly, not cold and disdainful. His mouth curved in a smile, not in a cruel sneer.

'Fine,' she said. 'I think Mr Scarsfield is pleased with my work.'

'He is,' Adam nodded. 'That's what I've come to tell you. Your appointment is confirmed. You're no longer on trial.'

'Thank you, sir. Thank you very much.'

He leaned closer, speaking above the noise of the machinery, yet only for her to hear. 'I'd like it if you called me Adam. And would you . . . would you come out with me some evening?'

She stared at him, wide-eyed for a moment. And then quite suddenly, like a revelation, she saw her way to get revenge on Edmund Critchlow.

'I'd love to,' she said huskily.

'Saturday? You'll finish earlier on a Saturday afternoon.' He knew her hours better than she did. Hannah nodded.

'I'll meet you near the waterfall behind the mill. Do you know it?'

She nodded. She'd been here a month now. There'd been time enough for her to do a little exploring in the area. He wouldn't question it.

'I must go. See you Saturday.'

'Saturday,' she murmured.

'You gonner let me take you for a ride in Auntie's pony and trap on Sunday?'

Hannah nodded. 'That'd be nice, Ted. Where are we going?'

Ted shrugged. 'Where you like. Take you into Bakewell, if you like – if the old pony can manage the hills.'

'There won't be any shops open on a Sunday,' she said impishly.

'Oho, don't tell me you like the shops? Uh-huh! There I was, thinking I'd found me a nice girl and I find she's a spendthrift.'

Hannah laughed. 'I would be if I had the money, but I haven't.'

'Mebbe Sunday's the safest day to take you into town then.'

She chuckled. 'Mebbe you're right.'

'I'll come for you about three?'

Hannah nodded. 'Sunday it is.'

Who'd've thought it? Two young men in the space of two days. And what, she wondered, would each one say about the other when they found out?

And find out they surely would.

Saturday evening was dull with heavy April showers threatening. As she took the narrow path behind the mill and came to the footbridge across the river near the waterfall, she saw Adam waiting for her.

'I brought my father's big black umbrella,' he greeted her. 'It looks like rain.'

He took her arm and guided her along the narrow path at the side of the River Wye. On their right was the sheer face of the cliff. 'The village is on the top of this cliff. Millersbrook – it gets its name from the brook that runs in front of the mill. But I'm forgetting, you must know the village by now.'

She hesitated only a moment. 'Not – not ever so well. But I'm learning.'

'I presume you found some lodgings all right?'

'Oh yes, thank you.' Hannah bit her lip. She'd better be truthful about where she was living. 'I'm staying with the Grundys at Rushwater Farm.'

'Really?' Was she imagining a slight change in the tone of his voice at the mention of the Grundys' name? 'I didn't know they took in lodgers.' Then he murmured, so low that she could scarcely hear, 'Especially anyone working at the mill.'

'Don't they?' Hannah feigned surprise. 'Oh! Well, I don't know then. I only know that I first met them when I arrived here. I walked down the hill . . .' She was describing her arrival of years earlier, but Adam wasn't to know that. 'And I called to ask the way.' She glanced up at him. 'The carter just told us – I mean, me – that the mill was at the end of the dale, but when I came to the fork in the road, I didn't know which way to go, so . . .' She shrugged to indicate the simplicity of what had happened. 'I knocked on the back door of the farmhouse to ask the way, and this kind woman invited me in and fed me stew and dumplings.' She faltered at the memory of the four of them sitting around Lily Grundy's table, little knowing what lay in store for them. How innocent they'd all been then!

'And I suppose she liked the look of you.' He took hold of her arm on the pretext of steering her round a muddy puddle, but when they'd skirted it, he did not let go. Instead, he took her hand and tucked it through his arm. 'Can't say I blame her.'

They walked in silence, watching the ducks swimming and diving for food and the fish lying just below the surface, their heads facing upstream.

They had walked some distance when they came out of the trees overhanging the path. Before them was a building at the side of the river.

'Oh! Another mill!' Hannah exclaimed in genuine surprise. During her previous time at Wyedale Mill, she had heard tell of this one.

'Yes. This is Raven's Mill.' They stood looking up at the tall building, silent now on a Saturday evening. It was set in a narrow valley with nearby houses set beneath the cliff. 'It's strange,' Adam said, 'we have workers coming from this village to work at our mill, and I know there are one or two from Millersbrook who work here. They all use this path every day and must pass one another. I always wonder why they don't just swap jobs.'

'Mm,' Hannah was non-committal. In the past, she had heard rumours that there wasn't much to choose between the two mills as regards working conditions, but no doubt some workers believed one or the other to be better for some reason. Maybe, in the case of women workers, the owner of Raven's Mill was not a lecherous devil like Edmund Critchlow.

'Your father? Does he own Wyedale Mill?'

'Yes, but one day it will come to me.'

Hannah waited, willing him to explain. She wanted to ask about his grandfather, Nathaniel Critchlow, but she wasn't supposed to know of his existence. And yet, why not? Adam wasn't to know that she'd not heard about him from the other workers.

'Someone was saying,' she said carefully, 'that your grandfather started the mill?'

'Actually it was his father. My grandfather was a young boy when they found Wyedale together. He loved to tell the tale of how it all started.'

Adam was smiling fondly, but there was sadness in his eyes.

Gently, Hannah said, 'Is he . . . I mean . . .'

'He died almost three years ago.' It couldn't have been long after she left, Hannah thought. 'He took over the mill from his father, of course, and ran it – very successfully, I might add.'

Really? Hannah wanted to say sarcastically, but she bit her tongue.

'He had his first seizure about five years ago. There was a nasty accident. A little girl got her hair caught in a machine and she died. It really upset Grandfather. Then about three years ago there was the most terrible accident. A boy – well, a young man almost – fell into the water-wheel and was killed. There was an inquest, of course, but no one was to blame. Accidental death, they said. No one was supposed to tell my grandfather – they knew it would upset him – but,' his tone hardened, 'Josiah Roper used to come up to the Manor to see him and I think he let it slip during a conversation. I'm sure he didn't mean to, but it brought on another seizure – a bad one – and Grandfather died a few months later.' Adam's face was suddenly bleak.

'I'm sorry.' Hannah hoped her words sounded sincere. They were – for Adam. She was sure he'd been fond of his grandfather, and she couldn't really blame him for not knowing the truth about Luke's so-called accident. He hadn't been there.

'I don't think I've seen your father around the mill, have I?' It was difficult to pretend she didn't even know him, especially when his dark features were so vivid in her memory.

'No, he's away now. He left three weeks ago – just after you started. He's gone abroad for a few weeks. On business. Looking for new outlets, he said.' Now there was definitely an evasive, off-hand tone in his voice, as if the reason he was giving for Edmund's absence was not entirely the truth.

Hannah wondered if it had to do with the girl whose place she'd taken.

At that moment they felt huge spots of rain begin to fall and Adam put up the large black umbrella. 'We'd better go back.'

They were in sight of Wyedale Mill when the rain began to fall in earnest, drenching Hannah's skirt in seconds.

'Let's shelter beneath the cliff. You still have some way to go to get back to the farm.' Taking hold of her hand he pulled her beneath the overhanging shelf of the rock face. The rain was beating in the opposite direction and they were sheltered.

Adam shook the umbrella and closed it. 'I don't think it will last long,' he said, looking up at the lowering sky. 'The clouds are breaking up.'

She shivered suddenly and Adam put his arm around her. 'This wasn't a good idea. I should have taken you to some grand hotel and wined and dined you in luxury, but I was afraid you wouldn't come.'

Hannah looked up into his face, so close to hers. His brown eyes were so earnest, so open and honest that she couldn't resist teasing him a little. 'Not good enough to take to a fancy hotel, aren't I?'

Alarm crossed his handsome face. 'Oh, I didn't mean that. Please . . . please don't think—'

She laughed. 'I don't. I'm teasing you.'

There was no mistaking the look of relief on his face. 'So,' he whispered, bending closer, his lips only inches from her mouth. 'Will you let me take you out one evening?' But before she could reply, his lips touched hers and his arms were about her.

His kiss was gentle, undemanding, yet searching, questioning. 'You're so lovely, Anna,' he whispered. 'You will come out with me again, won't you?'

Hannah's mind was in turmoil. His use of her assumed name brought her sharply back to her reason for being here. She had almost been lulled into enjoying his company, into allowing herself . . . But now she remembered.

'I'd like that,' she murmured and held up her face, inviting him to kiss her again.

After the Sunday morning service that was still held in the now unused schoolroom, Hannah walked down the hill from the village, but instead of going along the lane back to the farm, she turned to the right and took the path behind the mill leading to the waterfall. She crossed the bridge and climbed the steep, rough-hewn rocky steps to the hillside above the mill.

She needed to be alone. She wanted to think and decide whether she could really go through with her daring plan. As she climbed, she stopped in surprise. A broad, flat pathway was being carved out of the hillside and it looked as if they were digging a tunnel through the hills. Whatever for? Hannah wondered. 'I'll ask Ted,' she murmured. 'He'll know.'

Just below the workings, Hannah sat down on the grass and looked down on the mill. Her gaze travelled to the line of houses set above the mill and the former apprentice house where she had lived for several years. Then higher still to the rows of houses, teetering on the hillside. Most of their residents gained their livelihood from the mill. Then further along still, above the path along which she had walked yesterday with Adam and set high on the cliff, stood the Critchlow mansion. Presumably, Adam lived there with his father. Before his death, Mr Nathaniel had lived there too. A house of men, with no women, except servants, within its walls. Then her gaze swivelled and travelled in the opposite direction down the dale until she saw the roof of the Grundys' farmhouse.

She sighed. She was not a conceited girl, but she knew that certain look that came into a young man's eyes when he looked at a girl who attracted him. She'd seen it first in Luke's eyes. And that had grown into love: a first love, an innocent love, pure and unsullied. She'd seen that sort of look in Edmund's eyes, yet his was tinged with selfish lust and depravity. He cared nothing for the object of his desire, only for his own gratification.

And now she was seeing that look again in Adam's

eyes. But which did his resemble? Luke's or Edmund Critchlow's? And then there was Ted. His was a teasing, flirting kind of look, but still, there was no doubting the admiration in his eyes.

Hannah sighed. Could she go through with it? Was her first love still so strong that she could give up all hope of future happiness to bring about her revenge on the man who'd robbed Luke of his life?

She pulled herself up and her gaze came roaming over the mill and then swivelled to the Critchlows' house. The answer was yes. Yes, she could devote the whole of her life, if needs be, to avenging the cruelty of the Critchlows, their deception, their callous treatment of others. It was not only Luke she was doing this for, but her mother and Nell and all the countless others who'd suffered at their hands. Maybe, she mused, even the girl whose machine she now worked.

Hannah looked about her again. It was such a beautiful setting. Who would guess that such inhumanity went on in such an idyllic place? But it wasn't the place, she reminded herself, it was the people. And most of the people who lived in this place were good, decent people. People like the Grundys and the Scarsfields and all the ordinary villagers who worked in the mill. People like the Bramwells – oh, she wished she knew what had happened to the Bramwells. It was only a few – a very few – whose powerful position and greed had corrupted them that spoilt this place. As the sun reached its zenith, casting its golden light over the hillsides and shining deep into the dale, Hannah hurried down the hillside. Ted would be waiting and, if no one else, she owed him an explanation.

*

'I thought you liked me,' Ted said dolefully, hurt in his eyes.

'Oh, Ted, I do.' Hannah touched his hand. 'That's why I'm being honest with you now. I – I don't want to hurt you.'

'You already have,' he muttered, avoiding her glance as they sat together on the wall at the very top of the hill on the road leading out of the dale. The proposed trip into Bakewell had been postponed as, once again, rain clouds threatened.

'You'll get soaked and catch yer death,' Lily had warned. 'Just go for a little walk, the pair of you, and you can come back here for your tea.'

But tea was the last thing on their minds at present.

'It's so difficult, Ted. Maybe I'm presuming, being conceited, reading too much into you asking me out . . .'

'No,' he sighed. 'No, you're not. I want you to be my girl. There, that's putting it straight. But you're saying "no".'

'Yes, no – I mean yes, I'm saying no. But, Ted, can't we be friends?'

'Huh!'

'Does that mean we can't be?'

The young man sighed heavily. 'Oh, Hannah, Anna – or whatever you want to be called now – I'd never do anything to hurt you and . . . and if you were in trouble, I'd always help you, but . . . but I can't think of you as just a friend. I love you, Hannah,' he ended simply, and the hangdog look on his face tore at her heart.

'I'm sorry, Ted, truly I am, but I've made up my mind. I came back here for one reason and one reason only. And I intend to carry it out – however much it costs me.'

Ted regarded her steadily as he said softly, 'And you don't care who you hurt in the process, eh?'

'I don't want to hurt you, Ted. You of all people, but I've been honest with you from the day I came back.'

'Yes, you have,' Ted acknowledged, 'but I didn't realize it would stop us . . . well, walking out together.'

Hannah bit her lip, embarrassed to tell him the whole truth.

They were both silent as they walked back down the hill, each deep in their own thoughts, so deep that they didn't notice the clip-clop of a horse's hooves behind them until it was almost upon them. Ted grabbed Hannah and pulled her to the side of the road, his arms about her to steady her. The rider reined his mount in and sat looking down at them.

Hannah drew in a startled breath and whispered, 'Oh no,' as she found herself looking up into Adam's face, his expression a mixture of anger and hurt. His eyes bore into hers and then turned cold. His glance swivelled away from her and met Ted's belligerent gaze.

Though not a word passed between them, a kind of war was silently declared between the two young men. And she was the cause.

Then Adam kicked his horse and urged it down the steep hill at a dangerous pace.

Ted released his hold and stared after him. 'What on earth was all that about?'

Hannah sighed, straightened her skirt. 'I went walking with him yesterday evening.'

Ted stared at her and then at the place where the cantering horse had disappeared round the bend in the road. They could still hear the beat of its hooves. He was thoughtful for a moment before he said quietly, 'And does Master Adam figure in this . . . this plan of yours?'

'Yes,' she said simply. 'I think he does.'

'Then I'd be very careful, Hannah, because even if you think you can take *him* for a fool, you certainly can't make one of his father.'

Forty

Tea at the Grundys' was strained, the two young ones hardly speaking to each other and avoiding each other's eyes. Lily, sensitive to the atmosphere, tried to make cheerful conversation, but when Ted left to go home, she confronted Hannah.

'What's going on between you two? Had a row, have yer?'

Hannah sighed. There was nothing else for it but to tell the truth. 'Ted wanted me to be his girl—'

'So?' Lily interrupted. 'He's a nice lad. A good lad. You could do far worse.'

'I know. He *is* a nice lad. That's why . . . that's why I can't. He shouldn't have anything to do with me.'

'Eh?' Lily was perplexed. 'Aw lass, don't put yourself down. Ted's not the sort to bother about your past. Who you are or where you came from or . . . or the fact that – well – you've got no dad. All families have got something.'

'It's not that,' Hannah put in hastily. 'Like I told him – I had to be honest with him, Mrs Grundy, and I'm being honest with you. If – when I've told you – you want me to leave, then I'll go. Find other lodgings, only, please, hear me out.'

'Go on.' Lily's tone was not encouraging.

'You know why I've come back. I've told you. I can't even think about . . . about Ted, not in that way, not until I've done what I came back to do. And . . . and he doesn't like what it involves.'

'What do you mean "what it involves"?'

Hannah lifted her chin determinedly and her blue eyes were as cold as steel. 'Being friendly – very friendly – with Master Adam.'

Lily's mouth dropped open and her eyes had the very same anxious look that Ted'd had. 'Aw, Hannah, mind what you're doing. You'll be the one ending up getting hurt, if you don't watch out.'

Hannah didn't see Adam for three days. She was sure that where before he'd sought her out, now he was deliberately avoiding her. On the fourth day, as she was leaving work in the evening, he was crossing the yard towards the mill.

'Adam,' she began, but he gave her a curt nod and carried on walking swiftly past her.

She ran after him and caught hold of his sleeve. 'Please – let me explain.'

Angrily, he shook her off. 'I have nothing to say to you, *Miss Morgan*.'

'Oh, have it your own way,' she cried, close to tears. 'There's nothing between Ted and me. I just wanted you to know that. He's the Grundys' nephew and they'd invited him to tea.' It was not quite the truth, but it was near enough. 'But if you don't *want* to believe me . . .'

Now it was she who turned away and, picking up her skirts, began to run across the yard.

'Anna – Anna. Wait. Don't go.' He caught up with her. 'I'm sorry.' He took her hands in his, not caring now who might see them together. 'Do you mean it? Is he nothing to you?'

'He's the Grundy's nephew. I can hardly ignore him, can I? He's a friend. That's all.'

Adam shook his head and his smile held disbelief. 'You really think that any young man in their right mind can look upon you as a friend?'

Keeping her expression innocent, she looked up at him with her wide, appealing blue eyes. 'Why ever not?' she said huskily.

'Oh, Anna – if only you knew.' She felt his grasp, warm and firm, holding her cold hands. She felt him squeeze them and knew what he was trying to say.

Pretending shyness, she dropped her gaze. 'Oh!' she breathed.

'We can't talk here. Not properly.' His eyes burned with desire. 'Meet me tonight. Please, Anna. Come back to the mill – no one will be here then. I have a key. We can go into the office.'

'All right,' she agreed, putting just the right amount of maidenly hesitancy into her tone. Her heart was beating fast, not with love or desire for him but with excitement that her devious and dangerous plan seemed to be working even better than she'd dared to hope. He was like one of the fish in the river and she was playing him on the end of her hook.

He raised her hands to his lips and kissed them both. Then he released her and continued his way across the yard. She stood, watching him, like any young girl would on the brink of falling in love with a handsome young man. At the door into the building, he turned, smiled and waved before disappearing inside. With a smile of satisfaction, Hannah skipped down the road towards the farm. And now, with only the sheep in the nearby field to hear her, she sang at the top of her voice.

It was almost dark when she slipped along the lane back to the mill. She'd had to steal out of the house without Mrs Grundy being aware of her going. If they'd gone to bed by the time she returned she knew where the spare key for the back door was hidden.

It was eerie walking into the mill at night-time: no one hurrying across the yard, no sound of the huge water-wheel, no clatter of machinery from several floors. Hannah, pulling her shawl closely about her, hurried across the yard and in through the door. The stairs were dimly lit and she felt her way up to the offices. Passing through the one occupied by Mr Roper during the daytime, she tapped on the inner door. It flew open at once, and Adam reached out for her and pulled her into his arms. Pushing the door shut with his foot, he began to kiss her. 'Sweet, adorable Anna . . .'

She returned his kisses. It was not difficult; he was a handsome young man. She liked him, but he was not Luke. And Luke had been the love of her life.

'Oh, Anna, Anna, I want you so. Let me love you. Please, let me love you . . .' With trembling fingers he began to fumble at the buttons of her blouse.

She stiffened and pulled back, smacking his hands away. 'No!'

He stared down at her, a mixture of anger and longing in his eyes. 'I won't hurt you. I promise. I'll be careful, I'll . . .'

Hannah shook her head firmly. 'No, I'm not that sort of girl.'

'Oh, Anna, I'd never think that about you. But I love you so much.'

'You hardly know me. You don't know anything about me.'

'I know enough to know I love you.'

'And what would your . . . your mother and father say? You consorting with a mill girl?'

His face was bleak for a moment. 'My mother's dead.' His tone became bitter. 'And my father is in no position to find fault.'

Hannah widened her eyes, feigning ignorance. 'Whatever do you mean?'

Adam looked uncomfortable. 'He . . . he "consorts" with the mill girls, as you so delicately put it.'

'Oh! I see.'

'No, no, you don't,' he burst out angrily. 'I'm not like him. I wouldn't tire of you and cast you off.'

Daringly, Hannah murmured, 'And if I were to get with child? What then?'

'Then . . . then I'd marry you. Of course, I would.'

'Then,' she whispered, 'marry me now.'

With a groan, he pulled her to him and buried his face against her neck. 'I would. You know I would. I'd give anything to marry you, but I can't. I daren't.'

'Daren't? Why "daren't"?'

'My father. He'd disown me. I'd lose my inheritance – the mill – everything.'

'But we'd be together. We'd have each other. We could work.'

Adam gave a wry laugh. 'Work? What do you suppose I could do? I've never lifted a finger to work in my life.'

'But you work here. You help run the mill. Surely you could get a job as a manager or an overlooker in another mill.'

'My father and Roper run the mill. I just put the time in. And not even that sometimes, if I'm honest.'

'But you must know something about what goes on? You come round the mill. You talk to the workers.'

'Even if I did what you say – even if I applied for a job somewhere else – how long do you suppose it'd be before my father found out where I was and got in touch with the owners? They'd sack me as soon as look at me, if my father asked them to. Perhaps you don't realize just how powerful my father is in the district. And beyond, if the truth be known.'

I think I do, Hannah wanted to say bitterly. If a man can be the cause of a boy's death and get away with it just because he has friends in high places, then anything is possible. Instead, she murmured, 'I hadn't realized,' adding sadly, 'then there's nothing to be done.'

'But I must see you. I must hold you. Please, Anna. I think about you all the time. I can't sleep at night for thinking about you.'

'We can see each other. We can meet.'

'But I want so much more. I want you.'

Was this how his father seduced the young girls? How he'd seduced Nell? With flattery and empty promises of love?

Hannah was resolute. 'Then put a ring on my finger.'

Adam's only answer was a deep groan. He buried his fingers in her hair and rained kisses on her forehead, her eyes, and lastly, her mouth.

*

It was as dark as pitch in the lane from the mill to the farm with no moon to light her way. She crept into the yard, closed the gate quietly and tiptoed across the yard. Near the back door, the Grundys' collie came out of his kennel.

'Shh, boy. It's only me,' she whispered, and the animal wagged his tail and licked her hand. The back door key was kept hidden just inside the dog's kennel and Hannah felt around until her fingers found it. With one last pat on the dog's head, she inserted the key in the lock, turned it and opened the door. To her horror, it only opened a few inches and then rattled against a chain.

Hannah had forgotten that last thing at night Ollie looped a chain across the inside of the back door.

'Serves you right if you was locked out,' was all Lily Grundy had to say next morning as Hannah appeared sheepishly through the back door, heavy eyed and with bits of straw in her hair from a night spent in the hayloft. Lily clicked her tongue in irritation and disapproval. 'I don't know what you think you're up to, lass, but you'll come to a bad end if you don't mind. Oh, go on with you. Into the scullery and get washed and come and get your breakfast.'

As she sat down at the table moments later, Ollie winked at her. 'I heard the chain rattle and I was coming down to let yer in, but 'er,' he gestured towards his wife with a nod, 'wouldn't let me.'

'I should think not an' all,' Lily said, banging a dish of thick porridge in front of Hannah. 'Coming home when decent folks are all in their beds. My Ollie works long, hard hours, m'girl. He doesn't want his sleep broken by you traipsing in at all hours.'

'No, Mrs Grundy. I'll mind it doesn't happen again.'

Lily sniffed and disappeared to the scullery. Ollie leaned over. 'Don't worry, lass. When I know you're out, I won't put the chain on. You know where key is?'

Hannah nodded. Ollie winked and tapped the side of his nose. 'What the eye doesn't see, eh? But just take care of yourself. I wouldn't want you getting hurt.'

'I won't, Mr Grundy, I promise you that. And I'm sorry for disturbing you.'

'That's all right. We'll say no more about it.'

And no more was said, but Lily was not quite so forgiving, and Hannah had the uncomfortable feeling that it was more to do with her rejection of Ted than with her late homecoming.

'You're wanted in the office.' One of the young girls approached Hannah at her machine. 'I'll take over here.'

'Who sent for me?'

The girl shrugged. 'Dunno.' She eyed Hannah, who was smiling. 'Don't know what you're looking so pleased about. We only get called up to the office if we've done summat wrong. What have you been up to?'

'Nothing,' Hannah said airily. But of course she had been up to plenty and with the young master. He was becoming more possessive, more ardent in his demands with each passing day, and she knew that her refusal to let him make love to her was driving him insane with desire.

As she hurried down the length of the workroom, she saw Daniel glowering at her. 'Can't wait till night, eh?' he mouthed at her. Folks who worked in the mills became expert at lip-reading, and whilst she couldn't hear his words, she knew exactly what he had said. She stopped and moved closer. 'What do you mean?'

'What I say. We all know about you and the young master. You can't keep secrets round here, Hannah, you should know that.'

'Don't call me that, my name's—'

'I'll call you whatever I like.' His eyes narrowed. 'I could think of one or two names that would fit you nicely.'

'How dare you?'

'Oh, I dare. D'you know something, Hannah – and I never thought I'd hear meself say such a thing – but I'm glad that my brother isn't alive to see it. To see how you're behaving. It'd've broken his heart.'

Tears sprang to Hannah's eyes as she blurted out, 'If Luke was still alive, I wouldn't be doing it.'

Then she whirled around and ran, and did not stop until she opened the door to the outer office and, breathless, almost fell into the room. Without taking any notice of Mr Roper, bent as always over his books, she ran towards the inner door. Her hand was on the doorknob when he spoke.

'There's no one in there,' came Josiah Roper's silky voice.

Hannah turned to face him, the tears of anger at Daniel's words still brimming in her eyes. 'What . . . what d'you mean? I was sent for. Adam—'

'Oho, Adam, is it?'

Too late, she realized her mistake. 'I mean Master Adam,' she stammered, but the damage was done.

Slowly, Josiah put down his pen, slipped off his high stool and regarded her for a moment over the top of his small oval spectacles perched on his beak-like nose.

'You needn't worry. Everyone here knows about you and Master Adam. Including me. Especially me.' He paused. 'But what no one else knows – except me – is . . .' He paused and then added with an ominous threat in his tone, 'Exactly – who *you* are.'

Forty-One

Standing in the office facing Josiah Roper, Hannah gasped, the colour fleeing from her face. 'What ... what do you mean? My name's Anna Morgan.'

'Don't play your devious games with me, girl. You're Hannah Francis. I knew you the minute you walked through that door.' He flung his arm out to indicate the office door. 'Think dying your hair that ridiculous colour is going to hide your identity? It's not quite as easy as that. Oh, I've no doubt you've fooled a few here. The ones who didn't know you that well. Master Adam, for one,' he added pointedly. 'But wait till Mr Edmund decides to come home. He'll know you. Oh yes, he'll know you all right.'

Hannah's shoulders slumped. 'So you're going to tell Adam?'

A sly look came over Josiah's face. 'No, actually, I'm not.'

Now Anna was surprised. 'You're not?'

He shook his head. 'I don't quite know yet what devious game it is you're playing or why – and I don't expect you're going to tell me.' He paused a moment as if giving her time to do just that. When she remained silent he gave a little shrug and went on. 'I assume you're setting your cap at Master Adam. And,' he raised his eyebrows, 'by all accounts, it seems to be working. Trying to get him to marry you, are you?'

'I . . .'

Josiah nodded. 'I thought so. Well, the master won't like that. He won't like that at all.'

'So,' Hannah asked carefully. 'Why aren't you going to tell Master Adam who I really am?'

'Because,' another pause whilst Hannah waited, holding her breath, 'it suits my purpose not to.'

'*Your* purpose? Whatever d'you mean?'

His thin smile did not reach his eyes as he said silkily, 'Because anything that *dis*pleases Mr Edmund *pleases* me.'

Hannah's eyes widened as she stared at him. 'But . . . but I thought . . . I mean you're Mr Edmund's lackey,' she blurted out. 'You're forever toadying up to him.'

Josiah's features twisted nastily. 'You know nothing, girl. Nothing about me.'

'But you told on me when you thought I was running away. Dragged me back here to be thrown in the punishment room. Why? If you're not bothered about Mr Edmund, why didn't you just let me go then?'

'Because it was my duty. Because it was what he expected me to do. What he pays me to do. Just as now I shall have to write and report to him that, in his absence, his son is keeping – er – undesirable company.'

Hannah was still puzzled. 'So this time you're giving me time to get away before he comes back?'

Josiah shook his head. 'Not at all. I'm giving you time to bring whatever it is you have to do to fruition. That's if you can manage it.'

Hannah shook her head wonderingly. 'Why? I just don't understand.'

'Why is my business,' he snapped. 'I'm just giving you fair warning what I'm going to do, that's all. I needn't write immediately,' he said. Now he was thinking aloud, laying out his plans. 'He's abroad, so the letter will take quite a while to reach him. Then it'll take him a few days to get back here. I reckon you've got about a month all told.'

Why, she wanted to demand again, but knew he was not going to tell her. 'Are you going to tell him in your letter who . . . who I am?' There was no point in her trying to carry on the deception further. At least, not with Josiah Roper.

Josiah didn't answer immediately. He turned and perched himself back on his high stool and picked up his pen. He twirled it between his fingers and than glanced back at her over his shoulder. 'No. I think it would be . . . amusing – see if he recognizes you for himself. Don't you?'

Then he turned back to the open ledger on his desk and calmly began checking a long column of figures.

Hannah stood staring at him in bewilderment for a few moments before she turned and went quietly out of the office without another word.

A month. For some devious, twisted reason of his own, Josiah Roper had given her a month to get Adam to marry her.

Hannah pondered how much to tell Adam. She didn't want him to know her true identity, and whilst she couldn't understand why he was doing it, she was grateful that Josiah Roper was for the moment keeping her secret. But there was another way she could put the pressure on Adam. Hannah smiled as she ran back across the yard to the workroom, another devious twist to her plan beginning to take shape.

'Darling,' she said, winding her arms about his waist as they stood together beneath the cliff on the narrow path beside the river. 'Everyone knows about us.'

Adam sighed. 'You can't keep secrets in a place like this.'

How true that was, Hannah thought ruefully. Even she had been unmasked by two people already and it was surely only a matter of time before either Daniel or Mr Roper told someone. Or someone else recognized her as a face from the past. She was surprised that Ernest Scarsfield hadn't realized who she was. He'd always been kind to her – as he still was, even though he thought she was a totally different person. And yes, she was a very different person to the innocent, naive child she'd been then. She shuddered, realizing with searing clarity that she did not like the new person she'd become.

Aloud, she said, 'What will happen when your father comes home? Because someone will tell him about us.'

'I don't know,' Adam said worriedly. 'I've been thinking about that. Roper will tell him for sure, if no one else does.' He was thoughtful for a moment before murmuring, 'I suppose I could sack Roper before Father gets back.'

'No,' Hannah said at once, afraid that if he did, the vindictive Josiah Roper would reveal her true identity. 'If Mr Roper doesn't tell him, someone else will.' She tried to be light-hearted. 'You can't sack everybody.'

She bit her lip and sighed dramatically. 'Your father will no doubt throw me out.'

'Then he'll have to throw me out too.'

'No . . . no, he wouldn't do that to you. Not his own son. Not if . . . not if you promise to give me up?'

'Give you up?' His arms tightened about her. 'I'll never do that. How can you even think it?'

Hannah pulled a wry face. 'You'll have to if you don't want to lose your inheritance.'

Adam groaned. 'I'd rather lose that than lose you.'

'You don't think he'd really do that, do you? Cut you off, I mean.'

Adam was thoughtful. 'He'd probably use it as a threat more than . . . than actually do it. You see, I'm the only heir there is. I've no cousins nor even more distant relatives that I know of.'

You have a little half-brother, Hannah wanted to say. Maybe more than one if the truth be known. But she held her tongue.

'And Father's very proud of the Critchlow family and its traditions. He wouldn't want to see the mill that my great-grandfather started pass into other hands. He'd do anything to stop that happening.'

'Well, I'm going to have to go when he comes back. I don't fancy ending up in the punishment room like—' She stopped, appalled that she had dropped her guard. Flustered she added, 'Like they say used to happen.'

Despite the seriousness of their conversation, Adam laughed. 'I can't imagine anyone being able to put a fiery redhead like you into the punishment room. Besides, it was only used when we had the pauper apprentices. And all that stopped a few years ago.'

Here was her chance to ask questions that had been puzzling her. 'The pauper apprentices? What do you mean? Who were they?'

'Oh, it was an old system whereby we took orphan children from the workhouse and gave them an apprenticeship here.'

He made it sound so philanthropic, as if the Critchlow family had been doing these poor, unfortunate children a favour. As he went on, Hannah realized that Adam thought that was exactly what they had done.

'We gave them a home and there was even a nice couple who ran the apprentice house. It was like one big, happy family for those poor kids. The kind of home that a lot of them had never known. I don't suppose being born and brought up in a workhouse could be much fun.'

No, Hannah could have answered. And it wasn't much fun being indentured to your family either. But in fairness, she thought, he was right about one thing. The Bramwells had been a nice couple. Carefully, she asked, 'So, where was this – what did you call it – the house?'

'The apprentice house. It's the one near the old schoolroom on the end of the row of houses directly behind the mill.'

'And do the couple who ran it still live there?' she asked deliberately, wondering if he knew any more than the Grundys.

'Oh no, the house is empty now. The Bramwells left. Went away somewhere. I'm not sure what they're doing now.' And he sounded as if he didn't really care either. The Bramwells had been thrown out of their job and their home and he didn't even know for sure what had become of them.

Hannah felt a cold chill run through her. Was Adam more like his father than she'd thought?

'Why did it finish? This . . . this apprentice system?'

'Laws were passed for shorter working hours for children, more schooling and such like. All very praiseworthy, but uneconomical from our point of view.'

Hannah had to bite down hard on her lower lip to stop the words bursting out. He sounded almost regretful at the ending of a system that had enslaved young children to fill the coffers of the already rich and powerful. She wondered if he'd ever realized just what the lives of the children had been like: the long hours of gruelling work, the punishments for any kind of misdemeanour, however trivial. The fines, the beatings and the punishment room. She said no more, relieved that her slip in mentioning the punishment room had not resulted in him asking awkward questions.

There was a long silence between them. They stood with their arms about each other watching the ducks swimming serenely on the river, the fish jumping . . .

As they walked home, hand in hand, Adam still had not said the words Hannah wanted to hear.

Three weeks later, Adam came into the workroom and, not caring now who saw them together, he walked straight up to Hannah at her machine.

'He's coming home. He'll be back here next week. I've had a letter. Roper's written to tell him about us. He's so angry, threatening, well, all sorts.'

'To throw us both out, you mean?'

Adam avoided her gaze. 'Well, sort of, but worse.'

'Worse? What do you mean – worse?'

'Look, we can't talk here. Come up to the office as soon as you can. I'll wait for you there. We'll have to decide what to do.'

Without waiting for her reply, he turned and walked away, his shoulders hunched, a look of desperation on his face.

As soon as she could, Hannah left her work and hurried after him. As she moved through the long room Daniel stepped out in front of her. 'Trouble in paradise, is there? He went out of here looking as if the world was going to end.'

'Maybe it is,' Hannah said tartly. '*His* world anyway.'

She side-stepped around him and would have hurried away, but Daniel caught hold of her arm. 'Be careful, Hannah. I mean it. Just be very careful what you're doing.' For the first time, there was genuine anxiety in his eyes. 'They're powerful people. They'll stop at nothing.'

Hannah nodded. 'I know,' she said huskily, touched by his concern. 'But you see, Daniel, there's nothing they can do to hurt me. Not now. Not any more.'

Roper was not in the outer office, and as Hannah opened the door to the inner room, she saw Adam sitting at the desk, his head in his hands.

At the sound of her entrance he looked up. 'Oh, Anna, what are we to do? What *are* we to do?'

Hannah bit her lip. She didn't want to be the one

to suggest it. She wanted the words to come from him.

He rose and came round the desk to her, taking her in his arms and burying his face against her neck. 'I love you, Hannah. I love you so much. I can't bear to lose you. And once my father comes home, that's what will happen. He ... he's threatening to have you arrested.'

'Arrested? Whatever for? On what charge?'

'I ... I don't know. But he'll think of something. He always does. And ... and he has friends who'll help him.'

I could have told you that, she thought bitterly, but aloud she said, 'Then I must leave, straight away.'

'No,' he clasped her to him as if he would prevent her physically from walking away from him. 'I won't let you go. We ... we'll get married. Now. Right away. Before he comes home. Then there won't be a thing he can do about it.'

Hannah was triumphant. She put her arms about him and pressed herself to his chest, hiding her face so that he should not read her feelings showing clearly on her face. 'Are you sure?' she whispered, injecting into her tone all the trembling delight and yet at the same time uncertainty that she could muster. 'You said yourself he's a powerful man.'

'When he's got used to the idea, when he's had time to meet you, to get to know you, he'll love you too. I know he will.'

Hannah said nothing.

'If only my grandfather was still alive,' Adam went on. 'He'd've been on my side. In his eyes, I could do no wrong.'

Hannah said nothing. Though Nathaniel had not

been quite so bad as his son, Edmund, she had vowed
to hate all Critchlows. With a vengeance.

It was all arranged with such speed that Hannah
wondered inwardly at the legality of it all.

'We've to go to a place in Yorkshire.' Adam
grinned boyishly. 'It's like a local Gretna Green. No
questions asked. It'll be quite a journey and we'll have
to stay there for a while. In separate rooms until
we're married,' he added hastily, in case she was
thinking he meant to seduce her and then not go
through with the marriage. 'Can you be ready
tomorrow morning? We'll leave early.'

Hannah's eyes shone, not with the happiness as
Adam saw it, but with victory. 'Oh yes,' she said. 'I
can be ready.'

'I'll be leaving tomorrow, Mrs Grundy. I just want to
thank you so much for everything you've done for
me. I know it hasn't been easy for you especially . . .
especially because you think I've been unfair to Ted.'

'I do,' Lily said shortly. 'Anyway, that's as maybe.
Least said, soonest mended, I suppose.' She eyed Han-
nah. 'So your fancy plans didn't work out then?
You're going back home, are yer? Back to
Macclesfield?'

Hannah shook her head. 'No,' she said quietly.
'I'm going away with Adam Critchlow. We're going
to be married.'

Forty-Two

They returned to Millersbrook Manor hand in hand to face Adam's father like two naughty school children caught stealing apples. But their sin was far greater than taking fruit from a neighbour's orchard.

'He'll be home by now,' Adam said as they walked down the hill and through the dale. 'He'll know.'

'Know what?'

'That we're married.'

Hannah's eyes widened. She had achieved what she'd schemed for, yet now that the moment had come to face Mr Edmund, her resolve almost failed her. She was still afraid, deep down, that he had the power to hurt her.

And her fear was mirrored in Adam's face.

It was almost dusk as they passed the Grundys' farm. Hannah was thankful that there was no one about; the last people she wanted to see at that moment were either of the Grundys or, worse still, Ted.

They climbed the steep hill through the village until they came to the driveway leading to the big house perched on top of the cliff overlooking the river flowing through the dale below.

'Well, here we are.' Adam turned to her and, forcing a lightness into his tone that she knew he wasn't feeling, he said, 'I suppose I ought to carry you over the threshold.'

Hannah laughed weakly. 'I don't think you'd better.'

'Oh, what the hell . . . ?' He dropped their bags to the ground and swung her into his arms. 'You pull the bell.'

They waited for what seemed an age, feeling rather foolish, until the heavy front door swung open and the Critchlows' butler stood there. For once, even the straight-faced manservant couldn't hide his surprise.

'Master Adam and . . . and . . .' he faltered not knowing how to refer to the girl being carried by the young master.

'And Mrs Anna Critchlow,' Adam said as he walked into the house and deposited Hannah on the floor. Ignoring the manservant's presence, Adam bent and kissed her. 'Welcome home, Mrs Critchlow.'

The butler coughed discreetly. 'The master is in the library, Master Adam. I . . . er . . . think he would want to see you straight away.'

Adam took hold of Hannah's hand. 'Come on, let's get it over with then.' He crossed the hall, pulling her along with him. Her heart was thumping painfully as he opened the door and they entered the room.

Edmund Critchlow was standing in front of the fireplace. Tall and broad, just as she remembered him. Yet, as she drew closer, she could see that there were noticeable differences even in the three and a half years since she'd last seen him. His dark hair was now flecked with white. His undeniably handsome face was florid, his skin blotchy. The excesses of the life he lived were beginning to take their toll and show on his features. But his eyes were just the same: hard and cruel and vindictive.

He scarcely glanced at Hannah and she kept her head lowered in submissive meekness. She left the talking – such as he was given chance to do – to Adam.

'You can pack your bags and be gone from this house.'

'Father—'

'You are a disgrace to the name of Critchlow. I never want to see you or this . . . this slut again.'

'She's no slut, she's—'

'Then pray tell me – who is she? Where does she come from and who are her family?'

The questions were genuine. He didn't know who she was – not yet. Hannah thought fleetingly of Josiah Roper. Whatever game of his own he was playing was certainly working to her advantage at the moment. He had not revealed her identity.

Adam faced his father squarely. 'She's the girl I love. She's my wife.'

Edmund stared for a moment, then threw back his head and laughed a loud, cruel sound. 'Ha! You silly young cub, you don't have to marry 'em just because you get 'em with child. If I'd married every one of them, I'd have a veritable harem.' He eyed Adam keenly. 'You mean you've actually been through a ceremony with her?'

Adam ran his tongue around his dry lips. 'Yes, a week ago. And – since you brought the subject up – she is not expecting my child. We . . . we didn't lie together until after the marriage.'

Now Edmund stared at his son in disbelief. 'Then,

boy, you are more of a milksop and a fool than even I thought you. Love 'em and leave 'em. That should be your motto. Far safer.'

Listening, Hannah was seething. She could scarcely contain her rage. All the years of bitterness and resentment, the years of hatred, welled up inside her. But now was not the time. She must wait. Whatever it cost her not to speak up right this minute, she must hold her tongue. This was only the beginning.

Edmund was pacing the hearth in front of the roaring fire in the huge grate. 'What am I to do with you, boy? Thank God your grandfather is not alive to see this day. It would have broken his heart. He lived only to see the mill pass down the generations. How could you do this to his memory, Adam? How could you do it to me? Everything I hold dear is wrapped up in this mill and in you. I have worked and schemed to pass on a great inheritance to you. And this!' He flung his arm out towards Hannah. 'This is how you repay me.'

'Father, I—'

Edmund held up his hand, palm outwards. 'Not another word, boy. Go to your room. I'll talk to you later – when I have decided what to do.'

Adam stood his ground. 'There's nothing to decide. I've thought it all out. I know exactly what I'm doing.'

'I don't think so—' Edmund began nastily, but Adam interrupted with surprising calm.

'I am your only *legitimate* son and heir.' The accent on the word legitimate startled Hannah. So, Adam knew about his father's philandering. A spark of anger ignited against her new husband. But then, she realized, what could a young man do against his own father? At least, Adam appeared determined not to follow in his sire's footsteps. That was a point in his favour. She listened now as he went on. 'If you wish us to leave, then so be it. But I hope you will reconsider. If you don't want us to live here – in this house – then we can move into the apprentice house. We can no doubt take in lodgers as well as work at the mill. That is – if we still have jobs at the mill.'

Edmund's only answer was a grunt as he still paced up and down the hearth. At last he said, 'Go. Get out of my sight. Leave me to think.'

'But if you'd only talk to Anna – get to know her.'

'I have no wish to get to know her. Go, Adam, just go.'

They went up to Adam's room to wait whilst their fate was decided.

'He'll come around,' Adam said confidently as he closed the bedroom door behind them and took her in his arms. 'It's just a shock for him, that's all.'

Hannah hugged him in return and buried her head against his shoulder. She was experiencing a strange, unexpected tumult of emotions. She'd achieved her goal – or almost. Edmund was beside himself with rage, and he'd be devastated when, to cap everything, he found out who she really was. She'd have achieved it all then. But revenge didn't taste as sweet as she'd anticipated.

She'd reckoned without Adam. He'd been but a pawn in her dangerous game. She'd not spared a thought for him. And she'd believed herself immune to any feelings of sympathy for him.

But as she'd watched him stand up to his formidable father, she realized that he was indeed prepared to give up everything for his love for her. The realization humbled her. And suddenly, without warning, she felt an overwhelming affection for him. She hugged him harder. He chuckled softly. 'Hey, what's this?' he asked, surprised but delighted.

She raised her face to look up at him and there were tears in her eyes.

'Oh, Anna, don't cry.' Gently, he smoothed away her tears with his forefinger. 'Please don't cry. It'll be all right.'

'Oh, Adam, I'm sorry – I'm so sorry if I've hurt you, I didn't mean that to happen. Please – believe me . . .' He couldn't know the full meaning behind her gabbled words as he kissed her gently. His kisses became more urgent and he had begun to draw her towards the bed when a knock came at the door.

With a click of impatience he released her and opened the door. The manservant stood there. 'Mrs Childs wonders if you'd like something to eat, master Adam. You and . . . er . . . Mrs Critchlow.'

Adam beamed at him – more because of the butler's acknowledgement of Anna as his wife than for the food he was offering. 'Thank you, Beamish, that'd be wonderful.'

The man, though always conscious of his position, leaned forward and smiled conspiratorially. 'I expect you'd prefer a tray up here, sir?'

'Thank you, Beamish. That's most thoughtful of you.'

The hours passed. They ate, made love and slept wrapped in each other's arms in the bed that had been Adam's since boyhood.

It was only now that she was here in his home that Hannah realized just how little she knew of the man she'd married. Apart from the fact that he had been away at school when she had lived here before, she knew nothing about his life. She had believed he would be another Critchlow: selfish, self-centred and with a cruel steak.

She was beginning to see that the truth might be very different.

Night came and there was still no summons from Edmund. A light supper was brought to them on a tray and a maid brought hot water to their room. At midnight they climbed into bed but now sleep eluded them and they both lay awake staring into the darkness and listening to the creaking of the old house. They fell into a restless sleep in the early hours and woke late to a knock on the door.

'Breakfast is served in the dining room, sir, and the master asks that you both should join him.'

'Right, Beamish, thank you.'

'Very good, sir. The maid will bring hot water for you both in a moment.' The butler gave a little bow and Adam closed the door and turned towards Hannah, who was still lying in the bed.

'There! You see? I was right. He wants us to join him for breakfast. He's coming round. I said he would. Come on, darling. Let's get dressed quickly and go down.'

'Oh, Adam, you go. I . . . I can't face him.'

Her reluctance was genuine, though Adam couldn't know the real reason. He thought she was just afraid of his father's temper, whilst the truth was that she was feeling the first stirrings of regret that she'd ever entered upon such a game of revenge. She certainly wished she'd not involved Adam. She wished now that she'd found some other way.

'Oh, please come down, Anna. We must face him together. I'll be with you. I won't leave you alone with him, I promise.' His face was so boyishly appealing that she couldn't hold out against him any longer. All her resolve, all her single-minded desire for revenge was melting away beneath Adam's charm and his genuine love for her.

What have I done? she asked herself silently. *Oh, what have I done?* But it was too late now – she had to carry on. As they descended the stairs hand in hand a few minutes later, she found herself praying the very opposite to what she had planned and schemed for weeks and months.

She was now hoping that Edmund Critchlow would not recognize her.

Forty-Three

He was sitting at the end of the long table. When they entered the dining room, he waved them to their places, one on either side of him. There was no welcoming smile. He didn't speak, not even to wish them good morning.

For him, Hannah knew, it was anything but a good morning.

The three of them ate in silence, though Hannah could hardly be said to be eating. She picked at the food set before her by a solicitous Beamish and kept her eyes downcast.

As the meal came to an end, Edmund rose and spoke for the first time. 'Adam, you will oblige me by joining me in my study.' As they both made to rise from the table and follow him, Edmund barked, 'Not you. I wish to speak to my son alone.'

Hannah sank back into her chair as Edmund marched from the room. Adam came around the table to kiss her. 'Don't worry. I'll stand up to him.'

She touched his hand and smiled weakly at him. 'Good luck,' she whispered, and was surprised to find that she really meant it.

When the study door across the hall closed, Hannah went back upstairs to Adam's bedroom. She couldn't think of it as 'theirs' for she doubted it ever would be. Sitting on the window seat overlooking the steep drop

405

down the cliff to the river below, Hannah leaned her forehead against the cool pane and sighed. They'd all tried to warn her: Auntie Bessie, Nell, the Grundys, Ted – even Daniel. But she hadn't listened. She'd been hell-bent on avenging the innocent life that Edmund had taken. She lifted her eyes and looked up above the river to the hillside opposite. She could see the narrow path that she and Luke had walked. And in her fanciful imagination, she could see herself and Luke – two youngsters walking along the path on a bright, sunlit day, hand in hand. So young, so innocent, so in love. A cloud hid the sun and the vision faded. She could no longer recall Luke's face clearly nor hear his voice in her head. Her memories of him were no longer so vivid. A tiny corner of her heart would always belong to him – her first love. But now, there was someone else who was pushing his way into her heart and her mind. Adam.

She chewed on her lip, wondering what was happening in the study. Had Edmund recognized her? Was he, at this very minute, telling Adam just who she was? And if so, what would Adam's reaction be? Would he love her still – or hate her?

It seemed an age before she heard footsteps in the passageway outside. Slowly, Hannah rose to her feet. Her heart was doing painful somersaults inside her chest as the bedroom door opened and Adam came in. He looked pale and drawn, but he was smiling.

He opened his arms to her and she ran across the room to him. She hardly dared to ask, yet she had to know. 'What happened?'

Adam took a deep shuddering breath and his voice was unsteady. 'He's disowning me. He's going to change his will and cut me out. I can work in the mill but I'm no longer to regard myself as his son. I'm to be an ordinary worker.'

Hannah gasped. It was not what she had expected at all. She couldn't believe that Edmund would cast his one and only legitimate son aside in such a callous manner, no matter what he'd done. She'd fully expected that he'd get rid of her. Have the marriage annulled, have her sent back to the workhouse – anything to break them up. But he'd keep his son. Oh yes, he'd keep his son close.

Her mind was working quickly. No, she didn't believe what Adam was telling her. Edmund was doing this only to teach Adam a lesson. It was his way of bringing his young pup to heel.

'And what about me? Am I to work in the mill?'

'He . . . he didn't mention you.'

'Not at all? Didn't he tell you to . . . to end it? To send me away?'

Adam looked uncomfortable. 'Well, yes, but I refused. That was when he came up with the alternative. I can work here, but that's all.'

Hannah shook her head slowly. 'I don't think it's all by any means,' she said quietly. 'He'll have other plans. He . . . he'll be up to something to get rid of me.'

Adam held her close. 'Oh, darling, don't think that. You make him sound an ogre. He's stern and strict with his employees – I know that – but he's not so bad. He'll come around. I know he will.' His eyes sparkled as he looked down at her. 'And if we give him a grandson – you'll see. I'll be restored to the family fold – and you along with me.'

Hannah stared at him, amazed at his naivety. He didn't know his father at all.

Edmund Critchlow would stop at nothing to rid himself of an unwanted daughter-in-law.

There was only one thing she could do that might yet save Adam. The very thing that she'd planned all along, but now it was with a very different purpose in mind. It was not only to exact her revenge upon Edmund, but now it was to save Adam too. She'd have to reveal her true identity herself. She'd do nothing yet, she decided. She'd bide her time and wait and see what happened. *But*, she thought, *I still have a trump card to play – if I have to.*

Her mind was spinning and she heard Adam's plans with only half an ear. 'We'll live in the apprentice house and take in lodgers. I know we don't have the orphans any more but we still get single young men and women coming to work at the mill and needing lodgings. You could do that, darling. Run it as a lodging house, couldn't you? There'd be no need for you to work in the mill any more. And when the family comes along . . .'

Adam was full of ideas, happily planning their future and confident that, in time, his father would come around.

Oh, how little you know of him, Hannah thought.

It was eerie to walk back into the apprentice house. So many ghosts lingered in the rooms. She could almost hear their voices: the Bramwells, Nell – and now Luke too. She fancied she could hear his laughter, teasing her. Calling up to her from below the window of the punishment room. Hannah shivered.

'I know it's cold and damp,' Adam said, throwing open all the doors and going from room to room, dragging Hannah in his wake. 'But we'll soon have it cleaned and warmed through. Perhaps some of the girls from the mill would help . . . Oh!' He stopped and his face fell. 'I was forgetting,' he murmured. 'I'm no longer the owner's son. I can't ask for help.'

'You could still ask,' Hannah said.

'I could, I suppose,' Adam said doubtfully, 'but I couldn't arrange for them to be paid, could I?'

'No,' Hannah said. 'No, I suppose not, unless . . .'

'Unless what?'

'How do you get on with Mr Roper?'

'Roper?' Adam was puzzled. 'Well, all right, but . . .' His face cleared. 'Oh, I see what you're getting at. Roper could arrange their pay.'

'Mmm.'

Adam shook his head. 'He wouldn't do it. He wouldn't do anything that would go directly against my father's wishes.'

Hannah said nothing. She was not so sure.

It was high time she had a word with Mr Roper herself. There were one or two matters that needed to be sorted out.

A week later, when Hannah heard that Edmund would be away on business for a few days, she crossed the yard and climbed the stone steps to the offices. She'd not been inside the mill since her marriage, but she knew the news would have travelled through the mill like a raging fire.

Josiah Roper was, as ever, sitting at his desk. As she opened the door and marched in, he looked up and smiled his thin, humourless smile as he saw who it was.

'Ah, the new Mrs Critchlow,' he said sarcastically. He laid down his pen and turned to face her. 'And to what do I owe this honour?'

Hannah smiled brightly at him. 'I've come to ask a favour, Mr Roper.'

'A favour? From me?'

'If Adam were to ask one or two of the girls to help clean out the apprentice house, would you arrange for them to be paid?'

For the first time that she could remember, Hannah saw surprise on Josiah's face. 'Arrange for them . . . to be paid?' he spluttered. 'For . . . for helping you?'

'Yes, Mr Roper.'

He stared at her and shook his head wonderingly. 'You've got some nerve, I'll say that for you. I always did admire your spirit. Grudgingly, of course.'

Hannah's smile widened. 'Of course.'

There was silence as they stared at each other. 'And how would you suggest that I justify such an action to Mr Edmund?'

Hannah put her head on one side. 'He's going away, isn't he?'

'Yes,' Josiah said slowly.

'And whilst he's away, you'll be in charge?'

'Mm.'

'Have you been told – officially, for I'm sure you will have heard the gossip – that Master Adam is no longer to be treated as son and heir?'

Josiah raised his eyebrows. 'Mr Edmund told me that his son's allowance was to be stopped. That he is to become an ordinary worker in the mill and treated as such.' He paused and then his beady eyes gleamed. 'But he said nothing about disinheriting him.' He was thoughtful for a moment before saying slowly, 'He didn't tell me that I was no longer to take instructions from his son – especially,' he added with emphasis, 'in his absence.'

'You're not afraid it'll cause trouble for you on Mr Edmund's return?'

His smile twisted wryly. 'I've never been afraid of Edmund Critchlow. Oh, I pander to him. To his every whim,' he added bitterly. 'And I expect I'm a laughing stock amongst the workers, but you see, Mrs Critchlow,' for some strange reason he seemed to delight in repeating her new-found title, 'I know exactly what I'm doing and why I'm doing it. And Mr Edmund trusts me. Trusts me implicitly. I'm the keeper of his secrets, you see.' He nodded meaningfully at her. 'I'm a very good keeper of secrets, Mrs Critchlow.'

'So – you'll do it?'

He turned back to his desk, dismissing her. 'Tell Master Adam to let me know the details of the young women involved and how much he wishes them to be paid.'

For a moment, Hannah stared at his hunched back. He was a complex, devious and mysterious character. She couldn't pretend to understand him.

When she told Adam what she had done, he put his arms about her. 'We'll make a great team, you and I. It's going to be all right. We're going to be so happy and everything will work out. I know it will.'

If only I could be as sure, Hannah thought.

Forty-Four

'So you've managed to hook him, then. What do you intend to do now?'

Crossing the yard after another meeting with Josiah Roper, to present him with the list of the names of the girls who were at this very moment scrubbing floors and flinging open the windows in the apprentice house, Hannah was met by Daniel, stepping out of the shadows to bar her way. She wondered if he'd seen her on her way in and had been waiting to waylay her.

'Daniel!'

'Ma'am,' he said sarcastically and doffed his cap to her.

How she wished now that she hadn't confided in Daniel! Her feelings had undergone a radical change. Whilst she still wanted to bring Edmund to justice in some way for causing Luke's death – that desire would never die – she wished she could do it without harming Adam. But it was seeming impossible now. Adam still respected his father, loved him, she supposed. Whatever she did to Edmund was bound to hurt Adam.

Now she faced Daniel. 'We're going to open up the apprentice house. Live there – take in young people working at the mill who need somewhere to live.'

'Starting up the pauper apprentice scheme again, are you?' His lip curled. 'Talk about poacher turned gamekeeper.'

'No, we're not. We're just going to offer a nice home to single folk.'

'Huh! I'll believe that when I see it. Well, I wish you joy.' He turned on his heel, pulled his cap back on and disappeared into the mill. Hannah stared after him. He wished her anything but joy. She could hear it in his tone: Daniel wished her nothing but ill.

She sighed and carried on out of the yard. In the lane she hesitated. There was one other person she ought to see. It had been praying on her mind and she'd better get it over with.

She would do it now. She would go and see Mrs Grundy.

'Oh, it's you.'

Lily Grundy's greeting was far from welcoming. She turned and went back into her kitchen without inviting Hannah in, but she left the door open as if expecting Hannah to follow. Hannah stepped inside and closed the back door.

'So, you're married to young Critchlow then?'

'That's right.'

'All part of the grand plan, was it?'

Hannah licked her lips, unsure how much to confide in Lily. But there was no one else. No Auntie Bessie, no Nell. Yet in many ways Lily reminded her so much of Auntie Bessie that almost before she realized what she was doing, she was sobbing out the truth.

'Oh, Mrs Grundy, I don't know what to do. I'm so confused . . . so mixed up. I . . . I wanted to get revenge on Mr Edmund – for everything he'd done. For the cruelty he inflicted on the child workers who were supposed to be in his care. For all the suffering and the deaths he caused. I didn't care how I did it or who I hurt in the process. Not Ted or Adam or anyone. I . . . I just wanted to make him pay.'

Lily stared at her for a moment and then, seeing that the girl's distress was genuine, she set her hot iron in the hearth and pulled a chair up close to Hannah. Putting her arm around the girl's shoulders, she said gently, 'Now, why don't you tell me all about it and then we'll see what can be done.'

So Hannah confided everything to her, how she'd made Adam fall in love with her but how the tables had now turned and she was finding herself falling in love with him.

'I don't think it's as simple as that, Hannah,' Lily said. 'You think you've made Master Adam fall for you. But you haven't. It either happens or it doesn't. He was going to fall for you anyway – once he'd set eyes on you, whether you wanted it or not. You can't make someone love you, lass, unless they want to.' She sighed. 'And I was wrong to go on at you about our Ted. I'm fond of the lad and I'm fond of you and I'd've liked nothing better than to see the two of you happy together. I thought you weren't giving him a chance, giving yourself a chance to like him, but I see now that if you were going to fall for Ted, then you would've done and you wouldn't have been able to help yourself. Besides,' she added, laughing a little sheepishly, 'I have to admit our Ted's a bit of a one for the girls. He's got his eye on a lass from the village already, so I don't think his heart is broken after all.'

Hannah smiled through her tears. 'I'm glad. I didn't want to hurt Ted and I hated you being angry with me. It was just that . . . that . . . well . . . even if I hadn't been bent on setting my cap at Adam, I still wouldn't have been right for Ted. I . . . I was believing myself still in love with Luke then.'

'You can't live in the past, love,' Lily said. She sighed. 'I s'pose I've been guilty of that. Never forgiving and never forgetting. Always bearing a grudge against them Critchlows because of our Lucy. But now, we'd best move on. All of us. Them days is gone. The apprenticing of young children has stopped – and a good thing too. I s'pect things is better up at the mill now, are they?'

'Not so's you'd notice,' Hannah said bitterly, thinking of the long working hours, the dusty, unhealthy atmosphere and the pitiful wage that most of the workers received. The punishment room might be gone, but workers were still fined for breaking the rules.

'If only—' She stopped, appalled to realize another consequence of her unremitting desire for revenge. 'If only Adam were in charge, things would be a lot better. He's kind and considerate and . . . and . . . oh, but I've put an end to all that, haven't I? He'll never have the chance to inherit the mill now. Oh, Mrs Grundy, what have I done?'

Lily squeezed the girl's shoulders but she could think of nothing to say that would bring any comfort.

By the time Edmund returned from his business trip, the apprentice house was looking much as it had done when Hannah had lived there before. Better, in fact, for most of the walls were freshly whitewashed and the whole house scrubbed from top to bottom. Two of the carpenters from the mills had put up partitions in the dormitories, dividing the space up into single rooms. And best of all, the dreaded punishment room had been turned into a cosy bedroom.

If only Hannah didn't feel such dreadful guilt hanging over her, she could have counted herself as happy.

'Roper. Roper! Come in here at once.'

Josiah laid down his pen, slid from his perch and ambled into his master's office. 'Sir?'

Edmund prodded the page in the open ledger lying on the desk in front of him. 'What is the meaning of this? These extra payments to some of the girls. And two of the men too. What was it for and who authorized it? Scarsfield? Because if so, he's exceeded his authority.'

Josiah went around the desk, pretending to look over Edmund's shoulder at the offending entries. 'Oh those, sir.'

'Yes, Roper. Those. Explain, if you would be so good?'

'It was work authorized by Master Adam, sir. On the apprentice house.'

'The apprentice house?' Edmund was growing steadily more purple by the minute. 'What on earth is he doing with the apprentice house?'

'Restoring it, sir, to it's – a-hem – former glory.' Edmund eyed Josiah, but decided to let the man's sarcasm pass. 'Master Adam and his good lady wife are living there, sir. But of course, you knew all that.'

'No, I didn't know all that,' Edmund roared, but Josiah didn't even flinch. Years of working for Edmund had immured him to his master's bursts of temper. In fact, Josiah revelled in bringing one about.

'Oh dear, have I done wrong, sir?'

'Done wrong? Done wrong? Of course you've bloody well done wrong.' Edmund thumped the desk. 'I've disowned my son, Roper. You know that full well.'

Josiah calmly shook his head. 'No, sir, on the contrary, I knew nothing of the sort.'

'But I told you – I *told* you that he was to work in the factory and treated as an ordinary worker.'

Josiah smiled obsequiously. 'Well, yes, sir, but I thought that was all part of the young man's training, so that when he takes over one day, he will have a true understanding of the workings of the mill. If I remember correctly, sir, you worked in the mill for a while – at your father's insistence.'

Edmund glowered. 'But I didn't marry a slut of a girl and try to bring her into our home.'

'No, sir. You didn't *marry* them, did you? But God alone knows how many bastards you have residing in various workhouses up and down the country.'

'Roper,' Edmund said menacingly. 'Watch your tongue.' But Josiah only smiled. Turning back to the matter in hand, Edmund frowned again. 'Nor did I give permission for them to live in the apprentice house.'

'I understand they are turning it into a lodging house for mill workers.' With measured mildness, he added, 'They're making a very good job of it, too, by all accounts. But then, I'm not surprised. Your son's bride is a very enterprising young woman.' He paused and licked his lips before saying with deliberate mildness. '*She always was.*'

Edmund stared at him. 'What do you mean? "She always was"?'

Josiah raised his eyebrows. 'Well, sir, you know who she is, don't you?'

Feeling a sudden, inexplicable fear sweep through him, Edmund shook his head. 'Tell me.'

'She's Hannah Francis. The girl you were chasing when that young lad fell in the wheel and was killed. I'm so sorry, sir. I could've told you weeks ago. I recognized her the moment I saw her. And I thought you were sure to have done so too. Oh, she's dyed her hair, tried to make herself look different. But she couldn't alter the colour of those magnificent eyes, could she?' As he saw the veins standing out on Edmund's forehead, saw his eyes take on a peculiar glazed look, Josiah thrust home his final barb. Edmund was now slumped in his chair, his hands shaking. 'She's come back and married your son. She's got her revenge all right, hasn't she?'

When Edmund had recovered a little from the shock, though his hands were still trembling uncontrollably, he gasped out, 'Get them. Fetch them here. Both . . . both of them. I want to see for myself. I know you, Roper. You're a lying toad . . .'

But Josiah only smiled at the insult and left the office. He sent one of the mill boys running to the apprentice house to summon Adam and Hannah.

When the message came, Adam was jubilant. 'You see, I told you, he's come around. He's been away and had time to think. Maybe all this work's been for nothing and he wants us to live at the Manor.'

'I'd rather live here anyway, Adam,' Hannah said swiftly.

'Yes, you're right. Time we stood on our own feet.'

Hand in hand they hurried to the mill, but as they

stepped into Edmund's office they were shocked by his appearance.

'Father!' Adam hurried round the desk to him. The man looked dreadful. His face was purple, his eyes bulged and his whole body seemed to be shaking. But he waved his son aside. His glare was fixed on Hannah standing helplessly in front of him. She was suddenly very afraid.

Mr Roper, she thought. *He's told him. I wondered why he never looked up as we came through his office.*

Edmund was levering himself unsteadily to his feet.

'No, Father, sit down. You're ill. I'll send for the doctor . . .'

With a surprising sudden surge of strength, Edmund swung his arm, striking Adam in the chest. 'Out of my way,' he said, his speech slurred. 'I want to see . . . her.'

He staggered round the desk like a drunkard and lurched towards Hannah. He stood before her, swaying slightly, but his gaze was intent upon her, boring into her soul.

'Look at me.'

Slowly, Anna raised her head and met his eyes. Suddenly, he raised both his hands and grasped her hair, pulling the pins from it. Then he pulled hanks of it apart so that the tell-tale line of recently grown blonde hair near her scalp was plainly visible.

'Father – you're hurting her. Stop it. Whatever's got into you?'

'Hurt her! I'll hurt the little trollop,' he spat. Saliva trickled down his chin and he swayed again. Hannah thought he was going to wrench the hair from her head and winced in pain.

'Father!' Adam shouted. 'Let her go.' Now, he tried to prise his father's hands open. 'Let her go!'

At last, Edmund loosened his grip. He stood swaying and if Adam had not been supporting him, he might have fallen.

'Sit down,' Adam said, and helped him back into his chair behind the desk. 'Now, what is all this about?'

Edmund jabbed a shaking finger at Hannah. 'Ask her. Ask your . . . your bride.'

Adam turned puzzled eyes on her. 'Anna?'

'She's not Anna,' Edmund spluttered. 'She's Hannah. Hannah Francis.'

Adam glanced from one to the other, still puzzled.

'She's been here before,' Edmund dragged out the words. 'She was here when . . . she was that . . . that boy's girl. Luke Hammond's girl.'

Forty-Five

Adam paled as he stared at her. 'Is it true?'

He had no need to ask for further explanation. He knew only too well who Luke Hammond was.

There was no point in further denial. Hannah nodded. Adam shook his head slowly. 'Why? Why did you come back, and why did you pretend to be someone else?'

Before she could think what to say, Edmund said, 'Revenge. That's what it is. Revenge on me – on us all. On all the Critchlow family.'

'No, I don't believe it,' Adam whispered, the colour draining from his face. 'Oh, Anna.' He still couldn't think of her by any other name. 'Say it's not true. Please, say it's not true.'

She opened her mouth to say the words he wanted to hear, but she couldn't speak. She could no longer lie to him. Whatever it cost her, Adam deserved better than that. He was the innocent in all this and he deserved the truth.

'I . . . I'll explain it all to you – everything. But not now. Not,' she nodded towards Edmund, 'not here.'

She saw the anguish darken Adam's eyes. He'd wanted an immediate denial and she hadn't been able to give him that. So now he thought the worst. He stared at her for a moment longer before saying flatly, 'I'd better get him home.'

Hannah moved forward, as if to help, but Adam said harshly, 'We'll manage. Go . . .' he hesitated, reluctant to use the word 'home' until he knew the truth, knew whether they had a future together – or not.

Hannah went back to the apprentice house to wait for Adam. He was a long time before he came back – a long time in which she had time to think how to explain it to him. But there was no easy way. There was no way around the shameful truth. And she was now deeply ashamed.

When he came at last it was growing dusk outside. She was sitting at the kitchen table – the same table where she had sat with Luke, Daniel, Nell and all the others whose ghosts still seem to haunt the rooms. A fire burned in the grate casting eerie dancing shadows around the room. She didn't move as he came and sat down opposite. She didn't even look up at him, not at first, though she could feel his gaze upon her.

'So,' he said in a tone that was not encouraging. 'Are you going to tell me?'

Slowly, Hannah raised her head and met his gaze. His eyes were wary and full of hurt.

'I'm going to tell you everything – right from the beginning. If you will hear me out.'

'Oh yes,' he said, and already there was a note of bitterness in his tone. She wondered what more his father had said. Had he already poisoned Adam's mind against her? 'I'll hear you out.'

'How is your father? Is he all right?'

Adam raised his eyebrows. 'Do you care?'

She stared at him. How swift and sudden was the

change in his tone. It was cold, devoid of love. She sighed and looked down at her hands lying limply on the table. 'I care – for your sake.'

'Really?'

There was a long silence before Hannah began to speak. She began at the very beginning – the beginning as far as she knew it. She told him how her mother had fallen in love with a married man, who, even when he became free to marry her, hadn't done so. She recounted her childhood memories living with her mother and her grandmother in the terraced house – her happiest time. But then, as she'd grown older, the cruel taunts about her bastardy. It all came spilling out – the workhouse and then the circumstances of her arrival at the mill.

'The Critchlows and Mr Goodbody, the master of the workhouse, had some scheme going. I think money changed hands for the supply of pauper apprentices. Children of twelve and younger who had to sign a paper binding them here for years until they were eighteen.' She looked up then and met Adam's gaze. 'How could a child of that age know what they are doing? They just did as they were told. They'd no choice. They weren't given a choice.'

Adam was silent, just staring at her as she went on, telling him about her life and the lives of the pauper children in the Critchlows' so-called care. She told him about their working conditions, the dangers, the accidents. She told him what had happened to Jane. Even though she knew he'd heard about the accident, now she spared him none of the gruesome details. And then, taking a deep breath she began to tell him about his father.

'There was this girl called Nell. She was so kind to

us all when we arrived. She showed us what to do, warned us about what not to do. If it hadn't been for Nell I might have spent half my life in the punishment room. I spent many an hour in there as it was. Most of us did at some time or another. There was one time when they thought I'd run away – I was only trying to go to see my mother because I'd heard nothing from her from the time I left the workhouse. I found out later that your father and the Goodbodys had hatched a plot to keep me happy. Mrs Goodbody wrote letters as if from my mother to make me believe she was still alive. But when I tried to go and see her for myself, Mr Roper caught me and dragged me back. No one would believe that I wasn't trying to run away, so I ended up in the punishment room for days after a cruel beating from your father. If it hadn't been for Luke sending me up food through the window, I might've starved. And he'd've earned himself a beating if he'd been caught.'

'I knew about the punishment room at the apprentice house. But beating? I didn't know about that. They . . . they beat the children? Girls too? You . . . you were beaten?'

'Oh yes.' She paused before continuing. 'Things were reasonable for a few years after that. We grew up, and Luke and I . . .' She ran her tongue over her lips. 'We liked each other. More than . . . more than liked. On Sundays, we'd go out for walks. We roamed the hills. We were happy together.'

'Were you lovers?' Adam asked bluntly.

Hannah shook her head. 'No. Not physically, if that's what you mean. It was all very innocent.' She raised her head and met his gaze. 'But I did love him with that first very special love. The love two children

424

have for each other that as they grow can either blossom into adult love or can wither and die. But we . . . we never got the chance, did we? We never got the chance to find out.'

Adam said nothing. If he knew little about the running of the mill when he had been away at school, he at least knew about Luke's death.

Hannah took a deep breath and said, 'Your father was a womanizer. He'd have his way with any of the girls from the mill – especially the pauper girls who had no one to turn to for protection. And they daren't refuse. How could they? The Critchlows ruled their lives. Even the Bramwells. I believe they did their best to protect the children in their charge, but even they couldn't do anything to prevent the cruelty. Not really.'

She glanced briefly at Adam, and now his face wore a disbelieving expression. It was going to be tough to convince him of his father's true nature. But Hannah told him all about Nell, ending, 'So, living in Macclesfield you have a three-year-old half-brother.'

'Really?' Adam said sarcastically. 'And I suppose once you'd hooked me and wormed your way into the family, they'll be along to claim his inheritance?'

Hannah shook her head. 'No. Nell is happily married now, to a policeman, and he plans to adopt Tommy legally. I shouldn't think she ever wants to hear the name Critchlow again.'

'We shall no doubt see,' he said tightly. There was a pause before Adam asked, 'And is that it? Is that all you've got to say?'

'No. I haven't told you what happened the day of the accident.'

'I know what happened—'

'No. No, you don't. And you promised to hear me out.'

'Go on, then.' His tone was not encouraging, but Hannah was determined that he should hear it all.

So, haltingly, painfully, she described the events of that terrible day which ended in Luke's death. 'After his funeral, I ran away. I just went.' She said nothing of the Grundys' involvement. She wanted to keep them out of it. Details of her escape were not important. 'I went back to Macclesfield. I daren't go back to the workhouse because Goodbody would have informed your father.' She went on, telling him how she had found Auntie Bessie and then Nell. 'She'd been sent back to the workhouse by your father when he found out she was carrying his child. But we got her out. She came to live with us. And then she met Jim and she's happy now.'

'So why weren't you happy too? Why couldn't you put it all behind you – like Nell?'

'Forget the lies and deceit? Forget that your father caused Luke's death and got away with it?'

'So you never forgive, you never forget, eh?' he murmured.

Now Hannah buried her face in her hands, her voice muffled as she said, 'That's how I felt then. Not now. Not any more.' Slowly she raised her head and looked directly at him. 'I don't expect you to believe me,' she whispered, 'but I love you. Oh yes, I admit I started out with the sole intention of wreaking revenge on your father – on the whole Critchlow family, including you. But . . . but you're so kind and good and . . . and you do love me, don't you, Adam?' He was silent, just staring at her as she finished simply, 'That I've fallen in love with you.'

There was a long silence before Adam spoke. His voice was hoarse with pain. 'You're right. I don't believe you. And as for loving you – well, I did. Very much. But at this moment, I loathe the very sight of you. I can't bear to be anywhere near you. I—'

What he might have gone on to say, tearing her to shreds, was never said. There was a knock at the door. An urgent knock. Without even waiting for an answer, the door opened and a boy stood there.

'Sir, they've sent word from the Manor. It's your father. They reckon he's had a seizure. You'd best come at once, sir.'

As Adam ran from the room, Hannah dropped her head into her hands. 'Oh no. No!' she whispered.

Now she had her revenge upon Edmund Critchlow. A more cruel and lasting revenge than even she had planned. But now it left a bitter taste. She'd hurt him just as she'd schemed, but she'd hurt Adam too. Adam, whom she now loved.

Forty-Six

Edmund Critchlow recovered slowly. The seizure had been a severe one. It had robbed him of his speech for a while. That returned slowly but left him slurring his words, like a drunkard. He was partially paralysed down his left side and had to be helped to dress, to walk, even to eat. Adam employed a nurse who moved into the Manor and cared for his father day and night.

Staying alone at the apprentice house, Hannah fretted, feeling sick with worry and remorse. She dared not go up to the Manor where Adam was now staying – not after the way in which they'd parted.

Her sickness got worse until she reached the stage where she didn't want to get out of bed in the morning. If only Adam would come home and talk to her. At least she would know what to do then. It was this waiting that was making her ill. Not knowing if he was ever going to forgive her. Not knowing if they had any kind of future together.

At last, she could bear it no longer. She rose, dressed and forced herself to eat a little Then she set off down the road to the farm

Lily Grundy would tell her what to do.

'So, I hear you got your way then? Edmund Critchlow's in a bad way I hear.'

Hannah nodded. 'I just wanted to make him angry – to give him a taste of his own medicine. Show him that he can't always have his own way. I . . . I didn't mean to make him ill.'

'Huh! It almost killed him, by what they say.' Lily laughed wryly. 'But I shouldn't waste your pity on him, lass.' Despite her earlier words, Lily Grundy was still unforgiving. 'It's no more than he deserves.'

'But it's Adam,' Hannah said, her eyes filling with tears. 'He hates me now. Oh, Mrs Grundy, what shall I do? It's making me ill. I feel sick all the time. Sick with worry.'

Lily regarded her steadily. 'Sick? When exactly?'

'All the time. 'Specially in a morning when I first get up.'

'When did you last have your monthly visitor?'

'Eh?' Startled Hannah looked up at her. Lily nodded, smiling grimly. 'You're expecting, Hannah. That's what. You're carrying a Critchlow.'

When she returned to the apprentice house, her head in a whirl, she found Adam in their bedroom collecting his belongings.

'Adam – please? Can we talk?'

'I've nothing to say to you.' He carried on pushing his clothes into a bag.

For a moment, biting her lip, she watched him, 'Are you . . . are you moving back to the Manor for good?'

'No.'

'No? Then . . . then what are you doing? Where are you going?'

He swung round to face her. 'I'm leaving.'

'Leaving?'

'Must you repeat everything I say? Yes, I'm leaving. I can't bear to look at you. I can't bear to be anywhere near you.'

She gasped and fell against the wall. She was trembling from head to foot and felt as if she was going to be violently sick any minute. She reached out a trembling hand to him, pleading, 'Oh, Adam, please don't go. If . . . if you don't want to stay here, then go back to the Manor.'

Bitterly he said, 'I'm not wanted there. Every time my father sees me he becomes agitated again. The nurse has advised me to keep away. So, I'm going. Right away.'

'What about the mill? You'll have to run the mill now.'

'Damn and blast the mill,' Adam shouted. 'I don't care what happens to the mill.'

'But it's your inheritance.'

'Not any more it isn't. Thanks to you.'

Instinctively, she put her hand protectively over her belly. 'But it's your child's inheritance, Adam.'

He stared at her. 'What child? I haven't any children. And now . . .' He stopped and stared at her as she nodded slowly.

'I'm expecting a child, Adam.'

She saw the conflict raging within him show clearly on his face. Then his features twisted. 'Another of your lies, Anna?'

'No, no, I swear.'

He picked up his bag and made to push past her. In the doorway, he paused. Close to her, he looked down at her as if taking in every feature of her face. 'Oh, Anna, you'll never know how very much I loved you. But I didn't *know* you at all, did I? I didn't know what

a scheming evil bitch you really are. I don't care if I
never set eyes on you again as long as I live.'

As he pushed past her, she caught hold of his arm.
'No, don't go, Adam. You stay. I . . . I'll go. I should
be the one to leave. You should stay here and run the
mill.'

His lip curled. 'Oh no, Anna. You stay. You run
the mill. It's what you wanted, isn't it?'

He pulled himself free and ran down the stairs, out
of the house and out of her life.

With heart-wrenching sobs, Hannah staggered to
the bed. She lay down, curling herself into a ball,
shivering and weeping uncontrollably. 'What have I
done? Oh, what have I done?'

She stayed in the house for two days, drinking water,
but eating very little. She had no appetite and felt sick
all day long.

On the morning of the third day, there was a knock
at the door. When she opened it Ernest Scarsfield was
standing there.

'Morning, Mrs Critchlow,' he said politely, though
a little awkwardly. He pulled off his cap and seemed
about to speak again, when he stopped and stared at
her. All thoughts of the difference in their positions
now fled as he said, his voice full of concern, 'Aw lass,
what a state you're in. Are you ill? Shall I send for the
doctor?'

Hannah shook her head, pulled open the door
wider. 'Come in,' she said hoarsely. As she moved
back to sit down near the cold range, he followed her.
In the mirror above the mantelpiece, she saw herself.
No wonder Ernest had been startled. She looked a

mess. Her eyes were swollen, her face blotchy. Her hair hung down in dirty, bedraggled lengths, the blonde at its roots showing clearly now that it was not fastened up. Her dress was crumpled and stained for she had not taken it off even to sleep at night.

'I . . . er . . .' Ernest began awkwardly. 'I came to ask where Mr Adam is? I need to ask him—'

'He's gone,' she blurted out. 'He . . . he's left.'

'Left?' For a moment Ernest was puzzled, then his face cleared. 'Oh, gone away on business, you mean? In place of his father?'

Hannah shook her head. 'No, he's gone away. For good. He won't be coming back.'

'Won't be—?' Now Ernest truly was shocked. 'But the mill? What'll happen to the mill? His father's in no fit state to run it. At least, not at the moment, so they say. It'll be a long time before he's fit enough.' His voice dropped as he muttered, 'If he ever is.'

'I don't know,' Hannah whispered, 'what's going to happen. Can . . . can you and Mr Roper keep things going, just for the moment and I . . . I'll . . . ?'

Without warning, a spark of her old spirit ignited. This was not like her. This was not Hannah Francis who fought whatever life threw at her, who sang no matter what. Whatever was she doing shutting herself away like this, moping and starving herself and her child?

Her child! She must think of her child. He – or she – was heir to the mill. Her child was a Critchlow, but it was Adam's child. It had a chance – a good chance – not to be like the old order of Critchlows. She could bring it up to be different, and one day it would own and run the mill. But in the meantime . . .

Hannah squared her shoulders.

'Mr Scarsfield, will you do something for me?'

The man was still dazed by the news that Adam had gone. He couldn't take it in. He couldn't believe that young master Adam would leave. Not now. Not of all times now when his father was incapable of running the mill. Surely . . . He dragged his attention back to what the new Mrs Critchlow was saying.

'Of course – anything, ma'am.'

She smiled at him. 'First thing, please call me Hannah.'

'Hannah? But I thought your name was Anna?'

She sighed. 'I can't explain it all now. I will soon, I promise. I'll tell you everything. I'd sooner you heard it from me than from anyone else. But there's no time now. Would you send word to the Grundys to have some provisions brought here? I've no food in the house. And then this afternoon, I'll come to the mill.'

'Very well.' He rose and then stood looking down at her for a long moment, then he murmured, 'You know, I thought there was summat familiar about you. You're that young lass that was here years ago, aren't you?'

Hannah nodded and held her breath, wondering what was coming next. But Ernest pulled on his cap and smiled. 'Well, I always did like that little lass. Loved to hear her singing about the place. I hope we'll hear you singing again, Hannah.'

With that, he gave a brief nod and left her. For a long moment, she sat staring after him. Then she too rose, squared her shoulders and lifted her chin. She put her hand on her belly and smiled softly. 'Come along, my little one. We've a mill to run.'

As she went to fetch paper and kindling and coal to light the fire in the range, Hannah was humming softly to herself.

About mid-afternoon, Hannah marched across the yard to the mill, her head held high and determination in every stride. She had washed, pinned up her hair and changed her clothes, and now she climbed the stairs and went straight to the offices. Without knocking, she strode into the outer office.

'Mr Roper.' She beamed at him. 'It's time you and I had a little chat.' She gestured with her hand towards the inner door. 'Please would you come into *my* office.'

There was no mistaking the emphasis on her appropriation of Mr Edmund's office. Josiah stared at her for a moment and then shrugged, put down his pen, slid off his stool and followed her.

'Please,' Hannah said as she moved around the desk and sat down in the well-worn chair behind it. 'Do sit down.'

Josiah sat in the chair placed for visitors in front of the desk. It was slightly lower than the chair in which Hannah was now sitting and she had the advantage of looking down upon him. It gave her confidence.

'Mr Roper, as you know, Mr Edmund is very ill and unable to undertake his normal work of running the mill. As you may not know – though I expect the gossip grapevine has already been busy – Adam has gone away. His father informed him who I really am.' She paused for a moment, looking Josiah straight in the eyes, leaving him in no doubt that she was well aware just how Mr Edmund had found out. Josiah dropped his gaze, but said nothing. 'He – Mr Edmund that is – has disowned Adam,' Hannah went on. 'It seems – even though he cannot run the mill himself for the time being – that he would sooner see the mill ruined than have his son in charge.' Hannah leaned towards Josiah. 'But, Mr Roper, we are not going to let that happen. We – and by that I mean you, Mr Scarsfield and me – are going to keep this place going.'

Josiah, for once, looked surprised. 'I'd've thought that was exactly what you wanted to see happen? The Critchlows ruined?'

Hannah sighed, rested her elbows on the desk and her chin in her hands. 'Yes. Once I did. Once upon a time I would have been singing with joy at the thought. But things have changed.' She hesitated briefly. It was difficult to talk to a man like Josiah Roper about affairs of the heart. She couldn't believe he would understand. She couldn't believe he had ever been in love. But he had to be told.

'You see, what started out as revenge against the Critchlows has rather rebounded on me. I . . . I fell in love with Adam.'

Josiah stared at her and then he smirked, 'Well, I might have known. Women can't keep up their desire for revenge. Not like a man. It takes years. It takes patience and single-mindedness. Women haven't got the stomach for it. They're too soft, too forgiving. Never forgive and never forget. That's my motto and I live by it.' His eyes gleamed with such relish that Hannah shivered. She couldn't understand Josiah Roper and probably never would, but she needed him. She needed his knowledge and his expertise if she were to run the mill – if she were to save it for her unborn child. Adam's child and Mr Edmund's grandchild.

'I haven't exactly forgiven and certainly not forgotten

what Mr Edmund did. But Adam was not to blame for any of it.'

'He's a Critchlow.'

Hannah regarded him steadily as she said, 'So's the child I'm carrying.'

For a moment, Josiah looked as if he too might have a seizure. He turned purple with rage. 'Another Critchlow bastard!' he spat.

'No, Mr Roper. Adam and I are legally married, if you remember. The child—'

'It might not be born a bastard legally, but it'll be one by nature. It'll have Critchlow blood in it.'

'Yes, but Adam's blood. He's a good man. Even you must agree with that.'

Josiah gave a non-committal grunt. 'But what,' he asked nastily, 'if it takes after its grandfather?'

Hannah grinned suddenly. 'Then I'll probably drown it.'

Of course she was not serious and Josiah knew it, but her statement relieved the tension. Even Josiah allowed himself a small smile. There was a long silence before he said, 'So, how do you intend to run this mill?' His tone was scathing. 'What do you know of business? Of dealing with suppliers and buyers?'

'Absolutely nothing. But, Mr Roper, you do, don't you?'

'Me?' He looked startled now. 'I've never been allowed to meet with buyers and such.'

'But you know what's done, don't you? There must've been times when meetings have taken place in this very office.' She leaned forward again. 'I'm sure that door is not so thick that you haven't been able to hear what's going on.'

He wriggled his shoulders. 'Well, yes, Mr Edmund had me in sometimes to make notes for him. Figures and such like.'

'So you do know how Mr Edmund conducted his business meetings?'

'Well, yes.'

'Then I suggest you and I – and Mr Scarsfield too, if he's willing – should meet such people together.'

Josiah's eyes gleamed. 'You're as crafty as a cartload of monkeys. I expect you'll pile on the charm and make out you're a weak and naive woman, whilst we drive home the bargains. That it, eh?'

Hannah smiled and her eyes twinkled merrily. 'Something like that, Mr Roper.'

'What about travelling abroad? Mr Edmund did quite a bit of that?'

Hannah put her head on one side. 'Was it always strictly business? Was it always really necessary?'

Josiah gave a bark of wry laughter. 'See straight through the old bugger, don't you? To answer your questions: no, it wasn't, but there were times when it was. Occasional trips abroad are very necessary.' He sighed. 'Especially now.'

Hannah frowned. 'What do you mean? Especially now?'

'You've heard about the war in America?'

'Vaguely.'

'There's a civil war going on in America. It started about three or four months ago. The north versus the south.' He reached for a newspaper lying on the desk, placed there every day for his master. 'There was an item in the paper. I kept it,' he murmured, scanning the small print. 'Ah yes, here it is.'

He came around the desk and spread the paper in front of her, jabbing at a paragraph with his bony finger. 'Read it for yourself.'

Hannah stared down at the tiny, close print. Whilst she was bright and had been a quick learner, her schooling had been spasmodic. She could read simple texts, write a neat hand and do arithmetic quickly in her head, but the tiny print and the long, complicated words baffled her.

'Er, you tell me what it says, Mr Roper.' She looked up at him and pulled a wry face. 'My learning doesn't go as far as the fancy words in *The Times*.'

For once, Josiah did not smirk derisively. He merely nodded briefly, picked up the paper to read the item again to refresh his memory whilst Hannah waited with impatient anxiety.

'The gist of it,' he began, 'is this. The majority of raw cotton that comes to this country comes from the Southern States of America. The people who do most of the work connected with the growing of cotton are black slaves belonging to the plantation owners. There's been a movement to abolish slavery, but of course the south don't want it because they want to keep their slaves – their cheap labour. But the people in the north believe it's wrong to snatch people from their homeland – that's Africa,' he added by way of explanation, 'and transport them to a far-off land and sell them to the highest bidder who'll probably work them to death . . .'

Hannah's face was grim. To her, there were echoes from her own life. Hadn't she been torn away from her mother and brought here to work at the mill for a pittance, made to sign a piece of paper she scarcely understood and been bound to the Critchlows for years?

As if reading her thoughts, Josiah Roper said softly, 'But there's no escape for them, Mrs Critchlow. Not ever. They're owned, body and soul, by the plantation owners. They even have to forget their own African names and live by whatever slave name their master chooses, taking his surname as their own.'

Hannah shuddered. She'd taken her master's name now, but the choice, for whatever devious reason, had at least been her own to make.

Josiah went on, warming to his tale now that he had such a willing listener. It was the one thing he missed since his aged mother had died – having someone to talk to about world affairs and political matters. Once – in the early days – Edmund had treated him almost as an equal and had occasionally indulged in such discussion. But of late, Mr Edmund had treated Josiah with the contempt he showed all his workers. Josiah Roper was now no more to Edmund that the lowliest floor sweeper in his mill. 'Now, the north and south are fighting each other over giving the slaves their freedom. It's called a civil war and it sets friend against friend, even brother against brother.'

Hannah gasped. 'Oh, how terrible!'

For a brief moment even the hard-hearted Josiah Roper spared a thought for the internal strife that must be tearing that great nation apart.

'So,' Josiah finished, 'we need to find other suppliers.'

'Could you do that?'

Josiah wrinkled his brow. 'Manchester's the place to go – or Liverpool. I could find out what's going on. It might even be necessary for me to go abroad. Rumour has it that we'll need to get Indian cotton, though some of that is inferior quality. It would need someone who knew what they were doing to make sure the brokers don't cheat us.'

'Would you be willing to go abroad? To seek out other supplies? All expenses paid, of course.'

For the first time a genuine look of pleasure crossed Josiah's face. 'I . . . I've always wanted to travel. See a bit of the world. Do . . . do you mean it?'

Hannah nodded, knowing instinctively that she'd won him over. 'I wouldn't be able to go – not with the child coming. And besides . . .' She put her head on one side, resorting to a little flattery to win him over. 'I wouldn't know where to start or what to do.'

'I'm sure you wouldn't be long in learning,' Josiah murmured with a wry smile. It was the nearest he would come to paying her a compliment. He was still looking thoughtful, but now there was a hint of admiration for her in his eyes. 'Do you know,' he said slowly, 'I think we could do it. The three of us together – you, me and Scarsfield. I really think we could keep this place going.'

'I'm sure all the workers will help.'

Now Josiah pulled a face. 'They'll be glad enough to keep their jobs, but as for actually helping, well, their hatred for the Critchlows goes deep.'

'But it won't be the Critchlows running it, will it? Not for a while, anyway.'

'You're a Critchlow now, don't forget,' he reminded her, though this time there was no malice in his tone.

Hannah pulled a wry face but then she laughed. 'Ah, but not by birth. That's the difference. And things are going to be very different, let me tell you. There are going to be a few changes around here, Mr Roper. Oh yes, in fact quite a lot of changes.'

Forty-Seven

Ernest Scarsfield sat with a bemused expression on his face as Hannah explained all that had happened and detailed her plans. 'Finally, you should know that I am expecting Adam's child. Whatever happens with Mr Edmund and ... and ...' her voice trembled a little, 'Adam, there's going to be an heir.' She glanced at both Ernest and Josiah now. 'So – will you both help me? Can we work together to save the mill?'

The two men glanced at each other.

'If you think we can do it, lass, well, yes, of course,' Ernest said.

'I'm sure we can. There's just one more thing,' she said as she stood up. 'I'll have to go and see Mr Edmund.'

'Well, I wish you luck,' Josiah said.

And almost beneath his breath, Ernest muttered, 'You're going to need it.'

'I'll go now,' Hannah said firmly, before her nerve failed. 'Get it over with.'

If the coming meeting with Mr Edmund hadn't been so nerve-racking, Hannah would have enjoyed the walk up the hill, through the village and into the grounds of the Manor. It was a hot, still day with only the sound of birdsong and the distant weir to disturb the peace.

Edmund was in his bedroom, sitting near the window so that he could look out, down the river valley. As she approached him, Hannah could see that the upper part of the mill was plainly visible. He was slouched to one side of his chair, a rug over his knee. The left side of his face was drawn down, giving him a lopsided appearance. But he recognized her at once, for he began to splutter. He raised his right arm and, with a trembling hand, waved her away, making strange, unintelligible sounds. Saliva dribbled from the side of his mouth.

He was a pitiful sight, yet Hannah hardened her heart. He'd been a cruel, ruthless man and even now, when he was helpless, he was still trying to turn her away.

Ignoring his feeble protests, she sat down in a chair opposite him.

'Adam's gone,' she said bluntly, sparing him nothing. 'You've driven him away.'

He made a noise and prodded his forefinger at her.

'Yes, I've no doubt you blame me. And you're right. I have much to answer for.' Another grunt from Edmund, but Hannah went on. She leaned towards him. 'But it's me you should have sent away – not Adam. You could have done. You were good at it once. Remember Nell Hudson?'

He dropped his gaze and let his hand fall back into his lap.

'Yes,' she whispered. 'I see that you do.' She paused and then added softly, 'I wonder just how many bastards you've sired.'

Now Edmund brought forth a growl of anger, but Hannah only laughed. 'You probably don't even know how many might come banging on your door one day to demand a share of their birthright.'

'Huh!'

'They'd get short shrift from you, I've no doubt. But Adam is your legitimate heir – and I am his wife and I intend to keep the mill running until he comes back to claim his rightful inheritance.'

Edmund shook his head and made angry noises, but Hannah went on, relentlessly, 'And here's something else for you to think about. I am carrying his child – his legitimate child – and your grandchild.'

With a great effort, Edmund reached out towards the small table placed beside him. A glass of water stood there and, thinking he wanted a drink, Hannah half rose from her chair to help him. But Edmund grasped the glass with his one good hand, picked it up and flung it at her. It struck her on the left-hand side of her forehead, just below her hairline, leaving an inch-long cut and spilling the water down her blouse and skirt. The glass fell to the floor and smashed as blood began to trickle down Hannah's face.

She did not move, did not raise her hand to touch her forehead. She stood there, quite still, staring at him for several moments, then slowly she turned and walked from the room, her resolve more steadfast than ever.

Hannah did not visit Edmund again, though she heard that he was improving slowly. She had plenty to occupy her at the mill.

For the first few months, the mill ran smoothly. There was still plenty of cotton in the storeroom and another delivery arrived, but the man who brought it was gloomy.

'Don't know when I'll bring you any more,' he told Josiah, who checked the paperwork assiduously. 'There's a mill in Lancashire threatening to close.

We're going to go through some hard times. You mark my words . . .'

Josiah did mark his words and passed on the man's dire predictions to both Hannah and Ernest, but Hannah refused to be downhearted.

Things were so much better. She'd arranged for the local doctor to visit the mill twice a month. Any worker who wished to consult him could do so. From the moment she'd suggested such a notion, Ernest had been all for the idea, but Josiah had shaken his head. 'It will cost too much. If we're facing hard times, we didn't ought to be letting ourselves in for extra expense.'

It was strange how quickly the three of them had assumed ownership of the mill and full responsibility for its running and the people who worked there. Hannah had even thought about releasing all the apprentices who were still tied to the Critchlow name – just like she hoped the poor slaves in America would win their freedom, so she wanted to set the bound apprentices free.

'Tell you what,' Ernest suggested, unwilling to see such a good idea quashed by the careful clerk. 'Why don't we ask all the workers to contribute a penny a week towards the scheme?'

Hannah stared at him. 'What – every week whether they need a doctor or not?'

Ernest nodded. 'I've heard of it being done in other places. It's not much, yet folk feel reassured that if they really need a doctor, they're not going to be faced with a huge bill to pay. And there's one mill I've heard of that has a visiting dentist as well. There's a room set aside with all the equipment in. A chair and everything.'

'Oh, now you are taking it too far,' Josiah said, but Hannah laughed.

'Now *I'll* tell *you* what,' she said. 'We'll sound out all the workers. See what they think, and if they agree we'll certainly have the doctor come regularly, and if the money will run to it, we can have the dentist come if anyone needs him.'

Ernest beamed and Josiah shrugged philosophically. As long as his books balanced, he didn't mind what the new mistress of the mill did.

And as for Hannah, she was happier than she had thought it possible to be. The mill was still working. As yet, they hadn't even had to put any of the workers on short time and now she was looking forward to the birth of her child in a few months' time.

Every month she wrote diligently to Auntie Bessie and Nell, and in return she received letters written by Jim – dictated to him, of course, by Bessie and Nell. Whilst they hadn't approved of what she had done, they nevertheless still assured her of their love and wished her well.

'Don't forget you've a home here with us if you ever need it. You and your little one,' Jim wrote in every letter.

Despite the threat of hard times to come hanging over them all, Hannah thrived and bloomed. There was only one thing that caused her deep sadness.

Not one word had come from Adam.

Sunday afternoon was the only time Hannah allowed herself some free time; the rest of the week was fully occupied with running the mill. On a surprisingly warm October afternoon, she walked along the narrow path across the footbridge over the waterfall and pulled herself up the steep, precarious path on the hillside opposite Millersbrook village and the Manor. Panting a little, she realized there would be not many more weeks when she would be able to tackle the climb. Smiling gently to herself, she ran her hand lightly over the swelling mound of her belly. 'You're growing fast, my little one.' And she felt a flutter of movement and believed the child she carried beneath her heart already understood. She walked on until she rounded the curve of the hill directly opposite the impressive manor house that stood on the edge of the cliff above the deep valley where the River Wye meandered. Sitting on the grass to catch her breath, she eyed the long windows glinting in the sunlight and wondered if Edmund was behind one of them, watching her.

Then her thoughts turned, as they always did when she came up here, to Luke. Her gaze roamed the hillside. She could almost see herself and Luke running up the hill, fancied she heard the echo of their young and innocent laughter. Tears filled her eyes and she pulled at the grass at the side of her. A lump came to her throat and a sob escaped her lips.

'Oh, Luke, if only you hadn't died,' she whispered. 'If only—'

'Hannah? You all right?'

Hannah jumped at the sudden sound of a voice. For one fleeting, foolish moment, she thought it was Luke.

Taking a deep breath, she lifted her head and squinted up against the sun to see Ted standing a few feet away, grinning down at her.

'Ted!'

He came and sat down beside her. 'Should you be up here?' he asked, genuine concern in his tone. 'Auntie Lily says you're . . . well, you know.' All of a sudden, the young man was embarrassed.

Hannah smiled and said, 'I'm fine. I'm only five months gone.' She pulled a wry face. 'But you're right. I won't be able to come up here many more times. It was a bit of an effort today, I must admit.'

'Well then, you're not to come up again,' Ted said firmly, but his bossiness was tempered by an affectionate grin. 'At least, not without me.'

'And what would your girlfriend say to that, eh?'

Ted laughed. 'Which one?'

'Oh, you!' Hannah laughed and punched his shoulder lightly.

'If you ever want any help, Hannah, you've only to say the word.' Now Ted was being serious.

'Thanks, Ted.'

She felt his gaze on her. 'There is something, isn't there?'

'Well . . .' She plucked at the grass again self-consciously.

'Come on, out with it.'

'It's just that there's two rooms at the apprentice house that we – that I – haven't got cleaned out and whitewashed. I can't really take in lodgers till I get them done. And I need to. Adam—' Her voice broke as she spoke his name, but she pulled in a deep breath and struggled on, 'was doing all that, but . . .'

'But he didn't get it finished before he went away,' Ted said gently.

Unable to speak, Hannah nodded.

'Consider it done.' Ted grinned. 'I'll—'

447

Whatever Ted had been going to say was cut off abruptly by an angry voice. 'Another poor sod in tow, eh?'

Startled, Hannah and Ted turned towards Daniel standing a few feet away, his hands clenched angrily by his side, his face thunderous. Ted rose to his feet and held out his hand to help Hannah up too. He knew who Daniel was, knew he was the twin of the boy who'd died years earlier, but that was all. He was unaware of the young man's bitterness, much of which was directed at Hannah. Knowing nothing of this, Ted thought that Daniel's interest in the pretty young woman was what any red-blooded young man's would be.

He grinned at Daniel. 'Jealous, a' ya?'

Daniel's frown only deepened and he spat crudely on the ground. 'I wouldn't want her if she was the last woman on this earth. You're welcome to her. But I'll warn you, she's bad news. She's trouble. And you,' he shook his fist at Hannah, 'you're no better than a whore.'

He turned and began to run along the narrow, precarious path.

'Daniel . . . !' Hannah cried, frightened that he would stumble and pitch headlong down the steep hillside.

Ted caught hold of her arm, fearful that she was going to go after Daniel. 'Let him go, Hannah.' He paused as they both stood watching until Daniel had disappeared around the curve of the hillside. 'What's eating him, then? Fancies you himself, I bet.'

If it hadn't been so serious, Ted's remark would have been funny. As it was, Hannah smiled but it was a sad smile. 'He hates me. He blames me for Luke's death.'

Ted was puzzled. 'How can he do that?'

'Mr Edmund was . . . was . . . well, Luke came to my rescue, if you know what I mean.'

Ted's face was grim. He knew all about Edmund Critchlow and his reputation with girls, especially the young girls at the mill.

Hannah sighed. 'That's when they fought and Luke fell in the wheel. I suppose . . . I suppose Daniel's right in a way. If it hadn't been for me, there wouldn't have been a fight and Luke would still be alive.'

'And you're still blaming yourself, aren't you, Hannah?'

Hannah sank to the ground and covered her face. 'Oh, Ted, I've been so stupid and . . . and wicked.' Tears flowed down her face.

'Oh, now come on, Hannah, love.' Ted squatted down on his haunches beside her. 'I can't bear to see you cry.'

She could see she was embarrassing him, so she sniffed and brushed away the tears with the back of her hand. She forced a tremulous smile.

Now she was calmer, Ted took hold of her hand and held it between his own. His touch was warm and comforting. 'Come on, tell Uncle Ted all about it.'

'I . . . I thought you'd've known. I told Mrs Grundy.'

'Oh, Auntie Lily wouldn't say a word to a soul. She knows how to keep a confidence. And so do I, Hannah.'

'I set my cap at Adam Critchlow – deliberately – to get revenge on his father.'

'Well, yes, I'd sort of guessed that, but I don't quite know why you had to go as far as marrying him. That did surprise me a bit.'

'Well, I had to. How else would it've really hurt Mr Edmund? He'd've just sent me away and that'd've been the end of it. But now, I've ended up hurting myself and . . . and the man I now love.'

'You mean, you *love* Adam Critchlow?'

Hannah nodded.

'Oh.'

There was a long silence between them until Hannah could bear it no more. 'So now you see why Daniel hates me, why Adam hates me and . . . and now I suppose you will too.'

'No,' Ted said at once. 'No, Hannah, because I can understand now how it's all come about. My family felt very bitter about our Lucy's death so if anyone can understand why you've acted the way you have, then it's me.' He gave a rueful laugh. 'When Lucy died I reckon me dad wanted to kill Edmund Critchlow with his bare hands. But he'd only have hurt all the family even more if he'd've faced the hangman for it, wouldn't he?'

Hannah nodded.

'And, like you say, it's you that's hurting now because you fell in love with Adam.'

Again, Hannah nodded silently.

'See.' Ted nudged her and winked, deliberately trying to lighten her mood. 'I said you should have married me.'

'Oh, Ted . . .' she was crying and laughing too now.

'Come on,' he said getting up and hauling her to her feet. 'It's time you were getting home, and next Sunday I'll come and whitewash those two rooms for you. Sunday's the only time I get. A right couple of slave drivers, me auntie and uncle are.'

It wasn't true about the Grundys, of course, but Ted's words reminded Hannah of the difficulties to come. Difficulties that arose because of the struggle half a world away to free those bound to real slavery. Despite all the hardship that might result because of it, she couldn't help but be sympathetic to the cause. And now, having unburdened herself to Ted and knowing that she still had his friendship, she returned home with a light heart and her resolve to save the mill and all its workers strengthened.

By the time Hannah gave birth, her hair had returned to its natural golden colour. She had cut it short and all trace of the dyed hair was now gone. But her baby son was born with wisps of black hair, and eyes that would soon become the dark brown of his father and his grandfather.

'What're you going to call him?' Lily demanded, the first of a surprisingly long line of visitors to the bedroom in the apprentice house where Hannah lay with her son in her arms.

Smiling down at the sleeping child, Hannah traced a gentle finger around the shape of his face. The baby slept on. 'I don't know. I . . . I'd like to call him Luke, but . . .'

'Best not. If Adam comes back one day, it's hardly fair, is it?'

'No,' Hannah murmured. 'No, it isn't.' She sighed. 'But I don't want to call him after any of the Critchlows, nor,' she added with an edge to her tone, 'my own father.'

451

'Well, just choose a name that doesn't mean anything. Just a name – the little chap's own name.'

'Well,' she said tentatively. 'I was wondering if . . . if Ted would mind if I called him after him. He's been a good friend – a real friend to me – these past weeks and . . . and he doesn't seem to have any hard feelings about . . . well, about what happened. And I . . . I'd like him to be one of the godfathers.'

Lily laughed. 'He'll be thrilled.'

'Then will you tell him?'

'You should ask him yourself, but I'll tell him you want to see him.'

Two days later, Ted stood at the end of her bed, twirling his cap through his fingers in nervous embarrassment, but beaming. 'I don't know what to say, Hannah. I've never been asked to be a godfather before. What do I have to do? I mean –' his face clouded for an instant – 'are you sure you want me? I'm only an ordinary chap.'

'You're just the sort of chap I want.' Hannah laughed. 'You're a good friend, Ted. I won't forget what you've done for me. All you have to do is come to the christening and make some promises and then see that I bring him up properly.' Her eyes became sad. 'If Adam doesn't come back, then you're just the sort of man I'd like my son to have in his life.' Huskily, she added, 'I can't think of anyone better.'

Ted puffed out his chest. 'Then I'd be honoured.'

'And we'll call him Edward?'

Ted nodded enthusiastically, but now he was unable to speak for the lump in his throat.

As soon as Hannah was well enough, she wrapped the baby in warm clothes and a copious shawl and set off up the hill to the Manor.

It was time that Edmund Critchlow met his grandson.

Forty-Eight

He was sitting in the huge window of his study overlooking the river. Like his bedroom, from here he could see the mill. The butler showed her in and as Edmund turned in his chair to look at her, she could see a vast improvement in him since the last time she had visited. The side of his face was no longer dragged down, and even in the simple act of turning in his chair, she could see that he had so much more movement in his limbs. And he no longer sat with a rug over his knees like an invalid.

His gaze was fixed upon her and the child in her arms as she crossed the room towards him. She stood before him and then bent down and placed the baby in the crook of his arm.

'I thought it time that you saw your grandson. His name is Edward. Edward Critchlow.' Deliberately, she emphasized the surname.

Edmund looked down at the child and Hannah was sure that his features softened.

'He's only three weeks old. So he's very tiny still,' she went on, 'but he's healthy and strong and he eats.' She laughed wryly. Her breasts were sore from her demanding son, but she didn't mind. She would put up with any discomfort for his wellbeing.

Edmund looked up and stared at her for a long moment. 'Please – sit – down.' He had fought hard to regain his speech, and though his words came out haltingly and a little slurred, he could at last make himself understood.

'Thank you,' Hannah murmured, drawing her chair close. Though she was determined to introduce Edward to his grandfather, adamant that Edmund should accept the child, she was still unsure of the man's reaction. But Edmund was holding the baby quite easily and tenderly. A slow smile spread across his face and he parted the shawl with a gentle finger to take a better look.

'He's – got – dark – hair.'

'Yes, just like you and Adam,' Hannah said.

'Sleeps well?'

Hannah grimaced. 'In between his feeds, every four hours round the clock.'

'You must – be tired. Have you – help? A nurse-maid?'

Hannah shook her head and said softly, 'No. I want to care for my son myself.'

'Then a – maid – to do housework?'

Again, Hannah shook her head.

'Take – Sarah – for a while. Just – just to help you.'

Hannah stared at him. He was making a gesture – she knew that – a gesture towards some kind of reconciliation.

'Thank you,' she said graciously. 'I would appreciate that.'

He nodded, but his eyes were still on the child.

They sat together for almost an hour, not speaking much, but there was no tension between them, no anger now. At last, the child began to stir and whimper, and Hannah rose and reached out for him.

'He's getting hungry. I'd better go.'

He let her lift the child out of his arms, but Hannah could read the disappointment on his face. As she settled the baby in her arms, she looked down at Edmund. 'Would you like me to bring him to see you again?'

'Please.'

'Very well then. In a few days.'

'Tomorrow?' His tone was pleading, no longer demanding.

She smiled. 'Very well. Tomorrow afternoon.'

As she turned to go, he said, 'The mill . . .'

She glanced back and waited, her heart beating a little faster, expecting the worst. But to her surprise and delight, he said, 'A good job – you've done a – good job.'

'Thank you.' She smiled.

'Roper – comes. Tells me – what's happening.'

'Yes, I know. I arranged that he should come up every week, show you the books and keep you informed.'

He nodded. 'Thank you – Hannah.'

They stared at each other and between them there passed a kind of truce. As she left the house, Hannah kissed her baby's forehead and murmured, 'You're a little miracle worker, my darling little Eddie, that's what you are.'

Life settled down to a comfortable routine. Hannah recovered quickly from the birth of her child; she was young and strong and healthy. Sarah came as her housemaid for a few weeks, but when Hannah told her she could return to the Manor, the girl burst into tears. 'I don't want to go back there. Cook's a tartar

455

and Beamish, the butler, he's never a kind word for anyone. And if I have to see the master, I shake from head to foot. Oh, madam, can't I stay here? I'll look after little Eddie. I love little ones and . . . and I am good with him, aren't I, madam?'

'You are,' Hannah agreed. She'd left the child in Sarah's care a few times whilst she went to the mill. She was quite happy that he was in safe hands.

Hannah was thoughtful. It would be a boon to have the girl work for her permanently. It would enable Hannah to resume her place at the mill. Since Eddie's birth, Josiah Roper had come to the house every Friday afternoon on his way back from his visit to the Manor, to lay his books before her and report on the week's activities at the mill. Ernest Scarsfield, too, came often, but he did not visit Mr Edmund.

'I'll leave that to old Roper, if you don't mind, Hannah. He's Mr Edmund's right-hand man.' He chuckled wickedly. 'I could think of other names to call him, but I won't be vulgar. Not in front of the little chap.'

Hannah laughed. 'I don't think he's quite ready to pick up bad language yet, Ernest.'

Ernest moved to the crib and tickled Eddie under the chin. 'By, he's like Master Adam, Hannah. Spitting image of him at the same age, he is. I remember his mother bringing him to the mill when he wasn't much older than this little feller.'

'Ernest – what happened to Adam's mother?'

'She died. About two years after Adam was born, I think it was. In childbirth. Little girl, but the poor little mite died too. Nice woman she was.' He glanced at Hannah. 'Too good for the likes of Edmund Critchlow,' he added in a low voice.

'He's changed. This illness seems to have – I don't know, what's the word? – cowed him.'

'Huh!' Ernest gave a wry laugh. 'Don't you believe it, lass. That one'll never change. Oh, he might not be able to shout and storm about the place like he used to.' His face was grim as he added, 'At least the girls at the mill are getting a bit of peace just now, but mark me, Hannah, he'll not have changed. Not in here, he won't.' He smote his own chest.

'But he seems to have taken to Eddie. He's quite upset if I miss a day taking him up there.'

'Oh aye, he will be. Eddie's his grandson. His eventual heir. He'll want him all right. And whilst the child's very young, he'll need you. But you watch out, Hannah. If ever he regains his health and strength, he'll be just like he always was. He'll want the child – oh yes, he'll want the child. But as for you – well, like I say Hannah, watch out.'

After Ernest had left, Hannah was thoughtful. She had thought that Edmund had mellowed, but like Ernest said, it could just be the debilitating illness that had curbed his ways. But he was recovering now. Hannah could see improvement almost daily.

And once Edmund Critchlow got his strength back, well, who knew what might happen then?

'Looks like he really has deserted you, then? That husband of yours?' Daniel was waiting to waylay her in the yard as she left the mill one evening, hurrying home to her baby.

'So it seems,' she said tartly.

'Luke wouldn't have done that.' He stood in front of her, barring her way. She was not afraid of him –

not physically – but every time she met him, she was reminded so sharply of Luke.

She swallowed hard, gritted her teeth and said, almost haughtily, 'If you'll excuse me, I have a baby to feed.'

'Oh yes, your son.' His face darkened. 'The child that should've been my nephew.'

She lifted her head and met his resentful eyes. 'Yes, Daniel,' she said, softening. 'He should've been. He should've been Luke's child. And I promise you, he would have been if . . . if . . .'

'If your husband's father hadn't killed him.'

'Oh, Daniel. Let the past go. Don't live your life with bitterness.'

'I'll never forgive and I'll never forget. And I thought better of you. I admired you, the way you were planning revenge on the Critchlows, but now, you're giving in to them.' His lip curled. 'Just like everyone else. Well, I won't. The only reason I've stayed here all these years is because of Luke. I can't leave him. He won't rest until he's been avenged.'

Suddenly, there was a strange look of madness in his eyes as he vowed never to forgive and forget. Hannah shuddered. They were the same words that Josiah Roper had used. They made a good pair, she thought.

'I must go,' she muttered, side-stepped around him and hurried away. But the conversation had left her feeling unsettled and strangely afraid.

Hannah did not forget either Ernest's dire warnings nor Daniel's continuing resentment, but there was one person who, surprisingly, did seem to have changed.

Josiah Roper was in his element. It was what he'd always dreamed of: holding a position of authority, his talents recognized at last. He, in turn, was courteous and mindful of Hannah's position, silently grateful to her that she was treating him with the credit he believed he deserved. And between Josiah and Ernest, who'd always disliked each other, there grew a mutual respect.

One Friday afternoon in March when they met in the inner office, both Josiah and Ernest entered to greet Hannah with glum faces.

'What is it?' she said at once. 'What's happened?'

They sat down and glanced at each other solemnly. 'Things are getting worse, Hannah,' Josiah began. 'As you know I was in Manchester yesterday. They say that the mills there are on short time.'

'Several have had to close,' Ernest put in, 'and workers are seeking public relief.'

'We've been lucky until now. We had a fair stock of raw cotton, but that's running low now and the price is rocketing,' Josiah went on. 'Since last October the brokers have been demanding one shilling and more a pound for the type we used to buy for eight pence. And prices are still rising. We can't absorb all of it and still make a profit.'

'Profit be hanged, Mr Roper. All we need to do is break even.'

Josiah raised his eyebrows and smirked, but Ernest laughed out loud. 'Well said, Hannah. Well said.'

'Mr Edmund won't like that.'

'Mr Edmund will have to lump it, if we're to save the mill,' Hannah said, grimly determined.

'We could ask the workers to take a cut in wages,' Josiah suggested, but Ernest snorted derisively.

'You'll have a strike on your hands if you do.'

'Was there *any* cotton to be had?' Hannah asked. 'What about Indian cotton?'

Josiah shrugged. 'Some, but only very inferior quality to what we normally use and the price of that has risen too.'

'But these aren't normal times,' Hannah said, trying to hold on to her patience. It seemed as if Josiah was loath to accept change. But change there would have to be if they were to survive. She turned to Ernest. 'Could we use inferior cotton?'

'We'll have to.'

Hannah smiled. At least Ernest was of the same mind as she was.

By April, Wyedale Mill had only very poor quality yarn to work with and the quantity Josiah could acquire for an acceptable price was not enough to keep the whole mill running. There was no alternative but to put the workers on short time.

Hannah called a meeting of all the workers. The warm, balmy evening mocked the grim faces. Some of the women were in tears. It was no more than Hannah had expected. The news from the cities and the mills in Lancashire was desperate. Families were facing starvation. They had burned every stick of furniture they had in an effort to keep warm. New-born babies were dying for lack of nourishment and children cried for food. And soon such hardship would reach Wyedale Mill.

Earlier in the day she'd walked down the lane to the Grundys' farm. Sitting in Lily Grundy's warm kitchen and sipping hot tea gratefully, she said, 'This is what I'm going to miss the most. Tea.'

'Bad as that, is it, lass?'

Ollie and Lily sat opposite, their solemn faces turned towards her, as Hannah nodded. 'I'm afraid it is and it's going to get worse. I've called all the workers together for a meeting tonight at the mill. We're going to have to put them on short time, even lay a few off. I thought I should come and tell you, because it'll likely affect you. You've always supplied the village folk and . . .'

She saw Ollie and Lily glance at each other. Then Ollie cleared his throat. 'Look, lass, me an' the missis've been talking things over. The mill and the villagers've given us our living for years. And a good living it's been too. Oh, it's not easy, farming. It's hard work and – ' he smiled a little – 'not many days off in a year, I can tell you. But it's a good life, a satisfying life. And now, we want to give a bit back.'

Hannah glanced from one to the other. 'I don't understand.'

'Well,' Ollie began, 'for a start I can take some of the fellers on to work on the land. If they're willing to do a few hours each, it'd help several families, wouldn't it. What I mean is, rather than take on one or two full time, they could sort of – sort of share the jobs out.'

'But do you need any more help? You and Ted have always managed.'

Ollie laughed. 'Mebbe we have, but that doesn't mean we wouldn't be glad of a bit more help.'

Tears sprang to Hannah's eyes. Ollie, Lily – and Ted must be in on it too – were creating jobs for the out-of-work millhands.

'With more help,' Ollie went on, 'we can grow more food for everyone.'

Hannah reached out and clasped their hands as the tears now flooded down her face unchecked. 'Oh, how good you are.'

Now, as Hannah stood on a box before a sea of worried faces, with Josiah and Ernest on either side of her, she began to explain the situation. 'We're all in this together.'

'You mean we'll all be in the workhouse together,' a voice from the back cried out.

Anger flashed in Hannah's blue eyes and she shook her fist in the air. 'Don't let anyone mention the word "workhouse" in my hearing. No one – *no one* – from this village will ever go into the workhouse.'

There was muttering amongst the crowd and shaking of heads. They couldn't believe her, however much they wanted to.

One of the men, Bill Ryan, who'd worked at the mill all his life pushed his way to the front to stand before her. He was tall, broad shouldered and strong. With a note of deference, he pulled off his cap, but he still addressed her as 'Hannah'. Now, they all knew exactly who she was, and whilst they were always courteous towards her, she herself had insisted that everyone should call her by the name they always had. She didn't want to be called 'Mrs Critchlow'.

'Hannah,' Bill began, 'we all know that you – and Mr Roper and Ernest here – have kept us going so far and we're grateful. And we also 'preciate you always being honest with us.' A low murmuring confirmed his words, 'But times is hard and they're going to get worse. Whole families work at the mill – you know that. Most of us have no other income except what we earn here, and soon we'll not have bread to feed our wives and families.' The proud man glanced around at his workmates and friends. 'And we're not going to sit idle about the house watching our families starve. If you've got to put us on short time or reduce our wages, then . . . then we'll have to look for other work or go on the parish, lass. I'm sorry, but there it is. And we can't even afford the penny a week for the doc no more.'

Hannah nodded. 'I know and I understand, but first, let me tell you what we have planned. For one thing, Dr Barnes has agreed to keep coming even if he doesn't get paid. "We must all pull together," he said.'

There was another murmuring, louder this time, at the doctor's kind sacrifice.

Hannah went on, raising her voice to be heard. 'I'm going to open up the schoolroom again. We'll start reading classes and—'

Before she could say more, a shout came from the back and a fist was raised in the air. 'That won't put food in our bellies. Reading! Pah!'

'*And*,' Hannah went on as if uninterrupted, 'there are to be sewing classes and shoemaking.'

The murmuring grew to excited chatter. Now they could begin to see the usefulness of the idea. Hannah stamped on the box for quiet. 'The Grundys at the farm are willing to take on hands to work on the land to help grow more food for all of us. And some of you might be able to find work on the hillside.'

The workings that Hannah had seen were for a railway that was to run through the dale all the way to Buxton. When she'd heard about it, Hannah had thought wryly, *It's come a few years too late for me. If there'd been a train then, Josiah might not have caught me.* Work on the track had been going on for months and it was rumoured that the line was due to open in the summer. At her suggestion, she saw several men turn to one another and nod their heads.

'And,' she went on, and now she was smiling broadly for she knew her last piece of news would be the best of all, 'whilst we are facing such difficulties, none of you will pay a penny in rent.'

A gasp of surprise rippled through the throng and Hannah heard Bill Ryan's deep laughter. 'I dare bet Mr Edmund hasn't approved that, Hannah.'

She smiled down at him. 'No, Mr Ryan, he hasn't, but we three have.'

She dared not look down at Josiah, for she knew he would be frowning. He hadn't agreed to the scheme, but he'd been overruled by herself and Ernest.

'We all have to make sacrifices,' Hannah had told him determinedly. 'Even the Critchlows.'

'I daren't think what Mr Edmund will say,' Josiah had muttered, but then a sly smile had appeared on his face that, for the moment, Hannah hadn't understood.

Forty-Nine

Late that evening, as Hannah was settling Eddie down for the night, she heard a knock at the back door.

'Sarah, see who that is, will you?' she called. 'There, there, my little man,' she crooned, her attention returning to her son. Distantly, she heard voices and then Sarah's footsteps running up the stairs.

'Oh, ma'am.' Her eyes were shining. 'They're back, they've come back.'

For a moment, Hannah's heart lurched with hope. Adam! He'd come home. But then she realized that the girl had said 'they' not 'he'. Her heart plummeted.

Levelly, she asked, 'Who is it, Sarah?'

'The Bramwells, ma'am. They've come home. You go down, ma'am, I'll stay with master Eddie.'

Hannah picked up her skirts and hurried downstairs and into the kitchen. They were standing awkwardly just inside the doorway, each carrying a bundle of belongings. Hannah gasped and covered her mouth with her hand, staring at them with wide eyes.

If Sarah hadn't told her who it was, Hannah doubted she would have recognized them. Although she hadn't seen them for several years, she was shocked by the change in them. Arthur was thinner and stooped. He looked an old man, his grey hair straggling almost to his shoulders, unkempt and unwashed. A grizzled, untidy beard covered the lower part of his face and his eyes were desperate. But it was the change in Ethel Bramwell that shocked Hannah the most. She was thin and gaunt, her cheeks hollowed, her skin sallow. Her eyes, sunk into dark shadows, were lifeless and defeated. Her shabby clothes were little more than filthy rags. To see the once neat and particular woman reduced to such poverty tore at Hannah's heart.

A sob escaped Hannah's throat as she stretched out her arms and rushed across the room to them, trying to embrace them both at once. 'Oh, Mrs Bramwell, Mr Bramwell. Come in, come in, do. Sit down. Here, let me take your things. Sarah,' the girl had followed her downstairs and was standing near the door, eyes wide with curiosity, 'Sarah make tea for us all.'

'Tea, ma'am?' Sarah hesitated. Tea was an even more precious commodity in these hard times. 'Yes, yes, tea. You, too. We shall all have a cup to celebrate Mr and Mrs Bramwell's return. Oh, how good it is to see you both. Come and sit down by the fire.' She urged them to sit close to the warmth, deeply anxious. They looked ill, both of them, but old habits die hard and she couldn't bring herself – not yet – to fire at them the questions that were whirling around her mind. To her, they were still Mr and Mrs Bramwell, superintendents of the apprentice house.

As they sat together, sipping the tea, Hannah began tentatively, willing them to tell her themselves how they came to be in such straitened circumstances.

'I heard you'd gone to Manchester after leaving here. Mrs Grundy told me.'

She saw them glance at each other, an awkward, embarrassed glance. Arthur cleared his throat. 'It's . . .

it's because of Lily Grundy that . . . that we've dared to come back.'

Hannah raised her eyebrows. 'Dared?' She was surprised by his choice of word. Then her face cleared, thinking she understood. 'Oh, there's nothing to fear from Mr Edmund, he's . . .' She stopped. Arthur was shaking his head.

'It's not him. It's, well, you can see for yourself how we are.' He gestured sadly towards his wife and himself and his voice broke as he said, 'Little more than beggars, Hannah.'

With shaking hands, Ethel placed her cup down and took up their sorry tale. 'Mr Edmund dismissed us when he stopped taking the apprentices. There were only a few with their indentures still running and he found lodgings for them in the village. Said there was no longer any need for the expense of the apprentice house. We begged to be allowed to stay, to turn it into a lodging house, that we could run and pay him rent. But no, he wanted us out, Hannah. Said we'd been a thorn in his side for years with our soft ways towards the children.' She faltered, her eyes filling with tears.

'Soft ways, he said,' Arthur put in. 'When I had to beat little lads for nothing except being normal, spirited youngsters and shut girls in the punishment room.' He shook his head. 'Whatever's happened to us, at least I'm glad I don't have to do that any more.'

Ethel sniffed and took up the story once more. 'We went to Manchester to try and get work in the mills there. We both used to work in the mills when we were young, so we weren't entirely without experience. We've been fine until . . . until this last year. They started by putting us on short time and then the mill closed and we were out of work.'

'There's no work to be had, Hannah. Not in Manchester. I tried road sweeping for a time – anything I could lay me hands to, but . . .' His voice faded away, defeated and hopeless.

'We wrote to Lily, asking what was happening here. Whether it had affected the mill here. And she told us about you coming back and marrying Master Adam and then about Mr Edmund being ill and all the wonderful things you've done here at the mill. We thought . . . we thought . . .' Her voice trailed away.

Hannah put down her cup and reached out to them both. Her voice was husky as she said, 'I'm so glad you've come back. I hadn't realized it, but I need someone just like you to help me. Oh, this is wonderful. Wonderful.'

The Bramwells glanced at each other, relief and thankfulness on their faces. Yet, their worries were not quite over.

'We . . . we've nowhere to live.'

'You'll live here, of course,' Hannah said at once and turned to Sarah. 'Make up a bed for Mr and Mrs Bramwell.' She laughed. 'You'll see some changes in the house. We've made the dormitories into smaller, separate rooms now. We'd hoped to run it as a lodging house for workers at the mill, but, of course, with all the trouble, we haven't anyone yet.'

'We . . . we can't pay you,' Arthur said hesitantly.

'No need,' Hannah said cheerfully. 'You'll be working for your keep.' She laughed as she added impishly, 'I'm not offering you charity, Arthur Bramwell. You'll earn your keep, believe you me.'

And with these few words she restored both hope and pride in the despairing couple.

'But first, you need some rest. Sarah—' She stopped as she turned to see the girl sobbing, the corner of her white apron lifted to cover her face. She put her arm about the young girl's shoulders. 'Whatever's the matter?'

'You'll not want me now. You'll send me back, won't you?'

'Oh, you silly goose. Of course I'm not going to send you back. I couldn't do without you, you know I couldn't. And Eddie certainly couldn't. You might have to look after him more, but you wouldn't mind that, would you?'

Sarah uncovered her wet face, but now her eyes were shining. 'Oh, I'd love it, ma'am. do . . . do you really mean it? You won't send me back to work for Mr Edmund?'

'I give you my solemn promise that whatever happens, I will never send you back there.'

The girl laughed and flung her arms around Hannah. 'Oh, thank you, thank you. I'll work ever so hard for you, ma'am. And I'll look after Master Eddie like he was me own.'

'I know you will,' Hannah said, giving the girl a quick hug and then saying briskly, 'Come along now, there's work to be done.'

At once, there was a stillness in the kitchen. Time seemed to tilt and it was Ethel's voice saying those very same words, exhorting the little apprentices to go about their chores.

Hannah broke the silence and, laughing, turned towards Ethel. 'You see, all your teaching did stick.'

And, suddenly, they were all laughing.

*

'Soup, that's what we need,' Ethel Bramwell said firmly. 'We can make enough soup to feed the whole village.'

The railway line had been finished and opened in the summer of 1862, but it didn't help the people of Wyedale unless they wanted a trip to Buxton, and now few had the money for the fare. But it was fascinating to see the engines steaming through the dale and hear the shrill whistle as they disappeared into the tunnel. The months passed and now another year on they were facing winter again. There was little work at the mill now but the whole community had pulled together with remarkable spirit. Even those who were not directly connected with the mill willingly became involved. The surrounding farming community, led by the Grundys, supplied food and took on workers whenever they could.

'Can't see folks starving,' one burly farmer delivering a cart load of potatoes to Hannah's door said gruffly. 'Can't sleep in me bed at night with a full belly whilst other folks is going hungry.'

'You're a good man, Mr Earnshaw,' Hannah said simply. 'Thank you.'

The big man's face reddened. 'Aye well, that's as may be, but as I hear it you're the real heroine in all this. But for you, folks'd be turned out of their homes to die on the streets.'

Now it was Hannah's turn to blush. 'Oh, I don't know about that. We're all pulling together.'

And indeed they were. The Bramwells' return had been like a talisman, a lucky charm. Once they had rested, eaten some good, wholesome food and washed themselves and their clothes, it was like they'd never been away. Arthur sought out Ernest, to be greeted like the old friend he was, and Ethel took over the running of the house once again whilst Hannah dealt with the pressing problems of the decreasing workload at the mill.

'I've heard all about what you're doing here, lass,' Farmer Earnshaw went on. 'Set up sewing classes for the women to turn old clothes into whatever's needed. And the fellers are learning cobbling,' he laughed, a great loud guffaw that made Hannah smile, despite her ever-present worries. 'I'll know where to come now when I wants me boots mending, won't I? Oh, I nearly forgot. There's a bundle of clothes in the front of the cart. The missis has been collecting 'em up from all round the district.'

'Oh, how good of her. These are wonderful – wonderful! Please, do thank your wife for all of us won't you?'

'Aye, lass, I will. Keep up the good work,' he called, climbing back onto the front of his cart. 'I'll see you again – soon as I can.'

Hannah stood with her arms full of the clothes and watched him trundle away. His shape became indistinct through the blur of her tears.

How good people were.

'So, how do we make this soup, Mrs Bramwell?' Despite their closeness, Hannah could still not bring herself to call the woman Ethel or her husband Arthur, but gradually the names got shortened to an affectionate Mr B and Mrs B.

Ethel picked up a piece of paper on which she had been writing. 'Whatever meat we can lay our hands on. Beef is the best, if we can get it. Barley, split peas, onions and salt.'

'My mouth's watering already.' Hannah laughed,

but behind her laughter the constant worry gnawed at her. How was she to keep the whole village fed through the winter?

The war in America had been going now for over two and a half years, and hard times had come to the mill towns of Lancashire during the first year of the war. Yet Wyedale Mill had struggled on, thanks to Josiah's clever dealings and Ernest's fair distribution amongst the workers of what work there was to be had. But now, the work had all but dried up and any meagre savings the workers had were gone. Already, folks were burning whatever they could to try to keep warm. As yet there had been no deaths in the village that could be directly contributed to the hardship.

That winter of 1863 was tough for the people of Wyedale, but they struggled through it together, and with the spring of the new year came more available work on the land. Every spare piece of garden or land was given over to growing vegetables. Every scrap of cloth that came from the generous donations of old clothes was carefully utilized. The wooded hillsides had been stripped of every dead tree. Anything that could be burned to give warmth was carried home in triumph by the village youngsters.

'You know, one thing surprises me,' Ernest mused, stroking his moustache as he sat in the kitchen with the Bramwells and Hannah on one of his frequent visits. 'We haven't had any thieving. I'd've laid money on it, if I had any, mind,' he added with wry humour, 'that we'd've had kids stealing from the orchards and fields roundabout. But no, far as I know, nothing.'

'There'd better not be,' Hannah declared, 'else they'll have me to reckon with.' She laughed out loud. 'I'd have to think about reopening up the punishment room.'

They all laughed, but more seriously Arthur said, 'Well, I reckon if there is a bit going on, folks aren't doing anything about it. Turning a blind eye, you might say.'

There was silence amongst them.

'I hope no one has got as low as that, though,' Hannah murmured, and to herself silently added, *not yet.*

Fifty

'I miss hearing you singing about the place,' Ethel remarked one morning as she stirred a huge pan of soup. 'It used to raise everyone's spirits to hear you, no matter how bad things got.'

Hannah sighed. 'To tell you the truth, Mrs B, I haven't felt like singing much lately. Not since Adam left, if I'm honest.'

'No word from him, then?' Ethel asked softly. She'd heard a little from Lily Grundy and surmised the rest for herself from the few words Hannah herself had said about him. But they were few. It seemed as if the girl had locked away the sadness in her heart, buried her misery deep whilst she filled her days with helping others. 'Hasn't his father heard anything?'

'I never ask him,' Hannah said shortly. 'I don't talk to him much if I can help it and then only about Eddie.'

Hannah still took her growing son up the hill to the Manor to visit his grandfather, though she never spoke of other matters to Edmund Critchlow – never discussed what was happening at the mill. That she left to Josiah Roper.

Eddie was two years old now, a sturdy, bright youngster who climbed on his grandfather's knee and chattered to him without inhibition or fear.

It amazed Hannah to see Edmund with his grandson. There was genuine love for the child in his face, she was sure of it. But the thought gave Hannah no comfort.

Instead it brought a chill of fear to her heart.

The day that Edmund Critchlow came back to the mill and took his rightful place behind his desk once more should have been an occasion for great rejoicing. But it wasn't.

They'd got through another spring and summer but now they all faced another hard winter, and how would Edmund Critchlow react to his silent mill and idle workers who were still living in his houses but paying him no rent?

They were not long in finding out.

He sat in his chair with Josiah's carefully written ledgers spread out on the desk before him.

On the opposite side of the desk, Hannah, Josiah and Ernest stood facing him. Ernest's brow was creased with worry and he tugged self-consciously at his moustache. Hannah bit her lip anxiously, but Josiah's face was an expressionless mask.

'So, I see that you three have all but ruined me . . .'

'That's not true,' Hannah burst out. 'We've saved the villagers from starvation—'

'Pah!' Edmund thumped the desk with his fist. 'The villagers! Idle wastrels, living on my charity. Charity be damned! It stops here. You—' he prodded his forefinger towards Josiah – 'you can go this very day and start collecting the rents again. And you'd better tell them I'll be collecting every back penny they owe me.'

Hannah gasped. 'How d'you think they can pay?

They're not earning. Only a few shillings here and there when the farmers employ them.'

Edmund leaned forward. 'They'll pay or leave. The choice is up to them.'

'And where do you suggest they go? To starve on the streets?'

Edmund laughed cruelly. 'I couldn't care less about what happens to the idle good-for-nothings. They've lived off me for years whilst I've been laid up. But I'm back now. And you two,' he pointed at Josiah and Ernest, 'had better watch out. I'm well aware that you've been aiding and abetting this strumpet.' He turned back to glare at Hannah. 'Well, what are you waiting for? You can go now. I'm back. You can go home and attend to your child.'

Hannah lifted her chin. 'I see your thanks didn't last long. You've no right to treat any of us in this way. We've worked well together. We kept this place running as long as we could. Longer than a lot of places. But for us, you wouldn't have a mill at all by now.'

Edmund's grim smile was still a little lopsided. 'I expect I've come back only just in time to save it from going under completely. What work is there, Scarsfield?'

'Very little, sir. We've some Indian cotton—'

'Indian cotton? Pah! That rubbish.'

'There's nothing else to be had sir and the prices of that are extortionate,' Josiah put in.

'Allow me to be the judge of that. You always were useless, Roper.'

'That's not true and you know it isn't,' Hannah cried heatedly. 'It's only thanks to Mr Roper's clever negotiations with the brokers. He's been to Manchester and Liverpool and even abroad—'

'Abroad? At my expense?' Edmund was growing red in the face. 'Is this true?'

'Well, yes, sir. I was trying to find new suppliers, open up new markets. America is closed to us. The blockades—'

Edmund leaned back in his chair. It was as if he'd never been out of it. 'So, I have you to thank, have I, for saving my mill? According to *her*,' he jabbed his finger at Hannah, 'it's all down to you and your wonderful negotiating skills.' His tone was heavy with sarcasm and Hannah winced. She wasn't bothered for herself, but Josiah and Ernest deserved his gratitude for the way they had pulled together to save his mill.

Hannah glanced at Josiah. His eyes were wary. Smoothly, he said, 'That's kind of her to say so, sir, but it's been the three of us. Scarsfield, myself and Mrs Critchlow. We – Scarsfield and I – couldn't have done it without her. She's taken all the decisions, led the way in the improvements.'

'Improvements? What improvements?' Edmund gripped the sides of his chair and leaned forward.

'We have a doctor visit regularly to look after the health of the workers and—'

'A doctor!' His face was growing purple. 'How much is that costing?'

'Well, before the work began to dry up, the workers contributed a penny each a week and we – I mean the company – doubled it. It covers the doctor's visits and any medicines he prescribes.'

'You mean to tell me that we're paying for their medicines?'

'In a way, but like I said, the workers are all contributing too. Well, they were. Since the American war, the doctor has given his services for free. But presumably he'll be hoping that we'll revert to that system again once the war is over.'

'Well, that won't happen, I can assure you. And I'll tell him so myself. You can't be soft with workers. They'll take advantage. Any kindness and they'll see it as weakness. Oh no,' he shook his head. 'This has to stop.' He thumped the arm of his chair. 'Now! Roper – see to it. And you, Scarsfield. You can tell the workers.'

'You're wrong,' Hannah spoke up. 'They appreciate it. They—'

'Appreciate it? Are you soft in the head, girl? They appreciate nothing. Employees need a firm hand. And, like I said, your presence here is no longer required. See to your child. You can keep that girl – what's her name? – Sarah. Ugly little thing, she is. Not the sort of girl I want around me. You're welcome to her. I'll make you an allowance and you can live in the apprentice house. Take in lodgers – do what you like – but I don't want to see you in the mill again. Clear?'

'Very,' Hannah said tightly. 'But I'm afraid you won't get rid of me as easily as that. Goodness knows why, but I care about the mill. Apart from the fact that it's my son's inheritance, I enjoy being involved, I—'

'I don't want you here,' Edmund interrupted. 'And you can send those parasites, the Bramwells, packing, too, and if you're not careful, you'll not be far behind them, though –' he smiled maliciously – 'your son would not be going with you.'

The blood drained from Hannah's face and she swayed, but Edmund took no notice. 'And you, Scarsfield, had better attend to the business of the mill. I'll soon have the wheel turning again, now I'm back. And as for you, Roper, you can go back to your pen pushing. No more fancy trips abroad for you at my expense.'

Josiah's eyes narrowed and his thin lips pursed. But he said nothing. No word of protest or pleading passed his lips. But Hannah could see that the bitterness and resentment from the old days were back in his eyes, one thousand fold.

Edmund Critchlow was making a mistake. A very serious mistake. He had revived all the enmity in Josiah Roper. And, when the news got around the mill, he wouldn't be the only enemy Edmund would make this day.

Banished to her home, Hannah paced the length of her sitting room waiting for Josiah and Ernest to arrive. It had been three days since Edmund's rash ultimatum and, hearing nothing, Hannah was fretting what was happening at the mill. So one evening after she'd seen Edmund leave to return home, she sent Sarah with a message asking Josiah and Ernest to come and see her.

'Please, come and sit down,' she said as they came in. 'Sarah, bring the gentlemen a tankard of ale each and a glass of milk for me, please. Now, tell me,' she said turning to the two men. 'What's happening?'

'Chaos, Hannah,' Ernest said, sitting down, placing his cap on his knee. 'He'll have a strike on his hands, if he doesn't watch out.'

'He's stopped the doctor coming, even though the man is demanding no payment until the troubles are over. He's ordered everyone to go back to work at once,' Josiah began.

'But he's reduced their hourly rate,' Ernest said.

'But . . . but there's no cotton. What are they going to work with?'

She saw Ernest and Josiah exchange a glance then Josiah shrugged. 'He's found some, Hannah. I don't know how or where from but he says he's got enough coming to start the mill up again.'

'He's demanding rent from all his tenants in the village,' Ernest said. 'And back payments.'

'Is he mad?' Hannah was still pacing the floor distractedly. 'How can they pay?' She stopped suddenly and turned to face them. 'Is that his way of getting rid of them? If they can't pay their rent, he's going to turn them out?'

The two men lifted their shoulders helplessly.

'Don't you upset yourself, Hannah. You've your little one to think of.'

'That's exactly who I am thinking of, Ernest. The mill is Eddie's future. If only . . .' She bit her lip. 'Tell me – and be honest with me – has anyone heard anything of Adam? Does anyone know where he is?'

Josiah and Ernest glanced at each other again. 'Well, we didn't know whether to tell you.'

Hannah felt as if her heart stopped. 'What? What is it?'

'We heard he's blockade running.'

Hannah drew in a frightened breath and her eyes were wide with fear. 'That's dangerous, isn't it? He . . . he could get arrested or . . . or even killed, couldn't he?'

'Aye, he could,' Ernest said bluntly. 'And if he does, it'll be greedy men like his own father who've sent him to his death in their demand for cotton by whatever means.'

Fifty-One

The mill was deathly silent once more. No wheel turning, no clatter of spinning mules and weaving looms, no sound of voices. The workrooms were deserted. But not now because of a lack of supply of raw material. Somehow, from somewhere, Edmund had obtained some cotton. Inferior quality though it was, it could have kept the water-wheel turning even if only for a little while. But there were no spinners, no weavers, no piecers or doffers. The great mill was empty, its workers on strike against the tyrannical owner. After the months of working together, of helping each other, joining together to fight the hardship that was none of their making, Edmund Critchlow's harsh demands had finally tipped the villagers over the edge. They had seen how the mill could be operated, glimpsed a promising future. Once the war was over and the raw cotton available again, life could be so much better. If they could just hold out, hang on until the war ended. But Edmund's return had dashed all their hopes and dreams. And worst of all, he'd taken revenge on the one person they all acknowledged had been the saviour of them all, of the mill and all its workers.

Hannah.

'They don't like the way he's treated you. Not after all you've done. And as for threatening you over little

Eddie, well, that's the last straw. Folks round here love the little chap. They see him as their hope for the future,' Ernest told her soberly. 'They're calling a strike, Hannah.'

'Oh no, Ernest. They mustn't. Not on my account, please.'

'It's not all about you, love, but even if it was, I wouldn't try to stop them even if I could. I'm with them all the way. I'm one of 'em.'

'But how did they find out. I mean, about me. About him threatening to send me away and keep Eddie here?'

Ernest grinned without a trace of embarrassment. 'I told 'em, lass. I told 'em.' He began to turn away, but hesitated to ask, 'What about the Bramwells?'

'Oh, they're not going anywhere. If we have to go, we're all going together. The Bramwells, Sarah, me – *and* Eddie.' She laughed suddenly. 'Don't forget, I'm the expert at running away from this place.'

'Aye, well, I hope it won't come to that, lass, 'cos it'll be a sad day if we all lose you again.' He turned away abruptly. A bluff, kindly man though he was, he wasn't one to hand out the compliments very often. It embarrassed him, yet he had to let this girl know exactly what she'd come to mean to him and all the villagers. If she went again, he believed there'd be a stream of folk following her up the hill.

By the time the chilly days of November were upon them with a vengeance, the only people at the mill now were a few men gathered near the gate, guarding the entrance to stop anyone going in to work. They stamped their feet against the cold and lit a brazier.

Yet they needn't have stood there in the snow and the biting wind; there were no strike breakers. Their action against Edmund was unanimous – at least amongst the spinners and weavers.

Only two people passed through the gate. Edmund Critchlow and Josiah Roper.

The first was greeted with morose silence, the second ran the gauntlet of questions and threats.

'We thought you was on our side, Roper.'

'You helped keep things going. Why're you siding with him now?'

'Reckons he'll fare better buttering up to the master.'

'We'll remember you, Roper. We won't forget.'

Josiah walked on, head lowered against the taunts. *No*, he thought, *and neither will I. I don't forget. If only you knew!*

On the evening of the third day of the strike, just as Josiah was about to leave for home, Edmund flung open his office door. 'I blame you for all this, Roper. You and Scarsfield and that blasted girl. Look where your pampering has got us. Kindness? To workers? They don't understand it. The whip hand, that's what they understand. That's what they fear and that's what keeps them in line.'

Josiah said nothing. He raised not one word of protest. His silence seemed to enrage Edmund even more. He jabbed his forefinger towards Josiah. 'You're sacked, Roper.'

Josiah didn't move, didn't turn round. He carried on writing slowly and clearly in the ledger. The only betrayal of emotion was a slight tremor in his hand and a line of uncharacteristic shaky handwriting.

'Make your own pay up. Leave tonight. I don't

want to see your face in this office again.' With that parting shot, Edmund slammed the door with such force that it shuddered on its hinges.

Josiah carried on writing for a few moments longer. Then slowly he closed the book, knowing it was for the last time. He put his head on one side, listening for any sound from beyond the door. No doubt Edmund was leaning back in his chair, indulging in his usual early evening tot of whisky, which he kept in his desk drawer.

Josiah put on his coat and stood listening again for a moment. Then he bent and from the very back of a cupboard he took out a slim ledger, which he slipped quickly into the copious pocket of his coat. With one last glance around the room where he'd spent the greater part of his adult life, he was about to snuff out the candle that burned on his desk, when he hesitated. His eyes gleamed as an idea began to form in his mind. He left the office closing the door soundlessly behind him and carrying the candle carefully, shading the flickering light with his hand so that the flame did not blow out.

He began to descend the stairs, then halfway down he stopped. The whole building was silent, yet drifting through the open door at the bottom of the stairs he could hear the voices of the men standing guard at the gate. Slowly, he descended the rest of the way, but instead of going outside, he went into the storeroom on the ground floor that was directly below the offices. No longer was it stuffed to overflowing with bales of raw cotton, but there was enough there for Josiah's purpose.

As he closed the door of the room moments later, the flames were beginning to lick at the few bales of cotton. Josiah hurried out into the yard. He hadn't long. It wouldn't take many minutes for the fire to spread through the whole room, and when that happened someone would be bound to notice, yet perhaps not as quickly as if the mill was still running.

'Here comes the scab,' Daniel sneered as Josiah pushed his way between them. For the first time he was physically jostled, as the five men congregated there surrounded him. He felt a moment's alarm, but he glared at them, betraying nothing of his fear in his eyes.

'Good day, gentlemen,' he said smoothly. 'I'd be obliged if you'd let me pass.'

'Aye, we'll let you pass this time, Roper. But no more. You'll not pass through this gate again. Not until this business is settled.'

Josiah gave a brief nod and they parted to let him through. As he hurried up the hill towards his lodgings on Prentice Row, Josiah was smiling. How prophetic! He had no intention of ever returning to the mill again.

Within twenty minutes, Josiah had flung his few belongings into a bag, collected his money and personal papers from a hiding place beneath the floorboards of his room, and was hurrying along the pathway behind the mill to the bridge over the waterfall and up the steep slope. It was growing colder as he emerged from beneath the trees and gained the narrow path leading up to the railway line. He slipped and slithered on the frosty ground as he climbed.

He glanced back just once at the building below. Already he could see the flames in the window two storeys directly below Edmund's office. With an evil smile he turned away and clambered up to the railway line. He glanced both ways, but it was silent. He peered down in the darkness and stepped onto the track. He trod heavily on an icy, uneven sleeper, and his foot slipped and twisted over. He felt a jab of pain in his ankle and dropped his bag. It fell open, scattering his possessions. Josiah cried out as he fell to his knees, the pain making him feel sick and faint. In the darkness, he scrabbled around for his belongings strewn around him, unaware of the train appearing out of the tunnel and bearing down upon him.

'Fire! There's a fire at the back of the mill.' Hannah had seen it from her windows at the apprentice house and now she came running pell-mell down the hill towards the men at the gate.

'Fire? Where?' Ernest Scarsfield demanded.

'I think it's in the storeroom where the bales are kept.' Breathless, she put her hand on her chest. Her heart was hammering painfully. Distantly, they heard a train, heard its whistle, but none of them was consciously aware of it.

'Is anyone in there?' Hannah demanded. 'Josiah – is he still working?'

'No, he left about half an hour ago.'

There was a brief silence. They all seemed frozen, unable to move.

'But Mr Edmund hasn't come out, has he?' Daniel muttered.

'Oh no!' Hannah gasped. Before anyone could stop her, she had picked up her skirts and was running to the door into the mill.

'Hannah, no!' Daniel cried and began to run after her.

Galvanized into action, Ernest began to issue orders. 'You – get to the village. Fetch all the workers – as many as you can round up. You – find as many buckets as you can. When more get here form a chain . . .'

Hannah had entered the building. But she didn't go to where the fire was, but up the stairs to the office. Already smoke was drifting up the stairwell and into the rooms on the first and second storeys.

'Mr Edmund,' she called, as she felt her way through the smoke, 'Mr Edmund – are you there?'

She almost fell into the outer office. The smoke hadn't reached here yet. Mr Edmund was probably sitting in his office, serenely unaware of the tragedy unfolding two floors below. She rushed across the room and opened the inner door. 'Mr Edmund—'

She stopped, aghast. Edmund was certainly still there, sitting in his chair with a half-empty whisky bottle on the desk. On the floor to one side lay a shattered glass and liquid spilt around it. Edmund was slumped awkwardly in his chair, the side of his face pulled down, his eyes glazed, his arms hanging down limply on either side of him.

She ran to him, lifted his arm and felt for his pulse. It was there, but erratic.

'Hannah, Hannah, where are you?'

'Daniel,' she cried out thankfully. 'In here. In the office. Quick. We must get him out.'

Daniel appeared the doorway.

'I think he's had another seizure. You must help me. We must get him out of here.'

Daniel stood transfixed in the doorway, staring at the helpless man.

'Daniel – come *on*.'

He half turned away, mumbling, 'I'll fetch help.'

'No, there's no time. You'll have to help me lift him. You get on one side.'

Reluctantly, Daniel moved forward. The paralysed man was a dead weight, but they managed to get him upright between them, looping his useless arms around their shoulders and grasping him from each side around his torso.

'We'll never manage him. He's a ton weight,' Daniel protested, but nevertheless he helped Hannah drag Edmund to the door, through the outer office and to the top of the stairs. The smoke was thicker here now and they began to cough. Slowly, they stumbled down the stairs, not daring to stop though their lungs were bursting with the effort and the smoke.

'We'll never make it. Leave him,' Daniel said. 'Why should we save this bastard?'

Hannah didn't answer – she hadn't the breath or the strength.

'Hannah? Daniel? Where are you?' A voice called through the smoke.

'Ernest,' Hannah gasped. 'We're here – on the stairs. Help us.'

In a moment, he was with them, steadying and guiding them to the bottom of the stairs and out into the blissful fresh air. 'Here, Hannah, let me take him.'

Gratefully, Hannah relinquished her hold and Ernest shouldered the weight. Two more men hurried forward, carrying a door on which to lay Edmund.

'Take him home and mind his man calls the doctor,' Ernest instructed. 'Now we'd best get this fire out.'

Hannah glanced around her. Figures were running everywhere, but already they were organized into a working team, though it took a while to get the flames under control. The storeroom was ruined, what little stock there was spoiled. The fire had only spread into the neighbouring rooms, but the smoke had permeated through most of the building.

When the fire itself was out, the exhausted workers stood around the yard in small groups, talking in low voices, glancing at Hannah, who leaned against the wall, breathing hard. Her dress was drenched with sweat, her hair hanging in bedraggled hanks.

'You look all in, lass. Get yourself home and—' Ernest began, but Hannah shook her head.

'No, I must get things organized, Ernest. I'm sure Mr Edmund has had another seizure. And if that's so,' she stood up, squaring her shoulders, 'then I – we – are in charge again. This foolishness has gone on long enough. Get word around all the workers.'

Ernest waved his hands towards the men and women standing about the yard. 'Most of 'em are here.'

Hannah nodded. 'Then call them together. I have something to say.'

In a few moments, Hannah was standing on a crate, the workers gathered around her.

'Thank you for saving the mill.' She glanced around. No one spoke and most of them looked as if they couldn't have cared less whether the mill was saved or not. Yet some inner instinct had driven them to come running when their place of work was endangered. They muttered morosely amongst themselves. Hannah raised her voice. 'I'm going up to the Manor to see how Mr Edmund is. Please – may I ask you all to come back here in the morning, when I shall have some news for you?'

Ernest held out his hand and she stepped down

from the box. 'I was going to tell them to go back to work – that everything would be all right – but I changed my mind. If Mr Edmund is not as bad as he looked and likely to return to work, then it's no good me making them promises that won't be kept, is it?'

'No, lass, it ain't,' he said soberly. 'I won't send a message to him, Hannah, because right at this moment I don't quite know what to think – or say.'

Hannah sighed and glanced around her. The workers were all drifting away now towards their homes, their futures hanging in the balance.

'It's a bad situation, Ernest,' Hannah murmured. 'How can you wish a man harm, and yet—?'

'I know, lass. I know just what you mean.'

There was a pause and then she said, 'I'll see you back here in the morning then.'

'Right you are.'

Fifty-Two

At home, Hannah washed and changed her clothes and then hurried to the Manor. Her breathing was laboured from the effects of the smoke and she would've liked nothing better than to lie down and rest. But she had to find out what had happened to Edmund.

As the butler ushered her into the hall, the doctor was coming down the stairs. His face was grave.

'A word with you, Hannah, if I may?' By now, Dr Barnes was a friend. He'd given generously to the villagers through their time of hardship and was beloved by them all.

'Of course.'

'If you would come this way, sir, madam.' The butler led them towards the morning room.

'How is he?' Hannah asked, as soon as the door closed and the doctor and she were alone.

Dr Barnes shook his head. 'It's a very bad one. It's touch and go if he'll even survive it. And if he does, I doubt he'll make any kind of reasonable recovery. I fear he will be paralysed and speechless this time.'

'I see.'

The doctor glanced at her keenly. 'I'm sorry to hear about the fire at the mill. Has it done much damage?'

'A fair amount, but with a lot of work I think we

can be up and running inside a week.' She pulled
a wry face. 'That's if we can get any raw cotton.'

'But the workers are on strike, aren't they?'

'Not for much longer, I hope. I've asked them
to meet me at the mill in the morning, but I needed
to know how Mr Edmund is before . . . before . . .'
She took a deep breath, but the doctor finished her
sentence for her. 'Before you could tell them that
the strike is over and that they can come back to
work.'

She nodded.

'Good,' he said, picking up his bag. 'Some of the
families are in a poor way. Their health would've
suffered before long and then it's a downward spiral,
isn't it? And all your efforts to keep things going
through these hard times would've been for nothing.'

Hannah nodded. 'Talking of their health, would
you be prepared to come to the mill again? Like you
did before?'

'Gladly.' Dr Barnes smiled. 'By the way, it's rumoured that the war in America is coming to an end.'

Hannah clasped her hands together. 'Oh, is it true?
Is it really true?'

'I think so,' he began, but as he opened the door for
her and they moved into the hall, the butler was
opening the front door to two men.

'Is the doctor here?' One began, but then, catching
sight of Dr Barnes, he pulled his cap off. 'Ah, there
you are, Doctor. Can you come? There's been a terrible accident on the railway track. Some poor devil
got hit by a train. It's a nasty mess, Doctor.'

'He's dead?'

'Oh aye. It must have hit him a glancing blow and

knocked him flying. He wouldn't've known much about it. I shouldn't think the train driver even realized he'd hit anything. He didn't stop.'

'Did you find the body?'

'Yeah. We work on the line, see?'

'I'll come at once. Have you called the police?'

The two men looked at each other. 'No – we didn't think of that.'

'Then could one of you go and find Constable Jacques and ask him to meet me up there?'

'We found these scattered around him.' The man held out a ledger and a wad of paper money.

'You really ought to have left it for the police,' Dr Barnes murmured.

'We never thought of that, sir, I have to admit. But it was blowing all over the place. We thought we ought to pick it up.'

Hannah gasped and moved forward. 'That's a fortune.' She glanced at the two railway workers. They'd been very honest in handing over the money.

'We couldn't think why anyone should be carrying all that, but we thought – well . . .' The two men glanced at each other. 'We thought he might have family that'd be glad of it.'

Hannah's glance was now on the book they were holding out. 'That . . . that looks like one of our ledgers.' She took it and opened it up.

The lines of figures, all in Josiah Roper's neat handwriting, danced before her eyes. 'Oh,' she gasped and swayed a little.

'And we found this too.' Now one of the men held out a smaller item. 'Maybe it's his.'

Hannah's hand trembled as she reached out to take

the battered wallet the man held. She opened it up, and in a flat voice said, 'It's Josiah Roper's.'

As Hannah had predicted, the mill was running again in under a week, though the supply of cotton – any cotton – was spasmodic. Once they knew that their jobs were safe for the foreseeable future and that Hannah and Ernest Scarsfield were once more in charge, all the workforce had worked around the clock to clean up the damage and get the huge water-wheel turning and the machinery running again.

There was only one mystery that remained: what had Josiah Roper been doing on the railway track with a large amount of cash and a bag containing clothing and personal belongings? Hannah, seated once more behind Edmund's desk, puzzled over the ledger.

'I don't understand it, Ernest. It's just a list of dates and figures. It starts years ago and it's all small amounts. Sometimes just a few shillings, even pence. I can't think what it can be.'

Ernest moved around the desk to stand beside her.

'That first date – there . . .' He pointed. 'That's the year he started here. I remember it, because he came just a month or two after I did.'

'Really?' Hannah turned page after page noting how the figures mounted up in the running total column. She came to the more recent pages. 'Look, he's deducted an amount here and here and – Ernest, those dates coincide with when he went abroad. I know they do, because he was away just before I had Eddie and . . . and I was worried he might not be back in time.'

Ernest leaned on the desk. 'You know what, Hannah,

I reckon he's been thieving from the Critchlows all these years – stashing it away. And then, when he got the chance, he's taken it abroad. I bet somewhere there's a bank with Roper's nice little nest egg.'

Hannah gasped. 'You're right.' She remembered Josiah's reaction when Edmund had put a stop to his trips abroad. 'And I bet this time he was going for good. Ernest, d'you think he started the fire?' She'd be relieved to be able to believe it was the embittered clerk. For a few dreadful moments she'd suspected Daniel, though she hadn't voiced her fears to anyone else.

'It's possible. In fact, I'd say it was probable.' Ernest stroked his moustache thoughtfully. 'But that's something we'll never know. Thank goodness you saw it in time before it got a real hold.'

'Yes,' Hannah murmured absently, her mind still on the book in front of her. She could hardly believe the evidence before her, and yet now the little remarks that Josiah had made over the years all seemed to fall into place. His bitterness and resentment against the Critchlows had festered for years and he'd taken revenge, only to have Fate deal him a final blow.

'I wonder if there's any way of finding out if he has got a bank account abroad somewhere?' Ernest murmured.

'There are some numbers at the back of the ledger. Perhaps there's a clue there, but it doesn't make any sense to me. I'm going to hand it all over to the police, Ernest. Let them sort it out – if they can.'

'Right,' he said, standing up. 'Then I'll be getting on. Oh, by the way, Daniel wants to see you. Shall I tell him to come up?'

Hannah nodded.

A few moments later, Daniel came into the office.

'Hello.' Hannah smiled. 'Are you all right? Have you recovered from the smoke?'

'Yes, thanks. You?'

'I'm fine.'

There was an awkward pause before Daniel cleared his throat and the words came tumbling out, as if he had been rehearsing them and now wanted to get them out before he forgot what he wanted to say. 'Hannah – I've been doing a lot of thinking and I . . . I've decided to leave. It's time I put the past behind me. Got on with my own life, but . . . but I can't do it here. There's too many memories. Too many ghosts.'

'What about Luke?' Hannah asked gently.

Daniel's chin quivered for a moment then he said hoarsely, 'I shall go to his grave – say "goodbye". I think he'll understand.'

'I'm sure he will,' Hannah whispered.

They gazed at each other. 'Would you . . . mind if I came with you?' she asked hesitantly, and then added swiftly, 'Say if you'd rather I didn't. I'll understand.'

He smiled. For the first time in years it was a real smile that lit up his eyes. In that instant he looked a young boy again, so like Luke that Hannah's heart turned over. 'I'd like you to come.'

'Sunday then? After the service?'

Daniel nodded.

Fifty-Three

Sunday was frosty but bright, and after the family service in the schoolroom, they walked to the cemetery, Eddie riding piggy-back style on Daniel's shoulders, and Hannah carrying a small posy of flowers. When they reached Luke's unmarked grave they stood together looking down at the place where the boy they'd both loved lay. Hannah knelt down and placed the posy on the grave.

'I'd've loved to have put a headstone up, but I couldn't afford it,' Daniel murmured. 'Maybe one day.'

'Would you . . . let me have one put up, Daniel?' Hannah asked tentatively, not wanting to destroy the growing understanding between them. 'If . . . if you tell me what wording you'd like, I'll see it's done.'

'Pay for it with Critchlow money, you mean?'

'Well – yes, I suppose it would be.'

Daniel was thoughtful for a moment before he nodded slowly and said, 'I reckon that's the least they could do.'

They were silent for a few moments before Daniel said haltingly, 'I'm letting go of it, Hannah. Like you said. Harbouring bitterness all these years, well, I've only hurt myself – not the man I wanted to. But I reckon Fate's taken a hand and done it for me. He's got his just deserts now.'

'Yes, Daniel, I think he has.'

'What about you? Are you staying here? Running the mill?'

She nodded. 'If I can.'

'Oh, you can, Hannah. I've seen that. It's as if you were born to do it.' He ruffled Eddie's hair. 'Look after yourself – and him. He's a grand little chap.'

'Thank you, Daniel,' she said huskily, taking her son's hand.

'Do you mind if . . . if I just have a few moments alone with . . . with Luke?'

'Of course not. Shall I see you again before you leave?'

Daniel shook his head. 'No, I'm off first thing tomorrow morning on the early train.'

'So . . . so this is goodbye then.'

They stared at each other, and then awkwardly, Daniel bent and kissed her cheek. 'God be with you, Hannah,' he whispered. 'And come and see Luke sometimes for me, won't you?'

'Of course I will. And don't forget to let me have the wording for the headstone. I'll see it's done. I promise.'

He nodded now, unable to speak.

She squeezed his hand and turned and walked away. At the gate, she glanced back, but he was kneeling on the ground, his head bowed, bidding his twin a final farewell.

Hannah set off steadily down the hill towards the apprentice house, slowing her walk to the little boy's pace. She was about to turn into the narrow path that ran behind the houses, when she saw a man standing near the big gate leading into the mill yard. He was tall with dark hair blowing in the wind, and the lower half of his face was covered with a dark, bushy beard. He was half-turned away from her, looking through the gate into the yard, but there was something about the way he was standing, the set of his shoulders . . .

Her heart missed a beat as she continued slowly down the hill towards him, hardly daring to breathe, hardly daring to hope . . .

Eddie pointed at the man, and in his clear, piping voice called, 'Hello.'

Hearing him, the man turned and looked up towards them. He stared for a moment, then wiped the back of his hand across his forehead, as if shaken by the sight of her. She stopped, her eyes wide, her mouth agape.

'Adam,' she whispered. 'Oh, Adam.'

Slowly, he came towards her until they were standing only a couple of paces apart. His gaze was on her face and he reached out and traced the line of her cheek with his finger.

He's safe, she was thinking, *he's safe and he has come back*. Her thoughts were a prayer of thanks.

'I thought you . . . I mean,' his deep voice was husky with emotion, 'we docked in Liverpool and I heard about the fire – that someone was hurt. I was so afraid that you . . .' His voice trailed away and his gaze shifted to the child, quiet now, staring in turn at the man who was a stranger to him. With a sad little smile, Adam squatted down in front of his son. His voice shook as he murmured, 'I should have believed you, Anna. Can you ever forgive me?'

'There's nothing to forgive. It's me who should ask forgiveness . . .' she began, but his attention was wholly on his son now. The little boy reached out his chubby hand and stroked the man's beard. It tickled his hand and Eddie chortled with delight.

'And what's your name, young man?'

'Ed-ward,' the little boy answered with careful deliberation.

Adam nodded and murmured, 'Edward Critchlow of Wyedale Mill. Yes, it has a good sound to it. And you're going to make a fine master one day, aren't you?'

She hardly dared to ask, but she had to know. 'Are you . . . are you back to stay? Have you come home, Adam?'

He straightened up and held out both his hands to her, palms upwards in supplication. 'If you'll both have me . . . ?'

And then she was in his arms and they were kissing and laughing and hugging, with Eddie clutching at their legs and laughing too. There was so much to say and yet there was no need now for anything to be said at all.

Adam was home.

Wish Me Luck

ACKNOWLEDGEMENTS

Many people have helped me in my research for this novel. I am especially grateful to Mick Richardson for his generosity in lending me the private papers and flying log book of his father, Sergeant W. J. Proffitt, the wireless operator of a Lancaster bomber, who was killed whilst on a bombing mission in March 1944.

My thanks also for his help to my brother-in-law Peter Harrison, who flew thirty missions as a wireless operator during the Second World War; to Mrs Lillian Streets and Mrs Barbara Brooke-Taylor for sharing with me their memories of their time in the WAAF; to Mike Smith, Curator of the Newark Air Museum, for answering my questions; to Fred and Harold Panton at the Lincolnshire Aviation Heritage Centre at East Kirkby for all the marvellous displays and wealth of information that have helped me so much, and to Michael Simpson, head of exhibitions at the Imperial War Museum North, Trafford Park, Manchester, for his advice and help.

I have also consulted numerous books in the course of my research, but special mention should be made of *A WAAF in Bomber Command* by Pip Beck (Goodall, 1989) and *Square-Bashing by the Sea (RAF Skegness, 1941–1944)* by Jack Loveday (J. Loveday, 2003).

Very special thanks to the members of my family who read and commented on the script: Robena and Fred Hill, and David and Alan Dickinson. As always, my love and thanks to all my family and friends whose support and encouragement means more than I can say. And not forgetting Darley and his Angels at the Darley Anderson Literary Agency and Imogen Taylor, my editor at Macmillan. To all of you – you're always there when I need you – thank you!

One

Fleur Bosley stepped down from the train, hitching her kitbag onto her back. The platform was in darkness, the blackout complete. She moved forward carefully. It was like stepping into the unknown. Behind her someone else jumped down from the train and cannoned into her, knocking her forward onto her knees. She let out a cry, startled rather than injured. At once, a man's voice came out of the darkness. 'Oh, I'm sorry, miss. I didn't see you.'

His hands were reaching out, feeling for her to help her up, but she pushed him away. 'I'm all right,' she said, feeling foolish.

A thin beam of torchlight shone in her face. She blinked and put up her hand to shield her eyes. 'D'you have to do that?' she asked testily, but the only answer coming out of the darkness was a low chuckle. 'I just wanted to see if whoever I knocked over was worth picking up.' A young man's voice, deep with a jovial, teasing note in it.

'Well, you needn't bother trying to pick me up.' She emphasized the words, making sure he knew she understood his double meaning.

His only answer was to laugh out loud. 'Come on,

1

the least I can do is buy you a nice cuppa. Let's see if there's a cafe or a canteen open somewhere nearby.'

'Shouldn't think so at this time of night,' she said, slightly mollified by his offer as she bent to feel around for her kitbag. Fleur hadn't had anything to eat or drink since midday and her throat was parched. Travelling from the south of the country had taken all day. There'd been delays all along the line because of air raid warnings and now she was stranded in Nottingham with no promise of further transport for the last leg of her journey. Fleur was hungry, thirsty – and cross!

'Here, let me . . .' The man shone his torch and picked up her bag, then ran the beam of light up and down her.

'Snap!'

'What?'

'You're a WAAF.' He turned the light on himself and she saw he was wearing RAF uniform. 'Come on, you can't refuse a cup of tea with me now, can you?'

In the darkness, she smiled. 'Oh, go on then.'

Minutes later, as she was sitting at a table whilst he went to the counter to fetch two teas, she was able to study him. Tall, with fair, curly hair; bright, mischievous blue eyes; a firm, square jaw and the cheekiest grin she'd ever seen. As he came back, set the tea on the table and sat down opposite her, she knew that he, in turn, was appraising her.

She took off her cap and laid it on the chair beside her. Shaking out her soft brown curls, she returned his gaze steadily with a saucy sparkle in her dark brown eyes. 'Will I do then?'

He took in her smooth skin, her small, neat nose and

perfectly shaped mouth that was delicately enhanced with just a touch of pale pink lipstick. 'Oh, you'll do very well, miss. It's usually little grey-haired old ladies I knock over, not pretty young ones. My luck must be changing.' He held out his hand across the table. 'Robert Rodwell, at your service. But my friends call me Robbie.'

She was about to answer tartly, 'How do you do, Mr Rodwell.' But something in his open face made her put her hand into his warm grasp and say instead, 'Fleur Bosley. Pleased to meet you – Robbie.'

As they drank their tea, he asked, 'So, where are you heading? Here in Nottingham?'

'No. South Monkford. It's a small town not far from Newark.'

Robbie nodded. 'Yes, I know it.' A slight frown line deepened between his eyebrows. 'I think we used to live there years ago, but my mother never talks about it much and we came to live in the city when I was little. But I seem to think my father – he died before I was born – ran a tailor's shop there.'

Fleur wrinkled her forehead. 'Can't think of a tailor's shop there now. There's old Miss Pinkerton's; she's a dressmaker and—'

'That's it. That'll be the one. Mother said once that a woman who was a dressmaker had taken it over.'

'Her and her sister run it. They sell women's clothes.' She giggled. 'They call it "Pinkertons' Emporium", would you believe? They're sweet old dears, but they're both a bit doddery now. And their shop is so old-fashioned. It's like stepping back in time when you walk in.'

'All corsets, wool vests and big knickers, eh?'

3

Fleur laughed and pretended to be coy. 'Really, sir, saying such things to a lady. And when we've only just met too. I do declare!'

They laughed together, feeling already as if they had known each other far longer than a few minutes.

'So – were you hoping to get to South Monkford tonight?' Robbie asked.

Fleur pulled a face. 'I was, but it's doubtful – there won't be a train out of here now. I could ring up and get my dad to fetch me, but I don't like to ask him to come all this way at this time of night. And using his precious petrol.'

'You've got a car? *And* a telephone?'

Fleur grinned. 'Yes. The car's called Bertha. It's a 1923 Ford and it's seen more "active service" down dirt tracks and across fields than many a tank. As for the phone – we live on a farm in the middle of nowhere. My mum insisted it was essential.' Her brown eyes twinkled. 'But I think it's just so that we've no excuse for not letting her know exactly where we are and what we're doing.'

'And do you?'

'What?'

'Let her know exactly where you are and what you're doing?'

Fleur laughed. 'Not likely!'

Trying to sound casual, but failing, Robbie asked, 'Er – who's "we"?'

'My brother, Kenny, and me. And Dad too. She likes to keep us all close.' There was an edge of resentment in her tone as she added, ' "Tied to her apron strings" is the phrase, I think.' Her face clouded and a small frown puckered her smooth forehead. She didn't know

4

why, but for some reason she felt she could confide in him. The words were out before she'd even thought to stop them. 'She . . . she didn't want me to volunteer. It . . . it's caused a lot of rows at home.'

'That's a shame,' he said gently. 'How long have you been in?'

'Oh, right from the start. I volunteered as soon as I could.'

His blue eyes twinkled. 'Me too. The day after Mr Chamberlain's "we are at war" broadcast.'

They stared at each other and then smiled, amazed that they'd both felt the same.

'Are they calling up women yet?'

'Don't know,' Fleur replied cheerfully. 'I didn't wait to find out.'

'And you live on a farm? You could've applied to be classed as a reserved occupation, couldn't you?'

Fleur grimaced. 'I know. That's why my mother was so put out. I could quite legitimately have stayed at home for one reason or another, but I didn't want to. I . . . I wanted to "do my bit" as they say.'

'But you're not regretting it, are you?'

'Not for a minute.' Her reply was swift and genuine. 'But it's still – well – difficult when I go home.' She sighed. 'But I'll have to go. I've just been posted and I've got three days' leave before I have to report there. It might be a while before I get any more.'

'Where are you going?'

She opened her mouth to reply and then hesitated, her smile causing two deep dimples in her cheeks as she said impishly, 'I'm not sure I should be telling you. Careless talk and all that.'

'Well, I'll be terribly careless and tell you exactly

where I'm going. Wickerton Wood just south of Lincoln. It's a new airfield. Parts of it are still being built, so they say, but it's ready enough to start flying.'

Fleur's eyes widened and she couldn't prevent a little gasp of surprise. Chuckling, he leant forward to say softly, 'Don't ever volunteer for special operations, will you? Your face gives you away. That's where you're headed too, isn't it? Wickerton?'

Feeling reprimanded, she nodded and murmured, 'Oh dear.'

'Don't worry,' he said cheerfully. 'Your secret's safe with me.'

'Is . . . is that where you're going now?'

'Yes, the day after tomorrow, but first I'm going home to see Ma.'

'What are you going to do at Wickerton Wood?'

'Ah, now that *would* be telling.'

'You're right. I'm sorry,' she said at once.

He laughed with a deep chuckle that was infectious and somehow endearing too. Don't be silly, Fleur, she told herself firmly, you've only just met him. He could be anybody. But already, she realized he wasn't just anybody. He was someone she'd like to get to know so much better. The thought surprised and shocked her.

Fleur regarded herself as a no-nonsense type of girl: down to earth and with no foolish romantic notions, especially now that they were plunged into war and all its uncertainties.

'I was only teasing.' The sound of his voice brought her back and she saw that his eyes were suddenly serious. 'You know,' he went on and now there was a note of surprise in his tone. 'It might sound daft, but I feel I could tell you anything.' Then, as if fearing he was sounding soppy, the mischievous twinkle was back and he leant towards her again. 'You're not a spy, are you?'

Now Fleur laughed. 'No. Like you say, I'd give the game away all too easily. Too honest for my own good, that's me.'

'Mm, me too.'

She hesitated, but then asked, 'Where've you been up till now?'

His face clouded. 'Down south. It's been pretty rough for the past few months, especially between July and October last year. The Battle of Britain, as Churchill called it.'

'Is that what you are?' she asked, filled with a sudden dread. 'A fighter pilot?' She knew all too well the average number of ops a fighter pilot was expected to survive and then . . .

But Robbie was shaking his head. 'No – no. I'm on bombers.' His smile crinkled his eyes. 'I'm a wireless operator.'

But Fleur wasn't comforted. She shuddered. 'Don't . . . don't wireless operators have to – have to fill in for other crewmembers if . . .' Her voice trailed away.

He was looking at her keenly. 'If one of them gets injured?'

Wordlessly, she nodded.

'I'm trained as an air gunner too. And yes, sometimes it happens, but not often.' He paused and then asked, 'How do you know so much?'

She took a deep breath. He'd know soon anyway if they were both going to be working on the same station. 'I've just finished training as an R/T operator. That's what I'm coming to Wickerton to do.'

'Ah,' he said, understanding. 'A radio telephone

operator? Yes, I'd heard a lot of WAAFs are being trained for that. One of the chaps was saying he thinks it's because a woman's voice is more high-pitched. Comes across the airwaves better.'

Fleur pulled a comical face. 'At least you know what we do. Most people just look blank when I tell them.'

'Will you be in Control?'

'I . . . I don't know yet. Maybe.'

He smiled. 'It'll make a nice change to have a lovely girl to talk us down when we come back from a raid . . .' He paused a moment and then added softly, 'Or who waits up all night for us if . . . if we're late?'

A lump came into her throat as she remembered how they'd all been warned during their training that that was exactly what they'd be expected to do. Wait and wait into the small hours until there was no more hope. 'Are you fixed up with a crew?'

'Oh yes. We met up at Operational Training Unit. They put us all together in a huge briefing room and left us to sort ourselves out. It's a very informal way, but it seems to work.' He laughed. 'That way, it's unlikely you end up flying with a chap you can't stand the sight of.'

Fleur nodded. 'I'd heard that's what happens at OTU, but . . . but doesn't it make it more difficult? Flying with people who become your friends?'

Robbie's face sobered as he shook his head. 'Strangely, no. I expect it's a bit like the "pals' regiments" they had in the last war. There's just something about going into battle with a "brother" at your side.' He paused and then added, 'I've been lucky. Tommy Laughton, the skipper, is a great bloke. You can't help but like him and the rest of the crew – well – I'll soon be getting to know them a lot better. But they seemed OK. We'll be flying Hampdens, we've been told. With a crew of four.' Robbie grinned, trying to lift the mood that was getting all too serious for his liking. 'We shouldn't be talking like this.'

'No.' She forced herself to return his smile. 'There's more than likely a policeman hiding behind the counter over there ready to spring out and arrest us for careless talk.'

As the cafe was now otherwise deserted – even the girl behind the counter had disappeared – they laughed together at the likelihood of anyone overhearing them. That they perhaps should not trust each other never occurred to either of them for a moment.

'What did you do? Before the war, I mean.'

'Worked in a bank.'

'Oh, very posh!' she teased.

He grimaced. 'It was a good job, I have to admit, but it was a bit too staid for me. I was always getting told off for cracking jokes or laughing with the customers. We're supposed to be very polite and formal. I agree with the polite bit, but—' He cast his eyes to the ceiling in mock despair. 'The formality got to me in the end. I couldn't wait to get out.'

'But there's lots of rules and regulations in the RAF surely. It can be very "formal". All that saluting officers and calling them "sir".'

'True, but most of them have earned the right to be treated with that degree of respect.' He leant forward. 'And there's always the compensation of nights out with the lads, *and* – best of all – flirting with a pretty WAAF.'

Fleur arched her eyebrows sardonically, but smiled nonetheless.

'So? What are you doing for the night then?' he asked.

'Bed down in the station waiting room,' she replied promptly. 'It won't be the first time I've done it.'

'Oh no, I won't hear of it. You're coming home with me. You can have my bed. I'll sleep on the sofa.'

Fleur suddenly remembered just how short a time she had known this rather nice young man. Her face sobered, but he read her thoughts at once. 'Of course, I've got an ulterior motive.' He pretended to leer at her, but then added, 'But there's not much a chap can do with his mother in the next bedroom. And my grandfather lives with us too. We'll be well chaperoned.' He pulled a comical expression, displaying mock disappointment. 'More's the pity.'

'But it's an awful imposition on your mother. Bringing a strange girl home in the middle of the night.' Impishly, she added, 'Or is she used to it?'

'Sort of. One or two of the lads have bunked down at our place when they've been stranded, but this'll be the first time I've taken a *girl* home. She'll not mind a bit, though. She helps out at the WVS and she's always picking up waifs and strays from the forces, taking them home and feeding them.'

'Well, if you're sure . . . ?'

'I am,' he said firmly as he got up and picked up her kitbag as well as his own. 'We've got a bit of a walk, though. Hope you're up for it?'

'Now if my drill sergeant could hear you even asking me that – I'd be on a charge!'

Laughing together, they stepped into the blacked-out street.

Two

'Let's get inside quickly,' Robbie said as he unlocked the front door of the terraced house. 'Our warden has got eyes like a hawk and if he sees the tiniest chink of light, he's down on us like a ton of bricks.'

Fleur giggled. 'That's an unfortunate turn of phrase, isn't it?'

Through the darkness, she heard his chuckle. 'Yes, I see what you mean. We might get a ton of bricks on top of us literally if Jerry sees a light when he's flying over.'

They were still laughing, his hand cupping her elbow as he guided her into the strange house in the darkness. 'This is Ma's best front room.' The door from the street had opened directly into it. 'Be careful, because she—' he began when the inner door opened and a light streamed in.

'Robbie? Is that you?'

'Hope so, Ma,' he called out cheerily, 'else you've got burglars.'

'Oh, you rogue! Come on in and let me see who you've brought home this time.'

Fleur drew in breath sharply and was about to kick his shins for having lied to her, but as he led her into the light of the next room, she saw the surprise on his mother's face and knew it was genuine.

11

'Oh! A WAAF!' The woman smiled a welcome and held out her hands. 'And what a pretty one too.'

'I bumped into her in the blackout, Ma. Knocked her over getting off the train as a matter of fact.' He put his arm about Fleur's shoulders with an easy familiarity that she was amazed to realize she didn't mind. 'You could say she fell for me there and then.'

Now Fleur did retort, muttering beneath her breath so that only he could hear, 'You should be so lucky!'

She heard – and felt – his laughter rising from deep within his chest. She glanced up to find him looking down at her, his face so close that she could feel his warm breath on her cheek. In just that brief moment she noticed the way his eyes crinkled at the corners when he laughed and the tiny, stray hairs at the end of his eyebrows. And his smile – oh, his smile – such white, even teeth with tiny spaces between them. She'd only to stretch just a tiny bit and she could've kissed his mouth . . . At the unbidden thought, she felt the blush rise in her face.

'The least I could do was bring her home,' Robbie went on smoothly as she felt him squeeze her shoulder. For one foolish moment she wondered if he could read what was in her mind. 'She can't get transport tonight to where she wants to be,' he went on, explaining to his mother. 'I couldn't let her sleep in the station waiting room, now could I?'

'Dear, dear,' Meg Rodwell tutted. 'Certainly not. Come in, love, and make yourself at home. You're very welcome.'

Now that Fleur's eyes were becoming used to the bright light after the darkness, she saw that Robbie's mother was slim and youthful looking. Her shoulder-length red hair, showing not a trace of grey, was swept back over her ears in curls and waves. Her green eyes smiled a welcome. She was wearing a fashionable patterned cotton dress with short sleeves and padded shoulders, its hem only just covering the knees of her shapely legs. Fleur couldn't help smiling at the contrast between this woman and her own mother, who, as a busy farmer's wife, had little time for 'titivating', as she would have called it. Fleur's mother wore her greying hair drawn back into a bun at the nape of her neck and dressed in plain blouses and skirts that were usually covered with a paisley overall. And sensible shoes were a must about the farm. At the thought, Fleur looked down at Mrs Rodwell's dainty feet. It was no surprise to see the high-heeled shoes with a ribbon bow at the front.

But the woman was smiling so kindly at her, drawing her further into the room and towards a chair beside the warm fire burning in the grate of the old-fashioned kitchen range. Fleur gave a start as she suddenly noticed a bent old man with a crocheted shawl around his shoulders sitting on the opposite side of the hearth.

Robbie let his arm slip from about her and moved towards him, putting his hand on his shoulder. 'Now, Pops. How are you?'

The old man looked up and reached out with a hand that was misshapen with arthritis, the knuckles swollen and painful. 'Mustn't grumble, lad, mustn't grumble.'

'You never do, Pops.'

To Fleur's surprise, the old man's eyes watered as his fond gaze followed Robbie's mother while she bustled between kitchen and the back scullery, setting food on the table. 'No,' he said in a quavering voice. 'Because I know how lucky I am.'

Meg came into the room carrying two laden plates. 'Come and eat. You must be starving. I'll just go and change the sheets on your bed, Robbie . . .'

Fleur roused herself. The warm fire was already making her drowsy. 'Oh, please, don't go to any trouble on my account. I can sleep on the sofa—'

'I wouldn't hear of it—'

'Certainly not—'

Robbie and his mother spoke together and the old man laughed wheezily. 'There you are, lass, outnumbered.' He tapped the side of his nose. 'And if you take my advice, you won't argue with m'lady here. Rules the roost, she does.'

'Now, Dad.' Mrs Rodwell stepped towards the old man, tucked the shawl cosily around him and planted a kiss on his white hair. 'You'll have this nice young lady thinking I'm a regular tartar.'

Robbie pulled a comical face. 'Well, you are.' He winked at Fleur. 'We'd better do as she says before I get my legs smacked.'

As Robbie towered over his mother by at least eight or ten inches, Fleur could not suppress a giggle at the picture that sprang into her mind of the grown-up young man hopping from one foot to another to avoid the chastising hand. They were all laughing now.

'Come and eat.' Robbie urged her to take a seat at the table. 'And then it's night-nights for you. You look as if you might fall asleep in the gravy.'

*

'What did you say her name was?' Meg Rodwell asked her son the following morning as she cooked breakfast.

'Fleur,' Robbie replied, his mouth full of fried bread. They had both been so tired the previous evening that, once they had eaten, Meg had shown Fleur to Robbie's bedroom and he had headed for the sofa set against the wall in the cluttered front room which his mother used, working from her home as a dressmaker. Despite the austerity of the war – or more likely because of it – there were still many calls on Meg's talents with her sewing machine. 'Make do and mend' was the order of the day. Whilst much of her work was now altering and re-styling second-hand clothes, it was a matter of pride to Meg that she was still able to support her family. And now that Robbie contributed some of his RAF pay whenever he came home on leave, she didn't have to work long into the night these days. Though she would gladly have worked around the clock if it meant keeping her boy safe.

Smiling brightly as she determined not to spoil their few precious hours together with her darkest fears, Meg turned to greet the young WAAF her son had brought home as the girl appeared in the kitchen. She looked rested this morning, but still a little self-conscious and perhaps feeling awkward now at having allowed herself to be taken home by a complete stranger.

'Come and sit down, love,' Meg greeted her warmly. 'What would you like to eat? I'm sorry I've no eggs—'

'Please, don't apologize. I don't want you to go to

any trouble. I feel very embarrassed, descending on you like that in the middle of the night and eating your rations.'

'Don't mention it. We were glad to help. Sit down, do.'

'What about the old gentleman?'

Meg laughed. 'Oh, he doesn't get up until later. You're not taking his place or his breakfast – I promise.' She returned to the stove in the scullery, but left the door open so that she could talk to them as they sat at the table. Dropping a single rasher of bacon into the frying pan, she said, 'Now, have your breakfast and then Robbie will walk you back to the station. Where is it you're going?'

Fleur sat down at the table. 'South Monkford.'

Meg was suddenly very still, staring at the girl. 'South Monkford,' she murmured, her eyes misting over. 'Fancy.'

'Robbie mentioned that you used to live there.'

Meg nodded slowly. 'A long time ago,' she whispered. 'A long time ago now.'

'My father had a tailoring business there, didn't he?' Robbie put in. 'And didn't you say someone called Pinkerton took the shop over from you? Well, Fleur says they're still there. Two old dears – sisters – running it.'

'Fancy,' Meg murmured again, prodding absentmindedly at the sizzling bacon.

'Maybe you know Fleur's family. Her surname's Bosley—' Robbie began, but he got no further as his mother turned sharply, catching the handle of the frying pan. It clattered to the floor, spilling hot fat and the precious piece of bacon over the tiles and splashing her legs. Meg's hands flew to her face and her eyes were wide, staring at Fleur. She swayed as if she might fall.

'Ma? Ma, what is it?' Robbie was on his feet and moving swiftly to catch hold of her. He helped her to a chair, whilst Fleur hurried to the tap in the scullery to get a glass of water.

'Here,' Fleur said gently. 'Drink this.'

Meg took the glass with shaking hands and sipped it. 'I'm sorry. How stupid of me.'

The young couple glanced at each other and then, concern on both their faces, looked back at Meg, but neither asked the questions that were racing around their minds. It had been Fleur's name – her surname – that had startled Meg so.

'I'm sorry,' Meg said, placing the glass of water on the table and taking a deep breath. 'It was just . . . hearing your name.' She looked up into the open face of the lovely girl standing in front of her, so smart, so confident in her WAAF uniform.

And now she looked more carefully she could see the likeness. The rich, brown hair and deep, dark brown eyes, watching her at this moment, with such concern.

'How is he?' Meg asked softly. 'How's Jake?'

Now it was Fleur who sank into a chair, staring at Robbie's mother. 'My dad? You . . . you know my dad?'

Meg nodded.

'He . . . he's fine.' Fleur waited a moment but Meg volunteered no more. 'How d'you know him?'

'I—' Meg hesitated. It was an ironic and cruel fate that had conspired against her to bring these two young people together. The past that she wanted to keep buried was doing its best to catch up with her. She must say nothing. It was not her place to be telling this girl things that perhaps her parents had never told her and most likely didn't want her to know. After all, she hadn't told her own son, had she?

Meg shuddered, and Robbie sat down beside his mother too, chafing her hand that was suddenly cold between his warm ones. He was willing Fleur not to ask any more questions that were obviously upsetting his mother. 'Are you all right, Ma?'

Absently, as if she had only just become aware of the pain, Meg rubbed her leg. 'The fat splashed, but it's nothing.'

'You ought to put something on it.'

'Don't fuss, Robbie,' she said sharply, her spirit returning, the colour coming back into her face. 'I'm all right.' Now she turned to Fleur. 'I'm sorry, my dear. How silly of me.' She was back in control of her feelings now and of the situation. But inside she was still quaking. I must be careful what I say, what I ask, she was thinking. Forcing a brightness into her tone, she said, 'It was just hearing the name after all these years. Of course I knew your father when we lived there. Both your parents.'

The two young people were aware that there was much more to it than just that. They glanced at each other, wanting to ask more, but afraid of distressing Robbie's mother again.

But in her turn and despite her desire to let secrets stay hidden, Meg could not stop herself asking, 'Are they still at Middleditch Farm? Still working for the Smallwoods?'

Fleur hesitated but, seeing Robbie's slight nod, she answered, 'Dad owns the farm now. The Smallwoods both died about eight years ago and they left the farm to my father and mother.'

Meg gasped and before she could stop herself, she blurted out, 'Not – not to their daughter?'

Fleur was puzzled. 'I didn't know they had a daughter.'

Meg closed her eyes and shook her head. 'I'm sorry, I shouldn't have said anything.'

Again Fleur and Robbie exchanged a glance, but their attention was brought back to his mother as she asked one last question. Was it Fleur's imagination or was there a slight hardening of her tone as Meg asked, 'And your mother? How is Betsy?'

Three

'So – what do you make of all that then?' Robbie said as he pulled the front door shut behind them and shouldered Fleur's kitbag. They began to walk side by side along the street towards the station.

Fleur frowned. 'I honestly don't know.'

'There's more to it than she's letting on,' Robbie said.

'Well yes, I thought so too, but I didn't like to say. I mean, it's none of our business, is it? Certainly not mine.'

He touched her arm. 'I'd like it to be. I'd like to see you again. We're going to be on the same camp. It shouldn't be too difficult. I mean – that is if . . . if you . . . ?' He was suddenly boyishly unsure.

She smiled up at him, surprised that he even needed to ask. 'Of course I want to see you again. That's if you want to be seen with a lowly ACW, Flight Sergeant Rodwell?'

'Mm,' he murmured absently as if the matter of rank was the very last thing on his mind at this precise moment. He squeezed her elbow. 'It's strange, but I feel as if I've known you years.'

'I know,' she said simply and without being conscious of what she was doing, she slipped her arm through his and they walked closely side by side, matching their strides.

They didn't speak again until they were standing on the platform. Robbie had put her kitbag in the carriage and now they stood facing each other. He put his hands on her shoulders, smiling down at her. 'I'll see you soon then?'

She nodded and now she did what she'd been wanting to do almost since they'd first met. She stood on tiptoe and kissed him. Not a chaste kiss on the cheek, but on his wide, generous mouth.

As she drew back, he laughed softly and murmured, 'You hussy . . .' Then his arms were tightly around her, his warm mouth on hers. Her arms wound themselves around his neck, her body pressed to his.

A whistle sounded and a merry, gruff voice said, 'Break it up, now. Train's leaving if you're catching it.'

They broke apart and turned to see the guard with the whistle in his hand, grinning at them. 'Sorry, folks, but the train can't wait.' The man's craggy face softened. 'Not even for you.' In his job he saw so many partings, so many tears. He often wondered what happened to all those youngsters whose poignant goodbyes he witnessed. Did they meet again or did those tears of 'sweet sorrow' become a deluge of grief?

But these two were laughing and blushing, and the older man guessed their love was new and young, just on the threshold . . . But his train couldn't wait – not even for love.

Fleur scrambled aboard and leant out of the window, clasping his hands. 'Come out to the farm later,' she invited rashly, 'and bring your mother.'

'I'll be there. Can't vouch for Ma, but I'll be there,' he vowed.

He stood watching the train out of sight, marvelling that in the space of a few hours he had found the girl

21

he wanted to spend the rest of his life with. However long or short, he thought soberly, that life might be.

'I wish you'd've let me know you were coming. I could've come to fetch you from Nottingham last night.' Jake Bosley frowned worriedly. 'I don't like the idea of you going home with a complete stranger. Even if he is in the RAF, he could be anyone.'

Fleur grinned as she dropped her kitbag to the floor, returned her father's bear hug and then dutifully kissed her mother's cheek.

Betsy sniffed. 'It's nice of you to remember you have a home.' There was a pause before she added, 'When are you going back?'

Deciding to ignore the barbed remark, Fleur responded gaily, 'Good old Mum. You always say the same thing. It sounds as if you can't wait to get rid of me again.'

Betsy's mouth tightened. 'You know very well that's not the case. We never wanted you to go in the first place. But you had to have your own way, didn't you? Couldn't wait to get away. Anyone would think—'

'Now, now, Betsy love. Don't spoil the precious time we've got with her,' Jake said, trying as he always did to quench the sparks that so easily flared between mother and daughter.

'I'm sorry, Mum. I was only teasing.' Fleur kicked herself mentally. She ought to know by now that her mother rarely took teasing from anyone – unless, of course, it was Fleur's younger brother, Kenny, doing the tormenting.

Fleur turned back to her father. He was still frowning anxiously. He was a good-looking man and middle age was being kind to him, for there were only a few flecks of grey in his thick, brown hair. His build was stocky and strong from years of farm work even though he walked with a stiff leg – the result of a wound in the Great War that everyone had believed would 'end all wars'. How wrong they had all been! But she saw now that the laughter lines on his face were deepening into anxiety and the look in his dark brown eyes troubled her, for she knew she was the cause.

He hadn't wanted her to join up. Neither of them had. Her mother had cried and stormed and demanded that she stay at home, whilst her father had gone about his work on the farm with a worried frown permanently on his face.

'You don't have to go. You're doing important work here on the farm,' he'd tried to insist.

'You'll be killed,' Betsy had wailed dramatically. 'I know you will.'

'Oh, Mum, girls don't fly. I'll just be on an aerodrome. In the offices or the canteen or – or something.'

'Airfields get bombed,' Betsy had persisted. She'd got Fleur dead and buried already before she'd even signed up. But for once Fleur had stood her ground. She wanted to do her bit, wanted to see something of life away from the farm, though of course she didn't tell them that.

'Kenny's still here.' She'd tried to soften the blow. 'He's too young to go.'

'That depends on how long this wretched war goes on,' her mother had said bitterly. 'He's seventeen now.'

'Only just,' Fleur said.

'What if it lasts another two years?' her mother

persisted. 'He'll get called up when he's nineteen. And I bet,' she added bitterly, 'it won't be long before they lower the age for call up.'

'But he'll work on the farm. Dad can apply for a deferment for him. He won't have to go,' Fleur had argued.

'But he *will* go.' Betsy's voice had risen hysterically as she'd said accusingly, 'Because he'll copy you. He idolizes you. You can't do anything wrong in his eyes.' There was more than a tinge of jealousy in Betsy's tone. It was she who idolized her son, and she made no effort to hide her possessiveness. Miraculously, the boy himself was unspoilt by her favouritism and Fleur enjoyed an easy, bantering relationship with her brother.

'It's the mother–son and father–daughter thing,' he'd once said laughingly, showing a surprising insight for one so young. 'You're Dad's favourite.'

But Fleur wouldn't allow that. 'No, he doesn't have favourites. You know that. But maybe he's a bit more protective of me because I'm a girl.'

Kenny had grinned. 'Nobody's ever going to be good enough for his little girl, eh?'

Fleur had laughed. 'Something like that.'

It hadn't mattered then – there'd been no young man she'd been serious about. But now . . . ? Well, now it was different.

'As a matter of fact,' she said carefully, 'the young man I went home with wasn't a complete stranger.'

Jake's face cleared. 'Oh, it was someone you know?'

'Not exactly,' she said carefully. 'Someone *you* know, or at least, used to know.'

The frown was back, but this time it was a puzzled look rather than a worried one that creased Jake's craggy features. And, strangely, there was a touch of wariness in his eyes.

'Do you remember someone called Mrs Rodwell and her son Robbie?'

Before Jake could answer a cry escaped Betsy and, her eyes wide, she pressed her hand to her mouth. And then to Fleur's utter amazement, Betsy began to scream. 'No, no, not her. Oh, not her. I thought she'd gone for good. I thought—' She clutched wildly at her daughter, her fingers digging painfully into Fleur's arm. 'You're to have nothing to do with him. Do you hear? He's a bad lot.'

Jake moved forward at once and put his arms about his wife. 'Now, now, Betsy love, don't take on so. Surely, after all this time—?'

Betsy twisted to face him. 'Leopards don't change their spots, Jake. She'll never change and her son'll be like her. Self-centred, devious, spiteful.' She rounded again on Fleur. 'What did she say? Does she know who you are?' Betsy was still like a wild thing, screaming questions at her daughter. Fleur stared at her. She'd seen her mother in some tempers, but never – in all her life – had she seen her quite like this. Completely out of control.

'Mum—' She reached out but Betsy slapped her hands away as if her daughter's touch was suddenly abhorrent.

Fleur let her arms fall to her side. 'Actually,' she said flatly, realizing that the tentative romance that had already begun between her and Robbie was doomed. 'She was as shocked as you are when she heard my surname, but she . . . she didn't react quite as . . . as . . .' Fleur faltered and her voice dropped to a whisper. 'Well, not like this.'

'She took you in, you say?'

Fleur nodded.

Betsy's voice hardened. 'So – what was in it for her?'

'Mum!' Fleur was appalled. She'd liked Robbie's mother. She couldn't believe the things her own mother was saying about her. Mrs Rodwell had been so kind, so welcoming. And the old man; she hadn't had much of a conversation with him, but he'd seemed a dear old boy.

Fleur sighed and said flatly, 'I don't know what you're getting at, Mum. But there was nothing "in it" for her, as you put it. She was just nice to me. Cooking breakfast for me. Apologizing because she had no eggs when there I was – a complete stranger – taking their rations.'

'But you're not a stranger.'

'I was then. She was doing all that before she knew my name. And Robbie says she works for the WVS. That she's always taking home waifs and strays. And she looks after the old man—'

'Ah! I knew it! She's got another poor old boy in her clutches.' Betsy was scathing now. 'Well off, is he?'

'An old man?' Even Jake was curious now, but Fleur was startled by the sudden bleak look in his eyes. 'Who was he? Her husband?'

'I . . . I don't think so. Robbie called him "Pops". And . . . and . . . yes, she called him "Dad".' Fleur looked from one to the other, puzzled and more than a little alarmed by their reaction. 'He must be her father.'

'Her *father*!' Now Jake was shocked. 'My God!' he murmured, and he was obviously stunned. 'Her father.'

'Huh!' Betsy pulled her mouth down at the corners. 'It'll more likely be a fancy man who's old enough to *be* her father.'

But Fleur was watching the strange, thoughtful look in Jake's eyes.

Betsy's voice was still high-pitched, demanding, 'I want to know what she *said*.'

'She asked how Dad was.'

'I bet she did. Oh, I bet she did!'

Fleur blinked under the vehemence in her mother's voice. She glanced at her father, but he was far away, lost in his own thoughts. She looked back at her mother, hoping to placate her. She couldn't know that it was entirely the wrong thing to say as she added, 'And she asked about you, too.'

'Wanted to know if I was still around, I suppose. Hoping I wasn't. Hoping I was dead and in my grave.'

'Mum!'

'Betsy!'

Jake and Fleur spoke together, shocked by Betsy's hysterical outburst. Jake went on, 'Now that's enough. You've no call to—'

'No call? No call, you say? Look at the lives she ruined with her . . . with her carryings on.' The venom was spitting out of Betsy's mouth. 'But you still love her, don't you? All these years you've never stopped loving her, and if she so much as crooked her little finger you'd go running.'

Fleur gasped and felt the colour drain from her own face as she listened to her mother's terrible accusations.

Jake's face was dark with anger, any sympathy and understanding gone from his expression. His wife was pushing him just a little too far now. 'That's not fair,

Betsy, and you know it. I've always loved you and our children. I've done my best to be a good husband and father, haven't I?' He turned his head slightly and now his question included his daughter. 'Haven't I?'

Fleur moved swiftly to his side and linked her arm through his, hugging it to her. 'Oh, Dad, of course you have.' She turned towards her mother. 'Mum—'

'You stay out of this.' Betsy's voice was still high-pitched. 'It's nothing to do with you.'

'Well, as a matter of fact, I think it has. You see – I'm sorry – but I invited Robbie to come out here to tea this afternoon. And . . . and I said he could bring his mother if . . . if he wanted.'

For a moment Betsy stared at her. Then she let out a chilling scream and began to pull at her own hair like someone demented. Jake released himself from Fleur's grasp to take hold of his wife, but she struggled against him, beating his chest with her fists, crying and screaming, even kicking out at him. Jake winced as the toe of her sturdy shoe caught him on the shin.

'Dad?' Fleur raised her voice above the noise her mother was making. 'Shall I fetch the doctor? Shall I call Dr Collins?'

There was a sudden silence in the kitchen as the screaming stopped abruptly. But then Betsy began to laugh – a hysterical sound that was more chilling than her crying.

'Oh yes, oh yes. Call Dr Collins – and his wife. Let them all come. Let them all meet. I'm sure Dr Collins would like to meet his—'

To Fleur's horror, Jake suddenly clamped his hand across Betsy's runaway mouth. 'That's enough,' he bellowed in a tone that brooked no argument.

Four

Middleditch Farm lay five miles from the small town of South Monkford amidst gently rolling countryside. Robbie – and his mother, if she came – would have to take the Nottingham to Lincoln train, get off at the Junction and catch the little train that the locals called 'the Paddy' out to South Monkford. Fleur hadn't dared to ask her father to meet the train. Not now. So, from the town railway station they would have to hitch a lift out to the farm. That afternoon Fleur walked down the lane some distance from the farmyard gate to waylay Robbie and – more importantly – his mother. Fleur frowned as she went over in her mind every little detail of her own mother's frenzied outburst. Her father was tight-lipped about it all. He would explain nothing.

Jake had released his hold on his wife, glared at her for a moment, then turned on his heel and gone outside into the yard, slamming the back door behind him. Betsy had stared after him, pressing trembling fingers to her mouth.

Fleur had stepped towards her, holding out her arms. 'Mum—?' But Betsy had let out a sob, turned her back on her daughter and run upstairs to her bedroom, slamming the door just as Jake had done.

Fleur had winced and stood alone in the kitchen, biting her lip. After a moment, she'd followed her father outside and found him leaning on the gate, staring with unseeing eyes at the spread of land before him that was now all his. She'd stood beside him, resting her arms on the top of the gate.

'Dad—?'

'Leave it, Fleur.' He'd sighed heavily, his anger dying as swiftly as it had come. 'It all happened a long time ago and it's best left buried. It's over and done with.'

'It doesn't sound like it as far as Mum's concerned,' she'd retorted. Immediately she regretted her words when she saw the bleak expression that flitted across her father's face.

'Oh, Dad,' she'd said, putting her hand on his arm and trying her most cajoling tone. 'Won't you tell me what it's all about?'

His hand had covered hers as he'd replied softly, 'I . . . I can't, love. They're not my secrets to tell.' And he'd refused to say any more.

For mid-April, it was surprisingly hot and still in the lane, sheltered from the light breeze by hedges on either side. Fleur spread her greatcoat on the grass and sat down beneath the shade of two huge trees, the branches rustling gently above her. She leant back against one of the trunks, her gaze still on the corner of the lane. She wanted to see him again – even wanted to see his mother again. She'd liked her. But part of her wanted them to stay away. For, if they did come, how was she going to explain that they weren't welcome at Middleditch Farm? She certainly couldn't risk taking them home. She didn't want her mother throwing another fit. Nor did she want to see that terrible haunted look on her dad's face.

Fleur loved her dad – loved both her parents, of course, but she was fiercely protective of her father. She didn't really understand why – couldn't have put it into words – but for as long as she could remember she'd sometimes seen a strange, sad, faraway look in his eyes and, even as a little girl, she'd felt the instinctive desire to shield him from hurt. Only the touch of her tiny hand in his had brought him back to his happy present, as he'd hugged her to him or ruffled her hair affectionately. As she'd grown older she'd thought his moments of melancholy were because of Betsy's preoccupation with Kenny, believing her father felt neglected and excluded. It had drawn her even closer to him.

But now, she wondered, was that sadness, buried deep, to do with Robbie's mother? If it was, the reminder of it had made her own mother hysterical . . .

There was something tickling her nose. Drowsily, she brushed it away, and then she heard his soft chuckle and opened her eyes.

'Sleeping Beauty,' he teased. He was lying beside her, leaning on one elbow and tickling her with a piece of grass.

She gave a startled cry and sat up. 'I must have fallen asleep.' She blinked and rubbed her eyes as she looked around her. 'Where's your mother?'

'She hasn't come.' For a moment, his eyes clouded. 'Said it wouldn't be right.' He shrugged. 'I don't understand why though.'

'I do,' Fleur said promptly. 'At least, part of it. I think I know why she hasn't come.'

She lay down, leaning on her elbow so that they were facing each other. 'There's something gone on in

31

the past between them all. I don't know what it is –
they won't tell me – but it must be something pretty
awful 'cos my mum threw a ducky fit.'

'A what?' He was laughing in spite of himself.

Now Fleur grinned too. 'Sorry. It's something one
of the girls I met while training was always saying. It
must be catching.'

'I take it your mother wasn't best pleased?'

'That's an understatement if ever there was one. I've
never – in my whole life – seen her act like that. Oh,
she gets a bit het up about things. Fusses and flaps
about anything and everything – usually about our
Kenny – but this morning she was screaming and
shouting and hitting out at my dad when he tried to
calm her down.'

'Good Lord!' Robbie frowned thoughtfully for a
moment and then said slowly, 'My mother was sort of
– well – odd. Not hysterical or anything, but you saw
how shocked she was when she heard your surname.'

Fleur nodded. 'Did she explain why?'

Robbie shook his head. 'No. Shut up like a clam.
She went very quiet and seemed lost in a world of her
own. I couldn't reach her, if you know what I mean.'

'Oh, I know exactly what you mean. I bet it's the
same sort of look my dad sometimes has. As if he's
lost in the past.'

'That's it. That's it exactly.' They stared at each
other for a moment before Robbie said slowly, 'You
. . . you don't think there was – well – something
between them, do you? Between your dad and my
mother? Years ago?'

Fleur nodded. 'There must have been because . . .
because in amongst all my mum's shouting and hyster-

32

ical crying she said, "All these years, you've never stopped loving her."'

'And you think she meant my mother?'

Again, Fleur nodded, but now she said no more. She couldn't for the heavy feeling growing within her chest, a feeling of ominous foreboding.

Robbie blew out his cheeks as he let out a long sigh. 'Crikey! Now I see why Ma wouldn't come with me today and why you're waiting for me in the lane.' His blue eyes were dark with disappointment. 'I take it I'm not welcome at your home?'

She shook her head, not trusting herself to speak for the lump in her throat.

He sighed again and sat up, resting his arms on his knees and linking his fingers. His back was towards her as he said flatly, 'So, you don't want to see me again?'

Fleur sat up too and touched his arm. Slowly, he turned to face her. They gazed at each other for a long moment before she said, 'I *do* want to see you again. I mean – that is – if you want to see me.'

'Of course I do.'

She smiled and felt a warm glow at the swiftness of his reply. 'But,' she went on, 'we've just got to realize what we might be getting ourselves into. We won't be able to visit each other's homes.'

'You can come to mine. Ma won't mind.'

'Are you really sure about that?'

'Well . . .' She could see the sudden doubt on his face.

'She was very kind to me last night,' Fleur went on, 'and even after she knew who I was, but that doesn't mean she'll want to see me again. Have me visiting, reminding her . . .' There was a long silence before Fleur said, 'So do you see why I say, "as long as we realize what we're getting ourselves into"?'

'Yeah,' Robbie's mouth tightened. 'Right into the middle of a Shakespeare play by the sound of it.'

Fleur laughed, stood up and held out her hand to pull him up. 'Just so long as you know I've no intention of committing suicide over you like Juliet.'

He stood close to her, still holding her hand and looking down into her dark brown eyes. 'And that's another thing.'

'What is?' she whispered, suddenly frightened by the serious look in his eyes.

'Death. Not by suicide, of course. But I face it every time we take off on a bombing run. And you're not in exactly the safest job there is, are you? Airfields are constant targets for the enemy.'

'I know,' she said quietly. 'But we're only in the same boat as thousands of others. We . . . we've all got to take our happiness when we can, haven't we?'

Robbie nodded. 'Damn right we have. And damn the past and all its secrets. We're living in the present.' Though he didn't speak the words aloud, as he took her into his arms and bent his head to kiss her Robbie was praying silently: Dear Lord, grant me a future with this lovely girl. Don't let me end my days in a burning plane, or her buried beneath a pile of rubble on a bombed-out airfield. Let us grow old together, with our grandchildren at our knees . . .

Five

'There's something else I want to ask you.'

'Fire away,' Robbie said, resting his elbows on the small table in the cafe where they were sitting. They were determined to spend the afternoon together, even if they were not welcome at Middleditch Farm, and had walked back to South Monkford, hitching a ride on a farm cart for part of the way.

'Who's the old gentleman who lives with you?'

'Pops?'

Fleur nodded.

'My grandfather.' There was a pause before Robbie asked. 'Why?'

Fleur stirred her tea, even though, with wartime rationing, she had stopped taking sugar in it. She avoided meeting his gaze. 'Your mother's father?'

Robbie nodded.

'Has he always lived with you?'

Robbie wrinkled his forehead. 'No. I must have been about eight or nine when he arrived out of the blue. I think – no, I'm sure – before that there was just me and Ma. My father died before I was born. I told you that, didn't I?'

'Mm.'

Slowly, as if he was reliving a memory he'd not thought about in years, Robbie went on, 'There was a knock at the door one day and I ran to answer it. You know how when you're a kid, you love to be the one to answer the door?'

Fleur nodded but did not speak. She didn't want to break his train of thought.

'This chap was standing there. I thought it was an old tramp asking for food. He was wearing scruffy clothes, had a full straggly beard and long greasy-looking hair.' He grinned. 'Mind you, it wasn't the first time I'd seen a gentleman of the road knocking at our door or sitting in our kitchen being fed.' He laughed. 'They reckon tramps leave signs for one another pointing the way to a house where they'll likely get a meal.' The smile faded and the thoughtful frown returned. 'But when Ma saw this particular chap, I thought she was going to faint. I do remember that. Then she hustled me away – sent me to my bedroom. Next morning the old boy was still there. Clean clothes, shaved, hair neatly trimmed. Ma's a dab hand with her scissors around hair as well as material. He was sitting in the chair by the fire just as if he'd taken up residence.' Robbie laughed again. 'And he had. He patted my head and said, "I'm your grandad, son." '

'And he's lived with you ever since?'

'Yup.' She felt his searching gaze on her face. 'Why all the interest?'

He'd seen through her. She laughed self-consciously. 'I can't hide anything from you, can I?'

'Nope.' His wide smile was back.

'It was just – well – when I mentioned him at home, my dad seemed flabbergasted.'

'Oh? I wonder why.'

'Mm. So do I.'

They sat in thoughtful silence drinking their tea,

until Robbie, leaning forward, whispered, 'Don't look now, but there's a woman over there who can't seem to take her eyes off me.'

Fleur giggled. 'Must be the uniform. There are some women who'll do anything for a man in uniform.' She held up her hand, palm outwards. 'And before you say it, I'm not one of them.'

Laughter crinkled his face and his bright blue eyes danced with merriment. 'Shame,' he murmured and his glance caressed her. She felt as if she were wrapped in his arms even though the table separated them. A pink tinge coloured her cheeks but she returned his gaze boldly. Fleur was no shrinking violet who simpered and tittered under a man's admiring eyes. She'd been a WAAF long enough to fend off ardent advances, but she had no wish to fend off Robbie Rodwell.

If only . . .

'Look out,' Robbie muttered suddenly, 'she's coming over.'

As the woman approached, Fleur looked up and then she smiled. 'Why, it's Aunt Louisa.' She jumped up and kissed the woman's cheek before pulling out a chair and inviting her to join them.

As she introduced her to Robbie, the young man stood up and held out his hand. Louisa gazed up at him as if mesmerized, allowing him to take her limp hand in his broad grasp. 'I'm pleased to meet you.'

'She's not really my aunt but I've always called her that. She's Mrs Dr Collins.' Fleur laughed. 'That's what folk call her, isn't it, Aunt Louisa?'

'Yes,' Louisa mumbled weakly, still unable to drag her gaze away from Robbie's face.

'And this is Robbie Rodwell. We only met last

ni . . .' Her voice faded away as she watched Louisa's face turn pale. The older woman seemed to sway and sink down into the chair Fleur had placed for her. But, still, she was staring up at Robbie.

'Aunt Louisa – what is it? Whatever's the matter?'

'Rodwell,' Louisa murmured. 'You're – you're Meg's boy, aren't you?'

Robbie, too, sat down. 'Yes, I am, and I'm very sorry if meeting me is distressing you in some way. It seems—' he glanced up at Fleur, seeking her permission to say more. Fleur gave a tiny nod and he turned back to face Louisa. 'It seems there are a lot of things that Fleur and I don't know about.'

Louisa was regaining her colour now and some of her composure, though her hands still trembled. 'Oh yes,' she said, a bitter edge to her tone. 'There are a lot of things you don't know. But I'm not the one to tell you.' She struggled to her feet and, automatically, Robbie and Fleur rose too. Robbie put his hand out to steady her, but she snatched her arm away as if she couldn't bear him to touch her. She stared at him for a moment and then said, 'You ask your mother, if you want to know. Yes, you ask her. Ask her . . .' She made a gulping noise that sounded suspiciously like a sob. 'Ask her about your . . . your *father*.' Then she swung round towards Fleur. 'But don't you go asking your dad anything – and certainly not your mother. Don't you go hurting my little Betsy. Not again.'

With that, Louisa turned and hurried from the cafe, her shoulders hunched and holding a handkerchief to her face. The young couple stared after her, concerned by the woman's obvious distress yet still mystified.

'Seems everyone knows what this is all about – except us,' Robbie said.

'Yes,' Fleur agreed slowly. 'It does, doesn't it?'

Robbie caught hold of her hand. She turned to face him and he put his hands on her shoulders. Looking down into her face, his expression was serious. 'You . . . you won't let this come between us, will you? Whatever it is?'

Fleur was anxious too, but she said firmly, 'No, I won't. *We* won't.'

And there, in the cafe, oblivious to onlookers, he bent and kissed her. Those around them who noticed merely smiled and turned away a little sadly. So many partings, they were thinking. So many young couples snatching brief moments together before the war tore them apart again. Not so long ago, such a public display of affection would have been frowned upon, but now no one said a word.

They walked back to the railway station, their arms around each other. It felt quite natural, even though they had only known each other such a short time. They were living in strange times – times when happiness had to be grabbed whenever and wherever it happened.

'There's only one thing I can think of.'

'I know.'

'It must be that your father and my mother were in love.' Robbie was the one to voice aloud what they were both thinking. 'Or at least that your dad was in love with my mother and your mum was . . . well . . .' He didn't like to say the word, but Fleur

39

finished the sentence for him. 'Jealous.' She was quiet for a moment before whispering, 'Do you think they had an affair?'

Robbie wrinkled his forehead and blew out his cheeks. 'Who knows? Let's face it, they lived through the last lot, didn't they? Maybe they met in the last war and . . . and felt just like we do now.' He turned and brushed his lips against her hair. 'Oh, Fleur, Fleur. I'm so glad I met you.'

'But my parents were married then. I was born just after the war ended.'

'So was I. Well – in the following June to be precise.'

Now they stopped and turned to face each other.

'You don't suppose—' Robbie began, as an appalling thought crept its way into his mind. So in tune with each other were they that Fleur ended the sentence yet again.

'That we're half-brother and sister?'

They stared at each other, stricken. They had promised each other that nothing would keep them apart. Nothing that had happened in the past was going to come between them. But now, with growing horror, they realized that there was something that could do just that.

'But my mother would've said if it had been that.' She paused and then asked doubtfully, 'Wouldn't she?'

'I don't think so. You said she was hysterical – like you've never seen her before?'

'Yes.' Fleur's voice was low.

'And she forbade you to see me again?'

'Yes.'

'And that woman in the cafe. She knows something.

She reacted just the same as my mother and your mother did.'

'But surely my dad would have said—'

Robbie shook his head. 'I bet your dad idolizes you, doesn't he?'

Fleur nodded.

'Then do you really think he'd want you to find out something like that about him?'

Mutely, Fleur shook her head.

'And there's something else too,' Robbie said solemnly. 'Something I should have realized before.'

'What?'

'Your dad's name? It's Jake, isn't it?'

Fleur nodded.

'That's my middle name. I'm Robert *Jake* Rodwell.'

'Oh no!' Fleur whispered.

He put his arms around her and held her close, trying to lessen the pain his words would bring. 'I really think we'd better find out what all these secrets are, don't you?'

Against his chest, he heard her muffled 'Yes.' Then she raised her head. 'But how are we going to find out?'

Robbie's face was grim. 'We'll have to ask them. I shall tell my mother that we've fallen in love.' For a moment he stroked her hair tenderly and kissed the end of her nose. 'And that we need to know. We have a *right* to know.'

'Would it be best if I asked my dad?'

He pondered for a moment. 'No, I'll ask my mother first. We've always been close. I think she'll tell me the truth. Your dad might . . .' He hesitated, not wanting to say what was in his mind, but uncannily she knew.

41

'You mean, he might not tell me the truth for fear of hurting my mum?'

Robbie nodded.

'Yes, you're right.'

'So I'll ask my mother. Don't worry, darling. I'm sure there's a simple explanation.'

But when they parted they were still both anxious and the kiss they shared was tentative, as if they were each holding back. Just in case . . .

Six

Louisa Collins sat in the darkness of her sitting room in the big, double-fronted house that was both their home and her husband's medical practice. The room to the right of the central front door was their private sitting room, whilst across the hall was Philip's surgery and dispensing room. Patients waited in the spacious hallway and Louisa, acting as her husband's receptionist, welcomed them with words of comfort and reassurance and ushered them into his room when their turn came.

The blackout curtains were drawn and the only light in the room came from the fire in the grate of the ornate fireplace, the flickering flames casting eerie shadows around the room, glinting on the heavy, old-fashioned but lovingly polished furniture. The light settled for a brief moment on the oil paintings on the wall and the delicate china in the glass cabinet and then flitted away again.

She sat perfectly still, yet her mind was busy with darting thoughts and fleeting memories and dark suspicions that refused to be buried any longer. She hadn't thought about all that for years. Only now and again when she saw Jake and Betsy was she reminded, but even then, as the years had passed, she had managed to stop her thoughts dwelling on those times they had all shared but never spoke of now.

She had loved Philip, body and soul, ever since she

had first met him. There had never been anyone else for her but him. Her only regret was that she had never been able to give him children. The sob rose in her throat and she pressed her fingers to her lips to stop the sound escaping, even though there was no one else in the house to hear. She had shed many tears over it through the years, mostly alone, but sometimes against her husband's shoulder whilst he held her and patted her and told her it didn't matter. They were happy, weren't they? Just the two of them? They had each other and more than likely it was all his fault anyway. Being gassed in the Great War had left its mark on him and he was sure that could be the reason. But Louisa knew that he was trying to be kind, trying to spare her the dreadful burden of being barren – of not being able to give him a child.

And now, today, she'd seen Meg's son. And – of all people – he'd been with Fleur. She'd seen the way they'd looked at each other and she shuddered. If ever she'd seen two people on the brink of falling in love, it had been those two. Then, stupidly, oh so foolishly, she had lost control of her emotions. She'd said far too much to them, far more than she should have done. A fresh panic swept through her. They would be sure to ask questions after the way she'd acted. He would ask Meg and – despite her plea – she was sure that Fleur would ask her parents too.

Now she groaned aloud to the empty room and dropped her head into her hands.

'Oh, what have I done?' she whispered. 'What *have* I done?'

*

At Middleditch Farm, Betsy, too, was sitting in the dusk beside her bedroom window. There was no light in the room behind her so the blackout blinds were not drawn. She looked down into the yard, watching Jake finishing the evening milking and driving the cows out of the byre, through the gate and down the lane back to the field.

She should have been helping him. With Fleur gone, he was always short-handed nowadays, even though Kenny lent a hand whenever he could. And that was another worry. Where was Kenny? He should have been home from school hours ago. They had persuaded their son to stay on at school into the sixth form, with the hope that he might go on to university afterwards. Anything to try to keep him out of the war for as long as possible.

Betsy craned her neck, trying to see further up and down the lane through the gathering gloom. She opened the window and leant out, straining to hear the sound of his whistling. Kenny was always whistling as he rattled homewards on his bicycle. She'd hear him long before she saw him . . . But the evening air was still, the only sounds the occasional bark of their dog as he helped herd the cows along the lane.

And Fleur – where was she? She'd not come back since going out to meet that boy. Meg's boy. Betsy had watched her go from this very window – had seen her walk down the lane. Watched her turn the corner until she was out of sight.

The very lane that Meg had walked down all those years ago as she left with her baby. The day that Jake had said 'goodbye' to her for ever. The day he had chosen to stay with Betsy and their daughter, and they had stood together in the yard and watched Meg walk away.

Betsy sank back into the chair, her arms resting on the sill, and dropped her head onto her arms. It was as if the intervening years had never happened. As if all the love and care Jake had lavished on his children and, yes, on her too, she had to admit, had never happened.

It seemed like only yesterday that she'd stood beside him as he'd waved goodbye to Meg.

'I'll drop you at the main gate for you to book in at the guardroom,' the driver of the RAF lorry that had met them at Lincoln railway station told them, as he drove through Wickerton village and turned into the gateway of the RAF station. Robbie and Fleur had met up on the Nottingham to Lincoln train as they had planned and travelled the last few miles together.

'Here we are, then,' the driver said as he slowed the vehicle to a halt just in front of the barrier. Whilst they waited for the sentry to approach them, he added, 'You'll need to report in at the main guardroom here first, but all the living quarters are set well away from the actual airfield itself. The Waafery's that way, miss.' He pointed along the road to the left. Fleur giggled inwardly at the nickname given to the WAAF buildings.

'That's where you need to go and they'll tell you where to go from there, but you, sunshine' – he nodded at Robbie – 'will have a bit of a walk.' His grin widened as he added, 'I reckon they've built the fellers' quarters as far away from the lasses as they can.'

Robbie laughed. 'I shouldn't wonder!'

'Over there, see.' The driver jerked his thumb to the right, towards several buildings of all shapes and sizes, scattered across a vast area some distance away. 'That's the men's quarters. There's the CO's quarters, officers' mess, sergeants' mess, airmen's mess, NAAFI, gym, chapel and the sick quarters. Let's hope you don't see much of that place, though.' He winked at Robbie. 'I wouldn't mind meself. There's a couple of nice nurses there, so I've heard.'

Robbie jumped down and held out his hand to help Fleur. 'Home for the next few months at least.'

As the lorry drove off further into the camp with a series of splutters and bangs, they looked about them.

Fleur shaded her eyes against the setting sun beyond the distant airfield, its huge, camouflaged hangars black silhouettes against the golden glow. A little nearer several aircraft stood in a silent row.

'What are those?' Fleur asked. Though she'd studied pictures of various aircraft, she'd never been so close to one.

'Hampdens,' Robbie murmured. 'I wonder if one of them's ours.'

Fleur gazed at the planes and shuddered. Soon Robbie might be flying night after night in one of them. And she would be left watching and listening and waiting.

'Come on,' he said, picking up his belongings and Fleur's kitbag too. 'We'd better do as we've been told and then I suppose we'll have to go our separate ways.' The regret in his tone mirrored her feelings.

'But we'll see each other, won't we? About camp, I mean?'

He grinned at her through the gathering dusk. 'Just

let 'em try to stop us.' But his hearty tone was forced now. The worry was still in both their minds. Should they even be meeting at all?

When they'd reported in, they stood together for another few minutes, in the middle of the road, both reluctant to make the final move to part.

'There doesn't seem to be anyone about,' Fleur said. 'I thought the place'd be teeming with activity.'

'You'd think so, wouldn't you? Maybe it's supper-time or something.'

'That'd explain it.'

'Or maybe they're flying . . .'

Again, a silence, but neither of them moved.

Robbie nodded towards the WAAF buildings. A few were obviously still under construction. 'I'd heard this was a newish station. Looks like it's not finished yet.'

Fleur looked about her and then said reluctantly, 'We . . . we'd better go, hadn't we?'

Robbie grinned. 'Trying to get rid of me already, are you?'

'Course not.' Fleur pretended indignation that he could even think such a thing. 'I just don't want you in trouble on your first day. I . . . I'm not quite sure how they'll view the men and women mixing, especially different ranks. You know . . . ?'

Robbie laughed aloud. 'Shouldn't think they'll be able to stop it even if they try.' His blue eyes twinkled at her through the gathering dusk. 'Not with us they won't. Will they?'

'Not likely,' Fleur grinned, then she sighed. 'I'd better report in at the Waafery.'

'And I'd better go and find the rest of the chaps, I suppose,' Robbie said and handed over her kitbag. 'So – this is it then?'

Fleur nodded and tried to smile. 'Looks like it. I . . . I'll see you around, then.'

'You most certainly will even if I have to break into the Waafery at night.'

'Don't you dare . . .' she began and then realized he was teasing. Instinctively, she knew he wouldn't do anything that would get her into trouble, even if he didn't mind for himself.

As she moved towards the WAAF buildings, Fleur glanced over her shoulder and waved as Robbie's long strides took him along the road in the opposite direction further and further away from her. At the same moment, he turned and raised his arm in the air and then strode away, quickening his pace.

With a small sigh, Fleur shouldered her heavy kit-bag and walked towards the Waafery. As she did so, a WAAF came out of the nearest building, slamming the door behind her. As she drew nearer, Fleur could see that she was short and round, her uniform buttons straining to stay fastened across her ample bosom. She was a good few years older than Fleur and her plump cheeks were florid, her small eyes almost lost in the fatness of her face.

The woman – a Flight Sergeant – would have walked straight past without even glancing at her had not Fleur said, 'Excuse me. I've just arrived. Could you tell me where I have to go?'

The WAAF stopped, looked Fleur up and down, and then snapped, 'Name?'

Fleur reeled off her number, rank and name.

'You're late. Supper's nearly finished, but you'd best go to the dining room.' She nodded towards the building she had just left. 'You might get something.' She didn't sound very hopeful and seemed to care even less. 'Find Morrison. You're billeted with her. In the village. And report to Flight Sergeant Watson in Control in the morning. They work a system of shifts in the watch office: a four-hour and then an eight-hour, times varying of course, so between all the operators, the twenty-four hours are covered, with always at least two on duty. More sometimes, when they're flying. The rota's posted on the board in the office. Because you work a twelve-hour day and often through the night, the time off is very generous.' It sounded as if she heartily disapproved of the WAAFs being given any time off. No doubt she was a great believer in the 'idle hands' saying.

'Thank you,' Fleur said carefully.

The older woman eyed her critically. 'Your hair's too long. It's touching your collar. Either mind it's tied up properly under your cap or get it cut.' Then she turned and marched away.

'Well,' Fleur murmured as she watched her go. 'I hope the other girls are a little friendlier than you!'

Seven

As Fleur entered the dining room, the noise of chatter and laughter hit her. She stood, blinking in the bright light, and looked around her, not sure what to do.

Catching sight of her, a plump, merry-faced girl with unruly fair curls rose from her seat at one of the long tables and came bouncing towards her. 'Hello there. Come and sit with us and I'll get you something to eat. Leave your gear there. We'll sort it out in a mo.'

She caught hold of Fleur's arm and pulled her towards the place where she'd been sitting. 'Budge up, you lot. Room for a little 'un. Sorry about the squash. We're having to make do with trestle tables at the mo, though they keep telling us that proper dining tables and chairs are on order.' Then she rushed away towards the counter where the food was being served.

As they shuffled along the bench seat to make room for her, the other girls smiled at her. 'Just arrived, have you?'

Fleur nodded. 'Yes. Thanks,' she added, as she squeezed into the space they'd made for her. The girl who'd greeted her arrived back carrying a plate of cheese on toast and a mug of tea. 'There. Get that down you. Bet you're hungry. Come far, have you?' She hardly paused for breath as she sat down again.

'I'm Ruth Morrison, by the way, and you'll be with me. We're billeted in the village. Most of the girls are.' She nudged Fleur and winked. 'Don't reckon they trust us to stay on the camp with the fellers.'

'It's nothing of the sort,' a fair-haired girl sitting opposite retorted. 'Don't listen to her. I'm Peggy Marshall.' She held out her hand across the table and Fleur took it.

'Fleur Bosley. Hello.'

'And don't believe a word our Ruth tells you. Truth is, they haven't got the sleeping quarters finished yet, so most of us are billeted out . . .'

'Not all of us.' A dark-haired girl further down the table remarked. There was a distinct note of resentment in her tone, though, as Fleur glanced at her, the girl winked. 'Some of us,' she went on dryly, 'have to put up with sleeping in a draughty hut on hard biscuit beds and eat forces' fare whilst the rest of you languish in feather beds and are plied with delicious home cooking by the locals.'

There were cries of derision and someone threw a dry biscuit at her, but the girl just smiled, her dark eyes sparkling with mischief.

'That's Kay Fullerton, by the way. As you can see, she's a corporal,' Ruth said. 'The rest of us are just lowly ACWs.'

Fleur nodded. 'Me too.'

Ruth nodded towards Kay as she added, 'She doesn't mean it – about the sleeping arrangements, I mean.'

'Oh yes I do. Why should all the newcomers get the best billets, I'd like to know?'

Fleur looked up and met the girl's belligerent expression. 'Well, I don't mind sleeping here if you want to swap,' she offered.

Kay stared at her for a moment until someone else put in, 'Kay's all talk. She'll not leave camp – she's already got her eye on one of the new pilots that's just arrived.'

The remark was greeted by loud guffaws and even Kay smiled sheepishly. 'No, you're OK, but – thanks for the offer.'

As there was a general movement to get up from the table, Kay came up to Fleur and held out her hand. 'You're the first one to do that.'

Closer now, Fleur could see that the girl had the most unusual dark blue eyes – so dark they were almost violet. Her skin was smooth and flawless, and her black hair was so shiny it seemed to glint in the light as she moved. She was really very pretty.

'She gives all the new ones a hard time over it,' Ruth explained, 'just to see how they react.'

Kay laughed. 'Most of them go all red and embarrassed, but none of them have ever offered to swap. You're all right, Fleur Bosley. In my book anyway.'

Now it was Fleur's turn to look a little embarrassed at the unexpected compliment.

'Not one to hold back is our Kay. You'll get it straight John Bull from her,' Ruth said. 'If she likes you, she'll tell you so. And if she doesn't – well, she'll tell you that an' all.'

'What job will you be doing? Do you know?' Kay asked.

'R/T operator.'

Kay's eyes lit up. 'Oh, then you'll be with me in Control. That's good. Welcome aboard, Fleur.' Then she spun on her heel, adding, 'Must go. Things to do, people to see. See you tomorrow.' And before Fleur could say a word, she had marched down the long room and out of the door.

Ruth spluttered with laughter. 'She's a caution, that one, as my mother would say.'

Fleur smiled. She was feeling very much at home already. She liked Ruth and had taken to the girl she now knew would be working with her. She wondered if she'd be working with Ruth too. 'What do you do, Ruth?'

'I'm in intelligence. I help at briefings and then debrief the crews when they come back from a raid.'

'That must be tough,' Fleur murmured sympathetically.

Ruth's hazel eyes clouded for a moment. 'It is a bit. An RAF intelligence officer usually asks the questions and I write down their answers. But if it's been a rough one and the crews are dog tired, sometimes their stories take a lot of unravelling. Still, it's an interesting and – I think – worthwhile job. Though you're right, it's harrowing at times.'

Fearing she had touched on something sensitive, Fleur changed the subject swiftly. 'So – how do I find this billet we're sharing?'

Ruth's expression lightened at once. 'I'll take you. I'm not on duty for a couple of hours or so when the first planes start coming back.'

'There's a raid on tonight then?'

'Mmm. Not a very big one, just a gardening run . . .' She grinned. 'Mine-laying, you know, but we still have to go through the routine, of course. Come on. Let's get your gear. We're only a few yards down the road on the outskirts of the village. With a widow.

She's a nice old dear. Fusses a bit, but then I think she's lonely. Her husband died a few years ago and all her chicks have left home. Oh, you'll get the full family history within the space of ten minutes, believe me.'

As they walked out of the main gate and along the road, following the pencil-thin beam from Ruth's torch, she chattered. 'I'm from Lincoln. I live with me mam and dad and two sisters. They're younger than me and keeping their fingers crossed that the war's going to last long enough for them to join up.' She pulled a face. 'Selfish little devils – fancy anyone wishing such a thing!' But Fleur heard Ruth's soft chuckle through the darkness. The girl linked her arm through Fleur's as she confided, 'Mind you, it could be my fault. I'm always telling them what a great time we have and how we're surrounded by all these handsome chaps.' Then her voice faltered as she added sadly, 'I can't bring myself to tell them the truth, see. Of course, we do have fun, but . . . but it's no fun, is it, when you wave all the bombers off at night and know what they're going to face? And then, when they come back, counting them all. One by one. Only they're never all there, are they? They never *all* come back, do they?'

Fleur shook her head. 'Not very often.'

Ruth squeezed her arm and forced jollity back into her tone. 'Hark at me, getting all serious. As if I need to tell you. You've worked on another operational bomber station, haven't you?'

Fleur nodded. 'Yes, down south, but I applied to remuster as an R/T operator and hoped I'd get a posting a bit nearer home and here I am.'

'Me too. I was up north for a while straight after training and I've been very lucky to get a posting so near home. What about you? Did you manage it?'

'What?'

'To get a posting nearer home?'

'Oh yes. I live at South Monkford. Do you know it?'

'Near Newark, isn't it? Well, you should be able to get home on leave easily enough. Even on a forty-eight-hour pass. You might have to hitch, but we're really lucky. Some of the girls are hundreds of miles from home. Peggy's from Newcastle. And Kay's from London. They can really only get home about once every three months.'

At the mention of Kay, Fleur remembered what had been said at the table. 'Has ... has Kay got a boy-friend here then?'

'Yes, she has,' Ruth said with a snort that sounded very much like disapproval. 'Silly mare!'

'Why do you say that? Haven't you got one?'

'Me? Oh no. Fancy free, me. And I mean to stay that way.' Again there was a sniff. 'It doesn't do.'

Alarmed, Fleur said, 'What do you mean? Isn't it allowed?'

'Well, you have to be careful, but they can't stop it, even if they'd like to. No, what I mean is, you're stacking up a load of heartache for yourself if you let yourself get close to anyone.'

Fleur thought she detected a note of real pain in the girl's tone and she was about to ask gently if she had lost someone close to her, but before she could form the words, Ruth said brightly, 'Here we are. Rose Cottage. "Home, Sweet Home".'

She pushed open the wooden gate and they crunched up the narrow cinder path.

'Watch yourself. The garden's so overgrown the

long grass falls onto the path. When it's wet, your ankles are soaking by the time you reach the door.'

In the wavering torchlight, Fleur caught glimpses of the neglected front garden. The grass looked so long it would need a scythe to cut it now, she mused. As if answering her unspoken question, Ruth said softly, 'Poor old dear loves her garden. Her old man used to keep it immaculate, she says, but since he's gone it's got topside of her. She's got a huge back garden with an orchard at the end of it. Used to grow veg and all sorts. But she's got arthritis, see, and can't cope with it. But she won't move. Says she came to this cottage as a young bride and she'll die here.'

Briefly, Ruth flashed the torch over the low, oblong shape of the cottage. 'Typical "roses-round-the-door cottage" we all dream of, eh? But she really got it.'

'Mm,' Fleur murmured. 'No wonder she doesn't want to leave it.' Even before she had met Mrs Jackson, she knew she was going to be a sweet old lady who'd lived a lifetime of love in her little cottage. Fleur had a sudden mental picture of a young bride being carried over the threshold to start a long and happy life with her groom in the idyllic little house. However, the image in her mind's eye was not of the unknown Mrs Jackson but of herself and Robbie.

'I'm surprised the authorities haven't been on to her about her garden,' Fleur said, dragging herself back to the present. ' "Dig for Victory" and all that.'

'I think they did try. Got some local boy scouts to come and dig the back garden, but they made a right pig's ear of it.' She giggled in the darkness. 'There was even talk of them building her an Anderson shelter, but after a couple of spadefuls, they gave up, so she says.'

'Not got a shelter and living so close to an airfield!' Fleur was shocked. 'Well, we'll have to see about that.'

'Come on, then,' Ruth urged. 'We'll go round the back. Tell you the truth, the front door's stuck and she can't open it.'

They followed the narrow path round to the back, brushing through long wet grass so that by the time they arrived in the unevenly paved back yard their ankles were quite damp, just as Ruth had predicted. She shone the torch and nodded towards a brick building a few steps across the yard from the back door. 'That's the lav.' She leant closer and whispered, 'It's a bit basic. No indoor facilities, but the old dear cooks like a dream.' Ruth patted her stomach. 'Makes up for a bit of discomfort in other areas. 'Sides, she provides us with a potty under the bed so we don't have to come tripping out into the back yard in the dark.' Ruth giggled again as she added, 'She calls it a "jerry". I always imagine I'm piddling on Adolf's head if I use it in the night.'

Fleur laughed softly. 'Home from home, Ruth. It's what I'm used to. We've no inside lav either.'

Ruth's eyes widened. 'But I thought you said you lived in South Monkford? It's a town, isn't it?'

'A small one. But I live on a farm about five miles from the town itself. Right out in the wilds.'

'You're a country girl, then?'

'Born and bred.' Fleur moved carefully across the cobbled yard towards the rickety little gate leading into the back garden. As her eyes became accustomed to the darkness, she could see the shapes of trees silhouetted against the night sky. Ruth came to stand beside her and shone the torch and now Fleur could see that the whole area was as overgrown and choked with weeds as the front one.

'There's raspberry and gooseberry bushes and all sorts down the bottom there. The old dear said they even had a strawberry patch once. And you can see the fruit trees. There's a lovely old apple tree with a little bench seat under it. It's where her and her Arthur used to sit on a summer's evening, she said.'

'You know,' Fleur suggested, 'we could help her in our spare time.'

'Hey, hang on a minute. I'm a city girl. Born and bred in Lincoln. That's why I chose the WAAFs instead of the Land Army. You're welcome to go grubbing about in Mother Earth but don't ask me to join you.' The words could have been tart and dismissive, but they were spoken with such a warm humour that Fleur laughed.

'We'll see,' she teased, as Ruth grabbed her arm and pulled her towards the back door. As she pushed it open, it scraped and shuddered on the uneven floor.

'Coo-ee, Mrs Jackson. You in?' She turned and whispered. 'She hardly ever goes out, 'cept to church on a Sunday and sometimes as far as the village shop, but her legs are getting that bad, poor old thing. She walks with a stick as it is, though she can move about the house without it. Come on in. Mind the blackout curtain. It's a bit long and trails on the floor. It gets caught under the door if you don't watch out.'

They moved through the back scullery, which housed a deep white sink and wooden draining board with shelves of pots and pans above. There was also a cooker to augment the range that Fleur knew would be in the kitchen. Ruth flung open the door into the kitchen-cum-living-room where an elderly lady was struggling to lever herself up out of her armchair in the far corner of the room beside the black-leaded range that Fleur had expected to see. A fire burned in the grate and a kettle stood on the hob. It really was just like home, Fleur thought.

'Don't get up, Mrs Jackson,' Ruth was saying. 'I've brought another lodger for you. This is Fleur Bosley. She's just come to work in the watch office.'

The old lady sank back thankfully into her chair, but she beamed up at Fleur with such a wide smile that her rounded cheeks lifted her spectacles. She was a plump little woman, with her white hair pulled back and wound into a roll at the nape of her neck. She wore low-heeled lace-up shoes and lisle stockings, and her striped blouse and navy skirt were almost hidden by a paisley overall. Fleur smiled. It was identical to the one her mother wore. This woman could be Betsy in thirty years' time, she thought, though she couldn't imagine her mother welcoming complete strangers into her home the way this woman was doing. Her mother wouldn't even make someone she knew welcome, Fleur thought wryly, thinking of the uncomfortable last few hours she had spent at home. It was a sad fact – and it hurt even to think it – but she'd been glad to get away.

Fleur quickly scanned the room, taking in the other armchair on the opposite side of the range and the table with its white lace runner and two chairs set against the wall. On a small table beside the old lady sat a wireless with a polished oak cabinet, silk front and black Bakelite controls. It seemed out of place in the old-fashioned cottage, yet Fleur knew that the wireless had become almost a necessity in the homes of those anxious for news of the war.

Fleur crossed the room to stand on the pegged

hearthrug. 'Hello, Mrs Jackson. I'm pleased to meet you.'

'You're very welcome, lass,' the old lady said, her faded blue eyes smiling up at Fleur. 'Mek yourself at home. Ruth'll show you your room upstairs. I can't get up there now.'

'Mind your head,' Ruth warned, as she led Fleur up the narrow staircase to the two attic bedrooms under the eaves. 'There's only us here. We have a room each. I'm in the bigger room with the double bed and you'll be in here . . .' she said, opening the door into a small room that only had space for a single iron bedstead, a wardrobe and narrow dressing table. But the bed was covered with a cheery patchwork quilt and there was a pegged rug beside the bed to step onto instead of the cold floor.

'Do you mind?' Ruth glanced back over her shoulder.

Fleur smiled reassuringly. 'Course not. Don't be daft. It's fine. It's not much smaller than the one I have at home. Honest.'

'The old dear sleeps downstairs in her front parlour now. Bless 'er. I'll show you when we go down.'

As Ruth helped her unpack her belongings, hanging her clothes in the narrow wardrobe with a creaking door, she pulled a face and said, 'At least staying here we don't get those dreadful kit inspections every morning. Mind you, I'll warn you now. Ma'am has eyes like a hawk so it pays to keep your uniform spick and span. And she has been known to make an unannounced inspection of our billet now and again.'

'Is she very strict?'

Ruth turned surprised eyes towards her. 'Who? Mrs Jackson? Heavens, no!'

'I didn't mean her.' Fleur laughed. 'I meant the WAAF CO. I mean, are we allowed to meet the RAF lads?'

Ruth stared at her for a moment. 'Well, of course we meet them at work. And there's the dances on camp, usually in the men's NAAFI or sometimes in the sergeants' mess. Then there's the Liberty Bus on a Saturday night.'

'What on earth is the "Liberty Bus"?'

Ruth grinned. 'A bus laid on to take us into Lincoln. To dances or the pictures.'

She was silent a moment, watching Fleur sort out her underwear and put it away in one of the drawers in the dressing table. Then Ruth said quietly, 'Why all the questions? Do you know someone on camp? Someone – special?'

Fleur felt the blush creep up her face and knew she couldn't hide the truth. 'Well, sort of. I've only just met him. We bumped into each other – literally – on Nottingham station. He's just been posted here an' all. That's how we met.'

'Oh, Fleur!' Ruth flopped down onto the bed. The springs protested loudly, but neither of the girls noticed. 'Don't get involved with someone – with anyone. Not if he's a flier. He is, I take it?'

Fleur nodded. 'He's a wireless operator on bombers.'

Ruth groaned and then sighed heavily, regarding her new-found friend with a hangdog expression. 'I don't suppose anything I say's going to make any difference, is it?'

Fleur grinned. 'Not a scrap.'

Ruth heaved herself up. 'Well, my shoulder's ready when you need it.'

'Don't you mean "if"?'

Ruth stared at her for a long moment before she said seriously, 'No, love. I'm sorry, but I do mean "when".'

Eight

As Fleur approached the control tower early the following morning, her heart was beating faster. Although she had been thoroughly trained and had been briefed on how to cope with every emergency possible, she was still a little apprehensive. This was her first posting as a fully fledged R/T operator and she knew that 'the real thing' would be very different. Mistakes in training hadn't mattered. Now they did.

She stepped into the ground floor of the watch tower. The concrete steps leading to the upper floor were on her right, but first she was curious to see what else the building housed. The first room on the left was the met office, with maps spread out on the waist-high table against the wall. A WAAF sat at a telephone switchboard; another stood in front of a teleprinter, which was noisily chattering out a message. A nearby desk was cluttered with telephones, a black typewriter and papers. Next door to the met office was the duty pilots' rest room. It was empty and silent, newspapers flung down untidily amongst the battered easy chairs. Dirty mugs, an overflowing ashtray and dog-eared books littered the table almost hiding the telephone. It seemed, even here, there was no escaping the call to duty. Near the door was the compulsory sand bucket – the ever-present reminder of the war and all its dangers.

Fleur climbed the stairs to the upper floor. The smell from the freshly painted cream and green walls reminded her that this was a new station, still in the process of being built. She peeped into the signals' room with its wirelesses, typewriters and teleprinters. For a moment she stood listening to the morse code blips that filled the room, mentally translating a few words in her head. Directly opposite the signals' room was the rest room, but Fleur ignored this for the moment and, taking a deep breath, moved to the end of the narrow passageway and opened the door into the watch office.

This was the largest room in the building. Directly in front of her was the long desk where the R/T operators sat. In one corner the duty officer sat at his desk, overseeing all that was happening. Flight Sergeant Bob Watson was in his mid forties, Fleur guessed. He was tall and thin and had dark, Brylcreemed hair and the usual moustache that was fast becoming the trademark of the RAF. Fleur was to notice that he stroked it continuously when the tension mounted in the watch office and that he would pace up and down behind the operators as the aircraft took off one by one and again when they landed.

As she entered the room, Bob Watson greeted her informally with a friendly smile. 'You must have made an impression already. Fullerton has already asked if you can work with her.'

Fleur smiled and felt a faint blush creep into her cheeks. 'I'd like that, Flight, if it can be arranged. I think we'd work well together.'

He eyed her keenly. 'You think so? Some of the younger girls find her – well – a bit abrasive. She doesn't suffer fools at all – let alone gladly, as they say. Mind you,' he said arching his eyebrows, 'neither do I, but I suppose they expect it from me.'

Fleur remained silent. He stroked his moustache thoughtfully. 'Well then, I'll adjust the rotas so you work with Fullerton. And in that case, you'll be on from tonight, but only if they're flying. Come on duty a bit early and we'll show you the ropes – how we do things in this watch office.'

'Thank you, Flight.'

So, she thought, as she went down the steps, I've the rest of the day off. I wonder what Robbie's doing.

Ruth brought her the news in the NAAFI at midday. 'I don't think you'll see much of him for the next few days. The new crews are getting to know one another. They might even get a few practice flights in to make sure they gel before they're sent on a mission. Mind you, they could be flying tonight if Tommy thinks they're ready. He's done quite a bit of flying on Hampdens already evidently and . . .' But Fleur was no longer listening. She was far too wrapped up in her own disappointment that she wouldn't be able to see Robbie and – worse still – there would be no chance for him to get home on leave for quite a while. No chance for him to ask his mother some very delicate – yet to them very important – questions.

With time on her hands, Fleur went back to the cottage and changed into civvies – a pair of old trousers and a thick sweater.

'Are you hungry, dear?' Mrs Jackson asked as Fleur came downstairs.

'No, thanks. I ate in the NAAFI, but I wouldn't mind a cup of tea, if you can spare one.'

'Of course. I get extra rations with you two here.'

'I'll make it. You sit down.'

The old lady sank thankfully into her chair and took up her knitting. 'Socks for the troops.' She smiled. 'A nice WVS lady brings me the wool and collects them. It gives me something to do and I feel I'm helping.'

'You're helping a lot already, putting up with us two.'

Mrs Jackson's face creased into smiles and her spectacles wobbled. 'Oh, that's no hardship, dear. I enjoy the company.'

Fleur set a cup of tea on the small table beside the old lady. She was about to sit in the chair on the opposite side of the hearth when she paused and asked quietly, 'Is it all right for me to sit here?'

There was the slightest hesitation before Mrs Jackson said, 'Of course, dear. My Arthur would have been tickled pink to think that a lovely young WAAF was sitting in his chair.'

Fleur sat down, balancing her cup carefully. 'When . . .' she began tentatively, thinking that this was as good a time as any to broach the subject of the garden, 'When did your Arthur . . . ?'

The old lady's face dropped into lines of sadness. 'Three years ago next month. Very sudden. Heart attack. Out there in the garden.' She smiled fondly. 'But it was just the way he'd've wanted to go. With a spade in his hand, doing what he loved best.'

'And the . . . er . . . um . . . garden?'

Mrs Jackson sighed deeply. 'It makes me so sad to see it like that. Poor Arthur. All his hard work overgrown and so quickly too. Who'd have thought it could've gone wild in only three years?'

'Would you mind if I worked on it when I'm off duty? I mean, if you'd rather I didn't,' she began, fearing she might have upset the old lady, but Mrs Jackson's face was alight with joy.

'Oh, my dear, that would be wonderful. Really wonderful.' Her face clouded. 'But do you really want to? I mean surely a young lass like you wants to be out enjoying herself. And besides, I mean, do you know much about gardening?'

Fleur laughed. 'Born and bred on a farm, Mrs Jackson. What I don't know already my dad will tell me.'

The old lady laughed along with her. 'Well, you won't have to go very far for a bit of advice, love. Old Harry next door will be only too pleased to help. In fact' – she smiled – 'you'll have a job to stop him.'

'Right then,' Fleur said jumping up, glad to have something physical to do. With her first duty looming and maybe with Robbie flying with his new crew for the first time, she needed something else to concentrate on. 'No time like the present.'

Mrs Jackson's garden shed in the back yard was cluttered; there was hardly room to step inside it.

'Another job for a rainy day,' Fleur murmured as she unearthed some rusty gardening tools. There was a sickle but no scythe, and cutting the grass at the front of the cottage and the overgrown kitchen garden would be a long and back-breaking task on her hands and knees.

'Mrs Jackson?' she said, going back into the house. 'Do you know anyone who's got a scythe?'

The old lady washing up at the deep sink in the small scullery turned in surprise. 'Whatever do you want a scythe for?'

'To cut all the overgrown grass back and front. If

I get it dug over there's still time to plant some vegetables.'

Mrs Jackson's eyes were filling with tears. 'D'you know, when Arthur was alive I never 'ad to buy vegetables all year round.'

'You'll have to tell me what he used to grow,' Fleur said gently. 'I'm sure he'd be pleased to think we'd got it like it used to be.'

'Oh, he would, he would.' Mrs Jackson wiped the corner of her eye with the back of her hand and sniffed, but she was smiling through her tears. 'A scythe, you say? Harry next door might 'ave one or 'ee'd know someone who has.'

'Right then.' Fleur began to turn away but then paused to ask, 'What's his surname, Mrs Jackson? I can hardly call him "Harry".'

The old lady chortled. 'Oh, Harry wouldn't mind. He's a one for the pretty lasses.' Her face fell into sad wrinkles. 'He's on his own like me now. His wife, Doris, died two years ago. His name's Harry Chambers.'

Fleur went through the front gate and along the lane to the next-door cottage. She walked round to the back and as she turned the corner of the house, she gasped in surprised delight. The layout was the same as Mrs Jackson's cottage and garden, but there the similarity ended: beyond Harry Chambers' back yard lay a lovingly tended kitchen garden. But after her initial pleasure, Fleur frowned. If he could do his own garden, why didn't he help the old lady next door? The way Mrs Jackson had spoken of her neighbour, they were friendly, so why . . . ?

As she lifted her hand to knock tentatively on the

back door, Fleur bit her lip, wondering, after what Mrs Jackson had said, just what she was going to have to deal with. But she needn't have worried. When Harry Chambers opened the door, she saw that he was as old and bent as her landlady, yet there was a mischievous twinkle in his rheumy eyes and a wide, toothless smile.

'By heck – have I died and gone to heaven? A pretty young lass knocking at my door. Come away in, lass.' He turned away and shuffled back into the kitchen. Smiling inwardly, Fleur followed. Now, the question in her mind was not why he didn't help his neighbour, but how on earth did he manage to keep his garden so immaculate? As she stepped into the kitchen, she saw the answer. The inside of his home was like a rubbish tip. The range was dirty, the floor filthy and every surface was littered with newspapers and unwashed pots. The old man swept aside a pile of clothes on a chair. 'Sit down, sit down,' he insisted, beckoning her forward.

Thankful that she was wearing her old trousers, Fleur sat in the rickety chair. The old man let himself down into the dusty armchair near the range and beamed at her. 'A' you one of them lasses at Mary's?'

'Yes. I only arrived yesterday. I'm just getting settled in, but I'd like to make a start on getting the garden in order for her.'

'Aw lass . . .' To Fleur's horror, tears filled his eyes. But at his next words she realized they were tears of joy too, just like Mrs Jackson's had been. 'That'd be wonderful for 'er. I'd've liked to have kept it right but I've more than I can manage with me own bit.' He wiped the back of his hand across his face. 'Her ol' man, Arthur – we was mates.' He laughed wheezily.

''Cept when it came to the village show and we was both entered for the biggest marrow competition. Then it was "gloves off" time. Eee, lass, but I miss him. You don't know how much I miss our little chats over the fence.'

Fleur smiled but didn't know what to say so she let the old man ramble, reliving happier times. But he was laughing along with his tears. At last, he came back to the present.

'So what can I do for you, lass?'

'Mr Chambers, have you got a scythe I can borrow?'

He gaped at her. 'A scythe, lass? Aw now, I don't know if I should let a young lass like you loose with a scythe. Them's dangerous things if you don't know what you're doing . . .' He leant towards her, screwing up his eyes in an effort to see her better. Then he chuckled. 'I can see by the look on your face – you *do* know, don't you?'

Fleur nodded, her eyes brimming with mischief. 'If my dad could hear you, Mr Chambers, he'd say, "No daughter of mine's going to grow up without knowing how to use a scythe." I was born and brought up on the farm.'

The old man blinked. 'Then what are you doing here? In the WAAFs? I'd've thought they'd've needed you at home.'

Fleur sighed as she felt a sudden stab of guilt. 'They do,' she admitted, 'but I wanted to get away. To see something of the world outside me dad's stackyard. I still want to do my bit, but . . .'

The old man watched her for a moment as she bit her lip. 'I can understand that,' he said gently. 'I volunteered for the last lot even though I could have stayed safely at home 'cos I was getting on a bit for service life. My Doris begged me not to go, but I would have me own way.'

'So did my dad. I think he understands why I wanted to join up, but me mum . . .'

'Aye well, she's your mother, lass,' was all he said as if it explained everything. There was a moment's silence between them and then he began to chuckle. 'And now here you are, wanting to dig up Mary's garden. Seems you can't get away from it, eh, lass?'

Fleur spluttered with laughter. 'Just serves me right, doesn't it?' And they rocked with merriment.

'Ee lass, you've done me a power of good. I don't know when I last laughed so much. It's the best medicine, they say. I'll be throwing all me pills away if you're staying long.'

'I'm staying.' Fleur nodded as her thoughts turned to Robbie. 'Oh, I'm staying, Mr Chambers.'

'Right then, lass,' he said as he levered himself up from the battered chair. 'Then you'd best start calling me "Harry". I don't know who on earth you're talking about with all this "Mr Chambers" business. Now, let's go and see if I can find this 'ere scythe for you.'

When he opened the door of his shed, Fleur could not prevent a gasp of surprise escaping her lips. All the gardening tools were neatly stacked against the walls or lined up in order along the shelves or hanging from hooks. Each item had been cleaned and oiled before being put away. She almost laughed aloud to see the contrast between the old man's garden shed and the state of his house. But, she reflected, the smile dying on her lips, this was his domain; the house had been his wife's and he'd lost her.

''Ere we are,' Harry said, carefully unhooking the

huge scythe from its nail. 'It's a big 'un, lass. Sure you can manage one this size?'

Not wanting to sound boastful, Fleur said, 'I think it's the same size as me dad's.' She took it from his hands, feeling the weight. 'Yes, I'm sure it is. Anyway, I'll soon know.'

'Just you be careful, lass.' Harry was still anxious.

'I will,' she smiled. 'And thank you.'

'Don't mention it. There'll be no one more pleased than me to see old Arthur's garden looking a picture again. I just wish . . .' His voice faded away and a sad, faraway look came into his old eyes as he glanced back towards his own house.

'What do you wish, Harry?' Fleur prompted softly, but he sniffed and forced a smile. 'Nothing, lass, nothing at all.'

But as she walked past the open back door and saw again the cluttered state of the old man's kitchen, she thought she knew what he had been going to say.

Of course, as she thought might happen, Harry leant on the fence between the two gardens to watch her taking the first few sweeping strokes. Soon she was into a steady rhythm. When she paused for a breather, she looked up to see him nodding at her.

'Aye lass, you're right. You can do it. Never seen a lass frame so well, I haven't. In fact' – his expression was comical – 'I can't say I've ever seen a lass scything afore.' He levered himself off the fence. 'Well, can't stand here all day chatting. I'd best be getting on with a few jobs mesen.'

'Harry, before you go, could you pass the sharpening stone over? I'm going to need it.'

'Right you are, lass. Ah, and here comes Mary with a cuppa.' Fleur turned to see Mary Jackson tottering along the mud path down the centre of the garden. Laying down the scythe, Fleur hurried towards her. 'Oh, you shouldn't have bothered,' she scolded the old lady gently, but reached with eager hands to take the mug. 'Mind you, it's thirsty work. I'm ready for it.'

'Any left in the pot, Mary?' Harry called out and the old lady chuckled.

'Course there is, Harry. Think I'd forget you?' And she turned to walk stiffly back towards the cottage.

'Don't you be struggling out again, lass,' Harry called. 'I'll come round.'

Fleur stifled her giggles to hear the old lady called 'lass', but maybe they'd lived side by side for years and that's how he still thought of her.

Before long the two elderly people were sitting on a couple of old stools in the back yard chatting amiably – Harry's jobs forgotten – whilst Fleur worked herself into a sweat cutting the long grass. She was still at it when Ruth appeared round the corner of the cottage.

'Well, it's all right for some. 'Ello, Harry – Mrs Jackson.' She shaded her eyes and looked down the garden. 'What on earth is she doing?'

'Cutting the grass. Mekin' a good job of it an' all,' Harry said with a note of pride, almost as if he had trained Fleur himself.

'Then what's she goin' to do?' Ruth turned wide eyes on Harry. 'She's never going to dig that lot?'

Harry began to chuckle and Ruth cast her glance skywards. 'Don't tell me! She is.'

At that moment, Fleur, red faced and breathing hard, paused and looked up. Seeing Ruth, she waved.

'I've got a message for you,' Ruth shouted. 'From

Flight Sergeant Watson and . . .' Her eyes were full of mischief. 'From lover boy.'

Fleur dropped the scythe and pushed her way through the long grass, her eyes anxious. 'What is it? There's nothing wrong is there?'

Ruth shook her head. 'Far from it. Flying's cancelled tonight. Low cloud over the target.' She pulled a face. 'Wherever that was. So he's got the night off.' She grinned. 'And so have we, 'cos we're not needed if they're not flying. A gang of us – including your Robbie – are going to the Mucky Duck in the village.'

Fleur's eyebrows rose. 'The Mucky Duck? What on earth is that?'

She heard Harry's deep, rumbling chuckle and saw Mrs Jackson's smile. 'It's the locals' name for our pub – the White Swan. It's been called the Mucky Duck for as long as I can remember.'

'Right,' Fleur said. 'I'll just clean the scythe and—'

'No, no, lass,' Harry said, pulling himself up off the stool. 'I'll see to that. You get off and enjoy yourself.' He seemed about to say more, but then cleared his throat and, instead of whatever he had been about to say, added, 'You've earned it.'

'Thanks, Harry. Can I borrow the scythe next time I get some time off?'

'Course you can, lass. Any time. Just come round and help yoursen out o' me shed.'

'And I'd better get you girls a bite to eat if you're going out.' Mary was struggling to pull herself up. Ruth and Fleur held out their hands to haul the old lady to her feet. 'Thank you, my dears. Now off you go and make yourselves pretty.'

'That won't take too long to do,' Harry laughed. 'Pretty as a picture already, they are.'

75

'By the way,' Ruth said. 'Sorry, but we have to wear uniform. Ma'am's orders.'

Fleur shrugged. 'I don't mind. I'm proud to wear my uniform.'

'You might change your mind when you see all the local girls in their pretty dresses being chatted up by all the fellers.'

'There's only one I want to be chatted up by and he'd better not be looking at other girls while I'm around – uniform or no uniform.'

The two girls laughed and hurried into the house to wash at the sink in the back scullery and change their clothes.

The two old people watched them go. Quietly, Harry said what he had stopped himself from saying earlier. 'Aye, let 'em enjoy themselves, eh, Mary? While they can.'

Nine

The moment Fleur and Ruth stepped into the public bar of the pub, she spotted Robbie with three other airmen. Kay and Peggy were already sitting with them. Robbie must have been watching the door for he rose at once and threaded his way around tables to reach her. He didn't kiss her, but took her hands in his and squeezed them warmly. 'Come and meet the rest of the crew. They're great lads.'

He pulled her behind him, weaving his way through the crowded bar room, and made the introductions. He reeled off the names. 'This is our skipper, Tommy Laughton. And these two reprobates are Alan Hardesty and Johnny Jones.' Then Robbie waved his arm to encompass other airmen sitting in small groups around the bar room. 'We'll no doubt get to know a lot of the other chaps on our Flight in time. They all seem a great bunch.'

Tommy unfolded his lanky frame and shook her hand warmly. He was thin faced with sharp eyes that missed nothing and he sported a moustache that stuck out on either side of his upper lip like a stiff, bristly shaving brush.

It was a merry evening. The beer flowed as did the conversation and laughter. They talked about anything and everything. Everything, that is, except the war.

But Fleur was acutely aware that perhaps the jollity was a little forced, the laughter just a little too hearty.

'Fleur, you must meet Bill Moore, the landlord.' Tommy Laughton, the pilot of the newly formed crew, got up and held out his hand to her. 'Come on. You can help me get the next round in and I'll introduce you.'

Fleur glanced at Robbie, who stood up to let her move past him.

'Bill,' Tommy called to the middle-aged man behind the bar. The landlord was dressed casually in a collarless striped shirt, the sleeves rolled up above his elbows, and a black waistcoat. His strong arms pulled pint after pint effortlessly. What hair he had left was dark, yet the pate of his head was bald, and he sported a black moustache that drooped over the corners of his mouth.

'This is Fleur Bosley. She's come to work in Control. She's the lovely voice we'll hear when we're coming home. And a very welcome voice it'll be too, I can tell you.'

'Of course, it could be mine,' Kay chipped in. 'You'd better be able to tell the difference or there'll be trouble.'

As Tommy grinned briefly over his shoulder at Kay and winked, Fleur realized that the newly arrived pilot that Kay had 'got her eye on', as Ruth had said, must be Flying Officer Tommy Laughton.

'Pleased to meet you, love.' Bill Moore enveloped her hand in his huge paw. She felt the calluses on his work-hardened hands – strong, capable, reliable hands. The sort of hands you could trust . . .

'Pleased to meet you, Mr Moore.'

'Eh now, lass. None of that there "mister" stuff. Bill's the name.'

Standing behind the bar amongst the pumps, the bottles and the glasses sparkling against the polished wooden surface of the bar, Bill Moore was master of all he surveyed. Fleur smiled. The man was just like Harry had been when they had first been introduced. No standing on ceremony. What a friendly bunch these locals were. Actually, she was surprised. She would have thought that the locals would resent having the airfield quite so close to their village. Despite the custom that came the pub's way and maybe to the local shop too, she was sure the disadvantages of noisy aircraft day and night and the danger of attacks, not to mention having a lot of strangers milling about the place, would far outweigh any advantages.

But it seemed she was wrong. The locals – young and old alike – were mingling freely and in a friendly manner with the RAF boys. Especially, Fleur noticed with a wry smile, the local lasses, who were being very friendly with the handsome RAF lads in their smart, blue uniforms. And the only looks of resentment were on the faces of one or two local youths not in uniform and obviously feeling that their noses had been pushed very much out of joint.

As Fleur began to ferry the drinks back to their table, Johnny jumped up and said, 'I'll give you a hand, Fleur.' He went to stand beside Tommy, but at once a young blonde girl in a short-skirted dress sidled up to him and tapped him on the arm.

'Hello, Johnny.'

'Hello, Kitty. Would you like a drink?'

'Ta. Don't mind if I do.'

Johnny bought her a drink and they stood at the bar chatting.

'I reckon we could have trouble from one or two of the local lads,' Fleur whispered to Robbie as she took her seat beside him again. 'See that lad in the white shirt and sleeveless green pullover? Over there – near the fire.'

Robbie glanced casually around him. 'I see him. What about him?'

'Well, just keep your eye on him for a few moments. He's watching Johnny talking to that lass, and if looks could kill, Johnny would be feeling decidedly ill.'

Robbie didn't seem perturbed. 'I expect the girl old Johnny's chatting up is the lad's girlfriend.'

'Did you ought to warn Johnny, 'cos I don't think he's noticed?'

Robbie chuckled. 'No. He's otherwise occupied, isn't he? And Johnny can take care of himself. Besides, there's plenty of us here if—'

As if on cue, the youth in the corner got up and brushed back the flop of hair from his face. Then he stumbled his way between the tables, knocking against a chair and then someone's arm.

'Watch it, young 'un. You're spilling me beer.'

But the young lad took no notice. His eyes, bleary with drink, were fixed on the girl who was now sitting with Johnny and cuddling up to him quite openly.

'I really think you should do something, Robbie,' Fleur muttered.

Robbie put down his beer and unfolded his tall frame. He held out his hand. 'You're right. I should get you out of here before any trouble starts.'

'I didn't mean that. I meant—' Fleur began, but at that moment the landlord's thunderous tones cut through the chatter and laughter. 'Now then, young Alfie. I want no trouble in my pub.'

Alfie stopped in his tracks and stood swaying unsteadily in the middle of the bar-room floor.

'Go home, lad, an' sleep it off. Kitty's doing no harm. She's only being friendly, like.'

'A bit too – friendly,' the lad slurred his words. 'Kitty! You're my girl. You come here this minute.'

Now all eyes were turned towards Alfie or on Kitty sitting with her blonde head against Johnny's shoulder. She raised it briefly and waved her hand towards Alfie as if brushing him away. 'Oh, go home, little boy.'

Incensed by her dismissive taunt, Alfie launched himself towards the pair, knocking over drinks and tables.

'Steady, lad.'

''Ere – watch what you're doing.'

With one accord, the rest of the crew – including Robbie – rose to their feet and moved together. Tommy and Alan caught hold of the youth's arms and Robbie grasped his kicking legs.

'Calm down, mate, calm down,' Johnny said. 'No offence meant. If she's your girl, then—'

'I'm not his girl,' Kitty piped up. 'Only he'd like to think so. Tek no notice of him. He's nowt but a kid. Ought to be in uniform, he did. He's old enough.'

There was a brief silence whilst the locals glanced at each other uncomfortably.

'Now, now, Kitty,' Bill said gently. 'No need for that sort of talk. The lad works on a farm. He's doing a good job.'

Kitty said no more, but her lip curled disdainfully.

'So why aren't *you* in uniform?' Alfie spat back at her, struggling to free himself, but the young airmen

were holding him fast. 'Like that lass there.' He nodded towards Fleur, who felt embarrassment creep up
her face. 'Or are you "doing your bit" another way?'

His crude meaning was obvious to everyone listening and a gasp rippled around the room. But Alfie
turned his attention to the young men holding on to
him. He glared into the face of each one of them and
then, slowly and deliberately, he said, 'And I hope
your bloody plane crashes.'

Now there was a shocked silence through the whole
bar. For a moment, no one moved. Then Fleur leapt
to her feet, her eyes blazing. 'That's a wicked thing to
say!'

'Steady on, lass. He doesn't mean it—'

'Oh yes, I do,' the youth muttered.

'He's had one too many – he dun't know what 'ee's
sayin',' Bill said and moved from behind the bar to
step between the airmen and take firm hold of Alfie
himself. The burly man held the lad quite easily. 'Time
you was going home, Alfie Fish. You've said quite
enough for one night. More than enough. Now, I
don't want to 'ave to bar you from my pub, but if you
can't behave ya'sen, I will. Mek no mistake about that.
These lads' – he nodded towards Robbie and the rest
– 'and those lasses there an' all' – now he included
Fleur and the other girls too – 'are all here for a very
good reason. They're fighting this war for us. They're
in the front line, as it were. Now, to my mind, we're
all doing our bit. You're working on the land, providing us all wi' food. I'm doing my bit, giving these
young 'uns a bit of fun on their time off. So, we're all
doing our bit one way or another. Everybody here.'
Now he swept his arm wide to include everyone sitting
in the bar room. 'So let's have no more fighting

amongst oursens. We've got enough on, fighting old Adolf. And as for Kitty – well – you're hardly going to keep her with this sort of behaviour, now a' ya?'

Suddenly, the fight seemed to go out of the young man and he slumped against Bill. The older man took his full weight and the airmen released their hold. With a shake of their heads the locals resumed their conversations and took a swallow of their beer, whilst Bill helped Alfie from the bar room out into the night.

As Bill returned, he nodded towards Robbie and the others. 'Sorry about that, lads. Just give him a minute or two to get hissen down the road home afore you leave.' He winked at them meaningfully. 'I 'aven't got so much authority on the public highway and PC Mitchell's nowhere to be seen when you want him.' He laughed heartily. 'Mind you, it's a good job sometimes if I'm a bit late closing.'

After about fifteen minutes, Tommy said, 'We'll have to get going, chaps, else we'll be late back at camp. 'Specially if we've to escort these lovely young ladies back to their billets.'

'No need,' Ruth said brusquely. 'We'll be fine.'

'And I, of course,' Kay remarked dryly, 'am going the same way as you lot anyway. Back to my biscuit bed in a draughty hut.' She cast a mock resentful glance towards Ruth and Fleur, who merely grinned in return, refusing to rise to her bait this time.

'Right then. Time to go,' Robbie said, standing up and holding out his hand to Fleur. As they moved towards the door, calling 'goodnight' to Bill, and out into the darkness, none of them noticed the three youths who had been sitting with Alfie in the corner rise to their feet and follow them out.

The youths came at them out of the blackness,

launching themselves at their perceived enemies with the same ferocity as any trained solder with a bayonet in his hand.

'Look out!' Fleur's cry came too late and, as she found herself pushed to her hands and knees on the rough road, Robbie and the rest were under attack.

It was an unequal fight, even though it was four against four. Alfie too had appeared out of the shadows. The airmen, though fit from drill and gymnastics on camp, were no match for the brawny strength of the young farm workers. Fists flew and solid punches found their mark. Grunts and shouts filled the night air, whilst the four girls peered through the gloom, watching helplessly.

'Ouch! You little sod!'

It was Robbie's voice that galvanized Fleur. 'Stop it! Stop it this minute!' she cried and then launched herself at the youth attacking Robbie. She clung to his back and wound her arm around his throat. Suddenly, all the play-fights she had ever had with her younger brother came back to her. She hooked her leg round Robbie's attacker and pulled him backwards so that he lost his balance and fell to the floor.

'Ruth!' she yelled. 'Come and sit on this one.'

'Attagirl!' Ruth whooped and threw herself bodily across the prone figure, satisfied to hear his weak groan of futile protest as her weight knocked the last ounce of breath from his body.

Squinting through the darkness, Fleur saw that Tommy was taking a real battering.

'Come on.' Now she heard Kay's voice at her side and together they launched themselves against Tommy's assailant. A moment later, he too was lying on the ground with Kay sitting astride him.

With both Robbie and Tommy now free, Alan and Johnny's attackers were soon dispatched. They fled into the darkness and only then did Ruth and Kay release their captives.

Panting heavily, the airmen and WAAFs stood in the lane listening to the pounding feet growing fainter in the distance.

'Now we'll be for it,' Tommy muttered. 'Fighting with the locals. We'll be on a charge and no mistake.'

Ten

'Well, I'm going to say I fell over in the dark. That'll explain my laddered stockings,' Ruth declared next morning. 'What about you?'

Fleur bit her lip. She'd never liked telling lies. She'd always owned up to any misdemeanour either to her parents or to her teachers. But now, others were involved and she didn't want to get anyone else into trouble. 'I wonder how the lads are faring.'

'It's a clear forecast for tonight – so Peggy was saying,' Ruth told her as they left the dining room together after breakfast. 'They'll be flying for sure. I doubt a word will be said as long as no one from the village makes trouble. And I don't think they will. You heard what Bill Moore's attitude is. And I reckon most of the villagers feel the same.' She laughed wryly. 'More likely those lads will get a leathering from their dads for being such idiots.' She nodded wisely. 'The station brings a lot of trade to this area to say nothing of the little treats that find their way from our NAAFI onto the tables of the villagers.' She tapped the side of her nose. Fleur laughed, hoping fervently that Ruth was right.

As she climbed the steps to the watch office that evening, Fleur found her heart was hammering inside her chest and she felt sick. Already, the vehicles were ferrying crews out to their aircraft as she took her place beside Kay. Although she'd spent four hours earlier in the day familiarizing herself with how things were done in this particular flying control, this was her first time on duty during a mission. Kay was a good teacher, brusque and to the point as was her manner, but in no way irritable or impatient. Fleur, meticulous as she had always been since the day she'd signed up, welcomed the other girl's professional attitude. Bob Watson was on duty that night. He smiled and nodded at Fleur as she took her seat, rearranged her writing pad and pens in readiness for the notes and lists she would be required to jot down through the busy night. She adjusted her headphones and the microphone around her neck for comfort as, behind her, other members of the team readied themselves too.

On the walls around the room were maps and clocks, and blackboards giving local weather conditions and target information. The most interesting one to Fleur was the operations blackboard with 'WICKERTON WOOD' painted in white at the top. Beneath it, the station's call sign 'Woody' and the numbers of the two squadrons operating from Wickerton Wood with their respective call signs, Lindum and Pelham. In the centre of the board was the word 'RAID' with a space for the name of the target to be chalked in each time. Below that was a white painted grid where Peggy was already filling in all the details of each aircraft and the pilot's name for tonight's raid. As each one took off she would fill in the time. And then, lastly, there was the blank column that everyone watched most anxiously: 'RETURN'.

Fleur glanced over her shoulder to see Peggy writing

in Tommy Laughton's name. Now there could be no mistake. Robbie was definitely on tonight's raid.

She glanced out of the window, criss-crossed with tape, in front of the long desk where the R/T operators sat with all their instruments and telephones overlooking the airfield's runways. Her heart skipped a beat. In the distance she could see the airmen climbing into their planes. She strained her eyes but could not pick out Robbie. Good luck, darling, she said silently. Safe home.

One by one, dozens of engines burst into life, their throbbing filling the night air and almost shaking the ground as they taxied from the various dispersal points, forming up to take off at orderly, timed intervals. At the end of the runway each aircraft waited for the controller's red light to switch to green before, revving its engines, it began its cumbersome, breath-holding take-off. One by one the Hampdens, heavy with fuel and bombs, lumbered down the runway.

On take-off and until the aircraft reached the target there was radio silence, unless in a dire emergency. Landing back at base, when security no longer mattered quite so much, was when the girls in the watch office would have radio communication with the aircraft. But they were all on duty for take-off, listening in, ready to help if needed.

'Right, ladies and gentlemen,' Bob Watson said. 'Let's see these lads into the air.'

There was a clatter of footsteps outside and the door burst open. A breathless Ruth came to attention in front of Bob's desk. 'Permission to go up to the roof, Flight?'

With a small smile, Bob nodded and Ruth rushed out of the room.

Fleur blinked and turned questioning eyes towards Bob Watson, who said shortly and with a trace of sarcasm, 'Your friend seems to think it vital that she waves off every mission from the roof of the watch tower. Some silly superstition of hers. She comes in even when she's not on duty herself and, if she's on leave, she makes someone promise to do it for her.'

Fleur said nothing. She understood about superstition and 'good luck' charms that the airmen carried. Why, at this moment, one of her initialled handkerchiefs nestled in the breast pocket of Robbie's uniform. No, she didn't blame Ruth one bit for her 'silly' superstition.

It was a long night. Once the flurry of activity of watching all the aircraft get safely airborne was over, there was nothing for the team in Control to do but wait.

'You girls can take it easy for a while. It'll be several hours before they're back,' Bob said. 'Get a cup of tea in turns . . . er . . . write letters, knit or do some . . . er . . . mending . . .' Fleur noticed that Bob was looking hopefully at Kay, who was studiously avoiding his eyes.

Fleur chuckled. 'I think Flight has a job he'd like you to do, Corp,' she said, pretending innocence.

'Then he can think again,' Kay said tartly, but Fleur caught the twinkle in the girl's eyes and she sent Fleur a surreptitious wink. She was toying with Bob, who looked crestfallen. Suddenly Kay swivelled round on her chair. 'What is it this time? Socks? Shirt buttons?'

'Actually – it's a button on my jacket . . .'

'Oh, now that is serious,' Kay mocked. 'Just think

if you were called to the CO's office with a button missing on your jacket. Tut-tut.' She winked at Fleur. 'You any good with a needle, Fleur?'

Fleur caught the mischief in Kay's eyes and shook her head. 'Terrible! My mother despaired of me.' She could hardly stop the giggles that were welling up inside her from spilling out. The truth was that Betsy had brought her up to sew, mend and make do. She was quite expert with her needle and thread and no slouch with a sewing machine either.

Now the two girls dissolved into laughter whilst Bob stood looking at them helplessly. Peggy joined in the conversation. 'You're rotten, you two.' She turned to Bob. 'I'd offer, but I really am useless at needlework. I bet that one' – she jabbed her finger at Fleur – 'is pulling your leg. She's been brought up on a farm and I bet she could knit you a jumper straight off a sheep's back.'

Fleur wiped the tears of laughter from her eyes, thankful that for a few moments she had been able to put aside her anxiety over Robbie. 'Not quite, Peggy, but I am teasing. Yes, I can sew. My mother would have a ducky fit if she heard me denying all her teaching. Hand it over and I'll see what I can do.'

As she fished in her bag for her 'housewife' with, amongst other items, its sewing needle, blue thread and tiny pair of scissors, Bob brought his uniform jacket to her, holding out the shining button in the palm of his hand. 'Lucky I didn't lose this.'

'Well, on your own head be it, Fleur,' Kay remarked. 'Don't say I didn't warn you. Word will go round this place like wildfire that you've set up as the camp seamstress. You'll have all these ham-fisted fellers beating a path to your door.'

'I should be so lucky!' Fleur quipped as she threaded her needle.

'There's just one thing,' Bob said seriously. 'Don't let the CO catch you. He's a stickler for the rulebook.'

'Then you'd better keep an eye out.' She grinned up at him. 'At least while I'm doing *your* jacket.'

'I'll get us some tea,' Peggy offered, whilst Kay turned back to study her notes and the jottings she had made during take-off.

The hours of waiting seemed interminable, especially on the eight-hour night watch, but Fleur was glad to be here. It helped her to feel closer to Robbie, even though she had a hollow, sick feeling in the pit of her stomach that she knew would not go away until he had landed safely. But tomorrow she could look forward to a day off after the long night duty. She hoped Robbie would have some time to spend with her.

As the time drew near for the aircraft to return, the relaxed atmosphere in the watch office disappeared and became businesslike once more. Just as the voice from the first homecoming aircraft came crackling over the airwaves, a red air-raid warning came in and at once the runway lights went out. Hurriedly, but with surprising calm, Kay gave warning to the homecoming crew about what was happening.

Though her hands were shaking, Fleur managed to speak calmly into her own microphone, warning each aircraft as it called in of the danger. They were all given the command to orbit at a certain height, though several were already low on fuel and wouldn't be able to circle for long. Fleur bit her lip, her ears tuned for the call sign of Robbie's plane, D-Doggo.

Then they heard the incendiary bombs falling.

Thud! A silence and then another thud. Closer now. Another, even closer, and then came a thunderous boom very close to the control tower. The whole room seemed to shake and the glass rattled, but Kay continued to speak calmly into her microphone. 'Hello, G-George, this is Woody receiving you, strength niner, over . . .' Then she wrote rapidly on her notepad, her hand moving smoothly over the page, without any telltale shake.

Fleur took a deep breath. 'Hello, P-Poppy, this is Woody . . .' She was gratified to find that her voice was level and calm too, but her heart was pounding so loudly in her chest, she was sure they could hear it over the airwaves.

They waited for the next bomb to fall, convinced it would be a direct hit on the watch office. Well, there's one thing, Fleur thought irrationally. If I'm to die so soon, my mother will have been proved right!

But no more bombs fell and in a few moments the all-clear was declared.

'Just a lone raider dropping a stick of bombs, I expect,' Bob said, smoothing back his hair, which had become distinctly ruffled during the last few minutes. The landing lights came on and, as soon as the runway was declared damage free, instructions to land began at once.

Later Fleur was to learn from Ruth that one or two aircraft had landed on almost empty tanks.

One of the last aircraft to land was D-Doggo. Finally, Fleur could breathe again. Robbie was safely back.

If every night was going to be as bad as this one had been, Fleur wondered how she would cope. But cope she would; she had to for Robbie's sake. It wouldn't help him if she let him see how dreadfully anxious she was. And yet she needed to let him know how very much she cared for him, how very much – already – she loved him.

She smiled. But he knew that, just as she knew how much he loved her.

There were no doubts between the two of them about their feelings for each other. If only he had been able to talk to his mother . . .

Eleven

'Hi, Sis. Thought I'd bike over and see how you're getting on.'

'Kenny! What are you doing here this time of the morning? Whatever time did you set off?'

He was waiting for her as she came off duty after the long night. She wouldn't see Robbie until later – they both needed to sleep. Kenny had arrived at the guardroom at the main gate and a message had been sent to Fleur.

'There's nothing wrong at home, is there?' Fleur was still anxious.

Kenny grinned. 'No more than usual. Mum's still going on about you joining up and me following you. I shan't wait till I'm called up, though. I shall volunteer as soon as I can.'

'Oh, it'll all be over by the time you're old enough,' Fleur said, hoping she sounded more convincing than she felt.

'Hope not,' Kenny said cheerfully with the thoughtlessness of youth. 'I want to see a bit of the action myself.'

Fleur sighed heavily but couldn't prevent a smile. 'And you know who'll get the blame if you do "see a bit of the action"?'

'You will.' He grinned, draping one arm around her shoulder and wheeling his bicycle with the other hand as they began to walk down the lane towards Rose Cottage. Although five years younger than Fleur, he was already a head taller.

'Exactly!' she said with wry humour, but then her tone sobered. 'But seriously, Kenny, I couldn't bear it if something happened to you. No more than Mum and Dad could. You do know that, don't you?'

He gave her shoulder a squeeze. 'Course I do,' he said softly, but then teased, 'now don't start getting all soppy on me. But I'll tell you now, if the war is still going on, I shall join up. I'm not having anyone calling me a coward.'

'Oh, Kenny, they wouldn't. Farming's acknowledged as a reserved occupation.'

'I know, and *I* don't blame those who stay, but you've seen for yourself the looks that young, unmarried fellers get.'

Fleur was silent, thinking of Kitty's scathing remark about Alfie. She'd seen for herself now how hurtful such comments could be.

'And it's not your fault either. I'd've gone anyway, whether you had or not, and I shall tell Mum so when the time comes.'

Fleur slipped her arm around his waist and laid her head against his shoulder as they walked side by side.

'It makes no difference whether Mum blames me or not, love. I shall blame myself.' There was a pause and then she said, 'I just wondered why you're here so early, that's all.' She sighed. 'It's a sign of the times. I immediately thought something was wrong.'

'I just thought I'd like to spend the day with you. I've no school today and Dad said he'd manage the morning milking on his own, so I set off at the crack of dawn.'

'How long does it take you?'

Kenny wrinkled his forehead. 'Couple of hours, I suppose. Bit more, p'raps. I use all the back roads and lanes, cutting across country. It's quicker.'

'Well, it's great to see you,' she said, giving his waist a quick squeeze.

As they rounded the last corner towards the two cottages, Fleur glanced up and saw Robbie waiting by the gate, arms akimbo, watching them approach. His fair hair was ruffled by the breeze, his jacket and shirt collar undone, his tie hanging loose. She pulled in a sharp breath and Kenny looked down at her.

'What is it, Sis?' Then, as he saw the brightness in her eyes, he followed the line of her gaze. 'Oho,' he said softly, 'so this is the feller all the trouble's about, is it?'

'Yes,' Fleur breathed. 'That's him. That's Robbie.'

'Then you'd better introduce me and I can report back to Mum.'

'It won't make any difference,' Fleur murmured sadly. 'There's something that happened in the past, but we don't know what and no one will tell us. Look, Kenny, be a dear. Don't say anything in front of Robbie, will you?'

'Course not if you say so.'

They were too close now to be able to say more without him hearing, so, releasing herself from Kenny's arm, Fleur ran towards Robbie.

'What's this?' he said, smiling down at her. 'A rival already, have I?'

'Absolutely! This is the man I've loved all his life. Robbie – this is Kenny, my . . . my brother.' For a brief moment her voice faltered and they exchanged a stricken glance.

96

What if . . . oh, what if . . . ?

But then Robbie had mastered his expression and was turning towards Kenny, his hand outstretched. 'I'm very pleased to meet you,' he said warmly, but Fleur was still battling to control her runaway emotions. What if she were at that moment introducing half-brothers to each other?

A shudder ran through her and it was Robbie's arm that now tightened around her, silently encouraging her to stay strong.

Kenny held out his hand. Although he favoured their mother's colouring – fair hair and blue eyes – there were times, like now, when his face creased in smiles just like their father's did when he laughed. 'Pleased to meet you.' The younger man looked Robbie up and down. 'Smart uniform, though I was thinking of the army mesen – when the time comes.'

'You'll probably see more of the world than I will stuck up there in a plane. But I fancied the flying.'

Kenny nodded. 'Yeah. Now you come to mention it,' he said thoughtfully, 'it must be thrilling, though I think I'd prefer fighter planes. Bit more exciting, that one-to-one stuff.' And they laughed together, comrades already.

Fleur stepped between them and linked her arms through theirs. 'Right, now I'll take you to meet Mrs Jackson and Harry – if he's about. And Ruth should be home soon.'

'Well, I'd come to tell you that I'll give you a hand this afternoon with this overgrown garden you were telling me about,' Robbie said. 'I felt like some fresh air and a bit of real work when I've had a few hours' kip.'

'Me too,' Fleur agreed. She was delighted to see

Kenny, but after the long night of anxiety she felt she could fall asleep standing up.

'But I needed to come and make sure you were all right after the air raid.'

'Air raid? What air raid?' Kenny asked at once before Fleur could even reply.

'Oh, it was nothing, just a lone raider dropping a stick of incendiaries,' Fleur said airily, as if it was a daily occurrence and nothing to get excited about. She squeezed Robbie's arm, warning him not to make too much of it.

Catching on at once, Robbie adopted a light, bantering tone. 'Well, it was just an excuse to see you really.'

Kenny glanced at Robbie above Fleur's head and, despite Robbie's affected nonchalance about the raid, Kenny could still see the worry in his eyes. The young man knew that they were both trying to make light of the incident in front of him.

Softly, he said, 'You can tell me the truth, you know. I won't go running home to tell Mum. I know an airfield's a dangerous place.' He looked down at Fleur. 'You've been on duty all night, haven't you? And you,' he said, glancing up again at Robbie, 'have been flying?'

Robbie laughed softly. 'Seems there's no keeping any secrets from this brother of yours, darling.'

Fleur smiled ruefully. 'No,' she said wryly. 'I don't think there is. Not about anything.'

'So, you both need to get some sleep,' Kenny began, but Fleur cut in saying, 'Well, yes, but don't go. I've the rest of the day off. In fact, I'm not on duty until the afternoon shift tomorrow.'

'And our aircraft's out of action until tomorrow. We encountered flak coming back across the coast and there are a few holes here and there.' Again, he was trying to make light of it. 'We'll just need a couple of hours and then we can spend the afternoon with you, Kenny.'

'Right-o,' Kenny said cheerfully. 'In the meantime, I can maybe make myself useful. What's all this about a garden?'

Fleur laughed. 'Careful – I might set you on.' Swiftly, Fleur explained about the state of the old lady's garden. 'It must have been a wonderful kitchen garden when her old man was alive, but now . . .' She shrugged. 'Well, you'll see the state of it for yourself. I scythed about half of it yesterday and then it'll want digging over. There's a lot of work, but it'll be worth it if I can get it right. And it's still only April. There'll be time to plant a few veggies.'

They went in by the front gate and around the corner of the house and then moved to the little gate leading into the back garden. The two men stood looking at the neglected ground.

'Grow a lot of stuff, that would,' Kenny mused. 'And the government's shouting for us all to use every spare bit of ground. I'm surprised they haven't sent a couple of sturdy Land Army girls to do it for her. Dad's got two coming, since you left.'

Fleur laughed. 'Now there's a compliment! Takes two to replace me, does it?'

Kenny grinned. 'That's about the size of it, Sis.'

'It's a lot to tackle on your own,' Robbie said. 'Is Ruth helping?'

'She's a city girl. Wouldn't know a 'tatie from a

turnip. Mind you' – Fleur's eyes sparkled with mischief – 'I've got another little job lined up for her – though she doesn't know it yet.'

'Well, I don't mind lending a hand when I'm off duty. Be good to get my hands dirty for once,' Robbie promised.

'Maybe I could bring you some tools—' Kenny began, but Fleur shook her head. 'No need. What Mrs Jackson hasn't got in her shed, Harry'll lend me. Come on in and meet my landlady.'

Fleur led the way into the kitchen and watched the old lady's eyes light up at the sight of the two handsome young men. The introductions over, Fleur made tea whilst Robbie sat down opposite Mrs Jackson with Kenny next to her. From the back scullery, Fleur heard them all laughing. It was the first time she had heard the old dear laugh aloud and when she carried the tea tray into the room and set it on the table, she saw that Mary's face was pink with pleasure.

'Coo-ee, it's only me,' a voice shouted as the back door was thrown open and Ruth appeared like a whirlwind. 'Why didn't you wait for me—?' she began as she stepped into the kitchen, but she stopped short as she saw the two young men. She'd met Robbie during the evening at the local pub, but her eyes widened as she spotted Kenny. Her mouth twitched with amusement as she said with mock severity, 'Well, I can see why now. Wanted to keep this handsome pair to yourself, did you? I call that greedy, don't you, Mrs Jackson?' She stuck out her hand towards Kenny. 'Hello. I'm Ruth. Fleur's very *best* friend.'

Kenny scrambled up, the colour rising in his face. 'H-hello. I'm Kenny. Fleur's brother.'

Fleur watched with mixed feelings as her little brother – not so little now, she noticed with a pang, for he towered over Ruth – took the girl's hand in his, his gaze fastened on her pretty face. Ruth smiled, the dimples in her round cheeks deepening. She took off her cap and shook her wayward curls. 'Nice to meet you, Kenny.'

She let go of his hand and turned towards the table. 'Any tea in the pot? I'm parched.'

Kenny sank back down into the chair, but his gaze never left Ruth as she busied herself freshening the pot and pouring herself a cup. She sat in a chair near the table, crossed her shapely legs and smiled round at everyone.

They sat chatting for several minutes until a knock came at the back door, which then opened. 'You there, lass?' came Harry's voice. 'I saw you come in. I've brought you the scythe round.' He reared the implement against the wall and stepped into the house. 'Oh, sorry. Didn't realize you had company.'

The old rascal, Fleur thought. If he saw me come home then he must have seen the lads with me. He's just come round to see what's going on. Then, remembering how lonely the old boy must be, she introduced him to Robbie and her brother.

Harry nodded at them in turn. 'How do?'

'How d'you do?' Robbie said, getting up. 'You must be Mr Chambers. Fleur has told me about you.'

'Call me 'Arry, young feller. Everybody does.'

'Well then, pleased to meet you, Harry.'

'Well,' Fleur gave an exaggerated sigh. 'I'd best get me head down for a couple of hours and then into me gardening clothes. You're a hard taskmaster, Harry, an' no mistake.'

101

'No, no, lass, if you've got company, I'll take the scythe back again.'

'It's OK,' Kenny said at once. 'I'll have a go while Fleur has a sleep. I'll do all the grass under the fruit trees and bushes at the bottom of the garden. Have you got a sickle I could use as well, Mr Chambers?'

'I have, lad, and I'll fetch it round for ya, but only if you call me "Harry".'

'And I'll be back this afternoon,' Robbie promised. 'And we'll all do a spot of digging.'

Kenny, red to the roots of his hair, said, 'You know I could bike over now and again and lend a hand, if you like, Sis.' But she noticed that his eyes went to Ruth as he made the offer.

Struggling to keep a straight face, Fleur said, 'That'd be great.'

'Well, young feller,' Harry put in, 'if you're as handy with me scythe as your sister, you should get that grass cut by the end of the morning.'

'You're on, Harry.' Kenny grinned.

That afternoon, Robbie returned. As he took off his jacket and hung it on a nail in the shed, he glanced down the garden to where Kenny was mowing the last patch of long grass, with Ruth sitting on the bench under the old apple tree, watching him.

'You know,' he said softly to Fleur, 'I think your little brother is smitten with Ruth.'

'Mmm, I noticed. But he's not so little now, is he?' she added wistfully and felt a shudder of apprehension at the thought that in the short space of a year her beloved Kenny would be old enough to enlist. 'Come on,' she said, determined not to let thoughts of the war spoil this sunny afternoon. 'Let's go and help.'

'What do you want me to do?'

Fleur grinned at him. 'How are you at digging?'

Twelve

It was a happy afternoon. Robbie and Kenny tackled the digging – a tough job, for the ground was hard and the grass and weeds had taken a firm hold – whilst Fleur finished the last bit of scything.

Harry sat in the house, chatting to Mary Jackson in between making little forays into the garden to see how the work was progressing, whilst Ruth kept everyone supplied with tea.

'The old dears have fallen asleep,' Ruth said about the middle of the afternoon. 'Harry's snoring with his mouth wide open. But they look so sweet,' she added fondly. 'You'd think they were an old married couple instead of just neighbours.'

Kenny, his face red from exertion, took a breather leaning on his fork. 'Thanks,' he said, the colour on his face deepening as he took the mug of tea from Ruth.

Hands on her hips, Ruth surveyed their work. 'Well, I feel like a spare part. But I wouldn't know where to start.'

Fleur rested on the scythe for a moment. 'You could rake this grass up if you like, but mind you don't get near me.'

'Huh! Not likely when you're wielding that thing.'

'Well, you're doing a great job keeping us supplied with tea for today. It's thirsty work.'

'I'll stick to that then. Mind you, I suppose I could do a bit of raking. Seems easy enough.' She was about to move away to rummage in the conglomeration of Mrs Jackson's shed to find a rake when she turned back and eyed Fleur suspiciously. 'What did you mean "for today"? Sounds as if you've got something else lined up for me. I told you, I'm a city girl.'

'I know – but how are you at housework?'

Ruth's eyes lit up. 'Oh, I'm a dab hand at that. I like everything spick and span.'

'I know,' Fleur said ruefully. 'I've seen your bedroom.' She was having a hard time keeping her own room as neat and tidy as her fellow WAAF's.

'We live in a council house back home,' Ruth went on. 'And me mum keeps it like a little palace.' She frowned. 'But Mrs Jackson's cottage is spotless. I don't see—'

'I wasn't thinking of here.' She paused, leant towards Ruth and lowered her voice. 'Have you seen Harry's place?'

Ruth stared at her and shook her head. 'Harry's place?' she repeated. 'No, I've never been inside.'

Fleur laughed. 'Well, take my word for it. It's a tip.'

'But – but he keeps his garden immaculate.'

Fleur nodded. 'I know, but I reckon that was his domain and the house was his wife's, and since she's gone . . .'

'Oh, I get you. Not much of a housewife, is he?'

'That's an understatement, love,' Fleur said wryly.

'But – but how can I offer to help? I mean, I don't want to hurt the old boy's feelings. He's a pet.'

'Go back into the house and say you feel a bit – well – a bit useless out here.'

'Oh, thanks!'

'You know what I mean. You've got to lay it on with a trowel.'

'I told you – I'm no good with trowels.'

They laughed, sparring with each other, until Ruth nodded and said, 'I'll go in and ask Mrs Jackson if there's anything she wants doing. I know she'll say "no" 'cos I've asked her before and there's only so many times I can clean my bedroom from top to bottom. And then I'll turn to Harry and ask him if he wants any ironing doing or the washing up. That'd be all right, d'you think?'

'Perfect,' Fleur grinned.

'Right.' Ruth took a deep breath. 'Here we go, then.'

The grass forgotten, Ruth headed for the cottage and a few moments later she emerged, her arm linked through Harry's. Behind his back she gave Fleur the 'thumbs up' sign and called, 'Mrs Jackson's taking over tea-making duties. Let her know when you want another.'

At the sound of her voice, Kenny looked up. 'Where's Ruth going?'

'Just next door. Give Harry a bit of a hand. She's not one for the outdoor life, it seems.'

'Oh.' His disappointment was clear to see. 'Will she be back before I have to go?'

'I expect so, but if not, you can nip next door and say "cheerio".'

The grin was back on his face as he attacked the solid ground with his fork. Unseen by Kenny, Robbie winked at Fleur just as Mrs Jackson appeared in the back doorway with a plate of scones in her hand to go with the tea Ruth had brought out.

As they stood leaning against the outer wall of the cottage, drinking tea and eating scones, Robbie declared, 'D'you know, I'm a townie like Ruth, but I have to say I'm enjoying a bit of physical work.'

'You'll suffer for it tomorrow.' Fleur grinned. 'You'll ache in muscles you didn't know you'd got.'

Robbie pulled a face. 'Quite likely, but it'll be worth it. It's good to get away from camp and to concentrate on something other than what we've got to do at night. And that reminds me.' He glanced at his watch. 'I'll have to go in about half an hour. There's a final briefing in an hour's time and even though I'm pretty sure our crew's not flying tonight, I'd better be on hand just in case.'

'Yes, and I'll have to report in too. Someone might have gone off sick and I'll be needed to take their place. Ruth too.'

As she collected the cups and plates, Kenny said, 'Look, you two go off – for a walk or summat. Have a bit of time to yourselves. I'll carry on with the digging here. I can stay till you have to go, Sis.' He glanced at the cottage next door.

'Right you are, Kenny. Thanks.' Deliberately casual, she said, 'And don't let me forget to give Ruth a shout. We'll both need time to get back into our uniforms.'

Kenny grinned. 'No, I won't forget.'

'I bet he won't.' Robbie laughed softly as they walked, hand in hand, out of the squeaking gate and a little way down the lane to where the houses stopped and the countryside began. They headed for a little copse at the edge of a field that would afford them a bit of privacy. Climbing over the gate, they headed for the shelter of the trees.

Robbie took her in his arms, but Fleur was stiff, afraid to respond. 'Oh, Robbie,' she whispered, tears filling her eyes. 'Did we ought to?'

He sighed heavily and rested his cheek against her hair. His arms were still about her but comforting rather than desirous. 'Darling, I'll try to speak to Ma as soon as I can. I promise. Maybe I could wangle a day's leave on compassionate grounds. I got a letter from her this morning and she says Pops has a very bad cold and it's gone on his chest. She's quite worried about him, I think.'

Fleur pulled a face. 'I doubt you'll manage it unless the weather gets bad and you can't fly.'

So much taller than Fleur, Robbie kissed the top of her head. 'Then we'll just have to pray for snow.'

Fleur laughed, despite the worry clouding their time together. 'What? In April?'

'It's been known. Pops reckons he remembers it snowing in the middle of May in nineteen hundred.'

'Really?'

'So he says.'

They stayed for the half-hour, just happy to be together, and yet they dared not kiss – it felt wrong until they knew for sure.

'Oh I wish we knew. I wish we knew the truth,' Fleur moaned as they walked back to Mrs Jackson's cottage. Robbie squeezed her hand. 'I'll find out as soon as I can. I promise.'

The snow that they'd wished for didn't arrive and there were operations on each of the following three nights. The watching and waiting didn't get any easier and Fleur breathed a sigh of relief each time D-Doggo landed safely. On the fourth night, however, there was a weather report of bad visibility over the target area that cancelled the mission. All aircrews were stood down and Robbie went at once to see Tommy Laughton.

'Skip, is it absolutely definite that we won't be flying? Because, if it is, I could do to nip home for twenty-four hours.'

'It's definite, old boy, so it should be OK. Mind you fill in a two-nine-five.' Tommy reminded him to submit the usual application form. 'But can you be sure to be back by thirteen hundred tomorrow? If there's flying tomorrow night, briefing's likely to be at fourteen hundred.'

Robbie nodded. 'I'll hitch if the trains don't fit up. Folks are very decent about picking up servicemen.'

Tommy stroked his bristly moustache thoughtfully. 'Tell you what, nip along to MT. They might have a lorry going your way.'

'Thanks, Skip. I will.'

When he went in search of Fleur, it was to find that she too had been given permission to go home for a brief visit because there was no flying that night. He squeezed her arm. 'I've got a lift all the way to Nottingham. I'll ask the driver if he can take you too.'

They parted in Newark.

'Could you drop me outside Castle Station, please?' Fleur asked. 'I rang home and my father had to come into Newark anyway today so he said he can pick me up there.'

'What if he sees me?' Robbie asked worriedly.

The WAAF driver smiled knowingly, but made no comment as Fleur said cheerfully, 'I don't care if he does. You've got to meet each other some time.'

The lorry came to a halt and Fleur leant over and kissed Robbie's cheek before climbing down. As the vehicle pulled away, she turned towards the station to see Jake standing beside his battered Ford. She caught her breath. He must have seen Robbie. When she got closer she was shocked by the look on her father's face. Even though he was tanned by the outdoor life he led, the colour had drained from his face and his eyes were haunted. He looked as if he had just been dealt a devastating blow. The thought terrified Fleur. Had her father believed he was looking at his own son for the first time?

Her voice shook as she said, 'Dad? What is it? What's the matter?'

He was breathing heavily. 'Is that him? Is that Meg's boy?'

'Yes,' Fleur said hesitantly. 'He . . . he couldn't stop now. He's on his way home. His grandfather's ill. He—'

'Are you *sure* it is his grandfather?' There was still disbelief in Jake's tone.

'Yes. I asked him. It's his mother's father.'

Jake shook his head as if he couldn't believe what she was saying. 'You do surprise me,' he murmured, but he was speaking more to himself than to her.

Fleur took a deep breath and put her arm through her father's. 'Dad – Robbie and I – well, we've fallen in love, and unless you tell me that there's a good reason why we can't see each other—'

'Isn't upsetting your mother good reason enough?' he demanded harshly.

Fleur kept her voice calm. 'No – not on its own. I'm sorry, but it isn't.'

'Don't you think she's got enough to worry about

with you gone and Kenny just waiting for the day when he's old enough to join up without you taking up with someone – with someone – unsuitable?'

'But *why* is he unsuitable, as you put it? If only you'd tell me then perhaps I could understand.'

Jake's mouth was a hard, unyielding line. 'I've told you once and I won't tell you again.' It was as if she were small again and he was chastising her for some childish escapade. 'It's not my secret to tell.'

'Are you sure?' Fleur cried passionately, no longer able to stay calm. 'Are you quite sure it has nothing to do with you?'

The bleak look on her father's face tore at her heart and when he pulled himself free of her grasp, picked up her bag and marched towards the car, she knew it would be fruitless to ask any more questions.

'I just hope Robbie's having better luck with his mother,' she muttered angrily as she followed Jake.

They drove all the way from Newark to South Monkford in an uncomfortable silence. As he drew the vehicle to a halt in the yard, Jake said, 'Not a word to your mother about all this. You hear me?'

If she didn't want to spoil her leave completely, Fleur gave the only answer she could. 'Yes, Dad.'

Thirteen

'Oh, it's you.'

'Well, that's a nice greeting, Mum, I must say.'

'What do you expect?' There was no smile from Betsy, not even a hug. 'It was bad enough you leaving us in the lurch, but now Kenny's taken it into his head to come cycling over to see you every spare minute instead of helping your father.'

'Mum, he's been over *once* . . .'

But Betsy was in no mood to listen. 'He *says* it's to help some poor old dear with her gardening.' She gave a disapproving click of her tongue. 'But there's more to it than that.' She wagged her finger in Fleur's face. 'He's done nothing but talk about a girl called Ruth. Who is she, I'd like to know?'

Fleur took off her uniform jacket and hung it up on the back of the door. The teapot – as ever – was standing on the hob in the range. She picked it up, moved to the table and poured herself a cup of tea.

'Well,' Betsy demanded impatiently.

Fleur sighed as she sat down at the table. 'She's the other girl in the billet with me and the old lady is our landlady. She's a sweet old dear, but she's crippled with arthritis. Her husband used to keep the garden lovely, but since he died three years ago, it's been neglected. I just thought I'd help tidy it up in my spare time, get some veggies growing. You know, like the government's always telling us to do.'

'It's here you should be helping.' Betsy prodded her forefinger towards the floor. 'Not digging some stranger's garden *and* enticing your brother away from his duty too.'

'I didn't *entice* him, as you put it,' Fleur said wearily. 'I didn't even ask for his help. He came over to visit me and saw what I was doing.'

'Huh! And I expect you're trying to set him up with this Ruth girl? He's far too young to be thinking about girls. He's still at school, for heaven's sake.'

'Only because you've made him stay on. Still want him to go to university, do you?'

'No,' Betsy said promptly. 'Agricultural college.'

Fleur raised her eyebrows. 'That's a new idea. I've not heard that before. When did you think that one up?' Her eyes narrowed thoughtfully as she stared at her mother. 'Oh, I get it. You think it will keep him out of the war, don't you?'

Betsy wriggled her shoulders. 'Can't blame a mother for trying.'

Fleur was about to say, No, though you're trying much harder to stop Kenny going than you ever did with me. But she bit back the retort. It was the mother/son thing. She knew that. She sipped her tea in the tense silence.

Almost as if she had read her daughter's thoughts, Betsy blurted out, 'I'd've thought you'd have done what your dad wanted, even if you'd take no notice of me. But no, you had to go, didn't you?' Tears filled Betsy's eyes. 'And now there'll be no stopping Kenny.' Her voice rose hysterically. 'He'll go and it'll be all your fault. If you'd stayed here at home, he would've done an' all. But now . . .'

Fleur set down her cup with deliberate care. 'I know you won't believe me, Mum, but I've asked him not to go. But I don't think anything any of us can say will make any difference. And – and he said he'd go anyway – that it has nothing to do with me . . .' She saw her mother's sceptical glance but ploughed on. 'He doesn't want to be thought a coward. He says he gets some funny looks even now because he's not in uniform – because he's so tall for his age.'

Now Betsy leant over the table towards Fleur, almost menacingly. 'I'd rather him be thought a coward,' she said slowly, emphasizing every word, 'put in prison for it even – if it keeps him alive.'

'Oh, Mum!' Now Fleur's eyes filled with tears as she felt an overwhelming pity for her mother. 'That's not our Kenny. Can't you be proud of your son that – that he wants to do his duty for his country?'

Betsy banged the table with her fist. 'His duty's here. Helping his father on the land. Why else would the government make farming a reserved occupation? He'll be helping his country just as much. More, if truth be known, than becoming cannon fodder.' Fleur gasped as her mother ranted on. 'I've been through all this before, you know. Your father was in the last lot. Oh, he married me before he went – so that I would get his pension.' Her face twisted. 'His pension! What good is a pension compared to a lifetime of loneliness?'

'But Dad came back.'

'Aye, he did. I was lucky . . .' For a moment her eyes glazed over and she was lost in the past. 'I was lucky he came back – that he came back to *me* – that he stayed with *me*.'

Fleur felt as if ice-cold water was running down her spine. 'Mum – what d'you mean – came back to *you*?'

Betsy blinked, back in the present. 'Eh? Oh – oh nothing. Nothing.' She bit her lip and turned away, murmuring, 'Yes, you're right. I was lucky.' And then adding ominously, 'That time.'

The atmosphere lightened noticeably when Kenny breezed in from school, slung his satchel in the corner, hugged Fleur and then lifted his mother in a bear hug and swung her round. Betsy laughed and slapped him playfully. 'Oh, you bad boy! Put me down, put me down. I've your tea to get . . .'

She bustled about the kitchen and scullery with renewed vigour, a smile on her face now that her beloved son was home. She placed an overloaded plate of hot food before him, fussed around him, stroking his hair and patting his shoulder.

How does he put up with it? Fleur thought, gritting her teeth, realizing that she was glad she was not her mother's favourite if that was what she would have to put up with. She glanced across the table at her father, but Jake was eating his meal, outwardly placid, his face expressionless. But she wondered what exactly he was feeling inside.

'How's Ruth?' Kenny mumbled, his mouth full of meat and potato pie.

Before Fleur could answer, Betsy, sitting down next to Kenny, said, 'Don't talk with your mouth full and never mind about her. Did you see the careers master today? Did you ask him about agricultural college like I told you?'

Kenny stopped chewing and laid his knife and fork

down on his plate, though his meal was only half eaten. He swallowed.

'Mum,' he began, his face unusually serious. He put his arm along the back of her chair and touched her shoulder. 'I don't want to go to college or university or anywhere. Not yet. When I leave school, I'm going to join the RAF. I want to be a pilot. A fighter pilot.'

For a moment there was complete stillness in the room until the air was rent with Betsy leaping to her feet, pointing at Fleur and screaming. 'See? See? I told you. It's all your fault. If it hadn't been for you, he'd never even have thought of the RAF. If – if he's killed, it'll be your fault. All your fault.' She swung round towards Jake. 'And you're no better. You should have forbidden her to go. But you're too soft, too – too . . .' Betsy couldn't find the words to describe what she felt about Jake. She sank back into her chair, covered her face with her hands and broke into noisy sobbing.

'Oh, Mum, don't.' Kenny hugged her awkwardly, but it was to no avail.

Above the noise, Jake said, 'Betsy, now that's enough. You know I won't interfere with what either of them wants to do. I went myself last time, didn't I? I can hardly start playing the heavy-handed father this time round. Besides, if you want the truth, I'm proud of them. Proud of them both that they want to do their bit.'

Fleur and Kenny gaped at him, a mixture of emotions on both their faces. Gratitude for his under-standing and because he'd spoken up in their defence, but at the same time shock because it was the first time they'd ever heard him criticize their mother. At least, in front of them. What perhaps passed between their parents in private they weren't to know.

Betsy's sobs subsided and she let her hands fall away from her face. In a flat voice she said, 'Then you don't care if they get hurt or even killed?'

'Of course I care.' Jake's voice was rising in anger now. 'How can you accuse me of not caring? But the whole country is in the same boat. Every mother's son is in danger.' He looked at Fleur and added, 'And a lot of fathers' daughters too.'

'I don't care about anyone else,' Betsy said and now her quiet tone was more frightening than her screaming. 'I only care about my own.' And she leant towards Kenny to emphasize just where her concerns lay.

'Then that's very selfish of you, Betsy.' Jake pushed back his chair and rose. As he was about to turn away, his wife said, 'I bet *she's* only bothered about her own precious son.'

Jake was very still and Fleur held her breath. Slowly he turned back to look down at Betsy. There was sadness on his face, a sorrow that was far deeper than disappointment in his wife's attitude. He was struggling to hold his tongue, to end the argument, but he lost the battle as he said quietly, 'He's a fine boy.'

Betsy stared up at her husband, her eyes wide with shock, whilst Fleur and Kenny could only watch in silence, mystified by what was being said. 'You've seen him?' she whispered. 'You – you've met him?'

'No, but I saw him – at a distance.' Without thinking, his glance went automatically to Fleur. It was enough for Betsy.

'He was with her? At the station? You saw him there? Today?'

Jake sighed. After all his warnings to Fleur, it was him who'd let the secret out. 'Yes, he was.' His eyes were hard as he held his wife's gaze. 'He's a fine-looking boy, Betsy.'

'I bet he is. Oh I bet he is.' Tears ran down her face once more. 'I expect he's just like his *father*!'

There was a breathless pause before Jake said, with surprising calm now, 'Yes, Betsy, he is. He's the spitting image of his father.'

Fourteen

'I seem to say nothing but "I'm sorry, darling", don't I?' Robbie said ruefully.

They had arranged to meet in Newark and travel back to Wickerton Wood together.

'So – I take it you didn't get to ask your mother?'

Robbie shook his head. 'I felt very guilty asking for compassionate leave when the old boy had got no more than a cold, but in actual fact, when I got home, he was in hospital. Pneumonia, they say.'

Fleur gasped. 'Oh no! Will he be all right?'

'I hope so. Ma will be devastated if anything happens to him. Specially now with me . . . You know?'

There was no need for him to say more: Fleur knew exactly what he meant. If anything happened to Robbie, then the old man was the only person his mother would have to cling to.

Interrupting her thoughts, Robbie said, 'I just couldn't worry her at the moment.'

'Of course you couldn't.' Fleur was quick to reassure him. 'But there is a glimmer of hope.'

'Really?' His eyes lit up.

Over their tea, Fleur recounted the strange, mystifying argument between her parents. 'And when Mum said she expected that you're just like your father, Dad said, "Yes, he is. He's the spitting image of his father."' She reached across the table and clasped his hands, leaning towards him to say earnestly, 'But you're nothing like my dad. You're fair and he's dark. He's starting to go a bit grey now, but he has brown hair. You've got blue eyes – really bright blue eyes – and his are brown. You're tall. He isn't particularly. So, where's the resemblance? I can't see it. Admittedly, your face creases up when you smile, a bit like his does, but then so do a lot of people's.' She paused and laughed. 'Old Harry's does, for a start.'

Robbie's face creased as he chuckled. 'Yeah, but he's got a lot more laughter lines on his face than I've got at the moment.'

'At the moment'. How poignant that simple phrase was. In these dangerous days how many handsome young men would never grow old enough to have a wrinkled face like Harry's?

Fleur deliberately tried to lighten their thoughts. 'Laughter lines, you call them?' she quipped. 'Nothing's that funny!'

Returning to the comparison between Robbie and her father, she went on, 'You've got a much squarer jaw than my dad and . . .' Suddenly, her voice faded away as she stared across the table at Robbie.

'What? What is it? Grown another nose, have I?'

Fleur shook her head, but she was still staring at him. 'You know, you do remind me of someone. Not my dad,' she added hastily, 'but someone . . . But for the life of me, I can't think who.'

Robbie grinned. 'Some handsome film star, I've no doubt.'

Fleur laughed out loud so that one or two folk at nearby tables smiled fondly. It was good to see two young people in uniform enjoying themselves.

'Of course,' Fleur teased. 'That must be it.'

They rose from the table, put a tip beneath the plate for the waitress and left the cafe, their arms about each other, suddenly a little freer to let their feelings show. And yet, they wouldn't be certain, not absolutely certain, until Robbie had spoken to his mother. Not until then would they allow themselves to be real girlfriend and boyfriend. Until then, they must act like the brother and sister that – God forbid – they might really be.

'You really are a grand pair of lasses to be helping us old folk like you are,' Mrs Jackson said as she shuffled across the room to set the table in time for an early tea. Both Ruth and Fleur were due to report back to camp for the evening shift. The lads – including Robbie – were flying tonight.

'It keeps us out of mischief,' Ruth laughed. 'I mean, if we weren't doing that we'd only be down the pub—'

'Or dancing—'

'Or shopping—'

They glanced at each other in mock horror.

'What *are* we thinking of?' Ruth said and Fleur giggled.

Ruth put her arm round the old lady's ample waist. 'Don't you fret, Mrs Jackson. I'm one of these strange people who actually enjoy housework. And – if I'm not mistaken – Fleur is going to get a lot of satisfaction when she sees leeks and potatoes and whatever else she's going to grow in that garden of yours.'

Fleur nodded. 'I've got it all planned out. I was asking my dad for advice when I was home at the weekend and he's given me a list of what to plant and when to plant it. I've written it all down in an old diary. I'm going to plant carrots, potatoes and cauliflowers, maybe leeks and onions too. And that rhubarb patch we unearthed when we cut the grass needs looking at. And I'll start a compost heap in the far corner. And in the other corner, I'm going to build you an Anderson shelter, Mrs Jackson.'

'Oh, don't worry about that, love. I don't think I could get there quick enough anyway. Someone did come a while back, but I told 'em I'd go round to Harry's if we got a bad raid.'

The two girls stared at the old lady. 'But . . . but Harry hasn't got a shelter either,' Ruth said.

Now Mrs Jackson looked suddenly sheepish. 'No, I know. He wouldn't accept any help from anyone and he promised the authorities he'd build one himself.'

'But he never did.'

Mrs Jackson shook her head. 'I don't think he ever intended to, the awkward ol' devil!' She smiled fondly.

'Well, you really ought to have one,' Fleur said firmly, 'especially living so close to the airfield, so we'll build one for the two of you. We'll put it in the corner of your garden nearest his and cut a hole in the fence for him to get through and you can share it. All right?'

Mary Jackson smiled. 'If you say so, dear.'

'Right – that's settled then,' Fleur said firmly. 'I'll make enquiries as to how to get hold of what we need to make one.'

'The local ARP people might know,' Ruth suggested.

'That's a good idea. Only thing now is – I could do to find a farmer nearby with a lot of pigs, and maybe cows and chickens as well.'

'Pigs!' Ruth exclaimed. 'You're not thinking of keeping pigs at the bottom of the garden, are you?'

'Mr Clegg at Top End Farm keeps pigs,' Mrs Jackson put in. She was smiling as if she'd already guessed what Fleur was talking about. 'All the villagers keep their scraps for pigswill for him. He collects two or three times a week.'

Fleur's face lit up. 'Great!'

'But what do you want them for?' Ruth persisted. 'You're not seriously thinking of having some here, are you?'

'I don't actually want the *pigs*, I just want what they produce. For the garden.'

'What they—?' Ruth's face was a picture as realization dawned. 'Oh my! Well, now I've heard it all!'

The bombing mission that night was a difficult one and the planes encountered heavy flak both over the target and along the route home, especially near the enemy coast. Fleur was careful to hide her anxiety as the bombers limped home, some with aircraft so badly damaged that it was a miracle they got back at all.

Anxiously, she waited for the call sign of D-Doggo. At last, she heard, 'Hello, Woody, this is Lindum D-Doggo. One engine u/s and wounded on board . . .'

At once, Bob Watson was standing behind the operators. 'Kay, call up number four and tell him to overshoot. Fleur, tell D-Doggo he has straight in approach. Corporal—' Bob called to the airman who manned the internal telephone. 'Call up the ambulance and fire tender.'

Fleur took a deep breath. 'Hello, D-Doggo, you are

number five to land, straight in approach, runway two-zero . . . switch to channel B.'

Calmly, her instructions were repeated and then they heard the drone of the aircraft as it approached the runway.

'His other engine doesn't sound too healthy,' Bob said. Everyone was holding their breath, trying to see out into the darkness. The aircraft touched down, the noise fading as it ran towards the end of the runway.

The radio crackled again. 'Hello, Woody, this is number five. Turned left off runway, but second engine now u/s. Over.'

From the clipped message, Fleur knew that the aircraft had been able to turn off the runway, but now it seemed that the second engine had given up on them and the plane could taxi no further under its own power.

'Help is on its way, number five,' she said into her microphone. 'Well done. Out.'

Now Fleur could breathe easily again and at once began to call up the aircraft waiting to land. It had been a close call for Tommy Laughton and his crew. The rear gunner was injured, but at least they were all home. Five planes failed to come back. Debriefing revealed that one had been seen to crash in enemy territory.

'I did see parachutes, though,' one of the pilots told Ruth.

Three aircraft had ditched in the sea, though the fate of the crews was unknown and one plane couldn't be accounted for at all.

D-Doggo was badly damaged and would be out of commission yet again for two or three days whilst the mechanics worked on it frantically. Several more planes in the same squadron needed extensive repairs before they would be airworthy.

'I've got a seventy-two, so I'm going home. And this time, I really will speak to Ma,' Robbie promised Fleur. 'What about you? Can you get any leave?'

She shook her head. 'No. Sounds like there's a big op on for tomorrow night. We're on duty.'

A fleeting look of regret crossed Robbie's face. 'And I'll miss it,' he murmured. Fleur looked at him incredulously, shaking her head slowly. She said nothing, but she was wondering just what it was about these young men that made them want to be in the thick of danger. Was it the excitement? And was that excitement all the more thrilling because it was dangerous? She didn't know. All she knew was that Kenny craved that same kick.

Robbie put his arm about her waist. 'I'm sorry you can't get leave too. We could have met up. Spent some time together.'

'I know,' she said softly, anguished at the thought of not being able to spend every precious minute with him. 'But maybe it'll be worth it if you do get a chance to talk to your mother.'

'I'll make sure I do this time. I promise.'

Fifteen

Fleur attacked the gardening work with a vigour born of anxiety and frustration. Anything, to keep her mind from wandering to Robbie and what was being said between him and his mother.

She double dug an area down one side of the garden ready for planting potatoes, then levelled an area nearby to plant carrots and cauliflowers. After that she carefully weeded the rhubarb patch. Then she marked out the oblong shape for the Anderson shelter and began to dig out the hole. The ground was hard and the effort back-breaking.

Taking a break about mid morning, she went into the house to find Mrs Jackson standing at the kitchen table rolling out pastry. Beside her was a container of shrivelled-looking rings.

'What on earth are those?' Fleur asked.

Mrs Jackson chuckled. 'Dried apple rings.'

'Dried? I've never heard of doing that.'

'Oh, they come out quite well if you soak them and then use them in a pie.'

'My mum always bottles all her fruit. She's got a cooker as well as the old range and she uses a huge metal container. A big box-like thing . . .' Fleur demonstrated its size with her hands. 'It holds about eight bottles at once. And she packs all the fruit into them with syrup and then boils them for – oh, I don't know how long.'

Mrs Jackson was nodding. 'Yes, I used to do something similar in the oven with Kilner jars, but since Arthur went I haven't had the heart. Truth is, I found it too hard to get the fruit picked.'

Fleur put her arm around the old lady's shoulders. 'Well, this year we'll harvest it all and we'll see what we can do then, eh?'

Mary Jackson smiled. 'That'd be lovely, dear. My Arthur would be so thrilled to think all his hard work hadn't been wasted. He planted those fruit trees, y'know, when we was first married. There's two apple trees and a Victoria plum as well as raspberry canes and gooseberry bushes. Just before our Eddie was born, it was. And he built that bench under the apple tree so's I could sit down there with the pram.'

'Eddie? Who's Eddie.'

The old lady's face fell into lines of sorrow. 'Our boy. Our son. Our *only* son.'

'And – er – where is Eddie now?' Fleur held her breath. For some reason she feared the answer.

'He was killed in the last war. On the Somme.'

'Oh, Mrs Jackson, I am sorry.' She paused, before asking tentatively, 'Have – have you any other children?'

'Two daughters. Phyllis and Joyce.'

Fleur waited for Mrs Jackson to volunteer the information herself. 'Phyllis is married and lives down south. She . . . she doesn't get home much, but she writes every week.'

Fleur nodded. She had seen the letters arriving regularly and had posted replies for the old lady, although she hadn't known they were addressed to Mary's daughter.

'And . . . and Joyce?'

Mrs Jackson was silent for a moment, concentrating on rolling out the pastry for the apple pie. Her voice was husky with sadness when she did answer. 'Joyce was only seventeen when she started courting a lad from the village. She . . . she got herself into trouble.'

Fleur said nothing, knowing that in such a small community the gossips would've had a field day.

'They got married but . . . but she died having the bairn. She was only just eighteen.'

Fleur's eyes filled with tears. 'Oh, Mrs Jackson, how sad. I'm so sorry. And . . . and what happened to her baby?'

'A little boy, it was, but his daddy – the whole family, in fact – moved away. They've kept in touch and I've seen him a few times while he's been growing up. I've always sent him a little something at Christmas and on his birthday.'

How sad that must be for the old lady, Fleur thought. The boy's birthday would also be the anniversary of his mother's death.

'He . . . he's seventeen now.' Mrs Jackson's expression was suddenly anxious. 'I expect he'll be called up when he's old enough. If . . . if it's not over by then.'

'Same age as Kenny.'

'That's right. Your Kenny reminds me of Simon in some ways. Same cheeky grin.' Now she smiled fondly.

'Do you mind Kenny coming here? I mean, I wouldn't want it to upset you if he reminds you—'

'Mind? Heavens, no, dear. I like him to come. He's a lovely lad.'

'Has Phyllis any children?'

Mary laughed fondly. 'Oh yes. Four. Two boys and two girls. Clever, wasn't she?'

Fleur laughed too, glad to move on to a happier note. But still, even with her other grandchildren, it seemed Mary had worries.

'One of the girls is in the WAAFs like you and the other is in the Land Army. The eldest boy is a fighter pilot. We were very worried last year when the Battle of Britain was going on. He was in the thick of it. But he's all right, thank the Good Lord. And the youngest boy, well, he's only thirteen. I hope it'll all be over by the time he reaches call-up age.'

'Oh, my goodness, let's hope so,' Fleur said fervently.

There was a silence between them as Mrs Jackson shaped her pastry to fit the pie dish.

'Has Harry any family?'

'Not now. They only had one child – a boy – and he was killed an' all in the last lot. Ypres, I think it was.'

Fleur couldn't think of anything to say. How sad it was for these lonely old people and now they were being plunged into another terrible war. Hearing about Mrs Jackson's loss and old Harry's made Fleur understand her mother's fears a little more. What she couldn't understand was Betsy's vehement hatred of Meg and her son. Surely, in such troubled times past animosities and feuds should be laid aside, forgotten and forgiven. Whatever could have happened to make her mother so bitter and resentful against Robbie's?

Outside again, Fleur eyed the area she had marked out for the Anderson shelter with a frown. She'd made a start but was getting tired now, and she had to remember that she still had a full eight-hour night shift to do.

'I'll do a bit in the front garden,' she decided. 'The ground might be a bit softer there.'

She hadn't been digging for many minutes when she heard the familiar, 'Hi, Sis.'

Fleur looked up at the sound of squeaking brakes as Kenny slithered to a halt at the gate. He jumped off his bike, reared it against the fence and straddled the gate without bothering to open it. Fleur grinned and leant on her fork. 'Hello. What brings you here?'

'To see my sister, of course.' Kenny grinned and the twinkle in his eyes told the rest.

'Really?' Fleur teased with a wry note of disbelief in her tone. Then she capitulated and laughed. 'It's good to see you – whatever the reason. But shouldn't you be at school?'

'Nope. Our school's sharing with another that got bombed out. So we go in the morning and they have the afternoons. And before you say anything – yes, I have taken this morning off to get here, but don't tell Mum, will you?'

'You bad lad!' Fleur laughed again, but Kenny knew she wouldn't give him away.

'What are you going to do here?' He changed the subject, pointing to the newly turned earth at her feet.

'I thought runner beans. I'll get them planted and then build a frame from canes for the plants to climb. I've seen a bundle in Harry's shed.' She lowered her voice. 'And Mrs Jackson said that her Arthur always used to grow her a row of sweet peas. They're her favourite flowers. I'd love to grow some for her, but I don't think I dare.'

Kenny frowned thoughtfully. 'Wait a minute. What

about . . . ?' He moved to the corner of the cottage furthest away from Harry's cottage and pointed at the end wall. 'Down this narrow border here. It's not much use for anything else, and behind that big bush she's got there near the fence, it won't be easily seen from the road. I reckon you could get away with it there. And if the authorities say anything . . .' he shrugged. 'Then you'll just have to rip 'em up again.'

Fleur beamed at him. 'You clever old thing. That'd be perfect. It'd just take a narrow frame, wouldn't it?'

'And it'll get a bit of sun,' Kenny added. 'Not much, but enough. Mind you, you're a bit late now for getting sweet peas sown, aren't you?'

'Dad's got some seedlings, hasn't he?'

Kenny's face cleared. 'So he has. I'd forgotten. I'll bring you a trayful next time I come.'

'Meantime, I'll get that narrow border dug over and a cane frame built, but not a word to her.'

'Won't she see it?'

Fleur shook her head. 'Doubtful. She only comes out once a week to go to church and then she walks round the other end of the cottage and down this front path.' She stood a moment and glanced towards the other end of the building. 'No, she'll not see it. Not unless she goes that end deliberately – and I don't think she will.'

'Mum's the word then, until you present her with a bouquet of sweet peas.'

Fleur hugged herself. 'I can't wait to see her face.' Then her expression sobered. 'Talking of "mum" – is everybody all right at home?'

Kenny laughed. 'Right as they'll ever be. She's still adamant that if I apply for college, I won't be called up, and nothing we say will persuade her any different.'

He pulled a face. 'I reckon when the time comes, she'll march into the nearest recruiting office and tell them I'm not going and that's it.'

Fleur wasn't laughing. 'You know,' she said seriously, 'she might very well do just that.'

'Eh?' Kenny looked scandalized. 'I was only joking. Oh, Sis, she wouldn't really, would she?'

'She'll do anything to stop you going. Anything she can. She'll use the "reserved occupation" argument and anything else she can think of. She certainly might apply to the local War Agricultural Executive Committee for your exemption.'

'But it wouldn't work, would it? I mean – they wouldn't take any notice of a chap's mother, would they?'

'If she makes a proper application as your employer, then, yes, I think they might.'

'Does she know that?' he asked worriedly.

Fleur shrugged. 'If she doesn't yet, she'll soon make enquiries and find out. You can be sure of that.'

'Fleur, I want to go. Just like you.'

'Oh, don't say that, Kenny.' Fleur groaned. 'You make me feel so guilty.'

Kenny shook his head. 'That's not what I mean. I'd go anyway – I've told you that already – even if you hadn't volunteered.'

Fleur looked at him, wanting to believe him but not sure she could. She had set an example to her younger brother and he didn't want to be outdone by her. If anything happened to him . . .

'Right then, where do you want me to start?' Kenny interrupted her maudlin thoughts with his ready grin and willing pair of hands. 'By the way,' he added, trying to sound nonchalant, 'Ruth here, is she?'

'She'll be home later. She should be back before you go. But, yes, I would be glad of your help.'

Kenny grinned. 'More digging? I thought you'd've got it finished by now.'

'It is – more or less – but I want to build an Anderson shelter that both Mrs Jackson and Harry can share. Down the bottom of the garden. I've made a start, but the ground's so hard.'

'Right-o. I'll help you dig out the foundations.'

'Actually, there's something else I'd rather you helped me with today, if you would.'

'Oh yes. What's that then?'

'I've made arrangements to go up to Top End Farm and see about some manure. If I can get some for this afternoon, I was hoping to get it dug in tomorrow. I'll be off all day after tonight's shift. In fact I'm not on again until the day after tomorrow in the afternoon, so I'll get a good long go at it. But now you're here.' She smiled archly at him. 'You could help me dig it in this afternoon. I was going to ask Robbie, but his plane's grounded for repairs and he's gone home to see his mother, so I thought I might twist Ruth's arm to lend a hand.'

Kenny guffawed loudly. 'I don't think you'll get either of that pair of townies to deal with a pile of—'

'Careful, Kenny,' Fleur laughed. 'Mrs Jackson's a lady. It's "manure" to her.'

Her brother's grin widened. 'I'll try to remember, Sis. She's a sweet old dear. I wouldn't want to upset her. She reminds me of Gran.'

They were both silent for a moment, remembering

with affection their father's mother who had lived with them for the last two years of her life.

'She is a bit, I suppose. Gran had arthritis just like her.'

'And she's round and waddly – just like Gran.' After another brief pause, Kenny said, 'Right then, what about this – manure? How are we to get it here?'

'I saw the farmer. Mr Clegg. He said if I went up today, I could have one of his horses and his cart. I've to do the loading up that end and the unloading this end and take the horse and cart back before I go on duty.'

'Sounds as if it's a good job I've come then.'

'Bro, you don't know how glad I am to see you.'

'You only want me for my brawn,' Kenny teased, flexing his muscles.

'Absolutely!' she retorted, but brother and sister smiled at each other with deep affection.

They walked the half-mile through the village until, a short distance after the houses ended, Fleur pointed to a rough track leading down a slight incline towards a farmhouse and outbuildings nestling in a natural shallow vale. Kenny glanced around him. 'Is this what they call the Lincolnshire Wolds?'

'I'm not sure. I think they're a bit further east. More in the centre of the county. And then there's the Lincoln Edge. Not so flat as people think, is it? I think it's flatter to the east – towards the sea and in the south of the county.'

'Oh yeah. What they call the fens down there, isn't it? Mind you, you can see why it's ideal for all the airfields they're building, can't you? I heard someone call it "bomber county" the other day.'

'Really?' Fleur was thoughtful for a moment. 'Well,

yes, I can see why they might call it that. Right,' she said more briskly as they reached the farm. 'Now, where is Mr Clegg?'

'Well, there's his horse and cart standing over there near that pile of . . .' He grinned. 'Manure. And if I'm not mistaken, someone's already started loading.'

As he spoke, a forkful of manure flew up in the air and landed with a thud on the growing pile in the back of the cart. As they approached, Fleur stroked the horse's nose and patted his neck. 'Now, big feller,' she murmured.

Hearing her voice, the man at the back of the cart straightened up. 'Na' then, lass. Thought I'd mek a start for ya.'

The farmer was a big man, tall and broad with iron muscles standing out on his arms. He wore heavy workaday boots, dark green corduroy trousers that had seen better days, a striped, collarless shirt and a checked cap. Mr Clegg nodded towards Kenny. 'Brought reinforcements, I see. Yar young man, is it?'

'My brother.'

'Pleased to meet you, young feller.'

Kenny stuck out his hand, 'Kenny Bosley, sir. Pleased to meet you, an' all.'

The farmer blinked down at the young man's outstretched hand. 'Oh, I don't think I'd better shek yar hand, lad. Not with my mucky 'un.'

Kenny laughed. 'We're used to it, Mr Clegg. Born and bred on a farm. Never afraid of good, clean dirt, our dad always says.' He nodded comically towards the manure heap. 'And especially not this that's going to do Mrs Jackson's garden a power of good.'

The big man laughed loudly. 'Ah well, in that case, lad, put it there.' And the two shook hands.

'It's very good of you to let us have it,' Fleur said.

'Pleased to get rid of some of it. I keep pigs, cows an' chickens so there's plenty to go at. Mind you, you'd be surprised at the number of folks asking for it nowadays. Now then, if I can hand over to you, I must get on wi' me other work. Just mind you have old Prince here back for 'is tea, else 'ee's likely to get a bit cussed and take off on his own. Trouble is,' he added, laughing, 'he knows 'is way home so 'ee won't think twice about it.' He paused and eyed Kenny again, his gaze running up and down him as if assessing him. Bluntly, though not unkindly, Mr Clegg said, 'Home on a spot of leave, a' ya, lad?'

The flush rose in Kenny's face at once. 'Well, no, actually . . .'

'Ah, reserved occupation, is it? On yar dad's farm?' Now there was the tiniest note of disapproval in his tone.

Fleur caught and held the big man's gaze. Quietly, she said, 'Kenny's only seventeen, Mr Clegg.'

'I'll be joining up next year,' Kenny put in. 'Soon as I can.'

Mr Clegg smiled. 'That's the spirit, lad. Pleased to hear it.' His face sobered. 'Same as me own boy. He joined up, though his mam wanted him to stay wi' me on the farm. But I was in the last lot. Two years in the trenches, I was, and never a scratch.' He paused before saying in a low voice, 'I was lucky, though. I know that.'

Fleur nodded. 'Our dad was too. He was wounded and has a stiff leg, but at least he came back.' She bit her lip before she added quietly, 'A lot from the town never did.'

'Aye,' the big farmer sighed heavily. 'Bad business,

it was. And now they've no more sense than to get us involved in another one.' He sighed. 'Aye well, I wish you luck, young feller. When you go. Good luck to you.'

Kenny nodded. 'And I hope your son's – all right.'

'Aye, so do I, lad. So do I. He's all we've got. If owt happens to him, the missis will never forgive me.' His voice was low as he added, 'Won't forgive mesen, if it comes to that.' Then briskly he shook himself and smiled. 'Aye well, let's not dwell on all that. Not when there's work to be done. Look, I tell you what, you carry on here now loading up and if I've got me own work done, I'll see if I can come with you. Give you a bit of a hand, like.'

'Oh, Mr Clegg. Are you sure? You must have such a lot to do, 'specially if you're on your own now.'

'Aye, there is. But I'm never too busy to help a neighbour. Old Arthur Jackson used to work for me, see? Good man, he was. Worked on this farm most of his life – well, the latter part of it anyway. I'd like to help his widow.'

Fleur and Kenny grinned at him. 'Then we'll gladly accept your offer,' Fleur said.

'Right you are, then. Come and find me when you're ready to go. In fact, come to the back door of the house. I'm sure the missis will find you a drink and a bit of summat to eat.'

'There you are, you see,' Kenny said, as the farmer moved out of earshot. 'What did I tell you? Even a nice man like Mr Clegg questions why a big lad like me isn't in uniform.'

'Yes, but you soon will be, won't you?'

'Yeah,' Kenny said, firmly. 'And the sooner the better.'

137

At that moment, a cloud crossed the sun and a sharp breeze brought a chill to the bright day. Fleur shuddered, then snatched up the fork and attacked the pile of manure as if her life – and Kenny's too – depended upon it.

'By heck, you've done a grand job with this back garden,' Mr Clegg said three hours later as he stood surveying all their hard work.

'My sister's done most of it,' Kenny said and then, as Fleur walked away from them to fetch mugs of tea, he added slyly, 'when she's not on duty at the airfield.'

The farmer's eyebrows rose. 'Yon lass? She's in the forces?'

Kenny nodded. 'She's a WAAF. She's an R/T operator. Talks to all the aircraft when they land. That sort of thing.'

Mr Clegg pulled a face. 'Tough job. Specially if you get to know the airmen, like.'

'There's one she's particularly close to,' Kenny confided.

'Not the best place to be then,' the big man murmured, but as Fleur came back their conversation ceased.

'How are we going to get it all round to the back?' she asked, handing out the mugs of tea.

'Tell you what,' the farmer suggested. 'I'll take it round into the field at the bottom of her garden and tip it there. It'll be easier to chuck it over the fence.'

Fleur eyed the grass field where cows grazed contentedly. 'Will the farmer who owns that field mind, d'you think?'

The big man laughed. 'Shouldn't think so. Them's my cows and it's my field.'

When Ruth arrived home, she stood staring in astonishment at the farmer on top of a pile of manure in the neighbouring field, rhythmically flinging forkfuls over the fence into the garden. Then at Fleur and Kenny, who were moving it and spreading it over the surface of the garden and digging it into the earth. All three of them were red faced and sweating, but they worked on as a team.

Kenny looked up and grinned at her. 'Hi, Ruth. Come to lend a hand?'

Fleur looked up and grinned mischievously. 'There's another fork over there.'

'Not on your nelly!' Ruth was horrified. She wrinkled her nose. 'Pooh, what a pong.'

Fleur closed her eyes and breathed in deeply. 'Nothing like it. Best perfume in the world.'

'Dead right there's nothing like it, but I don't know about the last bit. *Eau de cochon*? No thanks! Count this townie out. Tell you what, though, I'll make you all a nice cuppa. Will that do?'

There was a heartfelt unanimous chorus of 'Yes, please', and Ruth held up her hand, fingers spread out. 'Give me five minutes to get out of my uniform.'

'Sounds heaven,' Fleur called.

The promised minutes later, they stood in the tiny back yard, drinking tea, eating scones and admiring their handiwork.

'What a' ya thinking of planting, lass?' Mr Clegg looked to Fleur as the leader of the venture.

'Potatoes, carrots, leeks, cabbages. Runner beans in

139

the front garden. Oh don't let's forget to take some of the manure round the front.'

'It'll cost you a fortune to grow all that lot,' Ruth exclaimed.

'Dad's promised me some seeds.'

'Now mebbe I can help you there,' the farmer put in. 'I'll have a word with the locals and see if we can put a bit of a collection together. Not money, lass,' he added hastily. 'But a few seed 'taties, an' that.'

Fleur's eyes filled with tears. 'Oh, how kind of you. That'd be wonderful.'

'Aye well,' the man said gruffly, touched by her gratitude, 'we've all got to pull together. All got to do our bit. There is—'

And they all chorused together, '. . . a war on, you know.'

Sixteen

Later the following morning, after a few hours' sleep, Fleur reluctantly returned to digging out the foundations for the Anderson shelter. She'd managed to dig the oblong shape to a depth of about a foot when the curved sheets of corrugated steel arrived for the shelter.

'Ya'll need to be another three foot down, luv,' the man who made the delivery advised, nodding his head towards the hole.

'I know. It's harder than I thought. This ground hasn't been dug over for some time and certainly not four-foot deep.'

'Ah, well, I wish I could give you a hand but I've still three more shelters to deliver today. I'd best be getting on . . .'

'Would you like a cup of tea?' Fleur asked.

'Nah, lass, ah'm all right. Had one at the last house.' He set off back along the narrow garden path, having deposited his delivery near where Fleur was working. 'Good luck, lass. I reckon you're going to need it.'

'Thanks!' Fleur muttered wryly but she gave him a cheery wave.

She'd dug for another ten minutes and then sat on the edge of the hole for a breather when she heard the chugging sound of an engine that sounded vaguely familiar. 'Can't be,' she muttered. The noise died away and she shrugged, stood up and, with a sigh, picked up her spade once more.

She'd dug five more spadefuls when a voice said, 'You look as if you could use a little help, love.'

Fleur stopped, looked up and then dropped her spade with a squeal of delight. She flung her arms wide as she scrambled out of the hole. 'Dad! And Kenny too! Whatever are you doing here?' Her face clouded. 'Oh, there's nothing wrong, is there? Is Mum all right?'

'She's fine,' Jake laughed as he gathered his daughter, earthy hands and all, into a bear hug.

'Then why are you here?'

'A little bird told me you were planning to put up an Anderson for the old folk to use and finding the digging a bit tough.' He shrugged. 'So, here we are. We thought a little help wouldn't come amiss.'

'Come amiss!' Fleur echoed. 'You're heaven sent!'

'Right,' Kenny grinned. 'I'll go and get the tools out of the boot while you take Dad to meet Mrs Jackson. And I've no doubt Harry will be popping his head over the fence any minute now . . .'

Right on cue, as they moved towards Mrs Jackson's cottage, the old man appeared round the corner with his usual greeting, 'Now then, lass.'

Fleur and Kenny leant against each other, unable to stem their laughter, but Jake merely smiled broadly and moved towards the old man, his hand outstretched. 'You must be Harry. I've heard a lot about you. I'm Jake Bosley, Fleur and Kenny's dad.'

Harry beamed as he shook hands. 'I'm real glad to meet you. You've a fine couple o' bairns, Mr Bosley.'

'Jake – please.'

If it could, Harry's beam widened even further. 'Have you met Mary yet?'

'No. We were just on our way in to say "hello" before we get digging.'

'Ah. Come to give the lass a bit of a hand have you. It's a big job on her own and I'm afraid I'm past that sort of digging mesen else I'd've . . .'

'Of course,' Jake said and put his hand on the old man's shoulder.

'Well, come and meet Mary. I'll introduce you. She'll be glad to meet you an' all. Thinks a lot of yon lass, an' that lad o' yourn an' all. Tells me he can't wait to join up.'

Jake's face sobered. 'Aye.'

Harry stopped on his way towards the back door of the cottage and faced Jake in surprise. 'You don't sound too pleased about it.'

Jake sighed. For some reason he couldn't at this precise moment fathom, he felt he could confide in the old man. 'It's not me, it's his mam. She . . . she wants to keep her chicks safely at home and because we live on a farm she can't understand why they even want to go.'

'Were you in the last lot?'

'Aye. I volunteered.'

'Then *you* know why they want to be involved?'

Jake nodded. 'Oh yes. I know why.'

'We lost our lad in the last war. Nearly broke my Doris's heart when the telegram came. But we were still proud of him. To this day, I'm proud of him. The only sad thing is that these youngsters have got to do it all again now. Don't seem right, does it?'

'No. It doesn't. But they'll do it. They'll do it all right.'

'Oh, I know that. Whilst we've got young 'uns like yourn there . . .' He nodded towards Fleur and Kenny. 'And that young feller of hers, then we'll win. No doubt about that. It's just – well – what we might lose along the way, eh?'

Now Jake couldn't speak for the sudden fear that arose in his throat, so he just gently squeezed the old man's shoulder.

Harry nodded understandingly and then opened the door and called cheerily, 'Hello, Mary, love. Got a visitor for you. Fleur's dad.'

Mrs Jackson was standing at the kitchen table, her hands floury as she rolled out pastry. She looked up and smiled a welcome as Harry opened the door and ushered Jake into the room.

'Sorry I can't shake hands but come in, do. You're very welcome.' She glanced beyond him. 'Is your wife with you?'

'Er – no. She stayed to mind the farm. But Kenny's here.'

Mrs Jackson's beam plumped up her cheeks so that her glasses rose. 'He's a lovely boy. So helpful. Please, Mr Bosley, do sit down. I'll make a cup of tea.'

'No, no, don't trouble just now. We've come to help Fleur with the shelter for you both.'

Mrs Jackson gasped and pushed up her glasses to wipe a tear away, leaving a smudge of flour on her face. 'How kind you all are.'

At that moment Kenny pushed open the back door and deposited a box on Mrs Jackson's table. 'Just a few eggs and a bit of butter from our dairy. And I think there's a chicken in there.' He grinned. 'Plucked and dressed with my own fair hands.' He nodded towards Harry. 'It's for you both. And we killed a pig last week. Dad's got a licence, of course. So there's some sausages and a piece of pork. Oh, and a couple of rabbits as well, but I haven't had time to skin them. But Fleur can do them for you.'

'Oh, I don't know what to say. I really don't.' Mrs Jackson was lost for words.

'You're looking after Fleur for us, Mrs Jackson. It's the very least we can do,' Jake said softly. 'Now, where's that pick we brought, Kenny? We'd best get cracking.'

The earth yielded willingly to Jake's experienced wielding of the pointed pickaxe. When he paused for a breather, Kenny shovelled out the broken-up earth whilst Fleur ferried mugs of tea down the path. The hole sank steadily deeper. 'Don't make yourself late, Dad. You ought to get home before milking time.'

'Just a few minutes more, luv, and I think it'll be deep enough. Can you manage to put up the shelter?'

'Yes, Robbie and Ruth will give me a hand with that as soon as they can.'

'Where is Ruth? Is she due back soon?' Kenny asked, pausing for a breather and mopping his forehead.

'No, sorry, she's on duty.'

Kenny's face fell. 'Oh well, give her my love, won't you?'

Jake climbed out of the hole and brushed the earth from his trousers. 'There. I think that'll do.'

As they gathered the tools together to take back to the car, Fleur said, 'Where've you built one at home?'

'I haven't.' Jake laughed. 'I can't see us getting bombed in the middle of nowhere, can you? It's different for these folk here, though. They're likely to catch a few stray bombs being aimed at the airfield.'

145

'Oh, Dad, I think you should build one. You never know.'

'But we can't even hear the sirens, love. Only very faintly in the distance and then only if we happen to be outside. If we're in bed asleep, we'd never hear them anyway. Besides, your mam'd never use it. "Can't waste my time sitting in here when there's work to be done," she'd say. You know she would.'

'You might have to build one if you're going to have Land Army girls.'

'I don't think I need them. Old Ron says he'll lend a hand when he can.'

Old Ron, as Jake now called him, and his family had lived in a cottage on Middleditch Farm for as long as Fleur could remember. He'd worked for her father and for the Smallwoods before that until his retirement a few years earlier. He was still fit and healthy and liked to help out at lambing and at harvest time.

'You will when I go, Dad,' Kenny said, throwing the spades into the back of the car.

Jake sighed. 'Aye well, I'll think about that when the time comes.'

'You off, then?' Harry hobbled round the corner of the cottage and stood beside Fleur as they all said their goodbyes.

'Well, I think so, unless you can come back with us, Fleur? Kenny said he didn't think you were on duty until tomorrow afternoon. Will it be all right? We could be sure to get you back tomorrow morning.'

Fleur forced a smile. Part of her didn't really want to go home, didn't want to face more antagonism and censure from her mother, yet she could see that both Jake and Kenny wanted to snatch another few hours with her. 'I'll risk it. I'll just get my things . . .'

As she ran upstairs she was thinking: at least it might keep my mind off Robbie; but in her heart she knew it wouldn't. Oh I wonder if he's asked her yet, she couldn't help thinking as she slipped out of her workaday clothes and back into her uniform. I wonder if he knows already . . .

Seventeen

'Mother dear . . .' Robbie began, using the more formal address he'd adopted as quite a young boy when he was trying to wheedle his way around her.

Meg smiled archly at him. 'Oho, and what is it you're wanting now?'

He took her hand and led her to sit on the sofa in front of the fire. 'I need to talk to you.'

He'd been at home for two days and was due to return to camp the next morning. He was glad to have been there for he'd been on hand to help his mother bring his grandfather home from the hospital. The old man was much better, glad to be home and tucked up warmly in his own room upstairs. And now was Robbie's last chance to talk to his mother.

'Oh dear, this sounds serious,' Meg said gaily. 'What have you been up to now? Have I got to write an apologetic letter to your commanding officer – just like I had to so many times to your headmaster?'

Robbie forced a laugh, though at this moment he didn't feel like laughing. His mother, sensitive to her beloved son's feelings, said softly, 'What is it, love? Something's troubling you, I can see that.'

'Ma – I want to ask you about my father.'

He heard her pull in breath sharply and her green eyes were suddenly round, dark pools of anxiety.

My God, Meg was thinking. He's heard something.

They've told him something. It must have been that day just after he'd first met her. He must have gone to the farm, met Fleur's parents . . . They must have said something.

I should have tried to stop him seeing Fleur, she thought in panic. But how could I, she asked herself, her mind in a turmoil, when they're stationed on the same camp? She licked her dry lips and said unsteadily, 'What about your father?'

'There's no easy way to put this, Ma, so I'll just come right out and say it.'

'Don't you always?' she murmured, though her heart was thumping madly in her chest. Her son was one of the most honest, reliable and straightforward people she had ever known in her life. Even more so than Jake.

Jake, oh Jake! What did you say to him? Are you still so bitter after all this time that you would wreak such a revenge on me?

Clasped in his huge, warm hands, Meg's own hand trembled. Robbie felt it. 'It's all right, Ma. I don't want to upset you, dearest, but I have to know. It's important to me. To me and Fleur.'

Meg's head shot up. 'You – and Fleur?'

'Uh-huh. We . . . we want to go on seeing each other, but there's something going on that we don't understand. That we don't know about. Ever since we met, it's . . . it's been very . . .' He sought for the right word. 'It's been very strange. In fact, it started that very first day when you were so surprised to hear Fleur's name.'

Meg tried to pull her hand away from his, but he held her fast, though gently. She gave a huge sigh and sagged against his shoulder. She closed her eyes for a moment and two tears squeezed their way out from under her eyelids and ran down her face, making a salty rivulet down her carefully applied face powder.

'Oh, Ma, don't cry. I hate to do this, but we *have* to know.' Gently, he wiped her tears away. It was so like Jake's tender gesture all those years before – the very last time she had seen him – that her tears just flowed all the harder. 'And then when you thought it best if you didn't go with me to Fleur's home. And you were right. When I got there – well, to tell the truth, I didn't even get as far as the farm. Fleur met me in the lane and said that when she'd told her parents about me, her mother had become hysterical, shouting and screaming and saying all kinds of – well – odd things. Things that Fleur couldn't understand.' He paused but his mother was silent, trying to put off the dreaded moment for as long as possible.

I'll lose him, Meg was thinking. If he finds out the truth, he'll have nothing more to do with me. Oh, and I've tried so hard over the last few years to make amends for all the wicked things I did. I've tried so hard, Jake, I truly have. She took a deep breath and said, 'All right. What is it you want to know?'

'Was . . . was Percy Rodwell my real father?'

Meg raised her head slowly and looked into his eyes – her dearest, darling boy who'd been conceived in a few moments of passion with a man she now realized she'd never truly loved. A man who, though infatuated with her, had been too afraid of losing his standing in the eyes of the community. A man who'd deserted her when she had needed him most. There was only one man she'd ever really loved in her whole life, only she had been too blind, too grasping, too afraid of living a life of poverty, to recognize it. And now this son of hers, who'd grown up to be such a wonderful human being, the son whom she had almost given away to that dreadful woman, was going to find out all about her. All her sins were going to be revealed and she would have to pay the price. This was to be her punishment.

She was going to lose him.

His hands tightened around hers until he was hurting her. 'Who is my father, Ma?' he demanded harshly. 'Is it Fleur's dad? Are we . . . are we half-brother and sister?'

'Jake!' The relief flooded through Meg. So this was what it was all about. 'Oh no, no, it wasn't Jake.' She laughed, light-headed with relief.

He was still holding her hand tightly, but now she didn't mind. 'Is that really true? We're not related in any way? Me and Fleur, I mean?'

Meg shook her head. 'No, you're not.'

His grip on her relaxed and he let out the longest sigh she'd ever heard as if releasing all the tension inside him.

She swallowed and tried to ask casually, 'Whatever gave you that idea?' She was regaining her composure now enough to pretend offence. 'And fancy thinking such a thing of your mother.'

'Oh, Ma, I'm sorry.' He drew her into his bear hug and she stayed there, closing her eyes with thankfulness. 'It's just . . . it's just some of the things Fleur's mother said when she was having her "ducky fit" as Fleur called it.'

An inner voice was telling Meg to let it lie, to ask no more, but before she could stop the words coming out, she'd said, 'What did she say?' And when he told her, she closed her eyes again. Was it true? Had Jake loved her all these years, just as she had loved him? But Robbie's voice was dragging her back to the present and now his words filled her with dread once more.

'And there was something else funny happened. We met a woman in a cafe in the town and she seemed about to pass out at the sight of me. Fleur called her "Aunt Louisa". She was the local doctor's wife.'

'My dear, what is it? You don't seem yourself? Are you ill? I could prescribe something for you if—'

'Don't fuss, Philip. I'm perfectly all right.'

Philip Collins blinked. It was so totally out of character for his wife to snap in such a way. Louisa was usually so calm, serene and in control of herself. She was the perfect wife for a doctor, for any man, if it came to that. And yet . . . He sighed inwardly. She was beautiful. She dressed elegantly and was a perfect receptionist for his patients. She soothed them and marshalled them with a gentle hand. She smoothed his path through life and had supported him in everything he had ever done.

So why, oh why, could he not forget the red-haired firebrand with whom he'd once fancied himself in love? He'd almost given up everything for her; his infatuation for the passionate, persuasive young woman had nearly been his downfall. But he'd not had the courage, if that was the right word to apply to what would have been such an act of betrayal. Betrayal of his wife, his upbringing and his vocation. It would have meant the end of his career as a doctor, and he'd realized that he loved that more than any human being. More even than *her*.

So he had turned his back on his mistress and her son and for the last twenty-two years he'd lived a model life as the caring doctor, the dutiful husband with a perfect wife. There was only one thing that disappointed him and now it was never spoken of between them. It was the tragedy of their lives that he and Louisa had never been blessed with children. Was it a punishment, he had so often wondered, because he had not been man enough to shoulder his responsibilities, as a man of honour would have done?

He had always loved Louisa – of course he had, ever since he'd met her when she was a lowly school-marm, struggling to support her widowed mother. But he had to admit now that he'd never quite loved her with the unbridled passion he'd felt for—

Louisa was reaching out to him across the dinner table. 'I'm so sorry, Philip dear. I didn't mean to be snappy. It's just this war. All the privations, the anxiety I see on the faces of all your patients, especially those with husbands or sons or sweethearts in the services. I . . . I . . .' She hesitated, about to touch on something which had always been a painful subject between them. 'I never thought I'd say it, Philip,' she whispered. 'But I'm almost glad we didn't have children, if that's the heartbreak it brings.'

Philip patted her hand and smiled thinly. His blue eyes were kindly yet shadowed with hidden thoughts and memories, but he said nothing. Whatever he was thinking, he kept it to himself.

She couldn't tell him the truth, the real reason for her bout of bad temper; she was worried sick in case he ever came face to face with the young man she'd seen with Fleur Bosley. Robbie Rodwell. Meg's boy. What would happen if Philip saw him? She felt sick at

153

the thoughts that tumbled around her mind in a riot of fear. Would he see the likeness? Of course he would. It would be like turning the clock back and looking into the mirror of his youth. She wondered if he'd always known. She remembered Meg coming to the house once with the child in her arms, but what had passed between doctor and patient remained a secret behind the surgery door.

Had Philip known Meg's boy was his son? Perhaps he had and he'd kept the secret from her, his wife, all these years. So, Louisa thought bitterly, the whispered gossip all those years ago had been true. There had been something between Philip and Meg. It was obvious now and, surely, neither of them could deny it any longer. You only had to look at the boy to see the truth.

She wasn't sure which hurt her the most. The fact that her husband had been unfaithful to her, had had a son all this time, or the fact that he had never told her about any of it.

So, Meg was thinking at that very same moment, Louisa has seen him. Mechanically, she tucked her father in bed and saw that the lamp and the glass of water were in easy reach on the bedside table, but her mind was elsewhere. She was so thankful her father was home from hospital and out of danger, but he'd need careful nursing for some time. Kissing the old man's forehead, she turned off the light and went downstairs. Robbie was in bed and sleeping soundly now that she had given him the answer he wanted. He'd be up early in the morning and on his way back to camp, back to the girl he loved. Fleur Bosley.

Meg sat down in front of the dying embers of the fire. She kicked off her shoes and sighed heavily. Why Fleur? Why *Jake's* daughter? Of all the people in the world, why did Robbie have to meet her? And fall in love with her?

Fate had played a dirty trick on Meg. Yet, she was honest enough now to admit that perhaps she deserved it. She wasn't proud of some of the things she'd done as a girl, yet she'd tried to make amends. From the moment of Robbie's birth she had changed. For the first time in her life she'd loved someone more than she cared about herself. From the moment he'd stared up at her with those bright blue eyes, she had adored him, worshipped and idolized him. She'd never loved anyone quite like that before. Not even Jake, though she now knew that he'd been the love of her life up until the time her son had screamed his way into the world and wound himself around her heart.

She stared into the glowing coals. How strange life was, she mused, that her son and Jake's daughter should meet and fall in love. How ironic. And how catastrophic, for she knew without a doubt that Betsy would never agree to such a union. And yet she hadn't been able to lie to her son. It would've been so easy to tell him that, yes, they were half-brother and sister, that they couldn't – mustn't – be together. Yet she couldn't do it. She'd had to tell him the truth. There'd been enough lies and deceit in the past. It was time now for the truth to be told, whatever the consequences might be.

Much as she might have wished it all these years, Jake was not Robbie's natural father. But then, neither was her dead husband, Percy Rodwell. She shuddered afresh as she remembered Robbie's final words.

'We met a woman in a cafe in the town and she seemed about to pass out at the sight of me.'

Well, she would, wouldn't she? Meg closed her eyes and groaned aloud. Louisa would see the likeness at once.

Robbie's likeness to her own husband.

Eighteen

With trembling fingers, Louisa reached for the telephone receiver. Her heart was racing. What she was about to do was unethical, and if Philip were to find out . . . But she had to know. Years ago, when she'd heard the gossip about her husband's frequent visits to the little cottage near the church, she had dismissed them. She'd trusted Philip completely. But seeing Meg's son – the image of Philip as a young man – she feared now that the rumours had been true.

Louisa bit her lip, pulled in a deep breath and began to dial the first number on the list in front of her.

When a woman's voice answered, Louisa said, 'I'm sorry to bother you. This is Dr Collins' wife from South Monkford. My husband . . .' She faltered for a brief moment over the deliberate lie she was about to utter. 'My husband has asked me to try to trace a former patient of his. She left the district without informing us and we . . . we still have her medical records here. We know she moved to Nottingham . . .' Louisa was babbling now, a nervous note creeping into her voice. She tried to calm herself again.

The woman's voice on the other end of the telephone was stiff and uncooperative. 'The usual way is for the new doctor with whom the patient has registered to send for their records.'

'Yes, yes, I know, but . . .'

The woman unbent a little. 'Well, I will have a look and see if the patient has registered with us. Of course, there are several other doctors in the city.'

Louisa glanced down at the rather long list on the desk in front of her, hoping it wouldn't prove necessary to phone every one of them. 'Yes, yes, I realize that,' she said.

'What name is it you're looking for?'

'Meg Rodwell. Mrs Meg Rodwell.'

'Hold on one moment.'

There was a lengthy silence whilst Louisa grew more and more agitated. She glanced nervously towards the window. Philip was out on his morning rounds, but that didn't mean he might not arrive back home at any moment.

'I'm sorry.' The woman's voice sounded again in her ear. 'But we have no one of that name recorded with us.'

'Thank you for your time,' Louisa said. 'Goodbye.'

She tried four more numbers and was met with a similar reluctance to give out information. Two even refused to look for the name in their records. 'I couldn't possibly divulge such information. You could be anyone ringing up . . .'

Louisa almost slammed the receiver back into its cradle in her frustration.

On the sixth attempt a young girl's voice answered merrily, 'Good morning. Dr Gough's surgery.'

Louisa repeated her request and gave Meg's name.

'Hold on. I'll look for you.' The girl voiced no concern and Louisa felt a sudden stab of guilt that she might be getting her into trouble. But within moments the girl was back on the line. 'Yes, we have a patient of that name.'

Louisa held her breath, willing the girl to give her Meg's address without her having to ask outright for it, hoping the young receptionist wouldn't realize that Meg had been their patient for years and the story of the 'lost notes' was nothing but a ruse.

As if the gods were now smiling kindly, the girl rattled off the name of the street and even the number of Meg's home in the city.

'Thank you, thank you very much,' Louisa said weakly. As she was about to replace the receiver, the girl said, 'So you'll send her notes through to us, will you? Have you got our address?'

'Oh – oh yes. Yes, I have it here.' It was on the list in front of her. 'Thank you for your help.'

'Don't mention it,' the girl said gaily, oblivious to the fact that she had given out confidential information to a stranger.

Louisa replaced the receiver slowly. She had not even bothered to write down Meg's address. She would remember it only too well.

When Meg opened her door, it was perhaps one of the biggest shocks of her life to see the woman standing on her doorstep.

'My God!' she breathed. 'Louisa.'

The two women stared at each other until Louisa said calmly, 'Good morning, Meg. May I come in?'

Meg looked nervously up and down the street. Robbie had gone into the city, but he could be back at any moment. The last thing she wanted was for him to run into Louisa. He might start asking more awkward questions. But neither could she make Louisa unwelcome.

159

'Oh yes, I'm sorry. Of course.' Meg pulled the door wider and gestured for Louisa to step inside straight into the front room of the terraced house. 'Please excuse the mess. This is my workroom – as you can see.'

Louisa looked around her. The room was strewn with paper patterns, materials and pins. On the table in the centre of the room stood a Singer sewing machine.

'I make my living as a dressmaker,' Meg explained, gesturing nervously with a hand that still shook from the surprise. She tried to calm her whirling thoughts.

'So,' Louisa was saying smoothly. 'Your husband taught you well, did he?' She was much more in control. But then it was she who had chosen to come here. She had had time to marshal her thoughts and her emotions.

'May I offer you a cup of tea?' Meg said, ignoring the remark and playing for time. But she guessed the reason for this visit. 'Please come through to the back room. We'll be more comfortable there.' She led the way through and Louisa seated herself in front of the range whilst Meg went through into a back scullery.

As she listened to the rattle of cups and saucers, Louisa glanced about her. There was little in the room that gave any indication of Meg's former life. No photographs, no obvious relics from Percy Rodwell's house. Perhaps the only thing she had kept had been his sewing machine. No doubt, Louisa thought bitterly, it wasn't her own husband whom Meg wished to remember.

Meg came back into the room and set the tray on the table. She poured a cup of tea and offered her visitor a biscuit.

'They're rather dry, I'm afraid.' She pulled a face. 'The war, you know.'

Louisa smiled thinly and shook her head. 'No, thank you. The tea is fine.'

Meg sat down opposite, but she was still on edge, listening for any sound that heralded Robbie's return. As they sipped their tea the two women regarded each other. They each saw in the other's face the changes the years had brought.

They were each thinking that the years had been kind to the other. Louisa was dressed in smart clothes, well tailored and expensive. Whilst Meg wore a fashionable dress, she had made it herself from a length of material bought on a market stall. Louisa's complexion was smooth and well cared for. She was the epitome of a doctor's wife – serene and sweet and caring. Her hair, still black, was smoothed into a chignon and showed no sign of grey.

And Meg's too belied her age. Her luxurious red hair was swept up into waves and rolls and her figure was still slim; her legs beneath the short hem of her dress were shapely and she wore silk stockings. I wonder how she can afford those, Louisa thought uncharitably.

She was the first to speak. 'I met your son recently.'

Meg felt a sudden flush through the whole of her body and her heart was pounding so loudly she was sure Louisa must hear it. 'Oh?' Her voice was unnaturally high and she fought again to control her feelings.

'He was in a cafe in South Monkford with Fleur. Fleur Bosley.' She laid emphasis on the name.

'Oh yes.' Meg forced a smile and set her cup and saucer on the tray. She was so afraid that her trembling hands would give her away. 'Robbie brought her home. They'd bumped into each other – literally – on the station. In the blackout. She . . . she couldn't get transport home that night so . . . so Robbie brought her here.'

'What a coincidence!'

'Yes, wasn't it?'

There was an uncomfortable pause before Louisa, staring hard at Meg, said, 'He's a very good-looking young man.'

Meg managed to hold down the fear climbing into her throat and said, 'I think so, but then I could be biased.'

And then the question she had been dreading came.

'He's not like Percy, is he? Or you. So who does he take after?'

Louisa was looking directly into her eyes, holding Meg's gaze. It was so obvious that she had seen the likeness to her own husband in the young man's features. As he had grown, Robbie had become even more like his natural father. It had been Meg's ever-constant fear that one day someone from South Monkford would meet her son. And of all people it had to be Jake's daughter.

What a cruel and devious mistress fate was.

Meg felt suddenly calm. She knew what she must do. She had thought she could tell the truth now and, as the saying went, 'shame the devil'. But she found she couldn't do it. Once Robbie had the answer he wanted, he hadn't pushed to learn more. And now, Meg doubted he would. So, for all their sakes, she must tell the biggest lie of her life and she must make Louisa believe it. She smiled, serene now in her decision. 'He's like my father.'

Louisa looked startled. 'Your father?'

Meg nodded, growing more confident with each minute that passed and warming to her story. 'Yes. He was fair haired and blue eyed, just like Robbie. Of course,' she added, feigning innocence, as if she had just realized, 'you never knew my father, did you? He lives with us now.' She gestured to the room above them. 'But he's very frail. He doesn't get up until dinnertime. Mind you.' Meg forced a laugh. 'You'd be hard pressed to see the likeness. He's white haired and crippled with rheumatism. And he's just home from the hospital. A nasty bout of pneumonia. We're lucky he's survived it.' Silently, she prayed that her father would not choose this morning to get up earlier. There was no likeness to see between grandfather and grandson. Never could have been. Her father, Reuben, had had brown hair and eyes.

'No,' Louisa was saying, 'I never met him.' She was surprised to hear that the old man was living with his daughter. Had Meg really forgiven him – the man she had vowed never to see again? My goodness, Louisa thought, Meg really must have changed. She was tempted to ask more, but it was Meg's son who interested Louisa. If what Meg was telling her was true, then perhaps she'd been wrong. Perhaps the gossip about Philip's friendship with this woman all those years ago was unfounded. Maybe he'd been what he always said he'd been to Meg. Just a friend.

Louisa set her cup down and clasped her hands in her lap. The whiteness of her knuckles was the only sign of her inner turmoil. Her voice was quite steady as she said, 'We never had children, you know. It has been a great disappointment to us both, especially to Philip.' She stared directly into Meg's eyes as she added deliberately, 'He'd have loved a son.'

Meg returned her gaze. 'I'm sorry,' she said gently. In those simple words there was a world of apology for everything that had happened in the past between them. All the misunderstandings, all the hurt. In the briefest of moments there passed between them a flash of understanding of the truth, though they both knew that neither of them would ever voice it. And Meg emphasized this again as, choosing her words carefully so that she gave nothing away but implied everything, she added, 'It has always been my greatest sorrow that poor Percy did not live. *Robbie's father would have been so proud of his son.*'

They stared at each other for what seemed an age, before Louisa dropped her gaze and said, 'Yes, I . . . I'm sure he would.'

After a few moments, she stood up and took her leave. The two women kissed each other's cheek awkwardly. At the door, Louisa said solemnly, 'Goodbye, Meg.' Then she turned and walked up the street, her head held high. From the doorway, Meg watched her go, knowing it was unlikely that they'd ever meet again. Nor would she ever meet Philip again. Louisa would see to that.

Louisa's step was lighter. She would never tell Philip about her meeting with Meg. She knew, in her heart, that Robbie Rodwell was Philip's son, but Meg had given her a credible story: a story she herself would use if it were ever needed to confound the gossips. But strangely the truth was easier to deal with than the terrible doubts. Not knowing had been far worse.

Louisa smiled. Now she knew what to do. When

the war ended – and surely the end must come soon – she would encourage Philip to take a well-earned retirement and move away.

The south coast perhaps, Wales or Scotland. She would let him choose. Just so long as it was miles away from South Monkford.

Nineteen

Fleur was counting the hours until Robbie got back from his leave and praying that, this time, he would be able to talk to his mother.

The first night had passed quickly enough as she'd been on duty and now, on the second night, she had come home with her father and Kenny, and the time seemed to tick by so slowly. She said nothing to her parents, did not even mention Robbie's name, but she was edgy and distracted, her thoughts miles away. Her forced gaiety, punctuated by long, uneasy silences, alerted both Jake and Betsy.

'She's still seeing him. I know she is.' Betsy was threatening to become hysterical again.

Jake tried to calm her. 'Maybe so, love. But there's nothing we can do to stop it. And you know what they say, the more parents try to stop their offspring doing something, then the more they'll want to.'

'Don't I know it? Just look at them both. Won't listen to a word we say, will they? What's the world coming to, Jake? Just think what it was like for us as kids. They don't know they're born today.'

They exchanged a glance. Their shared past was something they never spoke of – not even their children knew anything about their parents' childhood.

Jake sighed. 'It's not easy for them, love. Not with this war on.'

'We lived through a war, didn't we? We had to cope. You with the terrible life in those trenches. Me worrying every minute of every day, dreading the telegram or seeing your name in the casualty lists in the paper.'

'I know. But this one's different. It's so much closer to home with the bombing. In the last lot most of it happened abroad, but this time it's on our doorstep.' He forced a smile. 'Come on, Betsy love, let's not spoil the precious few hours we have with her. We'll both take her to the station in Newark tomorrow morning and see her off. Then you can do a bit of shopping afterwards, love. How about that, eh? Time you had a trip out and a bit of a treat. Now, let's get the supper on the table and have a nice evening – all of us together, eh?'

'Well, maybe we could,' Betsy said tartly, 'if only Kenny would come home when he's supposed to. Where is he now, I'd like to know? Dashed off out as soon as you all got home. He's missed helping you with the evening milking again. I'll clip his ear for him when he gets back.'

'It's all right, love. Fleur helped me tonight. I think she quite enjoys keeping her hand in when she's on leave.' It was the wrong thing to say and Jake could have bitten his tongue off the moment he'd said it, for it prompted his wife to say tartly, 'She'd have been better "keeping her hand in" all the time instead of swanning off to become an officer's ground-sheet.'

'Betsy! I won't have you talking about our Fleur like that or any other WAAF, if it comes to that. They're a grand lot of lasses.'

Betsy pursed her lips and said no more but the loud

clattering of dishes in the scullery left Jake in no doubt of her feelings.

Supper was ready on the table by the time the back door opened and Kenny burst into the house, his face wreathed in smiles. 'I've done it! I've joined up!'

Betsy gave a little scream, covered her mouth with her hand and sat down suddenly, staring at him with wide, fearful eyes, but Jake and Fleur stared at him in puzzlement.

'What are you talking about, lad? You're not eighteen till next year.'

'I know.' Kenny was still beaming.

'But . . . but they won't take you till you're at least eighteen,' Fleur said.

Kenny's grin widened even further – if it were possible. 'No – but the Home Guard will. They'll take you at seventeen. I've joined the South Monkford Home Guard.'

Everyone in the room relaxed and Betsy was so overcome with relief that she almost fell off the chair. 'You bad boy – giving me a fright like that.' She pretended to smack him and then was hugging him and kissing him.

'Leave it out, Mum,' the young man said, red in the face whilst Jake and Fleur, relieved too, smiled at his embarrassment.

'So,' Betsy said gaily as they all sat down at the table and she began to serve out the rabbit pie, 'you won't need to join the forces now, will you? If you're in the Home Guard, you can stay here.'

There was a moment's silence as Kenny glanced at Jake and Fleur. 'It . . . it doesn't work quite like that,

Mum,' he told her quietly. 'I'm still going to volunteer for the RAF when I'm old enough.'

The plate Betsy was holding trembled slightly, and though she said no more, the light that had been in her eyes died instantly.

Determined to change the subject, Jake said, 'I think Blossom's going to calve any day now and I reckon she's carrying two.'

Robbie saw the three of them standing together at one end of the platform. Quickly, he shrank back into the carriage lest Fleur should glance in his direction. He sat well back, watching them. Strangely, it wasn't Fleur who captured his interest this morning, but her father. So this was the man who had perhaps loved his mother. He narrowed his eyes, trying to see him clearly, but the distance between them was too great. Robbie sighed. He'd dearly love to meet Fleur's dad, but . . .

The whistle sounded and uniformed men and women from all the services jostled each other good-naturedly as they rushed to board the train. Last farewells were said, hugs and kisses exchanged. Robbie stayed back until he saw Fleur look up and down the train, deciding which carriage to climb into. Then he moved to the open door of the carriage and leant out, calling her name and waving to attract her attention amongst all the hustle and bustle. She glanced round and, seeing him, hurried along the platform towards his carriage. Her father, carrying her bag, followed. Robbie held out his hand to her and hoisted her up into the carriage and then leant down again and held out his hand to take her bag. In that brief instant, he looked into the dark brown eyes of Fleur's father. Recognition was instant. Jake knew who he was. Robbie saw the older man catch his breath as, almost in a trance, he handed up the bag.

Fleur, standing beside Robbie, leant out too. ''Bye, Dad.' Then she waved to the woman standing like a statue on the platform, her gaze fixed upon Robbie. Fleur's wave faltered as her heart sank.

Her mother had seen him too.

The guard was moving along the platform, slamming doors and blowing his whistle. As the train began to move, there was no answering wave from her mother, nor, to Fleur's disappointment, from her father either. Though not together, they were both standing quite still, their gaze on Fleur, yet neither of them waved goodbye.

She ducked back into the carriage and sat down suddenly, her eyes filling with tears. Robbie sat beside her and took her hand.

'They didn't even wave,' she gulped.

'Darling – I'm so sorry. I should have stayed back out of sight. But . . . but I so wanted to travel with you. I couldn't wait a moment longer to tell you . . .'

Fleur's head shot up and her eyes widened as she saw that he was beaming, it seemed, from ear to ear.

'Oh, Robbie,' she gasped. 'Is it . . . is it really all right?'

He nodded and then she was in his arms, and behind them in the carriage there were whistles and catcalls and ribald laughter. But neither of them cared. They were laughing and crying and hugging each other.

As the train gathered speed and passed by the waving onlookers on the platform, through the window Jake saw it all. He sighed. Whatever Betsy wanted, he thought, nothing was going to keep those two apart. For a fleeting moment, he'd seen the joy on his daughter's face when she'd first caught sight of Robbie and hurried towards him.

It was the same joy he'd always felt when he saw Meg. And, deep in his heart, he knew that if she were to step onto the platform right this minute he would feel it again.

'What did you say to her? What did *she* say?'

As the train sped through the countryside towards Lincoln, Fleur was anxious for a verbatim report.

Robbie, all his anxiety gone now, laughed. 'This is like a debriefing. You sound just like Ruth.'

'True,' Fleur said, trying to adopt a stern tone. 'So get on with it Flight Sergeant Rodwell.'

He gave a mock salute. 'Yes, ma'am.'

Robbie recounted, word for word, what had passed between him and his mother. 'She pretended to be a bit indignant that I'd even thought such a thing of her, but I could tell she was only teasing me. It was strange,' he mused. 'When I first broached the subject she was very edgy, but when I asked her straight out who my father was – was it your father – she laughed. Yes, Fleur, she actually laughed, and like I said she pretended to be indignant.'

'But she denied it?'

'Oh yes – and it was the truth. I could see it was. But there was still – well – *something*.'

Fleur patted his hand. 'Maybe she doesn't like to be reminded of your father. Perhaps his death still affects her,' she said gently, referring to Meg's husband.

'Mmm. Maybe.' Robbie chewed his lower lip thoughtfully. 'She doesn't very often talk about him, come to think of it.' Then he smiled, determined to put it all out of his mind. They had the news they wanted – why worry about anything else? 'I'm sure you're right, sweetheart,' he murmured and, oblivious to the other passengers, he kissed her firmly on the mouth.

Twenty

Two weeks later, Fleur was busier than ever with the garden. The Anderson shelter had been constructed with the earth from the hole they'd dug placed back on top of it.

'Mek it a good thick layer, lass,' Harry had advised. 'And then you can plant summat on top.'

'Can I?' Fleur had eyed it sceptically.

'Aye, you can,' Harry had nodded. 'Lettuce or marrers. Summat that doesn't need a great depth of earth to grow in.'

So the area on top of the shelter was drawn in on Fleur's plan of the garden that she'd sketched out and kept on the shelf of the little table beneath Mrs Jackson's precious wireless.

The gifts of seed and small plants from the old lady's neighbours had been overwhelming, and now Fleur was anxious to get everything planted as soon as possible. 'These plants'll shrivel up if I don't get them in the ground,' she'd said, and had been working in the garden every minute of her spare time. Robbie still joined her whenever he could, but when a longer bit of leave came due, he said, 'Darling, I must go home and see Ma and Pops.'

'Of course you must,' Fleur said at once. 'And I should go home too, but I just can't leave here until everything's planted. I'm late with some of it now and

173

it'd be so unfair to all the people who've been so generous not to use it all. Plants and seeds are very precious just now.'

'I'm sure your mum and dad will understand.'

Fleur grimaced. 'Dad will, but I'm not so sure about Mum. Mind you,' she added as an afterthought, 'Dad did promise to come over sometime and see what I'm— Sorry' – she grinned – 'what *we're* doing.'

'I should think so too!' Robbie pretended indignation. 'Like you said I would, I'm still aching in muscles I didn't know I'd got.' His face sobered. 'But I hate not seeing you for days on end.'

They gazed at each other, their love spilling over. 'I know,' Fleur said, 'but we're luckier than most. We see each other nearly every day.'

'I know, I know. I shouldn't grumble. I'm not doing really, it's just . . .'

Now it was Fleur's turn to say, 'I know. I know just how you feel.' She reached up to touch him, but then, realizing her fingers were grubby, she smiled ruefully and dropped her hand.

'I can't bear to be away from you – not even for a moment. Fleur,' he said impulsively, grabbing her hands, oblivious of the earth clinging to her fingers. 'Fleur – let's get married. Now. Let's not wait any longer. Oh, darling, do say "yes".'

Fleur's eyes widened and she gasped in surprise. 'Are you – are you proposing?'

'Of course I am. Oh, I'm sorry – it's not the most romantic setting, but . . .'

Fleur's eyes filled with tears. 'Oh, darling, it is, it is.'

He dropped to one knee, not caring if his uniform

got dirty. 'Darling Fleur, I love you with all my heart. Will you marry me – please?'

'Oh yes, yes!' She flung herself at him, knocking him over so that they rolled on the ground together, laughing and crying and hugging each other.

''Ere, 'ere, what's all this, then?' Harry's voice came over the fence. 'Well, I nivver. I know the ground wants a bit of a roll when you've planted seeds, but I've never seen it done that way afore.'

Fleur and Robbie buried their faces against each other and roared with laughter.

'Come on,' Robbie said at last, still spluttering with mirth. 'We can't lie here all day.' Then he murmured against her ear, 'Much as I'd like to.' He got up and held out his hand to her to pull her to her feet, then drew her into his arms and kissed her tenderly. He turned towards the old man, still leaning on the fence.

'You shall be the first to know, Harry. This lovely girl has just consented to be my wife.'

The old man nodded and Fleur was touched to see tears shimmer in his eyes. 'That calls for a celebration, lad. You go and tell Mary to get the glasses out. I'll be round in a jiffy . . .'

'What's he up to now?' Fleur wondered.

'I don't know, but we'll do as he says.'

They went towards the house, hand in hand. In the back scullery, Fleur washed her hands quickly whilst Robbie brushed down his uniform. Before she could step into the kitchen to speak to Mrs Jackson, Harry was opening the back door with Ruth on his heels. She had been in his cottage ironing the old man's sheets.

'What's going on? Harry's dragged me round here

just when the irons are hot.' Ruth looked disgruntled. 'What's all the excitement?'

'Here we are then, lass,' Harry interrupted. 'Last bottle of my elderflower wine. Sparkling, it is. Nearest I can get to champagne.'

'It'll be better than champagne, Harry. But are you sure you want to use it? I mean . . .'

'Course I am.' He winked at her. 'Been looking for an excuse to open it up. I can always mek some more. I used to enjoy me wine making, but to tell you the truth, I haven't had the heart since Doris passed away. But now, well, I feel I might have another go. Now this lass has got me all straightened out in the house, I can see the wood for the trees, as they say. Come on, has Mary got the glasses ready?'

'I haven't had time to tell her yet.'

'Will somebody please tell me what's going on?' Ruth asked again, but Harry still ignored her, saying to Fleur, 'You go in and tell Mary and get the glasses ready. Come to think of it, I'd best open this outside. It might make a bit of a mess. Bring a glass, lass. Don't want to waste any . . .'

'What *is* going on?'

Shyly, Fleur said, 'Robbie's asked me to marry him and I've said "yes".'

Ruth stared at her. 'Oh no. You can't,' she burst out. 'Not now. Not while there's a war on. Oh Fleur!' She gripped Fleur's arm. 'Think about it. Please. What if—'

Fleur blinked. 'I don't need to think about it, Ruth,' she said stiffly, hurt that her friend didn't seem to be pleased for her. 'I love him and he loves me.'

'But . . .'

Squashed together in the tiny scullery, Harry could not help but overhear all that was being said. Gently, he touched Ruth's arm. 'Listen, love, I know what's troubling you. You're afraid that if anything should happen to that young man out there . . .' Harry jerked his head towards the back yard, where Robbie was still trying to remove the earth stains from his uniform. 'That she'll be terribly hurt. You're trying to protect her from that, aren't you?'

Ruth bit her lip and tears filled her eyes. 'I tried to warn her when we first met.' She glanced at Fleur. 'Didn't I?'

Fleur nodded. 'But it's too late for that now. It was even then. We'd already fallen in love. It happened so fast, I can still hardly believe it myself.'

Ruth sighed deeply as old Harry put his arm round her shoulders. 'Terrible times we live in, lass. I know that, but if you get a chance of a bit of happiness, you've got to take it. Grab it with both hands, 'cos you never know when you're going to get the chance again. Or . . . or . . .' He hesitated to say more, but it had to be said, 'Or how long it'll last.'

'I'm sorry, Fleur,' Ruth said contritely. 'It's just . . . it's just . . .' She took a deep breath. 'A few weeks before you came I got to know a bomber pilot. Got rather fond of him to tell you the truth and . . . and . . .'

She didn't need to say any more – both Fleur and Harry guessed what had happened. 'Oh, Ruth!' Fleur put her arms around her. 'Why didn't you tell me?'

'I'm not the only one,' Ruth said sadly. 'It's happening to countless wives and sweethearts. I just . . . I just wanted to stop you getting in too deep.' She smiled tremulously, the tears still shimmering on her eyelids. 'Seems I was too late. Oh, Fleur – of course I wish you every happiness. There's just one thing . . .'

'What?' For a moment, Fleur was apprehensive again.

'Can I be your bridesmaid?'

'Of *course* you can.'

Five minutes later it was a merry little party drinking Harry's sparkling elderflower wine in Mary Jackson's kitchen.

'Oo, it smells lovely, Harry,' Fleur said. 'Just like perfume. I don't know whether to drink it or dab it behind me ears.'

'So when are you getting married then?' Harry asked, his cheeks beginning to glow pink. His home-made wine was strong.

Robbie laughed and put his arm around Fleur's shoulders. 'I don't know. I suppose I'll have to ask her old man's permission.'

The words were said jokingly and everyone in the room laughed. All except Fleur. She was not smiling.

In the excitement, the joy of Robbie asking her to be his wife, she had not given a moment's thought to what her parents would say at the news.

Twenty-One

'I don't care what you say, Fleur.' Robbie was adamant. 'We're going to do this properly. I'm going to see your father.'

'Not without me, you're not,' Fleur retorted. 'There's no knowing what might happen. 'Specially if my mother's there – which she will be.'

'You really think he'd withhold his permission?'

Fleur pressed her lips together to stop them trembling. 'Yes, I do. Not because he wants to,' she added swiftly. 'But because Mum will be against it. Dead against it. And . . . and he'll not want to upset her.'

'I see,' Robbie said thoughtfully.

'Did you tell your mother?'

Robbie had just returned after a brief visit to Nottingham when ops had been cancelled because of poor visibility over the target. He shook his head. 'No. I didn't think it right until I'd spoken to your father. As soon as I – as soon as we – have seen him, then I'll try to see her. I want to tell her myself. I don't want to write to her. Not with this sort of news.'

'Will she . . . will she mind, d'you think?'

'Good heavens, no. She'll be tickled pink.'

'Really?' Fleur still wasn't so sure.

'Well, can we both wangle a forty-eight next weekend?'

Fleur nodded.

'Then we'll go together. First we'll go out to South Monkford and face your parents together and then – if there's still time – we'll go to Nottingham.'

'No – no, it'll be easier to go to Nottingham first and then come back here from South Monkford,' Fleur suggested. 'If the trains don't fit up, it might be easier hitching from there back to Lincoln.'

Robbie frowned. 'Yes, you're right. But I wanted to do it properly. To ask your dad first.'

Fleur smiled thinly. Much as she wanted to marry Robbie and as soon as possible, the days until the following weekend were filled with dread and, when the time came, she could not stop trembling and the nerves fluttering in her stomach made eating impossible. Fate, or perhaps the weather, smiled kindly upon them. There was no flying and they were both granted leave.

'There's no need to worry about Ma and Pops,' Robbie tried to reassure her for the umpteenth time as they stepped off the train and began to walk towards his home. 'I bet she offers to make you a wedding dress.'

'That's the least of my worries,' Fleur said. 'Besides, most people these days are getting married in uniform.'

'The fellers, yes. But I want to see you in the full works. Long white dress, veil and a huge bouquet of red roses from Harry's garden.'

Fleur stared at him. 'Harry hasn't got any roses in his garden. It's all vegetables.'

Robbie laughed. 'Haven't you been round the far side of his cottage?'

Fleur paused to think. 'Well, no, actually I haven't.'

The paths to the two neighbouring cottages were

side by side. Fleur had never had need to go to the other side of the old man's cottage.

'Ah, there you are then. Harry's got a bed of red roses at that end. Well hidden from the road, it is. He says they were his wife's favourite flowers and no way was he going to dig them up, not even for Potato Pete. He's already tending them with extra loving care so they're just right for your wedding day.'

'Really!' In spite of the ever-present worry, Fleur laughed. 'And does he know when that's to be then? Because if he does – he knows more than me!'

'Roses last a fair while. He reckons they'll still be in full bloom by the time we tie the knot.'

As they arrived at the end of the street where Robbie's family lived, Fleur pulled in a deep breath. 'Well, here goes then.'

They were welcomed with open arms by Meg, and the old man by the range smiled and nodded his pleasure at the sight of them both.

'How long have you got?' Meg asked, bustling about to set the table for a welcome home meal.

Fleur giggled, anxiety making her nervous. Meg paused, glancing from one to the other. 'What? What did I say?'

Robbie, too, looked at Fleur.

'Nothing – nothing,' she said hastily. 'Honestly. It's just that my mother always asks, "When are you going back?" The way you ask just sounds so much nicer. It . . . it sounds as if you really want us here . . .' Her voice trailed away. She was explaining herself badly and sounding very disloyal to her mother too.

Meg smiled gently. 'I'm sure your mother doesn't mean it to sound the way it does. We just want to know how to make the very best of the time we've got

181

with you.' She turned away swiftly and hurried out to the scullery, but not before Fleur had heard the catch in her voice and seen tears in her eyes. Meg Rodwell might be putting on a very brave face, but she was just as desperately anxious about her son as any other mother.

When she came back into the room, Robbie got up and put his arm about her shoulders. 'Ma, come and sit down for a moment. We've got something to tell you and Pops.'

Meg's eyes widened and the colour drained from her face. Fleur felt a tremor of fear. Had she really told Robbie the truth or had she lied to cover up her shameful past? Robbie must have noticed her reaction too, because he glanced at Fleur as he drew his mother to sit down. Still holding both Meg's hands in his, he knelt down on one knee beside her chair. 'Ma, Fleur and I are going to get married.'

Meg looked from one to another. Her mouth dropped open and she gave a little gasp of surprise, but it was relief that flooded her face. Relief and then a growing delight.

'Oh, how wonderful!' She flung her arms around Robbie's neck and kissed his cheek. Then she held out her arms to Fleur. 'It's wonderful news. Wonderful!'

In his corner by the range, the old man smiled and nodded and wiped away a tear running down his wrinkled cheek.

Gently, Robbie said, 'You looked frightened to death for a moment there, Ma. What did you think we were going to say?'

'I—' Now embarrassment crept up Meg's face. 'I just expected bad news,' she rushed on nervously. 'Nowadays – you know – I thought perhaps – there

182

was bad news from—' She glanced at Fleur. 'From home. That . . . that Jake . . . I mean that someone in your family.' She pulled her scattered wits together and smiled brightly. 'But I never guessed it would be that. I mean, you've only known each other just over a month.' She looked at them both again, searching their faces. And she could see the love there, knew they were right for each other and – because of the frightening times they were living in – knew they couldn't wait. A month, a year – ten years? When had love ever taken notice of time?

'You are pleased, Ma?'

'I'm thrilled. I—' Now she allowed tears of joy to run down her face. Gently, Robbie wiped them away with his finger. Then Meg looked across at Fleur again. 'Will you let me make your wedding dress for you?'

Fleur and Robbie exchanged a look and then both burst out laughing. 'I told you, didn't I?' Robbie spluttered. 'I told you so.'

'Well, that was easy enough,' Robbie said as they climbed on the train the next morning back to South Monkford.

'Yes,' Fleur said dryly. 'Now comes the difficult bit.' As they settled themselves in the carriage, she added, 'You know, your mother never asked if we'd told my parents, did she?'

Robbie, having stowed their small overnight bags on the rack, sat down next to Fleur. 'She asked me later. When you were out the back.'

'What did she say?'

'Just asked if we'd told them yet and I said, "No, but we're going to tomorrow."'

'And?'

'She just said, "Well, I wish you luck," but it was said with a sort of wry smile.'

'Mm,' Fleur nodded. 'She knows, doesn't she? She knows how they're going to react.' She paused a moment and then bit her lip. 'Robbie – you are absolutely sure she told you the truth. Don't get me wrong,' she added hurriedly. 'I love your mother – I think she's great – but, well, I just wondered if she'd been protecting you.'

Robbie smiled, put his arm around her and kissed her hair. 'I know what you mean.'

Fleur closed her eyes, marvelling at how understanding Robbie was. He reminded her so much of her father . . . Her eyes flew open in horror. It was still there. Would it always be there? This terrible fear that perhaps . . . She dragged her thoughts back to what Robbie was saying.

'I really don't think, Fleur, that my mother would have been so delighted to hear that we're getting married if there was the remotest possibility that your father is mine too. Now, seriously, do you?'

'Well – no – but . . .'

He hugged her to him. 'We've got to put all that right out of our minds.' He frowned. 'There *is* something in their past, though. That's obvious – but I don't think it affects us.'

Fleur was silent. She wasn't so sure.

As they walked along the lane towards the farm, Fleur's heart was thumping in her chest and her hands were clammy. As she pushed open the yard gate, she heard Kenny's voice.

'Hey, what are you two doing here?' He loped across the yard to envelop his sister in a bear hug and to shake Robbie's hand. 'Come on in. Mum and Dad'll be pleased to see you.' He paused and then, with a wry grin, added, 'Well, Dad will be.'

He led the way across the yard, flinging open the back door and shouting. 'Mum? Mum? Look who's here.'

They stepped in through the wash house and into the kitchen just as Betsy turned round from the sink, drying her hands on a towel. For a brief moment, she began to move towards her daughter, but then her glance took in Robbie standing behind Fleur in the doorway. Betsy dropped the towel and she gave a little cry. Then she opened her mouth and screamed. 'Jake! *Jake!*'

'Mum—' Fleur began, taking a step towards her and holding out her hands. 'Please . . .'

'Don't touch me. Don't come near me. And get . . . him,' she panted, 'out of here. Out of my house.'

Kenny was shocked, glancing helplessly between them. He'd heard Betsy ranting about Robbie, but he'd never seriously thought she would take it this far. To forbid the young man's entrance to her home.

'Mum . . .' he began helplessly but, at that moment, Jake opened the door that led from the kitchen into the living room, a newspaper in his hand. 'Whatever's the matter?' Then he spotted Fleur and, behind her, Robbie. 'Ah.'

'Dad – please . . .' Fleur began. 'We just want to . . .'

'Of course you do,' Jake said easily. 'Come in and sit down. Betsy, make us all a nice cup of tea, love, will you?'

'Tea? Tea? You want me to make tea?' Betsy's voice rose hysterically. 'You think a cup of tea's the answer to everything?'

'Now, Betsy.' Jake's voice suddenly held a note of firmness, a tone that all his family – including his wife – recognized at once.

Jake was an easy-going man. He liked a contented, peaceful life and rarely did he raise his voice or insist on things being done just his way. But once in a while, when he felt strongly about something, he put his foot down very firmly and all his family knew that he meant it. There was no arguing with Jake when his mouth was a firm line and his jaw hardened. Even his dark brown eyes lost some of their velvet gentleness.

He held out his hand to Robbie and shook his hand, indicating his own easy chair near the range for the young man to sit down.

'Thank you, sir,' Robbie said. There was a tension in his voice and a slight flush to his face.

Betsy stood a moment, staring at her husband, then at the young airman. Then, with a sob, she turned and fled from the room. They heard her footsteps pounding up the stairs and then the slam of the bedroom door.

'I'm sorry,' Jake said, his eyes troubled.

'Whatever's got into Mum?' Kenny was mystified.

No one answered him. Fleur just muttered, 'I'll make that tea.' And Jake sat down opposite Robbie, who leant forward, resting his elbows on his knees and linking his fingers together.

'Mr Bosley, I'm sorry to have distressed your wife. I wouldn't have come here at all, but . . .' He glanced at Fleur busying herself between scullery and range. 'We – I – have something to ask you. Something important and it wasn't fair to expect Fleur to do it.'

There was a moment's silence in the kitchen, and then Kenny let out a guffaw of delight. 'I know why . . .' he began, but earned himself a light punch on the shoulder from his sister.

'Shut up, our Kenny.' But she was smiling as she added, 'Let Robbie do it properly.'

So Kenny sat down on a chair near the table, folded his arms and looked backwards and forwards between his father and Robbie, a huge grin on his boyish face. 'Get on with it, then.'

Robbie cleared his throat and said formally, 'I'd like to ask for your daughter's hand in marriage, sir.'

Kenny tried to stifle a laugh but failed. 'Don't you want the rest of her?'

Fleur punched him again, but her gaze was on her father's face.

Jake stared at Robbie for a moment. Then slowly, his gaze came to rest upon Fleur's anxious face. 'Well, well,' he murmured at last, after what seemed an age. 'Meg's boy and my girl. Who'd ever've thought it?'

Fleur was holding her breath. She moved closer, beseeching him with her face. Their eyes met and held for a long, long moment. And then she saw the smile begin to twitch at the corner of his mouth. He rose and she flung herself against him, wrapping her arms around his neck, laughing and crying, 'Oh, Dad! Dad!'

Robbie rose to his feet as Jake held out his hand. 'It's not going to be easy, lad,' he said softly. 'I think you know that, but you have *my* blessing.' No one in the room could fail to hear his accent on the word "my".

Kenny sprang to his feet and slapped his future brother-in-law on the back. 'And mine. As if it makes any difference,' he added wryly.

'Of course it makes a difference,' Fleur cried, turning from her father to hug her brother. 'You might be the one to bring Mum around.'

There was an awkward silence until Kenny broke it by saying, 'Dad – what is up with Mum? She can't not like Robbie. She's never even met him before, has she?' He glanced at the other two. 'Has she?'

Fleur shook her head and looked to her father for an explanation. An explanation that she and Robbie needed too. But Jake shook his head. 'Don't you worry about it. I'll talk to her. Try to get her to see reason.' It should be the happiest day of their lives and Betsy was trying to rob them of their joy. He glanced sadly at the young couple as he added, 'But I can't make any promises.'

Twenty-Two

'I shan't go to the wedding, Jake, so you needn't expect me to. I don't know what you're thinking of – giving your permission. If you'd told her "no" she might've had the sense to think again.' Betsy sniffed. 'Mind you – I doubt it.'

'It was just a courtesy to ask, love,' Jake said mildly. His anger was gone now, but replaced by disappointment that Betsy refused to join in the happiness that such news should have brought. 'They don't need to. They're both over twenty-one.'

Robbie and Fleur had left and now only the three of them – Jake, Betsy and Kenny – sat around the supper table.

'Mum – why don't you like Robbie?' Kenny asked innocently. 'He seems a good bloke and he's besotted with our Fleur. And her with him. Why—?'

'It's nothing to do with you, Kenny. You're too young to understand . . .'

The young man flushed but he was not about to cave in. 'Mum – if I'm old enough to fight for my country, then I'm old enough to understand why—'

'You're not old enough to fight for your country.' Betsy's voice began to rise.

'Leave it, there's a good lad,' Jake said softly. There was no censure in his tone – just an infinite sadness.

There was a morose silence between them. Betsy's

189

blue eyes flashed from one to the other. She was rarely angry with Kenny, but now even he was included in her malevolent gaze. At last Jake said, 'You don't mean it, Betsy love, do you? You wouldn't really stay away from your daughter's wedding. Your *only* daughter's wedding.'

Tight-lipped, Betsy muttered, 'If she marries *him*, then, yes, I shall stay away.' Her eyes narrowed as she glared at her husband. Slowly and deliberately she added, 'And if you go, I shall never speak to you again.'

Shocked, Jake stared back at her. Slowly, he rose to his feet and stood looking down at her. Sadly, but firmly, he said, 'Then this house is going to be very quiet, Betsy, for I intend not only to attend the wedding but also to give my daughter away. No one – not even you – is going to deny me that.' He began to turn away, but Betsy sprang to her feet and caught hold of his arm.

'I'm not just thinking of myself, though God knows if I never saw Meg Rodwell again as long as I live, it'd be too soon. No – I'm thinking of Fleur. He'll break her heart. He'll be devious and ruthless and selfish, just like *her*. But you can't see it, can you? Where Meg Rodwell's concerned, you're blind. Always have been.'

Jake shook his head. Quietly, and with a patience that the watching Kenny – for once – believed his mother did not deserve, Jake said, 'I'm well aware of all Meg's faults, Betsy. But I do believe that when Robbie was born, she changed.'

Betsy snorted derisively. 'How do you know? You've not seen her since . . .' Her eyes widened as she added accusingly, '*Have* you?'

'No, of course I haven't.' Now, even Jake's composure was wearing thin. 'Don't you trust me better than that?'

'It's her I don't trust. No man's safe around her. What about him? What about Robbie's father? His *real* father? He couldn't be trusted, could he? Poor—'

'Betsy!' Jake thundered. 'We don't talk about that.'

Guiltily, Betsy glanced at Kenny as if – for a brief moment – she'd forgotten his presence. She had the grace to drop her head. 'No,' she whispered. 'You're right, Jake. I'm sorry. I don't want to hurt—' She bit her lip. 'Innocent people.'

But then her head shot up again and she tightened her grip on Jake's arm. 'But I meant what I said. If you go to their wedding, I'll never forgive you. Never!'

He stared at her for a long moment whilst Kenny held his breath. Then Jake shook himself free of his wife's grasp, turned on his heel and strode from the house, leaving both Betsy and Kenny staring after him.

'It's the last thing I wanted,' Robbie said as they sat together in the train, holding hands. 'To upset your family.' They'd been lucky. There was one bound for Lincoln just as they reached the station.

Fleur sighed. 'I know. But there was no other way to do it.' A faint smile touched her lips. 'Unless we eloped.'

He smiled too. 'Now, there's an idea. Why on earth didn't I think of that?'

She touched his cheek as she said seriously, 'Because you wanted to do it properly, and besides, we couldn't hurt your mum and Pops like that.'

'No, I wouldn't do that.' He sighed heavily. 'But it looks as if I've really caused trouble amongst your folks. The annoying thing is' – his eyes clouded – 'I don't know how or why. I wish I did. Just why is your mother so . . . so vitriolic against my mam? You see, Fleur, having seen her for myself now, I don't think it is actually against *me* personally. It's my mother.'

'I don't think we can worry about it any more. Dad said he'll come to the wedding and I know Kenny will.'

'And your mother?' Robbie's bright blue eyes were clouded with anxiety.

Fleur sighed. 'I don't think for a moment that she will come.'

Robbie's eyes widened. He was shocked. 'Not come to her only daughter's wedding?'

Fleur said nothing but just shrugged her shoulders.

'My God!' Robbie breathed. 'It must be something serious.'

For the rest of the journey, they were both silent, each lost in their own thoughts, yet those thoughts were much the same.

Just what on earth could have been so serious that Betsy's bitterness was so deep, her hatred of Meg so strong, that she would refuse to attend her own daughter's wedding?

'There's a notice on the board about a dance in the sergeants' mess on Saturday night. There's rather a shortage of females on station – so all ranks are invited. You going?'

'You bet!' Fleur grinned.

Ruth rolled her eyes. 'As if I needed to ask! And I expect you'll monopolize one particular chap all night and not give any of the rest of us girls a look in.'

Fleur grinned again. 'Of course. But there'll be plenty left for you.' She paused, wondering if she dare raise a rather delicate subject. 'Anyone in particular you've got your eye on?'

'Who me? Never! Safety in numbers. That's my motto,' she said, with a forced gaiety, and her mouth tightened as she added, 'now.'

'There's one thing,' Fleur said lightly, trying to steer the conversation away from thoughts that were painful for Ruth. 'At least we'll all be in uniform. We won't have all the civilian girls in their pretty dresses to contend with.'

Ruth laughed. 'You're right and there won't be any local yokels getting jealous either.'

Fleur pulled a face as she remembered the recent fracas at the Mucky Duck. 'You know we were lucky to get away with that. We could all have been in serious trouble if anyone had reported us. Especially Tommy.'

'I don't think they would. I think all the locals – apart from young Alfie and his mates – are friendly towards all of us.'

'Maybe you're right. They've certainly been generous giving me stuff for Mrs Jackson's garden.'

'You've done a grand job, Fleur. It's coming on a treat. Do you know, Mrs Jackson was in tears the other day?'

Fleur gasped. 'Tears? Oh no, why? Have I upset her?'

'No, no. Tears of joy, silly. She's so happy to see the garden like her Arthur used to keep it. Only thing she misses, she says, are her precious sweet peas.'

Fleur smiled. 'You haven't told her then?'

'Course not. And I've sworn old Harry to secrecy.

Mind you, when he comes round now, he uses the little gate you've made through the fence near the shelter. Not round the front path like he used to.'

'But he does know about them?'

Fleur had planted a row of sweet peas close to the sunny wall on the south side of the cottage, and the plants were already growing well and climbing the cane frame.

'Yes, but he'll not say a word,' Ruth reassured her.

'Do you think she'll see them before they're ready?'

'I doubt it. She hardly ever goes out now. She can hardly get across the back yard to the lavvy some days, her arthritis is that bad. Poor old dear. Harry says she used to love going to church every week but she hasn't even managed that the last two Sundays. Shame, isn't it?'

'Mm,' Fleur said thoughtfully. 'I wonder if we could get hold of a bath chair. We could wheel her to church.'

'You'd never get a bath chair down that narrow path, would you?'

'We could take her out of the front door.'

Ruth laughed. 'Her front door is jammed shut. Just like Harry's. I bet neither of them have used their front door in years.'

'How are you getting on with Harry? I was round there the other day taking some tools back he'd lent me and he took me into his kitchen. You've got it looking like a new pin.'

'Yeah, the house is clean from top to bottom now. There's still a lot of clutter I'd like to turf out, but I can't be too hard on the old boy. Do you know, he's still got all his wife's clothes hanging in the wardrobe? And she's been dead for two years, he was telling me.'

Fleur sighed. 'I expect he can't bear to part with them. Perhaps it helps him to feel she's still close. Still around, even.'

'Maybe. But nobody would ever want to wear them again. Not now, even though there are some lovely things amongst them. They pong to high heaven of mothballs. No, I've given that up as a bad job. But there's just one thing I haven't managed to do yet.'

'What's that?' Fleur asked innocently, and then dissolved into helpless giggles at Ruth's answer.

'Get that tin bath that's hanging in his shed on the hearth in front of the fire and get Harry in it!'

The dance was a great success. It was the first that Fleur had been to on the camp, though Ruth said there had been one or two before Fleur's arrival. Half the fun for the girls was getting ready together in their bedrooms at the cottage. There was much to-ing and fro-ing across the tiny landing.

'Have you got any shoe polish?' Fleur called.

'Only a tiny bit, but you can have it. I've done mine.'

'Have you got any Brasso? My buttons look a bit dull . . .'

And then, from Ruth, a mournful, 'I'm down to my last pair of silk stockings. Do you think it's worth risking them getting ruined?'

'That's up to you, but don't let Brown catch you or you'll be on a charge. Silk stockings aren't exactly classed as regulation uniform, y'know. I'm saving mine for a rather special occasion . . .' Fleur smiled at the thought. 'So I've only got my be-ootiful lisle ones.'

'Right then. Silk, it is. Even if only to show you up.'

'Thanks, *friend*!'

'Don't mention it,' Ruth called back gaily. A pause and then, 'Do you want this lipstick? It doesn't suit me. I'm better with paler colours, but it might suit you.'

Fleur trotted across the landing. 'Let's see. Ooh, yes. That's lovely.'

'You can keep it . . .'

Fleur grinned. 'No, tell you what. I'll borrow it. And I'll borrow it on my wedding day. That can be my "something borrowed".'

They went down the stairs, laughing and chattering, their spirits high at the thought of being able to forget the war for a few hours and into the kitchen for Mrs Jackson's inspection.

'It was just like listening to my girls getting ready when they were going out on a date. Now, have a good time, my dears, won't you?'

Impulsively, they both kissed her on her cheek. It was like having a loving granny watching out for them.

'Oh, she is an old duck,' Ruth said as they walked through the darkness back to camp.

'She is,' Fleur agreed readily, 'but with her arthritis so bad, I just don't know how we're going to get her to the wedding.'

'Oh, she'll get there. By hook or by crook. You'll see. She was only saying the other day that she'll manage it somehow, if she has to get all the village lads together to carry her.'

Ruth couldn't know how much her remark touched Fleur. To think, she mused, that an old lady who had only known her a few weeks was prepared to make the painful effort to get to her wedding, when her own mother was flatly refusing to attend.

'Here we are,' Ruth said, interrupting Fleur's troublesome thoughts as they walked into the large hall, where the tables and chairs had been cleared away. The air was filled with cigarette smoke and the smell of beer. Chatter, laughter and music shook the rafters. Already couples crowded the floor, dancing to the band.

Robbie, standing near the bar, had been watching for them and at once threaded his way around the edge of the dance floor, Johnny following in his wake.

'May I have the pleasure . . . ?' they chorused as Robbie held out his arms to Fleur and Johnny bowed courteously to Ruth.

'It was so nice,' Fleur commented as she and Ruth walked home through the darkness, their arms linked as they followed the tiny beam of Ruth's torch, 'to be just RAF personnel and weren't the band fantastic?'

An RAF band had been formed on camp – the girls had often heard the lads practising in a hangar, the music echoing around the silent aircraft.

'Mmm,' Ruth murmured. 'A pity though.'

'A pity? Why d'you say that?'

'There was a very good-looking lad on the drums, but of course he couldn't come and dance.'

Fleur spluttered with laughter. Ruth had been as good as her word. She'd not danced with the same man twice all the evening, yet had never been short of partners.

'What were you trying to do? Dance with every man there?'

'Something like that,' Ruth chuckled.

'Well, I was happy with just the one.'

'We noticed!'

Fleur smiled to herself in the darkness. It really had been a lovely evening. She'd been able to spend the whole time in Robbie's arms quite openly. The rumours of their engagement were already flying around the room. There'd been slaps on the back for Robbie and chaste kisses for Fleur.

Strangely, only Bob Watson had been disapproving. Fleur had tackled him about it at once. 'Do you mean I won't be able to carry on as an R/T operator after I'm married?'

He'd shaken his head. 'No, it's not that. I just don't hold with wartime marriages. 'Specially not with fliers. When he goes missing, it'll be the rest of us who have to mop up your tears.'

Fleur had been dismayed by his bluntness. And the worst of it was he had said 'when' not 'if'. That, more than anything, had shocked her. He was as bad as – worse than – Ruth. At least her friend was no longer disapproving, or if she was, then she was hiding it very successfully.

'Well, I'll tell you something, Flight, here and now. *If* it does happen,' Fleur had replied heatedly, emphasizing the word deliberately, 'then I promise you, you'll never see me cry.' And with that, she'd turned on her heel and gone in search of Robbie, who was at the bar getting drinks for them. By the time he returned to her, she'd calmed down and was able to smile and enjoy the rest of the evening.

But climbing into bed that night, Bob Watson's words came back to haunt her. Ruth seemed to have come round to the idea. She was her friend and, if the worst did happen, Fleur knew she could count on her, but there were still others who viewed a wartime wedding with scepticism and disapproval.

Including her mother. But that, of course, was for a very different reason. Whatever that reason was. Fleur only wished she knew the answer.

Twenty-Three

'I've got a darky,' Kay said calmly.

Fleur's heart skipped a beat. An aircraft in trouble. Bob sprang into action, issuing orders for the landing lights to be switched on and the crash crew to be alerted.

'Better let sick quarters know too,' he instructed Peggy, whilst Fleur threw aside her sewing and took her seat beside Kay.

Kay was speaking reassuringly to the aircraft in trouble. 'Hello, B-Beer. This is Wickerton Wood. You are cleared to land. Runway two-zero. QFE one zero two zero. Switch to channel B. Over.'

Faintly, everyone in the control room heard the intermittent noise of an engine.

'He's in real trouble,' Bob murmured, as Kay continued to talk the aircraft down. The spluttering noise came closer and closer and the crash crew, fire tender and ambulance were already moving as close as they dared to the runway. The black shape appeared suddenly, low over the perimeter hedge.

'God – he's only just missed it,' Bob muttered, straining his eyes through the darkness and pulling nervously at his moustache. 'I hope he doesn't block the runway just before all our lads are due back.'

Fleetingly, Fleur thought Bob was being callous, but then she realized the tough realism behind his remark.

With the runway blocked by a crash, their own returning aircraft would be endangered. Low on fuel, they might not be able to make it to another airfield.

Everyone seemed to be holding their breath, whilst Kay kept up a serene conversation with the stricken aircraft.

Lower and lower the plane came until, with a squeal of rubber, it touched the runway, bounced once and then stayed down, trundling past the control room where every head turned to follow its progress. When the aircraft slowed and came to a halt at the far end, there was a unanimous sigh of relief as the crash crew and fire tender raced after the plane.

'I think he's OK,' Bob said, still watching. 'Well done, Fullerton. Couldn't have handled it better myself.'

'Now there's a compliment,' Kay drawled. 'Could I have that in writing, Flight?'

As the crippled aircraft was towed away, the first call came from Wickerton Wood's own squadron and the control team swung into their practised routine.

'Coming to the pub tonight?'

It had been a busy week. The weather had been good and there had been flying almost every night. With one R/T operator off sick, Fleur and Kay had been required to work extra shifts and it wasn't until the Saturday, when there was no flying, that the friends had an evening off.

Fleur stared at Kay in surprise. 'Do you think we should?'

Kay, with a little smile on her mouth, shrugged. 'Why ever not? It's a free country.'

They glanced at each other, aware that that was the very reason they were all here. Fighting to keep that freedom.

'What about the locals? I mean we ... we don't want to antagonize them any more. We might not get away with it next time.'

There had been no repercussions from the fracas outside the White Swan – much to the surprise of everyone involved.

Kay's little smile became a smirk. 'Johnny's planning something.'

Fleur's eyes widened in fear. 'Oh no! He's not planning to round up a ... a posse, is he?'

Kay laughed, her dark violet eyes twinkling with mischief. 'Johnny? The responsible navigator of a Hampden? Really, Fleur. The very idea!'

'Then – then ... ?'

'Ah, now that would be telling. If you want to find out, you'll just have to come along, won't you?' She swung back in her chair to face her desk, adding, with a touch of sarcasm, 'Or are you chicken?'

'Is Robbie going?'

'Of course.'

'Then so am I.'

As she heard Kay's soft chuckle, she swung round and marched out of the room. There was half an hour before she needed to be at her desk to complete her morning shift. She wanted to find Ruth.

'What do you think Johnny's planning? Trouble?'

Ruth screwed up her face thoughtfully. 'Shouldn't think so. He doesn't seem the type to me.'

'Doesn't he?' Fleur was not so sure. Johnny had had no compunction in flirting with a local girl and causing her boyfriend to be jealous.

'Well, I'll come along too. Tell you what though. At the first sign of trouble we're out of there and I don't care if they do think we're chicken. I'm not incurring the wrath of the owd beezum for anyone else.'

Fleur laughed. She knew Ruth was referring to Flight Sergeant Brown rather than the Squadron Officer Davidson, who was the most senior WAAF officer on the station. Ruth was Lincolnshire born and bred, and though her dialect was not broad there were times when it came out strongly.

'What on earth is an "owd beezum"?'

'An old hag.'

Fleur laughed louder. 'Oh, that's priceless. I must remember that.'

'Well, don't let her hear you calling her it. You'd be on a charge for sure.'

Chuckling, Fleur returned to the control room. Only a few more hours, she was thinking, and she'd be with Robbie.

Later, as Fleur brushed her uniform and polished the buttons on her jacket until they sparkled, she felt butterflies of apprehension begin to flutter in her stomach. Downstairs she found Ruth and Mary Jackson listening to the wireless. Fleur stood quietly for a moment, holding her breath. Was it more bad war news? Then she let out her breath with relief. It was only one of Mrs Jackson's favourite programmes, *In Town Tonight*.

'Oh, sorry.' Catching sight of her, Ruth jumped up. 'Ready?'

'When you are.' Though Fleur was anxious to meet Robbie, part of her would have liked to stay here safely in the cottage, listening to Mrs Jackson's wireless.

'Now, you promise to go to the shelter if the sirens start, don't you, Mrs Jackson?' Ruth said.

'I don't think I could manage the path in the dark, my dears.'

'Harry's said he'll come and fetch you. Now I want your promise. Please.' Suddenly, Ruth bent down and kissed the old lady's wrinkled cheek. 'We don't want anything happening to you, you know.'

Tears filled Mary Jackson's eyes. 'You're such dear girls. All right, I promise I'll try.'

As the two girls walked down the dark lane, arms linked and following the thin beam of Ruth's torch, she murmured, 'I suppose that's the best we can hope for. That she'll try. But I very much doubt she'll venture down that path in the dark on her own.'

'But you said Harry had promised to go round.'

'Oh, he will, he will.' Ruth laughed wryly. 'He'll go round all right. But I bet they'll just sit there listening to Mrs J's wireless and gossiping while the bombs fall around them.'

'So all that digging was a waste of time, was it?'

'Not at all. We've tried. At least it's there.' She sighed. 'Now it's up to them. But we can't make 'em go in it if they really don't want to.'

They walked on in silence until they saw the blacked-out shape of the pub looming up in front of them.

'Now then, girls,' was Bill Moore's friendly greeting. 'The lads are already in the corner over there.'

Fleur glanced round and her heart skipped a beat as

she saw Robbie, but it was Johnny who rose to his feet from his place beside Peggy and came towards them. Draping his arms around their shoulders, he said, 'Now, girls, what are you drinking? I'm in the chair.'

As Johnny ordered the drinks, Fleur looked around her trying hard not to make it obvious that she was looking for someone. Then she let out a sigh of relief. There was no sign of Alfie Fish and his cronies. Fleur carried her drink across the room to sit beside Robbie.

'Hello, darling. All right?'

She nodded. She was feeling a little easier, but not entirely relaxed. It was early. There was still time for the local lads to make an appearance. And when Johnny came back and sat down, her fears increased again. He positioned himself so that he sat opposite the door and every so often he glanced up at the entrance.

He's watching for them, Fleur thought in horror. He really is planning trouble. Her heart began to pound and her hand, held warmly in Robbie's, trembled a little.

'Darling?' he said at once, full of concern. 'What is it?'

Fleur opened her mouth to blurt out the truth about what was worrying her, when she caught Kay's eyes. There was a gleam in those violet eyes. A gleam that seemed to say, I thought as much – I thought you were a scaredy cat.

Fleur closed her mouth and lifted her chin with a new determination. Right then. Let them come. Let them all come. She'd show 'em. She'd wade in with the rest of them and hang the consequences. It would likely be promotion out of the window, but what the hell?

She smiled brightly at Robbie and said, 'Nothing. It was just . . . just a bit cold walking here, that's all.'

As it was a warm May night, her excuse was feeble. Robbie looked deep into her eyes and such was their closeness already that he seemed to be able to read her very thoughts. He leant close and whispered against her hair so that no one else should hear. 'It's all right. I promise. Don't worry.'

As he drew back, he squeezed her hand. She gave him a small smile, not in the least surprised that he'd guessed what was troubling her. The time ticked on, with much laughter and jollity in their corner. The drinks flowed. Tommy sat with his arm around Kay. She snuggled up to him and Ruth was engaged in a verbal sparring match with the ebullient Johnny, while Peggy – the quiet one of the group – listened and smiled but did not join in the banter. Thankfully, the local girl, Kitty, was nowhere to be seen and neither – to Fleur's huge relief – was Alfie.

There was only half an hour left until closing time and Fleur was beginning to relax. Surely, the local lads wouldn't come in this late. She was laughing at something Johnny had said when, behind her, she heard the door to the public bar open and saw him glance towards it. She knew by his expression that this was the moment he'd been waiting for all evening.

They were here. She knew it. Without even turning round to see, she knew it. Alfie Fish and his pals were here.

Johnny rose and moved out from behind the table and towards them. Involuntarily, Fleur gripped Robbie's hand tighter. He returned it with a comforting squeeze, but Fleur found no reassurance in the gesture.

She leant towards him. 'Can't you—?' she began, but to her surprise, he put his finger to his lips and whispered, 'Just wait and see.'

Fleur glanced at Kay but her eyes were afire and a small smile played on her lips. The chatter in the bar room had fallen silent. Everyone was watching now. Sighing inwardly with resignation for whatever was about to happen, Fleur turned round slowly to see Johnny walking towards Alfie and his mates, his hand outstretched in greeting, a broad grin on his face. Then her eyes widened and she gasped in surprise, not just at Johnny's unexpected gesture, but at the sight of Alfie.

The young man and all his friends were dressed in Home Guard uniform.

'No hard feelings, lads,' Johnny was saying. 'I'd no idea the young lady was your girlfriend, Alfie. As far as I'm concerned, she's strictly out of bounds from now on.'

He still stood with his hand outstretched, waiting for Alfie to accept his apology and shake on it.

One of Alfie's friends guffawed. 'She ain't his girl. He'd just like to think so.'

His remark cost him a sharp nudge in the ribs from another in the group. 'Shut it, Tony.'

The smile on Johnny's face never wavered nor did his hand drop. 'That's as may be, but I meant what I said. I've no wish to upset any of you local lads, especially' – he laid emphasis on the words – 'fellow comrades in uniform.'

Alfie glared. 'Are you 'aving a laugh?'

For a moment Johnny's smile faltered. 'A laugh? No. Course I'm not. What d'you mean?'

'A' you 'aving a go at us 'cos we're not in the proper services?' His mouth twisted in a sneer. 'Not one of the Brylcreem Boys?'

Slowly Johnny let his hand drop now. It seemed Alfie had no intention of shaking it. His smile faded too. 'From what I hear,' he said in a last-ditch effort to heal the breech, 'the Home Guard is doing a great job. You – and all your mates – are doing just as much as us. Let's face it.' He nodded towards all of them. 'If old Hitler does get here, you'll be the ones on the front line. You'll be the ones fighting on the beaches and in the hills, like Mr Churchill warned. And we – well – if it gets to that, we'll have failed, won't we? So, no, I wasn't having a go.' He turned away from them to go back to his seat, but over his shoulder he called, 'Bill, set 'em up for these lads, will you? Maybe a drink'll make 'em realize there's no hard feelings. At least, not on my part.'

Johnny returned to his seat, picked up his glass and drained it. Near the bar the youths stood in an uncertain, embarrassed group.

'What'll it be then, lads?' Bill asked easily, though Fleur could see he was keeping a close eye on the undercurrent of tension still in the room. Then the one called Tony ordered himself a pint, and the atmosphere relaxed a little as the rest of the group followed his lead, until there was only Alfie who had not taken up the well-meaning offer. He was still glaring malevolently across the room at Johnny – indeed, at all of them, Fleur thought, quaking inwardly, though she was careful not to show apprehension on her face.

Bill had just pulled the second pint when the familiar wail of the air-raid warning siren sounded.

'Right, everyone in the cellar,' Bill roared above the din, but the Home Guard lads slammed their pints down on the bar and made for the door, Alfie in the lead, as the first bomb landed with a thud that rattled the windows and shook the doors. The rest of the locals were diving towards Bill's cellar.

'We'd best get back to camp,' Tommy said, taking the lead. 'Are you girls going down the cellar?'

Ruth glanced at Fleur. 'We ought to get back to Mrs J's. Her 'n' Harry are never going to go down the garden to the Anderson. I know they're not. Not unless we're there to drag them into it.'

'Right you are, then,' Fleur said at once. Strangely, she'd been more worried about a fight breaking out between the RAF lads and the local boys than she ever was about a few bombs falling.

'And where do you think you two are going?' Robbie said as Ruth and Fleur rose and began to head towards the door.

'Back to the cottage,' Fleur said. 'Those two old dears won't venture down to the shelter in the dark on their own.'

'Wouldn't they be safer to stay put?' Another thud, further away this time but nevertheless a warning. 'Now it's started.'

The two girls looked at each other. 'I still think we should get back to them. Be with them for once.'

'All right. I'll come with you,' Robbie said and as Fleur opened her mouth, he added, 'and no arguments.'

'Come on then,' Tommy said, 'whatever you're doing, we'd best get moving and let Bill here get down into his cellar.'

They all turned to the landlord, who was calmly clearing up, washing glasses and wiping down the smooth, polished bar top.

Another crump, a little closer again this time.

''Night, Bill,' Johnny called. 'We'll let you get down the cellar.'

'Oh, I don't bother,' the big man said calmly. 'Jerry didn't get me last time an' I doubt he will this.' He nodded towards them all. ''Night all. You tek care, now.'

They glanced at one another, shrugged and, chorusing 'Goodnight', went out into the noise of the air raid overhead.

Expecting to see the streets deserted whilst the enemy bombers wrought their havoc, they were startled to see figures running this way and that, illuminated by flames that were billowing from a building a little way down the lane opposite the pub.

Silhouetted against the bright orange flames licking the night sky was the black shape of a square tower.

'That's the church,' Ruth gasped. 'Oh, how terrible. A lot of the villagers use the crypt as a shelter.'

'Come on, lads,' Tommy said. 'We'll go and help. You girls go down to the cottage. You too, Kay. Don't try getting back to camp on your own. Not in this.'

But Kay shook her head. 'No, I'll come and help too.'

'We'll come back,' Ruth added, 'once we've got the old folk into the shelter.'

Robbie took hold of Fleur's arm. 'I don't suppose it's any good me asking you to stay in the shelter, is it?'

'Not a chance,' she retorted and grinned up at him, the light from the burning building flickering eerily on his face.

He squeezed her elbow swiftly. 'Take care, then. Give my love to the old folk. We'll all meet back here at the pub . . .' And then he plunged after Tommy, Johnny and the others.

Twenty-Four

'Come on, Fleur. Let's get the oldies into the shelter and then we can get back here. Else we'll miss the fun.'

Fleur swallowed a hysterical laugh. It was not quite what she would call fun, she thought, as she began to run down the lane after Ruth.

Bombs were still falling with a frightening regularity, but they were further away from the village now.

'That's the airfield,' Ruth panted as they ran.

'I know,' Fleur gasped. 'I just hope everyone's all right.'

'They'll be going for the aircraft on the ground and the runways to put the whole station out of action.'

They reached the cottage and pounded down the path round the end of the house and into the back yard. Opening the back door, Ruth called, 'Mrs Jackson? Are you there?'

There was no reply.

'Come in, Fleur, and shut the door before I open the one into the kitchen. If there's a light on, the last thing we want to do is attract Jerry's bombs here.'

With the back door safely shut, Ruth opened the door leading from the scullery into the kitchen. Light flooded out and they stepped into the room to see Mrs Jackson still sitting in her chair in the corner near the range and Harry sitting in the visitor's chair. Between them the wireless blared out a music hall programme. The two old people looked up guiltily.

'I thought as much,' Ruth said, as she stood on the hearth rug, her hands on her hips, looking down at them. 'Now come on, you two. We're going to get you down to that shelter Fleur's spent so much time digging and then we've to go. But we're not going anywhere till we know you're both safe. Come on, no arguments.'

She put out her hands and grasped Mrs Jackson's. With a sigh of resignation, the old lady allowed herself to be hauled to her feet. 'We'd better do as she says, Harry, else I'll never hear the end of it.'

With a chuckle, Harry levered himself out of his chair. Fleur picked up the emergency box containing candles and matches, a bar of chocolate and a bottle of fresh water, which Ruth religiously changed every day. In the box there was also a first aid kit which everyone hoped would never be needed, but it was there – just in case. It was kept in the scullery near the back door for just such an occasion as this.

'I'd better get you a couple of blankets,' Fleur muttered. 'You go on, Ruth. I'll catch you up . . .'

They lurched their way down the narrow garden path. It was a short but tortuous journey in the darkness, Ruth only daring to show the tiniest light from her faithful torch.

'Where are you two going? Back to camp? Can't you stay with us?' Mrs Jackson quavered as they got her settled on one of the battered old armchairs they had put in the shelter.

'No. We're going to help out down in the village. The church has been hit. It's on fire.'

213

'Oh no! Not the church. Oh Harry, that's where my Arthur and your Doris are.'

'They'll be all right, lass,' he said, reaching for her hand in the darkness. 'They'll be safe.'

As Fleur and Ruth climbed out of the shelter and pulled the sacking cover across the entrance, they heard the old lady say, 'And I'm missing *Music Hall*. It's one of my favourites.'

Giggling, the two girls hurried back along the pathway.

'What she'd do without that wireless of hers, I dread to think,' Ruth said.

'It's a pity we can't take it down to the shelter with her. It'd keep her happy.'

Ruth stopped suddenly and Fleur cannoned into the back of her. 'Now what?' she said a little crossly as she'd bumped her nose on the back of Ruth's head.

'Well, we can.'

'Eh? Can what?'

'Take her wireless down there. It's a battery-operated one.'

'Do you think she'd want us to?'

'It's probably the only thing that'll keep her down there.'

'Come on then. Let's make it quick . . .'

A few minutes later as they left the Anderson once more, it was to the sound of dance music blaring out into the night, accompanied by the distant sound of falling bombs.

The fire at the church had been put out, but at the west end of the building was a gaping, smouldering hole in the roof.

The fire-fighters, together with members of the ARP, the Home Guard and villagers, their faces and clothes

214

blackened and smutty, took a breather as the all-clear sounded. As the noise faded away, the RAF and WAAF contingencies found each other and made their way back to the pub, where Bill had opened his doors and was serving beer again as if nothing had happened.

'It's after hours,' Johnny said, picking up a welcome pint and taking a long drink before adding, 'won't you be in trouble with the local bobby?'

Bill laughed and nodded his head towards a figure sitting in the far corner of the bar room, his face blotched with smuts, his eyes wide with weariness, his uniform rumpled and his helmet missing. 'PC Mitchell turns a blind eye on such occasions.' Bill's deep chuckle rumbled again. 'Besides, he were first in the queue.'

'You look a sight,' Kay remarked, looking Ruth and Fleur up and down.

They grinned back as they retorted, 'So do you.'

Kay grimaced. 'I expect we're going to be on a charge when we get back.'

'Depends,' Ruth murmured.

'On what?'

'What's been happening there. I reckon there's been a lot of bombs fallen on the airfield. I expect that was their target.'

'That or Lincoln,' Tommy put in and, draining his glass, added, 'We'd better get back.'

'I just want to pop down the lane and see if the old folks are all right,' Fleur said to Robbie. 'But you go with the others. We'll be all right now.'

'Aren't you staying at your billet?'

Ruth and Fleur glanced at each other. 'No,' Ruth said. 'We might be needed on camp. We'll come back.'

'All right,' he agreed as he kissed her. 'Perhaps I'd better go with the lads, if you're quite sure . . .'

'I am,' she said firmly.

They were all moving towards the door when it burst open and Alfie and his cronies crowded in. For a brief moment the two groups stood staring at each other. Alfie's glance sought out Johnny and he took a step towards him and held out his hand, a wide grin breaking out over his boyish face. 'Thanks for your help tonight. Put it there, mate.'

With a laugh Johnny grasped the outstretched hand. 'Gladly.'

There were suddenly handshakes and back-slapping all round before Tommy said regretfully, 'Sorry we can't stay to have another drink with you lads, but we'd best get back to camp. We reckon it's taken a bit of a battering. We might be needed, but we'll see you all again as soon as we can.'

'Right you are,' Alfie said with a nod. 'And the drinks are on us next time.'

'You're on.' Johnny grinned.

'Oh, I do hope they're all right,' Fleur fretted as she and Ruth hurried back down the lane towards the two cottages. They were thankful to see that there was no damage to the two properties.

'They'll be back in the house, I bet,' Ruth said as they rounded the corner into the back yard and moved towards the back door. Her hand was already on the doorknob when she became still.

'Listen!'

Through the darkness the sound of dance music drifted from the Anderson.

'They're still down there. Come on, we'll help them back into the house and then go.'

But as they lifted the sacking over the entrance, above Billy Cotton's music on the wireless, they heard Harry's loud snoring.

Clutching each other and stifling their helpless giggles, they tiptoed away in the darkness.

They signed in quickly at the main gate.

'Do you know what's happened?' they asked the young airman on duty in the guardroom. His face was white, his eyes fearful. He's incredibly young, Fleur thought. He looks younger than our Kenny.

'Not really. I've been stuck here. It . . . it was pretty frightening. I think the runway's been hit and one or two buildings, but I don't know what.'

'I wonder where we'd better go,' Ruth wondered aloud. 'Where can we help?'

People were running to and fro and vehicles were rushing about putting out fires that still burned here and there.

'That's an aircraft.' Ruth nodded. 'I wonder how many we've lost.'

Fleur sighed. 'One or two I expect. But at least the crews will be safe.'

It was always annoying to lose aircraft on the ground. It seemed such a futile waste when they weren't even in battle, but it did mean the airmen were unharmed to fight another day, though they hated losing their aircraft. Some pilots and crews became attached to their own particular plane like a talisman.

'Come on. Let's see if we can find Kay.'

They found her eventually in the NAAFI, sitting at a table with her hands cupped round a mug of coffee, staring into space looking stunned.

'Kay? What is it? What's happened?'

Her eyes still didn't focus properly on them. 'She's dead,' she murmured hoarsely.

Ruth and Fleur glanced at each other.

'Get us a tea, Fleur. I'm parched.' The young girl behind the counter was calmly dispensing tea and coffee as if nothing had happened. She was even singing softly to herself. It was a particular kind of courage that Fleur always admired. Carrying on, no matter what.

When she returned to the table with two cups of tea they both sat down opposite Kay.

'Now,' Ruth said firmly, but not unkindly. 'Tell us what's happened? Who's dead?'

It was strange to see the outspoken Kay looking lost. The girl blinked and suddenly seemed to see them for the first time, to recognize them.

She took a deep breath as if trying to rally herself. 'Flight Sergeant Brown – the one you call the owd beezum. She was in the sergeants' mess and . . . and it took a direct hit. There's her and three of the fellers killed and one or two more injured.'

'Why on earth didn't they go to a shelter? There's one near the mess.'

'There wasn't time. The bombs started falling almost as soon as the siren started.'

'That's true. They did.' Ruth nodded.

'What can we do to help?' Fleur touched Kay's hand.

She shook her head. 'I – don't know.'

'Then we'll go to the watch office. Bob might be there. He'll know what we ought to do.'

Ruth and Fleur drank their tea quickly and stood

up. 'You coming?' Ruth said to Kay, who hadn't moved.

'What? Oh – oh, yes, I suppose so.'

As they moved out into the darkness, Fleur whispered to Ruth, 'Do you think she's all right? I mean, she looks stunned. Sort of – lost. I wouldn't have expected it of her. I mean, she's always so ... so ... well, I don't quite know what to call it, but you know what I mean. On top of things. I mean, when we had that raid when I was on duty with her, she was magnificent. She was calm as you like.'

'I don't know, but we'll keep her with us. She'll be all right. Maybe it's just shock.'

The three of them ran to the control room. Bob Watson was there ranting at the enemy.

'Would you believe it?' he raved. 'It's going to take days to put this lot right.' He flung his arm out to show them the glass littering the floor and paperwork scattered everywhere.

'Right,' Fleur said, as if metaphorically rolling up her sleeves. 'Let's get stuck in, girls. Kay, you fetch a sweeping brush. Ruth, you make some tea. Flight here looks as if he could do with a cup and I'll start sorting all this paperwork out.' She glanced at Bob. 'You here on your own? Where're the others?'

He sighed and sank down into a chair as if thankful to hand everything over to Fleur. 'Sick quarters. They both got cuts from the glass.'

'They're not badly hurt, are they?'

He shook his head. 'But I expect there'll be a few that are. Have you heard? I've been here all the time.'

Fleur nodded and repeated what Kay had told them. Bob Watson shook his head sadly. 'That's a shame.

Poor old Brown. I know she was a bit of a tartar to you girls, but she was doing her duty as she saw it. She had your best interests at heart really, you know.'

Fleur was thoughtful for a moment before she nodded slowly and said, 'Yes, yes, you're right. I think she had.'

Twenty-Five

There were five fatalities that night on the airfield – three airmen, Flight Sergeant Brown and a young WAAF who had been running across the airfield to the nearest shelter but hadn't made it in time. The dead were buried side by side in the local churchyard. It was sad and touching to see the five coffins all being buried at the same time. Fleur, Ruth, Kay and seven other WAAFs formed a guard of honour around the coffins of Flight Sergeant Brown and the young WAAF. It was a grey, miserable day befitting the mood of those attending the funeral, made all the more poignant by the gaping hole in the roof at the end of the nave. A cold, damp breeze filtered into the church, chilling the mourners. It was even colder standing in the graveyard.

Afterwards, as they were about to turn away towards the pub for something to warm them, Fleur said, 'You two go on. I just want a word with someone.'

'OK. You know where we'll be,' Ruth said and linked her arm through Kay's as they walked on.

Others moved away until there was only a couple standing forlornly by the graveside of the young WAAF – and Fleur. She gave them a few moments before moving quietly towards them.

'I just wanted to say how sorry I am,' she said

softly. The man turned to face her. There were tears on his face, yet he managed a smile. 'Thank you, miss. That's kind of you. Were you a friend of our Joyce's?'

'I'm afraid I didn't know her well,' Fleur said evasively. In truth, she couldn't even remember having met the girl at all. There were several WAAFs she only came into contact with on parade. She knew them by sight, but not by name. Perhaps Joyce had been one of them. Billeted off camp, Fleur really only knew the girls with whom she worked.

'She'd only just finished her basic training a month ago. This was her first posting,' his wife said, her voice tremulous. But she, too, was smiling. 'It's such a shame – a waste, but we were so proud of her for joining up—'

'We still are,' the man said quickly. 'I wouldn't want you to think we'd have it any different, even though this . . . this has happened.' His voice broke and he blew his nose loudly on a large handkerchief.

His wife glanced at him and then turned back to say, 'She volunteered on her eighteenth birthday, you know?'

Fleur didn't, but she nodded anyway. 'Are you coming across to the pub? Bill – the landlord – will have laid on refreshments . . .'

'That's very kind of you, miss, but we'd best be catching the bus back to Lincoln and then the train home. We've a long way. I don't expect we'll be home before nightfall.'

'Where—?' Fleur began, and then stopped. She had been about to ask where they were from. But then, she realized quickly, they would know she hadn't really known their daughter. She cleared her throat and swiftly changed what she had been about to say.

'Where will you get something to drink and eat? You ought to have a cup of tea at least.'

The man and woman exchanged a glance. 'All right, miss. You're right. We could do with something – even if it's only a cuppa.'

But half an hour later, Fleur was pleased to see them tucking into the sandwiches that Bill's wife always managed to produce when there was a particularly harrowing funeral. And today's certainly fell into that category, Fleur thought sadly. A little later she saw the couple onto the bus for Lincoln. The man – she still didn't know his surname – shook her hand warmly.

'It's been nice to meet you, miss, though I could have wished for happier circumstances. But it's a comfort to the missis and me to know that our girl had lovely friends like you. You've made today a lot easier. Thank you.'

Fleur couldn't speak for the lump in her throat. She would probably never meet these people again, but if she had helped ease their pain at all, then the little white lie that she had known their daughter was surely forgivable. As a salve to her own conscience she said impulsively, 'While I'm here, I'll look after Joyce's grave for you. Keep it tidy and that. I promise.'

The woman leant forward and kissed her cheek. 'How kind,' she murmured and dabbed away her tears.

'We'll arrange for a headstone. Perhaps you could see that it's done nicely?'

'I will,' was Fleur's parting promise to them.

Later that night, in Ruth's bedroom at the cottage, Fleur told her what had happened after the funeral and the promises she had made. 'And there's something

223

else . . .' Her voice dropped to a whisper. 'When we were in the graveyard I noticed poor Mrs Jackson's husband's headstone has been broken in two. The top half's lying on the ground. I bet the bomb did it.'

'Oh, crumbs, she'll be upset. It was the first thing she thought of when we told her the church had been hit. Are you going to tell her?'

Fleur shook her head. 'No, but I'm going to see if I can get it repaired for her. Maybe she won't need to know. I'll ask my dad. He'll know what to do.'

It was several days after the bombing before Fleur got a chance to go home for a brief, overnight visit.

'Dad?'

'Ssh, listen!' Jake was sitting in his chair near the range, his head against the wireless that sat on a shelf next to the range. 'Listen!'

Fleur bit her lip, waiting impatiently, until Jake reached and turned off the wireless. 'They've got the *Bismarck*. Can you believe it? Our lads have sunk the *Bismarck*!' Jake's face was alight with triumph for a moment, then he sobered swiftly. 'It's a great victory for us, but you can't help thinking about all those poor boys drowned or shot to pieces. They reckon there must be over a thousand men lost.' He shook his head sadly. 'And I bet half those young lads don't know what they're fighting for. You know, Fleur,' he said heavily, 'lots of folks wouldn't agree with me, but I reckon the ordinary German bloke doesn't want this war any more than we do. They've just been swept along in a tide of patriotism by a fanatic who's just bent on ruling the world.'

Fleur sat down beside him and touched his arm in a

gesture of understanding. 'You're right, Dad. And the loss of life on both sides, well, it's just sinful, isn't it? But what can we do? We've got to stop Hitler. We can't let him achieve his terrible ambition, now can we?'

'No, love, of course we can't.' He sighed heavily. 'But it's just so sad that all these innocent young lives are being wasted in the process. And only twenty years after the last lot. Another generation of young fellers.'

They sat in silence for a moment, until he pulled himself together and said, 'What was it you wanted, love?'

Fleur explained about the air raid and the damaged gravestone.

'Tell you what, love, I'll take you back tomorrow and see what I can do.'

'Oh, Dad, would you really? That'd be lovely – but not a word to Mrs Jackson, mind. We haven't told her. I'm just hoping no one else does before we can get it mended.'

'Aye, we'll have a family outing. Mebbe your mum'll come too. And Kenny.'

But Betsy was determined to play the spoilsport. 'I've too much to do to go gallivanting about the countryside. And you shouldn't be using petrol to go jaunting.'

'I've enough petrol to take my daughter back to camp without endangering the war effort and to do a favour for an old lady,' Jake replied, keeping his tone deliberately mild.

'You shouldn't be having to take your daughter anywhere. She should be here at home doing her duty. And now, because of her, I've likely got to put up with having strangers living here. Land Army girls, indeed.

And townies! What are they going to know about life in the country, I'd like to know.'

Betsy went back into her kitchen still muttering darkly, whilst Jake winked at Fleur. 'Well, I tried. She can't say she wasn't asked to come, now can she?'

It was a merry little party that set off in Jake's boneshaker of a car the following morning. Just the three of them – even Kenny had not been able to persuade Betsy to come along.

'You shouldn't be skipping school,' she admonished. 'Not if you want to get into agricultural college . . .'

Kenny opened his mouth to retort that he had no intention of going to college and never would have, but, guessing his intention, Jake cut in, 'Half a day won't hurt, love. And I really need his help.'

They bowled along, singing at the top of their voices, above the chugging of the noisy engine, but when they arrived at the churchyard their spirits sobered as they viewed the damage and saw the five freshly dug graves, side by side.

Kenny put his arm around Fleur's shoulders and gave her a quick hug. He said nothing, but his action spoke volumes. That could have been you, Sis, he seemed to be saying.

Jake cleared his throat and became suddenly brisk and businesslike. 'Right then. Where's old Arthur's grave, Fleur?'

She led them around the end of the church that had been damaged. They paused for a moment looking up at the gaping hole in the roof. 'That's going to take a bit longer than a day's work,' Jake declared. They moved on to stand before Arthur Jackson's headstone.

'Well, there's one good thing,' Jake said, after he

had examined it carefully. 'It's a clean break. I reckon a bit of cement will sort that out. You'll still see the crack, I'm afraid, but that'll maybe weather in time.' He glanced up at Fleur. 'Do you think she'll know yet?'

'Only if someone's told her while I've been away. Ruth won't, but Harry might if he finds out.'

'Right then, we'll see what we can do.' He straightened up and began to move back towards the car. 'Give us a hand, Kenny, will you?'

They carried all the paraphernalia that Jake had brought with him in the boot of the car through the gateway and set it all on the grass beside the grave.

'See if you can find us some water, Fleur. There's usually a tap somewhere in a churchyard.'

Fleur picked up a bucket and set off in search of water. She'd walked all the way around the church and arrived back at the main door when the vicar appeared from inside the church.

'Oh, hello, Vicar. Where can I find some water?'

'For flowers?' Revd Cunningham asked.

Fleur shook her head. 'We're trying to repair Mr Jackson's headstone. It got broken the other night and I know it'll upset poor Mrs Jackson if she finds out about it. I've just been home on a couple of days' leave so my father's brought me back and come to see what he can do.'

The man, who had led the most difficult funeral service only a few days earlier, beamed at Fleur. 'How very kind of him – and of you to think of it. The tap's over there, my dear, near the wall a little way along from the gate. I'll go and have a word with your father.'

Fleur followed the line of his pointing finger and saw the tap. 'Thanks, Vicar.'

When she returned, it was to find the three men talking and laughing together as if they had known each other for years.

'What a great bloke,' Kenny said when Revd Cunningham had excused himself and left them to their repairs. 'I thought all vicars were stuffy and superior. But he's a smashing chap.'

'He gave a lovely service last week,' Fleur said. 'At the funerals, I mean. It can't have been easy for him. But he seemed to know just what to say somehow. I can't remember a word he said now, but I know it was both moving and comforting at the same time.'

Jake had finished the mix of cement and had smeared it on top of the broken edge. 'Right, Kenny. Help me lift this up and when we've got it in place you can hold it whilst I put a couple of iron strips on the back of the headstone. Cement alone won't hold it. I don't know what it'll look like, but it's the best I can do.'

A little later they all stood back to assess Jake's handiwork. 'I'm afraid the crack still shows badly.'

'At least Arthur's got his headstone back,' Fleur said as they gathered everything up and reloaded the car.

'Now, do you think your Mrs Jackson could find us a cup of tea and one of those delicious scones she makes before we set off back?'

'Of course, she will. But not a word about what we've been doing.'

'Actually, love, I think we should tell her now. She's bound to hear about it and it'll soften the blow, perhaps, if we tell her what we've tried to do.'

Fleur sighed. 'Yes, I expect you're right.'

Mary Jackson not only made them a cup of tea, but

also insisted that they should share the stew she had made.

'We can't take your precious rations,' Jake insisted at first, but then from the back seat of the car he carried in a box of a dozen eggs, half a pound of butter and a wedge of cheese.

'How very kind of you,' Mrs Jackson said. 'Now I insist you stay for your dinner. Besides, Harry would never forgive me if I let you go without him seeing you again. Ah, that'll be him now. Come away in, Harry. We've got visitors.'

After the meal, whilst Fleur cleared the pots away and washed up in the scullery, Jake sat beside the old lady and, taking her hand in his, explained gently the reason for his visit.

'We've done the best we can, my dear. I'm afraid I can't say it's as good as new, though.'

Mrs Jackson dabbed her eyes with the corner of her apron, but she was smiling through her tears. 'How kind of you to come all this way to do that for me. You really shouldn't have, but I am glad you did. Thank you, Jake. Thank you very much.'

Twenty-Six

The next few weeks were a flurry of excitement, marred only by Betsy's obstinate mood. Meg, blithely ignorant of the depth of the trouble within Fleur's family, offered to make not only the bride's gown but also a bridesmaid's dress for Ruth. When the girls couldn't get to Nottingham for a fitting, Meg travelled by train and bus to the village where they were billeted, lugging a suitcase full of paper patterns and material samples with her.

Fleur hurried down the path to meet her. 'Oh, this is so good of you. Neither of us can get leave at the moment.'

'Don't mention it, love. It's nice to get away for a while.' She laughed gaily. 'Oh, don't get me wrong. I love Pops dearly, but with working at home as well I never seem to see anything but those same four walls.'

'I can guess what you mean. How is Pops? Is he better now?'

'As good as he'll ever be. He's got a bad chest and he's only to pick up a cold and it's bronchitis or even pneumonia. Hence the stay in hospital. Still, he's much better now the warmer weather's here. Edie, next door, is keeping an eye on him today. She'll fuss round him and he'll enjoy that.'

'Here, let me take that case for you . . . Goodness!'

Fleur exclaimed. 'Whatever have you got in here? It weighs a ton.'

Meg chuckled. 'You'll see.'

'Come along in and meet Mrs Jackson. She's a sweet old dear and getting so excited about the wedding. Did Robbie tell you, we've booked the church here for Saturday, the sixth of September? And we've both applied for a week's leave.'

Following Fleur down the narrow path and round the side of the house, Meg asked quietly, 'Don't you want to be married in South Monkford?'

Fleur paused, her hand on the back doorknob, and turned to glance back at Meg. 'No,' she said quietly. 'It'll ... it'll be easier here. We're resident in this parish and ... and ... well, it'll be better all round. Dad and Kenny can get here and ...'

Meg was staring at her. 'What d'you mean? Your dad and Kenny? What about your mother?'

Fleur kicked herself mentally. She hadn't meant to tell Robbie's mother yet. Of course, she'd find out eventually but ... Anyway, she'd said it now. She sighed and said flatly, 'She won't be coming.'

'Won't – be – coming?' Meg was scandalized. Then, after a moment's thought, she pursed her mouth. 'That's because of me, is it?' She sighed and shook her head in disbelief. 'I wouldn't have thought that Betsy's bitterness went quite so deep. So deep that she won't come to her own daughter's wedding.'

Fleur stared at Meg for a moment before she took a deep breath. 'I don't understand it at all. What *is* she so bitter about?'

Meg lifted her padded shoulders, but she was avoiding Fleur's candid eyes as she forced an offhandedness. 'My dear, I really have no idea.'

And there – for the moment – Fleur had to let the matter drop. She didn't want to risk upsetting Robbie's mother. She knew Meg was lying, or at least avoiding the truth, but she couldn't question her – not as much as Robbie would be able to do. And even he hadn't wanted to press matters any further than he already had done. He had his mother's reassurance that he and Fleur were not related and that was all he needed – or wanted – to know. As long as he could marry his lovely Fleur, that was all that mattered to him. So, Fleur took her lead from him, and instead of asking the awkward questions that still tumbled around her own mind, she smiled brightly and opened the back door. 'Come in. Mrs Jackson's so looking forward to meeting you. She's very fond of Robbie.' Fleur leant towards Meg to whisper. 'She gets all girlish when he's around.' She forbore to say that it was more that Mrs Jackson mothered him, perhaps remembering her own lost son.

Meg laughed. 'Well, he's a handsome boy, even if I say it myself.'

The awkwardness of a few moments ago was pushed aside, if not quite forgotten. At least, Fleur had not forgotten. Silently, she promised herself: one day I will find out what all the mystery is.

Very soon the old lady's kitchen table was spread with paper patterns and scraps of material.

'Now then,' came Harry's voice as he knocked on the back door, opened it and came in. 'What's going on here?'

'Harry,' Fleur called, winking at Mrs Jackson. She guessed the old man had seen Meg arrive and the sight of the pretty, smartly dressed stranger had aroused his lively curiosity. 'Come on in and meet my future mother-in-law.'

Harry stood just inside the doorway and stared at Meg. He stroked his white moustache and chuckled. 'You can't be young Robbie's mother. You're not old enough.'

Meg's eyes sparkled mischievously as she held out her hand. 'I assure you I am. And you must be Harry? I've heard a lot about you from Robbie – and from Fleur too. I'm very pleased to meet you.'

'Likewise, Mrs – er . . .'

'Meg.' Her eyes twinkled merrily at him. 'Please call me "Meg".'

Unbidden, her mother's words came into Fleur's mind. 'It'll be some poor old fool she's set her cap at.' Quickly, she pushed aside the unjust thought. She must not allow her mother's prejudice to influence her.

Bringing her thoughts back to the present, Fleur sighed as she fingered the pieces of silk and satin that Meg had brought. 'But how am I to raise enough coupons for any of these fabrics?' Fleur murmured. At the beginning of June clothing coupons had been introduced.

'Don't you worry about that,' Meg said. 'I've a trunk in the loft at home full of old dresses I've collected over the years. You know, when people have been getting rid of them. There are at least three silk dresses up there. I'm sure I can turn one of them into something for you if we can't raise enough coupons for new material. Only trouble is,' Meg said with disappointment, 'they're not white.'

'You can have my clothing coupons, dear,' said Mrs Jackson. 'I won't need them all.'

'And mine,' Harry put in. 'You can have all mine. Long as me good suit'll still fit me for the big day, I don't need no coupons for new clothes.'

Meg smiled at him archly. 'You'll have to try your suit on, Harry, and let me know if it needs any alteration.'

The old man chuckled, his eyes sparkling. 'Well now, I'm sure it'll need summat doing. It's a long time since I wore it.'

Fleur shuddered as once again her mother's words pushed their unwelcome way into her thoughts. Stop it! she told herself sharply. She's only being nice to the old boy. We all have fun with Harry. Even Mary Jackson teases him and Ruth positively flirts with him.

But now, Fleur could not help thinking, Ruth might have a rival for Harry's affections.

'That's very generous of you,' Meg was saying, pulling Fleur's thoughts back to the moment. 'But it's not only the coupons, it's finding the right material too.'

'Er . . .' Mrs Jackson seemed suddenly hesitant. 'Er . . . there is my wedding dress. It was white. You – you could have that, dear.'

Fleur stared at her. 'Oh, Mrs Jackson, no, I couldn't. It must hold such memories for you. I wouldn't want to . . .' Her voice faded away as Harry moved forward and put his arm around the old lady's ample waist. 'There now, Mary, that's a kind thought. A very kind action. And I'll match it. They can have my Doris's things, an' all. Time we stopped clinging to the past, eh, and let the young folks mek what they can of the present.' He wiped a tear from the corner of his eye. 'I reckon they're earning it, don't you? Besides' – he chuckled and winked at Fleur – 'Ruth'll be pleased to hear I'm getting rid of some more rubbish.' And they all laughed.

'You're right, Harry. My Arthur would agree and I know your Doris would have turfed all her old clothes out ages ago.'

The old man laughed again. 'She would that. I bet she's up there shaking her fist at me for letting the house get in such a mess. Anyway, thanks to young Ruth, it's bright as a new pin now. Doris'd've been pleased to help you, lass.' He nodded towards Fleur.

'And wouldn't Arthur be chuffed with his garden?' Mary Jackson was not quite finished with her reminiscing yet. 'And I owe that all to you, Fleur dear. So, yes, if Mrs Rodwell here . . .'

'Meg,' Meg interposed.

Mrs Jackson smiled. 'If Meg here can do anything with my wedding dress, you're very welcome to it.'

'And I'll get young Ruth to sort out all Doris's clothes and let you have them.'

Mrs Jackson was already moving stiffly towards the front room of the cottage that was now her bedroom. 'It's in here. In a trunk . . .'

But when they unearthed Mary's wedding dress, it was sadly yellowed and moth-eaten. The old lady fingered the material with tears in her eyes. 'What a shame. Such a happy day we had.'

Meg glanced at Fleur and at Ruth, who had now arrived home. Then she put her arm around the old lady's shoulders. 'It's a good job our memories last better than material, isn't it?' she said gently.

'But I thought it'd help Fleur . . .'

'Don't worry,' Meg reassured her. 'I know just what we can do. We'll scrape together enough coupons for Fleur to have a brand new dress.' She looked at Ruth.

'And I'm sure I can alter one of the dresses I've got, or one of Doris's, into a bridesmaid's dress for you. And some of the lace on this dress of yours, Mrs Jackson, is perfect. I can dye it to match whatever dress we decide on for Ruth.'

'Pink,' Fleur said.

'Blue,' Ruth insisted and fluffed her blonde curls. 'I look all wishy-washy in pink.' She made a moue with her mouth.

Meg regarded her thoughtfully. 'You know, Fleur, I think blue would suit her better, if you don't mind me saying so.'

Fleur smiled. 'Of course I don't. To tell you the truth, I don't care what anybody wears as long as Robbie turns up.'

They all laughed now, but Meg said very seriously, 'Oh, he'll turn up all right, I promise you that.' Though it was not spoken aloud, the thought was in everyone's mind. Just so long as he's able.

Twenty-Seven

'I'm here again,' Meg trilled as she opened the back door of Mary Jackson's cottage.

'Come in, love, come in,' Mary said, struggling to her feet.

'Please don't get up, Mrs Jackson,' Meg said as she heaved the huge suitcase through the back door. As the old lady sank back thankfully into the armchair, Meg added, 'But I could do with a cuppa. Mind if I make one?'

'Of course not, love. Help yourself.'

'I don't like using your precious tea.'

'Don't worry. The girls bring supplies from the camp. They're allowed to,' she added hastily, 'seeing as they've had to be billeted off the camp.'

Meg nodded. 'How're they getting on with building the WAAFs' quarters?'

Mrs Jackson smiled. 'Slowly.'

Meg chuckled. 'But I can see you don't mind about that.'

The old lady shook her head. 'Those two lasses have changed my life.' Her smile widened. 'And I'll be seeing a lot more of your boy too after they're married, I expect. He's a grand lad.'

Meg nodded. 'I think so,' she said earnestly, and then added with a smile, 'but then I could be biased.'

She glanced out of the window overlooking the back garden.

It was the third week in June already and all Fleur's hard work was beginning to pay off. Lettuces and radishes were sprouting up on top of the Anderson shelter and rows of green ferny leaves had appeared where she'd planted carrots. In the front garden, runner beans were climbing their frames, as too, unbeknown to Mrs Jackson, were the sweet peas at the end of the cottage.

'She's working so hard,' Mrs Jackson told Meg. 'Every spare minute she's out there dressed in her old clothes and her woolly hat when it's windy. And your boy, too, he comes whenever he can. They both helped me yesterday to bottle some gooseberries and make some strawberry jam. Harry's got a strawberry bed and he gave us some of the fruit. Don't forget – before you go – I'll give you a jar.'

'Oh, how lovely! Home-made jam. That will be a treat. Didn't you find it tiring? You mustn't overdo it,' Meg added with concern.

Mrs Jackson laughed. 'Oh, they did it all.'

Meg's eyes widened. 'My Robbie? Jam making?'

'Well, under Fleur's instruction. I didn't have to do much. I just sat here and topped and tailed the gooseberries. Her mother must have trained her well. She knew just what to do.'

Meg's eyes darkened as she said, 'Yes, I expect she did.' Her tone – though unnoticed by Mrs Jackson – hardened a little as she added, 'I expect her mother is the perfect farmer's wife.'

'Fleur's even saying,' Mrs Jackson went on, 'that she can't be away too long on honeymoon because a lot of the fruit and vegetables will be ready in September.'

Meg laughed. 'Well, I think Robbie might have something to say about that, don't you? But I can understand what she means. She doesn't want all her hard work – and the produce – to go to waste.'

'Oh, I think we can manage for a week. Harry will come round and do what he can and even Ruth's promised to help.'

Meg's voice was dreamy as she murmured, 'Perhaps Jake would come over.'

'I expect he's got enough to cope with on the farm,' Mrs Jackson said, knowing nothing of Meg's inner thoughts. 'But Kenny will cycle over, I don't doubt. We – Harry and me – think he's got his eye on Ruth.'

'So,' Meg said, turning away from the window. 'When will the girls be home?'

Mrs Jackson's face sobered. 'I don't know. There's some sort of flap on at the camp. I ... I ...' She hesitated to worry the young airman's mother, but she couldn't lie. 'I think there's a big raid on tonight. We're not supposed to know, but because so many of the personnel are living in the village at the moment, we ... we sort of get the feel that something's going on. They don't say anything, of course. Not a word. But we've got to know how to read the signs.'

'I see,' Meg said quietly. 'So ... so you think the girls might not be back today at all?'

Mrs Jackson shook her head.

Meg bit her lip. 'Well, I can't stay. I have to get back because of my father.' How she would love to have stayed – to have been here when the girls got home whatever time it was. To know at once that

Robbie was safely back. But she couldn't impose on Mrs Jackson and, more importantly, she couldn't leave her father for all that time. Since his spell in hospital, he was even frailer and needed a helping hand to climb the stairs to his bed. 'But I'll leave the dresses here. They can try them on and help each other with the fitting. Tell them I'll come back a week today and if they still can't be here, then they must pin them carefully and leave me instructions. We've still over two months to the big day, so there's plenty of time.'

Mrs Jackson nodded. 'You'll be surprised how fast the weeks go and with the girls working different shifts it's difficult for you to meet up with them. But I'll be sure to tell them what you've said. The big day will soon be here.'

Meg nodded, unable to speak. She was too busy praying that Robbie would be there.

She kissed the old lady's wrinkled cheek and let herself out of the back door. As she walked down the narrow path between the two cottages, she heard Harry's voice.

'Now then, lass. All right?'

She glanced up, and despite her sober thoughts, couldn't help smiling. To hear the old man call her, a woman of over forty, 'lass' always made her laugh. But, she supposed, to him she was 'no' but a lass'.

'Mustn't grumble,' she answered.

'Doesn't do any good if you do,' Harry chuckled. 'Nobody listens.'

He moved closer and leant on the fence running between the two pathways. 'I saw you arrive. I was just coming round. Are you off again?'

Meg nodded. 'Mrs Jackson doesn't think the girls are going to be home today.'

'Ah,' Harry nodded knowingly. 'So she said when I popped round this morning . . .' The idea of old Harry 'popping' anywhere, made Meg smile again. 'I'm very fond of them lasses, y' know. They're like me own.'

'Have you any family, Harry?' Meg asked, trying desperately to get her thoughts away from her own son and, for a few moments, to concentrate on someone else.

'Aye. Not now, lass,' his face clouded. 'Me an' Doris only had the one son and he were killed in the last war.'

'I'm sorry,' Meg murmured.

'What happened to Robbie's father then?' Harry asked, with the bluntness that old age seemed to believe it had a right to.

Meg gave a start and stared at him for a moment, then swallowed nervously. It was an innocent question. Of course, Harry couldn't know anything. This wasn't South Monkford . . .

'My husband,' Meg said carefully, 'was quite a few years older than me. He was too old for the last war, but he died in the influenza epidemic just after.'

Harry nodded sympathetically. 'Aye, I remember that. Took a few from this village. It were a bugger, weren't it? All them lads surviving the trenches to be hit by the flu when they got home. Bad business. Bad business.' He eyed her keenly. 'And you've brought that lad up on yar own?'

Meg smiled. 'It wasn't difficult. He's a good boy. And then my father came back – came to live with us. He worked a little at first. Here and there – just odd jobs, you know. And I've always been kept busy with my dressmaking.'

' 'Spect you're in demand now with all the shortages,' Harry nodded.

'Well, yes, I am. And I expect it will get worse – or better' – she smiled – 'depending on your point of view. Now they've brought in rationing, women want the clothes they've got altering to be a little more fashionable. Keeps their spirits up, you know.'

Harry looked her up and down. 'You always look so pretty and smart. Now I know why.' He paused, then cleared his throat and stroked his moustache with a quick nervous movement. 'Did you find anything useful amongst Doris's things?'

'Oh yes.' Meg was enthusiastic. 'There was a lovely long silk gown I've been able to make into a bridesmaid's dress. And it was blue – just the colour Ruth wanted.'

Harry nodded. 'Aye, I remember that.' His eyes misted over briefly. 'Doris looked a picture in that.' Then he chuckled. 'You might not think looking at me now, but I used to be quite a good dancer. Loved dancing, did the wife, and she always liked to dress up if we went to a proper dance.' He cleared his throat. 'Well, I'm real pleased if her things were some use to you. Ruth sorted 'em all out for me. She was real good, didn't make me part with anything I didn't want to, but she's right, it's high time I let go. Doesn't mean I'm going to forget my Doris just because I let her old clothes go, does it?'

'Of course not,' Meg agreed gently. 'And I've been able to make use of those two nice suits of your wife's. It was such good material. I've altered one to fit Mrs Jackson for the wedding. They must have been almost the same size. I hope you don't mind. I mean, it won't upset you, will it, seeing her wearing it?'

'I'll not let it,' Harry said stoutly. 'I'll just remember that my Doris would have liked that. They were big pals, y'know. 'Er and Mary Jackson. Big pals. Allus in and out of each other's kitchens. Borrowing sugar and a bit of flour. And swapping recipes. No, lass, she'd have been thrilled. And so will I be.'

Twenty-Eight

Life at Wickerton Wood had been fairly mundane for several weeks, if being involved with bombing raids could ever be described as mundane, but on the day that Meg came to visit a bigger mission than usual had been planned for that night and everyone on the airfield was tense.

Take-off, with more than the normal number of aircraft taking part, went smoothly and everyone in the watch office heaved a sigh of relief as the last bomber lumbered into the air and disappeared into the deepening dusk. The airfield was strangely silent after the drumming of dozens of engines. Yet for some reason the staff were unable to relax into their usual diversions for the waiting hours. Peggy made copious cups of tea until Fleur said, 'Do you know, when this war's over, I don't think I'll ever drink tea again.' She was trying to lighten the atmosphere, but failing. 'It's my landlady's cure-all and we seem to drink gallons of it here too.' Fleur, more than anyone, was feeling jittery. When she'd pricked her finger twice sewing a button on her blouse, she gave up and tried to read. But the words on the page blurred before her eyes and the light romantic novel seemed out of place when she was in the middle of a real-life drama.

The aircraft were late – all of them – and Bob began his restless pacing as he always did. At last, the first call sign came over the airwaves and one by one the planes limped home. And many of them had some damage. Several were landing on almost empty tanks. One plane had a damaged undercarriage and slithered off the runway to land on its belly on the perimeter track, the crash crews and fire tenders screaming out to it at once.

Then there were only three left to return, but the airwaves were silent. Fleur glanced up at the blackboard. Her heart missed a beat and then began to thump wildly.

Beside Tommy Laughton's name, the space was blank.

The minutes seemed to turn into hours whilst they all waited. The wireless crackled and a voice requested permission to land. But it wasn't Tommy and Robbie's aircraft. Kay snapped her answer. It was the first time Fleur had ever seen her colleague show any sign of stress whilst on duty.

The aircraft landed safely and then – there was silence once more. The tension in the watch office mounted. No one spoke as the minutes ticked by.

At last, when they were almost ready to give up hope, the radio crackled into life once more, and Fleur almost fainted with relief as she heard, 'Hello, Woody, this is D-Doggo calling . . .'

Fleur flew into his arms, not caring who saw them, not caring if she was reprimanded.

'I thought you weren't coming back. I thought we'd never get married. I thought . . .'

Though exhausted, with heavy dark rings under his eyes, Robbie could still raise a smile. 'Hey, what do you take me for?' He put his arm about her as they continued walking towards the debriefing centre. 'I'm not the sort of chap who leaves his girl standing at the altar. Not even Adolf is going to stop that.'

'Oh, Robbie . . .' She was crying openly now.

He paused a moment and turned to face her, taking her face between his hands. 'I have to go now, darling. You know that. But I'll see you tomorrow.'

She nodded. 'Get some sleep. You look all in.'

His eyes clouded. 'It was a bad one, Fleur. Our plane is badly damaged. But the one good thing is we won't be flying tomorrow. So I'll see you tomorrow night and you can tell me how all the plans are going. Love you . . .' He kissed her soundly on the mouth and turned to follow his weary crew into debriefing.

Suddenly, the tiredness washed over Fleur. Anxiety for Robbie had kept her going, but now that he was safe, the sleepless hours finally caught up with her. By the time she had walked to the cottage – it would be a while before Ruth could come home – Fleur had scarcely the strength to climb the stairs and fall into bed. So it wasn't until the following morning that Fleur heard from Mrs Jackson that Meg had visited.

'I told her I didn't think you'd be home yesterday, so she didn't wait, but she left the dresses for you to try on . . .' Mary Jackson repeated Meg's instructions about the fitting. Then she added anxiously, 'Fleur, I'm sorry, but I told her I thought there was something big going on at the airfield. I hope I didn't worry her.'

Fleur stared at her. She opened her mouth to say, *Of course you'll have worried her. You shouldn't have said anything. You shouldn't have said a word . . .* But seeing the troubled look on the old lady's face, her swift anger melted and instead she said, 'Robbie's back safely. I'll let her know somehow.'

'Don't send her a telegram,' Ruth said, her mouth full of porridge. 'That'll scare the living daylights out of her.'

Fleur bit her lip. 'But how can I let her know then? I can't go in person, we're on duty again tonight, aren't we?'

Ruth nodded. 'But Robbie probably won't be flying. His plane won't be ready for tonight.' She glanced up at Fleur. 'Did you see it?'

Fleur shook her head.

'Badly shot up, it was. One engine out of action and holes all down the fuselage. It was a miracle they got back at all, and even more miraculous not one of them was hurt.'

Fleur shuddered and sent up a silent prayer of thanks.

'I'll ring Mr Tomkins at the shop on the corner. He's the only one with a telephone in our street, but he doesn't mind taking messages for folks. 'Specially not now. And his little lad positively longs for the phone to ring.' Robbie laughed. 'The little tyke gets a few coppers from anyone he delivers a message to. More, if it's good news he brings.'

'I hadn't the heart to tell Mrs Jackson off, but she really shouldn't have said anything.'

Robbie pulled a face. 'Ma knows the score, I doubt she's any more worried than usual. But I will ring. There might be something on the wireless about it being a bad raid. Then she will worry.'

'Let's walk down to the phone box and do it now,' Fleur insisted. Although it wasn't her fault, she felt guilty that Meg had been burdened with extra anxiety. Though the worry would always be present, miles away in Nottingham she was usually unaware of exactly what was happening. But not this time.

As they walked down the lane, arm in arm, Robbie said, 'At least I've a bit of good news. My leave for the whole week after the wedding has been granted.'

Fleur grinned up at him. 'Mine too. I heard yesterday.' She hugged his arm. 'So where are you taking me on honeymoon?'

'Ah – now I haven't quite decided. But I'll tell you one thing. One of the chaps is lending me his sports car for the week, so as long as I can scrounge enough petrol we can go anywhere you like.'

'I don't care. Just as long as we're together.'

They reached the phone box and Robbie got through to Mr Tomkins. 'Just get your Micky to nip down the street and tell Ma and Pops I'm OK.'

'Right you are, lad . . .' Fleur, squashed into the box alongside him, heard the shopkeeper's voice faintly. 'Glad to hear you're OK. All ready for the big day, a' yer? All the best from me and the missis.'

'Thank you, Mr Tomkins,' Robbie said and turned to Fleur. 'Did you hear that?'

Fleur nodded as Robbie bent his head to kiss her. 'Oh, I'm ready for the big day all right.' Only the sharp rapping of someone on the glass window, anxious to use the telephone, finally disturbed them.

On a warm day towards the end of June, Fleur was at the end of the cottage tending the growing row of sweet peas. She sprayed the plants with water and then pinched out the side shoots. Pulling up one of the plants where the leaves had turned yellow, she said, 'You're not going to give Mrs Jackson any pretty flowers, are you, poor thing?'

'Fleur, Fleur – where are you?' She heard Mrs Jackson calling from the back door. Not wanting to give away what she was growing in secret along the wall, Fleur quickly moved into the front garden, paused a moment to inspect the row of runner beans and then went around the house by the pathway.

'Did you call?' she asked innocently as she rounded the corner.

'Oh, there you are, dear. Come in and listen to this on the wireless. We can't believe it!'

'What is it? What's happened?'

Mrs Jackson beckoned. 'Come and listen – you'll never believe it.' The old lady turned and hurried as fast as her legs would take her back to her seat beside the wireless. Harry was sitting in the chair on the other side and, as Fleur took off her boots and stepped into the kitchen, she saw the old couple, one on each side of the wireless, leaning towards it, straining to hear every word the news announcer was saying.

'What's happened?' Fleur asked again, to be answered with a 'Shh' from both of them.

Fleur listened but could make no sense of the final words of the bulletin and, as Mrs Jackson switched off the wireless, Fleur glanced at them in turn, the question on her face.

'Old Adolf's invaded Russia.'

'Russia?' Fleur was shocked. 'Whatever for? I thought he'd signed a non-aggression pact with Stalin?'

'He did. But he's broken it.'

Fleur sank down into a chair. 'But why? Russia's a massive country with an army of millions. How can he hope to beat Russia?'

''Cos he's a madman, that's why. Mind you, it'll probably be his downfall and while he's busy fighting that lot he won't be bothering us so much, now will he?'

Fleur wrinkled her brow thoughtfully. 'Maybe not.'

'If he tries to keep all his fronts going, he'll be spread too thin, see.' Harry stroked his moustache and beamed. 'What we want is for the Yanks to come in. Then we'd really see the end of Hitler.'

'I don't think they will. It's not their war, is it? You can't really expect them to do any more than they're doing,' Fleur said reasonably. 'I mean, I know we weren't exactly being attacked when war was declared, but we were certainly on his agenda, weren't we?'

'Aye, aye, I see what you mean, lass. It's just that – to my mind – with the might of America behind us, we couldn't lose.'

Fleur grinned at him. 'We can't anyway.'

Harry smile was tinged with poignancy. 'No, lass,' he said and his voice was husky with emotion. 'No, not whilst there's youngsters like you about, we can't lose.'

'Well, this won't get the hoeing done,' she said getting up. 'We're all going to a dance in Lincoln tonight, so I'll need a bit of time to get my glad rags on.'

As they climbed aboard the 'Liberty Bus' to take them into the city that evening, the chatter was all about the invasion of Russia and how it might affect Britain.

'It's got to take the heat off us, surely.'

'Well, I don't mind a bit of a breather, 'specially in September,' Robbie remarked, putting his arm around Fleur's shoulder. His statement was greeted with whistles and catcalls until Fleur blushed.

'Where are we all going?' she said, trying to divert attention from herself. 'It's too nice to sit in a cinema or a smoky dance hall, isn't it?'

'How about,' Robbie suggested, 'a row on the Brayford?'

'That's a good idea,' Tommy agreed. 'We could have a race.'

'Well, I'm popping home to see my folks,' Ruth said. 'But only for an hour or so. I'll meet you down there later.'

'Aw, come on, Ruth. Your folks won't mind for once, will they?' Robbie tried to persuade her.

'I won't be long, I promise.'

Robbie seemed disappointed. 'Where do you want the bus to drop you, then?'

'Monks Road near the school. I'll walk down to the Brayford from there. I'll only be about an hour.'

'My goodness,' Fleur exclaimed as they arrived beside the Brayford Pool. She shaded her eyes against the sun setting over the smooth expanse of water, the tall warehouses silhouetted against the golden glow. Sitting on a wall, three young boys dangled home-made fishing rods in the water. 'I've never been down here before. Oh, and look at all the barges. It's lovely.'

Boats were hired and soon everyone was out on the wide pool and heading towards where the Pool narrowed into the Fossdyke.

There was much shouting to one another and laughter and banter. A race of sorts developed until the airmen rowing decided the competition wasn't worth the risk of aching muscles the next day and they all rowed leisurely towards a pub set a little way back from the bank.

'We should have waited for Ruth,' Fleur said regretfully. 'She won't bring a boat out on her own.'

'Don't expect she'll be on her own,' Robbie said cheerfully.

'Really? Why? Do you know something I don't?' Fleur felt a little miffed. Ruth was her friend. Her best friend. Surely . . . ?

'You'll see,' was all Robbie would say.

Fleur lay back in the prow of the boat and trailed her hand in the water that shimmered with a myriad of colours in the setting sun. Through half-closed eyes she could see the fields on either side of the water and the cathedral standing proudly on the hill bathed in golden light.

The war and all its turmoil seemed miles away.

'There's a boat behind us.' Fleur shaded her eyes but couldn't make out just who was in the craft.

'That'll be Ruth,' Robbie said. He stopped rowing and rested on the oars. 'We'll wait for them to catch up.'

'Them?' Fleur teased. 'So you do know something.'

As the boat drew nearer, Fleur let out a gasp of surprise. 'Kenny! It's Kenny.'

Robbie's grin broadened. 'I know. I fixed all this up with him last time he was over to help you with the garden. He was to keep out of sight and meet us at the Brayford. And then Ruth had to throw a spanner in the works by going home to see her parents.'

Fleur laughed. 'I wondered why you were trying to persuade her not to go. You rogue! Trying your hand at a bit of match-making, are you?'

'Something like that.'

'Well, it won't work. Not with Ruth.'

'Oh, I don't know,' Robbie said, glancing across at the other boat where Ruth was waving excitedly and Kenny, though rowing hard to catch up with them, had a huge grin on his face.

The evening was a merry one, the landlord of the pub friendly and the regulars welcoming, and it was with reluctance that the party rowed back to the Pool as dusk settled over the waterway.

'Did you see?' Robbie was triumphant. 'Ruth sat with Kenny all night and he had his arm round her. And look at them now – laughing and talking as he rows her home. And I heard him insisting there was no room for anyone else in their boat when we all set off.'

'Mmm.' Fleur watched her brother and her best friend. She would've liked nothing more than to see them happy together, but soon Kenny would join one of the services, and the way he was talking these days, it sounded as if he was determined to become a fighter pilot.

And Ruth did not get close to fliers.

For a few hours they had been able to get right away from the war and all its anxieties, but now it was back with Fleur with a vengeance.

Twenty-Nine

Through July the bombing raids went on from Wickerton Wood, but now their targets were the docks and
ports on the coast of France. These were being used by
the enemy's shipping which was patrolling the seas
around Britain in an effort to sink the convoys bringing vital food supplies to the country.

At the beginning of August the day came that Fleur
had looked forward to: the day she could pick a huge
bunch of sweet peas and present the bouquet to Mrs
Jackson.

The old lady was dozing in her armchair, her cheeks
red from the heat of the day, little beads of sweat on
her forehead. Fleur crept into the room and stood
on the hearthrug. As if feeling her presence, Mrs Jackson opened her eyes. For a moment, she blinked rapidly
as if she couldn't believe the sight before her, and then
tears flooded down her face.

'Oh, Fleur! How beautiful! They're just like Arthur
used to grow for me. Wherever did you get them?'

Fleur chuckled. 'From the end of your cottage.'

'Eh?' Mrs Jackson was puzzled until Fleur explained
what she had been doing. 'I didn't think you ever went
round that end and it wasn't suitable for growing
much else. Runner beans, perhaps, but I've got those
in the front garden. So – I thought I would grow you

your favourite flowers. I'm sure the authorities won't clap me in irons for it.'

Mary Jackson clasped her hands together. 'Oh, I hope not, dear. I do hope not. You don't know what pleasure you've given me. They'll remind me so much of Arthur.' She started to struggle to her feet, but Fleur said quickly, 'Don't you get up. Just tell me where I can find a vase and I'll stand them on the table where you can see them.'

Minutes later, as she went back into the garden, Fleur left the old lady smiling gently at the delicate blooms and reliving her happy memories.

'Mum? You didn't really mean it about not going to Fleur's wedding, did you?' Kenny asked as he sat down to supper in the farmhouse, three weeks before the date in early September that had been set. Jake was in the scullery washing his hands before coming to the table.

'Oh yes, I did. And if you and your father really care about me, you won't go either.'

'But why? What on earth have you got against Robbie?'

Betsy was silent, struggling against blurting out the truth. 'I've got my reasons,' she said tartly at last.

'What?'

'You're too young to understand . . .' She glanced towards the door leading into the kitchen from the scullery and lowered her voice. 'Maybe I'll tell you one day. Oh yes, maybe when you're a bit older I'll tell you it all. But . . .'

At that moment Jake stepped into the kitchen and Betsy fell silent. Jake looked from one to the other, sensing that something had been said. He sighed. 'Now what's going on?'

Kenny avoided meeting his father's eyes, picked up his knife and fork and attacked the plate of food in front of him.

'Nothing,' Betsy said, but her tight lips and the angry sparkle in her eyes told Jake far more than a thousand words.

'I see,' he said as he sat down heavily. 'Like that is it? Getting in practice for three weeks on Saturday, when you won't be speaking to either of us forever more.'

Betsy slammed down Jake's plate in front of him, spilling gravy onto the pristine white tablecloth.

'You think it's a joke, don't you, Jake? Well, let me tell you—'

But Jake cut her short, raising his hand. 'No, Betsy. I don't want to hear whatever it is you've got to say. I've heard enough. More than enough. And if you think your attitude is going to stop either of us going to Fleur's wedding, then you'd better think again. Because it won't. Now, sit down and eat your supper and let's see if we can hold a civil, pleasant conversation for once.'

Betsy stared down at him for a moment. Then she gave a little cry, pressed her hand to her mouth, turned and rushed from the room.

'Obviously not,' Jake muttered as he took his first mouthful.

Kenny said nothing and they continued the meal in silence.

*

The evening before the wedding, Ruth tugged the tin bath from Mrs Jackson's shed into the kitchen and set it on the hearth, as she had done every Friday night since coming to live in the cottage.

'Like me to fill it with water for you, Mrs Jackson?'

'No, no, I can manage now.'

The hot water came from a tap at the side of the range, and the old lady was used to filling the bath with a jug before undressing in front of the warm fire and stepping into the water. She had done it all her life. The only thing she couldn't manage any more was bringing the bath from the garden shed into the house.

'Do you know,' Fleur said. 'I quite fancy a soak in there myself tonight. It'd . . . it'd remind me of home. It's what we did every Friday night. There's something very comforting about sitting in hot water in front of the fire. Would you mind, Mrs Jackson? After you, of course.'

'That's all right, dear. There's plenty of water. You can empty it after me and have some fresh.'

'What about you, Ruth?'

'Oh, I had a bath up at camp as usual. No, actually . . .' Ruth paused and a wicked gleam came into her eye. 'I was thinking of going next door. I've got the perfect excuse now.'

Mrs Jackson and Fleur exchanged a puzzled glance. 'An excuse? What for?'

Ruth's smile widened mischievously. 'To get Harry in a bath.'

Mrs Jackson and Fleur stared at her for a moment and then they both burst out laughing.

'I'll believe that when I see it,' Fleur spluttered.

'Oh, I don't think he'd let you watch!' Ruth

chuckled. 'But, you see, I've promised to trim his hair for him. Make him smart for tomorrow. His clean clothes are all ready for the morning. All laid out in his bedroom. Now all he needs is a bath.'

'You are good to him, dear.' Mrs Jackson was still laughing. 'But I don't think you'll get him to bath. Doris used to have a job. He's a "stand at the sink and wash up and down" sort of chap is Harry.'

'He'll love it – once he's in.'

'Ah – but that's the point,' Fleur laughed. 'It'll be *getting* him in!'

'Right then.' Ruth was determined. 'I'm going to give it a go. Wish me luck.'

'You're going to need it,' Fleur said.

They left the back door open. In the warm stillness of the September evening, they heard Ruth dragging the bath across the yard into the cottage. There was a moment's silence before they heard Harry come out of his back door as if a swarm of hornets was after him.

'Nah, lass. I dorn't need a bath. Only dirty folks need baths. You tellin' me I'm a mucky beggar.'

Fleur and Mrs Jackson stood together, peeping out of the scullery window. They could see Harry standing in the neighbouring back yard, his hair ruffled in panic. Mrs Jackson chortled.

'Eh, this is just like the old days. The times I've seen poor old Doris chasing him round the back yard on a Friday night to get him in the bath.'

Ruth appeared in the doorway of Harry's cottage, her arms akimbo. 'Harry, it's a special day tomorrow. A big day . . .'

'I knows that. Don't you think I knows that but—'

'But nothing, Harry. You said you'd let me cut your hair—'

'Me hair – yes. I dorn't mind that, but—'

'Well, when I've cut it, it'll look nicer if it's washed.'

'Aye – well – mebbe,' Harry agreed reluctantly, then added, with a gleam of hope, 'But old Bemmy never said to wash it after.'

'Old Bemmy? Who's old Bemmy?'

'Feller who used to cut me hair. Lived in the village, he did. Used to cut all the fellers' hair.'

'So do you want him to do it for you? But you've left it a bit late now.'

Despite his agitation, Harry laughed. 'Much too late. He's been dead nigh on six years.'

'Ah!' Ruth paused a moment and then said, 'Aw, come on, Harry. All that lovely hot water in front of a blazing fire. Height of luxury, I call that.'

'Well, you're welcome to use it. I don't mind, duck.' Harry's eyes were twinkling now. 'I'll scrub ya back for ya.'

Ruth laughed. 'I bet you would.' Then her eyes glinted. 'Right, you're on. You can scrub my back if you let me scrub yours.'

'Eh!' Now Harry looked positively frightened. 'I was only kidding. I didn't mean . . .'

Ruth fell against the door frame, laughing helplessly, whilst Mrs Jackson and Fleur, still watching from the scullery, stifled their laughter as they heard Ruth say, 'I'm only teasing you, Harry, you old dear. But I am serious about you having a dip. I'll fill it with lovely hot water and then make myself scarce. I'll cut your hair first and then you can wash it.'

Harry made one last plea. 'Can't I just have me hair washed? At the sink in the scullery?'

Ruth shook her head firmly. 'No, Harry, it's all or nothing.'

Suddenly, Harry capitulated disarmingly. He smiled and his eyes twinkled. 'D'you know, lass. It's just like having my Doris back.'

Ruth crossed the space between them and linked her arm through the old man's. 'That's the nicest thing anyone's ever said to me, Harry,' Fleur heard her say as they disappeared into the house.

She turned back from the kitchen window to say in surprise. 'Do you know, Mrs Jackson, I really think she's managed it.'

'Wonders never cease,' the old lady murmured, smiling as she began to ready herself for her own bath.

By the time Ruth returned from next door, Mrs Jackson was tucked up warmly in her bed and Fleur was sitting in the bath in front of the glowing fire.

As Ruth flopped into Mrs Jackson's empty chair, Fleur, soaping herself, asked, 'And did he let you scrub his back?'

'Yes, and wash his neck. It was just like dealing with a grubby little boy. He chuntered and grumbled the whole time. But I think he enjoyed it really – once he got in. He even let me cut his toenails for him.'

Fleur blinked. 'You're kidding me.'

'Nope. I had to go out into the scullery whilst he got undressed but once he was in, he shouted me in. Do you know, Fleur, it was a lovely cosy time we had together. He told me all about his family. He was born in that little cottage, y'know. He was one of ten kids. Where the heck they put 'em all, I can't think.'

'So, has he got a lot of family left?'

'No. Sadly. He was one of the youngest and there's only a sister left and she's in Canada.'

'And then he and Doris lost their only son, didn't they? How sad.'

There was silence in the kitchen, the only sound the ticking of the little clock on the mantelpiece and the coals settling in the fire. Ruth stirred and moved to kneel beside the bath. 'Here,' she said gently, 'let me soap your back for you.' Fleur leant forward whilst Ruth gently smoothed soap over her back.

'You've got a lovely skin, Fleur,' she said. 'I'm quite envious. My back's all spotty.'

It was warm and cosy and the two girls were feeling drowsy. 'Oh well, I suppose I'd better get out and empty this bath . . .'

'Well, you can get out and get yourself dry and up to bed, but I'll see to the bath.'

'Oh, but . . .'

'No "buts". I'm your bridesmaid. Remember? I'm supposed to look after you. And if I want to pamper you a bit, then I've every right.'

'Yes, ma'am.' Fleur grinned and gave a mock salute. As she stood up carefully, Ruth wrapped a warm fluffy towel that had been warming on the fireguard around her. As she did so, she held Fleur close and whispered, 'You do know I wish you every happiness, don't you?'

Fleur rested her head against the other girl's shoulder. 'Course I do.'

'I didn't mean to be hard on you when . . . when you first told me you'd got a boyfriend and when you said you were getting married. It's just . . .' She bit her lip, unable to continue for the lump in her throat.

'I know, I know,' Fleur sympathized. 'I didn't understand then, but I do now. You'd just been through it, hadn't you?'

'I let myself get very fond of Billy. I vowed I wouldn't. Right from coming into the WAAFs, I promised myself

261

I wouldn't let myself get fond of anyone, but then I had to meet Billy.'

There was another long silence before Fleur, pulling back a little, looked into her friend's face glowing in the dancing light from the fire and asked gently, 'Tell me honestly, do you wish you'd never met him?'

Ruth blinked and then slowly, with sudden understanding, shook her head. 'No,' she said huskily. 'No, I don't. "Better to have loved and lost" and all that, you mean?'

'Well, I didn't want to get all poetic on you, but, yes, I suppose that's what I do mean.'

'You're right.' Ruth sighed heavily. 'But – oh, Fleur, it hurt so much. So much. I just didn't want – you know.'

'Yes, I know.'

'But seeing you with Robbie – well, I suppose I've changed my mind a bit. Whatever happens, you'll have such happy memories. No one can ever take them away from you and . . . and despite everything – the war and even the trouble it's caused in your family – oh, everything, I still bet you don't wish you'd never met Robbie, do you?'

'No, I don't,' Fleur said emphatically.

Thirty

Fleur woke up on the morning of her wedding with a strange fluttering in her stomach. She lay a moment, trying to quell the unaccustomed nerves, and then she smiled and mentally castigated herself. What on earth am I nervous about? I've no doubts about marrying Robbie. So why? But she knew why. Today might mean the end of any sort of relationship with her mother. If Betsy did not attend the wedding, as she had threatened, then Fleur knew that her mother would carry out her threat to the letter. She would never speak to her daughter again. As she rolled out of bed, Fleur sighed. She just hoped her mother would not carry out the threat that extended to her father and brother.

For herself, she could cope with it. The relationship between herself and her mother had always been a strained one. Kenny had always been their mother's favourite; Betsy had never even tried to hide it. Luckily, it had not affected the love Fleur had for her brother, nor his for her. And Jake had always made up for Betsy's lack of demonstrative affection towards her daughter. Fleur just hoped that today was not going to cause a rift between herself and her father and brother. If they bowed to Betsy's demands and stayed away from the church today, then Fleur's day would be spoilt.

That – and only that – fear was what was causing her to feel nervous.

The service was set for midday, but Fleur was dressed and ready and standing nervously in Mrs Jackson's kitchen by eleven-thirty.

'My word,' Ruth teased. 'You don't intend letting him get away, do you?'

Fleur smiled nervously.

'You look fantastic,' Ruth said, standing back to take a final check on the bride's appearance. Mrs Jackson too nodded her approval.

'You look wonderful, my dear.' She stepped nearer and reached up to kiss Fleur's cheek and then dabbed a tear from her eyes. But the old lady's tears were tears of happiness. 'Now, I'll leave you. I'll go round to Harry's. He's borrowed a bath chair to take me to church.' She hesitated and then said, a little nervously, 'You – er – don't mind if he comes round? I know he . . . he wants to see you before you leave for the church.'

'Of course I don't,' Fleur said and almost added, I might have to ask him to give me away if Dad doesn't turn up. When the old lady had closed the back door behind her, Fleur burst out, 'Oh, Ruth, they're not coming, are they? They promised to be here by now.'

'Aren't they meeting you at the church?'

Fleur, pressing her lips together to try to stop the tears flowing, shook her head. Her voice was shaking as she said, 'No. Dad said he'd come here to take me to church.'

'He'll be here, don't worry.' Ruth tried to make her tone reassuring, but even she had begun to have doubts. 'And Kenny,' she added, hoping that Fleur's handsome brother, young though he was, would have the guts to stand up to his mother.

They heard a sound in the back yard and Fleur's heart leapt, but it was Harry who passed the window and opened the back door. He stood in the doorway. 'Eh, lass, you look a picture.'

Fleur raised a smile. 'Thanks, Harry.'

'But where's your bouquet, lass? You can't get married without a bouquet.'

'Well, flowers are so hard to come by. I thought I'd just carry a prayer book. You know . . . ?'

With a flourish as dramatic as any seasoned actor, Harry produced a bouquet of red roses from behind his back. 'I made it mesen,' he said proudly. 'Cut all the thorns off, lass, so's you don't prick yasen, and I begged a bit of fern from Mester Clegg to finish it off.'

'Oh, Harry. It's beautiful! I don't know what to say. Thank you – oh, thank you.'

Tears threatened again but Ruth was quick to rush forward and dab her eyes. 'Oh, Harry, you old dear. They're lovely, but if you make her ruin her make-up I'll chase you round the yard again.'

Laughing wheezily, Harry backed out of the door. 'In that case, I'll be off to get Mary to the church. See you there, girls.'

They heard his footsteps go round the end of the cottage and down the cinder path and then there was silence. The minutes ticked by and slowly the colour drained from Fleur's face until it was almost as white as her dress.

'What about Robbie's mum? Is she coming here?' Ruth asked, trying to turn Fleur's thoughts away, even if only for a few moments, but failing.

'No – she's going straight to the church. She . . . she said she . . . she didn't want to make matters worse by bumping into my family here.' Fleur's eyes filled with tears now. 'Looks like it wouldn't have mattered.'

'Look, love . . .' Ruth began, but at that moment they heard the sound of a noisy engine spluttering to a halt outside the cottage. The two girls stared at each other for a moment before Fleur's eyes shone. 'That's them. That's Bertha.'

'Bertha! Who the hell's Bertha?'

Fleur laughed. 'Our car. It's an old banger of a car. Now I know why they're late. Bertha's been playing up.'

'Mebbe your mother jinxed it?' Ruth laughed as she opened the back door and Jake, flustered and red faced, rushed in followed by a grinning Kenny.

'Fleur – I'm so sorry—' Jake began, but then he stopped short and his mouth fell open as he stared at his daughter in her wedding finery. 'Oh, Fleur,' he whispered. 'You look – beautiful.'

Now her tears spilled over and Ruth rushed to dab her cheeks with a clean handkerchief. 'Stop that – you'll wreck your make-up.'

Kenny grinned. 'Who is it, Dad? Surely it's not our Fleur? Where's her trousers and her woolly hat?' His teasing broke the poignant moment and they all laughed. Then Kenny held out his arm to Ruth.

'Come on, pretty lady. We'd better go ahead and see if the groom's been daft enough to turn up.' For a moment his glance lingered fondly on Fleur. 'You look great, Sis,' he said softly. 'We'll see you in church.'

As Kenny and Ruth left the cottage to walk the three hundred yards down the lane to the little church,

Jake stood once more just staring at his daughter, drinking in the sight of her.

'You look lovely, Fleur.'

'Oh, Dad,' Fleur said, now a little more in control of her emotions. 'Don't set me off again.'

'I just wish—' Jake began and shook his head sadly. 'I just wish your mother could see you. Maybe . . .' His voice trailed away.

'She . . . she's not come then?'

'No, love. I'm sorry. Nothing we could say made any difference.'

Fleur put her arm through his. 'But you and Kenny are here. Thank you for that and I'm so sorry if it's made things difficult at home. But I'm not going to apologize for marrying Robbie.'

Jake looked deep into her eyes. 'As long as you love him, Fleur, and you're sure he loves you . . .'

'I am.'

'Then that's all I need to know. And now, if Bertha can manage to carry us another few yards, we'd best be going.'

Bertha spluttered and coughed her way down the lane, pulling up to a thankful halt outside the gate of the old stone church, with its gently leaning square tower and arched porch. The path was so narrow that they had to walk in single file until they reached the door where Ruth awaited them. Adjusting Fleur's headdress and veil and straightening her gown, Ruth then fell into step behind the bride and her father.

'Ready, love?' Jake asked, huskily.

Fleur's eyes glowed as she turned to smile at him with unmistakable joy. Her love for Robbie shone out of her, and as Jake led her into the church and they turned together to walk down the aisle, he saw Robbie standing tall and handsome and proud at the altar steps.

Beside the groom stood Tommy Laughton, resplendent in his uniform, and behind them both, in the second pew back, were the other crewmembers from D-Doggo. And to Jake's surprise, the church was almost full. There were a few other RAF and WAAF personnel, but then all the spare seats were taken up by villagers. They'd come to see a pretty wedding, to try to forget the war, just for a few hours, as they turned their backs on the gaping hole in the roof at the back of the church and watched the beautiful bride and her handsome groom.

Jake's attention came back to the young man who was about to become his son-in-law. He saw the love in the young man's eyes as he watched his bride coming towards him and Jake was left in no doubt now. Fleur was doing the right thing. Whatever Betsy's feelings were, there was no mistaking this couple's love for each other. As they neared the steps, Fleur had eyes for no one but Robbie, but Jake could not stop his gaze roaming over the few guests in the front pews.

And then he saw her. For the first time after half a lifetime apart he saw Meg again.

Thirty-One

The service was over and Fleur and Robbie had stood just outside the porch as all the guests and villagers had filed past them, shaking Robbie's hand and kissing Fleur. Then the pictures had been taken with a great deal of laughter and amusement at the elderly photographer, who kept disappearing beneath the black cloth covering the square box camera which teetered precariously on a spindly tripod.

'Just look at him!' Kenny spluttered with mirth. 'Trampling all over the graves to get his antiquated camera in the right place. Is he allowed to do that?'

Robbie and Fleur were almost helpless with laughter.

'Well, I don't think the folks he's walking over are going to say much,' Robbie chuckled.

'I just hope there's none of their relatives watching though,' Fleur said, ever sensitive to the feelings of others. 'They might feel it's a bit . . . a bit – oh, what's the word?'

'Sacrilegious?'

'Something like that.'

'Well, I don't think there's anyone left much to notice.'

Fleur glanced around her. Most of the villagers who'd been in the church had gone, and only a few were left peering over the church wall to watch the goings on.

'Now I wonder where they've all rushed off to?' Kenny mused. 'You'd've thought they'd have stayed to watch the comedy. Mind you,' he added, nodding towards the little man waving his arms about to position his subjects and looking as if he were directing traffic, 'I reckon he's done it before. He seems to know just where he wants us to be.'

'You sure about that?' Robbie murmured.

'Smile please,' trilled the photographer and they all tried to straighten their faces into sensible smiles rather than wide, toothy grins and fits of giggles.

As the photographer declared, 'That's it, folks,' Robbie turned to Fleur. 'And now, Mrs Rodwell, we're off on our honeymoon. Your carriage awaits, m'lady.'

'I'll just have to go back to the cottage and get changed. I can hardly travel in this . . .'

'Why ever not?' Robbie pretended surprise as he bent to kiss her. 'I want the world to see my beautiful wife.'

'Now then, plenty of time for that later, you two lovebirds.' Harry hobbled up to them and held out his arms. 'I haven't kissed the bride yet.'

There were tears in the old man's eyes as Fleur leant forward so that he could kiss her on both cheeks. 'Eh, lass, but you're bonny an' no mistake. You're a lucky young feller . . .' he added, holding out his hand to shake Robbie's.

'Thank you, Harry.'

'Right then, we're all off to the pub. You will let me buy you both a drink before you go, now won't you?'

Fleur and Robbie exchanged a glance. They couldn't wait to be alone together, yet they didn't want to appear ungrateful to Robbie's mother, who had worked so hard on Fleur's gown and Ruth's dress, nor to Jake and Kenny, who had defied Betsy to be here. They owed it to their guests, to Harry and Mrs Jackson too, to spend a little time with them.

'Of course we will,' Robbie said. 'That's very kind of you, Harry.'

The old man beamed. 'Right.' Harry raised his voice. 'Everyone across to the Mucky Duck.'

There was a ripple of laughter.

'The what?' Kenny blinked.

Ruth hooked her arm through his. 'It's the White Swan, really, but all the locals call it the Mucky Duck. Come on, you can escort me. I'm supposed to walk with the best man – handsome devil, isn't he, in that uniform – but his girlfriend's here and I don't want to spoil the little bit of time they've got to spend together.'

'It's my pleasure,' Kenny said gallantly and the faint flush on his face told her that indeed it was.

The crew of Robbie's aircraft and six WAAFs, Kay and Peggy amongst them, formed a guard of honour down the pathway. Handsome young men in their smart blue uniforms that not only set the hearts of the young women in the village aflutter, but caused several of the older women to smile fondly and wish themselves forty years younger.

Then Harry led the way from the church across the road, pushing Mrs Jackson in the borrowed bath chair. 'Come on, folks, follow me,' he called, his excitement bubbling over as the wedding party fell into step behind them, with the vicar bringing up the rear.

'Dear old Harry,' Ruth murmured. 'He's loving this, isn't he?'

Kenny was thoughtful. 'D'you know, I reckon he's up to summat.'

'Eh?' Ruth's eyes widened. 'What d'you mean?'

'I dunno. Maybe he's got them a special present that he can't wait to give them. But there's something going on behind those twinkling eyes. And there's something else funny too.'

'What?'

'Well, I'd've thought there'd've been crowds to watch my beautiful sister come out of church, but there's hardly anyone about now. In South Monkford, I know it's a town and we've got a big church, but the street's usually lined with folk when there's a wedding going off. Anybody's wedding – it doesn't matter whose. They just like to have a nosy.'

'Mm,' Ruth mused. 'Funny that. Mind you, most of them were in church. Maybe they've seen all they wanted to.'

Harry was rushing on ahead as fast as his bent old legs would carry him and wheezing a little as he pushed the bath chair in front of him. Arriving at the main entrance of the pub, he parked the chair outside and helped Mary Jackson to stand up and walk inside. But instead of disappearing, he threw open the double doors and stood just inside, beaming at the bride and groom walking towards him.

As they approached, Bill Moore, dressed smartly in a black suit, white shirt and black bow tie, came to stand beside Harry to usher the wedding party inside.

As Fleur and Robbie stepped into the dark interior of the public bar, a huge cheer threatened to shake the rafters. It seemed as if the whole village was crammed into the room.

Fleur gasped and gazed around, stunned by the

applause that greeted them and the cries of 'Congrat-ulations' and 'Good Luck' on every side.

'So that's where they all disappeared to.' Kenny laughed.

'Come through, come through,' Harry said, leading the way into a large room just beyond the bar. He stood to one side and waved his arm to show them a table at the far end, laden with food. In the centre stood a magnificent wedding cake, complete with bride and groom figurines on the top.

'Everyone in the village has contributed. The women have been baking all week and . . .'

'Oh, Harry!' Now the tears flooded down Fleur's face. The kindness of all the villagers, some of whom she hardly knew, was overwhelming. Even Robbie had tears in his eyes. He held out his hand and shook Harry's hard. 'Thank you, Harry. This is wonderful. I really don't know how to thank everyone.'

'It's us who wanted to say "thank you", lad. To you and your lass here. To all of you really . . .' He nodded his head to include the best man in his RAF uniform and Ruth in her bridesmaid's dress. 'That's fighting this war for us. It's our way of showing our gratitude. But 'specially to you two and Ruth for all you've done for me an' Mary. You're . . . you're like family to us. No disrespect to your own families, like.'

'None taken,' Jake, standing just behind Fleur, murmured. He was touched by the villagers' obvious fondness for his daughter and for Meg's boy, as he still called Robbie in his own mind. He only wished Betsy was here to see all this and hear what was being said. Perhaps it would melt even her hard heart.

But he doubted it.

Robbie was nodding his thanks, but unable to speak for the lump in his throat and Fleur was still trying to stem her tears. But they were tears of happiness.

Just for a few short hours they could all forget the war and its tragedies and celebrate a happy occasion. A very happy occasion.

Of course the moment had to come. The moment when Jake and Meg came face to face for the first time in twenty-two years.

As the guests milled around, helping themselves to the food, chattering and laughing, Meg made her way through the throng to stand behind him.

'Hello, Jake. How are you?'

He heard her voice and, slowly, he turned to face her. The breath caught in his throat. She was even more beautiful than he remembered. He didn't see the tiny lines around her eyes; to him the years fell away and there before him was his flame-haired Meg with her heartbreaking smile.

He cleared his throat but his voice was still a little husky as he answered, 'Fine, Meg. And you? You . . . you look – wonderful.' He couldn't stop the compliment escaping his lips, even though he felt disloyal to the absent Betsy the moment the words were said. But Meg was smiling up at him, her green eyes gently teasing him. 'So do you.'

Jake pulled a face. 'I don't know about that. I've a lot more wrinkles and grey hairs.'

Meg's gaze never left his face. 'No,' she said softly. 'You haven't changed. You're still my – still Jake.'

There was an awkward pause before she went on,

making her tone deliberately light. 'Who'd've thought it, eh? Your girl and my boy. Must be fate taking a hand, Jake.'

Jake sighed. 'That's one way of putting it, I suppose. But is it a kind fate or a cruel one?'

Meg glanced across at Robbie and Fleur, who were touring the room, making sure they spoke to each and every person there to give their thanks.

'He's not like me, Jake. Just in case you're worried. He's got none of my badness. He loves Fleur dearly. He won't hurt her like I . . .' Her voice trailed away and Jake saw the tears shimmer in her eyes.

'Oh, don't cry, Meggie, I couldn't bear it,' he whispered and fished out the spotless white handkerchief from his top pocket. 'Here.' His use of the pet name he'd always had for her all those years ago was almost her undoing. For a moment the tears threatened to spill over.

'Thanks.' Meg dabbed carefully at her eyes. Then she handed him the handkerchief, which he stuffed back into his pocket.

'You weren't bad,' he told her softly. 'Just . . . just very young and you'd been so hurt by – well – by life. I said some very harsh things to you then, Meggie. I'm sorry.'

'I deserved them, Jake,' she said simply. 'But I want you to know, I've changed. Ever since that day when I nearly lost Robbie, when that dreadful woman tried to snatch him away from me, I've tried to make up for all the terrible things I did. I know I can't change the past, but I've tried to be a better person. Truly, I have.'

'Don't be so hard on yourself, Meggie. We . . . we all make mistakes. We've all done things we maybe shouldn't have.' She looked at him keenly, but he was avoiding her gaze now. 'Can I ask you something, Meg? Don't answer, if you don't want to.'

She knew a moment's panic, but then remembered. This was Jake she was talking to: Jake, who knew everything there was to know about her. She had no secrets from him. Nor did she want any. If there was one person in the whole wide world whom Meg could trust, it was Jake.

'Is it true that you have your father living with you?'

Meg laughed with relief. 'Yes, but I can see why you're surprised.' She smiled impishly now. 'That's all part of my reformed character, Jake. How could I continue to bear a grudge against him when I did things that were just as bad, if not worse?'

Jake pursed his lips. 'Well, it was because of what *he* did that made you like that. You were only searching for security. For someone to take care of you. You couldn't wait for . . .' His voice trailed away.

Meg shook her head. 'Don't try to excuse me, Jake. I . . . I should have had more faith.' Her voice was almost an inaudible whisper as she added, 'More faith in you.'

'How did he come back into your life?'

'Just turned up at my door one day. He'd been living rough. He was in a terrible state. How could I turn him away?'

'What happened to Alice Smallwood? The girl he ran off with?'

Meg shrugged. 'She'd found a bigger fish. Ran off with someone with money. Pops has never talked about her much, but I gather he tried to follow her, and the feller she'd taken up with got some of his cronies to beat Pops up. Nearly killed him. He'd still got a lot of the bruises by the time he found me.' She paused and then added softly, 'He's spent every day since trying to make it up to me and he's been wonderful for Robbie.' She glanced across fondly at her son. 'That's one thing I'm never going to apologize for, Jake. Having Robbie. Though I could have wished that his father—'

'Don't, Meggie, don't say it.' He reached out and took her hand. 'It shouldn't be spoken of. Not today of all days.'

'No, you're right.' She smiled up at him, her tears dried now. 'Today's a happy day. Let's just enjoy it. Let's just enjoy seeing each other again because I gather' – she looked around the room – 'that this might be the only chance we'll ever get.'

'Yes,' Jake said sadly. 'I'm afraid it probably is, Meggie.'

Thirty-Two

'Fleur,' Robbie whispered close to her ear so that no one else could hear. 'Don't look now, but your dad is holding my mum's hand.'

'Eh?' Startled, Fleur looked round quickly, her gaze seeking out Jake and Meg.

'No, no, don't look. Don't – spoil it. In a minute or two as we move round the room, take a look though. There's something between them. You can see it in their faces. Just look.'

Fleur tried to concentrate on what the woman in front of her was saying. 'My dear, you look lovely,' the little woman who helped her husband run the village bakery gushed. 'It's done us so much good to have such a pretty wedding in the midst of these dark times. Everyone in the village has loved planning this little surprise for you both. Of course, it was Harry's idea, but we've all chipped in. I made the cake. I'm so sorry it's covered with a cardboard decoration instead of real icing.'

'You've all been wonderful. You've made our day even more special. And the cake looks wonderful. You'd never know until you get right near it that it's not real. But the real cake underneath tastes delicious,' Fleur said and, impulsively, she leant forward and kissed the woman's cheek.

'Lots of people gave me fruit for it,' the little woman

went on, blushing a little. 'And Mr Clegg gave me the eggs.'

'How very kind everyone has been.'

Then, at last, Fleur was able to move away and take a surreptitious look across the crowded room towards her father and Meg. What she saw made her catch her breath in a gasp of surprise.

Close beside her, Robbie murmured, 'See what I mean?'

'Yes.' Fleur nodded slowly. 'Yes, I do.'

Jake and Meg were standing close together looking into each other's faces as if there was no one else in the room. They were oblivious to the chatter and laughter around them, completely lost in their own little world.

Fleur made an involuntary movement towards them, but Robbie touched her arm and said softly, 'Don't spoil it, Fleur. What harm can it do? Just this once. This may be the only time they'll ever have.'

Fleur bit her lip. Even from the other side of the room, she could see the raw emotion on her father's face, could see Robbie's mother's eyes shimmering with tears, and her tremulous smile.

'Yes, but what about my mum? What about her?'

'She was the one who chose not to come today.'

'Yes – and now we can see why, can't we?'

Robbie sighed. 'But if she had come, darling, that' – he nodded towards the couple – 'wouldn't be happening, now would it?'

'I suppose not,' Fleur agreed.

'I don't expect they'll ever meet up again. Let them just have these few moments, eh?'

Fleur nodded, a lump in her throat. She felt torn by divided loyalties: loyalty to her mother and yet now she understood a little more the reason behind the faraway look she had so often seen in her father's eyes.

'Kenny'll put a stop to it, though, if he sees.'

Robbie laughed softly. 'He's got eyes for no one but Ruth, darling. I don't think he'll even notice. Now, come along, I think we can be on our way without it looking too rude to all these kind people.'

They made another circuit of the room, saying goodbye to everyone and repeating their thanks.

Kenny pumped Robbie's hand. 'Look after my big sister, else I'll be after you.'

Robbie laughed. 'I will and thanks, Kenny, for today. I know it hasn't been easy for you.'

Kenny pulled a face. There was no need to pretend he didn't know what Robbie meant. 'It's Dad I feel sorry for. It's not long before I can join up and, believe me, I'm off the moment I can. But Dad'll be left there on his own with her.' He shook his head. 'I really don't know what's got into her. She never used to be like this. But maybe once this is all over, she'll settle down a bit. Come to terms with it, you know.'

'I hope so,' Robbie said, but as he turned away to go towards where Jake and his mother were still standing engrossed in each other, he thought, *but I doubt it*.

Meg and Jake broke apart, almost guiltily, as Robbie and Fleur arrived beside them at the same moment.

'You off now?' Jake said heartily. He held out his hand to Robbie. There had been no official speeches by the father of the bride or the best man. Only Robbie had stood up and thanked everyone present for the marvellous surprise reception. So now was the moment for Jake to say, 'I'm proud to have you as my son-in-law. Take care of each other . . .' He seemed about to say more, but his voice cracked and he swallowed as if having difficulty in holding back the tears.

Meg broke the moment by kissing Fleur on both cheeks and saying, 'And I already love you, my darling daughter-in-law. And I can't wait for you to make me into a granny.'

The tension was broken by Robbie saying, 'Hey, steady on, Mum.' But he enveloped Meg into his arms, giving her a bear hug. 'Look after Pops and we'll see you as soon as we get back.'

'Where are you going?'

'Now that's a secret. Even Fleur doesn't know. But I'll ring Mr Tomkins when we get there. I promise.'

After a lot more handshaking and hugs, Fleur and Robbie finally made their escape, running hand in hand down the lane, laughing together.

'I thought we'd never get away,' Robbie said.

'I know, but wasn't it a lovely surprise? How sweet of everyone.'

'It was. The perfect send off.'

Back at the cottage, Fleur changed quickly into her best outfit and Robbie loosened his tie and flung his cap into the back of the borrowed sports car as he stowed Fleur's battered suitcase in the boot space. He opened the passenger door for her to climb in and then he vaulted over the door on the driver's side.

'Ready?' He grinned at her and Fleur giggled, deliciously anticipating the week ahead. A whole seven days alone and away from the war.

As they passed the pub, a shower of confetti cascaded over them, thrown by the villagers who lined the lane. With shouts of 'Good Luck' ringing in their ears, they roared out of the village.

It was strangely quiet after the sound of their car had faded away, an anti-climax after all the frivolity. The villagers began to drift away back to their own homes, carefully carrying some of the food that had been left. It was too precious to waste. Jake and Meg stood awkwardly together, knowing the moment of parting had come. As Kenny came bounding towards them, Meg held out her hand.

'Goodbye, Jake. It's been lovely to see you, and Robbie will look after her, I can promise you that.'

Jake nodded. 'I know,' he said huskily. 'And . . . and you take care of yourself, Meggie.'

'Ruth's had to rush off. She's on duty later. So—' Kenny glanced from one to the other. 'Are you ready, Dad?'

'Just coming, just coming, lad,' Jake replied, yet he made no move.

It was Meg who turned to Kenny, held out her hand and said, 'It's been good to meet you, Kenny. Take care.'

'Can we give you a lift anywhere, Mrs Rodwell?' the young man asked.

'That's very kind of you.' Meg smiled. 'But I'll be fine.'

Then, before either of them could stop her, she turned and walked away from them without looking back. Jake stood a moment watching her until Kenny touched his arm and said gently, 'Come on, Dad. Time we were going home.'

*

'What's this, I'd like to know?'

Betsy thrust Jake's large white handkerchief towards him, shaking it under his nose. Even before he could look at it properly, she shrieked, 'Make-up, that's what it is. A woman's make-up. Whose is it, might I ask? As if I didn't know.'

Jake blinked and stared at the smear of pink on the white cotton. Keeping his face expressionless, he said mildly, 'It's Fleur's. Whose do you think it is?' He stared her straight in the eyes. 'She had a few tears, the lass did. And why do you think that was, eh?'

For a moment, Betsy was disconcerted. 'Over me, you mean?'

'Of course over you, Betsy. Doesn't every girl want her mother with her on her wedding day?'

'How would *I* know?' Betsy said bitterly. 'I never had a mother. At least, not one I can remember very well.'

'Then all the more reason why you should've swallowed your own resentment and thought of her – for once. But you'll just have to live with it now, Betsy, won't you? That you didn't go to your only daughter's wedding.'

Jake turned on his heel and slammed out of the house, leaving Betsy – for the first time – feeling a twinge of guilt.

Thirty-Three

They drove to the east coast, to Skegness, where they walked along the sea front and viewed with sadness the lovely scene scarred with rolls of barbed wire. Areas of the wide expanse of sandy beach were mined. Even there, the war could not be forgotten entirely.

'There's a lot of RAF chaps about. I wonder why?' Robbie mused. In the bar of the guesthouse where they were staying, they found out.

'It's a training centre,' the landlord, Jim Spriggs, explained and winked. 'Good place for square bashing, ain't it? All that drill along Grand Parade and Tower Esplanade. They're even using some of the quieter streets, an' all. It's a sight to see.'

'We saw them this morning,' Robbie said. 'We were trying to get on the pier, but couldn't. I wanted to see it from the ground.' He smiled. 'We often come over this way when we're setting off across the North Sea and Johnny – that's our navigator – uses your pier as a guide. Reckons he knows what course to set then.'

'Aye, I've heard that said afore,' Jim nodded. 'They've built an assault course near the pier and another in an overgrown area at the end of North Parade that the locals have always called "The Jungle". The RAF lads are billeted in the empty hotels on the sea front and their officers' mess is in one of the bigger hotels, the NAAFI in another.' He pulled a face. 'But I reckon a lot of the hotels are closed for the duration – to holidaymakers that is. Oh, we get a few, like yourselves, but not like we used to afore the war. The kiddies can't play on a mined beach, can they? There's even a gun position in the Fairy Dell.' His mouth tightened. The fact seemed to hurt him personally. 'But it's not the RAF being here we mind,' he said, as if fearful he might have given offence to his guests. 'We like having 'em, and, of course, we've got the Royal Navy just up the road. Taken over Billy Butlin's holiday camp. HMS Royal Arthur, they call it. Oh, there's a lot going on in Skeggy, I can tell you, but it's just this bloody war's altered everyone's lives, hasn't it?' He eyed them curiously. 'What about you two . . . ?' Then, guessing correctly, a broad smile spread across his face. 'Ah, honeymooners, eh? A wartime wedding?'

Robbie grinned back at him. 'That's right.'

'Oi, missis,' the man raised his voice. 'We've got a couple of honeymooners here, love.'

His wife appeared from the kitchen, drying her hands on a towel. 'Oh, how lovely. I'll cook you something special tonight, my dears . . .' And with a smile and a nod, his 'missis' disappeared back into her kitchen.

'Now, mebbe I shouldn't be telling you this,' Jim said with a teasing smile, 'seeing as you're honeymooners, but there is a very good show on this week at the local theatre.' He reached under the bar and pulled out the local paper. Opening it up, he jabbed his finger. 'Aye, here it is. "All Clear" they call it. Some clever acts, so I've been told. And then there's two very good cinemas in the town.' He sniffed with annoyance. 'Used to have three we did until the Luftwaffe decided to bomb one of 'em last January. The Central and then there's the Parade on the sea front.'

'We saw it this morning. It was advertising a Henry Fonda film, I think.'

'That's right. *Chad Hanna*. It's got Dorothy Lamour in, an' all. I like her. Bit of all right, she is.' He glanced archly at Robbie. 'Mind you, you'll not be noticing, will ya, lad?'

'Of course not,' Robbie said gallantly.

Fleur grinned saucily and said, 'Well, I don't mind you looking, as long as you don't touch.' To which remark the two men laughed heartily.

'Then there's *Pygmalion* on at the Central with Leslie Howard and Wendy Hiller . . .' Jim went on.

'I've seen that,' Fleur said.

'So' – Robbie grinned – 'Dorothy Lamour it is, then.'

The variety show they saw at the Arcadia Theatre later in the week was slick and professional, with a silent comedy routine, a witty comedian, and a clever dancing act. To top it all, the female singer, Elsie, each night picked a serviceman from the audience to assist her in her song 'Arm in Arm Together'.

Robbie, sitting three rows back, in his smart RAF uniform, the silver buttons sparkling in the lights, was a sitting duck. He cast a rueful grin at Fleur, who dissolved into helpless laughter to see him taken up on stage to be greeted by rapturous applause from the audience. At the end of the song, Elsie brought him back to his seat and planted a kiss on his cheek, leaving a perfect impression of her mouth in lipstick.

'I thought I told you you couldn't touch,' Fleur spluttered and Robbie spread his hands in mock helplessness.

They had a blissful week before they had to return and be plunged once more into the middle of the war.

'I've missed you so much.' Ruth hugged her the moment she walked through the door. 'The girl they brought in to work in the watch office whilst you've been away is thick as pig whatsit. Kay's never stopped grumbling about her and can't wait for you to get back.' She pulled a comical face. 'Eh, hark at me getting all countrified. And you'll never guess what?'

Laughing, Fleur shook her head. 'Go on, tell me.'

'Harry's even had me gardening out there.' She nodded towards the back garden. 'Said I'd got to keep it in shape for you and that stuff needed gathering and it'd go to waste otherwise and then all your hard work'd be wasted.' She held out her hands, palms upward, fingers spread. 'Just *look* at my hands.'

'I just hope you've not pulled out all the plants and left the weeds.'

'Oh no. Harry was there, leaning over the fence, telling me what was what. Actually,' she added, self-consciously, as if she was quite surprised at herself, 'I've quite enjoyed it.' For a moment her eyes were haunted. 'It . . . it gets your mind off this bloody war for an hour or two.'

'Has . . . has it been bad?'

Ruth bit her lower lip as she nodded. 'Mm. We've lost eight planes during the last week.'

Fleur gasped. 'And the crews?'

287

Ruth lifted her shoulders in a helpless shrug.

And suddenly, the war with all its catastrophes was back with a vengeance.

Ruth linked her arm through Fleur's. 'Now, come and see what else I've been up to – with Mrs Jackson's permission of course.'

Fleur stared at her. 'What . . . what do you mean?'

'Come upstairs. I'll show you.'

Mystified, Fleur followed her up the narrow stairs.

Instead of turning to the small back bedroom where Fleur normally slept, Ruth flung open the door of the large front room that had once been Mrs Jackson's and her husband's but was now Ruth's room.

'This is your room from now on. Yours and Robbie's, when he can get away from camp.'

'But . . . but it's your room.'

'Not any more, it isn't. I've moved into your room at the back. I' – she let out a wistful little sigh – 'have no need of a double bed.'

'But you might. You might meet someone and—'

Now Ruth pursed her mouth and shook her head vehemently. 'No, I've told you. I made the mistake once of getting fond of someone and he got killed. I'm not putting myself through that pain again.' She glanced ruefully at Fleur. 'Sorry, love, I don't mean to put a damper on things for you. It's . . . it's just how I feel for myself, that's all. Maybe it's me that's being stupid.'

'No,' Fleur said gently and touched her friend's arm. 'I can only guess how you must have felt, but I do know that if anything happened to Robbie, I wouldn't want to take up with anyone else. So, if you'd really fallen for this chap, then . . . then . . . I do understand.'

'Oh, it was only early days with Billy. Nothing serious. We weren't engaged or anything. Hadn't even got as far as discussing marriage before he – before he . . .'

'But you had the feeling that that's where it might have led?'

Again Ruth bit her lip as tears filled her eyes and she nodded. But then she wiped her eyes and smiled. 'Come on in and see what I've done.'

They stepped into the bedroom and Fleur gazed around her. 'I don't remember it being like this.'

'It wasn't.' Ruth laughed now. 'I've painted it. Or rather, Kenny did.'

Fleur's eyes widened as she stared at Ruth. 'Kenny? Kenny's been here?'

'Oh yes. Cycled over three times, bless him. He's been great. He did all the painting and your mother-in-law has made the curtains and bedspread. Aren't they pretty?' She grinned widely. 'It's the best we could do in the time to create a bridal suite for you both.'

'Oh, Ruth, it's wonderful.' Slowly Fleur turned and took in every detail. Then she glanced at Ruth again. 'Did Kenny say – how things are at home?'

'Not as bad as they'd expected. It's a bit frosty, but at least she's speaking to them both.'

'And . . . and me?'

'He's not said. Sorry.'

Fleur sighed and turned her thoughts away from her mother and back to the present. 'I don't know how to thank you for all this. I don't know how you've managed it and keeping up with the garden an' all.'

'Think nothing of it. It's been fun doing it. We've had a lot of laughs, me an' your little brother.'

'I think a great deal of it, Ruth,' Fleur told her. 'And I can't wait to tell Robbie.'

For a few idyllic weeks, the front bedroom in Mary Jackson's tiny cottage became their little hideaway from the war even though it was still going on so close to them. But then Ruth came home with news that threatened their love nest.

'The WAAF quarters are finished. We've to move onto camp.'

Fleur stared at her in horror. 'Oh no! Really?'

Ruth nodded.

'What about—?' she began but, not wanting to sound selfish, went on, 'What about Mrs Jackson's garden and old Harry? He'll never manage to keep his house straight without you, Ruth.'

Ruth bit her lip. 'We'll just have to come whenever we can. We'll go and talk to ma'am. She's a good sort. I'm sure she'll let us come down here on our time off duty. Especially if we tell her about your garden. After all, that's part of the war effort, isn't it? As long as we don't take advantage of it.'

'Could we get hold of a couple of bikes, d'you think? It'd only be a few minutes on a bike.'

'We could try, but bicycles are in short supply just now. Everybody's riding them to get about camp.'

'I've got one at home. Maybe I could get it here somehow.'

'Perhaps Kenny would ride it over and hitch back.'

Fleur laughed. 'I'm sure he would – if *you* asked him.'

'Mission accomplished, then.' Her face sobered. 'But what about you and Robbie? It'll put paid to . . .'

She pointed upwards to the floor above and the bedroom that they had made their own.

Fleur nodded but could not speak.

But Mary Jackson, it seemed, had other ideas. 'You can come here whenever you can. As long as you look after the rooms – wash the sheets, an' that.'

'But won't you want the rooms for other lodgers. Evacuees maybe?'

Mary Jackson laughed softly and shook her head sadly. 'I'd've liked nothing better, my dears, than to have a couple of youngsters here, but I couldn't look after them, now could I?'

'They might want the accommodation for a mother with a baby or a young child,' Fleur said, still unable to believe that nothing stood in the way. 'They send the mothers too sometimes. They did at the beginning of the war.'

'They might,' Mary agreed. 'But I think it unlikely now. The evacuation seems to have slowed down. In fact, a lot of children are going back to the cities.'

'That's true,' Ruth said. 'Though I think the parents are daft. Old Hitler might choose any big city to have a go at. Look what he did to Coventry. Why Coventry, for heaven's sake?' She paused and then clapped her hands. 'That's settled then. As long as we can get permission, we'll come here every spare minute. Stay the night whenever we can. Fleur and Robbie can do your garden and I can still help old Harry.' She beamed. It all seemed so easy. 'Now all we've got to do is persuade ma'am.'

Squadron Officer Caroline Davidson was, as Ruth had put it, 'a good sort'. When the two girls asked to see her, she welcomed them into her office and heard what they had to say without interruption. She was thoughtful for a few moments whilst Fleur and Ruth waited anxiously. Then she smiled. 'I don't see why not. Just so long as you're very careful never to be late back on duty, otherwise it would have to stop immediately.'

Both girls nodded at once. 'Yes, ma'am. We'll make sure of that.'

As they saluted smartly and turned to leave, she added, 'And I'll have a word with Flight Sergeant Rodwell's commanding officer. Just to make sure he's aware of the situation. How very valuable Robbie's help is for the old lady's garden on his time off. We're very anxious to help in the local community whenever we can, you know.'

Fleur turned back to stare at her and was rewarded with a broad wink.

'Thank you, ma'am,' Fleur breathed.

Thirty-Four

The last weeks of September passed in a haze of busy hours on duty and, in a way, even busier off-duty time. Kenny brought Fleur's bicycle over and the following week he came again, pedalling one that Jake had unearthed from the barn for Ruth.

'It's a bit of a bone-shaker,' Kenny said, 'but I've cleaned it and oiled it.'

'As long as it gets me from A to B, I don't mind. Thanks, Kenny. I'll give you a kiss at Christmas.'

Though a flush crept up the young man's face, he was at ease enough with Ruth now to say, 'I'll keep you to that! And now, are you going to help me pick those apples down the bottom of the garden? That poor tree is so laden down, you can hardly see the bench underneath it.'

Ruth chuckled. 'Fleur often sits there for a bit of a rest. Her and Robbie.' For a moment, Ruth's eyes misted over. So often, just lately she had seen them sitting there under the apple tree, talking or just holding hands and watching yet another glorious Lincolnshire sunset. It always brought a lump to her throat. Half of her envied her friend, but deep in her heart she feared for her too.

But now she smiled brightly at Kenny as she added, 'But I haven't seen them sitting there lately. I reckon they're afraid of getting clouted on the head with falling apples.'

'Well, we can soon put that right. The fruit are well ready for picking – I had a look at them last week. It's a shame to let them fall off and get bruised; they don't store so well then. And then they can have their love seat back. Where are they, by the way?'

'Having dinner in the NAAFI. They'll be here in a bit.'

Kenny had only just reared the ladder up amongst the branches, when Fleur and Robbie rounded the corner of the cottage.'

'Need any help?'

'Hi, Sis. Well, I suppose if you can find another ladder, we'd be done in half the time. I could do this side of the tree and Robbie the other.'

'Harry's got one in his shed.'

'I'll fetch it.'

Robbie was back in a few minutes with Harry following in his wake.

'Now mind how you handle them apples. They bruise easy.' The old man stood looking up into the tree and stroking his moustache. 'Fine crop you've got there. How're you going to store them?'

'Lay them out on newspaper under the beds,' Fleur said.

'Aye, mind they're not touching an' you'll be all right. Just unmarked ones, mind. Any fallers, Mary can use straight away or dry them.'

'I'm going to help her bottle some this year,' Fleur put in. 'She can sit down to peel them and I can do everything else.'

'Mum's busy doing it at the moment. I picked all ours earlier in the week.'

For a moment, Fleur felt a pang of longing to visit her home again. To see her dad and – yes – her mother too.

'Harry – Harry!' Mrs Jackson was calling him from the back door. 'Come away in and leave them youngsters to it. They know what they're doing . . .'

With a comical smile, Harry shambled back up the pathway and disappeared into the house.

'They'll be sat either side of the wireless now,' Ruth smiled. 'Listening to—'

'The news!' the other three chorused and they all laughed.

'It'll be *Workers' Playtime* in a bit.'

'Well, we've no time to be playing. Let's get cracking . . .'

With the beginning of October, summer was over.

'By heck, it's nippy this morning,' Ruth shivered as they hurried towards the NAAFI. 'We ought to see if we can get Mrs Jackson any more coal. This weather won't do her arthritis any good.'

'I know. Have you seen her poor knuckles? They're so swollen. I didn't want her to peel all those apples when we were bottling last week, but she insisted.'

'Mind you she's that proud of her shelf of bottled fruit, I think it was worth it for her. Made her feel useful again.'

'Oh, she's doing her bit, all right. She's still knitting for the troops and it must be painful for her hands.'

As they walked into the dining room for breakfast, the air was thick with chatter, more animated than usual.

'Hello,' Ruth remarked, glancing round. 'Summat's

up. Let's find Kay. She'll know. I reckon she sleeps with the wireless on all night so she doesn't miss the news.'

They took their places at one of the new tables that had recently been delivered – a table for four that they shared with Kay and Peggy. They were already there, eating breakfast, but talking rapidly too.

'What's up, Corp?' Ruth demanded, sitting down opposite with her loaded plate and reaching for the sauce.

'He's advancing on Moscow. That'll be the end of him. Fancy trying now! In October! Doesn't he know what the Russian winter is like?' Kay was excited by the thought. 'If Napoleon couldn't do it, I doubt Adolf can.'

'Well, if he's got other things on his mind, maybe he'll leave us alone for a bit.'

It did seem a little quieter at Wickerton Wood, but whether that was because the Germans were busy elsewhere or because of the atrocious winter weather that lay over the whole country, no one could be certain. But everyone was thankful for a little respite, whatever the reason. Life settled into something of a routine, with off-duty times for Ruth, Fleur and Robbie spent at Mrs Jackson's little cottage. Kenny still cycled over at weekends whenever he could, but now Jake never came and Fleur missed her father more than she ever admitted to anyone.

The weather worsened, the temperature dropped and a cold winter was forecast.

November fog caused disruption to flying. No one

minded too much if raids were cancelled, but the worst situation was if, after take-off, a swirling mist shrouded the airfield by the time the aircraft were due back.

'I hate it when they're all diverted,' Fleur muttered quietly to Kay on one such night as they waited in the watch office, the runway only a few yards in front of them completely blotted out. 'I like to know that D-Doggo is back – that they're all back safely,' she added hurriedly, in case she'd sounded selfish.

For once, Kay did not respond with a tart retort. Instead, she sighed. 'I know just what you mean. It's daft, but I feel just the same.'

'Do you?' Fleur couldn't stop the surprised question escaping her lips.

Kay smiled wryly as she glanced behind her to make sure that Bob Watson was out of earshot. 'Oh, I know I sound as if I don't give a damn most of the time, but inside – I do care.' Her voice was suddenly husky. 'I care very much. A lot of my . . . my attitude is just an act, Fleur. Bravado, if you like . . .' Her voice trailed away and then, suddenly, she was brisk and efficient and razor sharp as ever, 'But if you ever tell a soul I've said this, I shall deny it hotly. OK?'

'Naturally, Corp,' Fleur said and, though she gave a playful salute, her tone was sincere. The two girls, bound by their concern for the safety of the same aircraft, exchanged a look of complete understanding.

'Now, we'd better get ready for telling these boys that they can't come home tonight . . .'

Later, as they clattered down the steps from Control, they were met by the eerily silent fog-bound station. They stood a moment, listening, but there was absolutely nothing to hear. Fleur shuddered. 'Come on, let's get to bed. I hate it like this. It's . . . it's ghostly.'

'Mm,' Kay, in a strangely pensive mood, pondered. 'Makes you think, doesn't it? I wonder if the ghosts of all the boys we've lost come back here? To their station?'

'Oh, don't! I don't even want to think about it. Come on, Kay, let's see if we can find the WAAF quarters in this lot. I tend to lose my sense of direction in fog.'

After taking a couple of wrong turns and ending up near the main guardhouse, they found their quarters and fell into bed. Fleur was exhausted, but sleep eluded her for over an hour. She knew D-Doggo had landed safely at another airfield, but it wasn't the same as knowing he was sleeping only a few hundred yards away in the airmen's quarters. If only they'd hurry up and get the married quarters built, it'd be even better.

The squadron had been forced to go on to land at an airfield in Yorkshire, many of them dangerously low on fuel. Only one didn't make it and had to crash land in a field. Luckily, the crew only suffered cuts and bruises and came back to Wickerton Wood the following day indignantly travelling in the back of a RAF lorry. The rest of the aircraft flew in throughout the morning. Other than the unwelcome diversion, it had been a successful mission and all the crews were safe.

'Talk about brass-monkey weather,' Fleur shivered as she joined the other three at breakfast. 'D'you know there were icicles on the *inside* of the window this morning? I wish I was back at Mrs Jackson's in her nice feather bed.'

'It'll be even colder in Russia. It's the first of December tomorrow,' Kay remarked, wagging her fork towards Fleur. 'If Hitler doesn't take Moscow in the next few days, his troops'll never survive the winter.' Her interest in the news never waned. 'And I'll tell you something else I've heard on the grapevine. All single women between the ages of twenty and thirty are to be called up. So – we'd all have been in the services soon even if we hadn't volunteered.'

For a moment Fleur felt a rush of relief. Her voluntary entry into the WAAFs had been vindicated, but at Kay's next words she felt a shudder of apprehension.

'And they're lowering the call-up age for men to eighteen and a half and raising it to men aged fifty.'

So in roughly a year's time, Kenny – he would be eighteen next March – would have to go anyway. And what about her dad? He was still under fifty – just. Would he be called up? She had a sudden picture of her mother sitting at the table filling out numerous forms to stop her menfolk being sent to war.

Then Fleur remembered. Her dad still limped from an injury in the last war. He wouldn't be classed as fit enough now.

But Kenny would. Oh yes, Kenny would be A1 fit.

'We don't need a bloody wireless when you're around, Corp,' Ruth was saying, dragging Fleur's thoughts back to the conversation around the table. 'But could you give us a little light entertainment too, d'you think? Can you imitate Tommy Handley or sing like Vera Lynn?'

Kay enjoyed the banter. Both Fleur and Ruth gave

her back as good as she gave out, but Kay never 'pulled rank' though, as a corporal, she could have done. Only Peggy was the quiet one of the four and just listened to the sharp exchanges with a placid smile.

But a few days later everyone was appalled by the news that was going round.

'Oh, they've done it now.' Kay was jubilant. 'That's America in the war for certain now.'

'But it's Japan that's attacked them. They'll concentrate on them, won't they?'

'It's a world war now. They'll just fight everybody.' Kay grinned as she added, ''Cept us. Good to have a mighty friend on our side, isn't it?'

Fleur shook her head. 'But why? Why have Japan attacked Pearl Harbor? They must know they'd reap the whirlwind.'

'Don't ask me. I'm just glad we're on the right side of the whirlwind.'

A few days later, the news guru said, 'I told you so. I told you didn't I?'

'You tell us a lot of things, Corp,' Ruth remarked dryly. 'To which particular piece of your undoubted wisdom are you referring?'

'Oh well, if you don't want to know, then . . .' Kay retorted but then she caught Ruth's wink. 'Oh, you . . . !'

'Tell us, then,' Fleur said.

The three of them were sitting at their usual table in the dining room for dinner. Peggy was away on leave.

'The Russians are chasing Adolf out. They've recaptured some of the places that the Germans had taken and now Adolf's boys are on the run. I told you the Russian winter would defeat him – his troops can't withstand the cold. Can't get supplies through either, I shouldn't wonder. But the Russians know how to cope, don't they? They're used to it.'

'Do you think he'll try again? Next spring?' Fleur, too, was caught up with the staggering news of the last few days.

Kay shrugged. 'Not if he's any sense.'

'But he hasn't, has he?' Ruth put in, her mouth full of stew and dumplings.

'What?'

'Any sense.'

They were silent, each concentrating on their meal, until Ruth asked, 'So? What are we all doing for Christmas, then?'

'Oh, crumbs, I haven't got as far as that yet,' Fleur said.

'You still haven't come down off cloud nine since your wedding,' Kay teased, and gave an exaggerated sigh. 'Ordinary life has to go on for the rest of us. Like planning Christmas.'

'Have we got leave?'

Ruth pulled a face. 'Shouldn't think so for a minute. I think – though I don't know – that leave will be granted to those whose homes are a long way off. After all – to be fair – we do get home a lot because our families live relatively near. I mean, we can get home and back on just a twenty-four, can't we?'

Fleur nodded. 'I see what you mean.' She was silent for a moment. 'I wonder if they'd let us do something on camp to celebrate? Those of us who don't go home?'

'Oh, I'm sure there'll be a dance in the sergeants' mess and—'

'No, I meant something a bit more than that.' She

leant forward across the table towards the other two. 'I tell you what I'd really like to do.'

'What?'

'Throw a Christmas party for all the evacuee kids in the village – and the village kids an' all, of course.'

Ruth stared at her for a moment and then her face lit up. 'Fleur – that's a brilliant idea. Who do we have to ask?'

'Er – well, we could start with ma'am . . .'

Fleur's idea was taken up enthusiastically by everyone on camp and the date was fixed for the afternoon of Christmas Eve. A few days beforehand, willing hands – even those who would not be there on the day because they'd be on leave – helped to decorate the sergeants' mess.

'There's a bloke at the main gate asking for Fleur,' Johnny called from the doorway.

'Oho, Robbie,' Tommy shouted from the top of the ladder, where he was hanging paper chains across the ceiling. 'Got a rival already, old boy. Have to watch her.'

Johnny, grinning in the doorway, said, 'Well, he's a nice-looking bloke, I'll give you that, but he is old enough to be her father . . .'

Fleur gasped and her eyes widened. 'Dad? Here? Oh – I wonder what's wrong?' Before Johnny could say any more, Fleur had gone out of the mess and was running along the road towards the main gate, her hair flying loose, her jacket undone. She was lucky she didn't encounter any WAAF officers in her headlong flight, or she might have been on a charge and missed the children's party for which she'd worked so hard.

Jake was standing talking amiably to the guard commander as Fleur dashed up.

'What's wrong, Dad?'

'Oh, sorry, love, I didn't mean to worry you. Nothing's wrong. I've just brought you a Christmas tree. Kenny said you're throwing a party for all the kids in the village and I thought—'

'Oh, Dad, that's wonderful. We've only got a pathetic-looking thing made out of wire and green paper.' She turned to the guard commander. 'May he drive round to the sergeants' mess?'

Permission granted, Jake was greeted at the mess with open arms, quite literally, for Ruth ran towards him as he struggled through the door with the Christmas tree. 'Mr Bosley, you darling! We've got all these lovely tree decorations from Mrs Jackson, Harry and Bill Moore at the pub and no tree to put them on. Oh, that's perfect.' She clapped her hands. 'Now, where shall we put it?'

Already, Robbie, Tommy and Johnny were moving forward to help. 'How about over here in the corner? And then we can put all the presents for the kids under the tree.'

'Presents? My word, you have been busy,' Jake said.

'We've collected round the camp and we've managed to buy one present for each child.'

'And the CO has promised to dress up as Father Christmas.'

'Fleur,' Jake said softly, 'I tried to get your mam to make some extra puddings and a cake, but . . .'

'Don't worry, Dad,' she said, slipping her arm through his and hugging it to her side. 'This is absolutely great – you couldn't have brought anything better. And . . . and it's lovely to see you. I . . . I've missed you.'

His dark brown eyes regarded her soulfully. 'Why don't you come home any more? Surely you must have had a couple of days' leave some time since your wedding?'

Fleur ran her tongue round her lips. 'I . . . I wanted to. At least, if I'm honest, *part* of me wanted to. The other part – well – I didn't want to make matters worse than they already are.'

Jake sighed heavily. 'Well, they're not going to get any better unless you do come home from time to time and try to heal the breach.'

'All right, Dad. I will come. I promise.'

His face was bleak for a moment. 'Kenny's going in March, don't forget. He'll be eighteen then and he still seems determined to go even before he really has to.'

'I know,' Fleur whispered. She was hardly likely to forget that. It blighted her waking hours and some of her sleeping ones too.

'Have you heard?' Robbie's face was ecstatic. 'Tommy's just told the crew.'

'Father Christmas has landed on the runway?' Ruth volunteered.

'Better than that!'

'The war's over?'

'It soon will be now. We're getting the new Lancasters and they're arriving on Christmas Eve.'

All eyes turned to look at Robbie and then the excited questions began. 'How many?' 'Will we get a chance to train on them?' 'How many crew do they need?' 'What bombs can they carry?'

'Whoa, whoa there!' Laughing, Robbie held out his hands, palms outwards, fending off the volley of questions. 'We'll find out soon enough.'

The arrival of the new aircraft was amazing. Every vantage point was lined with station personnel and Fleur and Kay, on duty in the watch office, held their breaths as the first of the magnificent planes approached the airfield and landed smoothly.

'My word, what a beauty!' Kay said, her mouth open in wonder as she stared at the lines of the aircraft, strangely elegant in such a powerful machine.

'What a Christmas present!' Fleur laughed as another approached the airfield and she heard the wireless burst into life. 'Hello, Woody, this is J-Janie calling . . .'

And in they all came, one after another until they were all safely landed.

'And now we're going to party,' Kay said as they clattered down the steps from the watch office and headed towards the sergeants' mess.

The party was a great success, even though one or two children over-indulged at the sight of so much food and promptly threw up. 'Father Christmas' played his part and earned a new respect from those under his command.

'D'you know,' Johnny said later, 'I always thought the CO was a miserable old devil, but he was really good with those kids. Did you see? And he was great on Christmas Day too, wasn't he?'

The station had followed the usual tradition of all

the officers serving the lower ranks with their Christmas dinner. They had entered into the spirit of the occasion with great aplomb and accepted the ribbing with equanimity.

'No, he's a good bloke,' Robbie said. 'But, y'know, I think I'd be a miserable old devil in his position. I don't envy his responsibilities one bit. Sending crews off night after night, not knowing how many are going to come back. And just think of the dreadful letters he has to write when they don't.' Robbie gave a shudder. 'God – it must be a nightmare.'

Johnny's usual cheerful face sobered suddenly. 'Yeah, you're right, mate. I hadn't looked at it like that.' Then, his face crinkling once more into its usual grin, he punched Robbie's shoulder. 'Come on, let's go and play with our new Lanc.'

There would be no operations for a while from Wickerton Wood.

'We've to go on a course at a heavy conversion unit,' Robbie told Fleur. 'It'll be for about six weeks.'

'Six weeks! D'you mean I won't see you for six weeks?' She was staring at him in horror, but Robbie was grinning.

'It's only near Newark.'

Fleur let out a sigh of relief. 'That's all right then. You think you'll get leave now and then?'

Robbie shook his head. 'Probably not, but you should. There'll not be much going on here until we come back, I shouldn't think.'

Fleur pulled a face. 'I wouldn't bank on it. They'll find something for us to do, I've no doubt.'

The six weeks passed surprisingly quickly whilst the newly formed crews of seven instead of four under-went their training on the new aircraft: take-offs, circuits, landings and even flying across country at different heights to familiarize themselves with how the aircraft, heavier than they had been used to with its four mighty Merlin engines, performed. Whenever they met up, Robbie talked of nothing else.

When they all returned to Wickerton Wood, Robbie was enthusiastic about his new instruments.

'It's all right for you, you jammy devil,' Alan, the rear gunner, complained. 'You've got the hottest seat in the house.'

Robbie laughed, but Fleur was anxious. 'What's he mean?'

'He means it's the warmest place in the aircraft.'

'Oh, I . . . I thought he meant it was the most dangerous.'

'No. Actually, it's probably one of the safest places to be. I'm right behind the skipper and the back of his seat is armour-plated.'

'Really?'

'Yes, really.' He kissed her on the end of her nose. 'So stop worrying. It's a great aircraft.'

'It's the best Christmas present ever. Now we can get at 'em,' was the opinion of everyone.

Thirty-Five

'You know, you really ought to go home, Fleur. For a visit. Try to make it up with your mother,' Robbie murmured as they lay in each other's arms in the pale light of dawn after a blissful night of love. He kissed her hair. 'I don't like being the cause of a rift between you.'

It was February already and neither of them had been able to get home over Christmas or at New Year or since. Robbie because of the training course and Fleur because heavy falls of snow had given her the perfect excuse to stay at Wickerton. It was surprising that the crews had managed to complete enough flying hours on the course, but somehow they had.

Despite her father's plea, Fleur was still putting off the moment. 'I suppose you're right.' She sighed. 'But I don't want to miss any time with you.'

'Well, we're not always off duty at the same time,' Robbie pointed out reasonably.

'Mostly we are. Because ... because when you're flying, I'm usually in the watch office.' There was a pause before Fleur suggested, 'We could go together.'

'No, I don't think that's a good idea. Rather fuelling the flame, don't you think?'

'I suppose so.'

'Tell you what, next time we get a decent leave I'll

go and see Ma and Pops and you go to Middleditch Farm.'

'All right.' Fleur sighed again, knowing he was right, but feeling she would much rather visit the tiny terraced house in Nottingham with him. She would receive a warmer welcome from Robbie's mother than she ever would from her own.

'Good,' he said as he began kissing her. 'And now, Mrs Rodwell, before we have to get up and face the day . . .'

'Hello, Dad,' Fleur said softly, leaning on the top of the bottom half of the cowshed door. 'I thought I'd find you here.'

Jake straightened up from the milking stool. 'Fleur, love.' His smile was warm and loving. He picked up the bucket of milk and came towards her. 'Good to see you.' He looked into her eyes. 'I don't need to ask if everything's all right. I can see it is.'

'Oh, Dad, if only it wasn't for this wretched war, then life would be perfect.'

'Aye,' Jake's face clouded. 'Aye, it would.'

'But then, if it hadn't been for the war, I might not have met Robbie.'

'True, true,' Jake murmured absently.

Fleur glanced behind him into the shadows of the cowshed. 'Where's Kenny? Isn't he here? Helping you with the milking?'

Jake shook his head. Fleur searched his face. 'What is it, Dad? What's wrong?'

'He's gone. Kenny's gone.'

'Gone? Gone where?'

'Into the RAF. Seems he volunteered a while back

and he got his papers the day before yesterday and off he went.'

'But . . . but . . . he's not old enough. He's not even eighteen yet.'

Jake shrugged. 'He is next month. Seems it doesn't matter. He's in and that's all he cares about.'

There was a pause before Fleur said, 'He'd've been better in the army. Maybe they wouldn't send him abroad straight away, but the RAF. I mean once he's done his training he – they . . .'

'I thought it was the army he wanted too. It was – at first. But it seems . . . it seems as if he was influenced by – by . . .' His voice fell away as if he couldn't bring himself to say any more.

'By Robbie, you mean,' Fleur whispered.

Her father nodded. They stood awkwardly for a moment, neither knowing what to say. At last Jake said haltingly, 'You'd best go in. See yer mother.'

'No, no, I'll help you finish here.'

'You'll get yerself mucky,' he said, glancing at her uniform.

She pulled in a deep breath. 'Then I'll go in and find some old clothes. Unless, of course, Mum's thrown them all out.'

'No, no.' Jake sighed. 'Your room's just as you left it.'

'I won't be a mo, then.'

'Fleur—' Jake began but she was gone, running across the yard towards the back door. As she stepped into the scullery, her mother looked up from the sink.

'Oh, it's you. Well, I hope you're satisfied. He's gone. Joined the wonderful RAF.'

'Mum – I'm sorry. But it's not all my fault. He was determined to join up somehow.'

'It's your fault he's joined the RAF, though. Yours and – and *his*.'

Stung to retort, Fleur snapped. 'His name's Robbie.'

'Oh yes, I know what his name is all right. And his bloody mother's. Oh, I know *her* name all right. As if I could ever forget it. I wish to God I could.' Betsy slammed down the plate she was washing onto the wooden draining board with such force that it cracked in two. 'Now look what you've made me do. I've broken one of me best plates.'

'Mum,' Fleur said tiredly. 'Won't you tell me what all this is about? Don't you think we have a right to know? What has Robbie done for you to hate him so? You don't even know him.'

Betsy didn't answer but picked up the shattered pieces and dropped them into a bin at the side of the sink. 'It's not him. It's his mother.'

'Then why take it out on Robbie if it's not his fault?'

Betsy glared at her and avoided answering. Instead, she asked another question. 'Were they together at the wedding?'

Fleur frowned. 'Who? Robbie and his mother?'

Betsy gave a tut of exasperation. 'Your dad and her?'

Fleur blinked. 'Well – yes – they talked.'

Betsy held Fleur's gaze, as if daring her to look away. Fleur stared back boldly but her heart was thumping madly. She didn't want to lie to her mother, but neither did she want to admit that her father and Robbie's mother had stood close together holding hands and gazing into each other's eyes.

'Did they – did they go off together?'

Her heart rate slowed a little. 'Go off together? Of course not.'

'Hm.' Betsy sounded doubtful. She folded her arms in front of her and stepped closer to Fleur. 'Tell me – and I want the truth mind – did your father wipe your face with his handkerchief?'

Fleur gaped. 'Wipe my face? I don't know what you mean.'

'There was a woman's make-up on his handkerchief. He said it was yours. That . . . that you'd shed a few tears and he'd mopped your face. Is that true?'

Fleur's gaze didn't flicker, but she felt her heart begin to pound again. Slowly, she nodded. 'Yes, yes, he did. When he first got to the house. He was late and I thought he wasn't coming . . .' Her voice trailed away and she held her breath. Was her mother going to believe her? It was true she'd cried. It was true that someone had dabbed her face with a hanky. But that someone had been Ruth – not Jake.

After a moment, Betsy nodded. 'Very well then. But they did meet and they did talk?'

Fleur forced a laugh. 'Well, yes, of course they did. They could hardly avoid each other, now could they? But it was only at the pub afterwards and—'

'But you weren't there all the time, were you? You went off on your honeymoon. You don't know what happened after that, do you?'

'Well, no, but Kenny was still there.'

'Oh yes, Kenny. But he was so taken up with this . . . this Ruth that he wouldn't see what was going on under his nose.'

'Ruth had to go back to camp straight after we left. Kenny wouldn't have wanted to stay on then.'

'Oh.' Betsy was thoughtful for a moment then she turned away. 'Anyway, what have you come for?'

'I came to see if I could put matters right between you and me, Mum.'

'Well, I'm sorry you've had a wasted journey. While you're married to that lad and seeing his mother, I don't want owt to do with you. And now Kenny's gone . . .' She left the accusation hanging in the air.

'Then I'm sorry, Mum, very sorry. But I love Robbie and he loves me and if no one will tell us what this . . . this feud is all about, then there's nothing either of us can do. And I'm sorry about Kenny too. He would have gone somewhere – the army or somewhere – but yes, I agree, it is my fault he chose the RAF and I'm just going to have to live with that, aren't I?' Then she turned and fled upstairs, rushed into her old room and slammed the door behind her, leaning against it. She closed her eyes and groaned. Now she had two people she loved to worry about. Robbie – and Kenny too.

Ruth's reaction to Fleur's news that Kenny had joined the RAF was predictable.

'Stupid little bugger,' she railed. 'Why on earth didn't he stay out of it? He'd got the chance living on a farm and being in a reserved occupation. All quite above board. Why on earth does he want to play the hero?'

'Mum says it's all my fault. Because I joined up, he doesn't want to be left behind and have everyone thinking him a coward.'

Ruth let out a very unladylike snort. 'No one's going to think that. At least, not anyone with any sense.'

There was a pause before Fleur asked gently, 'Then

why did you join the WAAF? You could have done your bit some other way – in a factory or something.'

''Cos I was just as stupid when it all began. Fighting for my country and all that tosh.'

'So you wouldn't mind if Hitler walked in then?' Fleur said with deceptive mildness.

Ruth sighed heavily, her anger dying. 'Yes, of course I would. Oh, I know we've got to stop him. I know we've got to stop him coming here and we've got to help all these other poor folk he's already trampling over, but . . . but – oh, Fleur – you should understand if anyone does – what with Robbie and now Kenny too in danger every day.'

'Oh, I do,' Fleur said grimly, thinking of the sleepless nights she was having even when she wasn't on duty. The only time she felt at peace was when Robbie was lying beside her. But even that was spoilt because now she had Kenny to worry about. She didn't even know where he was or what he was doing. She didn't know which was the worst: knowing – or not knowing.

'I'm sorry.' Ruth put her arms around Fleur. 'It must be awful for you. And with your mum making it worse by blaming you. How's your dad taking it?'

'He's worried. Naturally.'

'But – but does he blame you?'

'I don't know. He hasn't said except to say that Kenny had joined the RAF because of Robbie. He'd never say outright, but . . . but maybe deep down . . .'

Ruth hugged her harder. 'Come on, girl. Chin up. Let's just pray they'll both stay safe, eh?'

Fleur rested her face against Ruth's shoulders and screwed up her eyes, trying to stem the tears.

She'd pray all right. Oh, how she would pray. But it was a lot to ask.

Thirty-Six

Towards the end of March, the RAF began a round-the-clock bombing campaign against the German arms' factories. Night after night the airmen at Wickerton Wood and their new Lancasters were involved, often escorted by Spitfires.

On a rare night off Fleur and Robbie spent the time at Mrs Jackson's cottage. Flying was still going on, so Ruth was on duty.

Robbie lay back on the bed, still in his uniform, his tie loosened, his hair ruffled. He closed his eyes with a weary sigh. 'Oh, Fleur, when is it all going to end and we can find our own little cottage with roses round the door and an apple tree we can sit under to watch the sunsets?'

She sat on the bed beside him, took his hand and kissed each finger. 'I don't know, but we're all doing our best to end it quickly. You especially.'

'But the end's nowhere in sight. At least, it doesn't seem to be. Two and a half years and we don't seem any nearer. In fact, it just seems to have got worse. What with Japan and America in it too now. Oh, darling, I just feel so . . . so tired. I . . .'

Fleur leant forward to kiss him, but then she hesitated. Robbie was asleep. She put the eiderdown over him and then undressed quietly and slipped into the bed beside him. But sleep evaded her.

She was worried. She had never heard Robbie talk like that. With a defeated air. He was always so positive with a 'get up and get at 'em' attitude. But tonight he'd seemed – well – beaten.

He's just so tired, she thought. He'll be all right tomorrow. And tomorrow, she reminded herself, is his very last mission. The four men from the original crew would have completed a full tour of duty and deserved a well-earned break. But one worry ate away at her. With the newly formed crews, would they want to break them up? Would they make Tommy and the other three carry on? She wasn't sure of regulations and Robbie refused to discuss it. It was as if he was superstitious about discussing the elusive thirtieth op. Only very few aircrews survived to even reach it and to mention it seemed like tempting fate . . .

The following morning, they rose late and ate a leisurely breakfast, which Fleur had gone downstairs in her dressing gown to bring up to their room.

They set the tray aside and Fleur climbed back into the bed.

'Feel better this morning?' she whispered.

'Yes. I'm sorry about last night. I don't know what got into me.'

She stroked his hair. 'You're tired. You're all tired. But only one more mission tonight and then . . .'

'I know. Maybe that's what's getting to me. What'll happen then, d'you think? D'you think we might get split up? Posted, even?'

'Oh, I hope not!'

Robbie grinned wickedly and took her in his arms, 'But we'd better make the most of this morning, just in case . . .'

'Fleur? Fleur, dear, are you there?' It was Mary Jackson calling from the foot of the stairs.

Robbie let out a groan and Fleur stifled her giggles against him, before she was able to lift her head and shout, 'Yes, Mrs Jackson. What is it?'

'Kenny's here, dear.'

'Kenny! How lovely! Oh—' She turned back to Robbie. 'I'm sorry, darling.'

Robbie smiled and kissed her. 'It's all right. Let's go down and see him.'

They dressed quickly and hurried downstairs. Fleur flung her arms round her brother, tall and resplendent in his RAF uniform.

'I've just got a spot of leave,' he said excitedly. 'Basic training'll soon be finished. Then it'll be passing out parade and I'm volunteering for fighter training . . . So, in the meantime . . .' He saluted smartly. 'Aircraftman Bosley reporting for duty, ma'am. Digging fatigues, is it?'

Fleur hugged him. 'We'll have a lovely day together, but we're on duty tonight. It's Robbie's last mission for a while.'

Kenny grinned and slapped his brother-in-law on the back. 'And there I was hoping to be escorting you in my Spitfire one of these days.'

'Oh, you'll get the chance. I've no doubt we'll be called on to do another tour before long.'

Fleur felt her heart plummet. Naively, she thought that Robbie's flying days would be over, that he'd be given a nice, safe desk job somewhere. In her wilder moments she'd even imagined him being in charge of the watch office, that they would be working together. But of course that would never happen. He was a trained wireless operator. Of course he would have to fly again . . .

But for today, she had both of them safely with her. They would make the most of today. 'So,' she said, forcing a bright smile onto her face. 'What are we going to do?'

'Well, I thought I'd help you in the garden a bit this morning – if you want me to, that is – and then this afternoon, I thought we'd go into Lincoln,' Kenny said. 'I'll treat you to a slap-up tea in Boots cafe. How about that?'

'You're on. A celebration tea.' She glanced at Robbie. 'Do you know what day it is?'

Robbie blinked. 'Er – Wednesday?'

Fleur smiled. 'Well, yes it is, but I meant the date. It's exactly a year ago today since we met.'

'Is it really? Fancy me forgetting.'

She reached up and kissed him lightly. 'You're forgiven. You've rather had other things on your mind just lately.'

'I'll make a stew for all of us for dinner and an apple pie,' Mrs Jackson said, struggling to her feet.

'We don't want to put you to any trouble, Mrs Jackson.' Robbie turned to her.

'No trouble, love.' The old lady patted his arm and chuckled. 'It'll make me feel useful.'

'Oh, I almost forgot, Mrs Jackson,' Kenny said. 'Dad's sent you some eggs and butter. I'll get them.'

As he opened the door, Ruth was coming round the corner of the cottage. Kenny's eyes lit up. 'Just the person I'd hoped to see. We're going into Lincoln this afternoon for tea.' He gave an exaggerated bow. 'Would madam care to join us?'

'Hi, Kenny. Fancy seeing you here. Got your wings yet?'

'Not quite, but I start training soon. Can't tell you where, of course.' He tapped the side of his nose. 'Careless talk, and all that, but it's somewhere down south.'

Fleur giggled. 'Oh, I think we're allowed to know where, Kenny. Else how will Mum know where to address all those food parcels she's bound to want to send you?'

He blinked and his young face wore a comical expression. 'Oh yes. I suppose so. I'm just not used to all this sort of secrecy. They dinned it into us so much that we mustn't say this and mustn't say that, that I'm not exactly sure what I can say and what I can't.' He grinned. 'So I thought it best just to say nothing.'

They all laughed, but Fleur said, 'I know what you mean. I felt that way too at first, but you soon find out what it's safe to say. You can tell your family where you're stationed but not the details about missions and so on.'

'But I'm going to train as a fighter pilot. That's a bit different, isn't it? We get scrambled when enemy aircraft are approaching, don't we?'

'I expect so.'

'And I suppose that's why I'm being sent down south. That's where the Battle of Britain went on, isn't it?'

Fleur felt a cold shudder of apprehension run through her as she imagined her baby brother up there above the clouds chasing after enemy bombers as they thundered towards England to rain death from the skies. She quelled the feeling swiftly and smiled up at him. 'Let's hope there's not so much going on now. Old Hitler seems to have other things on his mind.'

'Good job he has,' Kenny said with feeling. 'We were lucky he didn't invade in 'forty, y'know.'

'I do know. If he had done . . .' She said no more, but the same thought was in all their minds. If Hitler had pressed home his invasion plans in September 1940, what would life be like right now in Britain? It didn't bear thinking about.

'I wish Mum would see it like that,' Kenny murmured.

'How is she?'

Kenny pulled a face. 'Cross and then weepy. Hardly speaking to me one minute and then crying all over me the next.'

'Poor Mum,' Fleur said. 'It's not easy for her, Kenny.' She punched his arm gently. 'And for heaven's sake, take care of yourself. And, now,' she added briskly, 'this garden isn't going to dig itself.'

Ruth yawned. 'I'll just grab a couple of hours on my lovely soft feather bed upstairs and then I'll nip round to Harry's.'

The day passed all too quickly and then they were waving Kenny goodbye on the train back home. 'Well, I'll be off back tomorrow and then I'll soon be up in the clouds alongside you, Robbie. Wish me luck.'

The two men shook hands and Fleur hugged her brother hard. 'Oh, we do, we do. Good luck, darling bro.'

And then Kenny turned to Ruth. 'Goodbye, Ruth,' he said and suddenly he was boyishly shy.

'Good luck, Kenny,' Ruth said, giving him a bear

hug. As she drew back, she touched his cheek tenderly and looked into his eyes as she added earnestly, 'And take care of yourself.'

'I will. I'll . . . I'll see you soon.'

Then, with a last wink to Fleur, he boarded the train and leant out of the window waving until they could no longer see him. For several minutes, Fleur stood watching the receding train until Robbie put his arm around her shoulders and said softly, 'Come on, love, time we were all getting back. Last trip for a while – I can't wait for tonight to be over.'

Fleur shuddered. It was the first time she'd ever heard Robbie talk like that. He must be wearier than even she had realized.

In the control tower, Fleur stood alone staring at the blackboard with the names of the aircraft chalked up as they returned. There was one blank space left. One plane had not returned from the operation.

Robbie Rodwell's bomber.

Fleur lost track of the time she stood there, just staring at the blackboard, willing the radio to crackle into life, praying to hear the call sign. 'Hello, Woody, this is Lindum T-Tommy calling . . .'

But the radio was silent, the space left blank. She couldn't even have Ruth with her. She was already on duty at the debriefing. But she knew that T-Tommy had not come home. Maybe, at this very moment, Ruth was hearing what had happened to Robbie and the others. It had seemed a good omen at the time, that the call sign given to the new Lancaster they were now flying had, by coincidence, the same name as its skipper. Now, Fleur wasn't so sure.

Kay, too, had remained in the control room, hunched over her radio but unable to meet Fleur's eyes. Bob Watson carried on with all the necessary duties he had at the end of a mission, his face grim. He was studiously avoiding looking at either of the girls.

The room was silent, the airfield outside the window silent too in the early morning light. Though she strained her ears, there was no welcome sound of a damaged aircraft limping home.

She heard the door open behind her and for a moment her heart leapt. She spun round, her face suddenly alight with hope. There'd been a mistake! T-Tommy had landed and they'd missed it. Robbie had been safely home all the time . . .

It was her heart speaking, not her head. Control never missed a plane landing. It simply didn't happen. They were all too professional, too thorough. But terror and hope are strange bedfellows and forced the mind to play strange tricks.

Of course it wasn't Robbie who had stepped into the room, but Squadron Leader Tony Harris, whose aircraft had been the last to land. His face was sombre and her heart plummeted as she saw the sympathy in his eyes.

'I'm sorry, Fleur. One of the other pilots has reported at the debriefing that he saw a bomber with two of its engines on fire going down just off the coast. It looks like it could have been T-Tommy. It's the only one that hasn't come back this time.'

It was a good night's work. Even Fleur had to acknowledge that. Only one bomber missing. But why, oh why, did it have to be Robbie's?

The lump in her throat threatened to choke her, but she managed to ask, 'Did they see any parachutes?'

'It was too dark to see.'

'Thank you for letting me know, sir,' she said, shakily.

'There's still a chance, Fleur. We don't give up hope until we know for definite, do we?' Like her, the squadron leader was forcing an optimism he didn't really feel deep inside. He was not relishing the thought of the difficult letters that he would have to write to all the families of the missing crew, should the worst be confirmed. Fleur nodded, now not trusting herself to speak.

'I'll see Caroline – your commanding officer.'

If she hadn't been so distressed, Fleur might have smiled at the squadron leader's use of ma'am's Christian name. Rumour on camp had it that they were seeing each other on the QT. As it was, Fleur was quite lost in a flood of grief that she scarcely noticed. She couldn't allow herself false hope. She'd already seen too much of it. 'I'll see if she can arrange a spot of leave for you,' he went on. 'I expect you'd like to go home. See your own folks. And . . . and his mother. She's in Nottingham, I understand.'

Fleur nodded and managed to whisper huskily, 'Thank you.'

He moved across the room to have a word or two with Kay, who was still sitting in front of her microphone. He put his hand on her shoulder and bent down towards her, but Kay didn't speak, didn't even respond to his kindly gesture.

After he'd left the office, Fleur stood for a few moments longer just staring at the blank space on the blackboard. A space that would never now be filled in.

'Fleur . . .' She heard the scrape of a chair on the floor and heard Kay's voice, but she held out her hand, palm outwards. She closed her eyes for a moment and shook her head. She couldn't cope with sympathy – however well meant – at this moment. She was about to turn away, to run away as far as she could go, to deal with her anguish on her own, but then, even through her own pain, she remembered.

Tommy – Kay's Tommy! Of course! He was missing too. How could she have been so thoughtless, so selfishly wrapped up in her own grief that she had not given a thought to Kay?

'Oh, Kay – Kay . . .' She held out her arms and the two girls flew to each other, holding their friend tightly and crying against each other's shoulder. Quietly, his work finished, Bob Watson left the room.

The man felt guilty. There was nothing he could say. It would sound hypocritical. He'd never hidden his disapproval of wartime romances, let alone a wartime wedding. And now his fears had been realized and there was nothing he could say – or do. Not for the first time he silently cursed this blasted war!

After a few moments, Kay pulled herself free of Fleur's clinging arms. 'Right. This won't do any good. It's not what they would have wanted. Come on, get a grip, girl.'

Fleur was still hiccuping, overwhelmed by her grief, wallowing in a deluge of loss, despairing as to how she was ever going to cope with tomorrow and tomorrow and tomorrow. A lifetime of loneliness stretched bleakly before her. She raised her head and stared through her tears at Kay. She couldn't believe that the other girl was already being so callous.

With a sob she tore herself free and rushed from the control room. Once outside the building, she began to run and run until she felt as if her lungs would burst. Only when she could run no more did she sink down near the perimeter fence and lie, face down in the long, cold grass and weep.

'Oh, please, let him be alive,' she prayed wildly. 'I'll do anything, give anything – everything – if only you'll let him be alive.'

His poor mother, she was thinking. How is she going to take it? And his grandfather? News like that might . . .

I must go and see them, Fleur told herself. Once there's been time for the authorities to have informed them, I'll go.

She shivered; the damp coldness of the ground was beginning to seep through. She sat up and dried her eyes, but fresh tears trickled down her face. She couldn't stem the flow.

'Fleur? Fleur – where are you?'

Distantly across the open ground, she heard Ruth's anxious voice. She scrambled to her feet and through the pale morning light she could see her friend running up and down, calling her name. She waved and called weakly, 'Here. Over here.'

At once, Ruth was running towards her, 'Oh, Fleur – Fleur. I've just heard at the debriefing. I so hoped they'd just be late . . . But . . . I came as soon as I could . . .' She almost threw herself against Fleur and wrapped her arms around her, holding her tightly. 'It's my fault. It's all my fault,' Ruth was babbling against her shoulder. 'I didn't wave them off like I always do. After final briefing, Serg wanted me to deal with some paperwork. I lost track of time and, by the time I got down to the edge of the runway, most of them had taken off. Oh, Fleur – I'm sorry. I'm so sorry . . .'

Fleur clung to her, unable to give her friend any comfort, unable to exonerate her. She was drained, trembling with shock and weak with anguish. Deep in her heart, she knew it would have made no difference if Ruth had waved them off. It was just another superstition, but at this moment she was incapable of voicing it.

Against her, she felt Ruth draw in a deep breath. Somehow, the other girl found the strength to say, 'Come on, Fleur. You can't stay out here in the cold. Let's get you to the NAAFI . . .'

'I can't – I can't face anyone.'

'Don't be daft, Fleur,' Ruth said with brusque kindness. 'Everyone knows. Everyone understands. Most of us have been there at one time or another. You need to be with people who understand.' Ruth was saying almost the same as Kay, but somehow the words were not so harsh. She felt badly about Kay now. It was just her way. She must be hurting inside every bit as much as Fleur. For a moment, Fleur despised herself for her weakness. She wished she could be as strong as . . .

'Kay? Have you seen Kay?'

Ruth nodded. 'She came to find me. To tell me that you'd run off.'

'I'm sorry. She was only trying to help . . .'

'She understands. She was concerned for you, that's all.'

'She's so strong,' Fleur murmured. 'Look at me. I've gone to pieces. I'm a wreck. I'm – weak!'

'No, you're not. And Kay's not as tough underneath as she likes to make out. She'll be sobbing her socks off in bed tonight, you mark my words.' There was a pause before Ruth added shakily, 'And she won't be the only one. I feel so guilty. But we shouldn't give up hope. Not just yet.'

Sadly, Fleur shook her head. 'But someone saw a plane go down. It must have been them. And they didn't see any parachutes . . .'

Now Ruth had no answer.

Fleur sniffed. 'I . . . I want to go home. I want to see my dad.'

'Course you do. Let's go and see ma'am. I'm sure she . . .'

'Squadron Leader Harris came into the control room. He said he'd see her. Ask her if I could have some leave.'

'That's OK then. Let's go.'

'I can't. Looking like this.' She brushed ineffectually at the front of her uniform, blotched with wet grass stains.

'I'm sure she'll overlook it for once. You're usually the smartest of the lot of us.' Ruth took Fleur's arm firmly and urged her towards the buildings. 'You can't stop out here. You'll catch your death.'

With a laugh that was bordering on hysteria, Fleur said, 'You sound like my mum.' And at the thought of her mother, Fleur's tears flowed even harder.

Thirty-Seven

'Dad! *Dad!*'

Two days later, Fleur went home. Despite his disapproval of wartime marriages and romances, Bob Watson had quietly rearranged the rotas so that both Fleur and Kay were not on duty for four days following T-Tommy's failure to return. Kay went to her home down south, adding on a couple of days' ordinary leave that she was entitled to, and Fleur travelled to Middleditch Farm. She could not yet face Robbie's mother.

Dumping her bag near the back door, she ran round the yard, peering into the shadows of the cowshed then running into the barn, calling, 'Dad, where are you?' She didn't want to see her own mother, either. Not yet. She had to find her father. Fleur wanted her dad.

But it was Betsy who appeared at the back door, drying her hands on a tea towel. 'Whatever's the matter? Fleur? Is that you?'

Fleur stood a moment amidst the straw on the floor of the barn, summoning up the courage to answer her mother. She moved slowly to the doorway but she did not cross the yard. The two women stared at each other across the space between them and then Fleur saw her mother's hand flutter to her face to cover her mouth. Slowly, Fleur began to walk towards her.

'Well, Mum,' she said harshly as she neared her. 'You got your wish. He's gone. Robbie's—' She bit hard down on her lip to stop the tears. 'Robbie's missing, presumed killed.'

'Oh, Fleur, how can you think that of me? I didn't want you married to him. To have anything to do with him. But I wouldn't have wished him any harm.'

Fleur's eyes filled with the tears that were never far away. 'I don't know what to think. How can I when you won't tell me anything? What on earth can possibly have happened in the past to make you so – so – vitriolic against him? You didn't even know him.'

The bitterness of years was in Betsy's eyes again. Then she sighed deeply and gave a little shake of her head. Flatly, she said, 'Like I said before, it wasn't against him personally. Just his mother.'

'Why? What happened?'

Betsy's mouth tightened. 'She was a wicked woman. Devious, manipulating and utterly – utterly – selfish.'

'How? What on earth did she do?'

Betsy turned away. 'I don't want to talk about it. I *won't* talk about it.'

'You really hate her, don't you? Well, if you wanted some kind of . . . kind of revenge on her, then you've certainly got it now. She's lost her son. Her only son.'

Betsy just stared at her, her face expressionless, saying nothing.

'You really won't tell me?' Fleur tried again.

Betsy shook her head.

'Then I'll ask Dad. I'll ask him this very minute.'

'Perhaps it is time you knew,' her mother murmured and nodded, as if answering an unspoken question she was asking herself. At last she dragged out the words reluctantly. 'He's . . . away up the . . . fields with . . .

329

the sheep. You ... you'll find him in Buttercup Meadow.'

Fleur gave a brief nod and moved towards the back door. She picked up her bag and made to step into the house, but her mother didn't move aside. It was as if she was almost barring Fleur's way.

Fleur stared at her. 'I'll just change my clothes.' Her uniform was still a mess from her spasm of weeping in the wet grass the night she had heard that Robbie was missing. It would need sponging and pressing before she went on parade again. She would change into her old clothes before she went tramping through the fields to find her dad.

Betsy blinked. 'Can't you go as you are?'

'No, I can't. I need to change.'

'Well, you can't. I mean – you can't come in. There's ... there's someone here that ... that I don't want you to see. That you didn't ought to see.'

'What on earth are you talking about, Mum? What's going on?'

'Nothing. Nothing. I just don't want you to see her. Not just now. It'll be – awkward.'

'Who? Who is it you don't want me to see?'

Betsy bit her lip. 'You don't understand. I mean – I don't want *her* to see *you*. Not just this minute.'

'Who?'

Fleur was getting angry now. What was all the mystery and why – when Fleur was suffering the worst moment in the whole of her young life – was her mother acting so strangely? 'Mum – just tell me who it is you don't want me to see?'

Betsy sighed. 'Louisa. Your Aunt Louisa.'

'Aunt Louisa? Why on earth shouldn't I see her?'

'It's ... it's complicated. It's all to do with ... with

Robbie and his mother. You don't understand,' she finished lamely.

'No, I don't.' Now, Fleur pushed her mother aside. 'But I'm jolly well going to find out.'

'No, Fleur. Please don't. You don't understand – Fleur . . . !' Betsy tried to grab her daughter's arm, but Fleur shook her off and marched into the kitchen where Louisa was sitting at the table drinking tea.

'Fleur, my dear, how lovely . . .' Louisa began as she rose and held out her arms to hug Fleur, who submitted a little stiffly to the embrace. Then she stood back. 'My dear girl. What is it? What's wrong?'

Fleur stared into the older woman's eyes for what seemed a long time but was in fact only seconds.

'It's Robbie,' Fleur whispered at last. But before she could say more, Louisa took a step back. Her hand fluttered to cover her mouth and her eyes widened in horror. 'Oh, no!' she breathed. 'Don't say it – oh, don't say it!'

Fleur was puzzled. Despite the sorrow that anyone might feel to hear of a young airman's death and the sympathy Louisa, as a friend of the family, would naturally feel for the young bride so cruelly widowed, the woman's reaction was extreme.

'Aunt Louisa,' Fleur began, reaching out to take Louisa's hands. 'What is it? Whatever's the matter?' But Louisa snatched her hands away.

'No, no, don't. I must go. I can't stay . . .' She cast a beseeching, almost frantic look at Betsy who had followed her daughter inside. Then she snatched up her handbag and scarf and fled from the room. As the back door slammed behind her, there was silence in the room until Fleur moved woodenly and sank down into her father's chair by the range.

'What is it, Mum? What's it all about?'

Betsy sighed heavily and flopped down into the chair on the opposite side of the hearth, as if suddenly all the energy had drained out of her.

'Go and find your father,' she said flatly. 'Ask him,' was all she would say.

With sudden renewed vigour, determined to get to the bottom of the mystery, Fleur sprang to her feet. 'Then I will. I'll go now. This very minute.' She stood a moment, staring down at her mother, willing her to say something – anything. But Betsy was silent, just staring into the fire. She didn't move as Fleur hurried upstairs to change her clothes. When she returned, her mother had not moved. She was sitting just as Fleur had left her, staring silently and sadly into the flames.

'Mum?' Fleur said tentatively, but Betsy made no move, no sign that she had even heard her.

Fleur left the house and stood a moment outside the back door. She pulled in a deep breath. It helped to calm her, but nothing could assuage her terrible grief. She felt as if she would never smile or laugh ever again. The sun had gone out of her life. She thrust her hands deep into the pockets of her old coat and trudged across the yard, out of the gate and down the lane towards the field where she knew her father would be.

Even before Jake saw her, Bess, the black and white sheepdog, barked and came scampering across the field towards her.

'Bess!' Jake roared angrily, as the sheep scattered in fright. Then he saw Fleur and he grinned and began to walk towards her. But as he neared her, his smile faded. 'Aw lass, don't tell me. Is it Robbie?'

Tears choked her and all she could do was nod as

he limped towards her and put his arms around her, holding her close. 'Aw love,' he said huskily.

They stood for a long time until he said gently, 'Come on, let's go back to the house. Let's—'

'No, Dad. No. I want to talk to you. I *need* to talk to you.' She drew back, her eyes brimming with tears.

For a moment, he studied her face. Then he gave a deep sigh and nodded. 'All right. But first, tell me what's happened.'

'He ... he didn't come back from a mission the night before last. It's so ironic – so cruel. It was their thirtieth mission. A full tour, Dad. They'd done a full tour. At least, the four of them had.'

'Those lovely boys at your wedding? They're all missing?'

Fleur nodded. 'They – some of the other pilots – told Ruth at debriefing that they'd seen a plane go down with two of its engines on fire just off the coast. Tommy's a wonderful pilot, but . . .'

'Was that the one who was the best man?'

'Yes. But ... but even he wouldn't be able to do much if . . . if it was on fire.'

'Was it near our coast?'

She nodded.

'Then—' Jake began, with a tiny hope, but Fleur shook her head sadly.

'No one saw any parachutes. And there's been no word. We'd've heard by now if they'd been picked up.'

'Are you sure? There's been some dreadful bombing down south again. They reckon it's in retaliation for this round-the-clock bombing we've been doing.'

'It's no good having false hope, Dad. I've worked in the control room long enough, seen enough missions, to know that, nine times out of ten, when they don't come back that night then – then they don't come back at all. Oh, sometimes they do. The lucky ones. Their plane limps home late or lands at another airfield or they've parachuted out of the plane and been picked up. Even become prisoners of war, if it was over enemy territory. But . . . but this wasn't. It was over the sea.' She pulled in a deep breath. 'I've got to face it, Dad. He's gone. I've lost him.'

Jake shook his head, as if unable to believe the dreadful news, and yet it shouldn't really have come as a shock. Every day young men were dying for their country. Young men just like Robbie, young men just like Kenny.

'Have you . . . have you seen his mother yet? Have you seen Meggie?'

Fleur shook her head. Even now, she noticed he used the pet name for Robbie's mother that she'd never heard anyone else use apart from Pops. Meg's father called her that too. Maybe that's what she'd been called as a girl . . .

'But you will?' Jake was pulling her thoughts back to the present. 'You . . . you'll be going to see her?'

'Of course.'

'Then . . . then tell her I'm so sorry, won't you?'

Fleur raised her head and stared into his face. For a moment a shudder ran through her. The haunted look was back in her father's eyes and now it was ten-fold in its despair.

'Of course I will, Dad,' she said softly. There was a moment's silence before she added, 'Dad, will you please tell me what all the mystery is? Don't you think I have a right to know?'

Jake closed his eyes, sighed and shook his head.

'They're not my secrets to tell, Fleur love. If they were, then of course I would tell you. But . . .'

'But Robbie's gone. It . . . it can't hurt him now, can it?'

'No,' Jake said sadly. 'It can't and I can't tell you how sorry I am that that's the case. Poor Meggie. To lose her boy . . .' He wiped the back of his hand across his eyes and coughed to clear the emotion catching his throat. He sighed. 'Well, if I do tell you, you must promise me one thing first, Fleur.'

'Anything, Dad. I just want to know. I want to understand.'

He sighed heavily. 'You might not understand even when I've told you it all.'

'I'd like the chance to try. Mum and I have always clashed – you know that – but I don't want us to carry on like this – like we are now. It . . . it's tearing our family apart.'

Jake sighed. 'To be perfectly honest, I don't think your knowing about the past will help that. It's more this business with Kenny that's coming between you and your mum now.'

'What about you, Dad? Do you blame me for Kenny joining up?'

His answer was swift and certain. 'No, love, not for a minute. Like I've said before, I'm proud of him – and of you – even though I'm worried sick about you both. But your mother just wants to keep you safe. She doesn't even want to see the wider picture.' He gave a wry smile. 'I think she'd even rather Hitler marched in unhindered than lose either of you.'

Fleur shuddered. 'Well, I don't think any of us would last long if he did, do you? Can you imagine his jackbooted cohorts tramping through Britain?'

Jake shook his head. 'No, I can't and I don't even want to try. It doesn't bear thinking about.' He glanced at her, their faces almost on a level and so close. 'We can't let that happen, Fleur, and it's up to you and Kenny and all those wonderful young people just like you to stop it. Whatever it costs.'

'Yes,' she whispered. 'Whatever it costs.' Already it had cost her everything. It had taken away her future. There was no future for her now that Robbie was gone. Yet she had to summon up the courage to continue the fight Robbie had believed in so passionately. What would happen after the war was over, she dared not think. She couldn't face the thought of the empty years stretching ahead without Robbie.

Jake was speaking again, pulling her thoughts back to the present. 'I want your promise that even if you go on seeing his mother now and again – as I'm sure you will – you'll never breathe a word to her about what I'm going to tell you. It's not something she'll want to talk about or even like to think you know about. I don't want to hurt Meg any more than she's going to be hurt now. This is going to devastate her, Fleur. Oh, love—' He touched her arm. 'I don't mean to minimize your grief. But you're young. You've a whole life ahead of you—'

Fleur closed her eyes and groaned. 'But it means nothing without Robbie, Dad. Don't you see?'

'I know it feels like that now, but ... but in time—'

'No, Dad. You're wrong. Eternity wouldn't be long enough. I'll never get over this. He was all I ever wanted. The only man I'll ever love.' She lifted her head and stared him straight in the eyes. 'And now I want you to tell me about the past. I swear I won't breathe a word to his mother. But I have to know. I have to try to understand what it is that makes Mum so bitter that she can hardly bring herself to say she's sorry he's dead.'

Jake blinked as if that shocked even him. Then he sighed again as he said heavily, 'All right, then. I'll tell you. But you must promise me not to say anything to Meggie. Not a word. Not ever.'

'I promise, Dad,' Fleur said solemnly.

'I'm being dreadfully disloyal to her.' His eyes were full of pain at the thought, though Fleur wasn't sure if her father was referring to his wife or to Meg Rodwell.

There was a long silence before Jake, haltingly at first, began to speak.

'I'll go right back to the beginning. It's time you knew a few other things besides matters that concern Robbie. It's high time you knew about your mum and me too.'

He paused again and pulled in a deep breath as if he was about to launch himself over a precipice. Perhaps that's how it did feel for Jake to talk about things that had not been spoken of for years.

Thirty-Eight

They leant on the gate, watching the sheep, whilst Bess lay panting beside them, as Jake began to speak. 'You know the big building on the outskirts of South Monkford?'

'The one that used to be a workhouse? It's some kind of convalescent place for the forces now, isn't it?'

Jake nodded. 'That's where I was born. And your mum came into the workhouse as a young girl when her mother died.'

'You were both in the workhouse?' Fleur was shocked. She would never have imagined that the successful farmer owning Middleditch Farm and all its acres, the man who was well liked and respected in the neighbourhood, could have been born into such lowly circumstances. Then another thought struck her. 'But . . . but you had a mother. Gran.' She spoke of the woman who had lived with them for the last few years of her life.

'Yes.' Jake's voice was husky. 'But I didn't know I had until . . . until – well, all the bother happened.'

'All the bother?'

'Mm.' He was silent again.

Though she was impatient for him to continue, Fleur held her tongue. Quite literally, for she had to hold it between her teeth to stop all her questions tumbling out.

'All I knew as a lad was that I'd been born in the workhouse,' Jake went on as he gazed out across the rolling fields that were all his now. But he was seeing, Fleur knew, pictures and events from the past. 'I thought I was an orphan. A feller called Isaac Pendleton ran the place. He was what they called the master of the workhouse and the matron was his sister, Letitia Pendleton. *Miss* Letitia Pendleton.'

'But that was Gran's name. Except – well – I always thought it was *Mrs* Pendleton. I never knew that she was a . . . a "Miss". She was always just "Gran". I'm sorry, Dad. Go on.'

'As a young girl she'd fallen in love with Theobald Finch.'

Now Fleur gasped and before she could stop herself she interrupted his tale again. It was impossible not to show surprise or ask questions, so she gave up trying. 'The Finch family who live at the Hall?'

'Aye, but there's only Miss Clara Finch left there now. Mr Theobald' – he paused over the name, still unable to refer to the man in any way other than the name by which he'd always known him – 'died a while ago.'

'I do vaguely remember seeing him in the town. I think Mum pointed him out to me once.' She glanced sideways at her father but his gaze was still far away.

'Dad, was he – Mr Finch – your father?'

Slowly, he nodded. 'My mother loved him,' he said simply, 'but his family didn't think her good enough for him. At the time, Isaac – her brother – was running the workhouse with his wife. But she left him – so the rumour went. Isaac took me in as an orphan and Letitia became matron.' He smiled wistfully. 'She took the job so that she could be near me, yet she was not allowed to acknowledge me openly.' Now his smile broadened. 'As a lad I always wondered why she favoured me. She saved me many a beating from Isaac.' Now he chuckled. 'Though I still got plenty.'

'Oh, Dad!' Fleur rested her cheek against his shoulder, tears filling her eyes. Jake put his arm about her shoulders and held her close.

'Don't cry, love. It's all a long time ago now.'

'I know, but I can't bear to think of you as a poor little boy, believing yourself an orphan and being beaten and growing up in a *workhouse*. I mean, I know it's a magnificent building, but it was still a workhouse. Why, even now the old folk in the town fear it, don't they?'

'Oh yes. We all still live in the shadow of the workhouse. Those of us who grew up there.' He smiled gently. 'And even some of those who didn't. It's still a threat hanging over us all even if it isn't a workhouse any more.'

Fleur wound her arms tightly around his waist and nestled her head against his shoulder. She said nothing. The lump in her throat wouldn't let her, but her actions implied: you'll never go back in the workhouse, Dad. Not while I'm around.

'There, there,' Jake murmured, feeling her compassion. 'I was a tough little tyke. And then' – he smiled fondly – 'Meggie arrived at the workhouse. And she changed my life.'

He didn't need to elaborate. By the tone of his voice, Fleur could tell he remembered that time as very special. That Meg was very special.

'She was so – so *alive*,' he went on. 'So spirited and . . . and full of daring. D'you know, Fleur, I'd lived in that place all my life and I was— Let's see, I'd be about fifteen by the time she came and in all that time I'd never ventured out. Never asked to go out to seek work, never really gone out of my own accord. Oh, I knew *how* to get out. Several of the others did. There was a hole in the wall. And once or twice I went through the gates, but I never went more than a few yards.' He laughed aloud now. 'Not until she came and took me out with her one day. She went looking for her dad.'

'The old man? Pops?'

'Well, he wasn't old then, love. He was a young man and a bit of a rascal, by all accounts.' He gave her shoulder a squeeze. 'We were all young once, lass. Even me and Meg.'

'Oh, I think she still looks young, Dad. She looks years younger than Mum.' The words were out before she could stop herself. 'I'm sorry. I didn't mean . . .'

''S all right, love. There's only you an' me here.' He glanced down at the dog, dozing at their feet. 'And Bess won't say owt, now will she? But just think a minute. Your poor mam's a busy farmer's wife. She can't dress like Meg and wear those flimsy shoes, now can she?'

'No, of course not,' Fleur said hurriedly. Privately, she was thinking that her mother could still make a little more effort even if it was only now and again. 'But I don't think Robbie's mum's had it that easy. The front room at their house is her sewing room. She's worked to keep them all. Herself, Robbie and the old man.'

Again, Jake had a faraway look in his eyes as he continued with his tale. 'Her father, Reuben Kirkland – the old man as you call him – worked for the

Smallwoods and so did Meg. She worked in the dairy. And then, Meg's father had an affair with the Smallwoods' daughter, Alice.'

Fleur was shocked. 'Pops did?'

'Yes. Pops.' Jake was adamant. 'Of course, they dismissed him and his daughter, Meg, and then turned the whole family out of their tied cottage – the one old Ron lives in now. Reuben took his family – his pregnant wife Sarah, Meg and her little brother Bobbie – to the workhouse, promising to return to get them out when he'd found other work.'

Fleur was ahead of her father, guessing what had happened. 'And he never came back for them? He ran away with Alice?' She paused, taking in all the startling revelations. Then she asked, 'Did Meg know?'

'Not then. Not when she first came into the workhouse. She believed him, trusted him. She told everyone that they wouldn't be there long. That he'd come back for them. She didn't know why they'd been dismissed. For a while I think she blamed herself.' He smiled fondly again. 'She was a cheeky little tyke and she thought the missis – Mrs Smallwood – didn't like her friendship with her daughter.'

'*Her* friendship? Meg was friendly with Alice too?'

'Yes. Complicated, isn't it? So, you see, when she did find out about their affair, she felt doubly betrayed. By her father *and* by her best friend.'

'So how did Meg find out?'

'Her mam gave birth to a stillborn child in the workhouse and Meg went in search of her father to tell him. Of course, she didn't know about her dad and Alice then. She just went to try and find him to tell him about her mam. And she took me with her. We went to the racecourse. She thought her father might be trying to find work there. He was good with horses.'

Fleur nodded. South Monkford racecourse was famous, though sadly neglected since the war had begun.

'Did you find him?'

'Oh yes.' Jake's face was grim. 'He was with her. With Alice. Bold as yer like, walking round the racecourse with his arm around her.'

Fleur gasped. 'Oh, poor Meg!'

'Yes,' Jake said thoughtfully. 'D'you know, as far as I can remember, it was the only time I ever saw Meggie cry.' Again, he used the pet name as he spoke of her fondly. 'She was heartbroken and vowed never to forgive her father. Said she'd cut him out of her life for ever.'

'Well, she can't have done because he lives with her now.'

'She's changed. But back then, she swore that she'd never forget and never forgive.'

'Did she?' Now Fleur was surprised. 'She doesn't strike me as being like that.'

'No. Like I say, she's changed since then. Life changed her. I know now that she's sorry for everything she's done. I could see that when I met her at your wedding. I asked her about her father and she said, "How could I turn him away, when I'd been just as bad?"'

'But she hadn't done anything, Dad. It was her father's fault,' Fleur said, mystified. She still couldn't reconcile the picture of the sweet old man sitting by the fire in the little house in Nottingham with the heartless womanizer who'd dumped his family in the workhouse and run away with his mistress.

'I'm coming to that, love. But I want you to see the whole picture. And to do that, you have to hear what led up to – well – what Meg did.' Even now, though he had promised to tell her everything and had begun the tale, there was reluctance in his tone. He still didn't want to speak ill of Meg. Not even after all these years.

'Whatever did she do, Dad, that was so bad?'

He was silent for a moment, lost in memories in which Fleur had no part. Now, in short staccato sentences, he answered her question, explaining everything. 'After she found out about her father and Alice she became very bitter. The tragedies didn't end there. Her little brother, Bobbie, died. Then Isaac Pendleton – he was a one for the ladies, an' all – he took up with her mother. And that was the last straw for Meg. She never forgave her mother – called her some wicked names. And Meg herself became hard and calculating. There was only one person she cared about then. Herself. She left the workhouse and got a job working for Percy Rodwell.' Now Jake's mouth suddenly became a hard line. 'She wound him round her little finger and he fell for it. Poor sod!'

Fleur twisted to look up into her father's face. She saw his pain and, yes, now there was anger and disgust there too. 'Were you in love with her, Dad? Were you in love with Meg all those years ago?'

Jake stared down into his daughter's eyes. 'Oh yes. I loved her then and—'

There was a breathless silence until Fleur whispered, 'And you love her now, don't you, Dad? You've always loved her.'

'Fleur, love.' He squeezed her shoulders again. 'I know you feel now that you'll never love again. That

Robbie was the love of your life – and maybe he is. Who's to say? But you may well meet someone one day, fall in love, get married—'

'Never! I could never love anyone the way I love Robbie.'

'Listen to me, love.' Her father gave her a gentle shake. 'No, not in the same way, maybe you won't, no. I can understand that. He was your first love and that's very special. But you might love someone else differently. There are all kinds of love, Fleur. Passionate, overwhelming and for life. Then there's infatuation that seems like love, but isn't and dies as quickly as it flared. And then . . .' He paused again and took a deep breath before he said, 'And then there's the way I love your mother. After Meg went, I left the workhouse and I came to work for the Smallwoods here. Their daughter had gone, of course, and they never heard from her again as far as I know. A year or two later, Betsy came to work at the farm too. In fact, I sort of got her the job there. She'd spent several years in the workhouse. She was a shy little thing and I always felt protective towards her. The Smallwoods treated us both as their own and Betsy grew and blossomed. She was a pretty lass and – well – that's how it happened. I married her before I went to the war, and when I came back you were born and then Kenny.'

There was a long silence whilst Fleur digested all that he had told her.

'There's a bit more you ought to know,' Jake said at last.

'More!' Fleur forced a smile.

'When Meg went to work for Percy he was engaged to Miss Clara Finch – had been for years – and when he married Meg Clara sued him for breach of promise.'

Fleur gasped. 'Never!'

'Oh yes. There was a big court case and it was the talk of South Monkford for weeks.' His mouth twitched. 'You see, the judge found in Miss Finch's favour, but he awarded her damages of one farthing.'

Fleur stared at him for a moment and then burst out laughing, but Jake's face had sobered now. 'Clara was a bitter, dried-up old spinster, and after Percy Rodwell died, she tried to force Meg to hand over her baby – Robbie – because she believed in her twisted mind that the child should have been hers. Hers and Percy's. When Meg refused, Clara had her turned out of the shop and her home – the Finches owned both properties – and she tried to kidnap Robbie and have Meg thrown back in the workhouse. With the power the Finches wielded in South Monkford then, I doubt Meg would ever have seen the light of day again if . . .' He stopped and was silent.

Intuitively, Fleur whispered. 'You helped her, didn't you, Dad? You helped her get out.'

'She was locked in the punishment room and her boy was missing. We found him – Robbie – in the dead room in a coffin. Clara, in her twisted mind, had had him hidden there until she could take him home. Just think.' Jake tried to inject a note of lightness into their conversation. 'Your Robbie might have been a toff and brought up at South Monkford Hall.'

The dead room. The punishment room. Fleur shuddered. It all sounded like another world from the safe and happy childhood she had known.

'It was then I found out about my own mother –

just who she was. Maybe if all that hadn't happened, I might never have known.' For a long moment, Jake was silent, then he came back to finish his telling of the story. 'That was when Meg changed from her hard and calculating ways. Almost losing her son had jolted her because there was never any doubt about her love for him. After that . . .' Jake sighed softly. 'She left the district and I . . . I never saw her again. Not until your wedding day, Fleur.'

'I suppose poor old Clara Finch wanted something of her sweetheart's,' Fleur said with understanding. 'She wanted Percy's son.'

'Ah,' Jake said, 'but that's the irony of it all. You see, love, Robbie wasn't Percy's child.'

Her eyes wide, Fleur stared at him wordlessly. Surely, after all, her father wasn't about to tell her that he was, in truth, Robbie's father too?

'Perhaps you can't see it like I can, because you wouldn't remember his father as a young man.'

Her voice was husky as she asked hesitantly, 'Dad, just tell me. Who was Robbie's father?'

'The man you call Uncle Philip. Dr Philip Collins.'

'I can't believe it. I mean, how—?'

Despite the seriousness of their talk and all the long-held secrets he had just revealed, Jake laughed. 'Now surely I don't need to be explaining the facts of life to you, lass, do I?'

Fleur smiled briefly and shook her head. 'I mean, when did it happen? Before *he* married Aunt Louisa?'

Sadly, Jake shook his head. 'No, love, nothing so above board as that, I'm sorry to say. They had an affair.' His mouth hardened again. 'While Percy was ill with the influenza that killed him. Of course, Meg was able to make out the child was his, but there's no hiding it now. Not for anyone who remembered Philip in his younger days and then . . . saw your Robbie.'

'Oh, Dad.' Fleur clutched his arm. 'Auntie Louisa saw him. I introduced them. In a cafe in South Monkford. Just after I'd met him. You know – the day I invited them out to the farm and—' She bit her lip. 'Aunt Louisa seemed – well – odd. Now I know why. She . . . she must have guessed.'

Slowly, Jake nodded. 'I wondered at the time if she suspected. Poor Louisa, specially as she's never had any family herself.'

'Did Uncle Philip know he had a son?'

'I've no idea. But knowing Meg as she was then, I've no doubt she told him. Maybe—' He began to say something and then stopped himself. 'No, that's not fair to speculate. I shouldn't judge her.'

'No, none of us should. I certainly won't. She's Robbie's mum and she's been kind to me and . . . and she's suffering now. Whatever she did in the past, Dad, she's paying for it now.'

'Aye, love,' Jake said sadly. 'I know she is.'

And once more the haunted faraway look that Fleur had so often seen on her father's face was there again. But now, she understood exactly what caused it.

Thirty-Nine

'Oh, Philip – I'm so sorry. I shouldn't have . . . I mean
. . . I wish—'

'Now, now, my dear. What's the matter?'

Philip took her arm calmly and led her into the
front sitting room. The huge room was cold; no welcoming fire burned in the grate. They were trying to
economize on coal and only lit the fire when the room
was to be used for a lengthy period. Otherwise, they
now sat in the two easy chairs in the corner of the
kitchen, close to the wireless on which Philip loved to
hear the latest war news.

Louisa clung to him. 'Forgive me, Philip, oh, say
you forgive me.'

'I'm sure I shall, darling, if only I knew what it is
I'm supposed to be forgiving. Here, sit down. Let me
make us both some tea.'

'No, no, I should do that. That's my job.'

'Not just at this moment. I can see you're upset.
Sit down whilst I make it and then we'll talk about it.
Whatever it is.'

'But . . . but you've got surgery, haven't you?'

'There's no one out there at the moment. My
patients are remarkably healthy today, it seems.' He
smiled at her archly, trying to lighten her mood. 'I
must be a better doctor than I thought.'

'Oh, Philip, you're a wonderful doctor.' Her eyes

filled with tears. 'A wonderful man. I don't deserve you. I . . .'

'There, there, my dear. Please, don't upset yourself. We'll sort it all out – whatever it is.'

Philip was becoming increasingly worried about his wife. From being a calm, serene, perfect doctor's wife, she had in recent weeks become nervy and irritable and weepy. Had she been one of his patients, he would by now have diagnosed a nervous breakdown. And whilst he could scarcely believe – didn't want to believe – that that was what might be happening to his wife, ethics aside, it would be better for her to be treated by someone else. He was no expert in psychiatric cases.

He shuddered at the thought, but if that was the case, then it would have to be faced. She was such a tender-hearted person and even though they weren't experiencing particular hardship themselves, nor the loss of a close relative, still the community as a whole was being badly hit. And Louisa felt it, he knew. As he set her cup of tea on a small table beside her, he sat down opposite, leant forward and took her hands in his. 'Now,' he said in the kindly but firm tone he adopted when speaking to a distraught patient, 'tell me what is troubling you.'

Fresh tears spilled down her cheeks.

'Oh, Philip – he's dead.'

'Who's dead, my love?'

She raised her red-rimmed eyes to look into his face as she whispered, 'Meg's boy. He's – he's missing, believed killed.'

She felt his hands holding hers twitch involuntarily and saw the colour drain from his face. They stared at each other for long moments before, haltingly, Louisa broke the silence. 'You . . . you do know who he really is, don't you, Philip? Who . . . who his father is?'

The colour flooded into his face and she had her answer without him saying a word. Before he could speak, she rushed on. 'I wish you'd told me. I wish you'd had enough faith in my love for you to have told me the truth at the time. I presume you've always known?'

Wordlessly, Philip nodded.

'I know – I know you wanted to spare me the hurt.' Now it was she who was giving comfort. 'The fact that you'd been unfaithful to me – and with Meg of all people. But don't you see, if only you'd confided in me, perhaps, all those years ago, we could have adopted him? Brought him up as *our* son. Oh, Philip, I wish you'd told me then.'

He shook his head as he said heavily, 'No, my dear, it would never have worked. You . . . you say you'd have forgiven me, but you're speaking now with the benefit of hindsight. Back then, you didn't know that we'd never have children of our own. You didn't know that someone else's son could have filled the void in our lives—'

'But he was *your* son, Philip. I could have loved him, I could have—'

'Could you really, Louisa, have loved *Meg*'s son? Be honest now, since we're talking honestly. Let's be absolutely straight with each other.'

When she didn't answer, he added softly, 'No, I thought not.' He smiled wryly. 'Besides, Meg wouldn't let Clara Finch have him, would she?'

'Of course she wouldn't,' Louisa cried now. 'Meg knew – though Clara Finch didn't – that he wasn't

351

Percy's son. But if *you'd* wanted him, she'd've let him go.' Her lip curled. 'Remember how selfish she was, how self-centred? Oh, she'd've let you have him like a shot. Been glad to be rid of him, I dare say.'

'I think you're wrong, my dear. Whatever Meg may have been – and yes, I admit, she did some reprehensible things—'

'Reprehensible? Reprehensible, you call it. Unforgivable, I'd call it. Seducing poor Percy. Yes – yes – she seduced him, Philip. Poor, bumbling Percy Rodwell didn't know what had hit him when she batted her eyelashes at him and smiled so winningly.'

'My dear,' he said softly. 'We've all made mistakes. Especially me.'

Louisa held his gaze as she asked, 'Do you regret it, Philip?'

His answer was swift and he hoped that it sounded sincere. 'Of course I do. I wouldn't have hurt you for the world. Louisa, I've always loved you and I always will. You must believe that. Meg was just – was just a stupid, stupid mistake. An aberration. Please – please say you forgive me?'

'Oh, Philip!' Tearfully, she threw her arms around his neck. 'Of course I do. It's a long time ago. And . . . and you haven't seen her since. Have you?'

'No, no. I swear it.' That part, at least, was true. As for the rest, deep in his heart he couldn't be sure. He buried his face against his wife's neck and hugged her tightly, trying to block out the memory of that vibrant red-haired girl who had brought such passion into his life. Even though the affair had been brief, he'd never been able to put her completely out of his mind. And never a day had gone by through all the years since that he had not thought about the son she had borne him and wondered what he looked like.

And now he would never know.

'So now you know, do you?' Betsy asked, her mouth tight, as Fleur came back into the house. 'Heard the whole sorry story?'

Fleur sighed and said flatly, 'Yes. If that's what you like to call it. Yes, I think I've heard it all.'

'Well – it is a sorry tale. Your father loved her. I expect you've guessed that now, haven't you? Even if he hasn't admitted it.'

'He did admit it, Mum,' Fleur said simply. 'He loved her *then*. Not now. Not since he fell in love with *you* and married *you*.'

'Oh well, if that's what you like to think.'

'Look, Mum. Let's have all this out – once and for all. Just what is it that upsets you so much? Do you think Dad had an affair with her? Maybe you think it's been going on all these years. I mean, with all your insinuations you had us – me and Robbie, I mean – thinking that we were half-brother and sister.'

'*Wha-at!*'

'Oh, you can sound surprised, but look at it from our point of view. That first day you were screaming at Dad that he was in love with her and that he's loved her all these years. And you were so ... so vitriolic towards Robbie's mother. And him. It was something terrible. It was all we could think of.'

Betsy wriggled her shoulders. 'Well, I don't know, do I? Maybe they did have an affair. Maybe it has been going on all these years. He's had plenty of chances. All those supposed trips to market. How do I know where he *really* went?'

Fleur shook her head. It saddened her to think that, perhaps for the whole of her married life, Betsy had lived with the torment of imagining her husband was being unfaithful to her. For the first time, Fleur pitied her mother.

'Do you want to know what I think?'

'Does it make any difference?' Betsy snapped, recovering some of her spirit. 'I'm no doubt going to hear it anyway.'

'Dad was in love with Meg, yes, when they were kids in the workhouse.' She saw her mother flinch at the word that obviously brought back dark, unhappy memories. 'He owed her a lot. She had spirit. She gave him the courage to get himself out of there. To seek work here.' She pointed down at the ground, indicating their home, the farm, everything he now owned. Fleur paused a moment, letting her words sink in. And driving her point home she added, 'Just think, Mum, if he hadn't done that he – and you – wouldn't have everything you have now. Where would you have been, eh? Still in the workhouse?'

'It closed in 'twenty-nine,' Betsy murmured, but her protests now were without substance.

'But you wouldn't be here, would you? You wouldn't have been taken in and treated like the Smallwoods' son and daughter and left their farm because their own daughter had run away.'

A spark of sudden interest ignited in Betsy's eyes. 'Is it really her dad that lives with her?'

Fleur sighed inwardly. Still, her mother could not bring herself to speak Meg's name. 'Yes, it is. Evidently the girl he ran off with – Alice, was it?'

Betsy nodded.

'She left him and went off with someone else. He tried to follow her, but this chap got his cronies to beat him up.'

Betsy sniffed and her mouth hardened. 'Serves him right. And her? What happened to Alice Smallwood?'

Fleur shrugged. 'No one knows.'

'She was a bad 'un.'

'As bad as Meg?' Fleur put in slyly.

''Bout the same,' Betsy answered, refusing to give any quarter. 'Made a good pair, they did.'

There was a long silence before Fleur said softly, 'Meg's changed, Mum. She's not the girl you remember any more. Not, by all accounts, since she had Robbie. Having a baby changed her. She made some mistakes, did some terrible things. I see that now and I do understand how it must have hurt you to think that Dad loved her. But he chose *you*. He married *you* and he's stayed with *you*.'

'And that's supposed to comfort me, is it? When all the time I think he's been hankering after her.'

Fleur took in a deep breath. Although she knew that what Betsy said was perhaps true, she had to try to get her mother to get over it and move on. 'I think "hankering" is perhaps the wrong word. I think he remembers her with fondness. I ... I suppose you never forget your first love.' Her voice broke a little, but she carried on bravely. 'But it was a love between children, Mum. What he has with you is different. Very different.'

Betsy gave a sad smile. For once she knew her daughter was trying to help her, trying to get her to let go of the bitterness and resentment she'd held all through the years. But it was impossible. She couldn't expect the young girl who'd only loved and known the love of one man to understand. To understand the heart-wrenching pain of knowing that the man you love and live with is, every day, thinking of someone else. Living your whole life believing yourself to be second best. It was a pain that Betsy had lived with all of her adult life – an anguish that Fleur would never understand unless she experienced it for herself. There was only one person who might understand.

She wondered if Louisa Collins had suffered the same wretchedness.

But Fleur was living her own agony. A sharp, intense pain that would never quite go away, but would, Betsy believed, lessen in time even if Fleur could not believe it now.

With a supreme effort Betsy said, 'I'm sorry about Robbie. Truly. I can't help how I feel about his mother, but I wouldn't wish that on anyone. Not . . . not even on her.'

Fleur sighed deeply. It was no use. She couldn't get through to her mother. Betsy would never change.

Forty

Fleur had to face Robbie's mother, but she didn't know how she was going to do it. She almost wished now that she had not bullied her father into telling her the secrets of the past. Perhaps they would, as both Jake and Betsy had tried to tell her, have been better left buried. It had changed her view of Meg; she couldn't help but look at her differently now. It was difficult to imagine the pretty, smiling woman as a scheming temptress who had seduced two men and ignored the man who had always loved her. What puzzled her, though, was why her parents hadn't told her the truth from the outset when she had first met Robbie. If they had maybe—? No, Fleur was honest enough to answer her own question. No. Nothing they could ever have said would have stopped her. She had fallen in love with Robbie at that very first meeting on the station platform in the blackout and from that moment she'd known – they'd both known – that they had to be together.

The next morning, Fleur packed and came downstairs, ready to leave. She had sponged and pressed her uniform and washed her underwear the previous evening. Now she was ready to go back and get on with fighting the war. The war that had taken away everything she had ever wanted and yet, if it hadn't been for the war, it was unlikely she'd ever have met Robbie.

But she knew that to get back into the thick of it would help. It would help her to feel close to him still.

But, first, there was something else she had to do. She must go to Nottingham. She couldn't avoid it any longer.

'So, you're going back are you?' Betsy said to her as they sat at breakfast.

'I'll take you, love,' Jake began, but Fleur shook her head.

'I'm going to Nottingham first. I'm not due back at camp until tomorrow, but I don't know when I'll get any more leave. Ma'am has been very good, but . . . but I'm not the only one . . .' Her voice cracked and she stopped.

Jake cleared his throat and glanced briefly at his wife before saying, 'Then I'll take you there.'

Betsy opened her mouth as if to protest, but then thought better of it. She got up, clattered the breakfast dishes together and moved away into the scullery, but her shoulders were tense with disapproval.

'It's all right, Dad,' Fleur said gently. 'The trains fit up quite nicely, but if you could just run me to the station in town so I can catch the Paddy to the Junction . . .'

When Meg opened the door to her, the two women stood staring at each other for a long moment. At first sight, neither looked any different. Meg was still prettily dressed, with her face cream and powder carefully applied. There was even a pale tinge of lipstick on her generous mouth. And Fleur was smartly turned out in her WAAF uniform.

It wasn't until they each looked closely into the other's eyes that they could see the undeniable grief they shared.

'Oh, Fleur!' Meg opened her arms and Fleur fell into them, hugging the older woman.

'Oh, Ma!' was all she could say, poignantly using Robbie's pet name for his mother that brought tears to their eyes.

'Now, now.' Meg, dabbing at her eyes, tried to smile. 'He wouldn't want us to be doing this. Come in, come in . . .' she urged as she drew Fleur into the warm kitchen.

'Where's . . . where's Pops?' she asked at once as she saw the empty chair by the range.

'In bed. He's taken it very hard and, of course, at his age . . .'

She said no more, but Fleur understood. For someone of his age grief was a strange thing. Some old folk took bad news in their stride. Not that they didn't feel it, but life had conditioned them to deal with tragedies and, if not exactly immune to them, at least they had learnt resilience. But for others, such news was the last straw as if they had no strength left to field another blow. Fleur understood. With each morning, when she awoke, the full horror hit her afresh and she wondered how she would get through the day.

'I suppose,' Meg said as she handed Fleur a cup of tea and sat down in the old man's empty chair opposite, 'that we shouldn't hope.'

Fleur bit her lip. How could she answer? How could she say that every moment of every day she prayed that a miracle would happen? I'll give anything, she kept promising, if only he's alive. 'They – they say not,' she said at last.

Meg sat down opposite her. 'I've had such a nice letter from Wing Commander Jones already. I was surprised. I . . . I thought Robbie would have put you down as his next of kin now.'

Fleur smiled wanly. 'I think he must have forgotten to get it changed. Besides, the CO's like that. I think he'd have written to you anyway.'

'And he sent me the names and addresses of the next of kin of all the other members of the crew in case I wanted to write to them. Do you think I should, Fleur?'

'Yes, I've got that list too. Maybe . . . maybe we could both write in . . . in a week or so.'

Meg nodded. 'Yes – yes, that's what I thought too. Let a bit of time elapse. But . . . but I thought I'd like to write to Tommy's family and Johnny's too. All of them really. They helped to make your wedding day so special, didn't they? Such lovely boys . . .' Her voice trailed away.

Fleur was staring at Meg – she couldn't help it. All the things that her father had told her about this woman were whirling around her brain. And Meg was staring back.

Softly, she said, 'You know, don't you? Jake's told you.'

Fleur blinked and said quickly – too quickly. 'Told me? Told me what?'

'Don't deny it, Fleur. Lying doesn't suit you.'

Fleur felt her cheeks grow hot. How could she have been so foolish as to let her feelings show so openly on her face? It had always been her downfall and now she had let her father down. He'd never forgive her. She tried to salvage the situation by saying, 'I don't know what you mean.'

'Dear Fleur.' Meg shook her head, smiling gently. 'You've got such an open, honest face. You really shouldn't be trusted with secrets.'

Fleur closed her eyes and groaned. 'Please – don't be angry with my dad. It . . . it wasn't his fault. I . . . I bullied him into telling me.' She sighed. 'And now I wish I hadn't. He swore me to secrecy. Made me promise that I'd never say a word to anyone – especially to you. And now–' Tears sprang into her eyes. 'You've guessed and he'll be so angry with me.'

Meg reached across and, though there was a wistful note in her voice, she said, 'It doesn't matter now, Fleur. Nothing matters now.' There was a long pause before Meg added softly, 'Do you hate me?'

Fleur's eyes widened as she stared at her. 'Hate you? Heavens, no!' and was touched as she saw Meg's tremulous, grateful smile.

'I couldn't bear it if . . . if I never saw you again,' she said. 'You're . . . you're all I have left of Robbie. I don't suppose–' Suddenly, her eyes were filled with a fresh hope. 'I don't suppose there's any chance you could be carrying his child?'

Fleur pressed her lips together and shook her head. 'No,' she whispered. 'I only wish I was.'

A week later Meg opened the door, half expecting to see Fleur standing there again. She had promised to visit as often as she could and had said that her commanding officer was being very understanding. The girl had already written twice to her during the week, trying to give comfort even though her own heart was breaking. Meg loved her for that.

But instead of her daughter-in-law standing there, there was someone she had expected never to see again. She felt as if she had been dealt a blow just below her ribs and the breath had been knocked from her body. She clutched at the door for support. 'Philip! Oh my God!'

'Hello, Meg.'

He, of course, had prepared himself for the sight of her, but she'd had no such warning. 'May I come in?'

'Yes – well – yes, of course. But – but–' She stepped back to let him into the house. 'Why are you here? Why have you come? Now, of all times. Why have you come now?'

'I should have come years ago, Meg. I shouldn't have abandoned you and . . . and our son so callously.'

Meg gasped at his open admission, but he wasn't finished yet.

'If I'd been more of a man, I'd've acknowledged him. Been a part of his life. And now – I've left it too late, haven't I?'

'Oh, Philip,' she said. 'We both made a mistake but . . . but you know, I won't ever say I'm sorry for having Robbie. He's been the light of my life. He—' Tears filled her eyes and spilled down her cheeks as Philip clasped her hands. 'He was a wonderful young man. You . . . you'd've been proud of him.'

'So Louisa has told me.'

'Louisa? She . . . she's talked to you about it?'

Philip nodded soberly. 'Yes. Come – let's sit down and I'll explain. Is there – is there somewhere we can talk alone? I understand you have your father living with you?'

'Yes, I do, but he's still in bed. He – since Robbie – he doesn't get up until the afternoon. It . . . it's hit him hard.'

'And you, Meg. I can see you're putting a brave face on it, but you're devastated, aren't you?'

And now the tears that she had tried so hard to keep in check ever since she'd had the telegram flooded down her face and she let out a howl of anguish like a wounded animal. She'd held herself together for her father's sake, for Fleur's sake, but Philip's kind and understanding words had opened the floodgates of her grief.

'Oh, Philip . . . how . . . am I to . . . bear it?'

He put his arms around her and held her close as she sobbed against his shoulder. Even in this dreadful moment, he felt again the stirring of the feelings he'd had for her all those years ago. And though he knew that for her all the passion that had once been between them was gone, he was honest enough to admit that if she had at that moment led him up the stairs to her bedroom, he would have gone willingly, like a lamb to the slaughter. He felt a surge of shame that after his lovely wife's generous forgiveness, he could even think of being unfaithful again. Was it really possible to love two women at the same time? Once upon a time he would have dismissed such a notion as ridiculous, branding it as a man's excuse for philandering. Yet now, he was not so sure. If it was love he felt for Meg, then, yes, it was entirely possible, for he knew he loved Louisa. He always had done. But theirs was the love that deepened and grew through their years together, based on true affection for each other and caring for each other.

Yet Meg had wielded such a seductive power over

him. He'd been helpless against the consuming passion he'd felt for her all those years ago that had made him embark on a dangerous affair with her. He had believed, when it ended, that no one but the two of them had been hurt. He knew that she had kept her counsel, that she had told no one, not even her own son, who his father was. But it seemed that fate had had other ideas. In making their boy the spitting image of his father, there was no hiding the truth from those who'd known Philip in his younger days and had, more recently, seen Robbie.

There had been no hiding it – not even from his wife.

He let out a deep sigh and, above her head, he closed his eyes in anguish. He felt her pain and, even though he had never known Robbie, his own grief was for the lost years, the lost chances.

He felt ashamed of the flare of passion he was feeling for this woman, but now, all she wanted from him was comfort in her grief for the loss of her son. Their son. He held her tightly and stroked her hair and his heart was full of regret.

If only, all those years ago, he had been braver.

'Come, Meg. Sit down.' He urged her gently towards a chair. 'Have you any brandy in the house?'

Meg gave a hysterical laugh as she dried her tears. 'You, a doctor? Prescribing brandy.'

'Very medicinal on occasions,' Philip remarked dryly.

'Under the sink in the scullery,' Meg instructed.

As she sipped the amber liquid a moment later, she asked, 'Why have you come?'

'Louisa was at Middleditch Farm visiting Betsy

when Fleur came home with the news that Robbie had
been posted missing—'

'Presumed killed,' Meg ended flatly.

'They haven't said for sure though, have they?'

Meg shook her head and nipped her lower lip
between her teeth.

'Then – then he might be all right. He might
have—'

'Fleur doesn't think so,' Meg burst out. 'She's
amongst it every day. She should know.'

'Well, yes, but even if his plane was shot down,
maybe he baled out, maybe—'

'There were no parachutes.' She looked up at him,
her eyes brimming with tears. 'And it was over the sea.
I'm sorry – I know you're trying to be kind. But we
have to face it, Philip.'

'Oh, Meg,' he said softly. 'Still as brave as ever.'

She smiled wryly. 'That's not a word I've heard
used to describe me very often. Scheming, devious,
wicked, a temptress. Oh yes.' She put up her hand as
he made as if to argue. 'Yes, I was all those things,
Philip. Once. But not any more. Not since the day that
Clara Finch tried to kidnap my baby. I saw that as
my punishment and if . . . if it hadn't been for Jake,
I might really have lost him. It was Jake who found
him.'

Philip stared at her. 'And it's Jake you've always
loved, isn't it? I can see it in your eyes when you speak
his name. You love him still, don't you?'

'Yes,' she said simply, too weary to hide the truth
any longer. 'Oh, Philip, I was so wrong, so bad. To
seduce poor Percy into marrying me just so that I had
security . . .'

'Now, Meg, I won't have you blaming yourself for everything. Percy adored you and in the short time you were married to him, you made him very, very happy. You were loyal and . . .'

She raised her head and met his gaze. 'But not faithful, eh, Philip?'

'Well, no, but he never knew.'

She shook her head slowly. 'That doesn't excuse it.'

'Of course not, but – but what I mean is – you didn't hurt him.'

'But I hurt Louisa.'

'That was my responsibility. I betrayed my wife, not you. Meg, we share the blame for what we did. You don't carry the burden of guilt alone, you know. And, like I said, I should have behaved in a more gentlemanly way. I should have admitted everything at the time and stood beside you.'

Meg shook her head. 'No, no. You had everything to lose. Your career, your good name – and Louisa.'

'I might not have lost Louisa,' he murmured, as if thinking aloud. 'She says now that if I had told her at the time, she might have been willing to have adopted Robbie. It's been a great sadness to her that we have never had children.'

'But she didn't know that then, did she?'

'No – that's what I told her. It's how she feels now, but I very much doubt she would have felt that way back then.' He paused and then added, 'She told me she came to see you a little while back.'

'It . . . it was after she'd seen Robbie for the first time. In a cafe in South Monkford. It . . . it must have been a dreadful shock for her.'

'I wonder why she never said anything then?' Philip pondered.

Meg shrugged. 'I wouldn't admit that he was your son. I told her that my father had had fair hair and blue eyes, but I don't think she believed me. I think she had seen the truth only too clearly with her own eyes when she saw Robbie.'

There was a long silence between them before Philip said softly, 'And now she's regretting that she didn't give me the chance to meet my own son.' He caught and held Meg's gaze. 'Would you have let me see him, Meg?'

She was silent a moment more before saying slowly, 'Probably not. You see – I never told him the truth. Perhaps I should have done . . .' And she went on to tell Philip how Robbie, after meeting Fleur, had begun to ask questions. 'All he wanted was to know that Jake wasn't his father. And, of course, I was able to answer him honestly about that.'

'And he didn't probe any further?'

She shook her head.

'Yet someone or something must have put a doubt in his mind,' Philip said. 'About Percy not being his father, I mean.'

'It was Betsy. She became hysterical when she knew that Fleur had met Robbie and that they wanted to go on seeing each other. Wouldn't have him in the house and wouldn't say why. Naturally, the young ones wanted to know.'

'And so he asked you?'

'Mmm.'

'But you didn't tell him.'

'No. But Fleur knows now. Jake told her recently. Since . . . since Robbie was killed.'

'Why on earth has he told her now?'

Meg gave a small smile, thinking of her feisty

daughter-in-law and admiring her spirit. 'She said she bullied him into telling her the truth. She told him it couldn't hurt Robbie now and that she wanted to understand why her mother had behaved as she had.' Meg sighed. 'I don't blame her for wanting to know. I would have done in her shoes.'

Philip gave a wry laugh. 'You'd've found out months ago.'

And even Meg had to smile. 'I felt so sorry for her. She didn't mean to let it out that Jake had told her. He'd sworn her to secrecy. But I could see it in her eyes when she looked at me. Not disgust or anger or anything like that, but just . . . just something different. Just that – she knew.'

They sat together for several moments until Philip said, 'So – what now, Meg?'

'I don't understand. What do you mean "What now?"'

'What will you do?'

'Do?' She shrugged her shoulders helplessly. 'What can I do but carry on as best I can? Care for my father, hope that Fleur will still visit us now and again.'

'And Jake?'

'What about Jake?'

'Shall you – will you see him?'

'I very much doubt that I shall ever see Jake again. Betsy will see to that.' There was no bitterness or resentment in her tone, merely a calm acceptance of the inevitable, yet Philip could hear the desolation in her tone. She had lost her beloved son and the one man she had ever truly loved was also as good as lost to her.

As if seeing the sympathy written in his eyes, she reached out and touched his hand. 'I'm not the only one to lose my boy. There are so many of us – too many of us – all over the world grieving for the waste of young lives.'

'I know, I know,' he said gripping her hand. 'I'm just so sorry I never met him. But I'll tell you this, Meg, if by some miracle he is still alive, then by God I will see him. I will meet him and I will acknowledge him as my son. I promise you that. If I'm given a second chance, I will try to behave as a father to him.'

Forty-One

Fleur threw herself into her work. When she wasn't on duty she cycled down to the little cottage and attacked the garden as if it was personally responsible for Robbie's death. It was the only way she could think of to stop herself sinking into a dark abyss of grief and regret. Ruth was a tower of strength and even Mrs Jackson and old Harry played their part in helping her to cope.

'Time to plant carrots, love,' Harry told her, leaning on the fence between the two back gardens and jabbing the stem of his pipe towards the freshly dug ground. 'Fancy, it's a year since you came and started all this, lass. Least you haven't got all that grass and rubbish to get rid of this time, eh?'

'No, but I could do to go and see Mr Clegg again. See if his pigs are still producing what I need.'

Ruth came to the cottage too, as often as she could. She still helped keep Harry's house clean, his clothes washed and ironed. 'And he'll not have a bath from one month's end to the next if I don't personally drag the tin bath into that kitchen and push him into it,' she said as they were cycling down one afternoon.

The picture of Ruth pushing Harry into the steaming bath, probably fully clothed, made Fleur smile. She chuckled – the first time she had really laughed since

Robbie had been posted missing. 'It's only because he wants you to scrub his back for him.'

Ruth glanced at her friend, relieved to see a brief smile on her face. 'Well, at least now his hair's cut regularly. And his toenails. You should have seen them that first time I did them, Fleur.' She screwed up her face. 'Disgusting, they were. Almost curling round the ends of his toes!'

'No thanks,' Fleur said with feeling. 'I'll stick to my gardening.'

'Actually, if I'm honest, that sort of thing – Harry's mucky feet, I mean – doesn't bother me. My old grandad lived with us when I was a kid and the things my mam had to do for him – well, you don't want to know.' She shrugged. 'But she just accepted it and got on with it. Like ya do. And it was the norm for us kids.'

'You should've been a nurse,' Fleur remarked. 'You'd've been a good one.'

'Mm. Maybe you're right. Well, here we are again,' she said, squeezing the brakes on her bicycle to bring it to a squealing halt. 'You go and tackle Mrs J's garden and I'll tackle old Harry's toenails.'

Fleur laughed again. 'I call that a fair deal.'

Fleur had been working for a couple of hours under the warm sun. She straightened up, mopped her forehead, wet with sweat, and decided to take a breather. She dropped her fork and went to sit on the seat under the apple tree. Leaning her back against the trunk of the tree, she gazed out across the flat expanse of the airfield. It was silent today and she hoped it would stay that way. There hadn't been an air raid for a while now. They'd been lucky but there was an ominous kind of tension in the air as if any day they expected to see the Luftwaffe in the skies overhead again.

In the cottage, Ruth saw Fleur sitting beneath the tree. 'Breaks ya heart, doesn't it? To see her sitting there looking so lost and lonely.'

'It does,' Mrs Jackson agreed. 'And there's nothing any of us can do, is there?'

Sadly, Ruth shook her head. 'Not a thing. I'd go out and join her, but I think she'd rather be alone.'

'There are times when you just want to be by yourself,' the older woman said softly. 'Just to let go for a little while.'

'I know,' Ruth said, remembering only too well how she'd felt at Billy's loss and she hadn't even been married to him. She ached for the pain her friend must be feeling, yet she was helpless to comfort her. There was nothing she could say or do that would bring Robbie back and, right now, that was the only thing that would put a permanent smile back on Fleur's face. The only thing.

The days dragged interminably. Fleur couldn't believe that it was only just over a week since she had had news that Robbie was missing. And there was Kenny to worry about too. Now, he would be up there in the clouds, doing his training, hoping to be good enough to become a fighter pilot. Fleur sighed as she clattered down the steps from the control tower after another shift on duty.

I ought to go home again as soon as I can, she thought, but she shuddered at the thought of facing her mother. Betsy would be worried sick about Kenny and would turn her anger on her daughter. Yet Fleur knew her father would be feeling it keenly too. And she knew too that Jake would be sorrowful for Meg – a feeling he could never talk about with his wife. And I ought to go and see Robbie's mother again. See how the old man is too. It's what Robbie would have wanted me to do. But she shied away from the thought. Seeing Meg's grief only heightened her own.

As she was walking away from the control tower, she heard the dreaded sound of an air raid warning. Automatically, she turned to run to the nearest shelter, but then she remembered. She'd left Kay in the control room finishing off. She glanced back, hoping to see the girl emerging from the tower and running across the grass towards her. But there was no sign of the slim, dark-haired figure.

Fleur bit her lip. She was anxious about Kay. Since the loss of Tommy's plane, Kay had changed. She'd seemed very strong at first, but since she'd come back from leave, she'd been the one to sink into an abyss of misery. Fleur was constantly having to watch her at work to make sure she didn't make any mistakes, for Bob Watson had eyes like a hawk now and his disapproval of wartime romances was still evident every day.

Fleur turned and began to run back towards the watch office. She reached the foot of the steps as the first aircraft came swooping in, dropping incendiaries on the runway only a few feet from the control room.

'Kay! Kay!' Fleur shouted, but knew the girl wouldn't hear her above the noise. She almost fell into the room and then stopped in shock. Kay was standing in front of the long window overlooking the airfield, her arms outstretched, her head thrown back. She was laughing and crying hysterically and shouting, 'Come on. Get me! Get *me*! You've got him, now get me. Here I am . . .'

At that moment another plane screamed by, so low that Fleur fancied she saw the pilot sitting in the cockpit, could fancy she saw him press the button and pepper the ground with gunshot.

'Kay,' she screamed. 'For God's sake! Get down!' And she launched at the girl, bringing her to the floor and pushing her beneath the desk just as another aircraft dived towards them. The bomb landed just outside the tower, rocking its foundations, blowing all the windows into the room and showering the whole room with deadly shards of glass.

'Where's Fullerton and Bosley – I mean, Rodwell? Have you seen them?'

The raid was over, the all-clear wailing out and staff were emerging from their bolt holes. Bob Watson was first out, demanding of anyone nearby if they had seen 'his girls'. Bluff and disapproving though he might be of their private lives, nevertheless he secretly held them in high regard. Both were excellent in their work, and even though Fullerton had been a little preoccupied these last few days he'd found it in his heart to overlook it. Besides, he assuaged his duty-bound conscience, the other girl – Rodwell, as he must remember to call her – was emerging as the stronger of the two. He had noticed her keeping a keen eye on her colleague and leaping in to avert what could – in the hectic, tense atmosphere of Control – have been a disaster. Twice, to his certain knowledge, Fleur had prevented two aircraft being told to land at the same moment. Strange, Bob Watson couldn't help thinking to himself, how things turned out the way you didn't expect. He'd've laid money on it that the Rodwell girl would have cracked first, been a weeping wreck, whilst the outspoken Fullerton would have shrugged her shoulders, muttered, 'Well, that's war for you,' and moved on to the next handsome airman.

But it seemed, Bob was man enough to admit if only to himself, he'd been wrong.

Now, he was on the verge of panic himself as he realized suddenly just how fond he had become of those two girls, however much he tried to keep himself their aloof superior.

Ruth came running across the grass, shaking her fist in the direction the aircraft had disappeared.

'Bastards! Bastards! We'll get you. You wait till our fighter boys catch up with you . . .'

'Morrison,' Bob roared at the outraged girl. 'Have you seen Fullerton and Rodwell? Are they with you?'

Ruth stopped at once, her arm still in the air, her fist clenched. Slowly she let it fall to her side and turned to face him.

'Flight?' she asked stupidly and Bob repeated his question, watching her eyes widen in fear.

'No. I was in the shelter near debriefing. I thought – I mean – aren't they with you?'

'No.' Grimly, his glance went towards the tower. 'I left them in the watch office.'

The tower itself was still standing, but even from here they could both see that not a window was left whole in the building.

'Oh no!' Ruth began to run towards the tower, Bob Watson pounding close behind her. She flew up the steps and thrust open the door, the broken glass crunching beneath her feet, bracing herself for what she might find.

'Fleur! Kay!'

'Here. We're here – under the desk. Can you help me, Ruth? Kay's . . .'

She said no more but as Ruth bent down and offered her hand, she saw that Kay was as white as a sheet and shaking from head to foot. Tears were running down her face. Ruth's mouth dropped open. 'Kay?' she said in disbelief and again, 'Kay?'

'It's all right now, Kay,' Fleur was saying soothingly as Bob too arrived, panting heavily.

'Are they all right? Oh, good thinking,' he added as he saw they had taken shelter beneath the sturdy desk. 'Out you both come then. They've gone. Can't you hear the "all-clear"? But mind the glass, it's all over the bloody place.' He glanced round at the debris around him. Not only had the windows been damaged but radios and telephones. The blackboards hung drunkenly off the wall and papers had been scattered everywhere. 'Bloody 'ell,' he muttered. 'It'll take a month of Sundays to clear this lot up. And the runway's damaged. I reckon there won't be flying from here for a few days. Come on, you two, what are you mucking about at?'

'It . . . it's Kay. I think she's badly shocked,' Fleur said, crawling carefully out from under the desk. 'I can't get her to move.'

Kay was crouched beneath the desk, rocking backwards and forwards. 'Saved my life. She saved my life. Fleur saved my life,' she was muttering.

'Yes, yes, I'm sure she did, but come on out now,'

Bob snapped. Now he'd found they were safe, his patience was soon wearing thin.

'We'll sort her out, Flight,' Ruth suggested, standing up. 'Leave it with us. And we'll start and clear up here, if you like.'

'Ah well, yes. I ought to – er – yes, well. I'll leave you to it then.'

He left the room, and when they heard his footsteps clattering down the steps, Ruth breathed more easily. 'Right. Now he's out the way, we can sort her out.' She squatted down again and her tone softened, became cajoling, as she said, 'Come on, love. All over now. Give me your hand. Take her other hand, Fleur. Don't let her kneel else she'll cut her legs. God, what a mess!'

Whether Ruth was referring to the state of the control room or the state of their friend, Fleur could not have said.

'We'd best get her across to the doc's pronto,' Ruth muttered to Fleur and then again turned to Kay. 'Come on, love, that's it. There you go. Safe and sound.'

'Saved my life, she did.'

Kay emerged slowly from the makeshift shelter but she was still shaking visibly.

'It's the doc for you, Corp,' Ruth said, taking control. 'And you'd better come too, Fleur. You've had a shock an' all.'

'I'm fine. Honestly, but I'll help you take her across and then come back here.'

'Right-o. I'll come back and help you.'

The doctor – as they'd feared – was in great demand, but thankfully only for cuts and bruises.

No one, it seemed, had been killed or even seriously injured. The worst casualty seemed to be Kay and that was shock more than physical harm. She hadn't even a scratch though Fleur had cut the palm of her hand on some glass and had bumped her head as she'd dived for cover pushing Kay in front of her.

At last Kay was admitted to the sick quarters for observation. Ruth and Fleur, the cut on her hand bathed and dressed, returned to the control room to help tidy up. Already, there were plenty of willing hands sweeping up the glass, picking up pieces of paper and testing the radios. It would not take as long as Bob had feared to have the control room operational once more.

Fleur was very much afraid that it would take far longer for Kay to heal.

With the airfield out of action for a day or two, Fleur grabbed the chance of a couple of days' leave whilst repairs were carried out. Enough time to go home and to Nottingham.

For some reason she couldn't explain, this second visit to both places seemed more difficult than the first, but she couldn't put the moment off any longer. She ought to go to see Meg again and then she would have to go home. It was easier to get back to camp from her home than from Nottingham because if, for some reason, there was no train running at the time she needed one, her father would always bring her back.

But first she cycled down the road to make sure Mrs Jackson and old Harry were safe and unharmed. A few stray bombs had fallen in the village and she was anxious about the old couple.

But the two cottages looked unscathed and to her relief Harry was sitting drinking tea in Mary Jackson's kitchen.

'Now then, lass. All right?'

Although Harry's greeting was casual, Fleur could see her own relief mirrored in his eyes and Mrs Jackson said outright, 'Oh, love, I'm so glad to see you. We've been that worried. And Ruth? Is she all right?'

'She's fine. She'll be down to see you later, but I've got a forty-eight, so I'm . . . I'm going to see Robbie's mother and then going home.'

The old couple exchanged a glance and nodded. There was a pause before Harry, deliberately changing the subject, said, 'That there shelter in the garden you built for us came in handy.' He jabbed his finger towards Mary, teasing. 'And I got her in it, an' all. First time I've managed it on me own. But they was coming a bit too close for comfort yesterday. Don't mind admitting it.'

'We heard one or two had landed in the village. Was anybody hurt?'

Now Harry's face sobered and again he glanced at Mary Jackson. 'A couple of young lads playing down near the stream were killed. Fishing, I expect they were. Always been a favourite place for youngsters. Too busy to think of taking shelter, I dare say. Thought it would be just the airfield being targeted. Y'know?'

Fleur nodded. 'I'm so sorry,' she said.

'Three of Mr Clegg's cows were killed an' all. But that's nothing compared to the loss of a human life . . .' Old Harry's voice trailed away.

'No, of course it isn't,' Fleur agreed sadly. There was a pause and then she said, 'Well, if you're sure you're both all right, I'll be off. I'll come again as soon as I can.'

'Aye well, there's plenty to do in yon garden.' He jabbed towards the window with his pipe. 'There's a lot of planting to do and there's always hoeing needed. Weeds grow as fast as the plants, ya know.'

'Faster, if you ask me.' Fleur managed to raise a smile. 'But I'll be here.' Already she was looking forward to the peace and quiet of working alone in the garden. Of sitting under the apple tree – her quiet time to think about Robbie.

Forty-Two

Fleur hesitated outside the door, not really wanting to come face to face with Robbie's mother. Meg had seemed so strong when she'd seen her immediately after it had happened. But she'd seen now at first hand how easy it was for a seemingly strong person to crack. Who'd have thought Kay would be the one to end up a quivering wreck? Thankfully, she was already beginning to recover and, much to Fleur's embarrassment, was telling everyone how Fleur had saved her life.

Fleur took a deep breath and raised her hand, but before she could knock the door flew open and Meg was standing there, her face wreathed in smiles.

'Fleur! How lovely to see you. Come in, come in.' Meg reached out, grasped her arm and almost hauled her inside.

Fleur stared at her, anger welling up inside her. Well, she thought, it hasn't taken you long to get over your son's death. How can you be so cheerful? How can you be carrying on with your life as though nothing has happened?

'You got my message then?' Meg said as Fleur stepped into the cluttered front room and followed Meg's trim figure through to the back.

'Message? What message? No, I didn't get any message. All the lines have been down. We had an air raid the day before yesterday. No, I just came because . . .'

But Meg didn't seem to be listening. She was flinging open the door leading from the front room into the kitchen and announcing Fleur's arrival with a flourish and a beaming smile. 'Just look who's here . . .'

Perhaps she thinks I'm going to help raise the old man's spirits, Fleur thought. That's what all her cheerfulness is for. To try and buoy the old man up. Fleur tried to force a tremulous smile onto her mouth as she took a step forward past Meg and into the room.

The old man was indeed sitting in his usual chair, but there was someone else sitting in the chair on the opposite side of the hearth. Suddenly, the whole room seemed to spin. She swayed and clutched at the door-jamb. She felt the colour drain from her face and her legs felt as if they would no longer support her.

'Catch her, Ma. She's going to pass out. Damn this bloody leg . . .'

Fleur felt Meg's strong arms about her as she helped her to a chair near the fire. 'I'll get her some water . . .' were the last words Fleur heard Meg saying before everything went black.

Someone was bending over her and holding a glass to her lips. She opened her eyes and tried to focus on the beloved face close to her.

'She's coming round.'

Fleur felt clammy and cold and still dizzy, but she murmured, 'I'm all right now. It was just such a shock. I thought . . . I thought—' She reached up and touched Robbie's face, still unable to believe that he was really here. Her prayers had been answered. Robbie was alive and smiling down at her. 'I mean, I was told your plane went down in the sea.'

'It did.' Robbie was grinning at her. 'Hence this.' He tapped the plaster cast on his right leg.

'But no one saw a parachute.'

'No time. We were too near the water. But thanks to a brilliant bit of flying by our skipper, who managed some sort of belly flop with the plane – God knows how he did it – we all got out. We were picked up by the local lifeboat and here I am.'

'Yes,' Fleur said, grinning stupidly up at him. 'Here you are.'

Then she promptly burst into tears and clung to him, burying her face against him.

The rest of the afternoon was spent with laughter and tears, hugs and kisses. Tactfully, Meg left them alone with the excuse that she had a dress hem to finish.

'Now, come along, Dad. You can sit in the front room with me for a while. Let's leave these two young ones alone.'

Fleur watched as Meg helped her father to his feet and steadied him as he shuffled into the next room. 'Don't go without saying ta-ta to me, will you, lass?' he said in a quavering voice.

'I won't,' Fleur promised, a lump in her throat as she watched Meg's patient tenderness with the frail old man. Then she turned back to Robbie, still unable to believe the miracle that had really happened. 'Are you really all safe? Tommy too?'

'Yes, all of us. But, like I said, without Tommy's brilliant flying, we probably wouldn't be.'

'Oh, I can't wait to tell Kay.' Then she told him all about the air raid and Kay, and then for the rest of the afternoon they thought about no one else but themselves . . .

At five o'clock Fleur said reluctantly, 'I must go.'

'Darling, I wish I could come with you.' He grinned. 'But I really can't hop as far as the station and back – even on my crutches.'

'I'll be all right.'

'Just so long' – he tapped her playfully on the nose – 'as you don't let any strange young RAF types pick you up. Just remember, you're a married woman now.'

She wrapped her arms around him and held him close. 'I won't. I've got the only RAF type I want. And I'll come as often as I can. Are you staying here until your leg's healed?'

'I think so. They couldn't wait to ship me out of hospital as soon as they could. They needed the bed. Oh, darling.' His face sobered. 'I'm so sorry you've been worried. I can't understand why word didn't get through from Bournemouth.'

'Is that where you were? Bournemouth? Isn't that odd?' she murmured. 'Kenny's down south somewhere now.'

'Is he? Is he all right?'

'I hope so. He'll have started his flying training by now. He was so excited. Couldn't wait to start flying. Can't wait to get into the thick of it.'

'I hope he'll be all right,' Robbie said.

'I don't expect it's so bad for the fighter boys, is it? Not now? I mean – they did their bit in the Battle of Britain.'

Robbie smiled thinly and nodded. He couldn't bring

himself to disillusion her. That every day the fighter boys were in the air attacking incoming enemy bombers, trying to stop them reaching their targets.

Maybe Fleur hadn't heard the latest news and he didn't want to be the one to tell her. Hitler had issued orders for his air force to begin a series of attacks upon British cities. Exeter, Bath, Norwich and York had been targeted already and Robbie feared the German leader would turn his attention to the industrial cities of the Midlands next. But he said nothing of this to Fleur. Instead he said, 'I still can't understand why word didn't get through to you that we were all safe. I mean, I wrote to you from there myself, let alone the fact that the War Office should have let them know at Wickerton that all the crew were safe. I can't understand it at all. I think it must be something to do with the telephone lines being down. I tried to phone Mr Tomkins at the shop to let Ma know as soon as I could hop around again.' He tapped his leg again. 'And I tried ringing camp. But I couldn't get through to either of you.'

'Well, the lines are certainly all down now – since the raid. That is a fact.'

'And there I was thinking you were safe and sound.' He held her close. 'Oh, darling, do be careful.'

'I will,' she promised as she kissed him again and again, loathe to leave him. 'But I must go. I must go to Middleditch Farm. Dad will be so pleased to hear you're safe. And I must get back to camp first thing tomorrow morning.'

'Oh, I don't want to let you go,' he said, hugging her tightly to him as they stood at the front door saying their goodbyes. She laughed as she prised herself free and, planting a last kiss on his nose, began to run up the street, turning to wave once more before she turned the corner.

The house at Middleditch Farm was strangely quiet as she entered by the back door. The scullery was deserted, but as she stepped into the kitchen she saw her mother sitting motionless in the chair by the range, her head resting on her hand.

'Mum?'

Slowly, Betsy raised her head and stared for a moment at her daughter. Then with a low sound in her throat that sounded almost like a growl, she said, 'Get out! Get out of this house and don't ever come back.' Then she grasped the arms of the chair and pushed herself up. 'Don't ever show your face here again.'

'Mum—'

'Don't "Mum" me. You're no daughter of mine. I have no daughter. It's all your fault. He's gone because of you. My Kenny's gone. And it's your fault. All your fault.'

'Mum – I know he's gone. But he'll be all right. It's not like before when the fighter boys—'

'What d'you mean "He'll be all right"? He's gone, I tell you. Dead. Killed. His plane crashed when he was training. In *training*! He didn't even get to fly a Spitfire like he wanted.' Betsy shook her fist in Fleur's face. 'He's dead – and all because of you.'

For the second time that day, Fleur felt her legs give way beneath her. She felt as if the breath had been knocked from her body. The room swirled around her and she staggered forward towards her father's chair.

She sank down weakly, blinking and taking short, panting breaths, trying desperately not to pass out again.

'Oh no – no, you can't mean it. Not Kenny. Not my . . . little . . . brother.' The heartrending sobs came then, flooding out of her. She was shaking, feeling cold, so very cold.

Yes, her mother was right. It was all her fault. Kenny had only joined the forces because she had done so. He hadn't wanted to be outdone by his sister. But there was worse than that. Much worse than even her mother knew. Fleur had tried to bargain with God. What was it she had said? 'I'll give anything, if only You'll let him be alive.' So now, Kenny had been taken in his place.

Fleur was beside herself with anguish. From the heights of joy that Robbie was alive, she was plunged once more into the depths of despair. Her grief was a physical pain. She wrapped her arms around herself and rocked to and fro in the chair, sobbing in agony.

'Oh aye, you can shed tears now, can't you? Why didn't you think of that before? Why didn't you stop him going? Why did you ever—?'

'I did. I tried. I begged him not to go,' Fleur screamed. 'He'd've gone anyway, whatever I'd said or done.'

Neither of them heard the back door open and close, but suddenly Jake was in the room and hurrying towards Fleur. He knelt beside her chair and put his arms about her. Fleur hid her face against his shoulder, the sobs still racking her body.

'That's right. You comfort her. You comfort each other. But who's going to comfort me?'

Jake looked up at his wife, his own eyes bleak with

suffering, his face ravaged with loss. 'Fleur's had a double loss, Betsy love,' he said gently. 'First Robbie and now this. Can't you – just for once – feel for her?'

Betsy stared at them both for a moment, but instead of turning and running up the stairs as she usually did, she sank back wearily into her chair as if utterly defeated, without the will or the strength to argue any more.

Fleur raised her head slowly and whispered, 'No, Dad. That's . . . that's what I came home to tell you. Robbie's turned up. He's alive. The pilot managed to ditch the plane in the sea, just off our coast and . . . and they all got out. He's got a broken leg but—'

Betsy lay back in her chair and began to laugh and cry hysterically. 'Oh, that's good, that is. Her son is saved. It'd have to be *her* son that was saved, wouldn't it?'

Jake and Fleur stared at her, helpless to do or say anything.

Forty-Three

Early the following morning, before either of her parents were up, Fleur slipped away from Middleditch Farm. She hitched a lift into the town with an early milk lorry, but before going to the station Fleur slipped into the church in South Monkford. She sat down in a pew near the front and laid her cap, gas mask and bag on the seat beside her. She sat for a long time, just staring ahead at the altar. The tears ran silently down her face and she didn't even bother to wipe them away. She didn't pray. She didn't know how to now. She couldn't even bring herself to give thanks for Robbie's safe return. She didn't know what to say. Not now.

A man came out of the vestry. He crossed to the centre of the chancel, bowed to the altar and then turned and came down the steps towards her. He was dressed in a lounge suit, but in place of a shirt and tie he was wearing the collar of a clergyman. He wasn't the vicar she'd known since childhood: this man was a stranger. Old Revd Pennyfeather must have retired, she thought vaguely, but her mind was too numbed to even want to ask. The man hovered for a moment at the end of the pew where she was sitting. Then he sat down beside her, following the line of her gaze for a moment and staring, too, at the brass cross on the altar.

'You know it's a terrible thing to admit, but I really don't know what to say to people any more.'

Fleur said nothing.

He turned his head slightly to glance at her. 'But the good Lord will—'

Fleur held up her hand to silence him, but still she did not speak.

'Would you ... like to tell me what's troubling you?'

She let her hand sink back down to rest on her lap, but she just continued to stare at the cross on the altar. Still she did not answer him.

'Would you like us to pray together?'

Still, there was silence until, haltingly, Fleur spoke in a hoarse whisper. 'I have no right to pray.'

She held her breath, expecting him to come out with some trite remark. To her surprise, he just said, 'Why?'

Another long silence before she dragged out the words. 'Because ... I tried ... to bargain with God. And lost.'

'Ah.' The sound held a wealth of understanding and sympathy. Fleur turned her head slowly and looked at the man for the first time.

He was small and white haired with a kind face. She could imagine that normally his face would be wreathed in smiles, that he would have a lively, almost saucy sense of humour, but at the moment, the lines on his face drooped with sadness. 'Would you like to tell me about it, my dear? Perhaps I can help.'

'No offence, Vicar, but I doubt it.'

'Try me anyway.'

Several minutes passed before Fleur could bring herself to speak. At first the words came slowly and then faster and finally in a flood as she poured out her anguish.

'My husband – we'd only been married a few months – was posted missing, presumed killed.'

'Oh, my dear, I'm sorry—'

'No – no – he's come back. That's the trouble, you see.'

The man was naturally puzzled. Fleur rushed on trying to explain in short, staccato phrases. 'I'm sorry. I'm not explaining this very well. We met by accident. On a railway station. In the blackout. We didn't know it then, but our parents – well, my parents and his mother – had known each other years ago. There were – well – complications, and when my mother found out who he was she refused to meet him. Refused to let him come to our home. She . . . she didn't even come to our wedding. And then . . . and then there was my brother, Kenny.'

Fresh tears welled in her eyes. 'He was younger than me. When I joined the WAAFs, he made up his mind he was going to volunteer too. As soon as he was old enough. And . . . and he did.'

'Why do you say "volunteer"? He'd've been called up sooner or later.'

Fleur shook her head. 'We live on a farm.'

'Ah,' the vicar said, understanding at once. There was no need for her to say more.

For a moment, Fleur covered her face with her hands. Then she straightened up, brushed away her tears, sniffed and went on. 'When my husband was posted missing, I prayed. Oh, how I prayed. And . . . and that's where I made my mistake. You see, I said, "I'll give anything if only You'll let him be alive." And now . . . now He's given Robbie back to me but . . . but He . . . He's taken my brother in Robbie's place. Kenny's plane crashed while he was training. He never even got to fight the enemy. And that was what he wanted to do most of all. He wanted to help save his country.'

The older man laid his hand gently on her shoulder and said softly, 'That's not how the good Lord works, my dear. We've all, in our time, been guilty of doing exactly what you've done. Promising anything so that we get what we want. God hears, He listens – but do you really think He's going to take a scrap of notice of our – well, as you put it – "bargaining" with Him? I think not.'

'I feel as if I'm being punished.'

'No, no, you shouldn't feel that. You really shouldn't. God has His reasons.'

'What reasons? How can there be a God when all this is happening? How can He let it happen? All these young men – a whole generation – being wiped out. Again. Just like the last terrible war. Why?'

'Don't you think we all ask that? But I see it as a test. A test of our faith.'

'Huh! Some test!'

'I know, I know. That's why it's called "faith". We have to believe without question, without being given answers or reasons why things happen. We just have to put our trust in God. And you see, to God, your brother isn't dead. None of these brave young men are. They're in a far better place than we are right now. In the arms of Jesus.' He paused a moment, before asking quietly, 'Do you believe that?'

'I . . . I'd like to, but it's hard.'

'Oh yes.' The vicar gave a wry laugh. 'It's hard. I'll grant you that. I have to admit, I sometimes feel weighed down with all the suffering and heartache I see every day. I've railed against Him, but somehow He keeps sending me the strength to carry on giving comfort where I can.'

'My mother blames me for Kenny joining up,' Fleur burst out. 'She'll never forgive me. She . . . she says she doesn't want to see me ever again.'

'I'm sorry to hear that,' he said and Fleur marvelled that, yet again, he didn't make any kind of trite remark, saying that given time she would come round. Slowly, Fleur turned to face him. 'You've been very kind and understanding,' she said and added simply, 'thank you.'

'Would you like to pray with me now?'

Fleur nodded and together they slipped to their knees. The vicar began to speak in a soft, deep tone, making up the words of a prayer to suit. He asked for forgiveness and understanding for Fleur in her sorrow and for reassurance that she bore no blame. He prayed, too, for Fleur's parents in their grief and especially for her mother who found her loss so hard to bear. He ended by inviting Fleur to join him in saying the Lord's prayer.

As she left the church a little later, Fleur was surprised to find she felt a great sense of calm settle on her. It would be some time before she would be able to forgive herself, but with the help of the kindly clergyman she had made a start.

'Come back and see me any time, my dear. I'm always here.'

'Thank you,' she said and, as she walked away from

him down the path, she was already giving thanks in her mind that she had met him.

As she entered the main gate, Ruth came rushing towards her. 'I've been watching out for you. We've only just heard. Isn't it wonderful? Everyone's so delighted for you. And Kay. You must go and see her. She's almost back to her old self. I think they'll be letting her out of the hospital tomorrow. Have you seen him? How is he?' Her face was wreathed in smiles, but then she became aware that Fleur's face was not so joyous. 'What is it? Is he badly hurt?'

Fleur shook her head. Flatly, with no hint of the turmoil of emotion inside her that she was trying, desperately, to hold in, she said, 'No. Only a broken leg. Once that's mended, he – he'll be back.'

Ruth blinked, staring at her friend's face. Then, slowly, thinking she understood, she nodded. 'Oh, I see. Once he's well, he'll be flying again. Is that it?'

Fleur lifted her shoulders in a helpless shrug. 'Partly, I suppose.'

Ruth stepped closer and put her arm around Fleur's shoulder. 'It's more than that. I can see it is. Fleur, tell me what's wrong?'

Slowly, Fleur looked up into her friend's eyes. Hesitantly, she dragged out the words she had prayed never to have to speak. 'It . . . it's Kenny.'

Close to her, she heard Ruth's sharp intake of breath, saw her eyes widen in shock and fear. 'Kenny? Oh no!' She shook her head, refusing to believe it. 'Oh no! Not Kenny.'

'He crashed while training. In *training*, Ruth. How unfair is that?'

'Silly bugger!' Ruth muttered, but her eyes filled with tears. 'The stupid, stupid bugger.'

Her arm dropped from around Fleur. Her head lowered and she covered her face with her hands, her shoulders shaking. Now it was Fleur who comforted Ruth.

'I knew I shouldn't do it,' Ruth wailed.

'Do what?' Fleur asked gently.

'Let myself like him. I put a jinx on people.' She let her hands fall away and raised her head. Her face was wet with tears. 'Oh, Fleur,' she whispered. 'I'm so sorry. It . . . it's all my fault.'

Despite her misery, Fleur smiled a little. 'Darling Ruth, if anyone's to blame, it's me. He joined up because I had. That's what my mother thinks. And, of course, I blame myself too.'

Ruth wiped her face with a quick, fierce action. 'It's this bloody war that's to blame. Nothing – and no one – else. Not you, not me. Just the war.'

'You're right. It's not our fault.' Fleur sighed and murmured, 'But I can't help feeling so guilty.'

Ruth, a little more in control of herself, said, 'You ought to ask for compassionate leave. You ought to go home to be with your mam and dad.'

Fleur shook her head sadly. 'I've been. Mum's more or less told me not to bother going home again. Besides, I reckon I've used up all my leave on compassionate grounds. Ma'am's been very good, but just about everyone on camp has a good reason for asking for leave. I can't expect any more for a while now.'

'But what about Robbie? Won't they let you go and see him?'

'I doubt it. But d'you know something, Ruth? I don't

mind going weeks without seeing him, if it means keeping him out of this war for a while longer.'

Ruth pursed her lips and nodded. 'Well, I'm with you there.'

They walked slowly towards the WAAF quarters. 'Tell me what happened to Robbie,' Ruth asked. 'All we know is that they were picked up by the lifeboat and all the crew are safe, though there are a few injuries between them.'

Swiftly, Fleur told her all that Robbie knew. 'He said it was all down to the skill of their skipper. But for Tommy, none of them would be here.'

Ruth smiled. 'Yeah. Tommy's a great bloke. All of them are. I'm so glad they're all safe.' Her voice petered out and they were silent, both with their own thoughts of Kenny, the one they had both cared for. The one who hadn't come back.

Forty-Four

Fleur was wrong about having used up her entitlement to compassionate leave. Two days after her return to camp, she was summoned to see the WAAF commanding officer.

'I'm glad to hear your husband is alive, but I understand you have suffered the loss of a near relative. Your brother?'

'Yes, ma'am,' Fleur answered quietly.

'I'm surprised you haven't requested leave to go home.'

'I—' Fleur began and then faltered. She was about to admit that she believed she wasn't wanted at home. She bit her lip and then altered what she had been about to say. 'I thought – I mean – I didn't think I'd be entitled to any more. Not for a while, ma'am.'

Caroline Davidson looked down at the papers on her desk, appearing to consult them. 'Your friend, Morrison, has offered to cover your duties. She was trained in R/T work before remustering to become an intelligence officer. She feels – though she has not betrayed your confidence – that there are special circumstances in your case why a further period of compassionate leave should be granted to you.' She looked up again, her clear blue eyes boring into Fleur's. 'I expect your parents would welcome your support at this time?'

Fleur licked her lips. Her heart was beating painfully. She didn't like telling lies, yet if she agreed with her superior and was granted extra leave, she could go to see Robbie. Even if she was found out and punished, it would be worth it for a few extra precious hours with him.

Concentrating on her father's feelings rather than her mother's, Fleur was able to say truthfully, 'Yes, ma'am, I'm sure they would.'

Caroline leant back in her chair and smiled, her blue eyes twinkling with a sudden mischief. 'And, of course, if your transport arrangements should have to take you via Nottingham . . .'

Fleur stared at her for a moment, speechless. Really, she was thinking, sometimes their superior officers were capable of showing their human side.

Caroline straightened up and shuffled the papers on her desk with a brisk, businesslike movement. 'I can't let you go for a couple of weeks, I'm afraid. The forecasters think we're in for a spell of good weather and you know what that means.'

'Yes, ma'am.'

'So – we'll see in a couple of weeks' time. Come and see me then.'

'Thank you, ma'am.' Fleur saluted smartly and left the office, still unable to believe her luck. But, she realized, it wasn't so much down to luck as to her friend, Ruth. She went to find her to tell her what had transpired. Ruth listened with a wide grin on her face, particularly when Fleur reached the part about the transport arrangements.

'She's a nice old stick, really, though she can be a tartar if you kick over the traces.'

'Old stick!' Fleur laughed. 'She can't be much older than us.'

Ruth wrinkled her brow. 'No, I suppose not when you think about it. I expect it's just her rank that makes you think she must be as old as the hills.'

They laughed together and then Ruth's smile faded. She eyed her friend keenly as she said, 'Er, we're not on duty until six. I – um – reckon we ought to cycle out to Mrs Jackson's . . .'

Before she had finished speaking, Fleur was shaking her head. 'Oh no, I can't face her. Not yet. She was ever so fond of Kenny . . .'

'I know,' Ruth said softly and touched Fleur's arm. 'All the more reason why we should go and see her. And old Harry. If they've heard, they'll wonder why we haven't been to see them. And if they haven't been told, then . . . then it's us that ought to tell them.'

Fleur sighed deeply. 'You're right. I know you're right. It's just – just . . .'

'I know, I know,' Ruth said softly. 'But we'll go together. I'll be with you.'

Fleur was touched by her friend's thoughtfulness. Despite her adamant declarations that she would not allow herself to get seriously involved with anyone whilst the war was on, Ruth had allowed herself to become fond of Fleur's brother. And whilst she was strong, the same sadness that was in Fleur's heart was mirrored in Ruth's. Yet she was still sensitive to the feelings of others who had known – and liked – Kenny.

'You're right,' Fleur said firmly, summoning up her own strength. 'We ought to go. In fact, we'll go right now before I chicken out.'

Ruth smiled. 'Oh, you're not one to do that.' She linked her arm through Fleur's as they went in search of their bicycles.

'Oh, my dears,' Mrs Jackson held out her arms, trying to embrace them both as they let themselves in through her back door and stepped into the kitchen. Tears ran down her wrinkled cheeks. 'Harry only heard yesterday. He told me last night. We're so very sorry. Your poor mother . . .' She patted Fleur's arm. 'Sit down, dear. I'll make a cup of tea.'

'I'll do it,' Ruth said. 'Then I'll nip round to Harry's. And you' – she wagged her forefinger in Fleur's face – 'can get down to a bit of digging when you've drunk your tea. Do you good.'

As they sipped their tea, Fleur asked tentatively, 'You . . . you had heard about Robbie? That he's safe?'

The old lady nodded and smiled. 'Yes. Harry heard that at the same time.' She sighed. 'Dearie me, what terrible times we're living in. We were thrilled to hear that, but then the awful news about that lovely boy . . .' She wiped the tears from her eyes with the corner of her apron. 'It doesn't bear thinking about.'

Ruth returned a few minutes later with Harry in tow. The old man patted Fleur on the shoulder and just said, 'Now then, lass,' but the tone of his voice and his action spoke volumes. His sympathy and understanding, though not put into words, were very real. 'Plenty of work in the garden, lass. Need any help?'

Fleur smiled tremulously. Robbie was out of action for some time and Kenny . . . Poor Kenny. She'd never hear his cheerful whistle and see his broad grin again.

Oh, how she would miss him and not just for his help in the garden.

'I'd better get on. I – we – can't stay long today.'

'I'll bring your tea out to you then.'

Minutes later Fleur was digging in the garden. So many times Kenny had been here beside her, helping her. She had thought that the memory, the poignancy, would be upsetting, but in fact she found it comforted her. She kept glancing up, half expecting to see him a few feet away digging alongside her. Involuntarily, her ears strained for his merry whistle. But there was only the sound of the wind rustling in the apple tree and the sound of bird song.

When Ruth brought out their tea, the two girls sat together on the bench beneath the tree.

'Robbie'll soon be back here with you, sitting under the apple tree.' They smiled at each other.

Fleur nodded, though just at this moment she could not share her thoughts with Ruth. There was another thought that had just crept its way into her mind. I wonder, she was thinking, if Dr Collins has heard that his son is still alive.

Louisa was waiting at the front door when her husband drew his car to a halt in front of the house and climbed wearily out of it.

Oh, he looks so tired, Louisa thought. This war's almost as bad for him as the last one. She had been waiting on tenterhooks for hours, ever since she had heard the two pieces of news. One would bring him further sadness. And the other? Well, of course he would be glad that Robbie was safe. But with that piece of news would come further complications.

Louisa knew he had visited Meg. He had told her on his return from the city.

'There are to be no more secrets between us, Louisa,' he had said, taking her hands in his. 'You have been a dear, dear girl in being so understanding and – and forgiving – and the last thing I want to do is to cause you any more pain, but—' Here he'd paused, not knowing quite how to continue, so Louisa had squeezed his hands and said softly, 'Philip – I do trust you. As long as you promise to tell me everything, we can deal with whatever happens – together.'

'Oh, my dear,' he had said, taking her in his arms and holding her close. 'I don't deserve you.'

Then she had laughed, trying to lighten the emotion of the moment, and teasing him had said, 'No, you don't.'

And then they had sat down together, the glow from the fire in the grate giving them the only light in the room, whilst he had told her of his visit to Meg. He ended by saying, 'I shan't see her again, Louisa, I promise you that unless . . . unless by some miracle Robbie comes back. Because . . . because I told her that if he did then . . . then—' Again, he had faltered not wanting to hurt her.

But Louisa was not only forgiving, she was compassionate and she finished the sentence for him. 'You'd want to meet him and get to know him.'

He nodded, but he had such a hangdog expression on his face, like a naughty boy that had been caught scrumping apples, that Louisa had laughed aloud and touched his cheek. 'Oh, my dear, of course you would. He's your son.'

'You – you wouldn't mind?'

She had shaken her head. 'Not now, no. Once I

would've done. Once I would have minded dreadfully. You were right when you said that my idea that we could perhaps have adopted him was foolish. I was, as you so rightly said, only speaking with the benefit of hindsight. I've thought about what you said a lot since we talked and I've admitted to myself that, no, at the time I would have been far too upset to have even thought such a thing. But . . . but not now. I'm older and I hope a lot wiser. What happened in the past cannot be changed. He's your son. There's no denying that. I saw it for myself. Of course, if we'd had children of our own then it might have taken a little more thinking about, for their sake. It would have been a shock for them to discover they had a half-brother, but since we haven't . . .' Her voice trailed away.

Philip had squeezed her hand. 'I . . . I don't think Meg would let us see him very often. I mean I don't think she would want him to become – well – part of our family.'

Louisa had smiled softly. 'If the Lord is good to us and he comes back, then I don't think she will have any say in the matter. He's a grown man and he will make his own decision.'

Philip had sighed heavily. 'Only if she agrees to tell him that I am his natural father.'

Louisa's eyes had widened. 'You . . . you mean he didn't know? She never told him?'

Philip shook his head.

'Oh,' was all Louisa had said then and silence had fallen between them. They'd not spoken of the matter again but now, as she waited at the door to greet him, she knew they had a great deal to discuss. The miracle – and all that it entailed – had happened.

He was coming up the path towards her now, smiling as he approached. 'Hello, my dear.' Then, as he became aware of her anxious face, he added, 'Is something wrong?'

'No – yes, well – oh, come in, Philip. Your supper's all ready. We'll talk later.'

He glanced at her, seeing she was on edge, but he said mildly, 'Whatever you say, my dear,' as she helped him out of his coat and took his medical bag out of his hand.

Louisa picked at the food on her plate, eating so little that at last Philip leant towards her across the table and said, 'I think, my dear, you'd better tell me now, else you're going to waste all this lovely food you've spent hours preparing. And' – he smiled – 'you're making me so nervous that my appetite's disappearing by the minute. Now, tell me. What has happened?'

Louisa laid down her knife and fork and looked up at him. 'Firstly, I must tell you that poor Kenny has been killed. In training, would you believe? Isn't that cruel? I've been to see Betsy today and she's in a dreadful state. Poor Jake too. He's like a zombie. Just going through the motions of work but . . . but they're both devastated.'

Philip's face fell into lines of sadness and he let out a long, deep sigh. 'Oh dear. I'm so very sorry to hear that.'

There was silence between them whilst they each spared a thought for the boy whose life had been so cruelly snatched away before Louisa added, 'But there is good news.'

Philip smiled bleakly as if nothing could be counted as 'good news' after what she had just told him.

Watching his face, she said softly, 'Robbie is alive.'

His head jerked up and she saw the spark in his eyes and knew that, whatever it cost her, she had to let him get to know his son.

'Alive? How – I mean – what happened? Do you know?'

'Jake told me. He didn't mention it in front of Betsy, but he followed me out into the yard to tell me. Robbie's plane came down in the sea only just off the coast and the local lifeboat rescued all the crew. He has a broken leg, but apart from that, he's fine.'

Philip let out the breath he'd been holding in a huge sigh of relief whilst Louisa went on. 'It seems that Fleur didn't know until she arrived at Meg's house in Nottingham. She'd been granted compassionate leave to go to see his mother only to walk in and find him sitting there. It seems they didn't even know on the station until just before she got back. There'd been an air raid and all the telephone lines were down. And then, when she was so happy, she went to Middleditch Farm on her way back to camp only to hear that Kenny had been killed.'

'Good news one minute and bad the next, eh?' Philip said. 'Poor Fleur.'

'Betsy's turned totally against her. She's blaming Fleur for it happening.'

'For Kenny volunteering, you mean?'

Louisa nodded.

He sighed. 'I'll have to go and see her. Betsy, I mean. See if I can talk to her. I might be able to help.'

'Philip – there's something else.'

He glanced at her, waiting.

'Jake told me that after Robbie was posted missing,

presumed killed, Fleur pressed her father to tell her
about ... about the past.' She ran her tongue nervously around her lips but Philip finished her sentence
for her.

'And he did. He told her just who Robbie's father
is?'

'Yes,' Louisa whispered.

'And you think she'll tell Robbie?'

'Well – yes.'

'D'you think Meg realizes Fleur knows?'

Louisa shrugged. 'Jake says he swore her to secrecy.
Made her promise never to say a word to Meg, but, I
mean, now he's come back . . .'

'Who's to know what will happen?' he murmured
and, whilst his wife picked up her knife and fork to
finish her meal, Philip sat lost in thought.

Forty-Five

Two weeks later, having been granted special leave, the thoughts that now occupied Philip's waking hours also slipped into Fleur's mind. She didn't like having secrets from Robbie, but as her father had once said to her they weren't their secrets to tell.

She went straight to Middleditch Farm, but her mother would not speak to her, would not even acknowledge her presence and deliberately turned her back on her. Fleur stayed only an hour, talking with her father in the yard and then begging a lift to the station to catch the train to the Junction and then on to Nottingham, arriving late in the afternoon at the terraced house. She had, of course, written every other day to Robbie, so he knew about Kenny, but she had not mentioned anything about what Jake had told her. Nor did she intend to. She had made up her mind. It was Meg's place to tell her son, not Fleur's. She wondered if she had already done so. Though Fleur knew nothing of Philip's visit and the quandary Meg now found herself in, she did believe that Robbie should know the truth. But it wasn't her place to tell him.

'Well, if it's not Long John Silver.' She grinned as the door opened and Robbie stood there.

'Darling! How wonderful,' he said, pulling her inside, shutting the door and enfolding her in a bear-like hug all in one movement. 'However did you wangle more leave?'

'Ma'am's been very good. She actually called me to her office. This is supposed to be compassionate leave for Kenny, but I'm not really wanted at home . . .' And then she could say no more, because he was kissing her hungrily.

Some time later, they emerged into the light of the kitchen. 'Look who's here,' Robbie said, limping into the room.

'As if I hadn't guessed.' Smiling, Meg got to her feet and hugged Fleur. 'Darling girl, we're so sorry to hear about Kenny. How are your mother and father?'

Fleur pressed her lips together. 'Not good.'

'Here, come and sit by the fire. I'll make some tea.'

'I've been to the farm today, but Mum won't even speak to me. She blames me, you see.'

'Yes, you said before. I'm sorry. I wish I could help, but . . .' She left the sentence unfinished but they all understood.

Fleur glanced towards the old man's empty chair beside the range. 'Where's Pops? Is he all right?'

'He is now Robbie's safe. He's in bed, but he always goes early. He's fine. Better than he was.'

Fleur smiled with relief and sat down in his chair.

'There, love, drink that.' As Meg handed her a cup of tea, Fleur looked up and met the older woman's gaze. There was no mistaking the look of pleading in her eyes. Don't tell him, she was asking silently. Don't say anything. Unseen by Robbie, who had hopped out of the kitchen into the scullery in search of something to eat, Fleur smiled and gave a little nod.

Meg bent closer and whispered, 'I shall tell him, Fleur. I just . . . just haven't had the right moment.'

'It's all right. I promise I won't say—'

'And what are you two whispering about?'

'I was just asking your mother if you've been behaving yourself.'

Robbie laughed and pulled a face. 'I'm bored out of my skull.'

Meg, straightening up, laughed. 'We're not very exciting company, I'm afraid. Just me and the old man.'

'I didn't mean that, Ma. I love being with you. It's just that it's all going on without me.'

'Just be thankful it is for a while,' Fleur replied tartly. 'It's giving us all a bit of a rest knowing you're safe. Think about us for once instead of being the hero.'

There was silence until Fleur covered her face and said contritely, 'Oh, I'm sorry – I'm so sorry. That sounded awful. It came out all wrong. I just . . . I just – what with you going missing and we all thought you were dead and then Kenny . . .'

'Darling, it's all right.' Robbie hopped towards her, rescued the cup of tea that was in danger of slipping out of her grasp and then sat down close to her and took her hands. 'I understand. I know it's worse for you and Ma and Pops when I'm up there. You see, we've all too much to think about when we're in the thick of it, but you're just all waiting – and fearing the worst. It must've been dreadful for you the night we didn't come back.'

Fleur sniffed. 'It was. I stood for ages just watching the blank space on the board.'

'It's worse for Fleur than for us in a way,' Meg said gently. 'She's on the spot seeing what's happening.'

'Do you think you should apply for a transfer?' Robbie suggested, but before he had finished speaking Fleur shot back, 'No! I want to be there. I want to be near you. I *have* to be near you, even if it is tearing me apart. I'm not the only one: there are several girls on camp with boyfriends or fiancés – even one or two more are married like us. It's the same for them.' She pulled in a deep breath and forced a tremulous smile. 'No, I've just got to keep going but – just for a while – whilst you're laid up, I've got a bit of a respite. And, now you've done a full tour, you . . .'

Her voice faded away at the rather sheepish look on his face. Her heart sank. Without him saying a word, she knew that Robbie would get back on operations as soon as he could. But she said nothing more. She didn't want to worry his mother. At least she could let Meg stay in blissful ignorance if only for a while. She forced a smile as she added, 'Now you're grounded, we can all relax.'

She looked up at him and he smoothed her hair back from her forehead. 'Except that you've lost Kenny,' he murmured.

'Yes,' she said heavily. 'I've lost Kenny.' She closed her eyes and leant against him. Perhaps one day she would tell him about the heavy guilt that lay on her. How she had bargained for Robbie's life. But not just now. She couldn't speak of it just now. It was all too raw.

The hours of her short leave were over all too quickly. Her goodbyes said, she left the house as the air raid warning sounded. Fleur hurried along the street. I hope Robbie and his mother and Pops go to the shelter. Robbie can hobble that far on his crutches, she thought. And if I can make it to the railway station, I'll be safe there . . . She could hear the drone of enemy aircraft yet no bombs seemed to be falling on this part of the city. As she hurried along she was sure she heard thuds in the distance, and saw the night sky to the north of the city illuminated by exploding bombs.

Some poor devils are taking a hammering, she thought, but at least it's not us tonight. Reaching the station, she found that the trains had been delayed.

'Air raid Newark way,' the waiting passengers were informed. 'No trains running until it's over.'

And even when it was and the all-clear sounded, the announcement came that the line had been damaged and no trains would be running that night.

'Oh Lor',' Fleur muttered. 'I'm going to be in trouble. I'll be late back at camp. And I'm not even supposed to be in Nottingham. Oh heck!'

'You stranded like us, love?' a merry voice called out and Fleur turned to see three young men in RAF uniforms standing together.

'Seems like it.' She smiled and moved closer. 'Where are you heading?'

'A place called Wickerton Wood.'

Fleur's smile widened. 'Me too. I'm stationed there.' She held out her hand and the four of them exchanged first names. Then Fleur suggested, 'Shall we share a taxi?'

'A taxi? That'll be awfully expensive, won't it?'

'Not if the four of us chip in.'

'Righto – I'll see if there are any outside the station, though they might all have gone by now . . .' The youngest-looking one of the three men dropped his kitbag and loped off in search of transport.

The others stood together, feeling awkward, smiling in that embarrassed way that strangers meeting for the first time do. In only a few minutes the airman returned. 'There's just one left,' he panted. 'Says he'll take the four of us.' His grin widened. 'And he'll only charge us for the petrol. He's got a lad in the RAF down south. A fighter pilot. He's glad to help, he says. Hopes someone'll do the same for his lad if he's stranded anywhere.'

'Righto. Come on, love. Need any help?'

'I'm fine.' Fleur smiled. 'As long as he gets us back to camp, I'll ride on the running board.'

They laughed but they all squeezed into the car, three squashed in the back and the airman with the longest legs taking the front seat beside the driver.

'Now then, mi duck, what are you doing out with these young rascals?'

Fleur laughed. 'I've only just met them on the platform whilst we were waiting for the train. I've just been home to see my *husband*.'

There was a unanimous groan and one of the airmen said, 'Just my luck! And there I was thinking I'd met the girl of my dreams.'

In the darkness, Fleur smiled to think that that was just how she had met Robbie.

There was laughter before another asked, 'Your husband? What does he do?'

'He's a wireless operator on bombers, but he's on sick leave. A broken leg.' She stopped herself saying more. These boys looked incredibly young. They were probably just out of training. Maybe this was their first posting. It wouldn't do to talk to them about crash-landings.

'How did that happen?'

Fleur chuckled. 'You seem to be asking an awful lot of questions. I'm not sure I should be telling you.' And again, the car was filled with laughter.

412

They chugged along, going at a steady pace through the blackout with only the pencil-thin beams from the partially blacked-out headlights to illuminate their way. It wasn't until the early hours that they reached the gates of the camp.

'Now for trouble,' Fleur muttered as she clambered out. 'I'm about four hours late.'

'So are we,' one of the airmen said cheerfully. 'But it's hardly our fault Jerry decided to drop a few bombs – just to make us feel welcome.'

'Right, tip up, chaps. Let's pay this kind feller for bringing us. At least we've got here. If we'd waited for the train it could have been a week on Tuesday!'

Fleur fished in her bag to find her money but the airman said, 'No, love. We'll sort it. It'll be nice for us to have a friendly face about the camp. This is our treat. All right, lads?'

'Yeah, course it is. Where is it you work, Fleur? Canteen, is it?'

Fleur smiled to herself. Why did all men take it that the only job women could do was to serve them their meals?

'No. I'm in Control. I'm an R/T operator.'

'Really? That's great. It'll be good to know we've got you watching out for us when we're up there.'

Did she imagine it, or was there a tiny note of apprehension in the young man's voice?

Fleur was allowed straight into the camp, but she had to bid the others farewell whilst they waited for their identities to be checked and all the formalities for new arrivals to be gone through. Thankfully, Fleur slipped away into the darkness towards the WAAF quarters and crept into the room she shared with Ruth.

'Oh, thank goodness!' Ruth sat up in bed at once.

'I've been that worried. Are you all right? I've been ringing your home, but it seems the lines are down.'

'I'm not surprised,' Fleur whispered. 'There's been an air raid in the Newark area, but I was in Nottingham.'

Ruth's chuckle came out of the darkness. 'Now why doesn't that surprise me? Good job you've got back when you have, else you'd've been for it. How did you get back? Are the trains running?'

'No. I met three RAF lads coming here, would you believe, and we shared a taxi.'

'A taxi? Heavens! Have you come into a fortune?'

'No,' Fleur giggled softly as she climbed into her single bed. 'They paid. But the driver was very generous. Didn't charge us the going rate as we're RAF. His lad's serving down south.'

Ruth sighed and lay down. 'There's still some nice people about.'

They lay in silence for a few minutes and Fleur was just about to fall asleep when Ruth asked tentatively, 'D'you think your folks are all right? I mean, you said the air raid was in the Newark area, didn't you?'

'Mmm,' Fleur said sleepily. 'They'd be after the airfield there, I expect. But we live several miles from Newark. Right out in the country. There's nothing there worth bombing.'

'But the telephone lines are down.'

Fleur yawned. 'Well, they will be, won't they? But they'll be all right. Our farm's miles from anywhere. Right out in the wilds. Dad didn't even build a shelter . . .' And with that, she fell asleep.

But for some reason she couldn't explain, Ruth was left wide awake staring into the darkness.

Forty-Six

Meg read the news in the paper the next morning and her blood ran cold.

The bombing raid last night in the Newark area caused loss of life and severe damage to properties. Several of the bombs fell outside their target and a remote farmhouse some distance to the west of the town, which should have been considered relatively safe, received a direct hit. The farmer received extensive burns whilst trying to rescue his wife from the building, which was destroyed by fire. Sadly, his efforts were in vain and his wife perished. The man is in hospital and is thought to be in a critical condition. The names of the casualties have not yet been released as next of kin have yet to be informed.

'Robbie, oh, Robbie . . .' Meg was hurrying up the stairs to his bedroom, breathless as she pushed open the door. 'Oh, Robbie, it's Jake – it's Fleur's folks. I know it is.'

'What?' The young man sat up in bed and snatched the paper from her trembling hands. He scanned the newsprint whilst she sank down on the end of the bed, clasping and unclasping her hands in agitation.

He looked up at her. 'It doesn't mention South Monkford. It could be anyone. It doesn't even give the name of the farm. What makes you think it's them?'

Meg stared at him and pressed her hands to her bosom. 'But South Monkford is west of Newark. And I just know, Robbie. I feel it. In here. I know it sounds daft to you, but I just know.'

'Well, there's one way to find out,' Robbie said, swinging his legs out of the bed and hoisting himself upright. 'We'll ring the hospitals.'

'Oh, Robbie, can we do that?'

He looked down at her and tenderly touched her cheek. 'Anything, Ma, to take that devastated look off your face.'

Robbie spent half the morning in the phone box at the end of the street, feeding in coins one after another and hopping on his crutches between it and the corner shop for more change. After several calls – he lost count how many – he replaced the receiver slowly and pushed open the door of the box. As it swung to he leant against it briefly and his glance went to the front door of his home.

She was standing on the step, her hands clasped together, looking up the street towards him, but as he pushed himself away from the phone box and began to limp towards her, he saw her fingers flutter to her mouth. Then she turned and disappeared inside the house.

She knew already, from the droop of his shoulders, that he was about to bring her bad news.

The news was broken to Fleur by Caroline Davidson. How many more tragedies is this poor girl going to face? she was thinking as she said gently, 'My dear, we have just received information that your home was hit in last night's air raid.'

Fleur swayed momentarily, but remarkably she remained standing at attention. Silently, she was thinking, I was glad that it wasn't the city getting it last night and all the time . . . But aloud, all she said was, 'Are they dead, ma'am?'

'Your mother – I'm sorry – yes, but your father is in hospital. Evidently, he wasn't in the house when it was hit, but he tried to get into the burning building to save her. He's . . . he's very badly hurt, my dear, but he is still alive.' There was a pause and her unspoken words seemed to hang in the air. At the moment. 'He's in hospital in Nottingham. I need hardly say you are released from your duties immediately. I am issuing you with a seventy-two-hour pass on compassionate grounds . . .'

The journey back to Nottingham by public transport was impossible, but Caroline had pulled strings and arranged a lift for Fleur with an RAF vehicle due to go to the city that day. The journey seemed to take three times as long as normal. All the way, Fleur repeated the same prayer. 'Don't let him die. Oh, please don't let him die.'

This time she made no rash bargain with God, but just prayed simply and directly.

She reached the hospital late at night, and though their resources were already stretched the nurses found her a bed in an unoccupied side ward for the night.

'If we need it, we'll have to turf you out,' they told her cheerfully. 'Now, come along to the staff room and we'll get you something to eat.'

'How is he? Can I see him?' was all Fleur wanted to know.

'Best not tonight, love, he's sleeping now.'

'Can't I just see him? I promise not to disturb him.'

'I should wait until the morning, love.' The sister was gentle and understanding but there was a note of authority in her tone. 'You'll feel better able to cope after a night's rest.'

'Is he . . . is he . . . that bad?'

The woman's face sobered. 'He's not good, my dear. I can't lie to you, but the doctor will talk to you tomorrow.'

'Does he – my father, I mean – know about my mother?'

Sadly, the sister nodded. 'Yes.' More briskly, she went on, 'Now, a bite to eat, a sleeping pill and into bed with you, my girl.'

Exhausted by the journey, grieving for her mother and worried sick about her father, Fleur did not expect to sleep a wink. But the sister's pill knocked her out for a full ten hours and she might have slept even longer if a merry little trainee nurse hadn't bounced into the room, pulled open the curtains and woken her up.

'I've brought you some breakfast, miss,' she beamed. 'We don't do this for everyone, but your dad's a bit special.'

Fleur heaved herself up in the bed and rubbed her eyes. 'Oh?'

'Oh, yes. We've all been vying to be the nurse who looks after him.'

'Has he come round then?'

'He comes round for a bit and keeps apologizing for being such a trouble. But he isn't, miss, I promise you. Then he drifts off again. But he's a duck, ain't he?'

Despite her anxiety, Fleur smiled. She looked down

418

at the tray, not expecting to be able to eat a thing. To her surprise, she suddenly found she was very hungry.

'How is he?'

The little nurse's face clouded. She moved closer to the bed. 'It ain't my place to say, miss. You must ask the doctor or Sister, but' – she leant closer – 'he's still very poorly but I heard 'em say he's going in the right direction, if you know what I mean. But – please – don't tell 'em I said owt, will yer. I could get the sack.'

'Of course I won't. And thank you.'

'That's all right. See yer later.'

Fleur finished her breakfast, washed and dressed and stripped the bed. She knew it would have to be changed, and anything she could do to help the busy nurses she would do.

Now, she thought, taking a deep breath, I wonder if they'll let me see Dad.

He was in a small ward with three other seriously ill patients, each with their own nurse. Though she had tried to prepare herself, Fleur gasped when she saw her father swathed in bandages. She wouldn't have recognized him.

'He was badly burned,' the sister told her. 'But the medical profession are making huge strides in the treatment of burns. It's because of the war, you know. So many pilots, poor boys, get burned when they're shot down.'

Fleur shuddered. It could so easily have been Robbie she was coming to visit. Robbie lying in the bed . . .

She moved closer. 'Dad? It's me. How . . . how are you feeling?' It was a stupid question, but she didn't know what else to say.

He didn't answer her and she glanced up at the sister, a question in her eyes.

'Keep talking to him. We want to try to get him to regain consciousness fully. And you're the best person to get him to do that, Meg.'

Fleur stared at the sister. 'Why did you call me "Meg"?'

The sister blinked. 'Er – I'm sorry. I thought that was your name.' Obviously embarrassed, she looked first at her patient and then back to the girl.

'No, it isn't, but just tell me why you thought it was?'

'Er – it's the only name he's said when he's drifted in and out of consciousness.' The sister's face cleared. 'Oh, it was your mother's name, was it?'

Slowly, Fleur shook her head. 'No, as a matter of fact, it wasn't.'

'Oh dear, I am sorry. I shouldn't have said anything.' The sister was obviously upset and worried. 'I have put my foot in it, haven't I?'

The sister was only young for the post she held, little older than she was, Fleur thought. In all the forces, promotion came earlier and earlier and the nursing profession was every bit a fighting force as any of the others. They were all working round the clock for the same thing: the end of this war.

'It's all right.' Fleur touched her arm. 'Honestly. The thing is – I know who Meg is. And if he's calling for her then—?'

The sister nodded. 'Yes, if you could find her. It really might help him.'

'Oh yes,' Fleur whispered. 'I can find her.'

Forty-Seven

'Sit down, dear. There's something I have to tell you.'

'Oh no, it's not Fleur's dad, is it? You haven't heard something, have you, Ma?'

'No, no. Just – sit down, Robbie. Please.'

Robbie lowered himself into the old man's chair and waited whilst his mother settled herself on the opposite side of the fireplace. For a long moment, she stared into the fire, the flames dancing on her beautiful face. Robbie stared at her, marvelling at her smooth skin, at how young she still looked. It never ceased to amaze him that there wasn't a line of men beating a path to their door.

Slowly, she raised her head to meet his gaze. 'There's something I have to tell you. Something that – maybe – I should have told you years ago, but . . . but I couldn't bring myself to do it. I was so frightened of . . . of losing you.'

'Losing me!' Robbie leant forward, a little awkwardly because of the thick plaster on his leg still hampering his movements. Then he moved to sit on the hearthrug at her feet, taking her hands and holding them tightly. Earnestly, he said, 'Darling Ma, whatever it is, you couldn't lose me. Not ever. Not . . . not the way you're meaning.'

They stared at each other for a moment, each

knowing just how close they had come to Robbie being lost, but a different kind of 'lost'.

'When . . . when you were missing, Jake told Fleur and . . . and it's not fair of me to expect her to keep such a secret from you – from her husband.'

Robbie was silent, giving his mother time to tell her story. A story that was obviously difficult, maybe painful, for her to tell.

He stroked her hands tenderly. Those clever hands that had earned them a living all these years. Hands that had caressed him and nurtured him. Hands that lovingly nursed the old man now asleep upstairs.

Then slowly, haltingly at first, Meg began to tell Robbie about her past. Her shameful past. How she had once been a wilful, selfish girl, who had cared nothing for the feelings of others in her desire for security.

'You'll have to be patient with me, because I want to tell you everything. Right from the very beginning. I'll miss nothing out and then you can . . . can judge for yourself just what sort of a woman you have for a mother.'

He squeezed her hands encouragingly. 'I'm not going to judge you, Ma. Whatever it is.'

Meg lifted her shoulders in a tiny shrug. 'Well, we'll see,' she murmured.

Another silence before she took a deep breath and began. 'We were such a happy little family, Dad, Mam, Bobbie and me.'

'Bobbie? Who's Bobbie?'

Meg nodded and smiled a little. She was perhaps the one who was going to have to be patient with his interruptions. 'My little brother. You're named after him.'

'Your brother? I didn't know you had a brother.'

Meg nodded and her voice was husky as she went on. 'We lived in a small cottage on Middleditch Farm . . .'

Again Robbie could not keep silent. 'Middleditch Farm? But – but that's Fleur's home . . .' He stopped, realizing that the farmhouse now lay in ruins.

'Pops worked as a waggoner for the Smallwoods who owned the farm then. And I worked as a dairy maid for Mrs Smallwood.' A small smile twitched at her mouth as she added wryly, 'She was a tartar to work for. I was always in trouble with her. "You'll come to a bad end," she used to say to me.' Again she paused. 'Maybe she was right.'

'Oh, Ma, don't say that. You call this "a bad end"?'

'No, of course not. I'm content. At least . . .' She sighed inwardly. Was she about to jeopardize her contented life with her son when he heard the truth about her? Bravely, she pushed on. 'I was a bit cheeky and . . . and a bit of a flirt with the village lads. I was friendly with Alice Smallwood, their daughter. She was older than me and – if anything – it was her that was the flirt, but her mother thought *I* was the bad influence on *her*. Anyway, we jogged along quite happily, I thought, until one night my dad came home and said we'd both been dismissed without a reference and we were being turned out of our home too. It was a tied cottage, you see. It went with the job.' Meg bit her lip as if reliving the moment. 'I thought it was my fault. I thought I'd been cheeky to the missis once too often.'

'And was it?' Robbie asked softly.

Meg shook her head. 'No. It . . . it was Pops. He – well, I'll come to that in a minute. We had to leave the very next day and the only place we could go was the workhouse.'

'The workhouse?' Robbie was shocked. 'That big building on the outskirts of South Monkford?'

'You've seen it?'

He nodded. 'Oh, Ma,' he breathed sadly. 'You've lived in the workhouse?'

She smiled thinly. 'Dad took us there.' Talking of the times past, Meg referred to him by the name she had called him then, not 'Pops' as he was now known. 'Mam – she was expecting another baby – Bobbie and me. He left us there. Said he was going to look for work and that he'd come back for us . . .' Her voice trailed away for a moment, but then she took another deep breath and continued. 'But the weeks went by and he didn't come back. We had to work of course – in that place. Mam wasn't very well but they let her do mending and easy work. And they put me to work with the school marm. And for a while, I thought she was my friend. She was very kind to me. She was in charge of all the children and had to look after them all the time. One night, there was a little girl who was ill.' Meg glanced at Robbie. 'Actually, it was Betsy, Fleur's mum.'

Now Robbie was truly horrified. 'Fleur's mum was in the workhouse?'

Meg nodded. 'And so was Jake. He'd been born in there. So that's where I met them. Jake and I were friends even though we were segregated. Girls and boys, men and women. Poor Jake got a beating once for being seen with me.'

'And Fleur's mum? Were you friends with her?'

Meg ran her tongue round her dry lips. 'Not . . . not exactly. She was younger than us. Jake and me,

424

I mean. Anyway, this night she was ill, the school marm left me in charge of Betsy when Isaac Pendleton sent for her. He was the master of the workhouse – a lecherous old devil . . .' She paused and then put her head on one side thoughtfully. 'No, actually, that's not quite fair. And I am trying to tell you this very truthfully. He was a ladies' man, but he could be very kind.' She sighed. 'I didn't see it that way then, but now I have to admit that he was. In his own way. Well, at that time he had his eye on Louisa, the school marm—'

Again, Robbie could not help interrupting. 'That's not the woman Fleur calls Aunt Louisa, is it? Mrs Dr Collins?'

'Yes. She was working as the schoolmistress at the workhouse. I believe she had an elderly mother she was supporting. She was engaged to Philip Collins then, and was trying to avoid old Isaac as much as she could. So, this particular night, she left her watch with me and told me that after a certain time, I was to go and knock on his door and say that she was needed – that Betsy was worse. I did just as she said, but when we got back the watch was missing and she accused me of having stolen it. I hadn't, of course. Whatever else I may be, I'm not a thief. Anyway, it turned out that Betsy had it. She'd wanted to hear it ticking. It reminded her of her daddy, she said. Louisa apologized but I was impulsive and fiery in those days—'

'Must be the red hair,' Robbie teased and they both smiled.

'And I was unforgiving. Oh, Robbie, how unforgiving I was. I suppose, looking back, that was what caused all the trouble. If only I had been more willing to forgive and forget then maybe—'

'Go on, Ma,' he prompted gently as Meg seemed to get side-tracked. 'What happened?'

'I refused to work with Louisa any more. I couldn't forgive her for having accused me. And – quite wrongly – I bore Betsy a grudge too. I said I'd rather scrub floors than work with Louisa. And I did,' she added wryly. She sighed again and went on. 'Anyway, I'm getting a bit ahead of myself. Earlier that same day, my mother had gone into labour and the baby was stillborn.'

She saw Robbie wince but he said nothing.

'So a couple of weeks later I decided I should try to find my dad and tell him what had happened to Mam and the baby. And . . . and I just wanted to see him anyway. I got permission from the master to go in search of him, and Jake came with me.' Now she smiled. '*Without* permission.'

'Ooh-er,' Robbie said imagining the severe punishment he might have incurred.

'He didn't care. He wanted to be with me.'

'Did you find your dad? Pops?'

'Oh yes, we found him all right.' Meg's voice was suddenly hard as she relived that dreadful day. 'We went to the racecourse. He was so good with horses that Farmer Smallwood sometimes took Dad with him when he went to the races. And then we saw him, walking along, bold as you like, with his arm around Alice Smallwood.'

Robbie blinked. 'His arm? Alice Smallwood?'

Meg nodded and now there was no hiding the bitterness in her tone. 'My father had been having an affair with the daughter of his – of our – employers. They had found out and turned him and all his family

426

out because of it. So, it wasn't my fault as I had feared. It was his.'

'Pops? I can't believe it.'

Meg raised a smile. 'Oh, Pops wasn't always the frail old man you see now.'

'Well, no. When he first came to live with us he was still – well – quite sprightly.'

'When he was younger, he was a fine figure of a man, I have to admit.'

There was a long silence before Robbie asked gently, 'So – what happened then?'

'I went back to the workhouse, but from that moment on I cut him out of my life and vowed I'd never forgive him. It was up to me to take care of my mother. I went out into the town to seek work and I found it. With poor Percy Rodwell in his tailor's shop.'

'Why do you say "poor" Percy Rodwell?'

Meg sighed. 'He was a lovely man. A kind and generous man and I . . . I seduced him.'

'Oh, Ma! Whatever next?' Robbie began to laugh, but seeing his mother's serious face, he stopped. 'Mind you,' he added. 'You're still a stunner, so I expect the poor bloke hadn't got a chance.'

For a brief moment Meg's eyes sparkled with mischief. 'He hadn't.'

She explained about his long-standing engagement with the sour-faced Miss Finch and how, when Percy jilted her to marry Meg, he found himself in court on a charge of breach of promise. 'Poor Percy,' she murmured. 'He really didn't deserve all the trouble I brought to his door.'

'What happened to your mother and to your little brother?'

'Bobbie fell ill soon after I'd found out about my father.'

Robbie was intrigued by the way Meg kept referring to the man he knew affectionately as 'Pops' as 'my father'. It was as if she, too, couldn't think of them now as one and the same person.

'And he died. D'you know?' she said, the sadness still in her tone even after all the years. 'We buried little Bobbie on my sixteenth birthday.'

'And . . . and your mother?'

Meg's mouth hardened even more. 'She became Isaac Pendleton's mistress. I disapproved and refused to see her ever again. Jake tried to persuade me to go to see her. In the end I did, but I was told she had no wish to see me. I think it was a lie – in fact, I know it was now. I did go, truly I did.' She met his gaze, pleading with him to believe her. He gave her hands another little squeeze. 'But she fell ill and died before . . . before I could make it up with her.'

'So why did you think all this was so very dreadful, Ma? I mean, I know it's a shame you didn't make it up with your mother, but you were young and . . .'

'I haven't finished yet.'

'Ah.'

'I married Percy and the following year Louisa and Philip were married. Then the war came. Jake volunteered in 1916 and he married Betsy before he went. Then Philip went too. They were lucky – they both came back, but then we got that dreadful epidemic of influenza. Percy caught it.' She bit her lip. 'And I called Philip – Dr Collins. I . . . I'd always known he . . . he was attracted to me and . . . and I was lonely. Percy was ill – dying – and I . . . I mean we—'

'You had an affair with Dr Collins?' Robbie said gently, without any note of censure in his tone.

Meg nodded and tears filled her eyes. 'It was wicked of me. I . . . I still felt resentment against Louisa for believing I could have stolen her watch. You see? I never forgave anyone. And yet I did worse things myself than ever they'd done. Far worse.'

'How long did the affair go on?'

'Not long. When Percy died, Philip had an attack of conscience. It finished, but by then, of course, you'd been conceived.'

Robbie raised her hands to his lips and kissed them gently. 'So – Dr Philip Collins is my natural father?'

'Yes,' Meg whispered. 'But I want you to believe me, Robbie, that whilst I do regret so many of the things I did, I do not regret having you. Not for one moment. And if I hadn't had the affair, I wouldn't have had you. But it wasn't really until after you were born that I changed.'

Swiftly she recounted what Jake had already told Fleur about Miss Finch and her twisted belief that she had a right to Meg's baby boy. 'Angry and disgusted though Jake was with me – oh, he knew all about me. There was no hiding the truth from Jake – he still came to my rescue when I needed him. I suppose,' she ended reflectively, 'that's why Betsy has hated me all these years. From what Fleur says, Betsy believed that Jake still loves me.'

'Maybe he does, Ma,' Robbie said softly. There was a long silence between them until Robbie said at last, 'And what about – my father? Does he know that I'm his son? Has he always known?'

Meg nodded. 'He came to see me when he heard

you'd been posted missing. He . . . he said that if . . .
if a miracle happened and you came back that he
wanted to meet you. Get to know you.'

'Did he indeed? And what would his wife say to
that? Does *she* know, d'you think?'

'Yes. She does now. Perhaps – perhaps she's always
suspected, but now she knows for certain. You . . .
you're so like he used to be as a young man. Anyone
knowing him then and seeing you now . . .'

'So *that's* why she looked so startled that day I met
her in the cafe with Fleur. I thought she was going to
pass out.'

'It must have been a shock for her. Specially when
she found out just who you were.'

Again there was a long silence between them, before
she asked tentatively, 'Do . . . do you want to meet
him?'

'What do you want me to do?'

'Oh, it's not up to me. Not any more.'

'But will it cause you pain? I wouldn't want that,
darling Ma.'

She looked down into his upturned face, his handsome, open, loving face, and tears filled her eyes. 'You
. . . you don't hate me, then?'

'Oh, Ma!' Again he kissed her fingers. 'How could
you even think such a thing?'

'I . . . I thought you might be disgusted. I . . . I
wasn't a very nice person back then, Robbie.'

'You had a tough time.' He laughed gently. 'Because
of that old rogue up there. Who'd have thought old
Pops could do such a thing? The old rascal, him.'

Suddenly, Meg was frightened. She clung to Robbie.
'Oh, you won't say anything to him. Oh, please,
Robbie, don't—'

'Of course I won't. If you can forgive him, then I certainly can.'

'And . . . and you forgive me?'

'There's nothing for me to forgive where you're concerned. I'm still me, whoever my father is.' He paused and cocked his head on one side. 'Did you love him very much, Ma?'

Meg bit her lip. 'That . . . that's the worst part. I don't think I loved him at all. I was just lonely and . . . and he was handsome and besotted with me.' She looked him straight in the eyes then, meeting his gaze as she said solemnly, 'There's only one man I've ever truly loved, but I was too blind, too ambitious and too selfish to see it. And I've spent the rest of my life regretting that – through my own stupidity – I lost him.'

Slowly, Robbie nodded. 'You're talking about Fleur's dad, aren't you?'

Meg nodded and whispered, 'Yes. Jake was the only man I've ever really loved. And – once upon a time – I know he did love me. But I lost him. I lost my beloved Jake.'

Forty-Eight

Fleur knocked on the door of the terraced house and then waited for what seemed an age. At last, thinking they must be out, she turned away, disappointed. But she had only taken a few steps when the door opened and Robbie stood there.

'Sorry, it takes me a while to get to the door. Fleur, darling, how is he?'

'Oh, Robbie!' She rushed to him and was enfolded in his strong arms. He held her tightly, believing the worst had happened.

'Darling, I'm so sorry,' he murmured against her hair.

'No, no, it's not that,' she said, her voice muffled against him. She pulled back a little to say, 'He's all right. Well, he isn't – what I mean is, he's still alive.'

There was puzzlement in Robbie's eyes and she knew exactly what he must be thinking: then why aren't you with him?

'I've come for your mother,' Fleur was babbling in her anxiety. 'He's asking for her.'

'Asking for my mother?' Robbie was startled.

'Yes – yes. She will come, won't she? Is she here?'

'Oh yes, she's here, but as for coming to the hospital—'

Fleur's eyes widened. 'She won't refuse to come,

will she? Oh, she can't. She must come. It might help him. It *will* help him. I know it will.'

'It's not that, Fleur. But she . . . she's not well herself. Come in and see for yourself. She's just sat by the fire, not moving. She's been like that ever since yesterday.'

He drew her into the front room and closed the door. They did not move further into the house, but stood just inside the door whilst Robbie whispered, 'We had a long talk the night before last. She told me everything. All about what your dad told you.'

Fleur nodded. 'I'm glad you know. It wasn't my place to tell you but I hated having a secret from you. You do understand that, don't you, Robbie?'

'Of course.' He ran his hand distractedly through his hair as if, at this precise moment, that was the least of his worries. 'But ever since then, she's just sat there. She's not even been to bed for two nights. She's not eating or even drinking. I'm at my wits' end . . .'

'Let me see her.' Fleur pushed past him and almost ran through the front room and into the back part of the house.

Just as Robbie had said, Meg was sitting by the fire, her hands lying limply in her lap She was just staring into space, oblivious to everything around her. Across the hearth, the old man sat huddled in his chair, staring helplessly at his daughter. He didn't speak, merely nodded at Fleur and then wiped away a tear running down his wrinkled cheek.

Fleur knelt in front of Meg and touched her hand. It felt cold, almost lifeless. 'Mrs Rodwell,' she began gently, 'I've come to ask you a big favour.'

There was no response from the woman. She seemed unaware of Fleur's presence.

'See?' Robbie said as he limped into the room. 'I told you. I can't get her to do anything. She won't even speak to me. I can't get through to her.'

Taking both Meg's hands in hers, she said firmly, 'Mrs Rodwell, listen to me. My dad needs you. *Jake* needs you.'

Meg blinked and seemed to be trying to focus her eyes on Fleur. It was the name 'Jake' that had prompted a tiny response. Fleur latched on to it. 'Jake wants to see you. He's asking for you. Please, will you come and see him? Come and see Jake.'

Meg's lips moved stiffly and her voice was husky. 'Jake?'

'Yes – Jake. He's in hospital. He's drifting in and out of consciousness. I can't reach him. I've tried. I've been there all morning and he won't wake up. Not for me. And the only name the nurses have heard him say is "Meg". Oh, please.' She gripped the woman's hand even tighter and her voice was full of tears. 'Oh, please, say you'll come.'

Meg stirred as if she was awaking from a trance. 'Me? He . . . he's asking for me?'

'Yes.'

But Meg was shaking her head. 'I can't.'

'Why ever not?' Fleur cried passionately. 'Don't you want to help him? Surely – whatever happened in the past – you can put it aside to . . . to save his *life*, can't you?'

'You don't understand. It's not *me* who doesn't want to see *him* . . .' Her voice trailed away and tears trembled on her eyelashes.

'But he's asking for you.'

Meg shook her head. 'He doesn't know what he's

saying. He must be delirious. He – he won't want to see me. Besides, it wouldn't be right. With poor Betsy only just – only just . . .'

'It can't hurt my mother now,' Fleur insisted. 'She's gone. If she was still alive, then I wouldn't be asking you, but she isn't. Dad is and he needs you.'

'What will people say . . . ?' Meg asked. 'Folks have long memories.'

'Look,' Fleur cried passionately, 'I don't give a damn about what anyone might say. I don't care about what happened years ago. I don't even care that my mother hated the very sound of your name . . .' She saw Meg flinch and was sorry she had been so blunt, but she pressed on now. 'I don't care about any of that. All I care about is my dad and trying to keep him alive. I – I can't bear to lose him.' The final words ended on a sob and she buried her face in Meg's lap.

She felt the older woman's gentle touch on her hair and heard her say, 'Neither can I, Fleur. Oh, neither can I.'

The ward was quiet and peaceful in the middle of the afternoon. The morning flurry of doctors' visits had passed and the daily routine of work finished.

'It's not really visiting time,' the sister greeted them, 'but you, I take it, are Meg?'

Meg, still looking anxious as if she didn't feel she had the right to be there, nodded.

The sister turned to Fleur. 'There's no change, I'm afraid, since this morning. But maybe now . . .' She did not finish her sentence, but glanced hopefully back at Meg. 'Come this way.'

They followed the sister and, as she led them towards Jake's bed, Fleur heard Meg pull in a sharp breath at the sight of him, but she controlled her feelings and sat down in the chair beside him.

His hands and arms were bandaged and most of his face was covered with dressings. There was nothing she could touch. She couldn't hold his hand, couldn't kiss his face. All she could do was say, 'Jake, it's me. It's Meg. I'm here.'

Fleur and Robbie stood at the end of the bed, their arms around one another. They all saw Jake's eyes flicker open and he tried to turn his head towards the sound of her voice. Meg stood up and leant over him.

His eyes focused slowly and he saw her face as he remembered her. Her red flying hair, her smooth skin, her smile. Oh, her smile! That heartbreaking smile of hers. To him she was still the young girl he had met all those years ago. The girl whose strong spirit had lifted him out of the workhouse. The girl he'd loved and lost and who, despite his contented life with Betsy and his children, he'd never been able to forget.

'Meg, oh, Meggie. You came.' The words were faint and slightly slurred but understandable.

At the end of the bed, Fleur buried her face into Robbie's jacket and wept tears of thankfulness. He was going to be all right. Her dad was going to be all right.

'Yes, Jake,' Meg was saying simply. 'I came. I'm here to stay and I shan't leave you. Not unless you tell me to.'

He tried to lift his hand to touch her face, but winced with the pain. 'I won't do that, Meggie. Not ever.'

'Then just rest, Jake, and get well. I'll be right here. Always . . .'

If the past was not entirely forgotten, at least now it was all forgiven.